'**If only you could find a woman to marry who has no interest in actually being your wife, your problems would be solved.**'

She spoke flippantly, more to divert his attention from her own tragic situation than anything else, but Innes, who had been in the act of taking another sip of whisky, stopped, the glass half-way to his lips, an arrested look in his eyes.

'Say that again.'

'What? That you need to marry…?'

'A woman who has no interest in being my wife,' he finished for her with a dawning smile. 'A woman who is in need of a home and has no fixed plans, who might actually be looking for a respite from her current life for a wee while. You're right—that's exactly what I need. And I know exactly the woman.'

'You do? You cannot possibly mean…'

His smile had a wicked light in it. 'I do,' Innes said. 'I mean you.'

D0492191

AUTHOR NOTE

After I finished writing UNWED AND UNREPEN-TANT, which had a Clyde shipbuilder as its hero, I decided I wanted to stay close to home for my next story.

I started in Edinburgh, my favourite city second only to Paris, but the majority of Ainsley and Innes's story is set in Tighnabruaich, on the west coast of Argyll. I renamed it Strone Bridge, but anyone familiar with the area will recognise it. The view of the Kyles of Bute which Ainsley comes to love is one of my own favourites. Ostell Bay, with its golden sands and crystal-clear though icy sea, is a childhood haunt. And the weather— the wet, *driech*, grey west-coast weather—that's very true to life.

I hope that my love for the place where I was brought up, and where I now live and write, resonates in Ainsley and Innes's story. I hope it will inspire some of you to visit. More than anything, I hope that I've done justice to it, and that the romance of the place has enhanced the romance I've written.

Enormous thanks once again to all my Facebook and Twitter friends who have helped and encouraged me while writing this book. Thanks to all who suggested names for Ainsley's Agony Aunt alter ego, and in particular to Keira, who gave me Madame Hera, whose letters I had such fun dreaming up.

STRANGERS
AT THE ALTAR

Marguerite Kaye

All rights reserved including the right of reproduction in whole
or in part in any form. This edition is published by arrangement with
Harlequin Books S.A.

This is a work of fiction. Names, characters, places, locations and
incidents are purely fictional and bear no relationship to any real
life individuals, living or dead, or to any actual places, business
establishments, locations, events or incidents. Any resemblance is
entirely coincidental.

This book is sold subject to the condition that it shall not, by way of
trade or otherwise, be lent, resold, hired out or otherwise circulated
without the prior consent of the publisher in any form of binding or
cover other than that in which it is published and without a similar
condition including this condition being imposed on the subsequent
purchaser.

® and TM are trademarks owned and used by the trademark owner
and/or its licensee. Trademarks marked with ® are registered with the
United Kingdom Patent Office and/or the Office for Harmonisation in
the Internal Market and in other countries.

Published in Great Britain 2014
by Mills & Boon, an imprint of Harlequin (UK) Limited,
Eton House, 18-24 Paradise Road, Richmond, Surrey, TW9 1SR

© 2014 Marguerite Kaye

ISBN: 978-0-263-90997-5

Harlequin (UK) Limited's policy is to use papers that are natural,
renewable and recyclable products and made from wood grown in
sustainable forests. The logging and manufacturing processes conform
to the legal environmental regulations of the country of origin.

Printed and bound in Spain
by Blackprint CPI, Barcelona

Born and educated in Scotland, **Marguerite Kaye** originally qualified as a lawyer but chose not to practise. Instead, she carved out a career in IT and studied history part-time, gaining first-class honours and a master's degree. A few decades after winning a children's national poetry competition she decided to pursue her lifelong ambition to write, and submitted her first historical romance to Mills & Boon®. They accepted it, and she's been writing ever since.

You can contact Marguerite through her website at: www.margueritekaye.com

Previous novels by the same author:

THE WICKED LORD RASENBY
THE RAKE AND THE HEIRESS
INNOCENT IN THE SHEIKH'S HAREM†
  (part of *Summer Sheikhs* anthology)
THE GOVERNESS AND THE SHEIKH†
THE HIGHLANDER'S REDEMPTION*
THE HIGHLANDER'S RETURN*
RAKE WITH A FROZEN HEART
OUTRAGEOUS CONFESSIONS OF LADY DEBORAH
DUCHESS BY CHRISTMAS
  (part of *Gift-Wrapped Governesses* anthology)
THE BEAUTY WITHIN
RUMOURS THAT RUINED A LADY
UNWED AND UNREPENTANT

and recent books in the Mills & Boon® Historical *Undone!* series:

CLAIMED BY THE WOLF PRINCE‡
BOUND TO THE WOLF PRINCE‡
THE HIGHLANDER AND THE WOLF PRINCESS‡
THE SHEIKH'S IMPETUOUS LOVE-SLAVE†
SPELLBOUND & SEDUCED
BEHIND THE COURTESAN'S MASK
FLIRTING WITH RUIN
AN INVITATION TO PLEASURE
LOST IN PLEASURE
HOW TO SEDUCE A SHEIKH
THE UNDOING OF DAISY EDWARDS◊
THE AWAKENING OF POPPY EDWARDS◊

In the Mills & Boon *Castonbury Park* Regency mini-series:

THE LADY WHO BROKE THE RULES

and in M&B eBooks:

TITANIC: A DATE WITH DESTINY

†linked by character
*Highland Brides
‡Legend of the Faol
◊A Time for Scandal

**Did you know that some of these novels
are also available as eBooks? Visit www.millsandboon.co.uk**

HISTORICAL NOTE

Paddle steamers and the railways brought tourism to the west coast of Scotland at around the time when Ainsley and Innes decided to set up their hotel. Though the original and most popular destinations 'doon the watter' on the Clyde were Rothesay, Largs and Dunoon, Tighnabruaich (aka Strone Bridge) had its share of excursionists. The engineer David Napier, whose Loch Eck tours inspired Ainsley, built a pier on the Holy Loch in the 1830s, not far from my own home.

Numerous versions of the *Rothesay Castle* paddle steamer made the journey from Glasgow, Gourock and eventually Wemyss Bay railway terminals to the Isle of Bute. Today, the last sea-going paddle steamer, the *Waverley*, makes the same journey from Glasgow to Bute and down the beautiful Kyles all the way to Tighnabruaich.

Strone Bridge Castle is actually based on Panmure House, the seat of the Maules near Dundee, which was demolished in 1955. The story which Innes tells Ainsley of the locked gates following the 1715 Jacobite rebellion belongs to Panmure, details and pictures of which are in Ian Gow's beautiful book *Scotland's Lost Houses*. The chapel attached to Strone Bridge Castle, though, is based on the one belonging to Mount Stuart in Rothesay.

Agony Aunts existed, astonishingly, as far back as the seventeenth century, though they reached their peak in the mid-Victorian era—a little after Madame Hera was writing. There are some fantastic examples of their letters in Tanith Carey's book *Never Kiss a Man in a Canoe*.

As to the traditions and customs in this book—well, I must admit that I've let my imagination loose a wee bit. All the Hogmanay customs are traditional, but the Rescinding ceremony is not. I actually invented it for an earlier book set in Argyll, THE HIGHLANDER'S REDEMPTION, and I liked it so much I thought I'd start a tradition of my own and re-use it.

Chapter One

Dear Madame Hera,

The other day, while taking a walk in the Cowgate district of Edinburgh, I was approached by a young man who gave me some assistance with my umbrella. Since he was very well dressed, seemed most polite, and the rain was coming down in torrents, it seemed churlish of me not to offer to share my shelter. He accepted with some alacrity, but the small circumference of my umbrella forced us into a somewhat compromising intimacy, of which the gentleman was not slow to take advantage. He stole a kiss from me, and I permitted him to take several more while we found respite from the downpour in the close of a nearby tenement. By the time the rain stopped, we were rather better acquainted than we ought to have been.

We parted without exchanging details. Alack, when he left me, the young man took not only my virtue but my umbrella. It was a gift from another gentleman, who is bound to question me most closely when he discovers its loss. I fear he will not understand the peculiar effect the combination of rain, a good-looking young man and a very small umbrella can have on a woman's willpower. What should I do?

Drookit Miss

Edinburgh—June 1840

'I am very sorry, Mrs McBrayne, but there is nothing to be done. Both your father's will and the law are perfectly clear upon the matter. Could not be clearer, in actual fact, though if you insist upon a second opinion, I believe my partner is now free.'

'You, Mr Thomson, *are* my second opinion,' the woman said scornfully. 'I have no intentions of spending more money I don't have, thanks to that spendthrift husband of mine and that trust of my father's, simply to hear what you have already made perfectly plain. The law is writ-

ten by men for men and administered by men,
too. Be damned to the law, Mr Thomson, for it
seems to be forcing me to earn my living in a
profession even older than your own, down in
the Cowgate. I bid you good day.'

'Mrs McBrayne! Madam, I must beg you...'

The Fury merely tossed her head at the lawyer's outraged countenance and swept across
the narrow reception hall of the office, heading for the door. Innes Drummond, who had
just completed a similarly entirely unsatisfactory interview with Thomson's partner, watched
her dramatic exit admiringly. The door slammed
behind her with enough force to rattle the pane
of glass on which the names Thomson & Ballard were etched. Innes could hear her footsteps
descending the rackety stairs that led out into
Parliament Square. She was as anxious to quit
the place as he was himself. It struck him, as he
flung the door behind him with equal and satisfying force, how ironic it was, that they both, he
and the incandescent Mrs McBrayne, seemed to
be victims of very similar circumstances.

He reached the bottom of the stairs and
heaved open the heavy wooden door, only to
collide with the person standing on the step. 'I
am terribly sorry,' Innes said.

'No, it was my fault.'

She stood aside, and as she did so, he saw tears glistening on her lashes. Mortified, she saw him noticing, and scrubbed at her eyes with her glove, averting her face as she pushed past him.

'Wait!' Instinctively knowing she would not, Innes caught her arm. 'Madam, you are upset.'

She glared at him, shaking herself free of his reflexive grip. 'I am not upset. Not that it's any of your business, but I am very far beyond upset. I am…'

'Furious,' Innes finished for her with a wry smile. 'I know how you feel.'

'I doubt it.'

Her eyes were hazel, wide-spaced and fringed with very long lashes. She was not pretty, definitely not one of those soft, pliant females with rosebud mouths and doe-like gazes, but he was nonetheless drawn to her. She eyed him sceptically, a frown pulling her rather fierce brows together. She was not young either, perhaps in her late twenties, and there was intelligence as well as cynicism in her face. Then there was her mouth. No, not a rosebud, but soft all the same when it ought to be austere, with a hint of humour and more than a hint of sensuality. He noticed that, and with some surprise, noticed that he'd noticed, that his eyes had wandered down, over the slim figure in the drab grey coat, taking a rapid inventory of the limited view and wanting to see more, and that surprised him, too.

'Innes Drummond.' He introduced himself because he could think of nothing else to say, and because he didn't want her to go. Her brows lifted haughtily in response. For some reason, it made her look younger. 'A fellow victim of the law, of his father and of a trust,' he added. 'Though I'm not encumbered with a wife, spendthrift or otherwise.'

'You were listening in to a private conversation between myself and Mr Thomson.'

'Ought I to have pretended not to hear? The tone of your voice made that rather difficult.'

She gave a dry little laugh. 'A tone I feel sure Mr Thomson found most objectionable. Bloody lawyers. Damned law. You see, I can swear as well as shout, though I assure you, I am not usually the type who does either.'

Innes laughed. 'I really do know how you feel, you know.'

She smiled tightly. 'You are a man, Mr Drummond. It is simply not possible. Now, if you will excuse me?'

'Where are you going?' Once again, he had spoken without thinking, wanting only to detain her. Once again her brows rose, more sharply this time. 'I only meant that if you had no urgent

business— But I spoke out of turn. Perhaps your
husband is expecting you?'

'My husband is dead, Mr Drummond, and
though his dying has left me quite without resources, still I cannot be sorry for it.'

'You don't mince your words, do you, Mrs
McBrayne?'

Though he was rather shocked at this callous remark, Innes spoke flippantly. She did not
smile, however, nor take umbrage, but instead
paled slightly. 'I speak my mind. My opinions
may be unpalatable, but at least in expressing
them, there can be no pretending that I have
none.'

Nor, Innes thought, could there be any denying that a wealth of bitter experience lay behind her words. He was intrigued. 'If you are
in no rush, I'd very much like it if you would
take a glass of something with me. I promise
I don't mean anything in the least improper,'
he added hurriedly, 'I merely thought it would
be pleasant—cathartic, I don't know—to let off
steam with a kindred spirit—' Her astonished
expression forced him to break off. 'Forget it.
It's been an awful day, an awful few weeks, but
I shouldn't have asked.'

He made to tip his hat, but once again she surprised him, this time with a faint smile. 'Never

mind weeks, *I've* had an awful few months. No, make that years. The only reason I've not taken to drink already is that I suspect I'd take to it rather too well.'

'I suspect that you do anything well that you set your mind to, Mrs McBrayne. You strike me as a most determined female.'

'Do I? I am now, though it is by far too late, for no matter how determined I am to get myself out of this mess, in truth I can see no solution.'

'Save to sell yourself down the Cowgate? I hope it doesn't come to that.'

She gave him what could only be described as a challenging look. 'Why, are you afraid I will not make sufficient to earn my keep?'

'What on earth do you know of such things?' Innes asked, torn between shock and laughter.

'Oh, I have my sources. And I have an umbrella,' she added confusingly.

She spoke primly, but there was devilment in her eyes, and the smile she was biting back was doing strange things to his guts. 'You are outrageous, Mrs McBrayne,' Innes said.

'Don't you believe me?'

'I have no idea what to make of you, and right at this moment, I don't really care. You made me laugh, and honestly, after what that lawyer told me, I didn't think that was possible.'

Her smile softened sympathetically. 'It sounds like I am not the only one in need of a dram,' she said. 'Why not! I've nothing at home waiting for me except final demands and most likely a few bailiffs. Buy me a drink, Mr Drummond, and we can compare our woes, though I warn you now that mine will far outweigh yours.'

Ainsley McBrayne wondered what on earth had come over her. There had been ample time in the short walk from Parliament Square over the North Bridge for her to change her mind, but she had not. Now here she was, in a secluded corner of the coffee room at the Waterloo Hotel, waiting while a complete stranger bribed one of the waiting staff to bring the pair of them something stronger than tea.

She had surrendered her coat at the door, and her bonnet, too, for they were both wet with that soft, mist-like mizzle that was not quite rain, in which Edinburgh specialised. Her hair, which even on the best of days was reluctant to succumb to the curling iron, was today bundled up into a careless chignon at her nape, and no doubt by now straggling equally carelessly out of it. On a good day, she would tell herself it was chestnut in colour, for it was not red enough to rate auburn, and she was fairly certain there was no such thing as mahogany hair. Today, it was brown, plain and simple and the colour of her mood. At least her gown was one of her better ones. Navy blue worked with silver-grey stylised flowers formed into a linking pattern, the full skirts contrasted with the tightly fitted bodice, with its long narrow sleeves and shawl neck. The narrow belt showed off her slender waist; the crossover pleating at the neck was cut just low enough to allow a daring glimpse of bosom. It had been designed to be worn with a demure white blouse, but this morning Ainsley hadn't been interested in looking demure. This morning she had not, however, intended to take off her coat. Now, she tugged self-consciously at the pleated shawl collar in an effort to pull it a little closer.

She had been angry when she left the lawyer's office, though she should not have been, but it seemed, despite all, that she'd not managed to lower her expectations quite enough. There had been a tiny modicum of hope left in her heart, and she'd been furious at herself for that. Hence the tears. Stupid tears. If Mr Innes Drummond had not seen those stupid tears, he'd more than likely have gone on his way and she wouldn't be here. Instead, she'd be at home. Alone. Or in the company of yet another bailiff. And it wasn't going to be her home for much longer. So she might as well be here. With a complete stranger. About to imbibe strong liquor, just like one of the loose women she'd claimed she would become.

Not that that was so far-fetched either, given the state of things, except one thing she was absolutely sure about was that she had no talents whatsoever for that sort of thing. In fact, she had not even the skill to interest a man if he didn't have to pay, if her husband was anything to go by.

Ainsley sighed. Second to tears, she hated self-pity. Giving her collar a final twitch, she forced herself to relax. Mr Drummond was still conferring with the waiter, so she took the chance to study him. His hair, which was cut unfashionably short, was glossily black. He was a good-looking man; there was no doubt about it, with a clean-shaven jaw, and none of the side whiskers gentlemen preferred these days. A high forehead spoke of intelligence, and lines fanning out from his eyes and forming a deep groove from nose to mouth spoke of experience. He looked to be in his mid-thirties, perhaps five years older than herself. A confident man, and well dressed in his dark coat and trousers, his linen impeccably white. Judging by appearances, money was not one of his worries. But then, if one could have judged John by appearances, money had not been one of his worries either. Not that her husband had ever been at all worried by money—or the lack of. No, that was not true. Those sullen silences of his spoke volumes. And latterly, so, too, did his habit of simply disappearing when she challenged him.

Ainsley sighed again, irked with herself. She was absolutely sick and tired of thinking about John. Across the room, Mr Drummond, having concluded his business with the waiter, glanced up and smiled at her. His eyes, under heavy dark brows, were a deep, vivid blue. She felt it then, what she had ignored before, a tug of something quite basic. Attraction. It made her stomach do a silly little flutter. It made her pulses skitter and it made her mouth dry, that smile of his, and the complicit look that accompanied it, as if the pair of them were in cahoots. It made her forget her anger at the injustice of her situation, and it reminded her that though she might well be a penniless widow with debts so terrifying they could not be counted, she was also a woman who had not known the touch of a man for a long time. And this man, this Mr Innes Drummond, who was seating himself opposite her, this man, she was pretty certain, would know exactly how to touch her.

'So, ladies first.'

Colour flooded her face. She stared at him blankly, horrified at the turn her mind had taken, praying that none of those shocking thoughts were visible on her countenance 'I beg your pardon?'

'Your tale of woe, Mrs McBrayne. You tell me yours, and then I'll tell you mine, and we can decide which of us is worst off.'

He had very long legs. They were stretched out to the side of the table that separated them. Well-made legs. Not at all spindly. And really rather broad shoulders. *Well built,* that was the phrase she was looking for. Athletic, even. And yes, his face and hands were rather tanned, as if he spent a deal of his life out of doors. 'What is it you do?' she asked. 'I mean—do you—are you a resident here in Edinburgh? Only, you do have an accent, but I cannot place it.'

Instead of taking offence, or pointing out that she had changed the subject, Innes Drummond gave a little shrug. 'I'm originally from the Highlands, Argyll on the west coast, though I've lived in England most of my adult life. I'm an engineer, Mrs McBrayne.'

'A practical man.'

He smiled. 'You approve.'

'I do. It is none of my business, but—yes.' She smiled back. 'What do you build?'

'Railway lines. Tunnels. Canals. Bridges and aqueducts. There is a very high demand for all these things, thanks to the steam locomotive. Though I don't actually build the things myself, I design them. And even that— Business is very good, Mrs McBrayne. I am afraid I employ a rather large number of men to do most of the real work while I spend too much of my time in the boardroom, though I still like to think of myself as an engineer.'

'A very successful one, by the sounds of it. I did not think that money could be an issue with you.'

He gave her an enigmatic look before turning his attention to pouring them both a glass of whisky from the decanter that the waiter had deposited. *'Slàinte!'* he said, touching her glass with his.

'Slàinte!' Ainsley took a sip. It was a good malt, peaty and smoky, warming. She took another sip.

'I take it, then, that money *is* an issue for you,' Innes Drummond said.

She nodded. He waited, watching her, turning his glass round and round in his hand. One of the many things she'd learned from her marriage had been how to keep her own counsel—and how to keep her own secrets. Her failures, and the trusting, timid nature that had contributed to them, made her ashamed. She confided in no one, not even Felicity, and Felicity was the best friend she had. But confiding in this stranger, what harm could it do? Whatever had brought him to Edinburgh, he wasn't likely to be stopping long. If—however—he judged her, she'd be spared the pain of seeing it. Who knew, perhaps articulating her problems might even help her see a path to resolving them.

Catching sight of her wedding band, Ainsley tucked her left hand into the folds of her gown. 'It is money,' she said, 'it comes down to money, and though I tell myself it's not fair, for I did not spend the money, I know at heart it's just as much my fault as his.'

Mrs McBrayne took another sip of whisky. 'Dutch courage,' she said, recklessly finishing the amber liquid and replacing the glass on the table before straightening her back and taking an audible breath. Innes wondered what on earth was to come, and wondered if he should stop her confidences, but dismissed this idea immediately. She was steeling herself, which meant she wanted to talk. Besides, he was interested,

was under the misapprehension that if I'd be-haved differently I could have changed my hus-band,' she said. 'It took me some time to realise that since he would never change, then I must.'

She concluded with a small, satisfied smile that made Innes wonder how, exactly, she had changed and what, exactly, the effect had been on her spendthrift husband, but before he could ask, her smile had faded. She took a sip of whisky. Her hand was quite steady now. 'I remained with my husband, but matters between us were ex-tremely strained. John devoted himself to myr-iad schemes he found to lose money, and I—I pursued a new interest of my own which was distracting and made me feel not quite so use-less, but ultimately, I was burying my head in the sand. And then my father died, and his will dealt our marriage a death blow.'

'The trust?'

She nodded. 'I discovered later that John had asked him for money. Neither of them saw fit to inform me of that fact.' Her eyes blazed. 'My own father! I thought he trusted me. I thought— But there, I was wrong. Money is a matter for the man of the house, apparently.' The fire disap-peared from her eyes as quickly as it had come. 'To cut a long and tedious story short, my father changed his will so that my entire inheritance was put into trust for my first child. He did not specify the sex, so at least I should be grateful for that—not that it makes any difference, since there is no child. When John found out, he...' Her voice wavered, but she quickly got it back under control. 'He was furious. He wanted to break the trust. He wanted *me* to find a way to break the trust, to use the law to go against my own father's wishes. It was not exactly conducive to marital harmony. Not that there was much of that by then. When I wouldn't cooperate—well, it seems I didn't have to, for what was mine was actually my husband's. Fortunately for my father's wishes, though not so fortunately for my husband and his creditors, the trust could not be broken. And then my husband died.'

Her voice was hard. Obviously, the love she'd felt for the man she had married was long gone. 'How?' Innes asked, wondering fleetingly if she was about to confess to killing him. There was a bit of him that would not have been surprised. A bit of him that would have approved.

'Pleurisy,' she replied. 'They found him dead drunk down in the Cowgate, out cold in a puddle. Heaven knows how long he'd been there or where he'd been before. He had not been home for three days.'

Was that what she'd meant when she implied

she knew more than any respectable woman ought, about the women who plied their business in that scurrilous area? He wanted to ask, but he didn't want to distract her. Despite the sorry tale she'd told him, she was defiant, and he couldn't help but admire her for that. 'I take it then, that your husband left you with nothing?' Innes said.

'Nothing but debts. Not even my jointure, for it was to be sourced from investments that are now worthless. There is a mortgage on our house that becomes due in a month, a year after his death, and my father's trust is so watertight that, as Mr Thomson confirmed this morning, not even my utter ruin can break it. But you know, it's not even the money that bothers me. It's the extent to which I have been kept in the dark— allowed myself to be kept in the dark—not just by John, but by my father. It makes me feel about this size.' Mrs McBrayne held her thumb and index finger about an inch apart. 'That's how much of a say they gave me in my own life.'

'I am sure your father meant only to protect you.'

'Because I'm nothing but a frail female without a mind of my own?' she snapped. 'It made me wonder how many hundreds, thousands more of us poor wee souls there are out there, living life blindfolded.'

'You make it sound like a conspiracy.'

'That's because it feels like one, and not even Madame He…'

'Madame He?'

'Never mind.' Mrs McBrayne shook her head and picked up her glass, swirled the contents, then replaced it without drinking. 'I beg your pardon. I did not mean to become so emotional. I have made my bed, as they say, and now I must lie on it. Or not, for it is to be sold.' She smiled tightly. 'Like all sorry tales, this one comes with a moral. Whatever happens, I shall never again allow anyone to make my decisions for me. For good or ill, my fate will be of my own determination in the future. And now that is quite enough of me. It is your turn.'

He had a hundred questions, but she had folded her hands and her lips together, and was making a great show of listening. Innes was not fooled. Her eyes were overbright, her fingers too tightly clasped. She had taken quite a battering, one way or another. A lesser woman would have cried, or flung herself on some man's mercy. He could not imagine Mrs McBrayne doing either. He wanted to cheer her. He wanted to tell her she would be fine, absolutely fine. He was very tempted to offer her money, but she would be mortified, to say nothing of the fact that he was pretty certain she'd also see it merely as a transfer of obligation, and he didn't want her to feel beholden. What he wanted was for her to be free. It wasn't so much that he felt sorry for her, though he railed at the injustice of it all, but he felt—yes, that was it—an affinity.

'What have I said to make you smile?'

'Your situation, Mrs McBrayne, has struck a great many chords.'

'I do not see how. I don't know you, but you have told me yourself you're a self-made man and a success. Men such as you will never brook any interference in your life.'

'Actually, that's not true. Unfortunately, I know very well indeed what it's like to have someone else try to bind you to their rules, to dictate your life without you having a say.'

He was pleased to see that he had surprised her. 'What do you mean?' she asked.

'Did I not say at the outset that we are both the victims of fathers and trusts?' Innes replied. 'It's a strange coincidence, but I while you were consulting Thomson on the finer points of your father's will, I was consulting Ballard on the very same thing. I too have been left the victim of a trust fund, only my father's intention was not to protect me but to call me to heel, and un-like your trust, mine can be broken, though only in a very particular way.'

'What way, Mr Drummond?'

Innes smiled thinly. 'Marriage, Mrs McBrayne. An institution that I assure you, I abhor every bit as much as you do yourself.'

Chapter Two

Ainsley stared at him in astonishment. 'Your father's will sets up a trust that requires you to marry?'

'No, it establishes a trust to control the family lands that will remain in effect *until* I marry,' Innes replied.

'Lands?' She only just managed to prevent her jaw dropping. 'As in—what, a country estate?'

'A little more than that. I'm not sure what the total acreage is, but there are about twenty tenanted farms as well as the home farm and the castle.'

'Good heavens, Mr Drummond—a castle! And *about* twenty farms. Is there a title, too?'

He shook his head. 'My father was known as the laird of Strone Bridge, but it was just a courtesy.'

Laird. The title conjured up a fierce Highland

patriarch. Ainsley eyed the impeccably dressed gentleman opposite her and discovered it was surprisingly easy to imagine him in a plaid, carrying a claymore. Though without the customary beard. She didn't like beards. 'And these lands, they are in Argyll, did you say?'

When he nodded Ainsley frowned in puzzlement. 'Forgive me, Mr Drummond, but did you not tell me you had spent most of your life in England? Surely as the heir to such a substantial property—I know nothing of such things, mind you—but I thought it would have been customary for you to have lived on the estate?'

His countenance hardened. 'I was not the heir.'

'Oh?'

She waited, unwilling to prompt him further, for he looked quite forbidding. Innes Drummond took a sip of whisky, grimaced and put the glass back down on the table. 'Dutch courage,' he said, with a shadow of her own words and her own grim little smile. 'I had a brother. Malcolm. He was the heir. It is as you said—he lived on the estate. Lived and breathed it, more like, for he loved the place. Strone Bridge was his world.'

He stared down at his glass, his mouth turned down in sorrow. 'But it was not your world?' Ainsley asked gently.

'It was never meant for me. I was the second son. As far as my father was concerned, that meant second best, and while Malcolm was alive, next to useless, Mrs McBrayne.'

He stared down at his glass, such a bleak look on his face that she leaned over to press his hand. 'My name is Ainsley.'

'I don't think I've heard that before.'

'An old family name,' she said.

He gave her a very fleeting smile as his fingers curled around hers. 'Then you must call me Innes,' he said. 'Another old family name, though it is not usually that of the laird. One condition I have been spared. My father did not specify that I change my name to Malcolm. Even he must have realised that would have been a step too far. Though, then again, it may simply have been that he thought me as unworthy of the name as the lands.'

He spoke viciously enough to make Ainsley recoil. 'You sound as though you hate him.'

'Rather, the boot was on the other foot.' He said it jeeringly. She wondered what hurt lay behind those words, but Innes was already retreating, patently regretting what he had revealed. 'We did not see eye to eye,' he tempered. 'Some would call him a traditionalist. Everyone had a place in his world. I did not take to the one he allotted me. When I finally decided to forge my own way, we fell out.'

Ainsley could well imagine it. Innes was obviously a man with a very strong will, a modern man and an independent one who clearly thrived in the industrial world. It would be like two stags clashing. She wondered what the circumstances had been that had caused what was obviously a split, but curious as she was, she had no wish to rile him further. 'Tell me about the trust,' she said. 'Why must you marry, and what happens if you do not?'

Innes stared down at his hand, the one she had so abruptly released, his eyes still dark with pain. 'As to why, that is obvious. The Strone Bridge estate has been passed through the direct line back as far as records exist, and I am the last of the line. He wanted an heir.'

'But he only specified that you must take a wife? That seems rather odd.'

'We Drummonds have proved ourselves potent over the generations. My father no doubt assumed that even such an undeserving son as I would not fail in that most basic of tasks,' Innes said sarcastically.

'You don't want children?'

'I don't want a wife, and in my book, one must necessarily precede the other.'

This time Ainsley's curiosity overcame her caution. 'Why are you so against marriage?' she asked. 'You don't strike me as a man who hates my sex.'

'You don't strike me as a woman who hates men, yet you don't want to get married again.'

'It is a case of once bitten with me.'

'While I have no intentions of being bitten for a first time,' Innes retorted. 'I don't need anyone other than myself to order my life, and I certainly don't want to rely on anyone else to make me happy.'

He spoke with some vehemence. He spoke as if there was bitter experience behind his words. As there was, too, behind hers. 'Your father's will has put you in an impossible situation, then,' Ainsley said.

'As has yours,' Innes replied tersely. 'What happens to your trust if you have no children?'

'It reverts to me when I am forty and presumably deemed to be saying my prayers.' She could not keep the bitterness from her voice. She had loved her father, but his unwitting condemnation of her was still difficult to take. 'I have only to discover a way of avoiding my husband's creditors and surviving without either a roof over my head or food in my belly for the next ten years in order to inherit, since I have no intentions of marrying again.'

'Nor any intention of producing a child out of wedlock, I take it? No need to look so shocked,' Innes said, 'it was a joke.'

'A poor one.'

'I'm sorry.'

She forced a smile. 'I do not really intend to sell myself down the Cowgate, you know.'

Innes covered her hand. 'Are your debts really so bad?'

'There will certainly still be sufficient of them to pay off when I finally do come into my inheritance,' she said.

His fingers tightened around hers. 'I wish I could be of some help to you.'

'You have been, simply by listening,' Ainsley replied, flustered by the sympathy in his look. She no longer expected sympathy. She had come to believe she did not deserve it. 'A problem shared and all that,' she said with a small smile.

'It's a damnable situation.'

He seemed much bigger, this close. There was something terribly comforting in those broad shoulders, in the way his hand enveloped hers, in the way he was looking at her, not with pity at all but with understanding. Close-up, his irises were ringed with a very dark blue. She had never seen eyes quite that colour.

Realising her thoughts were once more straying down a most inappropriate path, Ainsley dropped her gaze. 'If my father had not left my money in trust, my husband would have spent it by now, and I'd have nothing to look forward to in what he clearly thought of as my forty-year-old dotage. The money might have postponed my husband's demise, but I doubt very much it would have been for more than a few years, and frankly I don't think I could have borne a few more years married to him.'

'I confess, at one point I thought you were going to tell me you had killed him yourself,' Innes said.

Ainsley laughed. 'I may not be the timid wee mouse he married, but I don't think I've become a monster.'

'I think you are a wonder.' She looked up, surprised by the warmth in his tone, and her pulses began to race as he lifted her hand to his mouth, pressing a kiss to her knuckles. There was no mistaking it for one of those polite, social, nothing kisses. His mouth lingered on her skin, his lips warm, his eyes looking deep into hers for long, long seconds. 'You are a most remarkable woman, Ainsley McBrayne.'

'Thank you. I— Thank you.'

'I really do wish there was some way that I could help you, but I know better than to offer you money.'

'I really do wish there was a way I could accept it, but—well, there we are, I cannot, so there is no point in discussing it. In fact, we have talked far more about me than you. I'm still not clear about what happens to your lands if you remain unmarried. What does this trust entail?'

She was pleased with how she sounded. Not a tremor to betray the quickening of desire his lips had stirred, and she hoped the flush she could feel blooming had not reached her cheeks.

However Innes Drummond felt, and she would have dearly liked to have known, he took his cue from her. 'A trustee appointed by that lawyer, Ballard, to manage them, and all monies associated with them banked. I can't touch a penny of it without a wife,' he replied, 'and even with a wife, I must also commit to living for a year on Strone Bridge.'

'Is it a great deal of money?'

Innes shook his head. 'I've no idea, since I'm not even entitled to see the accounts, but the money isn't the point, I have plenty of my own. I haven't a clue what state the place is in at all. It could be flourishing, it could have gone to rack and ruin, for all I know.'

'So the fall out between yourself and your father then, it was…'

'More like a complete break. I told you, he was an old-fashioned man. Do as I say, or get out of my sight.'

Innes spoke lightly enough, but she was not fooled. 'How long is it since you were there?'

'Almost fourteen years. Since Malcolm— since I lost my brother.' Innes shuddered, but recovered quickly. 'You're wondering why I'm so upset about the trust when I've spent most of my adult life away from the place,' he said.

'I think this has all been much more of a shock than you realise,' Ainsley answered cautiously.

'Aye, mayhap you're right.' His accent had softened, the Highland lilt much more obvious. 'I had no inkling the old man was ill, and he'd no time to let me know. Not that I think he would have. Far better for me to be called to heel through that will of his from beyond the grave. I don't doubt he's looking down—or maybe up—and laughing at the mess he's put me in,' Innes said. 'He knew just how it would stick in my craw, having to choose between relying on someone else to run what is mine or to take up the reins myself under such conditions.

Be damned to him! I must find a way to break this trust. I will not let him issue decrees from beyond the grave.'

He thumped his fist on the table, making his glass and Ainsley jump. 'I'm beginning to think that your situation is worse than mine after all.'

'Ach, that's nonsense, for I at least don't have to worry about where my next meal is coming from. It's a sick coincidence, the way the pair of us are being punished by our parents, though,' Innes said. 'What will you do?'

'Oh, I'm beyond worrying right now.' Ainsley waved her hand in the air dismissively. 'The question is, what will you do? If only you could find a woman to marry who has no interest in actually being your wife, your problems would be solved.'

She spoke flippantly, more to divert his attention from her own tragic situation than anything, but Innes, who had been in the act of taking another sip of whisky, stopped, the glass halfway to his lips, an arrested look in his eyes. 'Say that again.'

'What? That you need to marry…'

'A woman who has no interest in being my wife,' he finished for her with a dawning smile. 'A woman who is in need of a home, and has no fixed plans, who might actually be looking for a respite from her current life for a wee while. You're right, that's exactly what I need, and I know exactly the woman.'

'You do? You cannot possible mean…'

His smile had a wicked light in it. 'I do,' Innes said. 'I mean you.'

Ainsley was staring at him open-mouthed. Innes laughed. 'Think about it, it's the ideal solution. In fact, it could almost be said that we are perfectly matched, since you have as little desire for a husband as I have for a wife.'

She blinked at him owlishly. 'Are you drunk?'

'Certainly not.'

'Then I must be, for you cannot possibly be proposing marriage. Apart from the fact that we've only just met, I thought I had made it plain that I will never—absolutely *never* again—surrender my independence.'

'I'm not asking you to. I'm actually making it easier for you to retain it, because if we get married, I can pay off all those debts that bastard of a husband of yours acquired and then you really will be free.'

'But I'd be married to you.'

'In name only.'

'I owe a small fortune. I couldn't take it from you just for the price of putting my name on a bit of paper.'

'You'd have to come with me to Strone Bridge. The clause that specified my spending a year there doesn't actually include my wife, but all the same, I think you'd have to come with me for a wee while, at least.'

'That would not be a problem since, as you have already deduced, I'm going to be homeless very shortly, and would appreciate a change of scene, but I simply couldn't think of accepting such a huge amount of money and give so little in return.'

'What if you saw it as a wage?' Innes asked, frowning.

'For what?'

'A fee, paid for professional services,' he said, 'and a retainer to be paid in addition each year until you are forty, which you could pay me back if you wish, when you eventually inherit, though there is no need.'

'But I'm not a professional.' Her eyes widened. 'You cannot possibly mean— I told you, I was joking about the Cowgate.'

Innes laughed. 'Not that! I meant a business professional.' She was now looking utterly bewildered. Innes grinned. 'The more I think about it, the more I see how perfect it is. No, wait.' He caught her as she made to get up. 'I promise you, I'm neither drunk nor mad. Listen.'

Ainsley sat down, folding her arms, a sceptical look on her face. 'Five minutes.'

He nodded. 'Think about it as a business proposal,' he said. 'First of all, think of the common ground. To begin with, you need to pay off your debts and I am rich enough to be able to do so easily. Second, you are a widow, and I need a wife. Since we are neither of us in the least bit interested, now or ever, in marrying someone else...'

'How can you be so sure of that?'

'How can you?' He waited, but she made no answer, so he gave a satisfied nod. 'You see? We are of one mind on that. And we are of one mind on another thing, which is our determination to make our own way in life. If you let me pay off your debts, I can give you the freedom to do that, and if you marry me, you'll be freeing me to make up my own mind on what to do—or not—about my inheritance.'

'But we'll be tied to one another.'

'In name only, Ainsley. Tied by a bit of paper, which is no more than a contract.'

'Contracts require payment. What *professional* services can you possibly imagine I can provide?'

'An objective eye. An unbiased opinion. I

need both.' Innes shifted uncomfortably. 'Not advice, precisely,' he said.

'Because you do not like to take advice, do you?'

'Are you mocking me?'

'Another thing you're not used to, obviously.' Ainsley smiled. 'Not mocking, teasing. I'm a little rusty. What is it, then, that involves my giving you my unbiased and objective opinion without advising you?'

'When you put it like that!' He was forced to smile. 'What I'm trying to say is, I'd like you to come to Strone Bridge with me. Not to make my decisions, but to make sure when I do make them, I'm doing so without prejudice.'

'Is that possible? It's your birthright, Innes.'

He shook his head vehemently. 'That's the point. It's not. It pains me to admit it, but I don't know much about it, and I haven't a clue what I want to do with it. Live there. Sell it. Put in a manager. I don't know, and I won't know until I go there, and even when I do—what do you say?'

'That's the price? That's the professional services I'm to render in order to have my life back?'

'You think it's too great a cost?' Innes said, deflated.

Ainsley smiled. Then she laughed. 'I think it's a bargain.'

'You do? You understand, Strone Bridge is like to be—well, very different from Edinburgh.'

'A change from Edinburgh, a place to take stock, is, as you pointed out, exactly what I need.'

'I'm not asking you to stay the full year. A few months, until I've seen my way clear, that's all. And though I'm asking you to—to consult with me, that does not mean I'll necessarily take your advice,' Innes cautioned.

'I'm used to that.' Ainsley's smile faded momentarily, but then brightened. 'Though being asked is a step in the right direction, and I will at least have the opportunity of putting my point across.'

Glancing at the decanter of whisky, the level of which had unmistakably fallen by more than a couple of drams, Innes wondered if he was drunk after all. He'd just proposed marriage to a complete stranger. A stranger with a sorry tale, whose courage and strength of mind he admired, but he had met her only a couple of hours ago all the same. Yet it didn't seem to matter. He was drawn to her, had been drawn to her from that first moment when she'd stormed out of the lawyer's office, and it wasn't just the bizarre coincidence of their situations. He liked what he saw of her, and admired what he heard. That he also found her desirable was entirely beside the point. His instincts told him that they'd fare well together, and his instincts were never wrong. 'So we are agreed?' Innes asked.

Ainsley tapped her index fingers together, frowning. 'We're complete strangers,' she said, reflecting his own thoughts. 'Do you think we'll be able to put on enough of a show to persuade your people that this isn't a marriage of convenience?'

'I'm not in the habit of concerning myself with what other people think.'

'Don't be daft. You'll be the—their—laird, Innes. Of course they'll be concerned.'

She was in the right of it, but he had no intentions of accepting that fact. He was not the laird. The laird was dead, and so, too, was his heir. Innes would not be branded. 'They must take me—us—as they find us,' he said. Ainsley was still frowning. 'Strone Bridge Castle is huge. If it's having to rub shoulders with me on a daily basis you're worried about, I assure you, we could go for weeks without seeing each other if we wanted.'

'That is hardly likely to persuade people we're living in domestic bliss.'

'I doubt domestic bliss is a concept that any laird of Strone Bridge is familiar with. My ancestors married for the getting of wealth and the getting of bairns.'

'Then that puts an end to our discussion.' Ainsley got to her feet and began to head for the door of the coffee room.

Innes threw down some money on the table and followed her, pulling her into a little alcove in the main reception area of the hotel. 'I don't want either of those things from you. I don't want to be like them,' he said earnestly. 'Can't you see, that's the point?'

'This is madness.'

He gave her arm a little shake, forcing her eyes to meet his. 'Madness would be to do what you're doing, and that's walking away from the perfect solution. Stop thinking about what could go wrong, think about what it will put right. Freedom, Ainsley. Think about that.'

Her mouth trembled on the brink of a smile. 'I confess, it's a very attractive idea.'

'So you'll do it?'

Her smile broadened. The light had come back into her eyes. 'I feel sure there are a hundred reasons why I should walk very quickly in the other direction.'

'But you will not?' He was just close enough

for her skirts to brush his trousers, to smell the scent of her soap, of the rain in her hair. She made no attempt to free herself, holding his gaze, that smile just hovering, tempting, challenging. Tension quivered between them. 'You would regret it if you did,' Innes said.

'Do you know, Mr Innes Drummond, I think you may well be right.'

Her voice was soft, there was a tiny shiver in it, and a shiver, too, when he slid his hands from her shoulders down her arms, closing the space between them and lowering his mouth to hers. It was the softest of kisses, the briefest of kisses, but it was a kiss. A very adult kiss, which could easily have become so much more. Lips, tongues, caressed, tasted. Heat flared and they both instinctively recoiled, for it was the kind of heat that could burn.

Ainsley put her hand to her mouth, staring wide-eyed at him. Innes looked, he suspected, every bit as shocked as she. 'I'm sorry,' he said.

'Are you?'

'Not really, but I promise *that* was not in any way part of the bargain I'm proposing.'

She slanted him a look he could not interpret as she disentangled herself from his loose embrace. '*That* was merely the product of too much whisky on top of too much emotional upheaval.

It was like a—a valve to release the steam pressure on one of those steam engines you build bridges and tunnels for, nothing more.'

He laughed. He couldn't help it, because she was right in a way, and she was quite wrong in another, but in every way she was wholly unexpected and a breath of much-needed fresh air. 'I'm thinking that my return to Strone Bridge is going to be a source of constant emotional upheaval,' Innes said. 'We might need to do a lot of kissing.'

'You're an engineer,' Ainsley replied primly, though her eyes were sparkling. 'I suggest you invent a different kind of safety valve for yourself.'

'Ainsley, what a nice surprise.' Felicity Blair, editor of the *Scottish Ladies Companion*, greeted her friend with a warm smile, waving her into the shabby chair on the other side of the huge desk that dominated her tiny office. 'I've just been reading Madame Hera's latest advice. I am not at all sure we can publish this reply, not least because it's rather long.'

'Which one is that?' Ainsley asked.

In response, Felicity picked up a piece of paper from the collection that Ainsley recognised she'd handed in to the office a week ago, and began to read:

'Dear Anxious Miss,
Simply because you are more mature than
the average bride-to-be—and I do not consider two-and-thirty to be so old—does not
mean that you are exempt from the trepidation natural to one in your position. You
are, when all is said and done, setting sail
into unchartered waters. To put it plainly, no
matter how well you think you might know
your intended, you should be prepared for
the state of matrimony to alter him significantly, for he will have secured his prize,
and will no longer be required to woo you.
This might mean calm, tranquil seas. But it
might prove to be a stormy passage.

My advice is to start the way you mean
to go on and take charge of the rudder!
Give no quarter, Anxious Miss; let your
husband see that he cannot set the course
of the matrimonial vessel to suit only himself. Do not allow yourself to be subsumed
by his nature nor his dictates simply because you have assumed his name. Do not
allow your nerves, your maidenly modesty
or your sex to intimidate you. Speak up for
yourself from the first, and set a precedent
that, if not immediately, will, I am sure,
eventually earn your husband's respect.

As to the more intimate matters with which you are concerned. You say your intended has indicated a lack of experience, and you are worried that this might—once again, I will revert to the seafaring metaphor—result in the becalming of the good ship wedlock. First, I would strongly advise you to muster your courage and have a frank chat about the mechanics of your wedding night with a married lady friend, thus eliminating the shock of the complete unknown. Second, I would advise you equally strongly to give your husband no inclination that you come to the wedding night armed with such information, lest he find it emasculating. Third, remember, if he really is as innocent as he claims, he will be as nervous as you. But he is a man, Anxious Miss, and thus a little flattery, some feminine admiration and a pliant female body, will ensure the success of your maiden voyage.

Good luck!

Madame Hera'

Ainsley smiled doubtfully. 'I admit, the sailing metaphor is rather trite, but if I had not used it, I would have been forced to invent something else equally silly, else you would have deemed it too vulgar to print.'

'At least you did not surrender to the obvious temptation to talk about dry docks in the context of the wedding night,' Felicity replied acerbically.

'No, because such a shocking thing did not occur to me,' Ainsley replied, laughing. 'Though to be serious for a moment, it is becoming quite a challenge for Madame Hera to advise without entirely hiding her meaning behind the veil of polite euphemisms. The whole point of the column is to provide practical help.'

Felicity set the letter down. 'I've been pondering that very issue myself. You know how limited the space is for Madame's column each month, yet we are now receiving enough correspondence to fill the entire magazine.'

'Aren't you pleased? I know I am. It is proof that I was absolutely right about the need for such a thing, and you were absolutely right to take the chance to publish it.'

'Yes, the volume of mail is a true testament to the quality of Madame's advice but, Ainsley, the problem is we can't publish most of it, for our readers would consider the subjects far too warm. Even with your shipping metaphor, that reply to Anxious Miss is sailing close to the wind. Oh, good grief, you've got me at it now!' Felicity adjusted the long ink-stained cuffs that protected her blouse. 'I'm glad you stopped by, because I've got an idea I'd like to discuss. You know it will be exactly two years since we launched Madame Hera's column next month?'

'Of course I do.' It had been the first step away from self-pity towards self-sufficiency Ainsley had taken. She remembered it vividly—the thrill of dreaming up the idea after one particularly dispiriting evening with her husband. 'It's funny,' she said to Felicity, 'at first it was the secret of Madame's existence that I enjoyed most, knowing I had something all mine that John knew nothing about. But these days, it is the hope that some of Madame Hera's advice actually helps the women who write to her that I relish. Though of course, one can never really know if one has helped.'

'You do,' Felicity said firmly. 'You know you do, just by providing an ear. Now, as I said, there are a great deal more people asking for Madame's advice than we can cover in our column, which brings me to my idea. A more personal service.'

'What on earth do you mean by that?' Ainsley wondered, for a startled moment, if her friend had somehow heard of her remark about earning a living in the Cowgate the other day.

Felicity gave a gurgle of laughter. 'Your face! I do not mean anything immoral, never fear. I mean a personal *letter* service. For a price, of course, for matters of a more sensitive nature, we can offer a personal response from Madame. We'll split the fee between the journal and yourself, naturally. Depending on how many you can answer in a month I'd say your earnings from the journal could triple at least. What do you say?'

'I'm getting married,' Ainsley blurted out.

Felicity's dark brown eyes opened so wide as to appear quite round. 'You're doing what?'

'I know, it's a shock, but it's not what you think. I can explain,' Ainsley said, wondering now if she could. She'd hardly slept a wink these past few nights wondering if she had been an idiot, and coming here this morning had been a test she'd set herself, for if practical, outspoken, radical Felicity thought it was a good idea…

Half an hour and what seemed like a hundred questions later, her friend sat back at her desk, rummaging absent-mindedly for the pencil she had, as usual, lost in her heavy chignon of hair. 'And you're absolutely sure that this Mr Drummond has no ulterior motives?'

'As sure as I can be. He's started the process of paying all of John's debts.'

'At least you'd no longer be obliged to call yourself by that man's name. Does he include the mortgage on Wemyss Place in the debts?'

Ainsley shook her head. 'Innes wanted to pay it, but as far as I'm concerned, the creditors can have the house. It has nothing but unhappy memories for me. Besides, I have every intention of repaying it all when I inherit my trust fund, and that mortgage would take up nearly all of it.'

'So, you are going to be a Highland lady. The chatelaine of a real Scottish castle.' Felicity chuckled. 'How will you like that, I wonder? You've never been out of Edinburgh.'

'It's only a temporary thing, until Innes decides what he wants to do with the place.'

'And how long will that take?'

'I don't know. Weeks. Months? No more, though he must remain there for a year. I'm looking forward to the change of scenery. And to feeling useful.'

'It all sounds too good to be true. Sadly, in my experience, things that are too good to be true almost always are,' Felicity said drily.

'Do you think it's a mistake?'

'I don't know. I think you're half-mad, but you've had a raw deal of it these past few years, and I've not seen you this animated for a long time. Perhaps getting away from Edinburgh will be good for you.' Felicity finally located her pencil and pulled it out of her coiffure, along with a handful of bright copper hair. 'What is he like, this laird? Are you sure he'll not turn into some sort of savage Highlander who'll drag you off to his lair and have his wicked way with you the minute you arrive on his lands?'

'There is no question of him having his wicked way,' Ainsley said, trying to ignore the vision of Innes in a plaid. The same one she'd had the first day she'd met him. With a claymore. And no beard.

'You're blushing,' Felicity exclaimed. 'How very interesting. Ainsley McBrayne, I do believe you would not be averse to your Highlander being very wicked indeed.'

'Stop it! I haven't the first idea what you mean by wicked, but...'

Felicity laughed. 'I know you don't,' she said, 'and frankly, it's been the thing that's worried me most about this idea of mine for Madame Hera's personal letter service, but now I think you've solved the problem. I suppose you've already kissed him? Don't deny it, that guilty look is a complete giveaway. Did you like it?'

'Felicity!'

'Well?'

'Yes.' Ainsley laughed. 'Yes, I did.'

'Was it a good kiss? The kind of kiss to give you confidence that your Mr Drummond would know what he was doing? The kind of kiss that made you want him to do more than kiss you?'

Ainsley put her hands to her heated cheeks. 'Yes. If you must know, yes, it was! Goodness, the things you say. We did not— Our marriage is not— That sort of thing is not...'

'You're going to be out in the wilds. You've already said that you're attracted to each other. It's bound to come up, if you'll forgive the dreadful *double entendre*. And when it does—provided you take care there are no consequences—then why not?' Felicity said. 'Do you want me to be blunt?'

'What, even more than you've been already?'

'Ainsley, from what you've told me—or not told me—about your marriage, it was not physically satisfying.'

'I can't talk about it.'

'No, and you know I won't push you, but you also know enough, surely, to realise that with the right man, lovemaking can be fun.'

'Fun?' Ainsley tried to imagine this, but her own experience, which was ultimately simply embarrassing, at times shameful, made this impossible.

'Fun,' Felicity repeated, 'and pleasurable, too. It should not be an ordeal.'

Which was exactly how it had been, latterly, Ainsley thought, flushing, realising that Felicity had perceived a great deal more than she had ever revealed. 'Is it fun and pleasurable for you, with your mystery man?'

'If it were not, I would not be his mistress.'

It was only because she knew her so well that Ainsley noticed the faint withdrawal, the very slight tightening of her lips that betrayed her. Felicity claimed that being a mistress gave her the satisfaction of a lover without curtailing her freedom, but there were times when Ainsley wondered. She suspected the man was married, and loved her friend too much to pain her by asking. They both had their shameful secrets.

Ainsley picked up the latest stack of letters from the desk and began to flick through them. What Felicity said was absolutely true. As Madame Hera's reputation spread, her post contained ever more intimate queries, and as things stood, Ainsley would be hard-pressed to answer some of them save in the vaguest of terms. She replaced the letters with a sigh. 'No. Even if Innes was interested…'

'You know perfectly well that he would be,' Felicity interjected drily. 'He's a man, and, despite the fact that John McBrayne stripped you of every ounce of self-esteem, you're an attractive woman. What else will you do to while away the dark nights in that godforsaken place?'

'Regardless,' Ainsley persisted, 'it would be quite wrong of me to use Innes merely to acquire the experience that would allow Madame Hera to dispense better advice.'

'Advice that would make such a difference to all these poor, tormented women,' Felicity said, patting the pile of letters. 'Wasn't that exactly what you set out to do?'

'Stop it. You cannot make me feel guilty enough to— Just stop it, Felicity. You know, sometimes I think you really are as ruthless an editor as you pretend.'

'Trust me, I have to be, since I, too, am a mere woman. But we were talking about you, Ainsley. I agree, it would be wrong if you were only lying back and thinking of Scotland for the sake of Madame Hera and her clients. Though I hope you've more in mind than lying back and thinking of Scotland.'

'Felicity!'

'Fun and pleasure, my dear, require participation,' her friend said with another of her mischievous smiles. 'You see, now you are intrigued, and now you can admit it would not only be for Madame Hera, but yourself. Confess, you want him.'

'Yes. No. I told you, it…'

'Has no part in your arrangement. I heard you. Methinks you protest just a little too much.'

'But do you approve?' Ainsley said anxiously.

Felicity picked up her pencil again and began to twist it into her hair. 'I approve of anything that will make you happy. When does the ceremony take place?'

'The banns are being called on Sunday for the first time. The ceremony will be immediately after the last calling, in three weeks. Will you come, Felicity? I'd like to have you by my side.'

'Will you promise me that if you change your mind before then, you will speak up? And if you are unhappy at this Strone Bridge place, you will come straight back here, regardless of whether you feel your obligations have been met?'

'I promise.'

Felicity got to her feet. 'Then I will be your attendant, if that's what you want.' She picked up the bundle of letters and held them out. 'Make a start on these. I will draw up the advertisement, we'll run it beside Madame's column for this month and I will send you a note of the terms once I have them agreed. Will you be disclosing your alter ego to the laird?'

'Absolutely not! Good grief, no, especially not if I am to— He will think…'

Felicity chuckled gleefully. 'I see I've given you food for thought, at the least. I look forward to reading the results—in the form of Madame's letters, I mean.' She hugged Ainsley tightly. 'I wish you luck. You will write to me, once you are there?'

Ainsley sniffed, kissing her friend on the cheek. 'You'll get sick of hearing from me.' She tucked the letters into the folder, which was already stuffed with the bills she was to hand over to Mr Ballard, Innes's lawyer.

'Just one thing,' Felicity called after her. 'I'll wager you five pounds that if your Highlander ever discovers that you are Madame Hera, he'll be far more interested in finding problems for the pair of you to resolve together than taking umbrage.'

'Since I shall take very good care that he never finds out, you will lose,' Ainsley said, laughing as she closed the door behind her.

Chapter Three

⁓⁓⁓⁓

Dear Madame Hera,

I have been married for three months to a man whose station in life is very superior to my own. Having moved from a small house with only two servants to a very large manor with a butler and a housekeeper, I find myself in a perfect tizzy some mornings, trying to understand who I should be asking to do what. My husband has suggested turning to his mother for advice, but she obviously thinks he has married beneath him and would see my need for guidance as evidence of this. As it is, I am sure the housekeeper is reporting my every failure in the domestic sphere to my mother-in-law. Only last week, when I committed the cardinal sin of asking the second housemaid to bring me a pot of tea, the woman actually chastised me as if I were a child. Apparently, such requests should be relayed through the footman, and I should not desire to take tea outside the usual hours, whatever these might be.

I love my husband, but I am being made to feel like an upstart in my new home, and I dare not tell him for fear he will start to take on his mother's opinion of me. Is there some sort of school for new wives I can attend? Please advise me, for I am beginning to wonder if my housekeeper would have made a better wife to my husband than I can.

Timid Mouse

Argyll, July 1840

It was cold here on the west coast. Despite the watery sunshine, a stiff breeze had blown up in the bay at Rhubodach. Innes shivered inside his heavy greatcoat. He'd forgotten how much colder it was here, and it would be colder still in the boat. Sitting on a bandbox a few feet away, Ainsley was reading a letter, clutching the folds of her travelling cloak tightly around her and staring out over the Kyles of Bute. These past three weeks there had been so much business to attend to they'd barely had time to exchange more than a few words. Standing before the altar beside him just a few days ago, she had been almost as complete a stranger to him as the day he'd proposed. Yet in a very short while, they'd be on Strone Bridge, playing the part of a happily married couple.

The dread had been taking a slow hold of him. It had settled inside him with the news of his father's death. It had grown when he learned the terms of his inheritance, then became subdued when Ainsley agreed to marry him, and even suppressed as they made their arrangements and their vows. But on the coach from Edinburgh to Glasgow it had made itself known again. Then on the paddle steamer *Rothesay Castle* as they sailed from the Broomilaw docks to the Isle of Bute it took root, and by this afternoon's journey from Rothesay town to the north part of the Isle of Bute where they now stood waiting, it had manifested itself in this horrible sick feeling, in this illogical but incredibly strong desire to turn tail and run, and to keep running, just as he had done fourteen years before.

He was Innes Drummond, self-made man of fortune and some fame in the business he called his own. He was a man who made his living building bridges, engineering solutions to problems, turning the impossible into reality. Yet standing here on the pebbled shores of Rhubo-dach bay, he felt as if none of this mattered. He was the second son, his father's runt, the upstart who had no right to be coming back to Strone Bridge to claim a dead man's property. The memories of his brother he had worked so long to suppress were lurking just across the water to claim him. On Strone Bridge, Malcolm's absence would make his death impossible to deny. Guilt was that sick feeling eating away at his stomach. Fear was the hard, cold lump growing inside of him. He had no right to be here. He was afraid that when he arrived, he'd be subsumed, that all he thought he was would be peeled ruthlessly back to expose the pretender beneath.

Innes swore under his breath, long and vi-ciously. And in Gaelic. He noticed that too late, and then swore again in the harsher, more famil-iar language of his construction workers. Pick-ing up a handful of pebbles, he began to launch them one after the other into the water, noting with faint satisfaction that they fell far out.

'Impressive.'

He hadn't heard her moving. How long had she been standing there, watching him? 'The boat is late.' Innes made a show of shading his eyes to squint out at the Kyles.

'You must be nervous,' Ainsley said. 'I know I would be, returning after such a long period of time. I expect you'll be wondering how much has changed.'

Her tone was light, almost indifferent. She was studiously avoiding his gaze, looking out at the water, but he was not fooled. She was an astute observer. One of those people who studied faces, who seemed to have the knack of reading the thoughts of complete strangers. 'Nothing will have changed,' Innes said with heavy certainty. 'My father prided himself on maintaining traditions that were hundreds of years old. You'll feel as if you've stepped back into the eighteenth century.'

Her brows lifted in surprise. He could see the wheels turning in her clever brain, but she chose merely to nod, and perversely, though he knew he would not like it, he wanted to know what she was thinking. 'Go on. Say it.'

'It is nothing. Only—you are very much a man of the nineteenth century.'

'You mean you're not surprised I left such a backward place.'

'Such a backward place must be crying out for a man like you.' Ainsley pushed her windswept hair out of her eyes. 'I meant that I am not surprised you and your father could not see eye to eye.'

She slipped her gloved hand into his, in the folds of his greatcoat. He twined his fingers around hers, glad of the contact. Ainsley Drummond, his wife. A stranger she might be, but he was glad of her presence, and when she smiled up at him like that, the dread contracted just a little. 'I think that's the boat,' she said, pointing.

It was, and he could see already that Eoin was at the helm. With a determined effort, Innes threw off his black mood. 'Are you ready?' he asked, sliding his arm around Ainsley to anchor her to his side.

'You sound like you're standing under the gallows, if you don't mind my saying.'

Innes managed a rigid smile. 'Judgement Day is what it feels like,' he said wryly, 'and I suspect it will be a harsh one.'

Looking out over the bay, Ainsley's nerves made themselves known in the form of a fluttering stomach as she watched the little boat approaching. Until now, she had lost herself in the bustle of arrangements, the thrill of the journey. Her first time on a paddle steamer, her first time on the west coast and now her first time in a sailing boat was looming. Then would be her arrival at Strone Bridge with the man who was her husband. She worried at the plain gold band on her finger, inside her glove. She still couldn't quite believe it. It did not feel at all real. She was now Mrs Drummond, wife of the laird of Strone Bridge, this stranger by her side whose dawning black mood had quite thrown her.

Innes didn't want to be here, though he was now doing a good job of covering it up. There was a lot going on below the surface of that handsome countenance. Secrets? Or was it merely that he had left his past behind and didn't want to be faced with it again? She could understand that. It was one of the reasons she'd been happy to leave Edinburgh for a while. Perhaps it was resentment, which was more than understandable, for unlike her, the life Innes was leaving behind was one he loved.

As he hefted their luggage down to the edge of the shoreline, Ainsley watched, distracted by the fluidity of his movements, the long stride over the pebbles, the smooth strength in the way he lifted even the heaviest pieces so effortlessly. She recalled Felicity's joke about him being a wild Highlander, and wondered if he would wear a plaid when he was back at Strone Bridge. He had the legs for it. A prickle of heat low in her belly made her shiver.

'Feasgar math.' The bump of the boat against the tiny jetty made her jump.

Ainsley stared blankly at the man. 'Good day to you, Mrs Drummond,' he repeated in a softly lilting accent, at odds with the curt nod he gave her before starting to heave the luggage Innes was handing him into the boat.

'Oh, good day,' Ainsley replied.

'This is Eoin Ferguson,' Innes told her, 'an old friend of mine. Eoin, this is my wife.'

'I'm afraid I don't speak any Gaelic,' Ainsley said to the boatman.

'Have the Gaelic,' he said to her. 'We don't say speak it, we say have it.'

'And there's no need to worry, almost everyone on Strone Bridge *speaks* English,' Innes said, frowning at the man he claimed for a friend, though Ainsley could see no trace of warmth between the two men.

'I have never been to the Highlands,' she said with a bright smile.

'Strone Bridge is not far north of Glasgow as the crow flies,' Eoin replied. 'If you're expecting us all to be wandering around in plaid and waving claymores, you'll be disappointed. Are you getting in or not?'

'Oh, right. Yes.' She could feel herself flushing, mortified as if he had read her earlier thoughts. He made no move to help her. Seeing Innes's frown deepen, Ainsley gave him a slight shake of the head, clambering awkwardly and with too much show of leg into the boat. Eoin watched impassively, indicating that she sit on the narrow bench at the front of the dinghy, making a point of folding his arms as she then proceeded to clamber over the luggage stacked mid-ship.

She tried not to feel either slighted or crushed, reminding herself she was a stranger, a Sassenach, a lowlander, who spoke—no, *had*—no Gaelic and knew nothing of their ways. Innes, his mouth drawn into a tight line, had leaped into the boat, and was deftly untying the rope from the jetty as Eoin tended the sail. She watched the pair of them working silently together as they set out into the water, the contrast between the harmony of their movements stark against the undercurrent of tension that ran between them. It spiked as Innes made to take the tiller.

'The tide is against us, and I know the currents,' Eoin said, keeping his hand on the polished wood.

'I know them every bit as well as you.'

'You used to.' Eoin made no attempt to hide his enmity, but glared at Innes, his eyes, the same deep blue as Innes's own, bright with challenge. 'It's been a long time.'

Innes's fists clenched and unclenched. 'I know exactly how long it's been.'

A gust of wind took Eoin's words away. When Innes spoke again, it was in a soft, menacing tone that made the hairs on the back of Ainsley's neck stand on end. And it was in Gaelic. Eoin flinched and made to hand over the tiller, but Innes shook his head, joining Ainsley in the prow, turning away from her to stare out at the white wake, his face unreadable.

The wind that filled the sail blew in her face, whipping her hair from under her bonnet, making her eyes stream. Innes had not worn a hat today, a wise move, for it would surely have blown into the sea. Though he was, as ever, conservatively dressed, his trousers and coat dark blue, his linen pristine white; compared to Eoin's rough tweed trews and heavy fisherman's jumper, Innes looked like a dandy. She had watched the other man noticing this when he docked, but couldn't decide whether the twitch of his mouth was contempt or envy.

The boat scudded along, the keel bumping over the waves of the outgoing tide. While the paddle steamer had felt—and smelled—rather like a train that ran on water instead of rails, in this dinghy, Ainsley was acutely conscious that only a few planks of wood and some tar separated her from the icy-cold strait. Spray made her lips salty. The sail snapped noisily. She began to feel nauseous, and looking up, catching a cold smile on Eoin's face as the boat lifted out of the water and then slapped down again, began to suspect that he was making their voyage deliberately rough.

'You're from the city, I hear. You'll not be used to the sea,' he shouted.

Ainsley gripped the wooden seat with both hands, determined to hold on to the contents of her breakfast. She wished she hadn't had the eggs. She mustn't think about the eggs. 'How did you know that?' she asked.

'Himself told Mhairi McIntosh, the housekeeper, in the letter he sent.'

Innes snapped his head round. 'Well, it wouldn't have done me any good to write to you.'

Eoin, to Ainsley's surprise, turned a dull shade of red, and looked away. Innes swallowed whatever else he had been about to say and resumed his staring out at the sea. The undercurrent of emotion that ran between the two men was as strong as the ebb of the tide that was making their entrance into the bay a battle.

The pier was old and crumbling, extending far out into the bay. The low tide forced them to berth right at the very end of the structure, where Innes threw the rope neatly over a post to make fast. It was only as he put one foot on the first rung of the ladder that Eoin spoke, putting a hand on his shoulder, making him freeze.

'You'll find the place much changed.'

'If you tell me once again that it's been fourteen years...' he said through gritted teeth.

'It's not that.' Eoin pulled his hand away, a bleak look in his eyes. 'You know Mhairi's got the Home Farm ready for you? The big house—ach, you'll see for yourself soon enough. Give Angus a shout; I can see he's there with the cart. I'll see to the luggage.'

Innes ascended the worn ladder quickly, then turned to help Ainsley. She was eyeing the gap between boat and pier with a trepidation she was trying—and failing—to disguise. Her cheeks were bright with the wind, her hair a tangle. She looked endearing. She was most likely wondering what the hell she'd let herself in for, with the enmity between himself and Eoin almost palpable. He swore under his breath. Whatever was going on in Eoin's head, there would be time enough to sort it out. Right now, he needed to get poor Ainsley, who might well be his only ally, out of that boat before she fell out of it. 'Put one foot on the bottom rung and give me your hand,' he said, leaning down over the end of the pier.

She looked at the seaweed-slimed lower struts of the ladder pier dubiously. 'I can't swim.'

Innes went down on his knees and leaned over. 'I can. If you fall, I promise I'll dive in right behind you.'

'And walk up the beach with me in your arms, dripping seawater and seaweed.'

'Just like a mermaid.'

Ainsley chuckled. 'More like a sea monster. Not the grand entrance that the laird and his lady are expected to make. It's as well we've no audience.'

'I told Mhairi—that's the housekeeper—that we did not want a formal welcome until we were settled. I must admit, I'm surprised she listened, though,' Innes said, looking about him. Save for Angus, making his lumbering way down the pier, there was not a soul in sight. Perhaps he'd maligned his friend after all. Eoin knew how much he hated the pomp and ceremony of the old ways that his father had gone to such pains to preserve. He looked over Ainsley's shoulder to thank him, but Eoin was busying himself with the ropes.

Shrugging inwardly, Innes held out his hand to Ainsley, pulling her up without a hitch and catching her in his arms. 'Welcome to Strone Bridge.'

She smiled weakly, clutching tight to him, her legs trembling on the wooden planking. 'I'm sorry, I think my legs have turned to jelly.'

'You don't mean your heart? I'm not sure what you've let yourself in for here, but I am pretty certain things are in a bad way. I'll understand if you want to go back to Edinburgh.'

'Your people are expecting you to arrive with a wife. A fine impression it would make if she turned tail before she'd even stepped off the pier—or more accurately, judging by the state of it, stepped through it. Besides, we made a bargain, and I plan to stick to my part of it.' Ainsley tilted her head up at him, her eyes narrowed, though she was smiling. 'Are you having cold feet?'

'Not about you.' He hadn't meant it to sound the way it did, like the words of a lover, but it was too late to retract. He pulled her roughly against him, and he kissed her, forgetting all about his resolution to do no such thing. Her lips were freezing. She tasted of salt. The thump of luggage being tossed with no regard for its contents from the boat to the pier made them spring apart.

Ainsley flushed. 'It is a shame we don't have

more of an audience, for I feel sure that was quite convincing.'

Innes laughed. 'I won't pretend that had anything to do with acting the part of your husband. The truth is, you have a very kissable mouth, and I've been thinking about kissing you again since the first time all those weeks ago. And before you say it, it's got nothing to do with my needing an emotional safety valve either, and everything to do with the fact that I thoroughly enjoyed it, though I know perfectly well it's not part of our bargain.'

'Save that it can do no harm to put on a show, now and then,' Ainsley said with a teasing smile.

'Does that mean you'll only kiss me in public? I know there are men who like that sort of thing, but I confess I prefer to do my lovemaking in private.'

'Innes! I am sure we can persuade the people of Strone Bridge we are husband and wife without resorting to—to engaging in public marital relations.'

He gave a shout of laughter. 'Good grief, I hope not. That makes it sound like a meeting of foreign ministers.'

'It does? Really?' They began to make their way slowly to the head of the pier.

'Really,' Innes said.

'Oh. What is your opinion on *undergoing a husband's ministrations*?'

'That it sounds as if the husband is to carry out some sort of unsavoury medical procedure. You may as well talk about performing hymeneal duties, which is the sort of mealy-mouthed and utterly uninformative phrase I imagine any number of poor girls hear from their mothers on the eve of their wedding. They probably think they're going to be sacrificed on the matrimonial altar. Whatever they imagine, you can be damned sure they won't be looking forward to it.'

'Oh, I couldn't agree more. The belief that innocence and ignorance must go hand in hand seems to me quite perverse. I wonder sometimes if there is a conspiracy by society to keep young girls uninformed in order to encourage them into marriages they would not otherwise make.'

The sparkle had returned to her hazel eyes, but it was no longer teasing. Rather, Innes thought, studying her in some surprise, it was martial. 'Are you speaking from experience?'

'My mother died when I was twelve, and I had no other female relative close enough to divulge the pertinent facts before my wedding night. It was a—a shock.'

He was appalled, but she was bristling like a porcupine. 'Perhaps there should be some sort of guidebook. An introduction to married life; or something of that sort.'

He meant it as a joke, but Ainsley seemed much struck. 'That is an excellent idea.'

'Though if what you say about the conspiracy is true, then mothers will surely forbid their daughters from reading it.'

'More likely fathers would.'

Most definitely martial. Intrigued, he could not resist pushing her. 'Since the shops that would sell such a thing are the kind frequented by men and not women, then your plan is defeated by the outset,' Innes said.

'That shows how little you know,' Ainsley said with a superior smile. 'Shops are not the only outlet for such information.'

Above them the white clouds had given way to iron-grey. The wind was picking up as the tide turned, making white crests on the water, which was turning the same colour as the sky. While they'd been talking, the luggage had been loaded onto the cart, where Angus was now waiting patiently. Of Eoin there was no sign. Reluctantly, Innes abandoned this intriguing conversation. 'Whatever else has changed,' he said, 'the weather is still as reliably fickle as ever. Come on, let's get out of this wind before you catch a cold.'

* * *

Ainsley woke with a start and sat up, staring around her at the unfamiliar surroundings. The room was panelled and sparsely furnished. It had the look of a place hastily put together, and it felt as if the fires had not been lit for some time. Shivering as she threw back the covers and stepped onto the bare floorboards, she could feel the cold begin to seep into her bones.

Though it was July, it felt more like April. She made haste with her ablutions. Without the help of a maid, she laced her corsets loosely and tied her hair into a simple knot before pulling a woollen dress from her trunk. The colours, broad stripes of cream and turquoise, made her think of a summer sky that bore no resemblance to the one she could see through the window. The narrow sleeves were long, the tight-fitting bodice made doubly warm with the overlapping kerchief-style collar that came to a point at her waist. Woollen stockings and boots completed her *toilette* in record time. Reluctantly, she abandoned the idea of wrapping her cloak around her, telling herself that a lesson in hardiness was in order.

The corridor outside was dark and windowless. The fading daylight darkened by the deluge that had erupted as she arrived yesterday had prevented her from gaining any perspective of her new residence. Exhaustion had set in once she had eaten, and Ainsley had retired almost immediately afterwards.

Start the way you mean to go on. Muttering Madame Hera's own advice like a charm, she stumbled her way towards the door where she had dined last night, cheered by the faint smell of coffee. The room looked much more attractive in the daylight, and the fire, which last evening had smouldered, today was burning brightly. 'Good morning,' she said.

Innes was seated at the table, staring moodily at his empty plate, but he stood when she came into the room. His jaw looked raw. Most likely he'd shaved in water as cold as she'd used to wash. Perhaps he simply wasn't a morning person. Ainsley hovered at the door.

'Are you staying or going?' Innes asked, and she gave herself a little shake.

'Staying,' she said, seating herself opposite.

'I didn't know if you'd want tea or coffee, so I had Mhairi bring both.'

'Coffee, thank you.'

He sat down and poured her a cup. 'There's crowdie and oatcakes, but if you'd prefer a kipper, or some ham or porridge?'

'No, that will be fine—at least— What is crowdie?'

'Cheese.'

'Thank you.' She took the oatcakes and creamy cheese. 'This looks delicious.' Innes poured himself a cup of tea. 'Have you eaten?' she asked, cringing as she spoke, for she had already noticed his empty plate, and she sounded as if she was making polite conversation over the tinkling of teaspoons in an Edinburgh drawing room.

'Yes,' Innes said.

Ainsley bit into an oatcake. The crunch was embarrassingly loud. She took a sip of coffee. It sounded like a slurp. This was ridiculous. 'Innes, would you prefer...?'

'Ainsley, if you would prefer...?'

He stopped. She stopped. Then he laughed. 'I'm not used to having company at breakfast. I don't know whether you'd prefer to be left in peace, or— What?'

'I don't know. I'm not any more accustomed to it than you. It's silly, I know it's silly, but it feels strange.'

'Would you rather I went?'

'No. Unless you'd rather—' She broke off, laughing. 'For goodness' sake, I'd like you to stay, and I'd like to talk, but not if we're going to make polite chit-chat for the sake of it.'

Innes grinned. 'I am more than happy to promise never to make polite chit-chat, though I would like to know if your bedchamber was comfortable—and please, give me the real answer, and not the drawing-room one.'

Ainsley chuckled. 'One does not mention a lady's bedchamber in the drawing room.'

'Actually, that very much depends on the drawing room,' Innes said, smiling. 'Let me put it another way then—did you manage to sleep, or were you frozen to death?'

'I slept, but I confess I dressed very quickly.'

'I'm sorry about that. It seems that my father had the main part of the castle shut up and took to living in just two or three rooms. This place is sound and dry enough, but it's been empty awhile, and Mhairi had little notice of our arrival, as you know. She gave you that bedchamber because it was the best of a bad bunch.'

'She apologised for the fact it was several rooms away from your own,' Ainsley said, flushing. 'I got the impression she was worried the effort it would take to walk the distance would put you off. I confess, it did not do my ego much good to think my husband would be so easily deterred.'

'If I thought I would be welcomed into your bedchamber for a bout of debauchery, not even a chastity belt would deter me,' Innes said wickedly.

''Tis a shame I cannot lay my hands on such

an item, else I would be tempted to test your resolve.'

'Don't be too sure, there are all sorts of things in the armoury,' Innes replied. 'Debauchery and chastity belts—who'd have thought that conversation over the breakfast cups could be so interesting?'

'*I* did not introduce the topic of debauchery,' Ainsley said, spluttering coffee.

'No, but you did say you didn't want to make polite chit-chat.'

'Innes Drummond, you should have considered entering the legal profession, for you can twist an argument better than any lawyer I've dealt with—and believe me, I've dealt with a few.'

He gave a theatrical sigh. 'Very well, we will change the topic, though it is your own fault, you know.'

She eyed him warily. 'I am very sure I should not ask what you mean by that.'

'Then do not.'

Ainsley took a sip of coffee. Innes folded his mouth primly. She took another sip, trying not to laugh, then finally cast her cup down in the saucer with a clatter. 'Oh, for goodness' sake, you win. Tell me what you meant.'

'No, for it is not true, it's not debauchery I

think of when I look at that mouth of yours, it's kissing.'

'Just kissing.'

'Not *just* kissing.' Innes leaned forward over the table and took her hand. '*Kissing.* There's a difference.'

He was teasing. Or was it flirting? She wasn't sure. She didn't think she was the kind of woman that men flirted with. Did she amuse or arouse? Was it possible to combine the two? Ainsley had no idea, but she knew he was not laughing at her. There was complicity in the way he was looking at her, and something in those beguiling blue eyes of his that made her tingle. 'What difference?' she asked, knowing she ought not, sure that if she did not she would regret it.

Innes lifted her hand to his mouth, just barely brushing the back of it with his lips. 'That,' he said, 'was *just* a kiss.' He turned her hand over. '*This,*' he said softly, 'is the difference.'

His lips were warm on her palm. His tongue flicked over the pad of her thumb, giving her the most delicious little shiver. When he enveloped her thumb with his mouth and sucked, she inhaled sharply. 'You see,' he said, his voice husky. 'There is only one problem with those kinds of kisses.'

She knew exactly what he meant. She was experiencing that very problem. 'More?' Ainsley said, meaning it as an answer, though it sounded like a request.

'More,' Innes said, taking it as a request, pushing back his chair, leaning across the table, doing just as she asked.

He hadn't intended to kiss her, but he couldn't resist, and when she did not either, when she opened her mouth to him and twined her arms around his neck with the most delightful little sigh, his teasing kiss became something deeper. She kissed him back. The tip of her tongue touched his, triggering the rush of blood, the clenching of his muscles, the shiver of arousal. He slid his hand down to her breast under the shawl that formed part of her bodice, only to find himself frustrated by the bones of her corset, by the layers of clothes. A knife clattered to the ground, and they both jumped.

He was hard. He was very glad that the table lay between them. Ainsley's face was flushed, her lips soft, eyes dark with their kisses. The urge to pull her across the table and ravage that sinful mouth of hers was unbearably tempting. What the devil was wrong with him that he couldn't seem to keep his hands off her! Sitting carefully back down in his chair, Innes thought ruefully that it had been the same right from their first meeting. Why hadn't he realised it would be a problem? Was it a problem?

'Mhairi could have come into the room at any moment,' Ainsley said.

Innes ran his fingers through his hair. 'Is that why you kissed me?'

She picked up a teaspoon and began to trace a pattern on the table. 'Actually, you kissed me, though I cannot deny that I kissed you back,' she said, looking at him fleetingly from under her lashes. 'I don't know why, save that I wanted to, and I haven't wanted to for... And ever since I met you I have and—and so I did.'

'I can't tell you how relieved I am to hear that, because it's been exactly the same for me.' Innes swallowed a mouthful of cold coffee and grimaced. 'I never was one to toe the line, you know. Maybe it's because our bargain precludes it that I'm so tempted.'

'You mean you want to kiss me because it is illicit?'

'Oh, no, I want to kiss you because you have a mouth that makes me think of kissing. But perhaps it's so difficult not to because I know it's not permitted, even though we're married.' Innes shook his head and jumped to his feet. 'I don't know. Maybe we should check the armoury for a chastity belt.'

'Maybe we should stop worrying about it, and discussing it and analysing it,' Ainsley said. 'We are adults. We are neither of us interested in becoming attached. There is no harm in us having some—some fun.'

'Fun? You say that as if you are taking a dose of Mr Rush's patented pills for biliousness.'

'I am sure that they too are healthful.'

Innes burst out laughing. 'You say the strangest things. Healthful! It's the first time I've heard it referred to in that way.'

'You think it's an inaccurate term to use?'

She was frowning, looking genuinely puzzled, just as she had yesterday, now he thought about it, when she'd mentioned—what was it—marital relations? 'I think it's best if we think about something else entirely,' Innes said. 'Delightful as this breakfast has been, the day is getting away from us. First things first, we'll start with a tour of the castle. I warn you, it's a great barrack of a place and like to be as cold as an icehouse.'

Ainsley got to her feet. 'I'll go and fetch a shawl.'

The door closed behind her. Innes gazed out of the window, though the view was almost entirely obscured by an overgrown hedge. It looked as if it had not been cut for a good many years. Like everything he'd seen at Strone Bridge so far, from the jetty to the stables, it was neglected. Eoin had warned him that things had changed. He wondered, if the state of the house and grounds were anything to go by, what had happened to the lands. He was surprised, for though his father had been old-fashioned, archaic even in his practices, he had never been negligent. He was also angry, though guiltily aware he had little right to be so. These were Malcolm's lands. If Malcolm was here, he would be appalled at the state of them. Yet if Malcolm were here, Innes would not be. If Malcolm was here, he would not have allowed the place to fall into decline, and Innes…

He cursed. He could go round in circles for ever with that logic. He was not looking forward to this tour of the castle. It wasn't so much the state of disrepair he was now certain he'd find in the rooms, it was the history in those rooms, all *his* history. He didn't want anyone to see him coping—or not coping—with that history, and Ainsley was a very astute observer. It had been fourteen years. Surely that was long enough for him to at least put on a show of disaffection. Yet here he was, feeling distinctly edgy and wondering how to explain it away.

The castle was just a building. A heap of stones and wood of dubious aesthetic value. There was no ancient law that said he must live there if he chose to remain on Strone Bridge after a year, which was highly unlikely. No, he would have the Home Farm made more comfortable, because nothing would persuade him to play the laird in the castle, not even for a few weeks.

The vehemence of this thought took Innes so aback he did not notice Ainsley had returned until she spoke his name. 'Right,' Innes said, sounding appropriately businesslike. 'Let's get on with it.'

Chapter Four

The sun shone weakly from a pale blue sky dotted with puffy clouds, the kind a child would paint. Following in Innes's wake along the narrow path of damp paving slabs, Ainsley could see that the gloom inside the Home Farm's lower rooms was largely due to the height of the untended hedge. Emerging through an extremely overgrown arch, she came face-to-face with Strone Bridge Castle for the first time.

They were standing at the side of a long sweep of carriageway with what must have been a huge lawn on either side, though at present it was more like the remnants of a hayfield, part long yellowed grass falling over, part fresh green pushing through. The building loomed over them, such an imposing structure she could not imagine how she had missed its hulk yesterday, though the stone was indeed the grey colour the sky had been.

Ainsley walked backwards to gain some perspective. 'This is the rear of the house,' Innes said. 'The drive meets the main overland road, which cuts over to the other side of the peninsula and Loch Fyne, though to call it a road… It's far easier to travel by boat in this neck of the woods.'

'We did not come this way yesterday?'

He shook his head. 'The front of the house faces down to the shore. We came up that way. I'll show you, we'll go in by the main entrance, but I wanted you to see the scale of this damned monstrosity first.'

Strone Bridge Castle was indeed enormous, and though it was not precisely charming, Ainsley would not have called it a monstrosity. An imposing construction with a large tower at each corner, and another central turret projecting from the middle of the main building, it was like a castle from a Gothic novel. The sturdy turrets had unexpected ogee roofs, adding a hint of the east into the architectural mix, each roof topped with tall spires and embellished with slit windows. The turrets looked, with their rugged masonry walls and stolid, defensive air, quite at odds with the central part of the building, which was considerably more elegant, mostly Jacobean in style, with four storeys of tall French-style windows, a low Palladian roof ornamented with a stone balustrade and a huge portico that looked as if it had been added on as an afterthought. The overall effect was certainly not of beauty, but it was striking.

'It looks,' Ainsley said, studying it with be-musement, 'as if someone has jumbled up three or four different houses, or taken samples from a book of architectural styles through the ages.'

'You're not far off,' Innes said. 'The main house was built about 1700. The roof and that central tower were added about fifty or sixty years after that, and my own father put those corner towers up. There's no rhyme nor reason to it. As I said, it's a monstrosity.'

'That's not what I meant at all. It is like nothing I have ever seen.'

'One of a kind. That, thank heavens, is certainly true,' Innes said grimly.

'You are not fond of it, then?' Ainsley asked. 'Though there must be some interesting stories attached to a building so old. And perhaps even a few ghosts.'

He had taken her arm as they made their way over the untended lawn around the building, and now slanted her a curious look. 'Do you believe in such things?'

'Honestly, I've never considered the question before, but looking at this place, I could easily be persuaded.'

'There is a tale of one of the lairds who went off to fight in the 1715 Jacobite uprising. He was for the Old Pretender. There's a set of gates, right at the end of the carriageway, which he had locked, so they say, and made his wife promise never to unlock them until his return.'

'What happened?'

'He died in the Battle of Sheriffmuir. His wife had the gates unlocked for his corpse to pass through in its coffin, but—' Innes broke off, shaking his head. 'No, there's enough here already to give you nightmares without adding a walking, wailing, clanking ghost to the mix.'

Ainsley stopped in her tracks, looking up at him in horror. 'Walking and wailing and clanking?'

He bent down to whisper in her ear. 'He rattles the chain that should have been kept around the gates. He walks just over there, on the carriageway. He wails for the treachery of his lady wife, who married his enemy less than a year after he was slain.'

She shuddered, looked over to where he was pointing, then looked back at him. 'Have you actually seen him?' Innes made a noncommittal noise. Ainsley narrowed her eyes suspiciously. 'Has anyone ever seen him?'

'None who have lived to tell the tale,' he answered sorrowfully.

She punched him on the arm. 'Then how can the tale be told! You made that up.'

He laughed, rubbing his arm. 'Not all of it. The first part was true. The laird at the time did fight, he did die at Sheriffmuir and he did have the gates locked.'

'Are there any real ghosts?'

His laughter faded as he took her arm and urged her on. 'Plenty, believe me, though none that you will see, I hope.'

His expression was one she recognised. *Don't ask.* Not because she wouldn't like the answers, but because *he* would not. This was his home, this place that he was mocking and deriding, this place that he called a monstrosity. She wondered, then, if he really meant the bricks and mortar. Yesterday it was obvious that Innes had not wanted to come back to Strone Bridge. It was equally obvious from this morning that he'd not expected the place to be in such a state of disrepair, but now she wondered what else there was to disturb him here. What was at the heart of the quarrel that had so completely estranged him from his father?

How little of Innes she knew. His formative
years had been spent here, yet he had left all of
it behind without, it seemed, a backward glance,
to make a new and very different life for himself. Why? It was all very well to tell herself it
was none of her business, but—no, there was
no *but*. It was absolutely none of her business,
Ainsley told herself rather unconvincingly. Yet
it was strange, and very distractingly intriguing,
like the man himself.

'You were a million miles away. I was only
teasing you about the ghosts. I didn't mean to
give you the jitters,' Innes said, cutting in on
her thoughts.

'You didn't.' Ainsley looked around her with
slight surprise. They had reached the front of
the house, and the prospect was stunning, for it
sat on a hill directly above the bay where they
had landed yesterday. 'My goodness, this is absolutely beautiful.'

'That's the Kyles of Bute over there, the
stretch of water with all the small islands that
you sailed yesterday,' Innes said. 'And over
there, the crescent of sand you can see, that's
Ettrick Bay on Bute, the other side of the island
from which we set sail. And that bigger island
you can just see in the distance, that's Arran.'

'I don't think I've ever seen such a wonderful

prospect. It is exactly the sort of view that one conjures up, all misty-eyed, when one thinks of the Highlands. Like something from one of Mr Walter Scott's novels.'

'Aye, well, strictly speaking Eoin was right in what he said yesterday, though. We're only a wee bit farther north than Glasgow here, and Arran is south.'

'As the crow flies,' Ainsley said. 'It doesn't matter, it feels like another world, and it really is quite spectacular. There must be a magnificent view from the castle.' She looked back at the house, where a set of long French-style windows opened out on the first floor to what must have once been a beautiful terrace at the top of a flight of stairs.

'That's the drawing room,' Innes said, following her gaze.

'How lovely to take tea there on a summer's day. I can just imagine the ladies of old with their hoops and their wigs,' she said dreamily.

'The hoops and wigs are like as not still packed away up in the attics somewhere. My family never throws anything away. Do you really like this place?'

'It's entrancing. Do you really *not* like it?'

Innes shrugged. 'I can see it's a lovely view. I'd forgotten.'

Without waiting on her, he turned on his heel and began to walk quickly up the slope towards the central staircase. 'Like someone determined to swallow their medicine as quickly as they can and get it over with,' Ainsley muttered, stalking after him.

'What was that?'

'This may be a monstrosity to you, Innes, but to someone accustomed to a terraced house in Edinburgh, it's magical.'

Innes stopped abruptly. 'Ach, I'm like a beast with a sore head. I'm sorry. It's not your fault.'

No, it was most definitely this place. Curious as she was, and with a hundred questions to boot, Ainsley had no desire to see him suffer. 'We could leave it for today. Or I could look around myself.'

'No,' Innes said firmly, 'it has to be done.' He took her hand, forcing a smile. 'Besides, you came here thinking you'd be lady of the manor— you've a right to see over your domain. I'm only sorry that it's bound to be a disappointment.'

'I did not come here with any such expectations. Aside from the fact that I know absolutely nothing about the management of a place this size, I am perfectly well aware that your people will regard a destitute Edinburgh widow without a hint of anything close to blue in her blood as nothing more than an upstart.'

Innes gave a startled laugh. 'You're not seriously worried that people here will look down their noses at you, Ainsley?'

'A little,' she confessed, embarrassed. 'I hadn't really thought about it until I arrived here yesterday. Then your boatman...'

'Ach! Blasted Eoin. Listen to me. First, if there's an upstart here, then it's me. Second, for better or worse, I'll be the laird while I'm here, and while you're here, I will not tolerate anyone looking down their noses at you. Third, the state of your finances are nobody's business but our own.' He pulled her closer, pushing a strand of her hair out of her eyes. 'Finally, though I have no intention of playing the laird and therefore there's no need for you to play lady of the manor, if I did, and you did, then I think you'd play it very well. And on the off chance you couldn't quite follow me,' he added, 'that was me saying you've not a thing to worry about.'

She felt a stupid desire to cry. 'Thank you, I will try not to let you down.'

'Wheesht, now,' he said, kissing her cheek. 'You'll do your best, and that's all I ask. Anyway, it's not as if *you* are stepping into a dead person's shoes. My mother died when I was eight years old.'

'And your father never remarried?'

Innes gave a crack of laughter. 'What for, he'd already produced an heir and a spare.'

'What about your brother. Did he…?'

'No.'

Another of those 'do not dare ask' faces accompanied this stark denial. And Innes would not be married either, were it not for the terms of the old laird's will. Were the Drummond men all misogynists? Or perhaps there was some sort of dreadful hereditary disease? But Innes seemed perfectly healthy. A curse, then? Now she was being utterly fanciful. It was this place. Ainsley gave herself a little shake. 'Well, then, let us go and inspect this castle of yours, and see what needs to be done to make it habitable.'

Everything inside Strone Bridge Castle was done on a grand scale. The formal salons opened out one after the other around the central courtyard with the Great Hall forming the centrepiece, heavy with geometric panelling, topped with rich fretwork ceilings like icing on a cake, or one of those elaborate sugar constructions that decorates the table at a banquet. Massive fireplaces and overmantels rose to merge the two, and everywhere, it seemed to Ainsley, every opportunity had been taken to incorporate heraldic devices and crests. Dragons and lions poked and pawed from pilasters, banisters and pediments. Shields and swords augmented the cornicing, were carved into the marble fireplaces and fanned out above the windows. It was beautiful, in an oppressive and overwhelming way.

The turrets that marked each corner were dank places with treacherous-looking staircases winding their way steeply up, and which Ainsley decided she did not need to climb. 'They serve no real purpose,' Innes told her. 'A whim of my father's, nothing more.'

After two hours and only a fraction of the hundred and thirty rooms, she had seen enough for one day. Back in the courtyard, she gazed up at the central tower, which was square and not round, and faced directly out over the Kyles of Bute. Bigger than the others, it seemed to contain proper rooms, judging from the wide windows that took up most of the sea-facing wall on each of the four stories. Ainsley wrestled with the heavy latch, but it would not budge.

'It's locked.' Innes made no attempt to help her. 'Has been for years. Most likely the key is long gone, for it's not on here,' he said, waving the heavy bunch of keys he carried.

Ainsley frowned at the lock, which seemed surprisingly new, and showed no sign of rust, wondering how Innes would know such a thing when he himself had not been here for years. 'The view from up there must be spectacular,' she said, looking back up at the battlements.

Innes had already turned away. 'We'll take a look at the kitchens.'

'There must be a door from inside the castle,' Ainsley said, frowning at the tower in frustration, trying to recall the exact layout of rooms that lay behind it. 'Is that the dining room? I don't recall a door, but…'

'The door isn't in the dining room.' Innes was holding open another door. 'Do you want to see the kitchens? I was hoping to get out to some of the farms this afternoon.'

He sounded impatient. Though this was all new to her, for him it was different. 'I can come back myself another time,' Ainsley said, joining him.

'I don't want you going up there,' Innes said sharply. 'It's not safe.'

She cast a dubious look at the tower, thinking that it looked, like the rest of the castle, neglected though sound, but Innes was already heading down the narrow corridor, so she picked up her skirts and walked quickly after him.

A few moments later she forgot all about the locked tower, gazing in astonishment at the table that ran almost the full length of the servants' hall. It looked as if it would sit at least fifty. 'Good grief, how many staff does it take to keep this place running?'

Innes shook his head. 'I've no idea. Even in my youth, most of the rooms were closed up, save for formal occasions, and there were few of those. My father was not the most sociable of men.'

They exited the servants' hall and entered the main kitchen, which had two bread ovens, a row of charcoal braziers, a stove the size of a hay cart and the biggest fireplace Ainsley had ever seen. Out through another door, they wended their way through the warren of the basement, past linen rooms and still rooms, pantries and empty wine cellars, and then back up a steep flight of stairs to another door that took them out to the kitchen gardens.

Innes turned the lock and turned his back on the castle. 'As you can see, the place is uninhabitable,' he said.

He sounded relieved. She couldn't understand his reaction to it. 'Is the building itself in such a poor state of repair, is it the cost of restoring it you're worried about?'

'It's sound enough, I reckon. There's no smell of damp and no sign that the roof is anything but watertight, though I'd need to get one of my surveyors to take a look. But what would be the point?'

'I have no idea, but—you would surely not wish to let it simply fall into ruin?'

'I could knock it down and get it over with.' Innes tucked the weight of keys into his coat pocket with a despondent shrug. 'I don't know,' he said heavily, 'and I think I've more pressing matters to consider, to be honest. Maybe it was a mistake to start with the castle. For now, I think it would be best if you concentrated on the immediate issue of making the Home Farm a bit more comfortable. Speak to Mhairi, she'll help you. I'll need to spend some time out on the lands.'

Ainsley watched him walk away, feeling slightly put out. He was right, their living quarters left a lot to be desired, and it made sense for her to sort them out. 'Whatever that means,' she muttered. The idea of consulting the rather forbidding Mhairi McIntosh did not appeal to her. Madame Hera had suggested that Timid Mouse appeal to her housekeeper's softer side. Ainsley was not so sure that Mhairi McIntosh had one.

Besides, that wasn't the point. She had not come here to set up Innes's home for him, but to provide him with objective advice. How was she to do that if she was hanging curtains and making up beds while he was out inspecting his lands? Excluding her, in other words, and she had not protested. 'Same old Ainsley,' she said to herself in disgust. 'You should be ashamed of yourself!'

Dear Madame Hera,

My husband's mother gave me a household manual on my wedding day that she wrote herself. It is extremely comprehensive, and at first I was pleased to know the foods my husband prefers, and how he likes them served. However, I must say that right from the start I was a bit worried when I read what his mother calls 'The Order of the Day'—and there is one for every day. I do try to follow it, but I confess I see no reason why I must do the washing on a Wednesday and polish the silver on a Saturday, any more than I see why we have to have shin of beef every single Tuesday, and kippers only on a Thursday. And as to her recipe for sheep's-head soup—I will not!

I tried to tell my husband that his mother's way is not the only way. I have many excellent recipes from my own mother that I am sure he would enjoy. I tried, with all my wifely wiles, to persuade him that I could run the household without following his mother's manual to the letter. He spurned my wifely wiles, Madame, and now he is threatening to have his mother, who has a perfectly good house of her own, to come and live with us. I love my husband, but I do not love his mother. What should I do?

Desperate Wife

Ainsley pulled a fresh sheet of paper on to the blotting pad. It was tempting to suggest that Desperate Wife invite her own mother to stay, and even more tempting to suggest that she simply swap abodes herself with her husband's mother, but she doubted Felicity would print either solution. Instead, she would advise Desperate Wife to put her foot down, throw away the manual and claim the hearth and home as her own domain. It was Madame Hera's standard response to this sort of letter, of which she received a great many. Mothers-in-law, if the readers of the *Scottish Ladies Companion* were to be believed, were an interfering lot, and their sons seemed to be singularly lacking in gumption.

Claiming this hearth and home as her own had turned out to be relatively easy. Yet looking around the room, which in the past ten days, like the rest of the Home Farm, had been made both warm and comfortable, Ainsley felt little satisfaction. Mhairi McIntosh had proved cooperative but reserved. She had not looked down her nose at Ainsley, nor had she mocked or derided a single one of her suggestions, which had made the task Innes had given her relatively easy, but it was not the challenge she had been looking forward to. She had, in essence, been relegated to the domestic sphere when he had promised her a different role.

Irked with herself, Ainsley tucked Madame Hera's correspondence into her leather folder and pushed it to one side of the desk, covering it with the latest copy of the *Scottish Ladies Companion*, which Felicity had sent to her. There could be no doubt that Innes needed help, but he had made no attempt to ask her for it. Though she rationalised that he most likely thought he'd fare better with his tenants alone, as the days passed, she felt more excluded and more uncomfortable with trying to address this fact. She was not unhappy, she was not regretting her decision to come here, but she felt overlooked and rather useless.

Standing on her tiptoes at the window, she could see the sky was an inviting bright blue above the monstrous hedge. Ainsley made her way outside, making for her favourite view out over the Kyles of Bute. Tiny puffs of clouds scudded overhead, like the steam from a train or a paddle steamer. It was a shame that the dilapidated jetty down in the bay was not big enough to allow a steamer to dock, for it would make it a great deal easier to get supplies.

She had to speak to Innes. She had a perfect right to demand that he allow her to do the task he had brought her here for. The fact that he was obviously floundering made it even more important. Yes, it also made him distant and unapproachable, but that was even more reason for her to tackle him. Besides, she couldn't in all conscience remain here without actually doing what she'd already been paid to do. She owed it to herself to speak to him. She had no option but to speak to him.

Mentally rehearsing various ways of introducing the subject, Ainsley wandered through the castle's neglected grounds, finding a path she had not taken before, which wended its way above the coastline before heading inwards to a small copse of trees. The chapel was built of the same grey granite as the castle, but it was warmed by the red sandstone that formed the arched windows, four on each side, and the heavy, worn door. It was a delightful church, simple and functional, with a small belfry on each gable end, a stark contrast to the castle it served.

The door was not locked. Inside, it was equally simple and charming, with wooden pews, the ones nearest the altar covered, the altar itself pink marble, a matching font beside it. It was clean swept. The tall candles were only half-burned. Sunlight, filtered through the leaves of the sheltering trees and the thick panes of glass in the arched windows, had warmed the air. Various Drummonds and their families were commemorated in plaques of brass and polished stone set into the walls. Presumably their bones were interred in the crypt under the altar, but Ainsley could find none more recent than nearly a hundred years ago.

Outside, she discovered the graveyard on the far side of the church. Servants, tenants, fishermen, infants. Some of the stones were so worn she could not read the inscription. The most re-

cent of the lairds were segregated from the r...
of the graveyard's inhabitants by a low iron rai...
ing.

Ainsley read the short list on the large Celtic
cross.

Marjorie Mary Caldwell
1787-1813, spouse of
Malcolm Fraser Drummond

This must be Innes's mother. Below her, the
last name, the lettering much brighter, his father:

Malcolm Fraser Drummond
Laird of Strone Bridge
1782-1840

The laird had married early. His wife must
have been very young when she had Innes. Ainsley frowned, trying to work out the dates. Seventeen or eighteen? Even younger when she had
her first son. Her frown deepened as she read
the lettering on the cross again. Above Marjorie was the previous laird. Nothing between her
and Innes's father. Innes's brother was not here,
and she was certain he was not mentioned in the
church. Perhaps he was buried elsewhere? What
had Innes said? His brother's death had been the

...ger for the split between Innes and his father,
...ne remembered that.

She could ask him. Taking a seat on the stone
bench by the main door, Ainsley knew she would
not risk antagonising him. She began to pick
at the thick rolls of moss, which were growing on the curved arm of the seat. Theirs was
a marriage of convenience. Her role as Innes's
wife was a public one—to appear on his arm at
church on Sunday—and not a private one. She
had no right to probe into his past, and she would
not like it if he questioned her on hers.

Which did not alter the fact that he was preventing her from helping, and he quite patently
needed help. She was bored, and she felt not only
useless but rather like an outcast. What would
Madame Hera say?

Wandering back along the path, with the sky,
not surprisingly, now an ominous grey, Ainsley
was thankful that Madame Hera had never been
consulted on such a complex problem. There
were a score of letters Madame Hera still had
to answer, including the one to Desperate Wife.
Was there an argument to defend the mother-in-
law's precious household manual? Perhaps there
were traditions, comforting customs, that Desperate Wife's husband valued or enjoyed, which
he feared would be lost if the manual were ig-

nored? Perhaps these very traditions were helping the husband adjust to his new life. Madame Hera rarely concerned herself with the men at the root of her correspondents' problems, but it must be supposed that some of them had feelings, too. Perhaps Desperate Wife might have better success with what she called her wifely wiles if she put them to a more positive use, to discover what parts of the dratted manual actually mattered to him? Though of course, there was always a chance it was simply the case that he simply did like to have kippers on a Thursday.

'I am glad one of us has something to smile about.' Innes was approaching the front door from the direction of the stables. His leather riding breeches and his long boots were spattered with mud, as were the skirts of his black coat. He had not worn a hat since he'd arrived at Strone Bridge, and his hair was windswept. 'What is so amusing, assuming it's not my appearance?' he asked, waiting for her on the path.

'Kippers,' Ainsley replied, smiling. He looked tired. There were shadows under his eyes. She had missed him at breakfast these past few days. 'You do look a bit as if you've been dragged through a hedge backwards. A very muddy hedge,' Ainsley said. 'I'll speak to Mhairi when we get in, I'll have her heat the water so you can have a bath. The chimney has been swept, so it shouldn't take long.'

Innes followed her down the hallway to the sitting room that doubled as their study. 'Thank you, that sounds good. Where have you been?'

'I came across the chapel. I saw your father's grave.'

He was sifting through the pile of mail that Mhairi had left on the desk and did not look up. 'Right.'

She wondered, surprised that it had not occurred to her until now, whether Innes himself had seen it. If so, he had made no mention of it. Another thing he would not talk about. 'I'll go and speak to Mhairi,' Ainsley said, irritated, knowing she had no right to be, and even more irritated by that fact.

When she returned, bearing a tea tray, Innes was sitting at the desk reading a letter, but he put it down as she entered and took the tray from her. 'I think half the population of Strone Bridge must now be in Canada or America,' he said. 'We've more empty farms than tenanted ones.'

She handed him a cup of tea. 'Why is it, do you think?'

'High rents. Poor maintenance—or more accurately, no maintenance. Better prospects else-where.' Innes sighed heavily.

'I know nothing about such matters, but even I can see from the weeds growing that some of the fields have not been tilled for years,' Ainsley said carefully. 'Is the land too poor?'

'It's sure as hell in bad heart now,' Innes said wretchedly, 'though whether that's through ne-glect or lack of innovation, new methods, what-ever they might be. There are cotter families who have lived in the tied cottages for decades who have moved on. I'm sick of hearing the words, "I mentioned it to the laird but nothing happened". My father's factor apparently left Strone Bridge not long after I did, and he did not employ an-other, though no one will tell me why. In fact, no one will tell me anything. They treat me like a stranger.'

'What about Eoin?' Ainsley asked tentatively.

'What about him?'

'You said he was your friend. Couldn't you talk to him?'

'Eoin is as bad as the rest. It doesn't matter, it's not your problem.'

Innes picked up another letter. As far as he was concerned, the conversation was over. *It's not your problem.* Ainsley sat perfectly still. The words were a horrible echo from the past. How many times had she been rebuffed by John with exactly that phrase, until she stopped asking any questions at all?

'Don't say that.'

Her tone made Innes look up in surprise. 'Don't say what?'

Ainsley stared down at her tea. 'It is my problem. At least it's supposed to be. It's what you brought me here for, to help you.'

'This place is beyond help. I can see that for myself.'

'So that's it? You've already decided—what? To sell? To walk away and let it continue to crumble? What?'

'I don't know.'

'So you haven't decided, but you're not going to ask me because my opinion counts for nothing.'

'No! Ainsley, what the devil is the matter with you?'

'What is the matter?' She jumped to her feet, unable to keep still. 'You brought me here to *help*! You have paid me a considerable sum of money, a sum I would not have dreamed of accepting if I thought all I was to do was sit about here and—and fluff cushions.'

'You've done a great deal more than that. I'm sorry if I have seemed unappreciative, but—'

'I have done nothing more than Mhairi McIntosh could have done. Oh, granted, I married you, and in doing so allowed you to claim this place, which seems to me to have been a completely pointless exercise, if all you're going to do is say that it's past help, and walk away.'

'I didn't say I was going to do that. Stop haranguing me like a fishwife.'

'Stop treating me like a child! I have a brain. I have opinions. I know I'm a Sassenach and a commoner to boot, but I'm not a parasite. I may know nothing about farming, but neither do you! Only you're so blooming well ashamed of the fact, though you've no reason to be, because why should you know anything about it when you told me yourself your father did not allow you to know anything, and—and...'

'Ainsley!' Innes wrested the teaspoon she was still clutching from her clenched hand and set it down on the tea tray. 'What on earth has come over you? You're shaking.'

'I'm not,' she said, doing just that. 'Now you've made me lose track of what I was saying.'

'You were saying that I'm an ignoramus not fit to own the lands.'

'No, that's what you think.' She sniffed loudly. 'If I could have got by without asking Mhairi for advice on this house, I would have, but I couldn't, Innes.'

'Why should you, you know nothing of the place.'

'Exactly.' She sniffed again, and drew him a meaningful look. Innes handed her a neatly folded handkerchief. 'I'm not crying,' Ainsley said.

'No.'

She blew her nose. 'I've never known a wetter July. I've likely got a cold.'

'It wouldn't surprise me.'

'I hate women who resort to tears to get their way.'

'I'm not sure it ever works. From what I've seen, what usually happens is that she cries, he runs away, and whatever it was gets swept under the carpet until the next time,' Innes said wryly.

'You know, for a man who has never been married before, you have an uncanny insight into the workings of matrimony.'

'I take it I've struck a chord?'

It was gently said, but she couldn't help prickling. 'Sometimes tears are not a weapon, but merely an expression of emotion,' Ainsley said, handing him his kerchief. 'Such as anger.'

'Stop glowering at me, and stop assuming that

all men are tarred with the same brush as the man you married.'

The gentleness had gone from his voice. Ainsley sat, or rather slumped, feeling suddenly deflated. 'I don't.'

'You do, and I'm not like him.'

'I know. I wouldn't be here if I thought you were. But you are shutting me out, Innes, and it's making me feel as if I'm here under false pretences. If you won't talk to me, why not talk to Eoin? There's nothing shameful in asking for help.'

Her tea was cold, but she drank it anyway. The silence was uncomfortable, but she could think of no way of breaking it. She finished her tea.

'I'm not used to consulting anyone,' Innes said. 'You knew that.'

'But it was your idea to have me come along here. An objective eye.'

'I didn't realise things would be so bad. As I said, it's obvious that it's too late.'

'So you're giving up?'

'No! I'm saving you the effort of getting involved in something that is next to useless.'

'Giving up, in other words,' Ainsley said.

His face was quite white. The handle of his

teacup snapped. He stared at it, then put it carefully down. 'I don't give up,' he said.

She bit her tongue.

'I'm not accustomed to— It's been difficult. Seeing it. Not having answers. That's been hard.'

Ainsley nodded.

'They are all judging me.'

She sighed in exasperation. 'Innes, you've been gone a long time. They don't know you.'

'I don't see how you can help.'

'I won't know if I can, if you don't talk to me.' Ainsley tried a tentative smile. 'At the very least, I would be on your side.'

'Aye, that would be something more than I have right now.' Innes smiled back. 'I'll think about it.'

'Please do. I have plenty of time on my hands.'

He tucked a strand of hair behind her ear, looking at her ruefully. 'You might want to use some of it to partition this place off into his and her domains. I'm like a bear with a sore head these days, though contrary to what you might think, I quite like having you around. And that's your cue, in case you missed it, to tell me you feel the same.'

Ainsley laughed. 'Would I have suggested helping you if I had wanted to avoid you?'

'True.'

'Perhaps you should consider having some sort of welcoming party.'

'Even though I'm not welcome.' He shook his head. 'No, I'm sorry, don't bite my head off.'

Ainsley frowned, thinking back to the letter she had been reading that morning from Desperate Wife. 'Sometimes traditions can be a comfort. Sometimes they can even help heal wounds,' she said, making a mental note to include that phrase in Madame Hera's reply.

'Sometimes you sound like one of those self-help manuals, do you know that?'

'Do I?'

'"Engaging in marital relations,"' he quoted, smiling. '"Undergoing a husband's ministrations." No, don't get on your high horse, it's endearing.'

'It is?'

'It is. What were you suggesting?'

'Didn't you say that there ought to have been a ceremony when we arrived?' There was a smut of mud on his cheek. She reached up to brush it away.

'A ceremony. I'm not very keen on ceremonies.' Innes caught her hand between his and pressed a kiss on to her knuckles.

Was it just a kiss, or a *kiss*? It felt like more than just a kiss, for it made her heart do a silly little flip. But his mouth did not linger, and surely knuckles could not be—what was the word, *stimulating*? She wanted to ask him, but that would give too much away, and he might not have been at all stimulated. 'A celebration, then,' Ainsley said. 'Lots of food and drink. Something to mark the changes. You know, out with the old and in with the new.'

'Mmm.' He kissed her hand again. 'I like that,' he said, smiling at her.

'Do you?' She had no idea whether he meant her idea or the kiss.

'Mmm,' he said, pulling her towards him and wrapping his arms around her. 'I like that very much,' he said. And then he kissed her on the mouth.

It was definitely not *just* a kiss. He tasted of spring. Of outdoors. A little of sweat. And of something she could not name. Something sinful. Something that made her heat and tense and clench, and made her dig her fingers into the shoulders of his coat and tilt her body against his. And that made him groan, a guttural noise that seemed to vibrate inside her.

One hand roamed up her back, his fingers delving into her hair, the other roamed down to cup her bottom and pull her closer. She could feel the hard ridge of his arousal through his trousers, through her skirts. She touched her tongue to his and felt his shudder, and shuddered with him, pressing her thighs against his, wanting more, wanting to rid herself of the layers of cloth between them, wanting his flesh, and then thinking about her flesh, exposed, thinking about him looking at her. Or looking at her and then turning his head away. Then not wanting to look at her. Like John. And then...

'Ainsley?'

'Your bath,' she said, clutching at the first thing she could think of. 'Your bath will be ready.'

'Is something wrong?'

'No,' she said, managing a smile, forcing herself to meet his concerned gaze, hating herself for being the cause of that concern, frustrated at having started something she had not the nerve to finish, frustrated at how much she wished she could. 'No, I just don't want the water to get cold.'

'The state I'm in, I think cold is what I need. What happened? Did I do something wrong?'

She flushed. Men were not supposed to ask such questions. Men hated discussing anything intimate. She knew that it was not just John who had been like that, because Madame Hera's correspondence was full of women saying that their husbands were exactly the same. Why did Innes have to be different!

'Nothing. I changed my mind,' Ainsley said, mortified, not only for the lie, but for knowing she was relying on Innes being the kind of man who would always allow a woman to do so. And she was right.

'A lady's prerogative,' he said, making an ironic little bow. 'I'll see you at dinner.'

Chapter Five

'Come and sit by the fire.' Innes handed Ainsley a glass of sherry.

'I thought it was warm enough to wear this without shivering,' she answered him with a constrained smile, 'but now I'm not so sure.'

Her dress was cream patterned with dark blue, with a belt the same colour around her waist. Though it was long-sleeved, the little frill around the *décolleté* revealed her shoulders, the hollows at her collarbone, the most tantalising hint of the smooth slope of her breasts. She sat opposite him and began to twirl her glass about in her hand, a habit she had, Innes had noticed, when she was trying to work up to saying something uncomfortable.

Her face had that pinched look that leached the life from it. Earlier, he'd suspected that she had pulled away from him because of her memories connected to McBrayne. Lying in the cooling bath water in front of the feeble fire in his bedchamber, Innes had begun to wonder what, exactly, the man had done to her. It was more than the debts, or even the fact that they were incurred without her knowing. He couldn't understand how she could be kissing him with abandon one minute and then turning to ice the next, and he was fairly certain it wasn't anything he'd done—or not done. When she forgot herself, she was a different person from the one opposite him now, twisting away nervously at her glass and slanting him timid looks.

Innes threw another log on the fire. 'I think I've solved one problem, at least,' he said, picking up the magazine that he'd been flicking through while he waited on her. 'This thing, the *Scottish Ladies Companion*. There's a woman who doles out spurious advice to females in here, and she uses that very same phrase of yours.' He opened the periodical and ruffled through the pages. 'Aye, here it is. "Make a point of extinguishing the light before engaging in marital relations"—you see, your very phrase—"and your husband will likely not notice your having so unwittingly misled him. Better still, retain your modesty and your nightgown, and your little deceit will never have to be explained." This

Madame Hera is either a virgin or a fool,' he said scathingly.

'What do you mean?'

'The lass has been stuffing her corsets with— What was it?'

'Stockings.'

'I see you have read it, then.' Innes shook his head.

'It was her mother's idea.'

'And a damned stupid one. Pitch dark or broad daylight, you can be certain the husband will know the difference. And as for the idea of keeping her nightgown on...'

'For modesty's sake. I am sure many women do.'

'Really? I've never come across a single one.'

'I doubt very much that the women you have— experienced—are—are— I mean— You know what I mean.'

'The women I've *experienced*, as you put it, have certainly not been married to another man at the time, but nor have they been harlots, if that is what you're implying.' She was blushing. She was unduly flustered, considering she was neither a virgin herself, nor as strait-laced as she now sounded. 'I'm finding you a puzzle,' Innes said, 'for the day I met you, I recall you were threatening to join the harlots on the Cowgate.'

'You know very well I was joking.' Ainsley set her glass of sherry down. 'Do you really think Madame Hera's advice misguided?'

'Does it matter?'

She bit her lip, then nodded.

Innes picked up the magazine and read the letter again. 'This woman, she's not exactly lied to the man she's betrothed to, but she's misled him, and it seems to me that Madame Hera is encouraging her to continue to mislead him. It's that I don't like. The lass is likely nervous enough about the wedding night without having to worry about subterfuge. Hardly a frame of mind conducive to her enjoying what you would call her husband's ministrations.'

'What would you call it?'

Innes grinned. 'Something that doesn't sound as if the pleasure is entirely one-sided. There's a dictionary worth of terms depending on what takes your fancy, but lovemaking will do.'

'You might think that innocuous enough, but I assure you, the *Scottish Ladies Companion* will not publish it,' Ainsley said.

'You are a subscriber to this magazine, then?'

She shrugged. 'But—this woman, Innes. Don't you think her husband will be angry if he discovers her deception? And anger is no more conducive to—to lovemaking than fraud.'

'In the grand scheme of things, I doubt it. Chances are he's not any more experienced than she, and like to be just as nervous. I'd say he's going to be more concerned about his own performance than anything else, something your Madame Hera doesn't seem to take any account of.'

'It is a column of advice for women.'

'And most of the letters in this issue seem to be about men. Anyway, Madame Hera is completely missing the main point.'

'Which is?'

'The lass thinks she's not well enough endowed, and Madame Hera is by implication agreeing by telling her to cover up. If she goes to her wedding night ashamed, thinking she's not got enough to offer, you can be sure that soon enough her husband will think the same.'

'So it's her fault?' Ainsley said.

'Don't be daft. If anyone's at fault it's that blasted Madame Hera—and the mother.' Innes threw the magazine down on the table. 'I don't know why we're wasting our time with this nonsense.'

Ainsley picked the magazine up, her face set. 'Because I wrote it,' she said. 'I'm Madame Hera.'

Innes laughed. Then, when she continued to look at him without joining in, his laughter stopped abruptly. 'I'll be damned. You mean it? You really do write this stuff?'

'It is not *stuff*. It is a very well-respected column. I'll have you know that in the past month, Madame Hera has received no less than fifty letters. In fact, such is the demand for Madame's advice that the magazine will from next month offer a personal reply service. Felicity has agreed a fee with the board, and I shall receive fifty per cent of it.'

'Felicity?'

'Blair. The editor, and my friend.'

'So all that correspondence you receive, they are letters to this Madame Hera.' Innes looked quite stunned. 'Why didn't you tell me?'

'Because it was none of your business.' Ainsley flushed. 'And because I knew you would most likely react exactly as you have. Though I am not ashamed, if that's what you're thinking. Madame Hera provides a much-needed service.'

'So why tell me now?'

Ainsley reached for her sherry and took a large gulp. She had not meant to tell him. She had been so caught up in worrying about how to explain away her earlier behaviour that Madame Hera had been far from her mind, though her advice would have been straightforward. *'Il faut me chercher'* was one of Madame's axioms.

is a business arrangement.' She wriggled back in her chair, because despite the thin calico of her gown, the heat from the fire was making her face flush. 'Now I suppose you want to know what she *is* interested in.'

Innes, who had been inspecting the sherry decanter, which seemed to have almost emptied itself, put it rather selfishly down on the table out of her reach. 'I do,' he said, 'but first I'd like to know why you confessed to being Madame Hera. You still haven't yet told me, in case you'd forgotten.'

'Aha! That's where you're wrong,' Ainsley exclaimed with a triumphant wave of her hand, 'because the two things are inexpressibly—no, inex—inextricably linked.' She picked up her glass, remembered it was empty and placed it very carefully back down again, because the side table had developed a wobble. Then, realising she had slumped unbecomingly back in her chair, she struggled upright, leaning forward confidentially. 'Those letters. The intimate ones to Madame Hera. They are all about marital—no, lovemaking. And—and the acquisition of womanly wiles. Felicity fears that I do not know enough about such things to be of any value, and I fear she is right. Are you perfectly well? Only your face has gone sort of fuzzy.'

Innes leaned forward. 'Better?'

Ainsley nodded. 'Do you know you have a charming smile?'

'Only because I am charmed by you.'

She giggled. 'Felicity said I should let you have your wicked way with me, and that you sounded like the kind of man who would not expect me to—to lie back and think of Scotland. And she said that we needed something to while away the long dark nights in this godforsaken place—though I don't think it is godforsaken, actually—and she said that I needed some lessons in—in fun. And pleasure. Do you have a kilt?'

'I do. Does Felicity's idea of fun and pleasure involve dressing up?'

Ainsley giggled. 'Not Felicity's idea—that was mine. I think you have a fine pair of legs, Innes Drummond. I would like to see you in Highland dress. But we are straying from the point, you know. Is there any more sherry?'

'No.'

Ainsley frowned over at the decanter. It seemed to her that it was not completely empty. Then she shrugged. 'Oh, well. What was I— Oh, yes, what Felicity said. She said that you would be well placed to teach me about womanly wiles and such—though I don't think she called

it that, zactly—*ex*actly—and I don't know how
she knew this, for she has not met you, and all I
told her was that you kissed very nicely, which
you know you do…'

'Only because you kiss me so very nicely
back.'

'Really?' Ainsley smiled beatifically. 'What
a lovely thing to say.'

'And true, into the bargain.' Innes took her
hand. 'So this Felicity of yours believes that you
need to be inducted into the palace of pleasure.'

'Palace of pleasure. I like that. Would you
mind if Madame Hera borrowed it?'

'I would be honoured.'

'What would you say if I told you that Felicity
also suggested I use you to assist me in finding
answers to some of Madame Hera's problems?'

'You mean, provide you with practical experience of the solutions?'

Ainsley nodded sagely. 'You would be insulted, wouldn't you? That's what I told Felicity, that you would be insulted.'

'Would you be taking part in this experiment
merely for the sake of obtaining better advice?'

'No.' She stared down at her hands. Despite
the tingling, and the fuzziness and the warmth
induced by the sherry, this was still proving
surprisingly difficult, but she was determined

to bring this embarrassing conversation to an end, one way or another. 'The reason I told you,' she said, 'about Madame Hera, I mean. It wasn't only that you were right about the advice I was dispensing, it was—it was—it was earlier. Me. When you kissed me. It was because I— Felicity says that he took away all my self-respect. John. My husband. Self-respect, that's what she called it. I don't know what to call it. I don't want to talk about it. But when you kissed me, it made me feel— I liked it. I liked it a lot. But then I remembered, you see. Him. What happened. Didn't happen. And it made me stop liking what you were doing and thinking about then, and him, and it wasn't that I think you're the same, you're so different, and he never, but— Well, that was it. That's what happened. Are you angry?'

She looked up. His eyes were stormy. 'No,' Innes said quickly. 'I'm not angry with you.'

She nodded several times.

'You don't have to say any more, Ainsley.'

'I want to finish telling you or I might not— I want to.' She clutched at his hand. 'I don't want to feel like this. I don't want to feel the way he made me feel. I want to feel what Felicity said, and what you made me feel before I thought about him. And that's why I told you about

Madame Hera,' she finished in a rush. 'Because when you kiss me, I want to—and because you know, we're not really married and it can't ever mean anything, so it's sort of *safe*. You can help me, and then I can be better at helping other women. That's why I told you. Because I want you, and I really want to be able to— If you do? So now you know.'

'Now I know,' Innes said, looking rather stunned.

'You can say no.'

'I'm not going to say anything right now. You've given me a lot to think about.'

'And you're not angry about Madame Hera?'

Innes laughed. 'Absolutely not. I am more than happy to discuss these intimate problems that Madame Hera has to answer. In fact, if you ever run short of problems then I'm sure I will be able to think up a few for us to discuss.'

'No!' Ainsley exclaimed. 'That's what Felicity said you would say. Now I owe her five pounds.'

Innes laughed. 'I am looking forward to meeting Felicity.'

Ainsley yawned, frowning at the clock. 'It's past dinner time. I shall go and find Mhairi.'

She got to her feet, swaying, and Innes caught her. 'I think maybe you'd be better in your bed.'

Ainsley yawned again. 'I think maybe you're right.'

'Thank you for telling me what you did. I'm honoured,' Innes said. 'I mean it.'

'I didn't want you to think I was a cock tease.' Ainsley grinned. 'Proof that I am not always so mealy-mouthed.'

Innes kissed her cheek. 'What you are is…'

'A porcupine.'

'A wee darling.'

She smiled. 'I like that,' she murmured. Then she closed her eyes, sank gracefully back onto the chair and passed out.

'The laird said that you'd be hungry, seeing as you missed dinner, so I made you some eggs, and I've cut you a slice of ham.' Mhairi laid the plateful down in front of Ainsley.

'Thank you. It smells delicious,' Ainsley said, repressing a shudder.

'Himself had to go out, but he said to tell you he'd be back by mid-morn at the latest. Here, I'll do that.' Mhairi took the coffee pot from Ainsley's shaking hand and poured her a cup. 'Do you want me to put a hair of the dog in it?'

'Is it so obvious?' Lifting the cup in both hands, Ainsley took a grateful sip, shaking her head, flushing. 'I don't normally— I hope you don't think I usually overindulge.'

'Oh, I'm not one to judge,' Mhairi said with a toss of her head. 'Unlike the rest of them.'

Sensing that the housekeeper was offering her an opening, and feeling that she had nothing much to lose, as she sat nursing her hangover, Ainsley smiled at her. 'Why don't you join me? It's about time we got to know each other a bit better. Please,' she added when the other woman demurred.

Mhairi studied her with pursed lips for a few seconds, then took a seat and poured herself a coffee, adding two lumps of sugar, though no cream. 'You're not at all what we expected when we heard Himself had wedded an Edinburgh widow woman,' she said.

'What were you expecting?'

'Someone fancier. You know, more up on her high horse, with more frills to her.'

'You mean not so plain?'

Mhairi shook her head. 'I mean not so nice,' she said with a wry smile. 'And you're not plain. Leastwise, you're not when you've some life in that face of yours. If you don't mind my saying.'

'I don't mind at all,' Ainsley said, buttering an oatcake, and deciding to brave a forkful of eggs. 'Am I a disappointment, then?'

'No one knows enough about you to judge.'

'Yet you said that people do judge—or that is what you implied just a minute ago.'

Across from her, the housekeeper folded her arms. Ainsley ate another forkful of eggs and cut into the ham. Mhairi McIntosh was younger than she had thought at first, not much over forty, with a curvaceous figure hidden under her apron and heavy tweed skirt. Though she had a forbidding expression, her features were attractive, with high cheekbones and a mouth that curved sensually when it was not pulled into a grim line. Her eyes were grey and deep-set, and she had the kind of sallow skin that made the hollows beneath them look darkly shadowed. But she was what would be called a handsome woman, nevertheless. She wore no ring.

'No, I was never married,' Mhairi said, noticing the direction of Ainsley's gaze. 'I've worked here at the castle since I was ten years old, starting in the kitchens—the big kitchens—back in Mrs Drummond's day.'

'So you've known Innes since he was a boy?'
Mhairi nodded.

'And his brother?'

'Him, too.'

'Is it because of him that people judge Innes

so harshly? Do they resent the fact that he is here and not Malcolm?'

Mhairi shook her head sadly. 'Himself should not have stayed away so long.'

'But surely people understand he had his own life to lead. And it's not as if— I mean, the state of the lands, the way things have been allowed to deteriorate... That was his father's fault, it was nothing to do with Innes.'

'He should not have stayed away,' Mhairi said implacably.

'Oh, for goodness' sake! It's not his fault.' Realising that recriminations were getting her nowhere, Ainsley reined in her temper. 'He's here now, and so am I, and what matters is the future of Strone Bridge.'

'It seems to many of us that Strone Bridge hasn't much of a future,' Mhairi said.

'What do you mean?'

'Himself has obviously decided that this place is not worth wasting his time on.'

'He hasn't decided anything. He's not even been here a month.'

'And not a single sign has there been that he's going to be remaining here another. He forbade the formal welcoming at the pier, and there's been no word of the Rescinding. Not that the castle is in any fit state to be used. And that's another thing. He's the laird, and he's living here at the Home Farm. It's obvious he has no plans to stay here. He'll be off as soon as he can decently go, back to building his bridges.'

There was no doubting the belligerence in the woman's voice now. 'Innes hasn't made any decisions about the castle. He's been spending his time looking at the land, because—'

'Because he plans to do what all the landlords are doing, break up the crofts and put sheep on them. Does he think we're daft? Sheep. That's what he'll do, that's what they all do. Get rid of the tenants. Bring in a bailiff. Out with the old, and in with the new. That's what Himself is doing, and then it will be back to Edinburgh or London or wherever he's been hiding these last fourteen years, and you with him, and he'll go back to pretending Strone Bridge doesn't exist because it's too hard for him to—' Mhairi broke off suddenly. 'Never mind.'

Ainsley stared at her in shock. 'He has made no mention of sheep, and he has no intentions of going anywhere for at least—for some time,' she amended, for she did not imagine that Innes would like the terms of his father's will made public.

A shrug greeted this remark. Ainsley risked pouring the pair of them another cup of coffee.

'What is this thing you mentioned? A restitution?'

'Rescinding.' Mhairi took a sip of her coffee. 'A forgiving and forgetting. After the burial of the old laird, a feast is held for all to welcome in the new laird. It is a wiping clean of the slate, of debts and grudges and disputes, a sign that they have been buried with the old. But since Himself was not here for the burial…'

'Can it not be held on another day?' Ainsley asked.

'To my knowledge it never has been.'

'Yes, but if it is held on another day would this Rescinding be invalid?'

Mhairi shook her head slowly. 'It's never been done. You'd have to consult the book. *The Customs and Ways of the Family Drummond of Strone Bridge,*' she said when Ainsley looked at her enquiringly. 'It's in the castle library.'

'Then I will do so, but do you think it's a good idea?' Ainsley persisted.

'It would mean using the Great Hall. I'd need a lot of help and good bit of supplies, and as to the food…'

'Yes, yes, we can see to that, but what do you think?'

The housekeeper smiled reluctantly. 'I think if you can persuade Himself, that it's an excellent idea.'

* * *

'A Rescinding?' Innes frowned. Ainsley had accosted him immediately when he had returned in the early afternoon. He had expected her to be sheepish, or reserved, or even defensive. He had not expected her to launch enthusiastically into some wild plan for a party. 'I'm not even sure that I know what's involved,' he said cautiously.

'It's a forgiving and forgetting, Mhairi says. She says that all debts and grudges are buried with the old laird to give the new one a clean start. She says that though it's customary to have it the day after the funeral, there is no reason why we cannot hold it on another day and combine it with a welcoming feast. She says that the chair that the laird uses for the ceremony is in the Great Hall. And there is a book in the library. *The Customs and Ways of the Family Drummond of Strone Bridge*, it's called.' Ainsley was looking at him anxiously. 'What do you think?'

'I think Mhairi has quite a lot to say all of a sudden. I wonder how she knows so much about it, for she cannot have seen one herself.'

'She has worked in the castle since she was ten years old. I suppose, these past few years while your father was alone here, he must have confided in her.'

'I can't imagine my father confiding in anyone,' Innes said drily. 'To be honest, I can't imagine him forgiving or forgetting either, Rescinding or no. He was not a man who liked to be crossed, and he bore a long grudge.'

'Were you always at outs with him, even before—before your brother died?'

'Yes.'

Ainsley was watching him. Innes could feel her eyes on him, even though he was studiously looking down at a letter from his chief surveyor. He wondered what else Mhairi had said. She was as closed as a fist, and always had been. It surprised him that Ainsley had managed to have any sort of conversation with her. He pushed the letter to one side. 'The old ways were the only ways, as far as my father was concerned,' he said, 'and for my brother, too.'

'Sometimes the old ways can be a comfort.'

'You mean the Rescinding?'

Ainsley nodded.

'A—what did you call it—healing of wounds?' He smiled. 'There can be no denying the need for that.'

'So you agree, it's a good idea?'

'It sounds like a lot of work.'

'I will handle that. With Mhairi. I am not too proud to ask for help.'

'Is that a dig at me?'

Ainsley hesitated only fractionally. 'Yes.'

Innes sighed. 'If I speak to Eoin, will it make you happy?'

'It would be a start. A forgiving and forgetting, that's what the Rescinding is. Perhaps you could do some of that before the ceremony.'

Innes threw his hands up in surrender. 'Enough. You've made your point. I will even write to your Miss Blair and invite her to attend. Unless you've changed your mind. Or perhaps forgotten that conversation entirely?'

'I was half-cut, not stotious!' Ainsley said stiffly.

'Ach, I didn't mean to bite your head off. At least I did, but don't take it personally. You make too good a case, and I don't want to hear it.' Innes got up from the desk and took her hand. He took her hand, pressing it between his own. 'Forgive me.'

Her fingers twined round his. 'It is I who should be begging your forgiveness. Last night, I propositioned you. In fact, I practically threw myself at you,' Ainsley said, flushing. 'You must not feel awkward at turning me down.'

'I have no intentions of turning you down, if you are not retracting your offer. I thought I'd made it clear, from almost the first moment I met you, that I find you very desirable.'

'You do?'

'I do.'

'I don't want to. Retract, I mean.'

'Are you sure? Yesterday, you turned to ice while I was kissing you.'

'It won't happen again.'

'I think maybe it will. I think, in fact, we should expect it. I wonder what Madame Hera would advise?'

'As you pointed out last night, Madame Hera would most likely provide quite unwise advice,' Ainsley said drily.

'I offended you. I'm sorry.'

'No,' she said, quite unconvincingly, and then she laughed. 'Yes, you did. I was upset.'

'If I had known that you and she were one and the same person...'

'I am glad you did not. It was a difficult lesson, but I hope that I have learned from it. I want Madame Hera to be helpful.' Ainsley opened the thick leather folder on the desk that contained her correspondence. 'These women are desperate enough to write to a complete stranger for help. They deserve honesty.' She replaced the folder and wandered over to her favourite chair by the fire, though she did not sit down. 'When John died, one of the things I promised myself was always to speak my mind, and that's what

Madame Hera has done. I didn't realise, though, that my opinions were so coloured.'

'I think that you're being very hard on yourself, but if it would help, I'd be happy to provide you with a counterpoint when you're writing your replies.'

'Would you?'

'I think I might even enjoy it.'

'What if we disagree?'

Innes pulled her round to face him, sliding his arms around her waist. 'Madame Hera has the final say, naturally.'

'And as to the—the other thing?'

Innes smiled. 'Your introduction into the palace of pleasures? I was thinking that it would be best if we started first with some theory.'

Her eyes widened. 'You have textbooks?'

'Good lord, no. I meant Madame Hera's correspondence. We could discuss it. I could explain anything you are not sure of. That way, you will be able to start answering some of your letters, and at the same time, you can accustom yourself to—to—before you have to—if you do. You might decide not to.' Innes stopped, at a loss for words, wondering if what he was suggesting was idiotic, or even repugnant.

But Ainsley smiled at him. 'You mean that

I become accustomed to what to expect?' she asked.

'And you can accustom me to what you want, too.'

'I don't know what I want.'

'Save that I must wear a kilt?'

Her cheeks flamed. 'I had forgotten that.'

'Do you dream of a wild Highlander?'

'No. Yes.'

'What does he do?'

'I don't know.' Ainsley's mouth trembled on the brink of a smile. 'He—he wants me.'

'You know I already do.'

'No, I mean he—he really wants me. He— No, it's silly.'

'He finds you irresistible,' Innes said, charmed and aroused. 'He wants you so much,' he whispered into her ear, 'that he carries you off, right in the middle of the day, and has his wicked way with you on the moor. Or would you prefer a cave?'

'A cave. In the firelight.'

He was hard. Innes cursed under his breath. He hadn't meant this to happen. He edged away from her carefully. 'You are a very apt pupil,' he said.

'Oh. I didn't realise— Is that what that was, a lesson?'

'It's all it was meant to be,' Innes said, 'but you are a little too good at this. Another minute and I'd be rushing off to find a kilt.'

'Oh.'

It was a different kind of 'oh' this time. She looked at him with the most delightful, pleased little smile on her face, and Innes simply could not resist her. He kissed her, briefly but deeply. 'I am already looking forward to the next lesson,' he said.

Chapter Six

A week later, Innes stared down at the Celtic cross, at the bright lettering of the new inscription and the long empty space below that was left to fill. His own name would be next, but after that, it would be a distant cousin, if anyone. He dug his hands into the pockets of his leather breeches and hunched his shoulders against the squally breeze, steeling himself against the wall of emotions that threatened to engulf him. Until now, he'd been able to ignore what had happened, tell himself that this was a temporary thing, that he was not really the laird, that his life was not inextricably tangled up in Strone Bridge. He'd been able to contain and control whatever it was that was building inside him, fence it in with resentment and anger, let the waste and destruction he saw every day tack it down, the hurt and the suffering gnaw at his conscience and prevent him from thinking about the reason he was here at all.

He'd arranged to meet Eoin here, but had arrived early, wanting some time alone. He'd come here telling himself that fourteen years had bred indifference, but he was wrong. It was like one of those seventh waves, building from the swell, scooping up memories and guilt and remorse, hurtling them at him with an implacable force. Innes screwed his eyes so tightly shut he saw stars behind his lids.

'It was all done properly, if that's bothering you at all.' He opened his eyes to find Eoin standing a few feet away. 'Your father's funeral. It was all done as he would have wanted it,' he said. 'Mhairi made sure of that.'

His father's housekeeper had been the one to arrange his father's funeral. Innes refused to feel guilty.

'She had me play the chief mourner.' Eoin came a few steps closer. 'I didn't want to, but she said someone with Drummond blood had to bear the laird's standard, and bastard blood from two generations back was better than none.'

It had been a joke between them when they were boys, that bastard blood. Malcolm had traced the line once, working out that Eoin was their half cousin twice removed, or some such thing. Their father had a coat of arms made for Eoin, with the baton sinister prominently displayed. Malcolm had dreamed up a ceremony to hand it over, Innes remembered. The laird had given them all their first taste of whisky. They'd have been ten, maybe eleven. He had forgotten that there were days like those.

'I didn't get the letter in time to attend,' Innes said tersely.

'Would it have made any difference?' Eoin demanded, and when Innes said nothing, he shook his head impatiently and turned away. 'I meant it to be a comfort to you, knowing that all had been done as it ought. I wasn't casting it up.'

'Wait.' Innes covered the short distance between them, grabbing the thick fisherman's jumper Eoin wore. His friend shrugged him off, but made no further move to go. Blue eyes, the same colour as Innes's, the same colour as Malcolm's, the same colour as the dead laird's, glowered at him. 'I wrote to you,' Innes said. 'After—I wrote to you, and you did not reply.'

'I live here, Innes, and unlike you, I've never wanted to leave. It was not only that I owed a duty to your father as the laird, I respected him. When you left, the way you left, you forced me to choose. What else was I to do?'

'I was your friend.'

'You were his son,' Eoin said, nodding at the Celtic cross. 'When Malcolm died, it broke his heart.'

'What do you think it did to me?' Innes struggled, eyes smarting, the sick feeling that had been lurking inside him since he'd arrived here growing, acrid, clogging his throat. He turned away, fists clenched, taking painful breaths, fighting for control, forcing back the images, the guilt, waiting desperately for the sound of Eoin's footsteps disappearing, leaving him alone to deal with it, to make it go away.

Eoin didn't move. When he spoke, his voice was raw, grating. 'I could hardly look at you the other day. All these years, I've told myself it was the right thing to hold my peace. All these years, with the laird letting things go, letting the place wither, I've told myself that if that was what he wanted and— No, not just that. I've told myself you deserved it. If you did not care enough to look after your heritage...'

Innes had intended this as a reconciliation. It felt as though he was being tried, and found wanting, by the one person here on Strone Bridge he had thought might be on his side. The disappointment was crushing. 'It was never meant for me,' he roared. 'It was never mine.'

His words echoed around the enclosed space,

but still Eoin stood his ground, his face grim, his own fists clenched. 'It is yours now. You've known for fourteen years that it would be yours.'

'And by the looks of it, for fourteen years my father has done his damnedest to run the place into the ground. Don't tell me I could have stopped him, Eoin. You of all people know he would never listen to me.'

There was silence. The two men glared at each other. Finally, as Innes was about to turn away, Eoin spoke. 'It's true,' he said grudgingly. 'I did blame you, and it was wrong of me. You've every bit as much right to choose your life as the next man, and it's obvious from the look of you that the life you've chosen suits you well. You're a rich man. A successful one.'

'Much good my successes will do me here. I know nothing about sheep, and certainly not enough to go clearing my lands to bring them in.'

'So you've heard that rumour, then?'

'And I'd be happy if you'd deny it for me.'

'I'll be delighted to, if it's the truth.' Eoin kicked at the ground. 'They do blame you, as I did. It's not fair, but that's how it is. Your father never got over Malcolm, and you're right, it was as if he was deliberately letting the place go to spite you. They think you should have put Strone Bridge first. They think if you'd have come back, you could have stopped him, so the longer you stayed away, and the worse it got, the more they blamed you.'

'Eoin, he wouldn't have listened to me. If I'd come back while he was alive I'd have ended up murdering him. Or more likely, he'd have murdered me.' Innes looked grimly at the cross. 'You know what he was like. I was the second son. He wanted me to study the law in Edinburgh, for goodness' sake! I was to be the family lackey.'

Eoin gave a bark of laughter. 'I'll admit, that was never on the cards.'

'No, but you know how hard I tried to do things his way—or more precisely, how hard I tried to make him see things my way. He couldn't care less about me. All he cared about was shaping my brother for the next laird in his own image, but he would not let me shape myself. I tried, but I was always going to leave. And when Malcolm— When it happened— How can you seriously think that would make me more likely to stay here?'

Eoin shook his head. 'But you could have come back, at least to visit,' he said stubbornly. 'You would have seen how things were going. Gradual it was. I didn't notice at first. And then— Well, like I said, I thought you deserved it. That was wrong of me. It's why I've been avoiding you. You're not the only one who feels guilty, Innes. I should have done something. I'm sorry. I should have done something, and now it's far too late. I truly am sorry.'

He held out his hand. Hesitating only a moment, Innes gripped it. 'I'm here now,' he said, 'and I need your help.'

Eoin nodded, returning the grip equally painfully. They sat together in silence on the stone bench. 'I did write,' Innes said eventually. 'Only once, but I did write to my father.'

'I didn't know that,' Eoin said. 'Mhairi would surely have told me, so she can't have known, either.'

'Why should she?'

Eoin looked surprised. 'She was his wife in all but name.' He laughed. 'You did not know?'

'No— I— No.' Innes shook his head in astonishment. 'He left no provision for her in his will.'

'Oh, he took care of that years ago. There's an annuity, you'll probably not have noticed it yet unless you've gone through the accounts, and she owns the farm over at Cairndow.'

'Then what the devil is she doing working for me when she does not have to?'

'Innes, for someone so far-sighted, you can be awfully blind. She's looking out for you. She's about the only one who is. She was ever on your side, you know, it's the one thing she and the laird had words about, but even she thinks you should have come back. I'm not saying it's right, I'm saying that's how it is.'

'I'm here now. Why can't they see that as a step in the right direction?'

'Maybe because they're wondering how long it will be before you go again.' Eoin got to his feet. 'Think about it from their point of view, Innes. The laird obviously believed he would be the last, else he would not have been so destructive.'

'He obviously thought I'd come back here simply to rid myself of the place. His will specifies I must remain here a year,' Innes conceded.

'The auld bugger obviously hoped being here would change your mind. Will you?'

Innes shook his head. 'I haven't a clue what I'm going to do,' he admitted ruefully, 'but I don't want to sell. I've spent every day, since I got off that boat of yours, going round the lands, making endless lists of things that need to be done.'

Eoin laughed. 'People think you've been sizing up the assets to sell.'

'For heaven's sake, why did no one tell me that?'

'Why didn't you say anything yourself, tell people your plans?'

Innes shook his head. 'Because I don't know what they are yet.'

'This is not one of your projects, where you have to have your blueprints and your costs and—I don't know—your list of materials all sorted out before you make your bid, Innes. Plans change, we all know that, but people would like to hear that they exist. They'd like to know you're not going to sell the roof over their heads.' Eoin got to his feet. 'I'm glad we talked. It's been eating away at me, the way we were when you arrived.'

This time it was Innes who held out his hand. 'It is good to see you, Eoin. I've not missed this place, but I've missed you. I would value your input to what needs done.'

'You know you have only to ask.'

'I wouldn't have, if it were not for Ainsley. She is the one who pushed me into this.'

Eoin smiled. 'Then I owe her. I look forward to meeting her properly.'

'You will do soon. She's planning a Rescinding.' Innes shook his head. 'Don't ask, because I'm not quite sure what it is myself, save that it will involve everyone.'

'Then I hope you will make sure not to let

the water of life run dry. I must go, but we'll talk again.'

Innes watched his friend walk away. He felt as if his mind had been put through a washtub and then a mangle. Striding along the path that led round the front of the castle, he spotted the ramshackle pier and came to a sudden halt. Here was something he could do, and it was something, moreover, that Strone Bridge urgently needed, for it would allow paddle steamers to dock. He couldn't understand why he hadn't thought of it before. Vastly relieved to be able to focus on a project that was entirely within his control, Innes made his way down to the bay and began a survey of the jetty with the critical eye of the engineer it had cost him and, it seemed, the people of Strone Bridge, so much to become.

Dear Madame Hera,
I am a twenty-eight-year-old woman, married with two small children and absolutely bored stiff. My husband is a wealthy man and insists that our house is taken care of by servants and our children by a nanny, but this leaves me with nothing to do. I try to count my blessings, but even that occupation has become tedious. One of my friends suggested taking a lover would

amply occupy my free afternoons, but lying convincingly is not one of my accomplishments. What shall I do?

Yours sincerely, Mrs A

Ainsley smiled to herself as she read this missive. Many of Madame Hera's correspondents complained of boredom, though none had suggested this novel answer. 'Take charge,' Ainsley wrote, 'of your children, of your housework, of your life!' She put the pen down, frowning. Mrs A's husband was doing exactly what was expected of him. More, in fact, than many could or would. Mrs A's friends might well even envy her. If Mrs A were to dismiss the nanny, or take over the housework, her husband would most likely be insulted. Or offended.

Ainsley looked at the clock. It was gone two. Innes had left before breakfast this morning, and she had not seen him since. Was he avoiding her? In the days since he had agreed to hold the Rescinding ceremony, he had continued with his visits to various farms and tenants, his poring over documents late into the night. True, she too had been very busy—too busy, in fact, to have any time to devote to anything else, but still, the niggling feeling that she was being pushed to one side would not go away.

With a sigh of frustration, Ainsley pushed Madame Hera's half-finished letter to one side and picked up the heavy bunch of castle keys from the desk, intending to consult the tome she had now christened the *Drummond Self-Help Manual* in the library once more, before taking another look at the Great Hall. Outside, as ever, it was blowy. There were several fishing boats in the bay. She paused to drink in her favourite view and spotted a figure down on the pier. Black coat with long skirts birling in the breeze. Long boots. All the Strone Bridge men wore trews and fishing jumpers or short tweed jackets. Tucking the keys into her pocket beside the notebook and pencil she had brought, Ainsley began to pick her way carefully down the steep path.

The tide was far enough out for Innes to have clambered down underneath the pier when she arrived. 'What on earth are you doing?' she asked, peering through one of the planks down at him.

'I was inspecting the struts,' he said, looking up at her, 'but now that you're here, there's a much nicer view.'

'Innes!' Scandalised, laughing, she clutched her skirts tightly around her.

Laughing, he appeared a few moments later on the beach, climbing up the ancient wooden supports of the pier fluidly. 'Do you always match your garters to your gown?'

'What kind of question is that?'

'One you needn't answer if you don't want to, I'm happy to imagine.' Innes picked a long strand of seaweed from the skirts of his coat and threw it on to the beach. 'I'm going to have this thing rebuilt.'

'Of course you are! I wonder you didn't think of it before.'

'Couldn't see the wood for the trees,' Innes said wryly. 'I don't suppose you've got a pencil and a bit of paper with you?'

Ainsley delved into her pocket and pulled out the notebook and pencil. 'Here, I was on my way to the castle when I saw you.'

'How are the arrangements progressing?'

She was about to launch into a stream of detail, but stopped herself, giving Innes a dismissive shrug instead. 'Nothing for you to worry about,' she said.

He had been scribbling something in her notebook, but he looked up at the change in her tone. 'I thought you wanted to take this on—have you changed your mind?'

'No.'

'Is it too much? Do you need help?'

'No, I told you, there's nothing for you to worry about. It's not your problem.'

Frowning, Innes stuck her pencil behind his ear. 'Aye, that was it. *It's not your problem.* I remember now, that's what set you off before.'

'I don't know what you're implying, but...'

'Actually, it's what you're implying, Ainsley,' he exclaimed. 'I'm not shutting you out deliberately. I thought we were dividing and conquering, not just dividing, for heaven's sake. Once and for all, I'm not the man you married, so stop judging me as if I am.'

She wrapped her arms tightly around herself. 'I know you're not.'

'Then what are you accusing me of?'

'Nothing.' She bit her lip. 'You don't talk to me. You don't value my opinion.'

'Well, that's where you're wrong. Do you know what I was doing this morning? No, of course you don't, for I didn't tell you—and before you berate me for that, I didn't tell you because I wasn't sure he'd come.'

'Who?'

'Eoin.'

Her latent anger left her. Ainsley smiled. 'You've spoken to Eoin?'

'I have. I met him at the chapel.'

'And?'

Innes laughed nervously. 'And it was difficult.'

He was clearly uncomfortable. If she did not press him, he would leave it at that. She was pleased, no, more than pleased, that he had taken her advice, though it would most likely result in her further exclusion from matters of the lands. 'Has Eoin agreed to help you?' Ainsley asked carefully.

'He has.'

Innes was staring down at his notes, but she was not fooled. 'And you've made your peace?' Ainsley persisted.

'We've agreed to disagree.' Finally, Innes met her gaze. 'He thinks I should have come back sooner. Though he understands why I left, he doesn't understand why I stayed away. Though he knows fine that if I'd come back, my father and I would have done nothing but argue, and my father would have carried on down whatever path he'd chosen regardless, still Eoin thinks I should have tried.'

'That's ridiculous. Then you would have both been miserable. Besides, you had no cause to think that your father would choose this path of destruction,' Ainsley said fiercely. 'You told me yourself, he was a good laird.'

'Aye, well, it seems you're the only person to see it my way,' Innes said despondently.

She put her hand on his arm. 'You brought me here so you'd have someone on your side.'

'And I've done my damnedest to push you away since we arrived.' He smiled ruefully down at her. 'I'm sorry. I did warn you. You need to speak up more.'

She flinched. 'I know.'

Innes cursed under his breath. 'That was unfair of me.' He kissed her fingertips. 'This marriage business, I'm not very good at it, I'm afraid. I'm too used to being on my own.'

'That's one thing you need to remember. You're not alone. May I see?' she asked, pointing at the notebook.

Innes had made several small sketches. He began to talk as he showed them to her, of tides, about the advantages of wood over stone, of angles and reinforcing. She nodded and listened, though she understood about a quarter of what he said, content to hear his voice full of enthusiasm, to watch the way he ran the pencil through his hair, reminded of the way Felicity did something very similar.

'That's quite enough,' he said eventually, closing the notebook. 'You're probably bored to death.'

'No. I didn't follow much of it, but it wasn't boring.'

Innes laughed, putting his arm around her.

'Do you think you'll be ready to announce the new pier after the Rescinding?' she asked. 'Perhaps you could show them a drawing. There's three weeks, would there be time?'

'I don't see why not. I could do the preliminary survey myself. It's what my trade is after all.'

Ainsley beamed up at him. 'If all the villagers and tenants see what a clever man you are, then perhaps they'll understand why you had to leave.'

'Atonement?'

'No, you've nothing to atone for. It is a gift. A symbol of the modern world brought to Strone Bridge by their modern laird.'

Innes laughed. 'I can just about hear my father turning in his grave from here.'

'Good.'

He pulled her closer. 'I saw it this morning at the chapel. The grave I mean, and yes, it was for the first time. I could see you just about chewing your tongue off trying not to ask. Eoin told me about the funeral. It seems I have Mhairi to thank for doing things properly.'

'We have a lot to thank Mhairi for,' Ainsley

agreed, enjoying the warmth of his body, the view, the salty tang of the air. 'She's at one with Eoin and everyone else in thinking that you should have come back here earlier, but now you're here, she's of the opinion that you should be given a chance.'

'That's big of her. Mhairi was my father's mistress,' Innes said.

Ainsley jerked her head up to look at him. 'Mhairi! Your father's mistress! Good grief. Are you sure?'

'Eoin told me.' Innes shook his head. 'I still can't believe it. He thought I knew. It seems everyone else does.'

'But—did he leave her anything in his will? You have not mentioned…'

'No. According to Eoin, he'd already made provision. A farm, an annuity. She did not need to stay on at the castle when he died.'

'But she did, so she must have wanted to. How very—surprising. It's funny, when I was talking to her over breakfast yesterday morning, I was thinking that she was an attractive woman and wondering why she had not married. There is something about her. Her mouth, I think. It's very sensual.'

'I believe I've said something similar to you.' Innes pulled her back towards him, tipping up her face. 'Infinitely kissable, that is what your mouth is, and if you don't mind…'

'I don't.'

'Good,' Innes said, and kissed her.

They took the path back up to the castle together. While the track used by the cart wound its serpentine way upwards, the footpath was a sheer climb. Out of breath at the top, Ainsley stood with her chest heaving. 'I don't suppose your engineering skills can come up with a solution for that,' she said.

'I will have my surveyor take a look,' Innes said. 'See if it can be widened, maybe change some of the angles so they're not so sharp. That way we can get bigger vehicles down to collect supplies.'

'And steamer passengers,' Ainsley said. 'Then you can build a tea pavilion up here on the terrace, where the view is best. Although there would be no need to build anything new if you set up a tearoom in that lovely drawing room. Then Mhairi could show the excursionists around the castle for a sixpence. She tells those ghost stories much better than you do, and she has lots more. There was one about a grey lady in the kitchens that gave me goosebumps.'

They began to walk together up to the castle.

'Mhairi's mother was the village fey wife when I was wee. A witch, though a good one, of course.'

'Better and better. She could make up some potions. You could sell them in the teashop. And some of the local tweed, too,' Ainsley said, handing Innes the keys to the main door, for they were going to inspect the Great Hall together. 'Before you know it, Strone Bridge will be so famous that the steamers will be fighting to berth at this new pier of yours.'

Innes paused in the act of unlocking the door. 'You're not being serious?'

She had forgotten, in her enthusiasm, how he felt about the place. Ainsley's smile faded. 'Don't you think it's a good idea?'

'I think it's a ridiculous idea. Besides the fact that I have no intentions of wasting my fortune having the place made habitable, it's a monstrosity—no one in their right mind would pay to see it.'

'Ridiculous.' She swallowed the lump that had appeared in her throat.

Innes looked immediately contrite. 'Don't take it like that, I didn't mean— It's not the idea. It's the place.'

'Why do you hate it so much? It's your home.'

'No. I could never live here.' He shuddered.

'There are more ghosts here than even Mhairi knows of.'

They were in the courtyard. Ainsley followed his gaze to the tower that stood at the centre. A huge bird of prey circled the parapet. She, too, shuddered, not because she thought it an omen, but at the look on Innes's face. She'd thought she was beginning to understand him, but now she was not so sure. That bleak expression could not merely be attributed to feelings of inadequacy or resentment. There was a reason beyond his quarrel with his father for Innes's absence from this place for fourteen long years. Ghosts. Who would have thought such a confident, practical man as Innes would believe in them, but he very obviously did. Something in his past haunted him. Something here, in this castle.

Above the tower, the sky was empty now. 'Come on,' Ainsley said, slipping her hand into Innes's arm. 'Let's go inside.'

She led him through to the Great Hall, their feet echoing on the stone flags. Innes seemed to have shaken off his black mood, and was now wandering around, sounding panelling, looking up with a worried frown at the high beams. 'I'll get Robert, my surveyor, to take a look at this while he's here. He'll be able to tell me if there are any structural problems.'

He said it hopefully, no doubt thinking that structural problems would give him the excuse to pull the place down. The castle seemed sound enough to her, no smell of damp, no sign of rot, but she was willing to admit she knew nothing about it.

Watching him out of the corner of her eye, Ainsley got on with her own measurements. 'I think we'll have to plan to feed about two hundred, including bairns,' she said. 'Mhairi is overseeing the work in the kitchens. I reckon we'll need to light the fires a few days in advance, once the chimneys are swept.' She scribbled in her notebook, which she had reclaimed from Innes, and began to tick items off from her list. Quickly absorbed in her task, she was struggling to pull the holland covers from what she assumed must be the laird's chair when Innes came to her aid.

'Let me,' he said.

A cloud of dust flew up, making them both choke. 'Good heavens, it's like a throne.'

Innes laughed. 'Now you can get some idea of the esteem in which the lairds of Strone Bridge have held themselves.'

Ainsley sat down on the chair. It was so high her feet didn't touch the ground. 'Mhairi would have a fit if she could see me. I'm probably

bringing any amount of curses down on myself
for daring to occupy the laird's seat.'

'I'm the laird now, and I'd be more than happy
for you to occupy my seat.'

'Innes!' He was smiling down at her in a way
that made her heart flutter. 'I don't know what
you mean by that, but I am sure it is something
utterly scurrilous.'

'Scandalous, not scurrilous.' He pulled her to
her feet and into his arms. 'Want to find out?'

'Do you even know yourself?'

He laughed. 'No, but I am certain of one
thing. It starts with a kiss,' he said, and suited
action to words.

The second kiss of the day, and it picked up
where the first had left off on the cold pier. Just
a kiss at first, his hands on her shoulders, his
mouth warm, soft. Then his hands slid down
to cup her bottom, pulling her closer, and she
twined hers around his neck, reaching up, and
his tongue licked into her mouth, and heat flared.

He kissed her. She kissed him back, refusing
to let herself think about what she was doing,
concentrating her mind on the taste of him,
and the smell of him, and the way he felt. The
breadth of his shoulders. Her hands smoothing
down his coat to the tautness of his buttocks,
her fingers curling into him to tug him closer,

wanting the shivery thrill of his arousal pressed into her belly.

Hard. Not just there, but all of him, hard muscle, tensed, powerful. She pressed into him, her eyes tight shut, her mouth open to him, her tongue touching his, surrendering to the galloping of her pulses, the flush of heat, the tingle in her breasts. Kissing. Her hands stroking, under the skirts of his coat now, on the leather of his breeches.

His hands were not moving. She wanted them to move. Took a moment to remember the last time, and opened her eyes to whisper to him, 'It's fine. I am— I won't.'

'Tell me,' he said then. 'What am I to do?'

She shook her head. 'Can't,' she mumbled, embarrassed.

He kissed her slowly, deeply. 'Tell me, Ainsley,' he said.

She was losing it, the heat, the shivery feeling, but not the desire. John had never asked what she wanted. Despite all the vague advice Madame Hera doled out about connubial bliss and mutual satisfaction, she had neither the experience nor knowledge of either. 'I don't know,' Ainsley said, sounding petulant, feeling frustrated. *You do it*, was what she wanted to say.

'You do know,' Innes insisted.

He kissed her again. He cupped her face, forcing her to meet his eyes. His own were not mocking, not cruel. Dark blue, slumberous. Colour on his cheeks. Passion, not anger or shame, though it was being held in check. She realised why, with a little shock, remembered how she had been the other night. 'I don't know what to say,' she said.

'Tell me where you feel it when I kiss you,' he said, putting his hand in hers, kissing her. 'Tell me where it makes you want me to touch you.'

'Here,' she said, putting his hand on her breast.

His hand covered the soft swell. Her nipple hardened. She caught her breath as he squeezed her lightly through the layers of her gown and her corsets. 'Like this?' he asked, and she nodded. He kissed her neck, her throat, still stoking, kneading, making her nipple ache for more, then turned his attention to the other breast, and she caught her breath again.

'You like that?' Innes said.

His thumb circled her taut nipple. 'Yes.'

'And that?'

Her other nipple. 'Yes.'

'What else?'

That smile of his. His hands teasing her. She wanted his hands on her skin. His mouth on her nipple. The thought shocked her and excited her and terrified her. Her breasts were so small. John had always said— But she was not going to think about John. And Innes had said— What had Innes said?

He was kissing her neck again, her throat again. And her mouth again. 'Ask me,' he whispered, nibbling on the lobe of her ear. 'Ask me to kiss you. Here,' he said, cupping her breast. 'Ask me to taste you. Tell me what you want, Ainsley. I want to please you. Tell me.'

'I want—I want you to kiss me. Here,' she said, putting her hand over his. 'I want you to— Innes, I want you not to be disappointed.'

'Ainsley, it is not possible. I absolutely assure you that I won't be disappointed,' Innes said, loosening her cloak and turning her around. Kissing the back of her neck, he began to loosen the buttons of her gown, just enough to slide the bodice down her arms. His hands covered her breasts, his body pressed into her back. She could feel his hard, rigid length against the swell of her bottom.

'You see,' he said, nuzzling the nape of her neck. 'You feel what you are doing to me?'

She wriggled, arching her back so that he pressed closer. Innes moaned, and she laughed, a soft, sensual sound deep in her throat, for it was potent, the effect she had on his potency, and it gave her a burst of confidence. 'Touch me,' she said, 'I want you to touch me. Your hands. Your mouth. On me.'

'It will be my pleasure.' He undid the knot of her stays, then turned her round. 'And yours, I hope.'

He dipped his head and kissed the swell of her breasts above her corset. His tongue licked into the valley between them, kissing, his lips soft on her skin. He loosened her stays and freed her breasts, cupping them, one in each hand. Her nipples were dark pink, tight. Innes's eyes were dark with excitement. 'I told you,' he said with a wicked smile. 'I told you.'

He dipped his head and took her nipple in his mouth and sucked. She jerked, the drag of sensation connecting directly with the growing tightness between her legs. He sucked again, slowly, and it was like the tightening of a cord. He kissed her. He traced the shape of her breast with his tongue and kissed his way over to the other one. Sucking. Dragging. She moaned. Sucking. Tension. She said his name in a voice she hardly recognised.

'What?' he asked, sounding just as ragged. 'Tell me what you want.'

'I can't.'

More sucking. Nipping. She clutched at his shoulders, for her knees had begun to shake. 'Tell me,' Innes insisted.

She felt as if her insides were coiling. She was so hot, and the heat was concentrated between her legs. There had been echoes of this before. She had forgotten that, but it had been further away, not like this, not so close. 'I don't know,' she said, frustration making her voice tense, her fingers digging deep into his shoulders. 'Innes, I really don't know.'

She thought he would stop. Or he would tell her what it was. That he would give her the words. That he would simply act. But he did none of those things. He smiled at her, his mouth curling in a way that made her insides tighten even more. 'Oh, I think you do,' he said.

His hand slid down, between her legs, and curled into her, through her gown. Instinctively she tilted up. 'Yes,' she said. 'Yes, I do.'

He caressed her, the flat of his palm against her skirts, her skirts and petticoats flattened, rubbing into the heat between her legs, and she realised that was what she wanted. 'More,' she said, helping him, arching her spine. 'More. No, less—no skirts.'

She pulled up her gown, her petticoats, shamelessly, not caring now, and put his hand underneath. Innes groaned. She pulled his face to hers and kissed him desperately. He groaned again. 'Innes,' she said, 'Innes I want— I think I want— Innes, for goodness' sake.'

He cupped her again, between her legs, only this time there was only the thin linen of her pantaloons between her and his hand. She was throbbing. There was a hard knot of her throbbing against his hand. And then he began to stroke her and the knot tightened, and throbbed, contracted and she thought she wouldn't be able to bear it, and for a few seconds she felt as if she were hovering, quivering, and then it broke, pulsing, the most delightful pulsing, making her cry out in pleasure, over and over, until it slowed, stopped, and she clung to him, her hair falling down her shoulders, panting, utterly abandoned, and for the first time in her life, utterly spent.

'I didn't know,' she said simply to Innes when she finally managed to let go her grip on him, surprised at her utter lack of embarrassment.

'Then I'm honoured.'

'Palpitations. That is how one woman described it to Madame Hera in a letter I read yesterday. "He does not give me the palpitations I can give myself."' Ainsley covered her mouth, her eyes wide. 'Good grief, does that mean that she…?'

'I reckon it does.'

She laughed. 'It is a whole new world. I thought the woman was talking about some sort of nervous condition. It's as well I've not replied yet.'

'I look forward to reading your reply.'

He was looking distinctly uncomfortable as he tried to arrange his coat around the very obvious swelling in his trousers. Catching Ainsley's eye, he blushed faintly. 'It's at times like this I can see the merit of a kilt.'

Were there rules that applied to this sort of situation? 'Should I do something to—to relieve you?' she blurted out, then flushed bright red. She sounded as if she was offering to bathe his wounds and not—not… She made a helpless gesture. 'I don't know the—the form.'

Innes burst out laughing. 'This is not a sport! Oh, don't go all prickly, I didn't mean— Ainsley, I would love you to *relieve* me, but there is no need. Well, there is, but I will— It will go away if we talk of something else.' He stroked her tangle of hair back from her face, his smile gentling. 'Your pleasure was very much mine, I assure you.'

Was he merely being nice? Polite? She eyed him dubiously. She had always suspected there was something missing even in the early days of her marriage before John began to find her body so repellent, but she had always been under the apprehension that the main event, so to speak, was a man's pleasure. Not that John had taken much pleasure latterly. A chore. Then a failure. Though he had not seemed to have any such problems alone. She shuddered, still mortified by that discovery.

'Ainsley, what is it?'

She was about to shake her head, but then she paused. 'Palpitations. The woman who wrote to Madame Hera, she gives them to herself because her husband does not—cannot. There is something wrong with her husband, then, is there not?'

'Ignorance, or perhaps he's just selfish. Is this another of Madame's problems?'

'It made me wonder,' Ainsley said, ignoring this question. 'Would a man—a husband— If he cannot, with his wife, I mean, but he can—you know, do that...' She swallowed. She did know the words for this, they had been thrown in her face. 'Bring pleasure to himself. If he can do that for himself, but he can't with his wife, then there is something wrong with his wife, isn't there?'

Innes looked at her strangely. 'I thought only women wrote to you?'

Ainsley managed a noncommittal shrug.

'Do you mean can't or won't?'

Were they the same thing? She forced herself to think back. No. John had tried, and it had shamed him. 'Can't,' Ainsley said sadly.

He touched her cheek gently. 'Poor wife. And poor husband. Though I'd say the problem was most definitely his.'

Chapter Seven

August 1840, three weeks later

Felicity threw herself down on the bed, careless of the creases it would put in the emerald-green gown she wore for the Rescinding ceremony. 'So tell me, since this looks like the only opportunity I'll have to get you to myself, how are you enjoying married life?'

Ainsley, still in the woollen wrapper she had donned after her bath, was perched on a stool in front of the dressing table. Her hair ought to be curled, but it would take for ever, and in the breeze that would no doubt be blowing outside, it would probably be straight again by the time they reached the church. 'We're not really married. I like it a lot better than my real marriage was.'

'I'm sorry I couldn't get here until yesterday.

I've been so busy. I've barely had a chance to talk to your Mr Drummond.'

'I've barely had a chance myself lately, there's been so much to do to get this ceremony organised, and when Innes has not been closeted with Eoin talking agriculture, he's been with his surveyor, Robert Alexander, talking engineering. They're finalising the plans for a new pier and road. Mr Alexander has made a model of the pier and the road out of paper and paste. It is quite realistic. Innes will unveil it today, after the Rescinding.' Ainsley picked up her brush but made no attempt to apply it. 'So I suppose it's no surprise that we've been like ships that pass in the night.'

'I'd have thought you'd be happy about that, not having to live in his pocket.'

'I am. I don't want to. You're right.' Ainsley put the brush down and picked up a comb.

'You don't sound very convincing. Please don't tell me you're falling in love with the man.'

'That is one mistake I won't make twice,' Ainsley said scornfully, 'and even if I did—which I assure you I won't—Innes has made it very clear that he will not.'

Felicity raised her brows. 'Has he, now? Why not?'

'He likes his independence too much.'

'Marriage makes no difference to independence for a man, they carry on just as they please, regardless of the little woman waiting at home. It is only a wife who is shackled by matrimony.'

'You sound so bitter, Felicity.'

'Now, that is definitely a case of the pot calling the kettle black.'

Ainsley nodded. 'Yes, but I have reason to be bitter. My marriage—you know what it was like.'

'I know what it did to you, even though you refused to confide the particulars.' Felicity's smile was twisted. 'And as you must have guessed, I know enough, from being the other woman, not to want to be the wife. But that is over now.'

'You mean your—your...'

'*Affaire*, why not call it what it was.'

'Why did you not say?'

'Because I'm ashamed, and because it has taken up quite enough of my life for me to wish to grant it any more,' Felicity said bracingly. 'I read Madame Hera's latest batch of correspondence last night, by the light of a candle that threatened to blow out in the gale that was howling through my bedchamber.'

Ainsley and Mhairi had been forced to put all

their visitors up in the west wing of the castle, which had latterly been the old laird's quarters. 'I'm so sorry,' she said. 'Were you freezing?'

'I certainly don't fancy being here in the winter. Though Madame's correspondence heated me up,' Felicity said with a saucy smile. 'I assume that you and Mr Drummond have not been ships that passed each other every night.'

Ainsley flushed. 'Well, I know now that palpitations are not necessarily the prelude to a fainting attack,' she said. 'The rest you can deduce from Madame Hera's letters.'

'Does he know that you're writing them?'

'Yes. And before you ask, you were right. I owe you five pounds. He thought it was fun.' Ainsley's laughter faded. 'He made me realise that some of my advice has been— Well, frankly, not the best, Felicity. I don't mean because I've been forced to modify my language to avoid offence—'

'I did notice a tendency to use rather less euphemisms and rather more—shall we say colloquial terms, in those personal replies,' Felicity interjected. 'I take it those were Mr Drummond's phrases?'

'Do you think they are too much?'

'I think they make it impossible for the recipients to misunderstand. We shall see. I have found in this business that while people rarely praise, they are very quick to let you know when they're not happy. But I interrupted you. You were saying, about your advice…'

Ainsley finished combing her hair and began to pin it up in what she hoped would be a wind-resistant knot. 'Looking back over my replies since Madame Hera came into being, I realised my advice has often been—defensive? No, sometimes rather combative. I assumed, you see, that the women who write are in need of— That they need to stand up for themselves. Madame Hera is very belligerent. She sees marriage as a battlefield.'

'In many cases she's right.'

'Yes.' Ainsley turned away from the mirror to face her friend, her hair half-pinned. 'Madame Hera was born of war. She ought to have been called Madame Mars, or whatever the female equivalent is.'

'Athena. No, she is Greek.' Felicity shook her head impatiently. 'It doesn't matter. Go on.'

'I've been thinking about John a lot these past few weeks. I blamed him for everything. I hated him, in the end, for what he did to me, for the constant undermining and the—the other things. I was furious about the debts, and about the mess he left me in. Much of it was his fault, of course.

He was weak and he was a spendthrift and he was completely gullible when it came to moneymaking schemes, but I wonder how different things would have been if, instead of blaming him and shutting him out, and setting off on my own vengeful path, I had shown him a little understanding.'

'None at all!' Felicity said scornfully. 'The man was a useless profligate and you are better off by far without him.'

'Perhaps he would have been better off without me.'

'What do you mean?'

'When things started to go wrong, I didn't try very hard to make them right. Oh, I challenged him about the money—but not really with the conviction I thought I had at the time. I think— this is awful—but I think I *wanted* him to be in the wrong, more than I wanted to make things right between us.'

'Ainsley, he *was* in the wrong.'

'Yes, but so, too, was I. I would do things differently if I got the chance again.'

'But you are getting the chance again. Don't tell me it doesn't count because you're not really married, Ainsley, you know what I mean. I hope you're not letting Drummond walk all over you?'

'Not exactly. I don't think he deliberately excludes me, but he's not in the habit of including anyone in his life. I told you, he is very attached to his independence.'

'Blasted men,' Felicity said feelingly. Looking down at the little gold watch she always wore on a fob on her gown, she clapped her hand over her mouth in dismay. 'Ainsley, we've to be at the chapel for the start of proceedings in an hour and you haven't even done your hair. Turn round. Let me.' Jumping to her feet, she gathered up a handful of pins. 'You could come back to Edinburgh with me after this, you know.'

'Thank you, but no.' Ainsley met her friend's eyes in the mirror and smiled. 'It's good for me, being here at the moment. It's helped me think.'

'Don't think too hard, else you'll be turning that John McBrayne into a saint, and that he was not,' Felicity said, pinning frantically.

'No, but I had turned him into a devil, and he wasn't that, either.'

'Hmm.' Felicity carried on pinning. 'I'm sorry I can't stay longer. You know how it is, being a female in a man's world. If I'm not back, they'll replace me.'

'It's fine. I know how important your job is to you. And to me. Madame Hera depends on you.'

'Madame Hera is becoming so popular that she doesn't need my support. There.' Felicity threw down the remainder of the pins. 'Let's get you into your gown.' She pulled the dress from its hanger and gave it a shake.

'I'm getting nervous,' Ainsley said as she stepped into it. 'I haven't thought about it until now. I've been too busy planning it, but it's a big thing, Felicity. It's really important for Innes that it goes well. I thought about asking Mhairi for a good luck spell, but asking her is probably bad luck. You've no idea how superstitious she can be.'

'The housekeeper?' Felicity was busy hooking the buttons on Ainsley's gown. 'Is she the witch?'

'Her mother was.'

'And she was the old laird's mistress, too, you tell me. You should ask her for a potion. You know, just to make sure that there are no consequences from the palpitations your husband is giving you.'

Ainsley's face fell. 'I don't think that will be necessary.'

'Oh, Ainsley, I'm so sorry. I didn't think.'

'It doesn't matter.' Ainsley managed to smile. 'Really. Are you done? May I look?' Ainsley turned towards the mirror and shook out her skirts.

'I do hope your Mr Drummond is making

sure he takes appropriate measures.' Felicity gave her a grave look. 'You cannot take the risk.'

'There is no risk, and even if there were, I am very sure that the last thing Innes would risk is such a complication.' Seeing that her friend was about to question her further, Ainsley picked up her shawl. 'We should go.'

'Wait. I brought you something.' Felicity handed her a velvet-covered box. 'A belated wedding present. It's not much, but it's pretty.'

It was a gold pendant set with a tiny cluster of diamonds around an amethyst. Ainsley hugged her tightly. 'It's lovely. Thank you.' She hugged Felicity again, then handed her the necklace to fasten. She stared down at her left hand, with the simple gold band Innes had given her more than two months ago. 'Do you think I'll pass muster. As the laird's wife, I mean?' she asked anxiously. 'I don't want to let Innes down.'

'That is exactly the kind of talk I don't want to hear. You will do your best, and that's all you can do. The rest is up to him. He's lucky to have you, Ainsley. Am I permitted to wish you good luck, or is that bad luck?'

'I don't know, probably.'

'Then I will say what the actors say. Break a leg. But make sure that you do not break your heart.' Felicity cast a quick glance at the mirror.

'My hair. As usual. Give me just a minute, for that rather gorgeous man who brought me over in his rather rustic fishing boat yesterday is to be one of your escorts, and I'd like to look a little less ravaged than I did the last time he saw me.'

'You mean Eoin?'

'That's the one. I am to be one of your Mr Drummond's escorts in the walk to the chapel. He asked me last night.' Felicity grimaced. 'Two virgins, it's supposed to be. I hope my lack of maidenhead will not bring you bad luck.'

Ainsley choked. 'I think what matters is that you are unmarried. Shall we go?'

'Are you ready?'

Ainsley kissed her cheek. 'As I'll ever be,' she said.

Innes hadn't thought about the ceremony until he was walking to the church between his escorts, with what felt like the entire population of Strone Bridge behind him. He was putting on a show, that was all. It was just a daft tradition; it meant something to the people who would be attending, but nothing to him. Except he felt nervous, and it did matter, and realising that made him feel slightly sick, because that meant Strone Bridge had come to matter, and that complicated everything.

It was not raining, which Eoin had assured him was a good sign. From somewhere behind him came the skirl of the bagpipes. On one side of him Felicity, Ainsley's eccentric friend, picked her way along the path, sliding him what he could only describe as assessing glances every now and then. He wondered what Ainsley had told her. He doubted very much that this very self-assured and rather sultrily attractive woman fulfilled the criteria expected of his escort. Of Mhairi's niece Flora's qualifications, he had no doubt at all.

They arrived at the door of the church, and the crowd behind him filtered in to become the congregation. Begging a moment of privacy, Innes made his way alone to the Drummond Celtic cross, not to commune with the dead man so recently interred there, but the one whose corpse lay elsewhere. In a few moments, he was going to have to stand at that altar, in front of those people, and be blessed as the new laird. It should have been Malcolm standing there. If things had gone as they had been planned, as his brother had so desperately wanted them to, Malcolm would have been standing at that altar fourteen years ago beside Blanche, taking part in another ritual.

Blanche. He never allowed her name into his

head. Until he'd come back to Strone Bridge, he rarely even allowed himself to think of Malcolm. Now, standing in front of the cross where Malcolm should have been buried, Innes felt overwhelmed with grief and regrets. If he could turn back time, make it all as it should be—Malcolm leading the Rescinding, Blanche at his side, and perhaps three or four bairns, too. Strone Bridge would be flourishing. The congregation would be celebrating.

'And you,' he hissed at the cross, 'you would have gone to your grave a damn sight happier, that's for sure. You never thought you'd see this day, any more than I did.'

Innes leaned his forehead on the cold stone and closed his eyes. If Malcolm could see what had happened to his precious lands, he'd be appalled. He could not bring his brother back, but he could do his damnedest to restore the lands to what they had been. 'No, I can do better,' Innes said to the stone. 'I will make them flourish, better than they have ever, and what's more, I'll do it my way.'

For better or for worse, he thought to himself, turning his back on the cross. The same words he'd said in front of another altar not so very long ago, with Ainsley by his side. For better or for worse, it looked as if he'd made up his mind to stay here, for the time being. He'd rather have Ainsley by his side than any other woman. 'For the time being, any road,' he muttered, squaring his shoulders and making his way towards the chapel.

She was waiting at the porch, with Eoin and Robert by her side. She looked so nervous as she made her way towards him, Innes was worried for a moment that she might actually faint. Her gown was of pale silk, embroidered with pink and blue flowers. The long puffed sleeves gave it a demure look, at odds with the ruffled neckline. She wore a pretty pendant he had not seen before.

Her hand, when he took it, was icy cold. Muttering an apology, Innes squeezed it reassuringly. Was she thinking as he was, how like a wedding this whole thing was turning out to be? Was she thinking back to the other time, when she had stood beside another man, in another church? It shouldn't bother him. He hadn't thought about it before, and wished he had not now. It shouldn't bother him, any more than the idea, which had only just occurred to him, that she would leave here soon. He might have committed to the place, but it had always been a temporary location for her. There would come a time when he'd be here alone. When things were clearer. They were very far from clear now. No need to think of that just yet.

Ainsley winced, and Innes immediately loosened his grip. 'Ready?' he asked. She nodded. She put her arm in his and prepared to walk down the aisle with him, and Innes closed his mind to everything save playing his part.

Standing in the church porch, offering her cheek to be kissed by yet another well-wisher, Ainsley felt as if her smile was frozen to her face. The Drummond ring that Innes had placed on the middle finger of her right hand felt strange. It was apparently worn by every laird's wife. A rose-tinted diamond coincidentally almost the same colour as the pendant Felicity had given her, surrounded by a cluster of smaller stones, it was obviously an heirloom. She felt quite ambivalent about it, for there was bound to be some sort of curse attached to anyone who wore it under false pretences. She would ask Innes. No, she decided almost immediately, she would rather not know.

The last of the men kissed her cheek. The church door closed and the minister shook Innes's hand before heading along the path to join the rest of the guests at the castle. 'They can wait for us a bit,' Innes said when she made to follow him. 'I haven't even had the chance to tell you that you look lovely.'

'Don't be daft. There's no one watching.'

'I know. Why do you think I kept you here?' he asked, smiling down at her. 'I believe the laird has the right to kiss his lady.'

'You already have, at the end of the blessing.'

He laughed, that low, growling laugh that did things to her insides. 'That wasn't what I had in mind,' he said, and pulled her into his arms.

His kiss was gentle, reassuring. He held her tightly, as if he, too, needed reassurance. Her poke bonnet bumped against his forehead, and they broke apart. 'I didn't think it would matter,' Innes said, running a hand through his carefully combed hair.

'Do you feel like a real laird now?'

She meant it lightly, but Innes took the question seriously. 'I feel as though I've made a promise to the place,' he said. 'I think— I don't know how I will manage it, but I owe it to Strone Bridge to restore it. Somehow.' He pulled her back into his arms. 'I know I was sceptical about the Rescinding, but I think it was a good idea, and it was your idea. So thank you.'

She was touched as well as gratified. Unwilling to show it, she looked down at the ring. 'Was this your mother's?'

'And my grandmother's and so on. Do you like it? Don't tell me you're worried that there's some sort of curse attached to it.'

She laughed. 'I don't appreciate having my mind read. I was worried that it would be bad luck to wear it, since I'm not really the laird's lady.'

'There's no need to worry, I promise you. Generations of Drummond men have married for the good of Strone Bridge before all else, and that's exactly what I've done,' Innes said. 'In our own way, we're carrying on a tradition. Drummonds don't marry for love.' His expression darkened. 'It's when they try to, that's when they become cursed.'

She wanted to ask him what he meant, but she was afraid, looking at his face. He could only be thinking of himself. It was so obvious; she couldn't believe she hadn't thought of it before. That was why he was so insistent he'd never fall in love. Because he already had, and it had come to nothing.

She felt slightly sick. She oughtn't to. The pair of them were even better matched than she had realised, both of them burned by that most revered of emotions. She should be relieved to finally understand. Actually, there was no cause for her to feel anything at all. Innes's heart was no concern of hers.

'We should go,' Innes said, dragging his mind back from whatever dark place he had gone to. 'I want to get the formal Rescinding out of the way before too much whisky had been taken. What is it? You look as if you've seen a ghost.'

Ainsley managed to smile. 'Just my husband, in his full Highland regalia, looking every bit the part of the laird. I have not told you how very handsome you look.'

He tucked her hand in his, smiling down at her wickedly, his black mood seemingly vanished. 'Do I live up to your expectations of a wild Highlander?'

Her own mood lightened. 'I don't know.' Ainsley gave him a teasing smile. 'It's a shame we have a party to attend, else I would say I was looking forward to finding out.'

A fire had been burning constantly in the huge hearth of the Great Hall for the past few days. The mantel was of carved oak set on two huge marble pillars, and the hearth itself was big enough to hold a massive log cut from a very old tree in one whole piece. The Great Hall was a long, narrow room done in the Elizabethan style, though it had been created less than a hundred years before. The walls were panelled to head height, then timbered and rendered, giving the impression of great age, as did the vaulted oak ceiling. Ainsley stood at the far end of the room, where a balconied recess had been formed with yet more oak, this time in the form of three arches rather like a rood screen.

The hall was full of people, very few of whom she recognised. Innes had not wanted anyone from his old life here. When Ainsley had enquired about inviting other local gentry, having heard the name Caldwell mentioned as the owners of the next estate, she thought he had flinched, though she could not be sure. 'We've enough to do, to win the hearts and minds of our own,' he'd said quickly. 'Let's keep it a Strone Bridge celebration.' Everyone present, save herself, Felicity and Robert Alexander had been born here, or had married someone who had been born here. Which for now included her, though she did not really count.

Innes was standing a few feet away, holding one of those intense conversations with his surveyor that seemed to require Robert Alexander to flap his arms about a lot. The model of the pier and the new road was to be revealed after the Rescinding. Mr Alexander was nervous. She could see that Innes was reassuring him.

The laird. Her husband, in his Highland dress, which he claimed to have worn just for her, though she knew he was only teasing. He had opted for the short jacket, and not the long, cloak-like plaid, of a dark wool that was fitted tight across his shoulders, the front cut in a curve, finishing at his neat waist. Under it, he wore a waistcoat and a white shirt. And below it, the kilt, a long length of wool folded into narrow pleats and held in place by a thick leather belt with a large silver buckle. When he turned, as he did now, granting her a delightful view of his rear, the pleats swung out. As she suspected, he had very shapely legs, not at all scrawny, but muscled. His long, knit hose covered what Mhairi called a fine calf, and Ainsley had to agree. There was a small jewelled dagger tucked into one of his hose, and another, longer dagger attached to his belt. The kilt stopped at his knee. He could not possibly be wearing undergarments.

He caught her looking at him and came to join her. 'I would very much like to ask you what you're thinking,' he said softly into her ear, 'but if you told me, I reckon I'd have to carry you off and have my wicked Highland way with you, and we've a lot of ceremony to get through, unfortunately.'

'And a party to attend afterwards.'

'Actually, Eoin was just telling me that it's customary for the laird and his lady to celebrate their new life alone.'

'I read nothing of that in the book.'

'It's known as the—the Bonding,' Innes said.

She bit her lip, trying not to laugh. 'You made that up.'

'It's one of the new traditions I'm thinking of establishing.' Innes smiled one of his sinful smiles that made her feel as if she were blushing inside. 'What do you say?'

'I would certainly not wish to break with tradition on a night like this. And I would not wish all that effort you've made with your Highland dress to go to waste.'

His eyes darkened. She felt the flush inside her spreading. 'If it were not for the Rescinding, I would carry you off right now.'

'I have gone to an enormous effort to get this Rescinding organised, Laird. You are not going to spoil it for me.'

'No. I would not dream of it. I'm truly grateful, Ainsley.' He kissed her cheek. 'But just as soon as it's over, my lady...'

'I know. A Bonding! Whatever that entails.'

'Haven't you imagined it? I know I have. Lots of times.'

'Innes! Let us concentrate on one ceremony before we start discussing another.'

He laughed. 'Very well. I see your Miss Blair conferring with Eoin. Again. Is she spoken for?' Innes asked.

'She's wedded to her career,' Ainsley replied.

'Do you know, you have a way of pursing up your mouth just at one corner when you fib, as if you're trying to swallow whatever it is you're determined not to say.'

'I was not fibbing.'

'You weren't telling the truth, either.' Innes smiled down at her. 'I suspect your Felicity is a woman of many secrets.' Innes put his arm around her waist, pulling her into his side. 'I'm not really interested in Miss Blair's private life, nor indeed Eoin's. I'm more interested in our own. But first, it's time for the Rescinding. Are you ready?'

'What if I forget something?' Ainsley asked, suddenly panicked.

'You've made the whole thing go like a dream so far. Now all you have to do is to remember all the promises I make, lest I forget any. And I must forgive and forget.' Innes rolled his eyes. 'I cannot believe my father did this and meant it.'

The chair, like most of the Great Hall, was carved in oak and had been polished to a soft gleam. The canopy that covered it was of the same faded green velvet as the cushion. After handing Ainsley into the much simpler chair by his side, Innes sat down. He felt part foolish, part—good grief, surely not proud? No, but it was something close. The ghosts of his ancestors had got into his blood. Or having all those eyes on him had gone to his head. Or maybe it was this chair, and the hall, which was only ever used for formal occasions. His father's birthday had always been celebrated here. The annual party for the tenants and cotters. His and Malcolm's coming of age.

No. This was a time to look forward, not back. Innes jumped up. The room fell silent. He picked up the sword that lay at his feet, the wicked blade glittering. The sheath lay beside it. Carefully, he placed the sword inside the sheath, a signal of peace, and handed it to Eoin, who was once again playing the part of the nearest living blood relative. All of this was prescribed in the book that Ainsley had shown him. *The Customs and Ways of the Family Drummond of Strone Bridge*, it pompously declared itself in faded gold script. Mhairi had been insulted when he'd laughed. Ainsley had apologised on his behalf. Later, she'd teased him, calling it the *Drummond Self-*

Help Manual. Now he was simply glad Ainsley had read it so carefully for him.

'Friends,' Innes said, 'I bid you welcome. Before we begin the ceremony, it is traditional to toast the departed.' He lifted the glass of whisky that lay ready, nodding to Ainsley to do the same, and waiting to make sure everyone watching had a glass. *'Slàinte!'* he said. 'To the old laird, my father. *Cha bhithidh a leithid ami riamh.* We'll never see his like again.' He drank, surprised to discover that the toast had not stuck in his craw quite as much as he'd thought it would. Perhaps it was because it was true, he thought to himself wryly. He was making sure of it.

Innes put his glass down. 'The laird has met his maker. With him must be buried all grudges, all debts, all quarrels. A forgiving and forgetting. A Rescinding. A new beginning. And I promise you,' he said, departing from his script, 'that it is not the case of sweeping the dirt out of one door and blowing it into the other. That is one change. The first, I hope of many. This Rescinding is an old tradition, but today it will be done in quite a new way. No recriminations. No half measures. No payback. That is my vow to you. Let us begin.'

He sat down heavily. Sweat trickled down his back. He never made speeches. The words, his words, had not been planned, but they were *his*, and he'd meant them. Scanning the room anxiously, he waited for the reaction. They were an inscrutable lot, the people of Strone Bridge. The lightest of touches on his hand, which was resting by the side of his chair, made him look over at Ainsley. 'Perfect,' she mouthed, and smiled at him. When she made to take her hand away, he captured it, twining his fingers in hers. He felt good.

Ainsley waited anxiously. Innes had been nervous making his speech. His palm was damp. He'd been treating the Rescinding almost as a joke, at the very least a mere formality, but when he spoke it was clear that he meant every word he said. Such a confident man, and such a successful one, she had assumed speech-making came easily to him. It was oddly reassuring to discover it did not. She couldn't decide whether she wanted there to be lots of petitioners or few, but she was vastly relieved when the first came forward, for none at all would have been a disaster.

The man was a tenant, and by the looks of him, one of long standing. 'Mr Stewart,' Innes said, 'of Auchenlochan farm. What is it you wish from me?'

The old man, who had been gazing anxiously down at his booted feet, straightened and looked Innes firmly in the eye. 'I petition the laird to forgive two wrongs,' he said. 'For my son, John Angus Stewart, who left two quarters rent unpaid on Auchenlochan Beag farm when he sailed for Canada. And for myself, for failing to inform the laird that the rent was unpaid.' Mr Stewart looked over his shoulder at the rest of the room, before turning back to Innes. 'The laird did raise the rents far beyond the value of the farms, it is true, and many of us here felt the injustice of that, but...' He waved his hand, to silence the rumbles of agreement emanating from behind him. 'But it was his right, and those of us who took advantage of his failing to collect were wrong, and they should be saying so now,' he finished pointedly.

Innes got to his feet, and said the words as specified in the Drummond manual. 'Angus Stewart of Auchenlochan, and John Angus Stewart, who was of Auchenlochan Beag, your petitions are granted, the debt is Rescinded.'

Mr Stewart nodded, his lips pursed. Before he had reached his wife, another man had come forward to proclaim another unpaid rent, and after him another, and another. Some went reluctantly, some resignedly, some went in response to Crofter Stewart's beady-eyed stare, but they all went. The debts Innes was waiving amounted to a large sum of money. Ainsley couldn't understand the old laird—the man was something of a conundrum—putting rents sky-high on one hand, then failing to collect them on the other. Since Mhairi assured her the laird's mind had not wandered, she could only assume that it must have been severely warped. *Twisted.* That was a better word.

As Innes continued to forgive and forget, the Rescinding began to take on a lighter note. A woman admitted to burying a dog along with her husband in the graveyard of the Strone Bridge chapel. 'Though I know it is forbidden, but he always preferred that beast's company to mine, and the pair of them were that crabbit, I thought they would be happy together,' she declared, arms akimbo. Laughter greeted this confession, and Innes earned himself a fat kiss when he promised the dog and the master's mortal remains would not be torn asunder.

Whisky flowed, and wine, too, along with the strong local heather ale. Innes was preparing to end the ceremony when a man came forward whom Ainsley recognised as Mhairi's taciturn brother, the father of Flora, the pretty lass who had been one half of Innes's escort.

'Donald McIntosh of High Strone farm.' Expecting another case of rent arrears, Ainsley's mind was on the banquet, which would be needed to sop up some of the drink that had been taken. She was trying to catch Mhairi's eye, and was surprised to see the housekeeper stiffen, her gaze fixed on her brother.

'Your father did wrong by my sister for many years,' Donald McIntosh said.

'Dodds!' Mhairi protested, but her brother ignored her.

'The laird took my sister's innocence and spoilt her for any other man. He shamed my sister. He shamed my family.'

'Dodds!' Mhairi grabbed her brother by the arm, her face set. 'I loved the man, will you not understand that? He did not take anything from me.'

'Love! That cold-hearted, thrawn old bastard didn't love you. You were fit to warm his bed, but not fit to bear his name. You were his hoor, Mhairi.'

Hoor? Shocked, Ainsley realised he meant *whore*.

Mhairi paled, taking a staggering step back. 'It's true, he didn't love me, but I loved him. I don't care if that makes me his hoor, and I don't know what you think you're doing, standing here in front of the man's son. This is a celebration.'

'It's a Rescinding.' Donald McIntosh turned back towards Innes. 'I beg forgiveness for the curse I put upon your family.'

Along with almost everyone else in the room, Ainsley gasped. Almost everyone else. Felicity, she noticed, was looking fascinated rather than shocked. What Innes thought, she could not tell. 'What particular curse?' he asked.

'That the bloodline would fail.' Donald spoke not to Innes, but to his sister. 'I had the spell from our mother, though she made me swear not to use it.'

'No. *Màthair* would never have told *you* her magic, Dodds McIntosh. No fey wife worth her salt would have trusted a mere man.'

'You're wrong, Mhairi. Like me, she felt the shame that man brought on our family.'

Mhairi's mouth fell open. 'And now she is dead it cannot be retracted. What have you done?'

Donald stiffened. 'I am entitled to be forgiven.'

'And forgiven you shall be,' Innes said, breaking the tense silence. 'The potency of the Drummond men is legendary. I refuse to believe that any curse could interfere with it.'

The mood eased. Laughter once more echoed around the hall, and another supplicant shuffled forward. Stricken, Ainsley barely heard his petition. Until she came to Strone Bridge, she had not considered herself superstitious, but Mhairi's tireless efforts to appease the wee people and to keep the changelings at bay seemed to have infected her. By some terrible quirk of fate, Dodds McIntosh's curse had come true. Ainsley felt doubly cursed.

Faintly, she was aware of Innes bringing proceedings to a close. Mechanically, she got to her feet while he said the final words. It didn't matter, she told herself. It would matter if she and Innes were truly married, but they were not. Innes did not want a child. He'd told her so on that very first day, hadn't he? She tried to remember his precise words. No, he'd said he didn't want a wife. *One must necessarily precede the other*, that was what he had said. But she was his wife. And she could not— But she wasn't really his wife. She could not let him down in this most basic of things, because he did not require it of her. She clung to this, and told herself it was a comfort.

'I declare the Rescinding complete, the door closed on the old and open on the new,' Innes was saying. 'It's time to celebrate. Mr Alexander here will fill you all in on the details of our plans for a new pier and a new road, too. There is food and drink aplenty to be had, but first, and most important, one last toast.' Innes lifted his glass and turned towards Ainsley. 'To my lady wife, who made this day possible. I thank you. I could not have done this without you.'

He kissed her full on the lips; the guests roared their approval and Ainsley's heart swelled with pride. She had done this. She had proved something by doing this. For the moment, at least, nothing else mattered.

Chapter Eight

It was dark, but the party was only just hotting up, thanks to the fiddlers. A bundle of bairns slept snuggled together like a litter of puppies, some of them still clutching their sugar candy. In the recess at the far end of the room, in front of Robert Alexander's model of the pier, Mhairi was holding court with a group of local wives. Miss Blair was dancing a wild reel with Eoin. This, Innes decided, was as good a time as any for them to make their getaway unobserved.

The night air was cool. He wrapped a soft shawl around Ainsley's shoulders and led her down to her favourite spot, overlooking the Kyles. Above them, the stars formed a carpet of twinkling lights in the unusually clear sky. 'It went well, didn't it?' she asked. 'Save for that curse Mhairi's brother made.'

'Stupid man. If he really was so ashamed, he

should have done something about it when my father was alive.'

'From what you've told me about your father, Mr McIntosh would then have found himself homeless.'

Innes considered this for a few moments. 'No. More likely my father despised Dodds McIntosh for not challenging him. His sense of honour was twisted, but he did have one.'

'Perhaps he did love Mhairi, in his own way.'

'My father never loved anyone, save himself.'

'Not even your brother?'

Ainsley spoke so tentatively, Innes could not but realise she knew perfectly well how sensitive was the subject. He hesitated on the brink of a dismissive shrug, but she had done so much for him today, he felt he wanted to give her something back. 'You're thinking that my father's wilful neglect of Strone Bridge is evidence of his grief for my brother, is that it?'

'Yes.'

'I'm not so sure. My brother loved this place. If my father really cared, why would he destroy the thing Malcolm loved the most? Besides, Eoin said it was a gradual thing, the neglect.'

'A slow realisation of what he'd lost?'

Innes shook his head. 'A slow realisation that

I was not coming back, more like. He destroyed it so that I would be left with nothing.'

'And you are determined to prove him wrong?'

'I'd prefer to say that I'm determined to put things right.'

'How will you do that?'

'I have no idea, and at the moment I have better things to think about.'

He kissed her in the moonlight, underneath the stars, to the accompaniment of the scrape of fiddles and the stomping of feet in the distance. She was not really his wife, but she understood him in a way that no one else did. He kissed her, telling her with his lips and his tongue and his hands not only of his desire, but that he wanted her here, like this.

'Are you sure someone won't come chasing after us to come back to the party?' Ainsley whispered.

'If they do, I'll tell them they're in danger of incurring a year of bad luck for interfering with the ancient and revered tradition of the Bonding,' Innes replied.

He felt the soft tremor of her laughter. 'Will you run up a special flag to declare it over, in the morning?'

'I haven't thought that far ahead. You know

that you can change your mind if you don't want to do this, don't you? You must be tired.'

'I'm not the least bit tired, and I don't want to change my mind,' she answered. 'I think we've waited long enough.'

He kissed her again. She tasted so sweet. Her skin was luminous in the moonlight, her eyes dark. He kissed her, and she wrapped herself around him and kissed him back, and their kisses moved from sweet to urgent. Panting, Innes tore his mouth from hers. 'I meant it,' he said. 'I am not expecting you to— We don't have to...'

'But you want to?' she asked, with that smile of hers that seemed to connect straight to his groin.

'I don't think there can be any mistaking that.'

And she laughed, that other sound that connected up to his groin. 'Good,' she said, 'because I want you, too.'

It was the way she said it, with confidence, unprompted, that delighted him most. He grabbed her hand, not trusting himself to kiss her again, and began to walk, as quickly as he could, towards the Home Farm. Ten minutes. It felt like an hour.

'Does this Bonding take place in the laird's bed or his lady's?' Ainsley asked as Innes opened the front door.

He kicked it shut, locking it securely, before he swept her up into his arms. 'Right now, I'm not even sure we'll make it to the bed.'

They did at least make it to her bedchamber. A fire burned in the cast-iron grate. Mhairi must have sent someone down from the castle to tend it. The curtains were drawn. A lamp stood on the hearth, another one on the nightstand, lending the room a pleasant glow. Ainsley stood, clasping her hands and wondering what she ought to do now. The excitement that had bubbled inside her dissipated as she eyed the bed, and memories of that other first night tried to poke their way into this one. She shivered, though it was not at all cold.

'You can still change your mind,' Innes said gently.

He meant it, too. A few days ago, Ainsley would have assumed that what he meant was that *he* had changed *his* mind. Even now, despite the fact that she knew how much he wanted her, she had to work to believe it. 'No,' she said. 'I don't want to change my mind. I don't.' She looked at the lamps, wondering.

'Do you want me to put them out?'

Like the last time. Like all of the last times.

She shook her head. She would not have it like any other time.

'Do you want me to leave you to undress?' Innes asked.

'I want…' She studied him, focusing on him, drinking him in so that he was the only one there in the room with her. 'I want you inside me,' she said, meaning in her head, not meaning it how it sounded, though when she saw the results, the leap of desire in his eyes, the way he looked at her, with such passion, she meant that, too. 'I want *you*,' she said, closing the space between them, 'and I want you to show me just how much you want me. That's what I want.'

Innes pulled her tight up against him, lifting her off her feet. 'I think I can manage that,' he said, and kissed her, and she realised that he already had.

He picked her up, but instead of laying her down on the bed, he pulled the quilt onto the floor and laid her down by the fire. Quickly divesting himself of his jacket, his waistcoat, his boots and stockings, he stood over her wearing just his plaid and his shirt. The firelight flickered over the naked flesh of his legs. She caught a glimpse of muscled thighs as he knelt down beside her, pulling her into his arms again to kiss her. There was heat inside her. There was heat on her skin from the fire. There were little trails of heat where he touched her. Her face. Her neck. His mouth on her throat. Kissing his way along the curve of her décolletage, his tongue licking the swell of her breasts, his hands splayed on her back, feathering over the exposed skin of her nape, the knot at the top of her spine, then down to pick open the buttons of her gown.

He kissed the tender spot behind her ears. He slid her gown over her arms, kissing her shoulders, the crook of her elbow, her wrists, tilting her gently back to work her gown down, over her legs. When he took off her shoes, he kissed her ankles through the silk of her stockings. And her calves. The backs of her knees. His mouth, thin silk, her skin. She watched him, her eyes wide open, not wanting to miss a moment, enthralled, astonished that simply watching could be so stimulating. His cheeks were flushed. His blue-black hair, grown longer since he came to Strone Bridge, was ruffled. She ran her fingers through it. Soft as silk. She pulled him down towards her, wanting the weight of him on her, and claimed his mouth. Hot, his mouth was. 'Sinful,' she murmured, lips against lips. 'I want to be sinful.'

Innes laughed, rolling to his knees again, pulling her with him to work at the ties of her stays.

His eyes were dark in this light, midnight blue, his pupils dilated. His shirt was open at the neck. The firelight danced over it, showing her shadows of muscle, making her ache to touch him. While he worked on her corsets, cursing under his breath at the time it was taking, she tugged at the shirt, pulling it free from the leather belt, sighing as her palms found his flesh, sighing again when he flexed and his muscles tensed. Flesh. Heated flesh. She pressed her mouth to his throat and licked his skin, feeling the vibration of his response. Then his triumphant growl as he finally cast her corsets aside and tore at her shift, leaving her in just her pantaloons and her stockings, the bright pink of her garters, which perfectly matched the flowers on her gown.

A fleeting urge to cover up her breasts faded as Innes devoured her with his eyes and then feasted on her with his mouth. Sucking. Nipping. Stroking. Setting up paths of heat, making her blood pulse and the muscles inside her contract. She fell back onto the quilt, tensing, heating, watching him kiss her, touch her, watching his hands on her skin, tanned, rough hands, covering her breasts, flattened over her belly, then pulling at the drawstring of her last undergarment. She looked so pale in the firelight. Her skin milky.

The curls between her thighs seemed tinged with autumn colours.

Innes smiled at her. She smiled back. Sinful. Sure. He pulled his shirt over his head, and she watched, clenching inside, the revelation of flesh and muscle, the smattering of dark hair on his chest, the thinner line from his navel to the belt of his kilt. The plaid tickled her thighs and her belly as he knelt over to kiss her. She could feel the tip of his shaft nudging between her legs. She tilted towards him, her fingers gripping into the muscles of his shoulders, and it touched her, the tensest part of her. 'Yes,' she said, not meaning to, not quite sure what she meant.

He sat up, still straddling her, and reached under his kilt, which was spread over the two of them. She could not see what he did, but she could see the intent in his eyes. Stroking, up and down, slick sliding, unmistakably not his hand, sliding. He was watching her. 'Yes,' she said, quite deliberately, 'again.'

Stroking. Sliding. She must be wet. She was tight. She was getting tighter. Stroking and sliding. And then more stroking. And more sliding. And she came. Suddenly. What she now knew was a climax, though it felt like an explosion. He lifted her, his hands under her, cupping the bare flesh of her bottom as she cried out, and the pulsing took her over, and he pushed his way inside her, thick, hard, pushing her apart, finding his way higher as her muscles pulsed around him, pulling him in, tighter, and higher and tighter.

He paused, his face tense, his breathing heavy. 'Ainsley?'

'Yes. Oh, yes.' She dug her fingers into his shoulder, remembering just in time Felicity's caution. 'But, Innes, be careful.'

'Of course. I promise. Always.' It pained her that he believed there was a need, then he tilted her farther, his hands cupping her bottom, and she forgot about it. She wrapped her legs around him, anxious, feeling anxious, not nervous, but like a runner, wanting to run, wanting to be off, wanting.

And then she was. Not running but better. He thrust inside her, and she met him, held him, thrust back. He thrust again, and she met him again. Not a race. But like a race. Inside her, tensing again, pooling, holding him tight. His chest was slick with sweat. The firelight danced over the planes of his chest. His eyes, midnight-dark eyes, were on her, watching her. She did not look away. She looked down at their bodies. At the dark, hard peaks of her nipples, at the shudder of her breasts as he thrust, and the entity that they were beneath his kilt, joined, flesh melding into flesh, heat and sweat. And then it happened, different but the same, a climax pulsing, and she heard him cry out, and pull away from her, chest heaving, as his climax took him, too.

Afterwards, she wanted to laugh with the sheer delight of it. Fun and pleasure, Felicity had said, and she had been right. 'Astonishing,' she said to Innes, and he laughed. 'I had no idea,' she said, and he laughed again, only it was a different kind of laugh. There was pride in it, and something proprietary. She would have minded that, under any other circumstances. Tonight, on what Madame Hera would no doubt call a voyage of discovery, Ainsley found that there was something rather exciting about a man in a kilt who looked as if he would like to mark every bit of her body as his own. She wanted to do the same to him herself.

She kissed him, tangling her tongue with his, pressing her breasts into the still-damp skin of his chest, relishing the *frisson* that the contact made, the roughness of his hair on the sensitive skin of her nipples. She straddled him in the firelight, as he had straddled her, and felt the stirrings of his member against her. Deciding that this time she wanted to see for herself, she undid the ornate buckle of his belt. The kilt fell open. She watched, fascinated, as he thickened and hardened before her eyes. She wanted to touch him, but this was quite new territory for her. Even the wanting was new.

Innes was leaning up on his elbows. She could see the ripple of his belly muscles as he breathed. His eyes on her. Waiting for her. 'Tell me what you want,' she said, an echo of what he had said, wanting to know, sure that what he wanted so too would she.

'Touch me.' She reached for him, running a tentative finger down the sleek length of him. He shuddered. She did it again. A finger, from the thick base of him, to the tip.

Innes's chest rose and fell. 'More,' he said.

She could guess what he wanted now, but she would not. 'Tell me,' she said.

He knew she was playing. She could see he liked it. 'Stroke me,' he said.

She did, feathering her fingers up and down the length of him. 'Like that?'

'No. You know what I want.'

She leaned forward again, brushing her breasts against his chest. Her nipples ached. 'Then tell me, Innes,' she said, nipping his earlobe. 'Tell me exactly what you want.'

'Put your hands around me, Ainsley.'

She was shocked, not by what he asked, but

by the effect it had on her. She sat up, sliding against him so that the soft folds of her sex touched his body, enjoying the separate *frisson* of pleasure this sent through her. Then she did what he asked. She wrapped her hand around his girth, and stroked. 'Like that?'

He groaned.

She did it again. 'Like that, Innes?'

'Yes. Oh, Ainsley, yes.'

'Not like this,' she said, squeezing him lightly.

He swore.

'Or like this?' She slid herself against him. Her skin on his, her hand, her sex. Different textures. Same heat. She stroked. 'Do you mean like this, Innes?' she persisted.

'You are a witch.'

'A white witch, or a black witch?' she asked, her fingers tightening and releasing, tightening and releasing.

He put his hands around her waist and lifted her, pulling her swiftly back down on top of him, entering her in one long, hard thrust. 'A very, very bad witch,' he said, pulling her down towards him and kissing her hard.

His kisses matched his thrusts. She matched his kisses first, and then dragged her mouth away to push back, to force him to match his thrusts to hers as she rode him, harder, faster and harder again, until they were both shouting, crying out. Hearing him, the change of note, feeling him, the thickening, feeling herself topple over the edge, she heaved herself free of him just in time to lie panting by his side on the quilt, by the fireside, utterly abandoned, utterly wanton, utterly satisfied.

'So did you enjoy your wild Highlander?' Innes asked her a few moments later.

'I did not know it was expected that a lady should compliment a laird on his performance.'

'Contrary to what you seem to think, we men like to know that we've pleased.'

Ainsley chuckled. 'You definitely pleased, as you very well know.'

'I'm glad you think so,' Innes said with a teasing smile, 'for I most certainly agree. In fact, it was so delightful I think we might even try it again in a wee while.'

'I'm extremely sorry to intrude, but I could wait no longer, and your housekeeper told me she would not be the one to interrupt you, so—so here I am.'

Innes, clad only in his hastily donned plaid, sketched Felicity a bow. 'I'll leave you to it.'

Felicity handed the breakfast tray to Ainsley, flushing. 'Never fear, I will not keep her long. I came only to bid you good morning and good-bye.' As the door closed behind him, she turned towards Ainsley. 'Not quite true, of course. I came to make sure you made it through the night unscathed. Did you?'

Ainsley, who had scrambled into the night-gown she had not worn last night, now pushed back the covers, blushing wildly, picking up her woollen wrapper from where it had fallen on the floor. 'You can see I did.'

Felicity put her hands on her hips. 'Well? Come on, I guessed after what you told me yesterday that it was your first time together.'

'You were right. *Again.* It was both fun and pleasurable. And that's all you're getting,' Ainsley said, sticking her nose in the air and trying to look smug. 'Is that coffee? Would you like some?'

'Yes, it is and no, I won't, thank you. That scary housekeeper of yours produced breakfast for everyone who was left up at the Great Hall hours ago. Eoin said it's true, her mother really was a witch.'

'Do you mean you were there all night?'

'Lots of people stayed. There's not been a ceilidh at the castle for years. Did you know that the old laird stopped holding the Hogmanay celebrations when—'

'The old laird! You've gone native, Felicity Blair. Was it Eoin who told you this, by chance?'

Felicity, to Ainsley's amazement, blushed. 'People used to look forward to the Hogmanay party for months,' she said. 'They're already wondering, after yesterday, whether Innes will be holding one.'

'And I'm wondering why you're avoiding answering my question.'

'Because I'm going back to Edinburgh today, and my life is complicated enough without adding a farmer who lives in the middle of nowhere into the mix,' Felicity said tartly. 'Sorry, Ains. Sorry.'

'What's wrong, Fliss?'

Her friend shook her head, blinking rapidly. 'Nothing. I am tired from all that dancing and too much whisky, probably, and I have to go and pack, for the steamer leaves Rothesay this afternoon and I can't afford to miss it.'

'But...'

'No. I'm fine.' Felicity spoke brusquely. 'Much more important, I can see that you are fine, so I can leave you without worrying too much. I've some more letters for Madame Hera. They're on the dressing table in my room at the castle. And I've got the ones you've written to take with me. I think that Madame Hera's latest venture is going to prove very popular. You are going to carry on with her, aren't you?'

'Of course I am,' Ainsley said. 'Why wouldn't I? This— You know I'm only here temporarily. I'll be back in Edinburgh soon enough.'

'Or sooner, if you are unhappy. You promised, you remember?'

'Yes, but…' Ainsley stopped, on the verge of saying that she could not imagine being unhappy. She'd thought that before. 'I remember,' she said.

Felicity hugged her. 'I'd better go. Just be careful, Ainsley, your Mr Drummond is a charmer. Don't let him charm you too much. Take care of yourself, dearest. I'll write.'

A kiss on the cheek, a flutter of her hands, the fainter sound of her bidding farewell to Innes and she was gone.

'It's bad luck to frown on the morning after the Bonding,' Innes said, closing the bedroom door behind him. 'What has Miss Blair said to upset you?'

'Nothing.' Ainsley poured the coffee. 'I don't know where we're going to sit for breakfast. There are no chairs.'

'We'll take it in bed.' Innes placed the tray in the centre of the mattress, patting the place beside him.

'I wonder what possessed Mhairi to send up a tray? She never has before.'

'Second sight,' Innes said flippantly, handing her an oatcake. 'She knew today was a holiday.'

'I suppose that's part of the tradition, is it?'

Innes grinned. 'It is now.'

Ainsley looked down at the oatcake, which was spread with a generous layer of crowdie, just exactly as she liked it. She wondered if Innes would return to his own room tonight. She took a sip of coffee. It had always been John who decided whether or not to visit her. She had never once been in his bed. He had never once slept in hers. She took another sip of coffee. Not even in the earliest days of her marriage had John made love to her twice in one night. He'd never asked her what she wanted. Never seemed to imagine that she could want something more. It had never been fun, and there had been very little pleasure. This was different in every way.

'What are you smiling at?'

Ainsley's smile widened. 'You'd think, after last night, that we'd want to spend the day in bed. Sleeping,' she clarified hastily.

Innes refilled their coffee cups, and cut into a slice of ham. 'Tempting as it sounds, I have other plans.'

'You've tired of my charms already,' Ainsley said, through a mouthful of oatcake.

'I said I didn't want to spend the day in bed, I did not say that I didn't want to experience more of your charms.'

'The palace of pleasures. There's more, then?'

'Keep looking at me like that and I'll show you more right now.'

'No, thank you, I'm much more interested in my breakfast,' Ainsley said primly.

Innes leaned across the tray to lick a smear of crowdie from the corner of her mouth. 'Fibber,' he said.

She touched the tip of her tongue to his, then pushed him away. 'You are not irresistible, Innes Drummond.'

'No, I'm not.' He pulled the oatcake from her hand and put it back down on the tray. 'But you are,' he said.

Ainsley leaned back, tilting her face to the sky. It was a guileless blue today, with not even a trace of puffy cloud as yet, and the sun was high enough to have some real warmth in it. The boat scudded along, bumping over the white-crested waves. The breeze was just sufficient to fill the red sail, to flick spray on to her face, but not enough to chill her. 'It's perfect,' she said.

Innes took her hand and placed it on the tiller on top of his. 'You're supposed to be helping,' he said.

'I am.' She smiled at him lazily. 'By not interfering. Besides, I want to look at the view, it's so lovely.'

They had sailed south down the Kyles of Bute towards the Isle of Arran, whose craggy peaks were such a contrast to the gentle, greener Isle of Bute, before veering east, round the very tip of the peninsula on which Strone Bridge was built, to follow the coastline north. 'It's only about fifteen miles overland from the castle,' Innes told her, 'but there's just the drover's roads and sheep tracks to follow.'

'This is much nicer.' Innes was wearing a thick fisherman's jumper in navy blue that made his eyes seem the colour of the sea. With his tweed trews and heavy boots, his hair wildly tumbled and his jaw blue-black, for he had not shaved that morning, he looked very different from the man she had met all those weeks, months ago, at the lawyer's office in Edinburgh. 'Your London friends would not recognise you,' she said. 'You look like a native.'

'A wild Highlander.'

She smoothed her palm over the roughness of his stubble. 'Is this for me, then? Is this the day you drag me off to your lair and have your wicked way with me?'

'Wasn't last night enough?'

'Didn't you say this morning that there was more?'

Innes caught her hand and kissed it. His lips cold on her palm, then his mouth warm on each of her fingers. 'Are you going to prove insatiable?'

'Will that be a problem?'

Innes gave a shout of laughter. 'It's every man's dream. There's plenty more,' he said, releasing her and hauling at the tiller to straighten the dinghy, 'but unless you want us to end up on the rocks, maybe not just yet.'

Ainsley shuffled over on the narrow bench. 'Where are we going?'

'Wait and see. This is Ardlamont Bay. We are headed to the next one round. You can see now that we've not really come that far. If you look straight across, you'll get a glimpse of the castle's turrets.'

The breeze began to die down as they headed into St Ostell Bay. Directly across, the Isle of Arran lay like a sleeping lion, a bank of low, pinkish cloud that looked more like mist sitting behind it and giving it a mysterious air. In front of them stretched a crescent of beach, the sand turning from golden at the water's edge to silver where high dunes covered in rough grass formed the border. Behind, a dark forest made the bay feel completely secluded.

The waters were very shallow. Innes pulled off his boots and stockings and rolled his trews up before jumping in and hauling the boat by the prow. Seeing that the water lapped only as high as his knees, Ainsley, who was wearing a skirt made from the local tweed, pulled off her stockings and shoes and followed suit. The little boat rocked precariously as she jumped over the side, and she gasped with the cold, stumbling as her feet sank into the soft sand.

The tide was on the ebb. Leaving the boat at the water's edge, they made their way up the beach, Innes carrying the basket that he'd had Mhairi pack. There was not a trace of a breeze. The sun blazed down on them, giving the illusion of summer. The air was heady with salt and the scent of the pine trees. Shaking out her dripping skirts, Ainsley stopped to breathe it in, gazing around her with wonder. 'It's just beautiful.'

'I'm glad you like it.'

They deposited the hamper and their shoes in the shelter of a high dune before picking their way along the stretch of the sands. 'I like your Highland outfit,' Innes said. 'I'm not the only one who would be unrecognisable to their friends.'

Ainsley's skirt was cut short, the hem finishing at her calf, in the local style, which gave her considerably more freedom of movement. She wore only a thin petticoat beneath, not the layers that were required to give fullness to her usual gowns, and a simple blouse on top, with a plaid. 'It took me hours of practice to get this right,' she said. 'You see how it is folded to form these pockets? The local women have their knitting tucked into them. They can knit without even looking, have you noticed?'

'Are you planning on making me a jersey?'

'Good grief, no. I'll wager Mhairi knitted that one.'

'She did.' Innes caught her as she stumbled, and tucked her hand into his. They headed down to the shoreline where the sand was harder packed and easier to walk on, but he did not release her. The wavelets were icy on her toes. In the shallows, flounders rippled under the sand. Spoots, the long, thin razor clams, blew up giveaway bubbles. At the western tip of the beach, a river burbled into the sea. 'The Allt Osda,' Innes said. 'There's often otters here. I don't see any today.'

It was only then that she realised he must have

come here as a boy. He talked about his childhood so rarely, it was easy to forget that he must
have a host of memories attached to all these
beautiful places, must have sailed around that
coastline countless times. It was obvious, when
she thought about it. The way he handled the
boat. The fact that he'd navigated almost without looking. As they followed the river upstream
on banks where the sand became dotted with
shale, Ainsley puzzled over this. She still had
no idea what haunted him, but she was certain
something did.

The river narrowed before twisting onto
higher ground. They crossed it, Innes holding
her close as her feet slid on the weed-covered
rocks, his own grip sure. It was odd, knowing
him so well in some ways yet knowing so little of his past. Strange, for they had shared so
much last night, yet she had no idea whatsoever
right now of what he might be thinking, no idea
of the memories he associated with this place,
save they could not be bad. No, definitely not
bad. He was distant but not defensive, simply
lost in his thoughts.

It was a different ache, she felt. Not the sharp
pang of feeling excluded, but something akin
to nostalgia. Like pressing her nose against a
toyshop as a child and seeing all the things she

could not have. Silly. Fanciful. Wrong. It was not as if Innes had any more idea of what she was thinking after all. Nor cared. She caught herself short on that thought. Last night had been a revelation, but it was fun and pleasure, nothing more. Surprising as it was, this discovery that she could be so uninhibited, that the body she had been so ashamed of could be the source of such delight, she would do well not to read anything more into it. She and Innes were, as luck would have it, extremely well matched physically. No, it was not luck. That connection had been evident right from the start. And that was all it was. She'd better remember that.

Innes left her to unpack the basket while he went into the forest in search of wood. The sun was so warm, and the dune in which they sat so sheltered, that Ainsley could see no need for a fire, but when she said so, he told her she would be glad of it when she had had her swim.

'You were teasing me,' she said later, watching him as he made a small pit in the sand and lined it with stones. 'The water is freezing.'

Innes began to kindle the sticks. 'That's why we need the fire.'

'I can't swim.'

'Do you want to learn?'

Ainsley looked at the sea. Turquoise-blue, and, she had to admit, extremely alluring, with the sun sparkling on the shallows, the little wavelets making a shushing noise. Then she remembered the shock of cold on her feet when they had first landed. 'No,' she said decisively. 'Perhaps another day, when it's warmer.'

Innes, feeding bigger sticks to the small flame, shook his head. 'It's nearly September, the end of the summer—it doesn't get much warmer, nor much colder, either.' He settled a larger piece of wood on the fire, before joining her on the blanket. 'We used to...'

The fire sparked. Innes put his arms around his knees, staring out at the sea. She waited for him to change the subject, as he always did when he stumbled on a memory, but he surprised her. 'Malcolm and I,' he said. 'We used to come here the first day of the New Year to swim. It was our own personal ritual, after the Hogmanay celebrations.'

'A cleansing?' Ainsley joked. 'Another form of a fresh start?'

'Aye, the Drummonds are fond of those, aren't they?' Innes said ruefully. 'Funnily enough, that's how my brother always put it. He was an awful one for dressing things up, but the truth is, a dip in water that cold is the best cure for a whisky head that I know.'

'Did you and your brother often have whisky heads, then?'

'Only on special occasions, and in truth, it was mostly me. My father believed that the laird should be able to drink everyone under the table. When he gave Malcolm his first dram, he made him drink the whole lot in one swallow. Malcolm was sick. He never could hold his drink, but he became very good at pouring it down his sleeve or over his shoulder, or on one occasion into a suit of armour.' Innes picked up a handful of soft sand, and watched as the grains trickled through his fingers. 'Since I was not obliged to prove myself, I could drink until I was stotious.'

'Like I was, on the sherry?' Ainsley said, blushing faintly.

'You were endearing. I fear that I was simply obnoxious, which is why I take good care not to drink too much these days.' Innes wiped the last few grains of sand from his palm and pulled his jumper over his head. 'Right, it's now or never.'

'You're not really going to swim?'

'I am.' Innes pulled off his shirt and got to his feet. 'I take it you'll not be coming with me?'

'I think this is one ritual you had better perform on your own,' Ainsley said.

Innes paused in the act of unbuckling his belt. 'I think I've told you before that you see a deal too much,' he said. Before she could answer, he grinned and began to unfasten his trews. 'Now, if you don't turn your back, you're going to see a great deal more.'

Ainsley looked up, deliberately running the tip of her tongue over her lower lip. 'I think the view from here is going to prove even more attractive than the one out there,' she said, waving vaguely in the direction of Arran without taking her eyes from Innes.

'If you keep looking at me like that, the view will be considerably more defined than it is right now.'

She got to her feet, unable to resist flattening her palms over the hard breadth of his shoulders, down over his chest, grazing the hard nubs of his nipples. Innes's eyes were beginning to glaze. Her own breathing was becoming rapid. He did not move. She slid her hands lower, to cup him through his trews. She trailed her fingers up his satisfyingly hard shaft. 'I do believe you are my idea of perfect Highland scenery.'

Innes pulled her to him roughly. 'Did I tell you that you're a witch?'

She wanted him. He was more than ready. His mouth was inches away from hers. All she had to do was tilt her head. Ainsley laughed, that soft, guttural sound she knew he found arousing. 'I think I'll be perfectly satisfied just taking in the view,' she said, freeing herself.

She turned away, but Innes caught her and hauled her back. His smile looked like hers felt. Teasing. Aroused. 'I'll be cold when I come out of the water.'

'And wet,' she said.

'And wet,' he said softly.

His hand covered her breast. Even through her corset, she felt her nipple harden in response. She shuddered. 'I'll keep the fire going.'

Innes nipped her ear lobe. 'I hope so, though I suspect that I'll need a little help with my blood flow.'

Her own blood was positively pulsing. 'What did you have in mind?' Ainsley whispered.

'I am sure you'll think of something.' His lips found hers in the briefest of kisses. 'Unless you've changed your mind and decided to swim with me?'

It was tempting, but she forced herself to wriggle free. 'The best things come to those who wait, isn't that what they say?'

'I just hope it's worth it,' Innes said, laughing, pulling off the rest of his clothes.

He stood before her quite naked, and completely aroused. Ainsley watched him making his way down the beach, long legs, tight, muscled buttocks, and thought she had never seen such a wickedly tempting sight in her life. 'Innes,' she called, waiting for him to turn around. 'It already is.'

Innes began to run down the beach, forcing himself to continue as he hit the shallows, knowing that if he stopped, if he turned around, he would immediately turn back. The water was freezing. He'd forgotten. With the tide out, the shallows went on for ever. He'd forgotten that, too. It had been a joke between them, he and Malcolm, that you would reach Arran before it was deep enough to swim.

It was over his knees now, and up to his thighs. He slowed, took to wading, his feet sinking into the soft sand, the flounder scooting out from under him the merest ripple of sand. When a wave hit his groin, he gasped and looked ruefully down. It wasn't just a whisky head the water cured. He dipped his hands into the water, and splashed water over his arms, his shoulders, then caught himself as he dipped his head down to throw more over his face. Malcolm, who always dived straight under, used to laugh at him when he did this. Innes stood up, closing his eyes and lifting his face up to the sun. It didn't hurt here. It didn't hurt to think of him. The memories here were all good. Looking over his shoulder, he saw that Ainsley had followed him down the beach and was standing in the shadows, clutching the blanket. He gave her a mocking salute and dived in.

When he emerged, fifteen minutes later, she was still there, holding the blanket open. Innes was shivering, and embarrassed at the effect the icy water had had on him. Instinctively, his hand moved to cover himself, but she was watching him, and her watching him was far better for his condition than the cold skin of his own hand. He waded out slowly, pushing his hair out of his eyes, relishing the rays of the sun on his back, his skin tingling from the salt. He liked to look at women naked, and he liked them to look at him, but it had always been in the privacy of a bedchamber, and it had never been like this. Ainsley found the idea of him as some sort of savage Highlander arousing, and he found that he liked playing the part. He'd never done that before.

By the time he reached her, the effect of the cold was definitely wearing off. Ainsley handed him the blanket, which he wrapped around his shoulders. 'Well?' he asked.

'The scenery was most elevating,' she said, then blushed. 'I did not mean...'

Innes laughed. 'Not quite, but it will be.'

'I don't know how it is, but when I am with you I say the most shocking things.'

'Delightful is what I'd call them. Why is it, do you think?'

'I will not pander to your ego by telling you.'

They had reached the dune. Innes put some wood on the fire. 'That's a shame, because I rather like the idea of you pandering to me.'

'What particular kind of pandering do you have in mind?'

'You could heat me up.'

'It's only fair, I suppose, since you got so cold at my request.'

'I did.' He made a point of shivering, and tried to look soulful. 'You could rub me down with the blanket.'

She eyed him speculatively. 'I could certainly rub you down,' she said, pulling the blanket from his shoulders and shaking it out onto the sand, 'but I don't think we need the blanket. Lie down.'

He did as she asked, his body already stirring in anticipation. Ainsley slipped off her undergarments, then sat on top of him. She was warm and wet. His shaft thickened, eager to be inside her, but she slid away from him, spreading her skirts around them, just as he had spread his kilt over the pair of them last night. Then she touched him, her hands forming a cocoon around him, and slowly, gently, delightfully, began to stroke.

He bucked under her. She gripped him with her thighs. He closed his eyes, praying for control. It was agonising, her touch feathery, the slightest of friction, not enough but almost too much. He dug his hands into the sand. He dug his heels in, but it was unbearable. With a guttural cry and a surge of desire he would have thought impossible after the night's exertions, Innes rolled her over onto her back, imprisoning her wrists above her head. 'Please,' he said, in a voice he barely recognised, 'say that you are ready, because I don't want to wait.'

'Then don't,' she said.

He kissed her, plunging his tongue into her mouth and entering her at the same time in one long, deep thrust. She met him, pushing up underneath him, clenching hard around him. He thrust again. Her mouth was hot on his, her kisses wild. She struggled to release her arms. When he held her, she dug her heels into his behind. He thrust again, and she met him with equal force, and he felt her tense, the sudden stillness before the crash that made him contract and sent the blood rushing, and he thrust again, hard, and again, deeper, with her crying out and holding him and digging her heels in and urging him on, to pound deep, deep inside her, so that when she came, pulsing around him, it took every ounce of his resolution to pull away, spilling onto the sand, then falling down onto the blanket, gasping, slick with sweat, panting, pulling her on top of him, the frantic beat of her heart clashing with his.

Chapter Nine

Dear Madame Hera,
I have been married for eighteen months. I love my husband very much, and relations between us have always been most satisfactory, him being a perfect gentleman, if you understand my meaning. Indeed, I had no cause at all to complain, until that fateful tea party with my three closest friends several weeks ago. It was my birthday, and I must confess that along with tea, we did partake of some strong drink. Conversation turned to intimate matters. I was shocked to discover that my husband's method of ministering to my needs was considered by my friends to be downright old-fashioned. Imagine my astonishment when they revealed the variety of other ways—well, I will draw a veil over that.

But the problem was that I could not. Draw a veil, that is. For my curiosity was aroused. Alas! Would that I had been content with what I had. When my husband came to my arms as usual on the following Saturday night, I tried to instruct him in one of these variations. It is true, I did fortify myself with a glass or two of his special port beforehand, but I rather think it was my inadequate instructions that were to blame. With hindsight, it is clear that his failure was not a cause for merriment, and that perhaps it was a mistake, after he had expended so much energy, to expect him to renew his efforts in the traditional way.

Now no amount of reassurance will convince my husband to repeat the attempt, despite the fact that I have obtained more complete instructions from my friends. Worse still, my husband assumes my desire to introduce an element of diversity into the bedchamber is actually implied criticism of his previous efforts, and has accused me of having simulated satisfaction in the past. As a result, my Saturday evenings are utterly bereft of marital comfort. What should I do?

Mrs J-A

September, 1840

Ainsley finished reading the letter aloud and looked enquiringly at Innes, seated at his desk and frowning as usual over the account books. 'There, I told you I'd find something to distract you. What do you think she means when she said that her husband is a "perfect gentleman"? I'm assuming it is not that he gets to his feet when she enters a room.'

Innes pushed his papers away and came to join her on the large, overstuffed sofa that sat in front of the hearth. 'She means that he ensures she is satisfied before he allows himself to complete his own pleasure.'

'Oh.' Ainsley grimaced, scanning the letter again. 'I had no idea. I hate to think how many times Madame Hera has quite missed the point of some of her letters.'

'What proportion of her correspondence do these sorts of problems form?'

'That's a good point.' Ainsley brightened. 'It is only since Felicity launched our personal answering service that they have grown. What do you think Madame Hera should advise Mrs J-A? Her poor husband is most likely imagining himself wholly inadequate. She will have to do something to reassure him.'

'Not so long ago, Madame Hera would have been pretty certain that the problem lay with that poor husband.'

'Not so long ago, Madame Hera wouldn't have had an inkling as to what Mrs J-A meant by variety,' Ainsley said drily, 'and she would most certainly never have believed that it was acceptable for a woman to make actual requests. Though perhaps it is not, in general, acceptable at all. I have no idea how other men feel about it. Are you an exception?'

She looked expectantly at Innes, who laughed. 'I have no idea, but I doubt it.'

'I do feel it's a shame that so many women know so little about the variations, as Mrs J-A calls them.'

'Because variety really is the spice of life?'

He was teasing her. She felt the now-familiar tingle make itself known, but refused to be drawn. 'Because it seems wrong that only men do,' Ainsley said.

'Not *only* men, else…'

'You know what I mean, Innes. Lots of women think it is wrong to enjoy what is perfectly natural, and downright sinful to want to enjoy it any way other than what this woman calls traditional.'

'So we are conspiring to keep our wives ignorant, is that what you're saying? Because I'd like to point out to you that you're my wife, and I've been doing my very best, to the point of exhaustion, to enlighten you. In fact, if you would care to set that letter aside, I'd be happy to oblige you right now with a—what was it—variation?'

'Really?' Ainsley bit her lip, trying not to respond to that wicked smile of his. 'I thought you were exhausted?'

He pulled her stocking-clad foot onto his lap and began to caress her leg from ankle to knee. 'I'm also dedicated to providing Madame Hera with the raw material she needs to write the fullest of replies.'

'You have provided Madame Hera with enough material to fill a book.'

'Well, why don't you?'

She was somehow lying back on the sofa with both of her feet on his lap. Innes had found his way to the top of her stockings and the absurdly sensitive skin there. Stroking. How did he know that she liked that? 'Why don't I what?' Ainsley asked, distracted.

'Write a book.'

His fingers traced a smooth line from her knee to her thigh, stroking her through the linen of her pantaloons. Down, then up. Down. Then up. Then higher. Finding the opening in her undergarments. Her flesh. More stroking. 'What kind of book?'

Sliding inside her. Stroking. 'An instruction book.' Sliding. 'A guide to health and matrimonial well-being, or something along those lines,' Innes said. 'Didn't you mention to me once that you thought it would be a good idea? Madame could offer copies to her private correspondents. I'm sure your Miss Blair would be more than happy to advertise something of that sort discreetly in her magazine.'

'I'd quite forgotten that conversation. Do you really think such a book would sell?'

'You're the expert, what do you think?'

She seemed to have stopped thinking. He was still stroking her. And thrusting now, with his fingers. And she was already tensing around him. Was it faster, her response, because of the experience of these past few weeks? Or was she making up for years of deprivation? Perhaps she was a wanton? Could one be a wanton and not realise it? The stroking stopped. Innes slid onto the floor. She opened her eyes. 'What are you doing?'

'Making sure your instruction manual covers every eventuality,' he said, disappearing under her skirts.

When he licked her she cried out in surprise.

Then his mouth possessed her in the most devastating way, and she moaned. Heat twisted inside her, and she began to tense, already teetering on the edge, as he licked and thrust and stroked. She gathered handfuls of her skirts between her fingers, clutching at her gown in an effort to hold on, but it was impossible. Such delight, such unbearable delight as he teased from her, that she tumbled over into her climax, shuddering, and shuddering again as he licked her into another wave, and another, until she cried out for him to stop because she really thought that the next wave would send her into oblivion.

'What is it in those account books that is causing you to sigh so much?' Several hours later, Ainsley was pouring their after-dinner coffee. The maid who helped out in the house had left, along with Mhairi, once dinner had been served, for the housekeeper preferred to sleep where she had always slept, in her quarters at the castle.

Innes stretched his feet out towards the fire and shook his head wearily. 'It doesn't matter.'

'It obviously does, else you would not have been sighing.'

'When it comes to sighing, I seem to recall there was someone else in this room doing their fair share earlier this evening. You didn't say whether you approved of that particular variation, now I come to think of it.'

'I thought it was obvious.'

'A man likes to know he's appreciated.'

'You are.'

'I'm looking forward to reading that particular chapter of your guidebook. I reckon it will tax even Madame Hera's newfound vocabulary to describe it.'

'So you were serious when you suggested that I write it?' Her smile was perfunctory.

Innes frowned. 'Why not? It makes perfect sense.'

'And it will give me something to do.'

Innes put his coffee cup down. 'Have you something on your mind?'

'It's been more than three weeks since the Rescinding. I don't have anything to do, yet every time I ask you how things are going with the lands, you find something else to distract me. I'm wondering if tonight's *variation*, as you call it, was simply a better tactic than telling me it was late, and that you were tired.'

'What's that supposed to mean?'

'Nothing.' She set down her cup. 'They are your lands,' she said, getting to her feet. 'You are the one who has set himself the task of making Strone Bridge better than it ever has been. You did not consult me before you made that decision. Why should I possibly imagine that you would think my opinion worthwhile now, when you obviously have no idea how to go about it?'

'Where on earth did that come from?'

'From being ignored! I have tried. I have tried several times now to remind you of the terms on which I agreed to come here, and you've ignored me.'

'But you have helped. The Home Farm. The Rescinding...'

'And I've entertained you, too, when you've found the real problems of this place overwhelming.'

'You're joking.'

He looked at her aghast, but she was too angry to care, and had bottled up her feelings for too long to hold them in. 'I don't know why I'm still here,' Ainsley said. 'I'm not serving any purpose, and I'm a long way from earning back that money you lent me.'

'Gave you.'

'It was supposed to be a fee. A professional fee. Unless you're thinking that it was the other sort of profession after all.'

'Ainsley, that's enough.' Innes caught her arm as she tried to brush past him. 'What has got into you? You can't honestly believe that I deliberately—what was it you said?—distract you by making love to you?'

Ainsley stared at him stonily.

'What?'

She shook her head. 'It doesn't matter.'

'Which means that it does,' Innes said wryly. 'You should put that in your book, you know, if you're including a section for husbands. Whenever your wife says it doesn't matter, you can be sure it's of dire importance.'

'I could write the same advice for wives.'

'I suppose I asked for that.' Innes held out his hand. 'Don't go, Ainsley.'

She hesitated, but she did not really want to run away, so she allowed him to pull her down on to the arm of his chair. 'I don't think it's deliberate,' she said, 'but when you don't want to talk about something, you—you distract yourself. With me, I mean.' She made a wry face. 'I am not complaining. I did not even notice it until tonight.'

'And you immediately decided that I was pulling the wool over your eyes. You should know me better.'

She flinched at the roughness in his voice. 'I do. That was not deliberate, either.'

Innes rested his head against the back of the

chair, closing his eyes with a heavy sigh. 'You do know me, better than I know myself, it seems.'

He looked unutterably weary. Ainsley slid off the chair to stand behind him, put her hand on his temples. 'Do you have a headache?'

'I do, but I'm not going to risk another excuse,' he said with a shadow of a smile.

'Why won't you talk to me, Innes?'

'Because despite my resolve to be the saviour of Strone Bridge, I can't see how it's to be done. There's nothing to discuss, Ainsley, and I'm gutted. That's why I've not wanted to talk to you.'

She pushed him gently forward and began to knead the knots in his shoulders. 'If the situation truly is irredeemable, you should turn your mind to something else more constructive, such as that pier of yours.'

'Now that Robert has started work on the foundations and we have most of the supplies in hand, that pier of mine needs little of my time.' Innes sighed. 'That's nice.'

Ainsley said nothing but continued to ease the tension in his shoulders, her fingers working deep into his muscles.

'It's different,' Innes said after a little while. 'The pier, the new road. I know what I'm doing with those. When things go wrong—as they no doubt will—I know how to put them right. You can't just pluck new tenant farmers out of thin air. You can't put heart back into the soil overnight. You can't make a soil fit only for oats and barley yield wheat or hops, and even if you could, you can't do anything about the rain or the cold. There's so much wrong, and every solution I think of causes another problem somewhere else. There isn't a solution, Ainsley. If the lands here were ever profitable, then it was a long time ago, and I will not clear the land just to turn a profit. I go round in circles with it all.'

'If it's any consolation, I do know how that feels,' Ainsley said drily. 'I also know from experience that bemoaning one's ignorance and endlessly reassuring oneself that it is both impossible and futile to act is not only fruitless but a self-fulfilling prophecy.'

'You are talking of your marriage.'

She gave his shoulders a final rub, then came round by the side of his chair to stand by the fire. 'Yes, I am. I was afraid to speak up because I thought it would make things worse. I was afraid to act because I thought it would make the situation irretrievable. So I said nothing and I did nothing and—and if John had not died, who knows what would have happened, but one thing is for certain, matters would not have miraculously cured themselves.'

'You're telling me that I'm dithering, and I'm making things worse.'

'I'd have put it a little more tactfully, but yes.'

'You're right,' he said with a sigh, 'I know you are.'

She settled in the chair opposite him. He was staring into the fire, avoiding her gaze. 'It is the not knowing,' he admitted. 'The ignorance. That's the hardest bit. I'm so accustomed to knowing every aspect of my own business, to being the man people turn to when there's a problem. As I said, if something went wrong with the pier, or the new road, I'd know what to do. Or I'd be certain of finding a solution. But here, when it comes to the essence of Strone Bridge, I'm—I'm ashamed. People ask me questions. They look to me for solutions. And I don't have answers. It's—it's— Dammit, Ainsley, I feel like a wee laddie sometimes and I hate it.'

'Did you imagine I would think less of you for admitting to all this?'

Innes rubbed his eyes. 'I think less of myself, truth be told. I don't know what to do, and I don't see how you can possibly help, for you don't know any more of the matter than I do. What's more, though the Rescinding bought me a deal of goodwill, in some ways it's made matters worse, for not only have I raised all sorts of expectations, I've had to write off a load of debt, and the poor, honest souls who have been paying their rent without fail are now resentful of the fact that defaulters have been let off the hook.'

'Oh. I hadn't thought of that.'

'Nor I. How could we have?'

Ainsley wrinkled her brow. 'I don't suppose you could simply balance the books somehow by writing the other rents off in advance. But no, that wouldn't really balance the books, would it? It would simply mean that you were in more debt.'

'It's not the money that's the problem, but...' Innes sat forward. 'You mean I could give the tenants who are up to date a rent holiday to even matters up?'

'Do you think it would work?'

'It's worth a try. Have you any other genius ideas in that clever wee head of yours?'

Ainsley tried not to feel too pleased. 'It was hardly genius. In fact it was pretty obvious.'

'So obvious it didn't occur to me. Does that mean that you're a genius or that I'm an idiot? And be careful how you answer that, mind,' Innes said, grinning.

'Thank you,' Ainsley said with a prim smile. 'I will opt for genius.'

* * *

Waking with a start to the distinctive sound of the heavy front door closing, Ainsley found herself alone. Innes's pillow was cold. She lay for a while going over their conversation this evening. She wished she hadn't lost her temper, but on the other hand, if she had not, she doubted she'd have found the courage to say some of those things to him. She had hurt him, but she had forced him to listen. Then when he had, she had been lucid. She had been articulate. She had not backed down.

She sat up to shake out her pillow, which seemed to be most uncomfortable tonight. And her nightgown, too, seemed to be determined to wrap itself around her legs. She had put it on because it had been laid out at the bottom of the bed, as it was every night. Almost every morning, it ended up on the floor. Some nights, she never even got so far as to wear it.

She pummelled at her pillow again, turning it over to find a cool spot. Where was Innes? Was he angry with her? He hadn't seemed angry. He'd seemed defeated. He was a proud man. Self-made. Independent. All the things she admired about him were also the things that made him the kind of man who found failure impossible to take, and talking about failure even worse. And she had forced him into doing just that. Was he regretting it?

She padded over to the bedroom window, but it looked inland, and there was no sign of Innes, who had most likely headed down to the bay and the workings that would become the pier. Hoping he had more sense than to take a boat out, telling herself he was a grown man who could look after himself and was entitled to his privacy, Ainsley crawled back into bed and screwed her eyes tight.

But it was no good. In overcoming her own reticence, she couldn't help thinking she had forced him to confront a very harsh reality without having any real solutions to offer. Maybe there simply weren't any. She sat up, staring wide-eyed into the gloom of the bedchamber, thinking hard. They were neither of them very good at discussions. She was too busy looking for signs that she was being excluded to listen properly, and Innes was too determined not to discuss at all.

Pushing back the covers, Ainsley knelt upon the window seat, peering forlornly and pointlessly out at the empty landscape. Innes was so determined to solve every problem himself, and it wasn't just because that was what he was used to. He'd admitted it himself, this very night, how small this place made him feel. 'Like a wee laddie,' he'd said. He was ashamed, that was what lay at the root of his inability to ask for help, yet he had not a thing to be ashamed of. There had to be a way to save this place without causing further hardship. There had to be.

Ainsley grabbed what she thought were a pair of stockings. Only as she pulled them on, she saw that they were in fact a pair of the thick woollen ones, which Innes had started to wear with his trews. Though he dressed more formally for dinner, he almost always wore trews and a jumper for his forays out on to the estate these days. Tying her boots around the stockings, she decided that one of those heavy jumpers would provide her with much better insulation against the night air than her own cloak, and pulled it over her head. It smelled of fresh air, and somehow distinctively of Innes. The sleeves were far too long, but they'd keep her hands warm, and the garment came almost to her knees. Smiling fleetingly as she pictured Felicity's face should she ever see her in such an outfit, Ainsley quit the bedchamber and made her way outside.

She found Innes sitting down in the bay, watching the ebbing tide swirl and eddy around the huge timbers that were the beginnings of the new pier. 'I couldn't sleep,' Ainsley said, sitting down beside him on one of the thick planks that lay ready for use, and which had been brought on to the peninsula on an enormous barge that had caused a storm of interest in the village.

He put his arm around her and pulled her close. 'I'm sorry.'

'No, I am.' Tempting as it was to simply leave it at that and give herself over to the simple comfort of his arm on her shoulders, her cheek on his chest, Ainsley sat up. 'I do judge you, Innes. I am too much on the lookout for reasons to judge you to listen to what you're telling me sometimes. I'm sorry.'

'I forget,' he said softly. 'You seem so strong-willed, I forget that there was a time when you did not dare voice your opinions.' He pushed her hair back from her face. 'I know it's not my business. I know you want only to forget, but—did he hurt you, Ainsley?'

'No.' She shook her head vehemently. 'No. Not physically, if that's what you mean.'

'It's what I mean.'

'Then, no.'

'Thank heavens. Not that I mean to belittle...'

'It's fine. At least it was not, but it will be.' Ainsley gave a shaky laugh. The breeze caught the full skirts of her nightgown, lifting them up to expose her legs.

'Are those my stockings you're wearing?'

'I thought they were mine, and then when I put them on they were so warm, I didn't want to take them off.'

'I'm glad you didn't. I had no idea they could look so well. Nor my jumper, for that matter.'

'I must look a sight.'

'For sore eyes.' He leaned over to kiss her softly. 'I'm glad you're here. I know we didn't really quarrel, but it felt as though we were at odds, and I didn't like it.'

The sky was grey-blue, covered by a thin layer of cloud. The distant stars played peekaboo through the gaps, glinting rather than twinkling. The sea shushed quietly, the waves growing smaller as the tide receded. Ainsley leaned closer to Innes, shoulder to shoulder, thigh to thigh, staring out at the water. 'It wasn't that he lifted a hand to me, not once, but I was afraid of him. Partly it was his fault, but partly it was my own. I told you that it was the debts,' she said, 'but it wasn't just that. When you feel worthless, it's difficult to have a say in other things, even when they concern you.'

'Why would you feel worthless?'

She hadn't planned this at all but it seemed

right, somehow, to match Innes's vulnerability by exposing her own. 'The obvious reason,' Ainsley whispered. 'I could not give him what he married me for.'

'You mean a child?'

She nodded, forgetting he could not see her. 'Yes.' She was glad of the dark. Such an old story, such an old pain, she had thought it long healed, but it seemed it was not. She could blame her tears on the wind, so she let them fall silently, biting her lip.

His arm hovered at her back. She could feel him, trying to decide whether to pull her closer or let her alone. She was relieved when he let it fall, let her wrap her own arms around herself, hug his jumper to her.

'Ainsley, forgive me, but I know from how you were with me at first. I know that things between you and—and him— They could not have been conducive to your conceiving.'

He did not ever say John's name, she noticed. He did not call him her husband. He was being absurdly delicate. If they had been discussing one of Madame Hera's letters, he would have been much more forthright. If she had been one of Madame Hera's correspondents, how much more of the truth would she have told? Ainsley shuddered. 'When we were first married,' she

said, 'things were—were normal between us.'
As normal as they were for many of the women
who wrote to her, though she was not as fortunate as Mrs J-A, for John's idea of traditional
ministering took no account of her pleasure. For
some reason, it was important that Innes know
this. 'Not as it is between us. He was not a—a
gentleman in the sense you explained.'

'No,' Innes said gently.

So he had guessed that much, too. Ainsley
tried to work out what it was she wanted to tell
him. Not all. The memory of Donald McIntosh's
curse made it impossible to say it all, for though
he had not actually cursed *her*, she felt as though
he had. And though she knew it did not really
diminish her, her flawed state, still she felt as
though it did, and she couldn't bear to reveal
herself in that way to Innes.

Ainsley felt for his hand, seeking comfort and
strength. 'He was not a cruel man, not really,
though some of the things he said and did felt
cruel,' she said. 'It was when I first discovered
the debts. That's when he accused me of failing him. Until then, I had thought—told myself—hoped—that it was just a matter of time.
Then, later, when our relationship deteriorated,
he could not— He could not perform.'

It was not easy, but she had the words now;

she understood so much more about herself now, and about men, since meeting Innes. 'He blamed me. The worse things got between us— He said I unmanned him, you see. But I knew I had not because I saw him. Alone. I saw he could be aroused, only not by me.'

'I remember now. You asked me about it, whether it was the wife's fault.'

'Yes. Don't be angry. He's dead. If he was not dead I wouldn't be here.'

She felt his reluctant laugh. 'Then I won't be angry, for I'm very glad you're here,' Innes said.

'Are you?'

She turned, trying to read his face in the darkness. It was impossible, but there was no need. He kissed her softly on the mouth. 'I thought it was obvious,' he said, borrowing her own words from earlier.

'We're neither of us very good at seeing that, are we?'

'Not very.' Innes touched her cheek, his fingers tracing a curve to her ear, her jaw, her throat. 'It's true, what you said earlier. There are times when I want to lose myself in you, to forget all the things I can't resolve, but it's you I want.'

'Truly?'

'You must not doubt it. You're thinking that

it's another way of doing the same thing, my wanting you, his not. That the end result is you're left out in the cold?'

'Yes. I hadn't— Not until tonight.'

Innes kissed her again. 'Never, ever doubt that I want you for one reason, and one only. Whatever it is between us has been there from the start. I have never met a woman who brings me more pleasure than you.'

'If you carry on kissing me, this thing, as you call it, will be between us again, and I'm trying to be serious.' Ainsley sat up reluctantly, pushing her tangle of hair from her eyes. 'I did not love John. I thought I did, but I did not. I thought he gave me no option but to ignore his—our— problems, but the truth is, I was relieved to be told they were none of my business, and when our marital relations broke down, I was relieved about that, too. What's more, what I've learned from being with you, Innes, has made me realise it wasn't just John who could not perform. I'm afraid my performance was pretty appalling, too. Partly it was because I didn't know any better. Partly it was because I didn't want to know. It was a mess I couldn't fix because there was simply no solution.'

'You can't possibly be sorry that he died.'

'That's what Felicity said. I would never have

wished him dead, but I don't wish I was still married to him. You see what I mean?'

'I'm not sure.'

Ainsley laughed drily. 'I know, I've told this in a very convoluted way. I couldn't give John a child, Innes.'

'You don't know that. It may not have been your fault. The chances are...'

Nil, was the answer. 'Slim,' Ainsley said, because she could not say it. 'It's not my fault, but it feels as if it is. Do you see now?'

'You mean my lands.'

'You could not help the fact that you were raised without any knowledge of them. You did not know what your father was doing—or not doing—in your absence.'

'My elected absence. Regardless of who is to blame, they are in a mess.'

'No, you blame yourself for the problem and for failing to fix it.'

'I'm not accustomed to failing.'

Ainsley laughed. 'Then we must make sure that you do not, but I don't think the solution lies with making your lands more fertile. What we need to do is think differently.'

'We?'

'Yes, we,' she said confidently. 'Between your stubbornness and my as-yet-untested objectivity, we shall come up with something. We have to. But right now it's very late, and it's getting very cold. We'll catch a chill if we sit here much longer, and you need to try to get a wee bit of sleep at least.'

Ainsley got resolutely to her feet, but Innes stood in front of her, blocking her path. 'I'm not stubborn.'

'You could have taken one look at the mess of this place and turned around back to your own life, but you have not. You've invested a lot more than money in the future of this place. What would you call that, if not stubborn?'

'Determined? Pig ignorant?' He pulled her into his arms, laughing. 'Have it your way. How do you fancy taking a stubborn man to your bed? Because fetching as you look in that rig-out, what I really want is to take it off you, to lie naked in bed with you.' He kissed her. 'Beside me.' He kissed her again. 'Under me.' And again. 'Or on top of me.' And again, this time more deeply, his hands on her bottom through the thin layer of her nightgown, pulling her up against the unmistakable ridge of his erection. 'You see, this is me consulting you. Over, under, beside—the choice,' he said, 'is yours.'

Chapter Ten

Dear Adventurous Wife,
I must tell you, and other readers of this column, how very refreshing it is to hear of a marriage that is still so happy and so fulfilled after twenty-two years. Instead of being ashamed of your continuing physical desires, you should celebrate them. I applaud your wish to explore new territory, as you call it. No matter how enthralling a favourite, well-thumbed book might be, no matter how satisfying the conclusion, it is human nature to wish to read other volumes, provided that you are prepared to find some of them less—shall we say enthralling? Their conclusions perhaps even less satisfying. What matters, Adventurous Wife, is the journey rather than the destination.

Ainsley laid down her pen, smiling to herself as she remembered some of the journeys she and Innes had taken in the past few weeks. The destination had never been anything other than satisfying, but Madame Hera was a cautious soul, and Ainsley was inclined to think Innes rather more talented than most husbands. Not that she would dream of boasting, though she had indeed, during one particular *adventure* involving a feather and the silk sash from his dressing gown, informed him that he had the cleverest mouth of any man in the world. But that had been under extreme circumstances, and he had returned the compliment when she had employed the same combination of mouth, feather and silken tie on him. She picked up her pen again.

Certain everyday items can, with a little imagination, be employed as secondary aids. Think of these articles as theatrical props. Provided that proper consideration is given as to texture and, it goes without saying, hygiene, and provided, naturally, that both adventurers are content with the selection, then I think you will find that your journey will be much enhanced.

I wish you *bon voyage*!

Ainsley signed Madame Hera's name with a flourish just as Mhairi entered the room. 'Excellent timing,' she said to the housekeeper. 'I've been wanting to have a word with you while Innes is out. He's with Eoin, so he's bound to be away most of the morning. Do you have a moment for a cup of tea?'

Mhairi smiled. 'I was just about to ask you the same thing. I've the tray ready. It's a lovely day, and we won't get many of those come October, so I thought you might fancy taking it outside.'

'Perfect.' Ainsley tucked Madame Hera's correspondence into the leather portfolio and followed Mhairi on to the terrace that looked out over the bay. The view was not nearly so spectacular as that from the castle terrace, but it was still lovely.

'I could never tire of this,' Ainsley said, taking a seat at the little wooden table.

'It's been a fair summer,' Mhairi said, 'better than the past few.'

'I hope a good omen for Innes's first summer as laird,' Ainsley said, pouring the tea and helping herself to one of Mhairi's scones, still hot from the griddle.

'Better still if the weather holds for the tattie howking in a few weeks, and better yet if there's more than tatties to bring in, for the land is not the only thing being ploughed, if you take my meaning.' Mhairi smiled primly. 'It would be nice if that husband of yours could see some fruits from all his labours.'

'Oh.' Flushing, Ainsley put down the scone, which suddenly tasted of sawdust. 'I see.' She tried for a smile, but her mouth merely wobbled.

Mhairi leaned across the table and patted her hand consolingly. 'It's early days, but it's well-known that the Drummond men carry potent seed.'

Ainsley took a sip of her tea, pleased to see that her hand was perfectly steady, studying the housekeeper over the rim of the cup. Mhairi spoke so matter-of-factly, though her words were shockingly blunt. 'But the old laird had only the two children,' she said.

'Two boys was considered more than enough. 'Tis easy enough to limit your litter if you don't service the sow.' Mhairi buttered herself a scone. 'I've shocked you.'

Unable to think of a polite lie, Ainsley opted for the truth. 'You have.'

'You must not be thinking I hold a grudge against Marjorie Caldwell. Poor soul, she was affianced to the laird when she was in her cradle. She can't have been more than seventeen when she married him and, knowing him as I did, I doubt he made any pretence of affection, not even in the early days. It was all about the getting of sons, that marriage, and once he'd got them—well, she'd served her purpose.'

'Innes said as much,' Ainsley said, frowning over the memory, 'but I thought his views highly coloured.'

'No, Himself has always seen the way things are here clearly enough. The laird thought the sun shone out of Malcolm's behind, as they say. Innes was only ever the spare, just as I was. The difference between us being that I stuck to the role he gave me and your husband went his own road.'

Mhairi stared off into the distance, her scone untouched on her plate. The insistent pounding of mallets on wood told them that the tide was low. The skeleton of the pier emerging beside the old one made the bay look as if it was growing a mouth of new teeth.

Mhairi stirred another cube of sugar into her tea, seemingly forgetting that she'd already put two in, and took a long drink. 'I loved that man, but that does not mean I was blind to his faults, and he had a good many. What my brother, Dodds, said at the Rescinding was true. I was fit to warm the laird's bed, but that was all. He never pretended more, I'll give him that. That annuity, the farm he made over to me, it was his way of making it right. Payment for services rendered,' she concluded grimly.

'But you loved him all the same.'

Mhairi nodded sadly. 'I'd have done anything for him, and he knew it. Until the Rescinding, I thought myself at peace with the one sacrifice I made, but now the laird is dead and buried, and I am too old and it's far too late, I resent it.'

Her fingers were clenched so tightly around the empty china cup that Ainsley feared it might break. Gently, she disentangled them and poured them both fresh tea. Though the late-September sun beat down, hot enough to have chased all the chickens into the cool of the henhouse, she shivered. 'A child,' she said gently, for it was the only explanation. 'That was what you sacrificed.'

Mhairi nodded. 'He would not have stood me bearing his bairn. Of course, the laird being the laird, it did not occur to him to have a care where he planted his seed. If it took root, that was my problem. He made that clear enough, so I made sure it never took root. I do not practise as my mother did, but I knew enough to do that.'

'The fey wife?' Ainsley's head was reeling. 'Do you mean your mother really could cast spells?'

Mhairi shrugged, but her face was anxious.

'She was a natural healer. Her potions were mostly herbs, but she did have other powers. The curse that Dodds made— Mrs Drummond, I have to tell you it's been on my mind.'

'That the bloodline would fail,' Ainsley said faintly.

'I made sure to bear no child. The old laird's only other child died fourteen years ago. There is only Innes, Mrs Drummond. You will think me daft to believe in such things, but I know how powerful my mother's gift was. You must forgive me for talking about such personal matters, but I can't tell you the good it does me, knowing that the pair of you are so—so enthusiastic about your vows, shall we say. And I was hoping—as I said, I know you'll think it's daft, worrying about a silly curse—but still, I was hoping you could maybe reassure me that we'll be hearing some good news soon. About the harvest I was talking about?'

Ainsley slopped her tea, and felt her face burn dull red. Mhairi was looking at her with an odd mixture of anticipation and concern. She believed in that curse, and as things stood she would be right to. Making a fuss of wiping up her tea with a napkin, Ainsley tried to compose herself. 'Silly me,' she said. 'I'm not usually so clumsy.'

'I've upset you.'

'No.' She smiled brightly. 'Not at all. Why would you— I was merely— Well, it is a rather embarrassing topic of conversation. Though I suppose it is perfectly natural that people are wondering...' She placed the soiled napkin on top of her half-eaten scone. 'Are people wondering? Is an heir really so important?'

Mhairi looked as if she had asked if the land needed rain. 'The estate has been passed from father to son directly for as long as anyone can remember.'

Innes had told her so, back in Edinburgh when they first met. He hadn't cared then, but he had not been to Strone Bridge then, and he had no notion of truly claiming his inheritance. It was different now. She thought back to the pain in his voice a few nights ago, when he had finally admitted how much it meant to him, and how desperately he wanted to make his mark on the place. It would not be long before he realised an heir was a vital element of his restitution.

Ainsley smiled brightly at Mhairi. 'As you said, it is early days.'

Mhairi was not fooled. 'Is there a problem?' she asked sharply. 'Because if there is a problem, I can help.'

Ainsley's poor attempt at a smile faded. 'What do you mean?'

'Just as there are ways to prevent, so there are ways to encourage.'

'Magic?'

'Helping nature, my mother always called it.'

A gust of longing filled her before she could catch it. It was like a punch in the guts, so strong she all but doubled over from it. Impossible not to wonder what difference such a spell would have made all those years ago. A spell! She gave herself a mental shake. She had the word of medical science, and no spell would counteract that. 'If nature needs assistance, it is not natural,' Ainsley said, pleased at how firm she sounded. Magic, white or black, real or imagined, formed no part of her life. She got to her feet and began to stack the tea things on the tray.

The next day Innes left early with Eoin for Rothesay, and then on to Glasgow where they had various meetings with paddle-steamer companies. Though she started missing him the moment he set out, Ainsley was relieved to have some time to spend alone.

She headed out of the Home Farm in the direction of the castle. Sunshine dappled down through the leaves of rowan and oak that bordered the path here. The bracken was high, almost to her waist and already beginning to turn brown, exuding that distinctive smell, a mixture of damp earth and old leather. Autumn was settling in. The sense of time ticking too fast was making her anxious. Though Innes had said nothing of her returning to Edinburgh, Ainsley had a horrible feeling that very soon she would have no option.

Peering down to the bay from her favourite spot on the castle's terrace, she could see Robert Alexander standing with a cluster of men, consulting their plans. The new road would be cut into the cliff. Innes was investigating the possibility of using a steam engine to help with the work. Since that night in the bay, they had spent a great deal of time together poring over maps and account books. She now fully understood his despair.

Crofting was still the tradition here, with each farmer producing enough to meet his own small needs, keeping a few cattle and sheep on the common grounds, and fishing to supplement his family's diet. The crofts were simply too small to grow more, and far too small to meet the huge demands from the growing metropolis of Glasgow, it seemed. The new road, the new pier, the paddle steamers that could berth there, would solve the transport problems, but the crofters of Strone Bridge simply could not produce enough to benefit from these markets. Eoin was encouraging Innes to merge some of the farms, but while many of them had been lying fallow, their former tenants having fled to Canada and America, hardly any of those lands lay together. Innes's farms were dotted about the landscape like patchwork, each a different size and shape. Innes was determined not to take the route that so many of the Highland landlords had done, which was to oust his tenants by fair means of foul, and to turn the lands over to sheep.

Despite the melancholy subject matter, Ainsley had revelled in these hours spent together. It wasn't only that she felt useful, that her opinion was valued, that Innes truly listened to what she said. She had felt included. And there was the problem. She was not part of this place, and never could be, but with every day that passed, that was exactly what she wanted. To belong here. To remain here. With Innes. She was close to letting Strone Bridge into her heart, and even closer, frighteningly close, to allowing her husband in, too.

She could love him. She could very easily love him, but it would be disastrous to allow herself to do so. Gazing out over the Kyles of Bute, watching the dark-grey clouds gather over the Isle of Arran, cloaking it from view, Ainsley forced herself to list all the reasons why it was impossible.

For a start, she was not the stuff that a laird's wife was made of. Not a trace of blue blood. Neither money nor property—quite the contrary. No connections. The Drummonds married for the name and the lands, and Ainsley contributed no good to either. She could not weave or spin or even knit. She knew nothing of animal husbandry, or keeping a house larger than the Home Farm. What she knew of the Drummond traditions Mhairi had taught her. In fact, Mhairi was far better qualified than she was for the role. No one could tell a tale of the castle's history and ghosts the way Mhairi did.

Then there was the fact that Innes didn't actually want a wife. It would be easy to persuade herself he'd changed his mind. He'd managed to overcome his precious need to be the one and only person in control of his life in so many ways. He even confided in her without prompting sometimes, and he made her feel that Madame Hera was every bit as important a venture as Strone Bridge. He had changed, and he had changed her. She was more confident. She was more ambitious. She no longer doubted her femininity, and she knew the satisfaction of pleasure and pleasing. She was cured of John for ever, but the role that had cured her was temporary. She was not a wife. A business partner. A lover. But not a wife. Innes did not want a wife, and Innes would never love her as a wife. She did not think that the mystery woman who had stolen his heart kept it still, but she was fairly certain he would not let it go again. But he would take a real wife because he would realise, very soon, that his commitment to Strone Bridge required him to produce an heir.

Which brought her to the biggest stumbling block of all. The one thing she could not give him. Swallowing the lump that rose in her throat, Ainsley decided to follow the path round to the chapel. It was cool here, in the little copse of trees and rhododendrons. She sat on the moss-covered bench in the lee of the chapel, idly watching a small brown bird wrestling with a large brown worm. She smiled to herself, remembering the woman at the Rescinding who had begged forgiveness for having her husband's dog buried beside him. His grave must be hereabouts. What was the name? Emerson, that was it. But as she crossed the path to start peering at the gravestones, Ainsley was distracted by the Drummond Celtic cross.

She read the old laird's name thoughtfully, and then his lady's inscription, too. Marjorie Mary Caldwell had been only twenty-six when she died, and if what Mhairi had said was true, she couldn't have had a very happy life. Caldwell. She remembered now—that was the name of the family who owned the lands that bordered Strone Bridge, somewhere north of here. Innes's nearest gentry neighbours. The ones he'd not wanted invited to the Rescinding, though they must be some sort of relation of his.

The atmosphere in the graveyard was only adding to her melancholy. It was very clear that she had no future here, but she did want to leave a legacy. Furrowing her brow, Ainsley made her way back to the castle. The Great Hall still smelled faintly of whisky fumes and ash. Though it was not yet October, Mhairi was already asking if the traditional Hogmanay party would be held here. It was a room made for great occasions. Parties. Banquets. Ceilidhs. Wedding feasts.

Would their marriage be annulled? Would Innes divorce her? She was fairly certain that the law, which was written by men and for men, would perceive her infertility as ample reason for either. Then some other woman with property and the right pedigree would benefit from the changes in Innes that had cost Ainsley so much. He would not love her, his real wife, but he would respect her, and he would confide in her, make love to her, rely on her to play the role of the laird's lady. And she would give him the son he didn't yet know he needed.

Ainsley dug her knuckles deep into her eyes. No point in crying. In the long drawing room, she gazed out of the French windows at her view. It was a pity more people could not share it, and fall in love with it. Excursionists from the paddle steamers that would be able to dock here within months. They could take tea here in the drawing room. Smiling, she remembered joking about that very thing the day Innes had decided to build the pier. Excursionists who would pay for Mhairi to show them round the castle and tell her ghost stories. Who would buy the local tweed, or the local heather ale.

She stood stock-still. Would they pay to spend the night here? Pay extra to spend the night in one of the haunted bedchambers? Her heart began to race. Innes had told her that the railway between Glasgow and Greenock was due to open next year. He had shares. The journey would be much easier than it was now, a quicker, cheaper escape from the smoke of the city to the delights of the country. There would be more excursionists able to afford the trip, perhaps wanting to take a holiday rather than merely come for the day. And there would be richer people, too, who would be willing to pay a premium to hire the castle for a family occasion. To marry in the chapel and hold their wedding feast in the Great Hall.

She hesitated, remembering the scorn Innes had poured on the idea when she had first, jokingly, suggested it. Ridiculous, he had called it. But that had been weeks ago, before he had decided to stay here. Before the success of the Rescinding, here in this very hall. He must have changed his mind about the castle by now. Certainly he had not suggested knocking it down again. And there would be jobs. The lands would provide enough produce to feed the visitors.

It could work. She just might have been right after all, when she'd said to Innes that they would have to think differently. Strone Bridge Castle Hotel. Ainsley's stomach fluttered with excitement. This would be her legacy.

Innes was gone ten days, during which Ainsley worked on her plan for the castle, determined to surprise him and equally determined not to dwell on the growing sense she had that her time on Strone Bridge was ticking inexorably to a close. He arrived with the morning tide, tired but immensely pleased to see her. Watching his tall, achingly familiar figure stride along the old pier towards her, she forgot all her resolutions and threw herself into his arms.

He held her tightly, burying his face in her hair, exchanging barely a word with Robert Alexander, telling the surveyor brusquely that he had business to attend to before rushing Ainsley back to the Home Farm, leaving old Angus and Eoin to take the cart and deal with the luggage.

They arrived breathless, and headed straight for their bedchamber. 'I feel like I've been gone an age,' Innes said, locking the door firmly behind him. 'I missed you.'

'Did you?' She felt as if she couldn't get enough of looking at him, and stood in the middle of the room, simply drinking him in.

'I missed having breakfast with you,' Innes said, putting his arm around her, steering her towards the bed.

Her heart was beating from the effort of climbing the hill, from the effort of trying not to let him see how very much she had missed him, and from anticipation, too. 'I'm sure you and Eoin had plenty to talk about,' Ainsley said.

Innes smiled. 'We did, but when Eoin smiles

at me over his porridge, it doesn't make me want to kiss him.'

'I expect the feeling is entirely mutual,' Ainsley teased.

'Did you miss me?' Innes kissed each corner of her mouth.

'A little.' She kissed him back, her words a whisper on his ear.

'Just a little?' He kissed her again, more fully this time, running his fingers down her body, brushing the side of her breast, her waist, to rest his hand on her thigh.

She shivered. 'Maybe a wee bit more than a little,' she said, imitating his action, her hand stroking down his shoulder, under his coat to his chest, his waist, his thigh. He was hard already, his arousal jutting up through his trousers. She slid her hand up his thigh to curl lightly around him. 'I can see you missed me a good bit more than a little,' she said.

Innes reached under her skirts to cup her sex. 'Do you want to know how much more?' he asked.

He had a finger inside her. She contracted around him. 'Yes,' she said. He started to stroke her. 'Oh, Innes, yes.'

They lost control then. She pulled him roughly to her, her mouth claiming his. He kissed her urgently. Their passion spiralled, focused on the overwhelming, desperate need to be joined. She had to have him inside her. He had to be inside her. There was no finesse to it. Speed, necessity, drove them. Innes struggled out of his trousers enough to free himself. He rolled onto the bed, taking her with him, lifting her to straddle him, her knees on either side of him. She sank onto him, taking him in so high, so quickly, that they both cried out.

Their kisses grew wild. She clung to his shoulders, then braced herself using the headboard, arching back as she drew him in, as he thrust higher, harder, furiously, until the deep-rooted shiver that preceded her climax took her, and he came, too, pulsing, shaking them both to the core, making them forget, in the utter satisfaction of it, that he was still inside her, clinging to her, holding her there, with his arms, with his mouth, though she needed no holding, clinging, too, her harsh breath mingling with is, his heart beating against hers.

She had not planned it, but the connection, having him deep inside her as he came, had been momentous.

A true joining.

A true mistake.

Her body had betrayed her. Ainsley felt as if

her world was shattering. She loved him. And even as she felt the truth of it settle itself inside her, she saw his face. Innes looked appalled.

'I'm sorry. Ainsley, I'm sorry. I don't know what— I didn't mean— I'm sorry.'

She shook her head, not quite meeting his eyes as she lifted herself free of him. 'It doesn't matter.' Though it did. It had changed everything.

Innes could not have made his feelings any clearer, but he seemed to want to try. 'It does matter,' he said, hurriedly adjusting his clothing. 'You asked me— I promised I would always be careful. I don't know why I...'

'It wasn't your fault. It was mine.' She would not cry in front of him, but she needed him gone. She gave him what she hoped was a reassuring smile. 'I told you, there is almost certainly nothing to worry about.' He was staring at her, horrified. 'It was simply— We were incautious because we had grown accustomed to more regular release,' Ainsley said, cringing at the words even as she spoke them.

She rolled off the bed. She couldn't look at him now. 'There are a hundred letters waiting for you, and Robert will be wishing to talk to you. Go on downstairs, I will rejoin you shortly.'

* * *

Ainsley held open the door, giving him no option but to leave her. Dazed, Innes did as she bade him and made his way downstairs to the sitting room. He sat at the desk, staring at the neat piles of correspondence, feeling as if he'd been punched in the gut.

He cursed long and hard, then poured himself a glass of malt. What had happened? He swallowed the dram in one. It burned fire down his throat and hit his belly too fast. He coughed, then poured himself another. *I'm sorry*, he'd said, but he had not been. That was the worst thing. It had felt so good, spilling himself inside her. He hadn't thought of the consequences. He hadn't been thinking of anything at all, save for his need to be with her. In all honesty, he couldn't have cared less about the consequences. But Ainsley had. Her face. *Stricken*, that was the word. She'd tried to cover it up, but he was not fooled.

Innes finished his second glass of whisky, feeling as if he'd just been given a death sentence. All he'd been able to think about these past few days was coming home to Strone Bridge and to Ainsley.

Home. Ainsley. The two words had somehow become connected, and as if determined to make sure his mind made the connection, too, his body had made it impossible for him to ignore. Which left him where, exactly?

He swore again, bitterly. Terrified and confused as hell, was where it left him. He could no longer trust himself, and Ainsley would no longer trust him. Things had changed fundamentally, yet some things would never change. He still carried the burden of the past with him. Whatever he felt for Ainsley, he had no right to let it flourish.

This was a warning, a very timely one. The truth would see to the outcome. He felt sick at the thought of it, but he didn't doubt it was the right thing to do. The only thing. He cared enough to want her to understand, which was a lot more than he'd ever cared for any woman since that first one. He cared too much. Far too much.

Checking the clock on the mantel, Innes saw that half an hour had elapsed. With a heavy heart but with his mind resolute, he set out to find her.

Ainsley was seated in front of the mirror, staring at her reflection as if it was another person entirely. She loved him. Did she really love him? How could she be so foolish as to have allowed herself to fall in love with him? Had she forgotten how miserable she'd been, married to John?

No. She had not loved John. Innes was not

John. This marriage was not at all like her first. 'Because it is not real,' she hissed at her reflection. 'Not real, Ainsley, and you have to remember that. This is not your life, it's a part you're playing, and that is all, so there is no point in hoping or wishing or dreaming that it will continue.'

Yet for a blissful few moments, that was exactly what she allowed herself to do. She was in love, and for those few moments, that was all that mattered. For those few moments, she allowed herself to believe that love would conquer all the barriers she had so painstakingly examined and deemed immovable. She was so overwhelmed with love, surely anything was possible. She loved Innes so much, he could not fail to love her back. They could not fail to have a future together, because the idea of a future without him was incomprehensible.

The knock on the door made her jump. Innes looked as if he was carrying the weight of the world on his shoulders. 'We need to talk,' he said, and not even her newly discovered love could persuade Ainsley that the words were anything other than ominous.

Fleetingly, she considered pretending that nothing momentous had happened, but looking at the expression on Innes's face, she just as quickly dismissed the notion. Feeling quite as sick now as he looked, Ainsley got to her feet and followed him out of the door.

To her surprise, he led them outside, along the path towards the castle. At the terrace they paused automatically to drink in the view. 'I went through to Edinburgh when I was away,' Innes told her. 'There were matters to tie up with the lawyers. I was going to call on Miss Blair. I know you'd have wanted me to let her know that you were well, but—you'll never believe this.'

'What?'

'Eoin,' Innes said, shaking his head. 'I wondered why he insisted on coming through to Edinburgh with me when the man never wants to leave Strone Bridge. It turns out that he and your Miss Blair have been corresponding, if you please. He went off to take tea with her and made it very clear I was not wanted. He was away most of the day, what's more, and not a word could I get out of him after, save that he was to pass her love on to you. What do you make of that?'

'I don't know what to make of it at all. I had no idea—she certainly has not mentioned this correspondence to me.'

'Do you think they'll make a match of it?'

'Oh, no.' Ainsley shook her head adamantly. 'That will never happen.'

'You seem very sure. I thought you'd be pleased. You would have been neighbours.'

'Innes, I will not be...'

'No, don't say it,' he said hurriedly.

'You don't know what I was about to say.'

'I do. I do, Ainsley.' His smile was tinged with sadness. 'Poor Eoin. But I didn't bring you here to talk about Eoin. I can see you're bursting to talk, but let me speak first. Then perhaps I will have spared you the need.'

Chapter Eleven

Ainsley had assumed they were going to the chapel, but when they got there Innes left the well-trodden path to push through a gap in the high rhododendron bushes in the nook forming the elbow of the graveyard, which she had not noticed before. The grass here was high, the path narrow, forcing them to walk single file. It led through the tunnel of the overgrown shrubs, emerging on a remote part of the cliff top looking not over the bay where the pier was being constructed, but over the far end of the Kyles, and the northern tip of the Isle of Bute.

'That's Loch Riddon you can see,' Innes said, putting his arm around her shoulder, 'and over there in the distance is Loch Striven.'

'It's lovely.'

'It was Malcolm's favourite view.' Innes took her hand, leading her to the farthest edge of the path. Here, the grass was fresh mown around a small mound, on top of which was a cross. A Celtic cross, a miniature of the Drummond one. And on it, one name. 'My brother,' Innes said.

Ainsley stared at the birthdate recorded on the stone in consternation. 'He was your twin! Oh, Innes, I had no idea.'

He was frowning deeply. She could see his throat working, his fingers clenching and un-clenching as he stared down at the stone. She was not sure if he was going to punch the stone or break down in front of it. She was afraid to touch him, and aching to. 'It's a very beautiful spot,' Ainsley said rather desperately.

'Aye. And it was his favourite view, but all the same he would not have chosen to spend eter-nity here. Malcolm...' Innes swallowed com-pulsively. 'I've said before, Malcolm— It wasn't just that he was raised to be the heir, Ainsley, he lived and breathed this place. The traditions meant as much to him as they did to my father. He would have wanted to be buried with the rest of them. Except they would not let that happen. No matter how much I tried to persuade them, they would not allow it.'

'Why not?' Ainsley asked, though she had a horrible premonition as to the answer.

'Consecrated ground,' Innes said. 'My brother killed himself.'

Shock kept her silent for long moments. Then came a wrenching pain as she tried to imagine the agonies Innes must have suffered. Must still be suffering. 'No wonder you left,' she said, the first coherent thought she had. Tears came then, though she tried to stop them, feeling she had no right, but his face, so pale, so stiff, the tension in the muscles of his throat, working and working for control were too much for her. 'Oh, Innes, I am so, so sorry.'

Seeking only to comfort, wordless, distraught, she wrapped her arms around his waist. He stood rigid for a moment, then his arms enfolded her. 'I'm sorry,' Ainsley said, over and over, rocking her body against him, and he held her, saying nothing, but holding on to her, his chest heaving, his hands clasping tighter and tighter around her waist, as if he was trying to hold himself together.

Gradually, his breathing calmed. Her tears dried. His hand relaxed its hold on her shoulder. 'I had no idea,' Ainsley said, scrubbing at her tear-stained cheeks.

'Why should you?' Innes replied gruffly. 'I made sure not to tell you anything. While I was away from here, I could pretend it had not happened.'

'That's why you never came back?'

'One of the reasons.' He heaved a deep sigh, tracing the inscription on the cross, before turning away. 'Come, there's a rock over there that makes a fairly comfortable seat. It's time you knew the whole of it.' He touched her cheek, then dipped his head to kiss her. A fleeting kiss, tinged with sadness. 'After this morning, we both know we can't carry on as we have been.'

She knew, but only when he said it did she realise that she still had not accepted it. She'd hoped. Despite all, she had hoped. Sitting down beside him on the huge chair-shaped boulder, her heart sank. Whatever Innes was about to tell her would destroy that hope for ever.

Innes was staring out at the sea, where the turning tide was making ripples on the summer blue of the surface. 'You know how things were with me here, when I was growing up,' he said. 'I can't remember a time when I didn't want to leave, but to leave without my father's permission would undoubtedly have caused a breach between myself and my twin. It would be an exile for me, unless I returned under the whip, and one that Malcolm would feel obliged to uphold. You must remember, in those days, my father was not so old. An enforced separation from my twin for years, maybe even decades, was not something I wanted to have to deal with.'

'And yet you left,' Ainsley said.

'I had planned to wait until after I came into an inheritance from my mother. I had persuaded myself that it would make a difference, my having independent means, that my father would not see it as a flaunting of his authority. As it turned out, I didn't have to put it to the test. Events— events took over.'

Ainsley's hand sought his. She braced herself.

'There was a woman,' Innes said.

He was still staring out to sea, his eyes almost the exact colour of the waters below. She loved him so much. A sigh escaped her, and he turned that beloved face towards her.

'You guessed?' he asked.

She stared at him blankly, her mind still trying to come to terms with what her heart had been trying to tell her for days now. Weeks? How long had she loved him?

'I suppose it was obvious,' Innes said. 'My being so dead-set against marriage—I always wondered what you made of that.'

'I thought…' What? What! She gazed at him, such longing in her heart, letting it flood her for just a moment. Just a moment. She loved him so much.

'Ainsley? You thought…' Innes prompted.

He must not guess she loved him, that was what she thought. Because if he guessed, he would send her away immediately, and she needed a few more weeks. Just a few more. 'I thought there must have been,' she said. 'A woman. I thought that's what it must have been.'

'Well, you were right.'

She waited, trying not to show what she was feeling. Was she looking at him differently? Innes was staring out to sea again, his throat working. Whatever was coming next, he was struggling with it. She didn't want to hear him talking about another woman, but he obviously needed to tell her. Ainsley ruthlessly thrust her own storm of feelings to one side. 'Go on,' she said. 'There was a woman. And of course she was lovely.'

'She was. She was very lovely.'

She hadn't meant him to agree with her. Now, perversely, she wanted to twist the knife, as if knowing how very different she was from his one true love would stop her loving him. 'No doubt she was graced with a fortune, too,' Ainsley said.

'She was rich. An orphan and an only child, she was brought to live at Glen Vadie when she was just a bairn.'

'Glen Vadie. That is the Caldwell estate?'

Innes nodded. 'Aye, she was a distant relative of my mother's. We grew up together.'

It was beginning to sound horribly like a fairy story, though without the happy ending, Ainsley thought. She already hated this rich, charming, well-born, beautiful woman.

Innes heaved a sigh. 'I'm sorry, I'm not being very articulate. The truth is, I can hardly bear to think of it, for even after all this time I'm ashamed, and I don't know what you'll think of me.'

'Innes, I could never think ill of you.'

He shifted uncomfortably on the stone and then got to his feet. 'Ainsley, you will.' His expression was deeply troubled, his eyes stormy. 'I could let you go without telling you. I considered it, but I did not want this all to end on a lie.'

'End?' He had said it. She had known he was going to say it, but she wished he had not.

'It was always going to end, Ainsley. We both knew that. It was what we agreed. You made it very clear you did not want anything else.'

Felled. Could a person be felled? She was felled. 'And you?'

She hadn't meant it to sound like a question. She couldn't bear the way he answered her with such finality. 'And me, too,' Innes said gently.

'Your being here, it was only meant to be for a wee while, to help me decide what to do with the place.'

'But you haven't decided,' Ainsley said, unable to disguise the desperation in her voice. She was clutching at straws, she knew that, and knew, too, that it was pointless, but she couldn't help herself.

'I've decided that I'm going to stay,' Innes said. 'Besides, you know that's not the point.' He was flushed, but his mouth set firm, and when he spoke, though the words were said softly enough, the tone was resolute. 'This morning I realised how much I have come to care for you, Ainsley. It's not only that it breaks the terms of our agreement that makes my feelings for you wrong, nor that I know you don't *want* the complication of any feelings at all, it's that I can't. It has to stop before either of us gets in too deep, for I will not allow myself to love you, Ainsley. I won't.'

It hurt even more than she'd expected. She bit her lip hard, dug her nails into her palms, telling herself that she was glad he had not guessed her own feelings.

'You'll think me arrogant,' he said, 'telling you I won't love you when you have no thought in your head of loving me.' He sat down beside her again and took her hand, which she quickly unfurled from its fist. 'This morning, we both got carried away. I could see from the look on your face afterwards that it—it shocked you as much as me. I don't know what it is between us, maybe it's spending so much time together that's…I don't know, intensified it, made it seem more than it is?' He shrugged. 'I do know that we neither of us want it, though. I do know that if I wasn't telling you that it's over, you'd be saying it to me, wouldn't you?'

She ached to tell him just how far off the mark he had been in his interpretation of her reaction, but she was not so foolish. It was not pride that stopped her telling him how wrong he was, but love. Heartsick, she could only nod.

'Aye.' Innes nodded slowly. 'I thought about letting you go without telling you, but I couldn't. I want you to know, you see, not only because I owe it to you but because I—I can't afford to allow myself to hope. This morning was like a glimpse of heaven and glimpse of hell at the same time.' He stopped, running a shaky hand through his hair, and drew her a very ragged smile. 'That's why I brought you here. To remind me why it can't go any further, and by showing you the worst of me, I'll be making sure that even if I kept on wanting what I am not entitled to, I could never have it.'

As he looked over his shoulder at the cross, beneath which lay his brother's mortal remains, goosebumps made Ainsley shudder. Her heart was clinging to Innes's confession of how much he had come to care for her, wanting to believe it would be enough to turn the situation around, to persuade him that he could care more. Hope, that treacherous thing she could not seem to extinguish, blew this tiny flame to determined life. All she had to do was tell him that she loved him. That was all it would take.

But her head was having none of this. Innes did not want her love. Innes *would not* love. Innes did not feel entitled to love. It was a strange word to use, but as he turned back to her, his face bleak, the question died on her lips.

'Her name was Blanche,' he said.

It was, as Ainsley anticipated, horribly like a fairy tale. Blanche, Malcolm and Innes, like brothers and sister at first, until Blanche changed, seemingly overnight, blossoming into a beauty. The brothers no longer felt at all filial towards her. Desire, lust, and with it competition, had entered into their Garden of Eden.

'But Blanche preferred you?' Ainsley said, because of course she would, and who would not?

Innes looked genuinely puzzled. 'How did you guess?' Fortunately, he did not wait for an answer. 'We tried to ignore it,' he said. 'How pathetic that sounds.'

'You were very young.'

'Old enough to know better.'

'But if you were old enough—and you and she— If you were in love, then why— I don't understand what the problem was.'

'The problem,' Innes said grimly, 'was that Blanche was betrothed to my brother.'

Ainsley put her hand to her mouth, caught Innes watching and made a conscious effort to wipe the shock from her face. 'But you were twins. Surely if Malcolm knew how you felt...'

'He did not. We made sure he did not. At least, I thought we did,' Innes told her, his mouth curled with disgust. 'Besides, you're forgetting that this is Strone Bridge. My father and Caldwell of Glen Vadie had signed the betrothal papers. A younger son would be no substitute for the heir.'

'But if Blanche was in love with you...'

'But Malcolm was in love with Blanche. And since Malcolm was my twin, I persuaded myself that I would be doing the honourable thing in giving her up, then I set about persuading Blanche that marrying Malcolm would not be so very different to marrying me. She and I enacted a most touching little scene, worthy of Shakespeare.' Innes's voice dripped sarcasm. 'The lovers renouncing each other. There were tears and kisses aplenty, though needless to say, there were more kisses than tears.'

He couldn't look at her. His hands were dug deep in his pockets as he stood before her, gazing over her shoulder at the cross on the grassy mound. 'Blanche refused to go along with it at first, but I was determined. Carried away with my own sense of honour, I thought I was,' Innes continued in a voice that poured scorn on his own youthful self. 'I pushed her. I was determined, and Blanche was in the end a pliant and a dutiful wee thing, so she agreed, and the betrothal was formalised at a party in the Great Hall. I thought myself heartbroken, needless to say, but I told myself that I'd done the right thing by my brother and I told myself that what she felt— Well, I told myself that I knew best and she'd come to realise it. I told myself a lot of things, all of them utter drivel. I was that sure I was right, it didn't even occur to me to ask what anyone else thought. What a fool I was.'

Ainsley made a sound of protest. Innes shook his head. 'No, I really was, and arrogant with it. If you give me a minute, I'm nearly done. I just need a minute.'

He took a deep breath, then another, obviously

steeling himself. Ainsley had no option but to wait, feeling quite sick at what he told her, and at what the telling of it was doing to him.

With a little nod, as if in answer to some internal dialogue, Innes continued brusquely, 'Blanche wrote to Malcolm. It hadn't occurred to me that she'd do that, that she'd want to try to explain herself—and me, too, in the process. She had the letter delivered after she'd fled. She had relatives in London. They were happy to take her and her fortune, I assume. I don't know. She ran, and Malcolm got her letter, and when he showed it to me, I am ashamed to say what I felt was anger. I'd done my best to make all right, and she'd thwarted me. I didn't think of her feelings or even his at first, only mine.'

Innes was speaking quickly now, the words tumbling out, as if they'd been packed deep inside him all these years. 'So I was angry with her. I think I even went so far as to tell Malcolm I'd get her back for him, persuade her to marry him. The arrogance of me! It was that word I used, *persuade*, that betrayed me. Malcolm had suspected of course, but he had not been sure. "What do you mean, persuade her?" he asked me, and you should have seen the look on his face. Even now I can picture it. "How could you persuade her? Why should you?" I felt sick. Then, when the accusations finally came, I tried to lie to him, but we could never lie to each other, Malcolm and I, I should have remembered that from the first. So finally I told him, trying to sound as noble as I thought I'd been, only in the face of it, seeing his face, seeing his hopes, his dreams, crushed—for he had loved her truly, you see. Unlike me. He really had loved Blanche. "I'd have given her up," he told me. "I only ever wanted her to be happy. How could you think I would marry her, knowing that she wanted you?"'

Ainsley sat as still as stone, her attention riveted on Innes, but he kept his eyes on the cross. His voice was cold now, as stripped of emotion, as his face was stripped of colour. Listening to him, she felt chilled.

'I told him it all,' he was saying, 'and Malcolm—Malcolm got quieter and quieter. When I asked him if he forgave me, he said there was nothing to forgive, but that he wanted to be left alone, and I was so racked with guilt that I wanted nothing more than to leave him. Then he said that I should go after her. That I should make her happy. He said again that all he ever wanted was for us to be happy, and then he closed the door on me, and—and those were the last words he ever spoke to me.'

Ainsley was lost for words, but Innes was not finished tearing himself apart. 'So you see,' he said, with a painful crack in his voice, finally meeting her eyes, 'my brother took his own life, but it was me who killed him. And now I have his lands, too,' he said with a bitter laugh. 'I have all of it, and I deserve none of it.'

'You do not have Blanche,' Ainsley whispered. 'You gave her up, though you loved her.' It was dreadful, but that was the thing that hurt the most.

'Don't go thinking there was anything noble about that,' Innes said with a sneer, 'because there was not. I didn't love her. That's why it was so easy to try to hand her back to Malcolm like an unwanted parcel, only I was so carried away with my own lofty gesture that I didn't notice that until later.' He rubbed his knuckles into his eyes, looking deeply weary. 'When it came down to it, what I really wanted was to give my brother a reason to side with me against our father. If Malcolm was beholden to me for the love of his life, then he'd take my part, he'd help force my father to let me leave Strone Bridge on my terms. Do you see, Ainsley?' Innes said earnestly, clasping her hands in his. 'I was selfish at every step of the way. It cost my brother his life. I owe it to Malcolm to restore the heritage I deprived him of. I can atone here for what I've done, but I don't deserve to be happy. This morning, I caught a glimpse of what that might be like. A timely reminder of what I deprived my brother of. I don't deserve it, but you do. Do you understand now, why I told you?'

Sadly, Ainsley understood only too well. He thought to drive her away. He thought to disgust her. She felt only unutterably sad, for his tragic confession changed everything and nothing. 'I understand that I can't make you happy,' she said, 'but if what you intended was to make me despise you, then you have failed. You were all so very young.'

'That is no excuse.'

His tone made it clear he would not be swayed. Only a few months ago, Ainsley would have accepted this. 'It is,' she said. 'We all make mistakes through lack of experience. If I had loved John as much as I thought I did, perhaps he would not have died.'

'That's ridiculous. You know—'

'I know *now* how much my own lack of confidence contributed to the—the deterioration of our marriage, but I did not know then,' Ainsley said heatedly. 'I know *now*, thanks to your encouragement, that I'm neither useless nor unattractive.'

'Ainsley, he did that to you—'

'No,' she interrupted him determinedly. 'I am not saying John was without fault, but nor was he entirely to blame. We were a—a fatal combination, but, Innes, how were we to know that?' She clutched tightly at his fingers, pulling him towards her. 'I have learned so much since I came here. I still feel guilty, and I still have regrets, but I am no longer eaten up with them. John is dead, and there's nothing I can do about it, save make sure I don't make the same mistakes again. You can do the same. Would not Malcolm want you to be happy?'

He held her gaze for a long moment, then flung her away, getting to his feet. 'That's not the point. I understand that you're trying to make me feel better, but you can't. You don't understand.'

'I do.' She got slowly to her feet, feeling quite leaden. 'You have made up your mind that I must go, and that is the one thing upon which we agree. I ask only that you allow me to remain here until I can— There are some things that I...'

'Of course. Obviously we must wait to ensure that there were no consequences from this morning.'

It took her a moment to understand his meaning, and when she did, another moment to control the tears that welled suddenly into her eyes.

Ainsley turned towards the sea, hoping to blame the breeze. 'A few weeks,' she said, thinking that would suffice to both torture her and accustom her.

'The end of the year,' Innes said. 'An ending and a beginning.'

She whirled round, thinking for an awful moment that he was making fun of her, but his expression was as bleak as she felt. The thought that he was finding this almost as difficult as she was, however, was no comfort at all. 'Until the end of the year,' she agreed.

They made their way back past the chapel in silence, each wrapped up in their own tortuous thoughts. It was not until they reached the terrace again, and both stopped of their own accord, that Ainsley remembered her plans for the castle, but immediately abandoned any notion of sharing them with Innes right now. Instead, she asked one of the two unanswered questions. 'What about Blanche? What happened to her?'

Innes stared at her blankly. 'I have no idea.' Did he care too little or too much? It seemed impossible that he should not know, for the Glen Vadie estate was less than twenty miles from here. 'She never returned to Scotland,' he added, presumably in response to her sceptical look.

'Don't you want to know if she's happy?'

Innes shrugged dismissively. 'I never sought her out, and she has never, to my knowledge, tried to get in touch with me for the same reason. Guilt,' he clarified. 'She will not wish to be reminded of those times any more than I do, and I have done enough damage, without dragging it all up for her. I know you think that's hard, Ainsley, but it's best left alone.'

'You are very sure of that,' she said.

'Yes. That's not arrogance. I've had fourteen years to make sure.' He pushed his hair back from his face and smiled very wearily. 'You do understand, Ainsley, this is how it has to be? I won't—I won't— I will sleep in my own bed-chamber from now on.'

'Yes,' she whispered.

He took a step towards her, then stopped. 'I must go and speak to Robert. Don't wait dinner for me.'

He turned away, but she caught his arm. 'Innes, I— Thank you for telling me. I won't— I promise I won't make it difficult for you.'

He enveloped her in a fierce hug. 'I never thought you would. I only want— I'm sorry.'

She watched him go, hurtling down the scar in the cliff that would be the new road, allowing the tears to run down her cheeks now that he could no longer see her. She stood for a long time, staring out at the Kyles of Bute, her mind numb, her heart aching. Then she scrubbed at her eyes with her sleeve and drew a shaky breath. Innes had done so much to help free her from the burden of her past. She had until the end of the year to do what she could to return the favour. Which meant she had better make haste if she was going to track down Blanche Caldwell.

Chapter Twelve

Dear 'Anna',
Your letter touched my heart. The love
you feel for this man shines like a beacon
from the page. I do not doubt that, as you
say, you have in him found your soul mate.
It therefore pains me all the more to tell
you that I can see no way for you to have
a future with him that could be anything
other than troubled. Were you a woman
of fewer principles, if you loved this man
less, then I would gladly tell you what you
so desperately want to hear, that love can
triumph over all. But, my dear, this can
only happen when that love is equally given
and received, and sadly, in your case, it is
not. This widower, you have made clear,
loves his three children before all else, and
these children have made their unequiv-

ocal opposition to his proposed marriage to you abundantly clear over a prolonged period. You have done all you can to win them round. Their opposition has increased rather than decreased over time, and now encompasses their dead mother's family, too. Frankly, if this man loved you as much as you love him, he would have made a stand by now. He will never put you first. The rights and wrongs of this make no difference, 'Anna', because you love him too much to endanger his happiness, and if you truly believed that this was with you at the potential cost of his relationship with his children, you would have acted accordingly. That you have turned to me for advice tells its own story, don't you think?

It is therefore with profound regret that I am forced to advise you this: you must leave him, for he will never let you go, but nor will he marry you while the situation remains as it is. I hope you will take strength from doing what is right for you. I pray, as I am sure all our readers will, too, that you will find the future happiness that you deserve.

With my very best wishes,

Madame Hera

Ainsley put down her pen and dabbed at her cheeks with her handkerchief. This was one letter that she would not show to Innes. It was now the beginning of December. Having bared his soul, he had retreated like a wounded animal, making it clear that he wanted neither comfort nor further discussion on the subject of Blanche and Malcolm. Or the date of Ainsley's departure from Strone Bridge, set for the first week in January.

She had been through the wringer of emotions, from shock to horror, from pity to compassion, sorrow and sadness, jealousy, anger, dejection, but she had not once doubted, since that day at Malcolm's graveside, that she must leave. Reading over Madame Hera's advice to 'Anna', Ainsley was confronted with how fundamentally her own feelings had changed in the face of Innes's determination not to allow himself to be reconciled to his past. She had not given up hope of contacting Blanche to help with this, but having had no response to her letter, and with only a few weeks left till the end of the year when she must leave Strone Bridge, Ainsley was not optimistic.

In one sense, it made no difference. Like 'Anna', she had found her soul mate, but unlike 'Anna', Ainsley could now see very clearly that her soul mate was not free to love her as she deserved to be loved, and also unlike 'Anna', Ainsley had grown to believe that she would settle for nothing less. It was strange and surprising, too, how much less important her inability to bear children had become. It grieved her deeply, but in a sense, she had been forced to acknowledge, she had been hiding behind it, pretending to herself that it was this that prevented her from declaring her love, telling herself that she was making a noble sacrifice in removing herself from Innes's life when in fact she must have known that it would have made no difference. He would not love her. He would not allow himself to love her. And Ainsley, having experienced second best, was not about to accept it again.

Lying wide awake and aching with longing at night, she could not decide which was worse: knowing that Innes wanted her so much, or knowing that he did not want her enough. She loved him, but in her time here she had come to love the person she had become, too. She knew he still wanted her, she no longer questioned her own desirability, but she would not use it to push them both into temporarily satisfying a passion that would ultimately make it harder for her to leave.

She longed more than anything to force Innes

to see his past more clearly, but she could not, and the woman who could do so remained incommunicado. So Ainsley concentrated on the one thing she could do to help, her plans for the castle, which today she had decided were finally in an advanced enough state for her to share with Innes. Putting Madame Hera's correspondence to one side, she hurried to her room to check her *toilette*. Her dress was of taffeta, printed in autumn colours. The bodice was fitted tightly to her waist, and came to a deep point. The fashionable oval neckline was trimmed with shirring of the same material, and the long sleeves, like the bodice, ended in a sharp point.

Though it was early December, the sun had a hint of unseasonable warmth as she made her way to the pier in search of Innes. He was in his shirtsleeves. He had lost weight since coming to Strone Bridge. Days spent in the fields and out here in the bay had sculpted his muscles. He would smell of sweat and the sea and the peaty air, and of himself. There was a spot, just where his ribs met, where she liked to rest her cheek and listen to his heartbeat and where she always imagined she could breathe in the essence of him.

'Ainsley? Did you want me?'

'Yes.' Too late, she heard the longing in her

voice. It was no consolation to see it reflected momentarily in his eyes, too. 'I mean, I was hoping to speak to you,' she amended hastily. 'I have something I'd like to discuss with you.' Innes nodded, pulling his heavy fisherman's jumper over his shirt. 'I thought we could go up to the castle,' she said when he looked at her expectantly. 'That way we won't be interrupted.'

The climb back up helped calm her flutter of nerves. She had worked so hard on her plans, but though she had been sure that it would be a pleasant surprise for Innes, it occurred to her belatedly that she had, by keeping her work a secret, contradicted her own hard-won wish to be consulted.

She opened the heavy front door with her keys and led the way through to the Great Hall. 'Do you remember,' she asked nervously, 'that I said the solution to Strone Bridge's economy would prove to be something other than modernising the crofts? In fact, you came up with the idea yourself, that first day you showed me round this place.'

Innes shook his head, frowning in puzzlement. 'I'm not sure I'm following you.'

'Napier did it a few years ago—the Loch Eck tour,' Ainsley said. 'I've been reading about it. He built the pier for the steamer and arranged the onward connections to places of interest. Do you not remember joking about it—a tea room, a gift shop for the tweed?'

'Vaguely, but I'm not sure…'

'And you told me yourself that the railway will run all the way from Glasgow to Greenock soon, so that there will be any number of people able to make the trip.'

'Excursionists. Is that what you're talking about?'

'More than that.' Ainsley smiled, excitement taking over from her nerves as she led him over to the table where she had laid everything out so carefully. 'Welcome to Strone Bridge Castle Hotel,' she said with a flourish.

Innes stared down at the plans, the drawings she and Mr Alexander had pulled together, the sketch she herself had made of the railway poster. He picked up the draft of the guidebook, leafing through it, and then the pages of costings she had so painstakingly worked on. 'You did all this?' he asked.

'I should have told you,' she said. 'I know I ought to have consulted you, but I wanted to surprise you.'

'You have.' He wandered round the table, picking up papers and putting them down again, the frown deepening on his face. 'Do you really believe people will pay to stay here?'

'Innes, I can't imagine anyone *not* wanting to spend the night here. I know you hate the place, but it's a real castle, for goodness' sake, with real turrets, and all these huge big rooms, and lots of pomp and splendour, and the views and— Yes, I really do think there would be any number of people willing to spend the night here. Or several. As you can see, I've even considered the possibility of leasing it out for weddings and the like. You can charge different prices, depending on which of the bedchambers people occupy, and more for the ones with ghosts in them.'

He was staring down at the railway poster. She had no idea what he was thinking. 'I thought that Mhairi would be the perfect candidate to run the place,' Ainsley continued. 'I thought it was the sort of restitution that would appeal to you, to have her installed as a chatelaine here.'

Now he did smile, albeit fleetingly. 'You were right about that. My father would be furious.'

'More important, there isn't anyone who could do a better job,' Ainsley rushed on. 'And there will be employment for any number of people here. Staff for the hotel, groundsmen. There's room for about forty or fifty guests at least, I'd say. And then there will be the food that can be provided direct from the crofts, and the tweed to sell, and—and it will mean that people don't have to emigrate to find a new life, Innes.' She laced her hands together tightly. 'What do you think?'

'I don't know.' He ran his hand through his hair. 'I can't believe you've done all this yourself.'

'Not myself. Robert has been helping, though I've sworn him to secrecy, for I did not want anyone else to know before you.' Still, Innes gave her no clue as to what he was thinking. 'You're worried it still won't be enough,' Ainsley rushed on. 'I wondered that myself, and also I was thinking that even fifty well-paying guests would not turn enough profit to justify the renovations for several years—you can see the rough figures—very rough, I'm no expert. So I thought— Well, actually it would be better if I showed you.'

'Showed me what?'

She led them through the Great Hall out into the atrium and produced the key that opened the hidden door. 'Wait till you see. I've got it all thought out, I...'

'Where are you going?' Innes stopped dead in front of the doorway.

'The tower. The view is magnificent, and it

is easier to show you what I'm proposing from there.'

'You've been up there?' He had his hands dug deep into his pockets. 'I told you not to go up there.'

He looked angry. 'It's perfectly safe, if that's what you're worried about,' Ainsley said. 'I had Mr Alexander look at it, and he said that it was structurally sound. I had him look over all of the castle, and in fact he said...'

'I'm not interested in Robert's opinion. I thought I'd made it very clear that this tower was off limits.'

'No, you didn't. You said the key was lost, and that it was unsafe, and since neither have proved to be the case—' She broke off, at a loss to understand his reaction. 'It's the cottages,' she said. 'The tied cottages that have been empty for several years. I was thinking we could renovate them and let them out to families who cannot afford to holiday in the hotel, and who—'

'Enough!'

Ainsley flinched at the fury in his voice. 'What is wrong?'

'I told you,' Innes roared. 'I said to you not to go up there.'

'You didn't. You're being quite unreasonable. You said...'

'Did you not ask yourself why the place was locked? For God's sake, did not Mhairi say anything?'

'Mhairi doesn't know anything of what I'm doing. No one does, save Mr Alexander. I— It was meant to be a surprise. Is it because I didn't tell you, Innes? Is that what's wrong?'

He gazed at her for a long moment, his eyes dark, his lips thinned. 'My brother died by throwing himself from that tower, that's what's wrong, and that's why all your plans must come to nothing.'

Innes turned the key in the lock of the hidden door, then detached it from the rest of the bunch and pocketed it. 'I'm sorry for all the hard work you've put into this, but you've wasted your time,' he said curtly before turning on his heel and walking away without a backward glance.

Chapter Thirteen

Innes did not return to the Home Farm until late that night, and he was gone for the rest of the next day. It was late and Ainsley had been lying wide awake for several hours, torn between fretting and anger, when she heard his footsteps in the corridor. They did not stop outside his room, but carried on to hers. She scrambled up in bed as the door was flung open. 'You couldn't leave it, could you?'

'I don't know what you mean.'

'This!' He strode over to the bed, waving a piece of paper at her. 'Don't pretend it wasn't your doing, for she mentions you herself, and even if she had not, I recognise some of your handiwork—or should I say Madame Hera's! "Take the opportunity to put the past to rest." That's one of yours,' Innes quoted, his voice heavy with sarcasm, 'and then there's "free to make a fresh start." One thing hasn't changed. Blanche's letters leave no room for misinterpretation.'

'Blanche?' Ainsley repeated. 'You mean Blanche wrote to you?'

'At your behest.'

'Yes, but— No, I thought she would write to me, but—Innes, what does she say?'

'That fourteen years is enough time to realise that love should conquer all and it's time we surrendered to the happiness Malcolm sacrificed himself to give us,' he said mockingly. 'Wouldn't your Madame Hera just love it if she did? Isn't that exactly what you hoped for when you interfered?'

His words were like whiplashes, deliberately and painfully cruel. The old Ainsley would have been intimidated, frightened, silent. The new Ainsley was hurt, but also furious. 'I hoped that you'd take the opportunity to at least listen to whatever she had to say,' she said through clenched teeth. 'What you call interfering was actually done through a genuine concern for your happiness, which, contrary to what you believe, I think you deserve. I hoped that you would credit me with actually caring about you, Innes, enough to risk meddling. Obviously I was wrong, and you are for reasons known only to yourself absolutely set on making the rest of your life as miserable as you can, though why you think that will make any sort of restitution when… Och, what the hell does it matter now what I thought! If you won't listen to Blanche, why would I think you'd listen to me?'

Innes crunched the letter into a ball and threw it at the grate. 'Dammit, Ainsley, it's you who won't listen! Why must you— I told you, I don't want you to care for me. I told you…'

She had had enough. Pushing back the blankets, Ainsley got out of bed and stood before him, hands on her hips. 'Do you think I could forget for a moment what you told me when it almost broke my heart!' she exclaimed. 'For goodness' sake, Innes, just because you want something to be so doesn't make it so! There are some things you can't control, and how I feel is one of them.'

'You think you're so damn clever! Can you not see, you annoying, interfering woman, that how I feel is another?' he said, yanking her into his arms.

He gave her no chance to respond, but covered her mouth with his. His kiss was passionate, dark and desperate. Exactly how she felt. Ainsley kissed him back with an abandon that left no room for thought. They staggered together, kissing, tearing at each other's clothes, kissing. Her back was pressed against the wall. His hands were on her breasts, her waist, her bottom. She wrapped one leg around him to steady herself. He pulled his jumper over his head and tore at the opening of her nightgown, groaning as he took her nipple into his mouth and sucked hard, making her moan, arch against him, thrust herself shamelessly against the thick bulge of his arousal.

She clutched at his behind, her fingers digging into the taut muscles of his buttocks. His mouth enveloped her other breast now, tugging at her nipple, making her ache and thrust and moan. Her fingers fumbled with the opening of his breeches. Her hands slid in, wrapping around the satin-soft length of him, sliding up to the hot, wet tip, and back down. 'Innes,' she said, the strain in her voice making her sound as if she'd run a mile.

'Ainsley,' he said raggedly, 'I need to be inside you.'

'Yes.' There was no hesitation in her agreement. She knew without a doubt that this was no beginning but an end, but she wanted him, needed to be part of him, this one last time. 'Yes,' she said, and when he hesitated, she arched against him. 'Yes, Innes, now.'

His face was dark, colour slashing his cheeks, his eyes deep pools. He lifted her onto the edge of the bed, pulling up the skirts of her nightgown. She wrapped her legs around his flanks, bracing herself on the mattress. He kissed her. He lifted her. He entered her. She started to come as he slid inside her. Tension, unstoppable, winding tighter and tighter as she thrust, pulsing around him as he thrust for the second time, her cries harsh, loud, demanding more and harder and more. Not enough, she didn't want it to stop, but she wanted him to have what she had. 'Come now,' she said. 'Innes, come with me.'

He did just as she asked, though he did not spend himself inside her, and panting, spiralling out of control, clinging, she did not regret that, because she knew he would, and this had to be it, the last time, the perfect time. She kissed him deeply, her lips clinging to his, her tongue touching his, touching, clinging, kissing, telling him with her mouth what she could not speak. There were tears lurking, but she would not shed those. Only she kissed him again. His mouth. His jaw. His neck. Nuzzling her face into the hollow of his shoulder, closing her eyes and trying to etch it all in her mind, as his heart thundered under her and his chest heaved, and his hands held her so tight, as if he would not let her go, though she knew he would.

Ainsley knew, even as they lay there, breathing heavily in the aftermath of their union, that it was completely and irrevocably over. Innes cared for her, but it tormented him. He had lost himself in her to stop that torment, and she had lost herself in him because she could not resist him. But she could not carry on this way, and she would not allow herself to be the means by which he escaped his past.

'I'm sorry.'

She dragged her eyes open as Innes rolled away from her, his expression troubled. 'What for?' she asked.

'Not this, but the way it happened. You meant well—the idea for the hotel, writing to—to her. You meant well, I know that. I shouldn't have lost my temper.'

But he wasn't going to change his mind. Ainsley got to her feet and pulled on her wrapper. 'I should have consulted you,' she said, turning her back to him to tend the fire.

'It would certainly have saved you a lot of effort.'

The final confirmation, as if she needed it.

He was standing behind her now. 'You must be tired,' she said. 'You should get some sleep.'

'Ainsley, I really am sorry.'

He looked quite wretched. She surrendered to the temptation to comfort him one last time and went to him, wrapping her arms around his waist, resting her cheek on his chest. He pulled her tight, almost crushing the breath from her. 'You do understand,' he said.

'I do, Innes.' She looked up, brushing his hair from his eyes, and kissed him gently on the lips. 'I understand perfectly,' she said. 'Now go and get some sleep.'

He went. He would have stayed if she had asked him, but she did not. Instead, she set about making her preparations to leave, packing a few necessities in a bandbox, leaving the rest to be sent on. She found Blanche's balled-up letter lying under the nightstand and smoothed it out. Her own words, quoted in the other woman's elegant hand, leaped out of the page at her, and at the end, a plaintive request from Blanche for a meeting. Nothing more. It was signed with a flourish, the first name only.

Innes had been joking when he suggested marrying Blanche would make all right, but there was still a chance it would. Blanche was his first love. His only one? How easy would it be for him to fall in love with her again if he could be persuaded his dead brother sanctioned the match? Blanche had always been intended to be the wife of the laird of Strone Bridge. She had been groomed for it. She had birth and money and beauty. She would be a laird's wife worth her salt. A woman who belonged here. A woman blessed by the last laird. No usurper. A woman who was perfect in just about every way, including, no doubt, her ability to pop out any number of the requisite heirs.

Feeling slightly sick, Ainsley folded the letter carefully. Pulling Innes's discarded jumper on over her nightclothes, she made her way softly down the stairs. Outside, the air was sharp with the first hint of frost. The stars were mere pinpricks, the moon a waning crescent, but she knew her way now, without looking. Up to the castle, along the path, to the terrace and her view. That was how she thought of it, though it would not be hers after today. Gazing out at the black shape that was the Isle of Bute, longing gripped her, tinged with anger. All her hard work had come to naught. When she was gone from here, there would be nothing of her left. Perhaps that was what Innes wanted, to forget all about her, and to immolate himself on the altar of the past. Tragic as it was, Ainsley was becoming impa-

tient with his determination to earn a martyrdom. She loved him with all her heart, and more
than anything, she wanted him to be happy, even
if he did decide to marry Blanche. He had lived
with guilt and regret for so long, she would not
add to that with tears, with long goodbyes, with
dragging out her time here.

Eyes straining into the inky blackness, she
sought to capture the view in her mind for all
time. Then she turned away and headed back to
the Home Farm to complete her preparations.
Before dawn broke she was tapping on the front
door of Eoin's croft, her luggage already left
waiting down in the bay.

Dearest Innes,
I am writing this as myself, and not Madame Hera, though the truth is, in my time
at Strone Bridge, I believe we have become
more or less one and the same thing. No
doubt reading this as Madame's advice will
make it easier for you to ignore. I expect
you will. I wish with all my heart that you
will not.

As you can see, I have rescued Blanche's
letter. I hope you forgive me when I confess
to having read it. Innes, please do as she
asks and meet her. If you cannot put your

own demons of guilt to bed, then perhaps
you can help her. The poor woman was but
a child when these tragic events that have
shaped both your lives took place—as indeed were you, though I know you do not
agree with me on that score. You are in the
unique position of being able to help each
other. I beg you to try to do so.

As to the rest. Robert Alexander can
answer any questions about my proposal
for Strone Bridge's future, which my doc-
umentation leaves unanswered. It is not
pride—well, only a little!—that leads me
to ask you to consider this, but a genuine
belief that it will help save your estates and
the people who live there. I'd like to think
I've left something of value behind. I hope
it's obvious how much I have come to love
the place and the people.

I leave it to you to manage the termina-
tion of our agreement in whatever way you
think best. I leave Strone Bridge a much
stronger person than the poor wee soul you
met at the lawyer's office all those months
ago. I leave it ready to do battle with whatever the future holds, and confident that
I can. You have helped me in too many
ways to list. I do not regret a second spent

with you. With all my heart I wish you happiness, because you're wrong, Innes, it is something you well and truly deserve.

A.

Innes finished reading the letter, then started all over again, as if a second reading would change the content. He looked up from the breakfast table to discover Mhairi was still there, watching him with such an expression of compassion on her face that he knew there was no point in pretending.

'Do you know when—or how—she left?' Innes asked.

'Eoin took her at first light. She left me a note asking to have the rest of her things sent on.'

'Where to?'

'It is a carrier's address in Edinburgh.'

Innes looked at the housekeeper helplessly. 'I don't even know if she's got any money. She has her allowance, but—I'll need to— I'll have to arrange to— She'll need a place to stay. I...'

'I think Mrs Drummond's more than capable of sorting that out for herself, if you don't mind my saying,' Mhairi interrupted drily. 'It seems to me that you'd better concentrate on sorting yourself out.'

'What do you mean?'

'Blanche Caldwell is back at Glen Vadie, did you know?'

Innes tore his eyes away from a third, fruitless reading of Ainsley's missive. 'At Glen Vadie? No, I didn't know. She wrote me a letter, though.'

'Does Mrs Drummond know?'

'About the letter?'

'About Blanche, Innes,' Mhairi spoke sharply. 'If that good woman has gone haring back to Edinburgh to leave the way clear for you to pick up where you never should have started with that Caldwell woman...'

'Dear God, do you think that's it?' For a moment, his heart leaped. If that was all it was, he could fetch her back. But for what purpose, and for how long? Innes slumped back miserably in his chair. 'What are you waiting for?' he demanded, seeing Mhairi, arms akimbo, was still there. 'She's gone, and she's made it very clear she won't be coming back, so go and pack her things and leave me in peace.'

But peace was not something Innes could find over the next few days. On the one hand, he was tracking Ainsley's journey in his mind, wondering where she was, who she was with, whether she was thinking of him, whether she was missing him as he ached for her. On the other, he was determinedly trying to put her firmly out of his mind and refusing to allow himself to think about what was staring him in the face— or, more accurately, fighting to be heard from his heart.

He did love her. He had, despite all his best efforts, fallen completely in love with her. He loved her in a way he had never loved Blanche, as if she were part of himself. Without her, he felt as if that part was missing. It did not help that every corner of Strone Bridge reminded him of her. It did not help, lying in her bed, the scent of her on the pillow. It did not help, avoiding her favourite view, any more than it helped forcing himself to stare at it. Mhairi's tight-lipped disapproval didn't help any more than her misguided attempts to comfort him, or Eoin's insistence that when he left her on the Isle of Bute, Ainsley had been 'very well', whatever that meant. Innes hoped she was very well. It was wrong of him to hope that she was as miserable as he, wrong of him to hope that she missed him as much, ached for him as much, loved him as much.

She had never said the words, but he was standing on the castle terrace looking out at the Kyles of Bute when he realised that she did love him, and it hit him then, how much he was wilfully throwing away. What was wrong with him?

Looking up at the tower, he remembered exactly what was wrong with him. Standing in front of Malcolm's grave a while later confirmed it. Guilt. The demons of the past. Ainsley was right.

Something glinted in the browning grass by the stone. Stooping to pick it up, Innes found a brooch. A simple thing of silver, with a name etched into it. He recognised it, for she had always worn it. So she had been here. He wondered how she'd managed it without his knowing, but it wasn't much of a puzzle. Mhairi or Eoin, or both.

Finally, Innes allowed himself to consider the advice Ainsley had left him in her letter. Heading back to the Home Farm, he read it again. And again. He found the keys on the desk where Ainsley had left them. The tower key, he still had in his coat pocket. In the Great Hall, all Ainsley's plans were still there as she had laid them out for him. So much work. He couldn't believe how stupid he'd been not to see the love that had gone into it. He felt sick to the back teeth thinking of how ungrateful he'd sounded, how much it must have hurt her to have it all thrown back in her face.

He lit a lamp and picked it up. At the doorway, goosebumps prickled on his arms. Mhairi always said there was no mistaking what she called a presence. It grew cold, she said, as if you'd walked into an icehouse, and you got a sense of it, like a breath of wind over your shoulder. Innes whirled round, but there was nothing there.

The lock turned easily. He climbed the stairs slowly, his feet remembering the twists and turns as if it had been yesterday, and not fourteen years since last he was there. Past the first-floor landing and then the second. The door at the top was closed. Heart pounding, he took a deep breath, pushed it open and stepped inside.

Nothing. Standing on the threshold, lamp held high, he felt absolutely nothing of his brother's presence. Mouth dry, he made his way over to the window. The view, in the gloaming, was as Ainsley had always said: spectacular. He opened the casement and forced himself to look down. The ground rose up to meet him, dizzying. Innes drew back hurriedly, looking over his shoulder, feeling like an idiot but unable to stop himself.

No Malcolm. Instead, he saw the table, so carefully set out. The scale model that Robert must have made of the castle and its grounds, the tied cottages, the newly landscaped gardens. Setting the lamp down, Innes pulled up a chair, picked up the sheaf of papers covered in Ainsley's distinctive scrawl and began to read.

Edinburgh, two weeks later

Ainsley put down the book she thought she'd been reading when she realised she'd been turning pages for the past half hour and could remember not a single word. Getting up from the nest of cushions and blankets she'd made for herself on Felicity's worn but comfortable sofa, she wandered over to the window. Outside, the streets of Edinburgh's New Town were quiet, for it was the Sunday after Christmas, and the church bells of St Andrew's and St George's were silent, the morning services well underway.

Felicity was spending the week with her family, so Ainsley had the flat to herself. While Felicity had been here, she'd forced herself to pin a smile onto her face and get on. With Felicity absent, Ainsley had allowed herself a few days to mope. Not that she was regretting what she had done, but she needed time to make sure it had sunk in. Innes hadn't been in touch. Though her luggage had arrived at the carrier, it had contained no note from him. Not that she'd been expecting it. She certainly hadn't been expecting him to rush after her, and even if he had it wouldn't have changed anything, so there was no point in wishing for such a stupid waste of effort.

Sighing, bored with the circles her mind was

running round, she pressed her forehead to the windowpane. Next week, the first of the New Year, she would start to look for a room. Even if she'd remained at Strone Bridge as agreed, that time would now be over. She wondered how Innes would see in the New Year. Ainsley— or Madame Hera—had been invited to a party hosted by the *Scottish Ladies Companion*. She knew she ought to go.

Outside, a post chaise pulled up on the cobbled street. Her heart did a daft wee flip, then sank as the door opened and a maidservant descended, followed by a young woman. Ainsley watched listlessly as the baggage was unloaded. Farther along the crescent, a man had appeared. Tall, dressed in black, he was making his way slowly along, checking the numbers on each of the doors.

It wasn't him. Why should it be him? All the same, Ainsley gazed down in dismay at her crumpled gown, put a hand to her hair, which was falling down from the loose knot she'd put it up in this morning. She dare not leave the window to consult the mirror over the fireplace. Not that it could possibly be Innes. Even though he did walk like Innes.

It *was* him. Her heart stopped and then began to race as she looked down into his face. Such blue eyes. He raised his hand in recognition. She couldn't move. He disappeared up the steps. The bell clanged. Still partly inclined to believe he was a figment of her imagination, Ainsley went down to open the door.

'It is you.' He looked tired. He looked— nervous? Afraid? 'Has something happened?' Ainsley asked, panicking. 'Is someone— Is everyone…?'

'Fine. They're all fine.'

'And you?'

Innes shrugged. He smiled, or he seemed to be trying to smile. 'I don't know. I'm hoping to find out. Can I come in?'

'How did you know I'd be here?'

'Eoin finally gave me Miss Blair's address.'

'She's not here. She's gone to her parents for New Year.'

'Ainsley, can I come in?'

She opened the door wider and Innes stepped through, following her up the stairs to the living room. She closed this door behind her, then simply leaned against it, unsure what to say, refusing to allow herself to think about what this might mean. It had been hard enough to leave him the first time. 'What is it?' she asked, and her voice sounded sharper than she meant, but it couldn't be helped.

Innes took off his greatcoat and put it over one of the chairs. His hat went on the table, and his gloves. He stood in front of the fire, hands clasped behind his back. Then he went over to the window, where she had been standing a few moments ago. Then he joined her at the door. 'I don't know where to start,' he said. 'I had a speech, but I can't remember it now.' He waited, but she could think of nothing to say. 'I've seen Blanche,' he said.

Ainsley's heart plummeted, even as she told herself firmly that this was good news. 'Good,' she said, as if saying out loud would make it so.

Innes nodded. 'Yes, yes, it was.' He took another turn round the room, to the fireplace, to the window, back to her. 'You were right. Or Madame Hera was,' he said with another of those lopsided smiles.

'Good,' Ainsley said again, this time with a firm nod. 'I'm glad.' She didn't sound glad. She sounded as if she were being strangled. 'Did it help?'

Innes ran his hand through his hair. He had had it cut. Suddenly she couldn't bear that he'd had it cut and she hadn't been there. She blinked furiously, but a tear escaped and ran down her cheek. She brushed it away quickly, but another fell.

'Ainsley...'

'It's nothing. I'm fine.' She pushed him away

and went to sit on the sofa, pulling the comforting woollen blanket over her, not caring how she looked or what he thought. 'Just tell me, Innes, and get it over with.'

'I thought you'd be pleased.'

'I am! I will be,' she said through gritted teeth. 'Would you just tell me?'

He stared at her in astonishment, and then he laughed. 'Don't tell me Mhairi was right.'

When she had nothing to say to this strange remark, Innes came to sit beside her. He was smiling, this time in a way that made her heart, which had become as wayward as her voice, start to do what felt peculiarly like a dance. 'Ainsley, you can't possibly be thinking that I would want Blanche?'

She shrugged, though the gesture was somewhat obscured by the blanket covering her. 'You did before,' she said, and though she sounded like a petulant child now, she couldn't help adding, 'You told me yourself that she is beautiful, rich, well born.'

'But I'm married to you.'

'Not really. I told you in my letter that I would cooperate with however you saw fit to end it.'

'And in the meantime, you don't mind if I'm bedding my first love, is that it?'

'No!' Though he had not raised his voice, he

sounded angry. Ainsley pushed back the blanket and got to her feet. 'You should not use a word like that in reference to your— To someone— To Blanche,' she said, picking up the poker and applying it furiously to the coals.

'Ainsley, I'm not bedding Blanche. I've no intentions of bedding her or even of making love to her. I can't believe you would think that. I'm married to you.'

'Not for much longer.'

The poker was wrested from her fingers. She was yanked to her feet, and held very tightly in an embrace. 'I came here in the hope of persuading you to make it for life. Please tell me I'm not wasting my time, Ainsley.'

Now her heart felt as though it was about to jump out of her mouth. The way he was looking at her, as if his life depended on her. But it did not. Surely it did not. She shook her head. 'I don't know what you're doing here.'

'I'm trying, in a very, very roundabout and long-winded way, to tell you that I love you. My only excuse for doing it so badly is that I've not said it before. Not like this. I've never meant it like this, and if you mention Blanche one more time…'

'It was you who mentioned her.'

He laughed. 'I was trying to show you that

I'd understood. That I'd done what you advised. That I'd taken the opportunity to "put the past to rest", to quote Madame Hera.'

'That was me, actually.'

'But, as you pointed out to *me*, they are become one and the same person.' Innes pushed her hair back from her face. 'I thought I had to prove myself worthy before I told you, but I think I did it the wrong way round. I love you, Ainsley. I love you with all my heart, and though I can live without you, I can get by with my guilt and my demons persuading myself that it's all I deserve, I don't want to. I want to be happy, and the only thing that will make me truly happy is you.'

She had never believed there was such a thing, but she could have sworn what she saw in his face was the light of love. She had so many questions, but right now all that mattered was that. 'I love you,' Ainsley said, 'I love you every bit as much, and I could do as you said, too, I could live without you, but, Innes, I really don't want to.'

'You don't have to. Dearest, darling Ainsley, you don't have to.'

He kissed her in a way he'd never kissed her before. Gently. Tenderly. Tentatively. He kissed her as if he was afraid she would not kiss him back. He kissed her as if he was begging that she would. 'Ainsley, I know it's all back to front, but I love you so much,' he said. And then he kissed her again, and she told him, with her hands and her lips, how very, very much his love was returned.

Later, Innes thought, kissing her. There would be all the time in the world for explanations later. What mattered now was that he loved her, and she loved him, and she was in his arms and he could finally admit just how much he had missed her and how close he had come to losing her. He kissed her, whispering her name over, whispering the words over, kissing her, touching her, pulling her so close there was no space between them. He never wanted to let her go. He wanted to make love to her right now. Make real love. Make love that he'd never made before. 'I love you,' he said. 'I can't believe how much I love you. I can't believe how daft I've been not to realise.'

He kissed her again. She laughed. She kissed him. She laughed. She kissed him. They fell, kissing, laughing with happiness, on to the sofa. And there, they made love. Laughter giving way to sighs, and then seamlessly to bliss. Love. Who would have thought it? Love.

'I meant to do this the other way round,' Innes said afterwards, lying splayed on the couch, with Ainsley draped languorously on top of him.

She giggled. 'Is this a new variation in the palace of pleasures you haven't told me about?'

'Hussy!' He grinned. 'I meant that I planned to tell you what's been happening since I read your parting letter before declaring myself, but if it's variations you're interested in, my wanton wife, then I am sure I can come up with something.'

'Really? Already?' Ainsley wriggled against him, her smile teasing. 'Are you trying to live up to the Drummond reputation for potency?'

Her face fell at her own silly words. Though she tried to hide it, he saw the flash of pain there as she moved away from him. 'Listen to me a moment,' Innes said urgently, pulling her right back to where she had been, lying over him. 'I love you exactly as you are. You need to believe me.' He touched her face gently. 'Strone Bridge is our legacy. It's all the legacy we need, and your love is all I need. I don't need you to prove it any other way than by being by my side, for better or for worse. I don't need a bairn, and I don't want you to go down the track of thinking that, or of thinking that you've somehow failed me if it doesn't happen. I need you to promise me that you believe me.'

A tear rolled down her cheek. 'Innes, you need to understand, I've been told by a doctor it's simply not possible.'

'And you need to understand that I mean what I say. I want you. That's all that matters to me. If it turned out I could not have a child, would you walk away?'

'Of course not!'

'Well, then, is this not a case of what's good for the goose being good for the gander?'

'Shouldn't it be the other way round?'

'Ainsley, I'm serious. I want you to be my wife. My real wife. My forever wife. My only love. I won't have this become an issue between us. I want us to have a fresh start in everything. I want us to be married. Will you marry me, my darling?'

'Again?'

'If that's what it takes.'

'Love me, that's all that it takes, and I promise, I won't let anything come between us.'

She kissed him softly on the mouth. Then she smiled at him, and Innes thought that maybe it was true what they said, that hearts could melt. He hugged her tightly, then he sat up, pulling her into the crook of his arm, wrapping the blanket around them. 'Now,' he said, 'I think I owe you a story. It's a long one, but I'll give you the gist of it now.'

He frowned, thinking back on all that had happened over the past two weeks. 'It wasn't finding the brooch that made me get in touch with her, or even her letter, but yours,' he concluded some time later, smiling fleetingly down at Ainsley. 'Your leaving like that brought to me my senses about how I felt for you. I'd always thought Strone Bridge was haunted by the ghosts of the past, but that was nothing compared to how it felt without you there. I kept expecting to see you at every turn. Especially at that view of the Kyles. Then there was Mhairi. And Eoin. And Robert—my goodness, that man went on and on about you. Everyone, asking me where you'd gone, when you'd be back.'

'Really?'

He laughed. 'You've no idea how much people have taken you to their hearts. It's not just me. You're part of the place, Ainsley.'

She kissed his hand, her eyes shining. 'It's part of me, too. I missed it nearly as much as I missed you.'

'Who'd have thought it?' He kissed the top of her head. 'It was when I was away the last time with Eoin I realised I'd come to think of it as home, and to think of you there, too. It scared the living daylights out of me.'

'That's when you told me about Malcolm?'

'Aye, there are no flies on you.' Innes kissed her again. 'That letter you left me—you said I deserved to be happy. That was the biggest problem, for I just couldn't see that I did. But then I was standing there in the tower looking at all the hard work you'd put into those plans, and I realised it wasn't just about me, but you, too. And Blanche—that point in your letter hit home, too. Was I actually glorying in my guilt, or so used to it that I couldn't see a way of escaping it? That turret room, I thought it held the bogeyman, but it was just a room with a view. You were right about that. It was there I began to think maybe you could have been right about other things. So I went to see her at Glen Vadie.'

Ainsley scrambled upright. 'And?'

'And it turns out things were not quite as I'd imagined,' Innes said wryly. 'Blanche ran away because she couldn't bring herself to marry Malcolm, as I told you. She wrote the letter to him, thinking that it was the right thing to do, to tell him, though she could not find the courage to do so to his face. She didn't think what it would do to him, because she didn't really think about what she'd said. That she didn't love him. That she couldn't marry him. She didn't say that she wanted to marry me, because she didn't.'

'What?'

'I know. It's farcical. Or it would be if it weren't so tragic. I'm not the only one who's been tying themselves in knots of guilt for the past fourteen years, nor am I the only one who swore off love, either.' Innes shook his head. 'I still can't believe it. She's been living in London unmarried all these years, until she met her man Murchison and fell head over heels at the age of thirty-two. So when your letter found her, out of the blue, she was delighted at the chance to finally come clean.'

Ainsley's jaw dropped. 'Blanche never wanted to marry you?'

'I know, love, it's unbelievable,' Innes said, grinning.

She slapped him playfully. 'You know what I mean.'

'I do.' He sobered. 'She said the same thing as you about Malcolm—that he'd have wanted us both to be happy. He thought, in his tragic, misguided way, that was what he was doing, clearing the way to make us so. It finally clicked with me, after you'd gone, that paying him back by making myself miserable was a stupid thing to do.'

'And Blanche?'

'Realised the same thing, not so very long ago, but all she did was confirm what you'd been telling me, Ainsley.'

'So she's as lovely on the inside as she is on the outside.'

He laughed. 'I expect she is, but there is no one as lovely as you for me. I thought I'd just proved that.'

'I hope you'll prove it again very soon.'

'Now, if you like.'

She smiled at him, the smile that sent the blood rushing to his groin, the smile he'd thought he would never see again. He kissed her on those delicious lips that were made for kissing. 'Now, and always,' he said, 'and for ever, too.'

Epilogue

Strone Bridge, New Year's Eve, 1840

Ainsley's gown for the first Hogmanay party to be held at Strone Bridge by the new laird and his lady, was of ivory silk. Cut very plainly, both the *décolleté* and the bodice were her favourite V-shape, showing her waist and her modest cleavage to advantage. The sleeves were short, puffed and trimmed with the same black lace that bordered the hem, and was formed into little flowers at the end of the ruched silk that ran in vertical stripes down the skirt, like waves on the sand.

The party was to be held in the Great Hall. She and Innes had arrived from Edinburgh only the day before, but it seemed Innes had left matters in Mhairi's capable hands beforehand. 'What if you had not found me? What if I had refused to come back?' Ainsley had asked him on the paddle steamer. Failure, he'd told her, was not an option. The look he'd given her then, aglow with love, made her want to kiss him then and there, on the blustery and freezing-cold deck of the *Rothesay Castle*.

It had begun snowing when they'd arrived at Strone Bridge, and it was snowing still. The last day of the year was spent making sure that the Home Farm was spotless, hanging rowan in the doorways for luck, and hazel to stop the bad spirits who'd been swept out getting back in again. Mhairi's advice, of course, but Ainsley had become so accustomed to pandering to good faeries and warding off bad that she'd almost started to believe in them.

She was making a final check in the mirror when the door opened and Innes entered the bedchamber. He was in the full Highland regalia he'd worn for the Rescinding. Her pulses leaped when he smiled at her. His hair was black as night. His eyes were the blue of the sea. She loved him so much.

'May I tell you, wife, that you look absolutely ravishing?'

'You may.' She dropped him a curtsy. 'May I tell you, husband, that you look absolutely ravishable?'

He laughed. 'I'm not sure that's a word, but I like it.'

'I think it's an excellent word, and I intend that Madame Hera makes it a popular one.'

'To keep a happy marriage, make sure your husband is ravishable at all times.'

'You see, it's perfect.' She put her arms around him and stood on her tiptoes to kiss him.

'Shall I prove how perfect?' he whispered.

She chuckled. 'Maybe next year. We have a ceilidh to attend.'

'A whole six hours, you're making me wait!'

'I'll make it worth your while, I promise,' Ainsley said with a meaningful look.

'I shall hold you to that,' Innes said with one of his devilish smiles. 'Did I tell you about the tradition of Reaffirming?'

'Is this another one of your invented customs?'

'It is.' He reached under the pillow and pulled out a leather box. 'I had this done in Edinburgh. Open it.'

Her fingers shaking, she did as she was bid. The rose-tinted diamond was the same, perfectly cut stone as before, but the setting was completely different. The diamond sat flat inside a very modern-looking circlet of gold, and the white diamonds that had encircled it were now also sunk inside the gold band. 'I've never seen anything like it,' Ainsley said. 'It's breathtaking.'

Innes slid the ring onto her finger, not where she had worn it for the Rescinding, on the middle finger of her right hand, but on her left hand, above her wedding band. 'A symbol of the passing of the old and the birth of the new,' he said. 'A reaffirming of what we promised, and a promise of so much more. I love you, Ainsley. I plan on loving you a little bit more every day.'

'A Reaffirming.' Her eyes were wet with tears, but she had never felt so happy. 'I think that might be my favourite custom yet.'

She had not thought she could be any happier, but as she stood by her husband's side in the Great Hall awaiting the bells that would herald the New Year, Ainsley thought she might burst with it. Looking around her at the faces, bright with the exertions of the reels and jigs, she couldn't help but compare it with the last time she had been here in this hall, a virtual stranger among them. Now she knew every person here by name. She knew which of the huddle of bairns at the far end of the hall belonged to which family and which croft.

But tonight, it was not only the people of Strone Bridge who were here to celebrate the

New Year. There were new faces, too, from as far afield as Arran and Bute. The laird of Glen Vadie was here, and so, too, was his ward. Blanche Murchison, née Caldwell, was every bit as beautiful as Ainsley had imagined. Her hair was golden blonde. Her eyes were cornflower blue. Her brows were perfect arches. Her lips were a perfect Cupid's bow. The gown she wore was of silk the same colour as those big eyes of hers, and the diamonds on her necklace were obviously not paste. She was slight, several inches smaller than Ainsley, and she was most infuriatingly curvaceous. She had a smile to melt a man's heart, and she had one of those bell-like voices into the bargain. Were she not so obviously besotted by the man whose name she bore, Ainsley might have been worried. Then she turned to her own husband, who had made the introductions, and saw the way Innes smiled at her, felt the pressure of his hand on hers and looked down at the diamond glinting on her hand, and she decided that she had no need to be worried about a single thing.

The bells rang for midnight. On cue at the last chime came a thumping at the door, and the first foot arrived, chosen for his coal-black hair, sheepishly bearing a bottle of whisky and a black bun cake. Glasses were filled, and the call for a toast went up.

Innes put his arm around Ainsley's waist and called for silence. 'I'll keep this short and sweet,' he said, 'for you've better things to do than to listen to me. At the Rescinding, we put the past to bed. Tonight, this first day of 1841, I want to talk about the future. The future my wife and I have planned here at Strone Bridge. The future I hope you will all share with us. Robert?'

He nodded over at the surveyor, who, with the help of several men, brought a long table into the centre of the room. 'This, I am proud to tell you, is all my lovely wife's idea,' Innes said. 'This is our promise to you. A Reaffirming,' he said, giving Ainsley a glowing look. 'A symbol of the passing of the old, and the birth of the new. Ladies and gentlemen, lads and lassies, I'd like you to raise your glasses to Strone Bridge Castle Hotel. *Sláinte.*'

* * * * *

MILLS & BOON®

Why not subscribe?
Never miss a title and save money too!

Here's what's available to you if you join the
exclusive **Mills & Boon Book Club** today:

✦ *Titles up to a month ahead of the shops*
✦ *Amazing discounts*
✦ *Free P&P*
✦ *Earn Bonus Book points that can be redeemed*
  against other titles and gifts
✦ *Choose from monthly or pre-paid plans*

Still want more?
Well, if you join today we'll even give you
50% OFF your first parcel!

So visit **www.millsandboon.co.uk/subs**
or call Customer Relations on 020 8288 2888
to be a part of this exclusive Book Club!

UBS_2014

MILLS & BOON®

Spend your Christmas at the Snow Crystal resort

Sarah Morgan's latest trilogy is filled with memorable characters, wit, charm and heart-melting romance! Get your hands on all three stories this Christmas!

Visit
www.millsandboon.co.uk/snowcrystal

1214_ST_7

MILLS & BOON®

Passionate pairing of seduction and glamour!

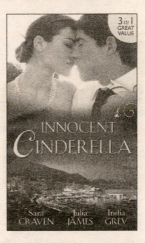

This hot duo will appeal to all romance readers.
Start your New Year off with some excitement
with six stories from popular Blaze®
and Modern™ authors.

**Visit
www.millsandboon.co.uk/mistress**

to find out more!

MILLS & BOON®

Exciting new titles coming next month

With over 100 new titles available every month,
find out what exciting romances
lie ahead next month.

Visit
www.millsandboon.co.uk/comingsoon
to find out more!

1214_ST_5

RUMER GODDEN

COROMANDEL
SEA
CHANGE

AND

SUMMER DIARY

With an introduction by Raffaella Barker

PAN BOOKS

First published 1991 by Macmillan

This edition published 2013 by Pan Books
an imprint of Pan Macmillan, a division of Macmillan Publishers Limited
Pan Macmillan, 20 New Wharf Road, London N1 9RR
Basingstoke and Oxford
Associated companies throughout the world
www.panmacmillan.com

ISBN 978-1-4472-1099-3

Coromandel Sea Change copyright © Rumer Godden 1991
'The Herbogowen' copyright © The Rumer Godden Literary Trust 2004
Introduction copyright © Raffaella Barker 2004

The right of Rumer Godden to be identified as the
author of this work has been asserted by her in accordance
with the Copyright, Designs and Patents Act 1988.

All rights reserved. No part of this publication may be
reproduced, stored in or introduced into a retrieval system, or
transmitted, in any form, or by any means (electronic, mechanical,
photocopying, recording or otherwise) without the prior written
permission of the publisher. Any person who does any unauthorized
act in relation to this publication may be liable to criminal
prosecution and civil claims for damages.

1 3 5 7 9 8 6 4 2

A CIP catalogue record for this book is available from
the British Library.

Printed and bound by CPI Group (UK) Ltd, Croydon CR0 4YY

This book is sold subject to the condition that it shall not,
by way of trade or otherwise, be lent, re-sold, hired out,
or otherwise circulated without the publisher's prior consent
in any form of binding or cover other than that in which
it is published and without a similar condition including this
condition being imposed on the subsequent purchaser.

Visit **www.panmacmillan.com** to read more about all our books
and to buy them. You will also find features, author interviews and
news of any author events, and you can sign up for e-newsletters
so that you're always first to hear about our new releases.

To Oscar – Sir Owain Jenkins –
my dear old 'enemy', who has done
so much to help me

'They come for the sea change,' said
Auntie Sanni and she might have added . . .
'into something rich and strange.'

CONTENTS

Acknowledgements

My sincere thanks are due to: Alan Maclean for his guidance over the book; my editor, Hazel Orme, for her constant care and patience; Tigger Stack for her expert help on Indian affairs and beliefs, also Shahrukh Husain whose books and advice have been invaluable; to Sir Owain Jenkins for his contribution of precious tidbits and, as always, to Ena Logan Brown and Sheila Anderson who typed and retyped without flagging.

R.G.

Introduction

I first read a novel by Rumer Godden when I was twelve. The book was *The Greengage Summer*, a story which perfectly describes both the misconceptions and the realities of adolescence – and which evokes a sense of place so strongly that I have only to read the title on my bookshelf now to be transported in my mind to the orchards and garden in France where the novel is set. I hold the children in the book as closely in my memories of childhood as I do my own friends and, like my friends, they helped me broaden my understanding of growing up.

Like *I Capture the Castle* by Dodie Smith and *The Constant Nymph* by Margaret Kennedy, *The Greengage Summer* is a timeless story, to be reread with as much pleasure as the first time. I have found this to be the case when returning to other novels by Rumer Godden, and it is her gift that she can intrigue a teenager with stories ostensibly about girls growing up which, when revisited by an adult, are also satisfying at more complex levels.

Rumer Godden had the ability to create a magical and vivid world and to people it with characters whose lives are visibly enriched by loving these places – and in doing this she has won her novels a loyal following. She has been highly praised for the subtlety of her characterization, and in particular her depiction of children; the young family in *The Greengage Summer* are humorous and arresting and very plausible. And she should also be remembered for her gift of interpreting the world through a voice that is both innocent and assured. Her life spanned most of the twentieth century, but her work remains timeless, retaining a quiet but constant humour which contributes significantly to its charm.

Coromandel Sea Change is one of the most captivating books I have read. Its subject matter is both personal and political, yet it never for a moment becomes anything but the lightest and most entertaining story to read. Set on the Coromandel coast in India, the backdrop for the novel is an eccentric and bohemian hotel, Patna Hall, which is presided over by the motherly and wise figure of Auntie Sanni.

Rumer Godden's relationship with India began when she was a child, living there with her family. Born in Sussex in 1907, her father's job with a steam-ship company kept the family in India and Rumer Godden returned to England to go to school only when she was twelve. Her love of India did not leave her, and she returned there after completing her education. Many of her novels reflect her knowledge of the culture and beliefs of the country, and *Coromandel Sea Change* is a significant example of this. Patna Hall offers an opportunity for many different aspects of Indian culture to be explored, with its guests ranging from diplomats to political campaigners, and both loyal Samuel and cocky, self-serving Kuku among the staff.

Hotels work well for Rumer Godden, and I don't mean any old hotel. A specific sort turns up frequently in her writing – the sort where people stay for weeks on end and return year after year. Godden uses that sense of continuity and permanence to colour the background and enhance the three-dimensional make-up of some of her characters. In *Coromandel Sea Change* the scene is set with a comic line-up of the hotel staff and arriving guests, which is supported by the entertaining yet loving depiction of post-colonial India.

One suspects that Mary St John, like Cecilia in *The Greengage Summer*, has much of Godden's own character in her. Mary is newly married to a pompous British diplomat; arriving at Patna Hall on honeymoon, she is delighted by southern India, the idiosyncratic charm of the hotel, and feels instantly at home with Auntie Sanni. Like other Godden heroines, Mary is young but self-assured. She begins to discover elements in her husband's character that she cannot accept, and in reaction and as salve she becomes increasingly involved in the hotel and in the elections going on in the state.

Rumer Godden is as subversively funny about politics and the hierarchy of power as she is penetrating about emotional relationships. There is something of Evelyn Waugh's mordant wit in her creation of the procrastinating Dr Hari Coomeraswamy, plump leader of the Root and Flower party's campaign and champion of the enigmatic and handsome Krishnan. Dr Coomeraswamy sails along on a cloud of his own hot air, buoyed by his belief in convention, which is punctured from time to time by Krishnan's flouting of it. The political story offers light relief from the unhappy marriage at the centre of the narrative, and is an elegantly used device for exploring Rumer Godden's great passion for India.

Many writers are able to create a rich new world for their readers, a place to lose themselves in for the duration of the story, but Rumer Godden's novels will stand the test of time not just for this quality, but more because she has done it so apparently effortlessly. This ease is what endears her work to every age group as her novels appear again for a new generation. Rumer Godden may depict a nostalgic world of never-ending summer and characters whose lives are played out light years from the frustrations and stresses of the twenty-first century, but her tone, her humour and her clear understanding of what it is to be young and passionate are qualities which all who come across the work will respond to. No one should limit his or her reading of Rumer Godden to just one novel. She offers too many treats and some precious and abiding memories.

Raffaella Barker

List of Characters

Auntie Sanni	Miss Sanni to her servants, owner of Patna Hall
Colonel McIndoe	her husband

Staff at Patna Hall

Samuel	butler and major domo
Hannah	his wife, housekeeper
Kuku	the young hotel manager
Thambi	lifeguard on the beach and general guard
Moses Somu	} lifeguards on the beach
Ganga	the wine waiter
Mustafa Abdul Ahmed	} waiters
Alfredo	the Goanese cook

houseboys, sweepers, a washerman, gardeners, etc.

For the election

Gopal Rau	candidate for the Patriotism Party
Mrs Padmina Retty	candidate for the People's Shelter Party
Krishnan Bhanj	candidate for the Root and Flower Party
Dr Hari Coomaraswamy	leader of the Root and Flower Party's campaign
Mr Srinivasan	his aide
Sharma	their young District Agent

| Ravi }
Anil } | young party workers |
| the disciples | other young men and women of the
Root and Flower Party campaign |

Guests at Patna Hall this week

Sir John and Lady (Alicia) Fisher	
Mrs Olga Manning	
Professor Aaron	leader of the International Association of Art, Technology and Culture
Professor Ellen Webster	lecturer to the group
Mrs van den Mar	leader of eighteen American lady archae- ologists, professional and amateur
Mrs Glover Mrs Schlumberger Dr Julia Lovat Miss Pritt }	archaeologists
Mr Menzies	
Blaise St John Browne Mary Browne }	on honeymoon

Others

Kanu	a small fisherboy
Shyama	Thambi's wife
Chief Inspector Anand	police officer
Krishna Radha Lakshmi }	gods and goddesses

Animals

Slippers	a donkey
Birdie	an elephant
Udata	a squirrel
Christabel	Auntie Sanni's mynah bird

Time

any time

Saturday

Saturday was change-over day at Patna Hall.

'Two hundred sheets,' shouted the *vanna* – the old washerman was close to weeping. 'Two hundred pillowcases *and* the towels. That is too much.'

'It is because of the election.' Auntie Sanni was unmoved. 'So many people coming and going besides our own guests.'

Usually guests, as Auntie Sanni liked to call them, stayed at least a week or ten days, two weeks sometimes three, even three months like Mrs Manning. Sheets were changed three times a week and always, of course, when a guest came or went but now, 'Too many,' wailed the *vanna*.

'It is for the good of your country.' Hannah, the Madrassi housekeeper, was always a reconciler; she also happened to be a strong partisan for the new and hopeful Root and Flower Party. 'Don't you care for your country?'

'I care that I can't wash two hundred sheets.'

'A contract is a contract.' Auntie Sanni was unrelenting. 'It does not say how many or how little. Take them and go.'

'And none of your ironing without washing them first,' sharp little Kuku put in.

'Wash them yourself,' said the *vanna* and left the bundles lying on the floor.

* * *

The three women in the linen room took no notice. They knew, as the *vanna* knew, that there were many *vannas* in Shantipur, even more in the port of Ghandara four kilometres away, all with swarming families, all poor; not one of them would let a contract with Patna Hall be taken from him. 'He will soon be back,' Hannah prophesied.

The linen room at Patna Hall was in a small cloistered courtyard built at the side of the main house for administrative offices and linen room, store rooms, a pantry or confectioner's room where Patna Hall's own specialist puddings and desserts were made with, nowadays, a refrigerating room. These were to be expected but Auntie Sanni's office was part business, part conservatory, part menagerie. The convolvulus blue of morning glory tumbled over the window, pots of canna lilies and hibiscus stood in corners; tame birds, cockateels and mynahs, flew round the room. One mynah, Christabel, had learned to call Kuku so cleverly that Kuku never knew if it were Christabel or Auntie Sanni. There were doves; bright green parakeets flew in from the garden and mingled with them all – often they perched on Auntie Sanni's desk, watching her fearlessly, their scarlet-topped heads on one side. It was not only birds: two cats, tabbies, slept stretched on a mat in the sun; a brown spotted goat was tethered outside while her kids wandered in and out, one white, one brown as if the colours had been divided. 'But don't let the monkeys in,' Hannah had warned Kuku, 'they take too many things.'

The monkeys were small, brown and wild; their brown faces and bright eyes peered from the trees. They ran across the courtyard on all fours, their tails lifted their small skinny hands quickly into anything – 'and every-thing,' said Hannah – and always, all through rooms and cloister, the soft Indian sea breeze blew bringing the sound of the waves crashing on the beach below.

* * *

2

Auntie Sanni — Miss Sanni to her staff and servants — was called Auntie because, in Eurasian parlance, that is the title given to any grown-up female whether she has nephews and nieces or not. Auntie Sanni had none by blood but, over the years, had acquired many — Auntie of the universe would have fitted her. She dominated the linen room as she dominated Patna Hall. 'Why?' Kuku often wondered. To her Auntie Sanni was only an unattractive massive old woman, nobody knew how old. 'No shape to her at all,' said Kuku, looking at her in one of her usual cotton dresses like a tent reaching to her feet, its voluminous folds patterned with blue flowers; Auntie Sanni called them her 'Mother Hubbards' from the garments missionaries used to hand out to the natives. On her feet were country-made sandals. Auntie Sanni's face looked young because of her head of short curls like a child's, their red still auburn. Her skin was true Eurasian, the pale yellow brown of old ivory against which her eyes looked curiously light, sea-colour eyes, now green, now blue, set wide, again like a child's but Hannah, even Kuku, could have told that Auntie Sanni was no child.

Hannah, almost her bondswoman, began piling the bundles tidily together, her silver bangles slipping up and down her arms. Hannah liked everything to be tidy, clean, exact, as did her husband, Samuel. They, for Auntie Sanni, were the twin pillars of Patna Hall.

Hannah was a big woman — though not beside Auntie Sanni. Kuku, when she was with them, looked wand slim, quick and brilliant as a kingfisher in her electric blue sari with its lurex border. Hannah had eyed that sari. 'Muslin for morning is nice,' she had said, 'and practical.'

'This, too, is practical,' Kuku had retorted. 'It is drip dry.'

Hannah herself wore a crisp white sari edged with red and an old-fashioned red bodice high in the neck, her scant grey hair pinned into a knob. In spite of this simplicity she was laden with silver jewellery: bangles; the lobes of her ears hung down with the weight of earrings; she had finger rings and toe rings on her gnarled bare feet; everyone knew where Hannah was by the sound of clinking. Kuku's *choli* stopped in a curve under breasts that were young and full, it left her midriff bare, supple and brown; her hair which could have made the usual graceful coil was instead frizzed into a mane that reached her shoulders; she had a flower over her left ear. 'Miss Sanni, why let her go about so?' Hannah often said to Auntie Sanni. 'That hair! Those nails! And a sari should be muslin, silk or gauze,' and Auntie Sanni always answered, 'I don't think Kuku has saris like that.'

Kuku was an orphan, brought up in St Perpetua's Home in Madras. 'St Perpetua's, very good,' Hannah had always maintained. She and Samuel were English-speaking Thomist Christians. 'St Thomas, apostle, came to Madras and is buried there,' they said. Kuku, though, was now proudly agnostic. No one knew what Auntie Sanni believed; perhaps all religions met in her as they met peaceably in Patna Hall; the gardeners were Brahmins, the sweeper women, untouchables, the waiters all Muslim while the head bearer, Colonel McIndoe's personal servant from Nepal, was a Buddhist. Nothing seemed to disturb any of them and, 'Yes, St Perpetua's is very good,' Auntie Sanni endorsed Hannah. 'It gives all its girls an excellent education and trains them for work but I don't think they get many saris.'

Kuku had been trained in hotel management. 'I didn't have to be trained,' said Auntie Sanni. 'I knew.'

Auntie Sanni's grandfather had started the hotel in the eighteen nineties but the house was older than that, 'Built by some nabob of the East India Company in the eighteenth century to catch the sea breezes,' she had told Kuku.

'Could they have come so far without cars or the railway?'

4

'Far from Calcutta but there were plenty of East India Company men in Madras. They would have had horses and palanquins.'

'What are palanquins?' asked Kuku.

'My grandfather made a fortune out of indigo in Bihar,' Auntie Sanni would tell the guests. 'That's why the hotel is called Patna Hall. Patna is the capital of Bihar.' She herself had never seen the acres of the leafy flowering shrub that brought such riches as, processed – 'My grandfather had his own factory' – the flowers turned from olive to orange and finally to the intense blue of indigo. 'All sailors' livery used to be dyed with it, all blue cloth until chemical dyes became rife.' 'Rife' as Auntie Sanni said it was a dirty word. 'My grandfather got out just in time. They were lovely colours, indigo, madder, sepia, those greens and turmeric yellows,' she said softly. 'It is seldom nowadays that you get colours like that.'

Patna Hall was the only substantial house on that stretch of the Coromandel coast; its stucco, as befitted the property of an indigo planter, was painted blue, now faded to paleness; it rose three storeys high to a parapeted roof. The porticoed entrance faced inwards towards the village of Shantipur with its palms and *simile* trees, their cotton flowers scarlet; behind them low hills, where coffee grew, cut off the horizon. There were servants' quarters, the courtyard offices, a gatehouse, a large vegetable garden, a small farm and poultry yard, even a private cemetery.

On the other side of the house facing the sea, a garden of English and Indian flowers sloped to a private beach that had a bungalow annexe. On every side dunes of fine white sand stretched away, planted with feathery casuarina trees; on the right the dunes led to a grove of mango and more *simile* trees; on the left they rose to a knoll that overlooked the demesne. On the foreshore of hard sand, the great rollers of the Coromandel Sea

5

thundered down, giant waves that rose to eight, even ten feet, before they crashed sending a wash far up the sand. Further out, by day, the sea was a deep sapphire blue.

The hotel beach was forbidden to fishermen or their boats; indeed, the sea there was netted to a distance of five hundred yards not only against fishermen but sharks; every night Thambi, the lifeguard, and his assistants, Moses and Somu, unfolded a high strong-meshed fence across the private beach padlocking it so that the beach was cut off from the sea. 'Unless there is bathing by moonlight,' said Thambi.

'Please,' Auntie Sanni would say seriously to each guest, 'please remember it is dangerous to go out alone to bathe. With the force and power of those waves, you must take a guard.'

Women bathers usually had to have a man each side to hold them and bring them up through the wave to ride gloriously back on its crest of surf. Thambi would let no one go into it without wearing one of the fishermen's pointed wicker helmets bound firmly under the chin; the helmet's peak would pierce the waves that otherwise might stun. 'Ours is not a gentle sea,' said Auntie Sanni, 'and please,' she said again to her guests, 'no one must swim unless Thambi is on the beach.'

Patna Hall looked tall from the beach, the blue of its stucco ornamented with decorations of scrolls and flowers like daisies, oddly inconsequential. The flat roof was bounded by its balustraded parapet, which had a wide ledge on which young adventurous guests liked to sit. At night the house lights shone far across the sea; a small glow came, too, from the gatehouse where Thambi and his wife Shyama lived. Thambi was another of Auntie Sanni's right hands, hotel guard as well as beach lifeguard; it was Shyama who was supposed to open and shut the gates but as they were always open she had nothing to

6

do except to cook a little, dry chillies in the sun and wash her hair. 'Lazy little slut,' said Kuku. 'Thambi ought to beat her.'

'I thought you were a feminist.'

'I am but I don't like to see her.'

'I do,' said Auntie Sanni with a vision of the scarlet of the chillies and the blue-black hair.

Overlooking garden and sea, verandahs ran the full length of the house above a basement of cellars and fuel stores that was half buried in sand. The lower verandah was the sitting place for the whole hotel, with cane chairs and tables, cane stools and old-fashioned steamer chairs with extended boards each side on which feet could comfortably be put up. There was a bar at one end; at the other, Auntie Sanni's swing couch had bright chintz covers and cushions; before lunch – which she called tiffin – and before dinner she liked to sit there and reign.

Inside, behind the verandah the rooms were high, floored with dark red stone which Samuel saw was polished; every morning a posse of village women came in to sit on the floor moving slowly forward on their bottoms as they pushed bottles, their ends wrapped in a waxed cloth until the stone shone. The upper air was stirred by *punkahs* – electric flat-bladed fans; when the sea breeze was strong they stirred by themselves. If the wind was too high, sand blew in over the floors to Samuel's grief.

There was a billiard room; though few house guests played billiards, gentlemen, chiefly Indian, came in from Ghandara to play and have drinks – there was a bar in the billiard room as well. The verandah was reserved for resident guests.

The drawing room, away from the sea, was immense, a double room; the stone floor here was green. It was so little used that the electric fans overhead creaked when they were switched on. 'So much empty space,' mourned Kuku.

7

'Which is always useful,' said Auntie Sanni, 'and makes for peace and health, two things that are uncommon in this country which is why people come.'

Hannah reigned over the bedrooms with, under her, not women servants but men, bearers or houseboys in brass-buttoned white tunics, white trousers, black caps, while Samuel was king of the dining room behind the verandah.

Samuel was regal, white-whiskered, white-bearded, his clothes immaculately white and starched, his turban huge with, round it, a red and gold band on which, in brass, was Auntie Sanni's family crest – 'My grandfather's crest.' The waiters wore modest imitations – woe betide any of them who had a spot or smudge on their tunics or trousers.

The food was delectable, the service unhurried; neither Auntie Sanni nor Samuel had heard of unions and, though luncheon was served at one, dinner at eight, the dining room kept no hours. The food was brought in from the cookhouse outside; in the magical way of Indian servants it was kept hot by the old-fashioned use of packing cases lined with zinc in which were gridded shelves with a brazier burning red below.

From the first day she came there had been battles between Kuku and Samuel. 'Always objecting. Never do as she is asked. Why not?' demanded Samuel.

'I suppose an orphan girl without money has to fight,' said Auntie Sanni. 'Poor little Kuku. She hasn't learned that the best way to fight is by not fighting. Also, we are getting old, Samuel, perhaps we need fresh blood,' and, seeing disbelief in his eyes, 'but I think Kuku will soon go on to something else, she won't be satisfied here. Besides St Perpetua's asked me to take her. Kuku needs a chance.'

'I think we are full up,' said Auntie Sanni in her office this Saturday morning.

'Full up! My God!' Kuku had brought the ledger from the reception desk in the hall. 'I don't know where to put them all.'

'Let me see.' Auntie Sanni opened the big register. There were, of course, permanencies, in chief Colonel McIndoe, Auntie Sanni's husband, though no one called her Mrs McIndoe. They had a suite on the first floor overlooking the sea. There was Kuku's small room on the floor above. 'The first room I have ever had of my own,' she had exclaimed in delight when she came. Samuel and Hannah had their own neat house, kept apart from the other servants' quarters by a hedge of poinsettias. 'Let me see,' said Auntie Sanni.

'Sir John and Lady Fisher?' Kuku peered over her shoulder.

'Number one,' said Hannah immediately.

'They are our oldest, dearest guests.' Auntie Sanni's voice dropped into a singsong which, like most Eurasians, she did not recognise as part Indian though it made Kuku wince – Kuku had tried to acquire an American accent. 'Sir John says they can only stay a week this time. You will put flowers in their room and fruit and order a taxi to meet the connection from Delhi.

'Professor Aaron and his ladies . . .'

'Eighteen of them,' added Hannah.

'One tourist professor, eighteen tourist ladies!' Kuku giggled but Hannah looked at her severely. 'This is Patna Hall,' said the look. 'We don't take tourists.'

Auntie Sanni explained, 'It is a cultural group. The International Association of Art, Technology and Culture. Professor Aaron brings a group every year, sometimes for archaeology, sometimes it is botany. Sometimes there are men but all are highly qualified. Last year the group was French, this year they are American.'

'Americans are the worst tourists,' said Kuku.

'You say that because you have heard it.' For once

9

Auntie Sanni was wrathful. 'What do you know about it? The British can be every bit as bad, also the Germans and you will not call these ladies tourists, do you hear? Some of them themselves are professors.'

'Old?' asked Kuku without interest.

'Usually middle-aged. Young people haven't the time or money – the tours are very expensive.'

'They come from all over,' said Hannah. 'They will bring books, notebooks, maps, binoculars, magnifying glasses, cameras, what all.'

'This time it is archaeology. They will visit the new diggings at Ghorāghat, also the cave paintings in our own hills but, especially, the great Dawn Temple at Ghorāghat, the temple of Usas, the Dawn goddess.' Auntie Sanni, who had never seen the Dawn Temple, still said it reverently, then, 'A single for Professor Aaron,' she said returning to the ledger. 'Nine doubles for the ladies, they will not mind sharing. They are usually not fussy,' she told Kuku.

'Mr R. Menzies,' Kuku read out. 'He does not say when he is arriving.'

'Well, then, we cannot meet him. Give him a first floor back and, later tonight, Dr Coomaraswamy and Mr Srinivasan will be here.'

'What again?'

'Of course.' Hannah at once grew heated. 'Isn't Dr Coomaraswamy the leader of our campaign? Isn't Mr Srinivasan his aide? Isn't this the week of the election? The campaign starts tomorrow. Of course they are all coming back.'

'Except Krishnan Bhanj, your candidate,' said Kuku.

That slowed Hannah. 'I do not know why,' she said, 'so often he has stayed here since he was a little boy, he and his parents, very good high-up people. He was here last month. Why not now?'

'No one knows but Krishnan,' said Auntie Sanni, 'and we can be sure he knows why.'

10

'God almighty Krishnan!' mocked Kuku. 'He's not going to win you know. It said so on the radio. Padmina Retty has held the seat for so long. Mrs Retty, Mother to the People of Konak.'

'Much good has it done them.' Hannah was fierce.

'Krishnan Bhanj is an upstart. They all say so.'

'Hardly an upstart,' said Auntie Sanni. 'Krishnan has been in politics since the day he was born, but in any case, I could not have had Mrs Retty here with Dr Coomaraswamy. He booked first. Also, with him', Auntie Sanni told them, 'will be at least ten, maybe twenty young electioneering assistants.'

'My God!' but Auntie Sanni was unperturbed. 'They will be out on the campaign all day and they can sleep in Paradise.'

Paradise was a line of cell-like rooms on Patna Hall's roof. Once upon a time European or American chauffeurs were put there, now and again ladies' maids. 'When we had people from the embassies,' said Auntie Sanni and, of the men, 'They are young. They can sleep three or four to a room. Buy *charpoys*,' she ordered Kuku.

'Mrs Manning?' asked Kuku.

There was a pause, then, 'She stays where she is,' said Auntie Sanni.

'Taking up two rooms when we are so full and she hasn't paid for a month!'

'I think she cannot pay at present,' said Auntie Sanni.

'Manning Memsahib is not like a memsahib,' said Hannah. 'She washes her own things in the bathroom to save the *vanna*'s bill.'

That seemed sense to Kuku. 'We were encouraged to do that at St Perpetua's.'

'You are you,' Hannah's look said plainly.

'Mrs Manning still orders whisky, your whisky . . .' Kuku came out against Mrs Manning. 'Olga,' she mocked. 'I thought only Russians were called Olga and showing off

11

with the piano.' If Kuku had admitted to what had hurt and rankled in her with Mrs Manning it was that Olga Manning had called her 'housekeeper'.

'The housekeeper is Hannah. I am hotel manager.'

'Indeed!' The hazel eyes had looked at her amused. 'How long have you been that?' and, 'Six weeks,' Kuku had had to say and now, 'Where is Mr Manning, I should like to know?' she asked.

'Kuku, we do not pry into our guests' affairs.'

'Perhaps better if we did and they are not guests, they are clients and supposed,' Kuku said defiantly, 'supposed to pay.'

Auntie Sanni did not choose to answer that. Instead, 'Mr and Mrs Browne,' she read out. 'They will not arrive until Sunday afternoon. Lady Malcolm recommended them. The girl is freshly out from England. They are, I believe, on honeymoon.'

'Aie!' said Hannah. 'They should have had the bridal suite.'

'Dr Coomaraswamy and Mr Srinivasan have booked the bridal suite long ago for the whole of the campaign.'

'What a bridal pair!' Kuku giggled again.

'Mr and Mrs Browne can have the second half of the bungalow,' said Auntie Sanni. 'So close to the beach and away from other guests, they should be happy there.'

That made Kuku brood again over Mrs Manning in the bungalow's other half, the half that had a sitting room.

'Miss Sanni,' she said, 'you will never make a profit.'

'Profit?' asked Auntie Sanni, as if to say what could she do with a profit. 'Patna Hall pays its way very nicely,' her singsong went on. 'Colonel McIndoe and I, Samuel and Hannah and Thambi have all that we want.'

Kuku's exasperation broke. 'You should put up one of those hotel notices on your gates, "Do Not Disturb".'

'That would be very nice,' said Auntie Sanni.

12

Professor Aaron and the cultural ladies, as Hannah called them, were the first to arrive, in time for luncheon; eighteen ladies. 'They can match with the young men in Paradise.' Kuku giggled again.

The big red-bearded Professor kissed Auntie Sanni, bowed to Hannah and introduced the group, which was led by Mrs van den Mar from Michigan – not with the waved blue-grey hair, Kuku had automatically expected. Mrs van den Mar wore hers in a plait round her head and, for all her elegance – 'I think she is rich,' whispered Kuku – was plump, comfortable, 'and I think comforting,' Auntie Sanni would have said. 'A good leader.' She introduced the most distinguished archaeologist of them all, Professor Ellen Webster, thin, earnest, brown hair cut in a fringe, spectacles. 'She is a senior professor in the Department of Archaeology at Yale University. She will give us our lectures,' said Professor Aaron. 'And who', he asked, 'is this charming young person?'

'Miss Kuku Vikram, who has come to help me,' said Auntie Sanni.

'You don't need any help,' the Professor said gallantly.

As Hannah had predicted they had much paraphernalia: satchels, shoulder bags full of notebooks, shooting sticks, camp stools, binoculars, cameras, dark glasses. To Kuku they seemed, too, all dressed alike; each carried a light raincoat; they wore cotton short-sleeved shirts, skirts or trousers in neutral colours, one or two in blue denim; some had eyeshades, others cotton-brimmed hats and all were eager, happy, intent. Impressed in spite of herself, Kuku murmured to Hannah, 'They must be very cultured.'

Mrs van den Mar's first eager question to Auntie Sanni, though, was anything but cultural. 'We're looking forward to your famous mulligatawny soup Professor Aaron has told us so much about. We hope it will be for lunch.'

'The soup of the day is vichyssoise,' Kuku said with pride.

Their faces fell. 'I can have vichyssoise in Michigan,' said Mrs van den Mar.

'I told you so,' Samuel hissed at Kuku, his moustaches bristling with fury. 'Do you think, after so many years butler at Patna Hall, I do not know what sahibs like to eat? You . . .' If Samuel had known the word 'chit' he would have used it, all he could say was 'upstart'.

'We shall have mulligatawny tomorrow,' and Auntie Sanni softened the blow further, 'Today we have our equally famous prawn curry, prawns fresh from the sea. Now, may Miss Kuku and Hannah show you to your rooms?'

Half an hour later, the ladies gathered on the verandah where Kuku served at the bar. 'Coffee, tea and soft drinks only,' Auntie Sanni had laid down. 'Indian young ladies do not serve hard drinks or wine,' but to Samuel's anger Kuku often transgressed, usurping what belonged to Ganga, the wine waiter. Now she served the cultural ladies with a favourite suggested by Professor Aaron, 'Gin and ginger beer, taken long, with plenty of ice,' but, 'Do you know how to make mint julep?' one of them asked Kuku. 'So refreshing!' Kuku, to her chagrin, had to ask Samuel. Some had iced tea. 'That's a very beautiful sari,' another said to Kuku, seduced by the colour. Samuel sniffed.

'Well, have you settled in?' Professor Aaron went from one to another.

'Indeed,' said a gentle Mrs Glover. 'We are charmed, Professor, truly charmed. We never expected anything like this.'

'I certainly did *not* expect anything like this,' an indignant voice came as a stout lady stumped on to the verandah. 'Have you *seen* the bathrooms?'

'They are primitive,' Mrs Glover had to admit.

14

'Primitive! Never did I think that to take a bath I should have to sit on a stool and pour water over me with a *pitcher*.' Mrs Schlumberger was the group grumbler. Now she looked up sharply. Kuku had not been able to restrain a giggle.

'Isn't it good to do as the people here do?' pleaded Mrs Glover.

'And it's far more hygienic than lying in a bath using the same water over and over again,' that was Dr Julia Lovat. 'The Indians say that we Westerners with our baths are like buffaloes wallowing in their own dirty water.'

'Julia! How can you?'

'All the same, I shall miss my shower.' Miss Pritt, the only unmarried one and handsome, tried to placate.

'We'll miss far more than that.' Mrs Schlumberger was not to be appeased. 'That sweet little manager agrees with me. Says the lady refuses to modernise.'

'Oh, come! There is air-conditioning . . .'

'No telephone in the rooms . . . no room-service . . . I wouldn't have come if I had known.'

'We can always arrange to send you back,' Mrs van den Mar said sweetly. 'Ah, lunch! I expect you'll feel better after lunch.'

Two large round tables had been set up for them in the dining room, Professor Aaron hosting one, Mrs van den Mar the other. 'For lectures they will use the drawing room,' Auntie Sanni had said, 'so open it properly,' she told Kuku. 'Put flowers.'

When opened the drawing room looked well with its Persian carpets — 'Kerman,' said Auntie Sanni — on the dark green floor. Potted palms stood in polished brass pots, also on the floor; chairs and sofas were covered in a sweet pea chintz. Around the fireplace, which had an enormous grate, a fire seat made a circle; the mantel above held Victorian china and over it was a painting, a portrait

15

of Auntie Sanni as a child with the same short chestnut curls; other paintings of the indigo plantations hung on the walls. There was an upright piano with pleated silk above the keyboard and brass candlesticks; antique as it was, Mrs Manning liked to play it in the evenings, even when the room was shrouded.

'Well, she can't do that while the conference is on,' said Kuku with satisfaction. Then an idea struck her. 'Couldn't she play something catchy for us during dinner? We could move the piano into the dining room. I will ask her.'

'You will *not*.' Auntie Sanni came down on Kuku like the juggernaut at the Dawn Temple which came out on festival days to carry the Goddess and could crush mere humans under its wheels. 'In our dining room people can still enjoy their food in *quiet*.' All the same, Auntie Sanni was uneasy about Mrs Manning's playing in the evenings. 'It sounds so lonely,' she had said more than once to Hannah.

'It is lonely,' said Hannah.

'You have not changed one i-o-ta.' Auntie Sanni greeted Sir John and Lady Fisher.

'Nor you.' Lady Fisher kissed Auntie Sanni. 'You never change.'

Sir John, on the verge of his sixties — 'I retire next year' — was, in Auntie Sanni's canny diagnosis, all that was elegant and excellent: still slim, upright, his voice was quiet and firm; his sun-tanned skin, after years in the tropics, contrasted oddly with his silvered hair, while Lady Fisher had kept a complexion that looked as if it had never felt a rough wind. 'I don't suppose it has,' said Auntie Sanni.

In any case Lady Fisher preferred not to go on the beach or bathe or lie in the sun. 'Then why does she come?' asked Kuku.

'To be with Sir John,' with which Lady Fisher and Sir John would have completely agreed.

'Have you never heard', asked Auntie Sanni, 'that men need rest? The more successful they are, the more in the public eye, the more they need it. There was never a more restful and calm person than Lady Fisher or one who listens more,' but now, 'I am sorry,' she told the Fishers as she led them from the hall to the verandah, 'sorry that the election should have come at this time. The house is so full, I am afraid you will have little peace.'

'I don't think it will disturb us,' said Sir John, while, 'Dear Aunt Sanni,' said Lady Fisher — she and Sir John gave her the dignity of 'Aunt' — 'with you there is always peace.'

'They have been coming here for fifteen years,' Auntie Sanni told Kuku. 'I am proud to say they are our friends, Colonel McIndoe's and mine.'

'A tinpot little election, how could it disturb them?' Kuku asked on the verandah that evening and was overheard by Dr Coomaraswamy.

'Tinpot!' He was indignant. 'An election that concerns at least a quarter of a million people?'

'Perhaps a million people,' put in Mr Srinivasan.

'There are too many people.'

Kuku seemed able to flirt even with the ends of her sari; Dr Coomaraswamy's brown eyes, already so prominent that they looked like a fish's or seemed, as a snail's, to have come out on stalks following Kuku's every movement. 'Yes, too many,' Mr Srinivasan was saying. 'If we have a million, soon there will be two million. Not long and there will be four. For-tun-ately one of the most important things in our Root and Flower Party's programme is restriction, the making popular of the use of condoms— '

'Srinivasan! Not in front of Lady Fisher and Miss Kuku,' cried Dr Coomaraswamy.

'I think, dear Doctor, both Kuku and I have heard of birth control,' said Lady Fisher.

Dr Coomaraswamy knew that he was elderly, as his wife Uma was always telling him; elderly and unlovely, he thought. He was bald, over-stout, obviously well to do, well dressed – his suits were made for him in London. He flashed gold, gold-rimmed spectacles, gold pocket watch on a gold watch chain that stretched tightly across his stomach, the diamond in his little golden finger ring. By contrast, Mr Srinivasan was a little man, thin and light as an insect, always anxious, dressed in an ill-fitting European suit and what seemed to be over-large shoes, meticulously polished.

With them had come a cohort of young men. 'No young women?' Auntie Sanni had asked in surprise.

'They are staying at Ghandara in our headquarters. Females', said Dr Coomaraswamy, 'do not mind discomfort so much – they are more dedicated, I think. Besides Krishnan has a special mission for them. At the moment he will not tell me what but they are to go among the women which is good – the women's vote is important to us.'

'Of utmost importance,' said Mr Srinivasan.

The young men were in national dress, 'For this week,' said Dr Coomaraswamy. 'And for our young women, I myself have provided for them saris in green and white edged with yellow, our Party colours. They are to go in sandals, marigolds in their hair. Padmina Retty's women go in trousers! We shall be traditional which, strangely, is nowadays more modern.'

Charming as the young men were, they threatened to overrun Patna Hall until they found Paradise. 'They will be out at Ghandara or in the country most of the day,' soothed Auntie Sanni. Besides providing *charpoys* and cotton quilts she had ordered braziers to be lit on the roof and she told Samuel, 'Send two of the waiters, Mustafa and Ahmed, up with pots and pans so they can cook.'

18

'Kebabs are not on the menu,' Kuku objected.

'They are now,' said Auntie Sanni.

Mr Menzies came late that evening in a small red car, appearing out of the dark. 'From where?' asked Kuku, trying to be friendly, at the reception desk. He did not answer.

It was the first time she had seen, in actual flesh, a gentleman wearing a hair ribbon, his hair tied back in a bow. Sometimes men wore them on television – 'Oh, why, why, won't Auntie Sanni allow television?' had been Kuku's moan – but those men were young; if Mr Menzies had known it he was, for Kuku, too old to be of any interest. She did not either like his over-pink complexion, yellow-pink, like the little crabs on the beach when they are cooked. Kuku could not suppress a giggle, though Auntie Sanni had impressed, 'Best manners only while you are at reception.' Still less did she like the way his eyes – again, as if from the beach, they reminded her of small grey pebbles – looked her over and at once dismissed her. She did not know that Mr Menzies was not interested in girls unless they were in society which would have made them, for him, likely fodder.

He gave a London club as an address. 'Savage Club?' Kuku could not believe it but, 'He must be respectable to have a club,' she said afterwards to Auntie Sanni. 'Club' to Kuku meant exclusiveness.

'For how long will you be staying?' she asked.

'I'll see. Don't bother to come up,' he said. 'The boy can show me.' The 'boy', one of the bearers, picked up his briefcase, typewriter and suitcase.

'I'm afraid there is not a garage for your car.'

'Doesn't matter. It's only borrowed.'

'Most clients not coming by car,' Kuku explained.

At that he smiled. 'Ah! But, then, I am not most clients.'

19

Sunday

Kuku was never to forget her first sight of the Brownes or, rather, Mr Browne: she hardly noticed the girl.

They arrived in the peace of Sunday's late afternoon when everyone and everything seemed quiet before the stir of dinner; it was as if the little dust of the new guests had settled. 'It always does at Patna Hall,' said Auntie Sanni.

Dr Coomaraswamy, Mr Srinivasan and the cohorts had removed themselves to the Party Headquarters at Ghandara – they had their own hired coach. Mr Menzies had followed them not long after. 'He must be something connected with politics,' Kuku had guessed. The cultural ladies and Professor Aaron had set aside Sunday for resting after their long journey and stayed in their rooms. Sir John and Lady Fisher were on the verandah, she stitching, he reading; they might never have been away. Mrs Manning was walking along the beach. All was quiet when the Shantipur taxi drew up.

'Browne with an e,' the young man instructed as he signed the register at the desk but Kuku hardly heard: she was gazing at his height, his fairness that was to her dazzlingly fair.

The young wife seemed no match for her husband – she was so slight, her over-large spectacles making her look like a schoolgirl – but she too was fair, grey-eyed with mouse-pale brown hair that fell to her shoulders and hid her face as it swung forward like a soft bell.

20

Both, though, had what Kuku called English complexions. 'Apple blossom,' murmured Kuku in despair.

Kuku was dark-skinned and had been schooled to think that, above all, fairness was desirable, all beauty had to be fair. The marriage advertisements in the newspapers showed that clearly: 'Educated England, returned young barrister seeks fair girl'. Sometimes it was the other way on: 'Highly educated, executive-positioned, fair Brahmin young lady wishes to contact eligible young gentleman in similar employment', or more naïve and old-fashioned: 'Wanted: young man, preferably in Government Service for fair good-looking girl. Knows music and knitting'. There did not seem much hope for the Kukus of this world.

He signed the register 'Blaise St John Browne'. 'Blaise! What an uncommon name!' Kuku dared to say. He looked at her with such surprise that she saw she had transgressed and flushed. The girl saw it too and stepped forward. 'You don't have to sign,' he told her. 'You come under me.'

Auntie Sanni, who had appeared in the doorway, caught the look she gave him; caught too, a sight of a small firm chin, when the hair swung back, as she firmly signed her name, 'Mary Browne'.

There was more to it than that. 'When my husband was born,' the girl told Kuku, 'his parents could not decide on a name uncommon enough for him, so they compromised with Blaise.'

'Mary!' He had turned crimson. 'For God's sake . . .'

But the clear voice went on. 'When I was born the nurses asked my father what I should be called – it had to be the nurses, unfortunately my mother had died. He said the first name that came into his head, "Mary." You can't wonder,' the girl would not stop, 'we were in Rome, you see, and Rome is full of Marys though there they say "Maria".'

'Mary, Reception isn't even remotely interested—'

21

'Oh, but I am, I am,' cried Kuku.

'All those churches: Santa Maria degli Angeli, Santa Maria dell' Assunta, Santa Maria Maggiore, Santa Maria Rotondo . . .'

Now what, wondered Auntie Sanni, could have provoked all that?

Mary could have told her: it was the journey from Madras. It had enchanted her, especially after three weeks spent in Ootacamund, 'Which might have been England,' she had said disappointed. 'It even has a vicar.'

'My dear child, most Indian towns of any size have an Anglican vicar,' Blaise had told her. 'Why not?'

'I . . . just didn't expect it.' Mary knew she sounded naïve.

From Madras the train had gone through forests where sun filtered between tall trees and creepers; villages, golden-thatched, the houses often on stilts, appeared and disappeared. Mary saw elephants, the first elephants she had seen working. 'Bumble, look. Do look' – she had always heard Blaise called Bumble – 'Look,' but he was reading the *Madras Times*.

The elephants pulled logs; the small brown men round them gesticulated as they fastened chains or goaded the huge animals, swaying in their strength to strip trees with their trunks or push against them with their foreheads. In the groves she saw flowers growing along the tree branches in festoons. 'Bumble, could those possibly be wild orchids? Come and look.'

Indulgently he had come but carrying his paper. 'I wouldn't know an orchid from a daisy.'

'You must do.'

'I know those big purple ornate things you buy in florists.'

'These are wild,' but he had gone back to his reading.

On ponds or village tanks, water lilies floated. Often monkeys, small and brown, swung away from the train

22

among the trees. When the railway left the forests to run along the shore, nets seemingly as fine as gossamer were spread on the white sand and there were boats. Mary had sat entranced by the colour and sun but she did not ask Blaise to look again.

Now, at reception, Auntie Sanni thought it time to intervene and sailed into the hall. 'Good evening. Welcome to . . .' but 'What's this?' Mr Browne was saying to Kuku 'Share a bungalow? An out bungalow! I booked for the main hotel.'

In agitation Kuku began hastily to turn the pages as if she were looking for another room but Auntie Sanni went on as if Blaise Browne had not spoken. 'Welcome to Patna Hall. I am Mrs McIndoe, the proprietor. The main hotel is full but, quite apart from that, we always put our younger guests in the bungalow if we can.' She made it sound like a favour. 'They like to be on the beach and so do away with formalities.'

'Yes, Blaise, it would be much nicer.' The girl's tone was conciliating, almost coaxing; obviously she did not want a scene.

'I booked——'

'I am sure you will find the bungalow most suitable.' Auntie Sanni put an end to the argument. 'Miss Kuku will take you there.'

'How handsome he is!' Kuku whispered to Auntie Sanni as the Brownes collected coats and hand luggage. Thambi picked up suitcases, tennis racquets, a big bag of golf clubs. 'So big and blond, like a young god. Is it Apollo?'

'Apollo?' Auntie Sanni looked sharply at Kuku.

Kuku took them down a small path that wound through what seemed a large garden; a path of white sand that glimmered in India's sudden dusk and was edged with shells and lit by old-fashioned lamp-posts. The sound of the sea grew louder as they came nearer. The bungalow

23

was almost on the beach, only separated by a narrow strip of garden from the foreshore; the roof was of palm thatch. The verandah rails shone white in the lamplight. Wicker chairs and a table stood on the floor of polished red stone. The bedroom had little but a wide bed, 'An *almirah*,' said Kuku opening the cupboard door to show hanging space and shelves, a chest of drawers with a looking glass and two chairs. *Durries* were on the floor.

To Mary it all gave a feeling of lightness and freedom but she could tell Blaise was not pleased, less pleased when he saw the bathroom, a dark little room, divided by a low kerb behind which was a single tap. 'Only cold water,' Kuku had to say in shame. Tall *gharras* were filled each morning from it, 'So that the water stays cool,' Auntie Sanni would have explained. Beside the *gharras* was a stool and an outsize zinc mug 'For pouring water over yourself,' but 'An Indian bathroom!' Blaise was as dismayed as Mrs Schlumberger.

'Our waterman will bring plenty of hot water', Kuku hurried to say, 'if you telephone.'

'At least we have a telephone,' said Blaise.

'Only a line to the house, I'm afraid,' Kuku apologised, but Mary could not think why they needed a telephone or hot water. 'We can bathe in the sea.'

'And there is a bar.' Kuku could show that in its small refrigerated cupboard with pride. 'You can help yourselves. There is ice but anything you want I shall bring.'

Blaise, who had not really looked at Kuku, said, '*Atcha*' as when dismissing a servant. Kuku, hurt, flushed darker, gathered up her sari and went. 'She hasn't even given us a key.'

'Why do we need a key?' asked Mary. 'It's all wide open.' Though the bungalow had heavy full-length wooden shutters to close against a storm, they were left folded back and the doorways had only half-doors

24

set midway; made of light wood and woven palm, they swung slightly in the breeze. Now Mary pushed through them on to the verandah and stood there looking.

From the moment they had driven up to Patna Hall she had known she loved it; it seemed to breathe a new air. In those three weeks at Ootacamund the time had dragged so they had seemed like three years. They had stayed at the club and only met the club people, retired English or else westernised Indians; Blaise had played golf; Mary walked round with him. In the evening there was bridge; she had sat beside him until, desperate, she had wheedled, 'For the last week of your leave couldn't we go somewhere Indian, in India?'

'Little silly. Ooty is in India.'

'No, it's *not*,' but she did not say it, only coaxed, 'Lady Malcolm says there is a hotel further north by the sea, "India unchanged," she says.'

Blaise frowned. 'Lady Malcolm is the only person I have not liked here in Ootacamund.'

Mary had looked at him startled. Lady Malcolm was the only person she had liked.

Now, out on the verandah, she felt the sea breeze which was strong but warm. In India, night falls quickly and now, as the bungalow lights fell on the beach, she could only make out the pale crests of the rollers. Their noise surprised her; as they crashed on the sand the whole bungalow shook. Looking along the beach and the wet sand she could see small lights, lanterns or fires under a darkness of trees. She lifted her face to look up at the stars, at one in particular which shone over the sea, Hesperus, Venus, the evening star. My star, thought Mary. Behind it was the shape of a growing moon. Suddenly, an immense happiness filled her. What does anything matter? thought Mary. I'm here.

'No hangers.' Blaise was walking about, peering into

25

the cupboard, opening drawers. 'This really is a run-down place.'

'It doesn't feel like that. I like it.' Mary did not say 'love'. 'Funny,' she said, 'I never heard you called Blaise until Bombay. I thought you were Bumble. We were Bumble and Merry.'

'I have always been Blaise.'

'Yes,' and she said sadly, 'I suppose we've gone public.'

'I should hope so. You're my wife.' Blaise came and gave her a swift hug but she sensed that he was stiff as he always was when he was embarrassed – Mary had already learned that. It seemed he did not want to remember a certain little hidden garden hut in Norway, a memory she had clung to all these days. 'They're much nicer before you marry them.' Who had said that? Lady Malcolm . . . But I wanted to marry, thought Mary.

The sadness was interrupted by a clip-clopping sound, like heavy horse hoofs on a hard road but, How can anything clip-clop on sand? thought Mary. Then she saw a small brown shape with a white nose: a donkey had come up on the verandah.

'Bumble, Bumble. There's a donkey on the verandah.'

'A *donkey*! Get it out at once,' but Mary had seen why it clopped: the donkey's hoofs had never been trimmed or cut so that they turned up like Turkish slippers.

'Oh!' cried Mary. 'Oh, poor thing. Bumble, come and look.'

Long ago when in Rome, the small Mary had had an Italian nurse, Giovanna. Darling Giovanna, thought Mary as she remembered now how Giovanna had told her that because Jesus Christ sat on a donkey colt for his entrance into Jerusalem – it was somehow mixed, in Mary's otherwise pagan mind, with palms – 'Ever since,' Giovanna had said, 'all donkeys bear stripes like a cross on their backs.' Mary had not known if the story were true but she had always honoured donkeys and here, on this one's back, was the striped cross, plain to see. 'Bumble, look. Do come and look. Poor little thing.'

A laugh came from behind a white painted wickerwork partition. 'He isn't poor. He's a perfect little pest.'

The laugh, the voice were musical and deep for a woman but it was a woman who appeared on the garden path below the verandah. In the gathering dusk Mary could not see her plainly but had the impression of someone tall, thin as the wrapped skirt of her dress showed – an elegant dress – of dark hair pulled back into a coil at the nape of the neck. Mary could not see her face. 'A pest?' she said. 'He's sweet.'

'He's not at all sweet. No one has ever been able to shoe him or even catch him. Yet he likes people. He's here all the time. He comes up the side steps.'

'That he won't.' Blaise appeared in the doorway but, 'What's his name?' asked Mary.

'He hasn't a name. He's one of Auntie Sanni's pensioners.'

'Auntie Sanni? Do you mean Mrs McIndoe?'

'Auntie Sanni to us. You'll see.' The woman – lady, Mary corrected herself – paused looking at them, taking them in. 'How do you do? I am Mrs Manning, Olga Manning. I have a sitting room. Come round and have a drink and I'll tell you all about everything.'

'Thank you,' Blaise said quickly, 'but we have to change for dinner or we'll be late. Come along, Mary.' Mary gave a defiant little shrug, went down the steps, round the partition to Olga Manning's sitting room. The donkey clopped after her.

'Tonight is the inaugural meeting of our campaign.' Dr Coomaraswamy, Mr Srinivasan behind him, had come out on the house verandah for a drink before the gong sounded for dinner and found Sir John and Lady Fisher already there.

27

'Our inaugural meeting,' repeated Mr Srinivasan.

'Would you not come, Sir John, and give us your blessing?'

'My dear man,' Sir John laid his hand on the Doctor's shoulder, 'the last thing I feel like is a political meeting.'

'That is a pity. I am to make my inaugural speech.' Dr Coomaraswamy smiled at the thought: he loved oratory. 'I must make it exactly explicit. This is a rural district—'

'The people are extremely rural,' put in Mr Srinivasan.

'So that everything has to be explained, but everything, in Telegu as well as Tamil. Fortunately I, myself, am multilingual.' Dr Coomaraswamy visibly swelled. 'In European languages as well . . . I shall begin . . .'

'Does Dr Coomaraswamy have to make his inaugural speech twice?' Kuku asked audibly. Fortunately the Doctor was called to the telephone.

'Constantly he is called to the telephone.' Mr Srinivasan scurried after him.

'Same dear old Coomaraswamy,' said Sir John when they had gone. 'But I should have been interested to hear young Krishnan.'

'So would I,' said Lady Fisher.

'Where is your candidate?' Sir John asked when Dr Coomaraswamy and his echo came back. 'Where is Krishnan?'

There was a pause. The Doctor and Mr Srinivasan looked at one another with a slight unease, then, 'Krishnan Bhanj has chosen to remain at our headquarters in Ghandara.'

'In Ghandara,' confirmed Mr Srinivasan and Dr Coomaraswamy gave a sigh, such a sigh that, clearly, it came from the depths of his being. 'I confess to you, Sir John, I am profoundly disturbed. We do not understand at all what Krishnan is doing.'

'Or not doing,' Mr Srinivasan said piteously.

'Yet I have to accede as if there were some mystery

28

force. For instance, only last week I allowed him, from party funds, to spend ten thousand rupees on umbrellas.'

'*Umbrellas?*'

'Precisely.'

'To be distributed,' explained Mr Srinivasan.

'In Konak?' asked Sir John.

'No, not in Konak. That I could have understood but Krishnan ordered as far away as possible, actually in Bihar. It has something to do with the mission of our young women but now he asks a further twenty-five thousand rupees which he needs to carry this project out. It looks as if', Dr Coomaraswamy was still more glum, 'I myself will have to supply that.'

'But an umbrella', said Sir John, 'is the symbol of Padmina Retty's Shelter Party.'

'I have told Krishnan that. Besides, of course, he knows it perfectly well.'

'Hmm,' said Sir John.

The knoll to the left of Patna Hall was an unexpectedly high mound, topped by palm trees whose fronds rattled in the wind; a small path went up to where, under them, Auntie Sanni had put a seat. Every evening, when she had bathed and washed her hair, she would put on another clean, freshly ironed Mother Hubbard dress, also her pearl necklace, the pearls real and beautifully matched, take her palm leaf fan from Hannah, who had attended her, and then come out on the wide verandah where Colonel McIndoe, dressed too for dinner in linen trousers, a cummerbund and jacket, waited for her. He would make an arm, she would put her hand in it and slowly, because of her weight, they would walk up to the knoll. 'Walk! She lumbers,' said Kuku.

From the knoll they could survey all that was Auntie Sanni's: the hotel, the demesne and the beach – she had to acknowledge she could not own the sea.

29

On the other side of the hotel, in the grove, the trees were dark against the white sand. The fishermen had shrines under the casuarinas and sometimes lit *dipas* there. They made the pricks of light Mary had seen.

Below, Patna Hall itself was lit into brightness, its lights, like a necklace, going down to the shore. A red light shone from the roof where braziers had been lit to make the barbecue for the cohorts – Sir John had nicknamed them 'the disciples'. Auntie Sanni could see smoke going up, pale in the dimness of the young moon and a sudden flame when the braziers were fanned. An answering glow came from the gatehouse where Shyama was cooking, Thambi keeping watch but, tonight, there was another glow, red and living from the mango grove. 'Someone has lit a fire there,' said Auntie Sanni. She looked towards the village where a drum was being beaten. 'Something is in the air,' said Auntie Sanni.

It was always a proud moment for Samuel when he sounded the gong for dinner.

Though dinner might go on being served until ten or eleven, the gong for the residents was rung punctually at eight. 'That is late for Americans,' Kuku had pointed out. 'In the Taj Hotel they begin serving dinner at half past six.'

'If they come to Patna Hall', said Auntie Sanni, 'they must do as we do.'

At five to eight, Samuel turned on the dining-room lights so that the starched white of the tablecloths was reflected in the polished dark red of the floor, which reflected, too, the white clothes of the waiters with their cummerbunds and turban bands of red and gold. The wine waiter, Ganga, an Ooriyah who served only wine and drinks, not food, was further distinguished by gold buttons and epaulettes. 'We have a wine waiter,' Samuel had told Kuku. 'He will fetch the drinks. There is no need for you to come from the bar.' Kuku still came, the end of her evening sari flowing as she moved between the tables, outdoing Ganga. Like Samuel, this was the best time of the day for Kuku.

At eight, everything was ready, the waiters at their stations, every table set, napkins fluted in the glasses, silver glittering, fresh flowers on every table. Soup was waiting in the hot cases where the small braziers shone red; final touches were being given in the kitchens. A small army of dishwashers was ready to run with hot food between kitchen and pantry. Samuel made a quick round of dining room, pantry, kitchens, pantry, dining room; then he sounded the gong.

The tables began to fill; Dr Coomaraswamy and Mr Srinivasan had darted in as soon as the first gong beat sounded. After them Auntie Sanni and Colonel McIndoe led the way; their table was nearest the verandah, Sir John and Lady Fisher's opposite. Professor Aaron and his ladies took their already familiar places at the two round tables; smaller tables at the back were for Mr Menzies, Mrs Manning and, a little secluded, a honeymoon table for the Brownes. Dr Coomaraswamy's table was midway between the Fishers and Auntie Sanni. 'Too close,' she said to the Colonel, 'I don't like politics in my dining room. Those two hardly waited for the gong!' She frowned: they were not eating, they were gobbling.

'Yes. Yes. We are in a hurry,' Dr Coomaraswamy told Samuel. 'We have to get to Ghandara. Tonight is our inaugural meeting.'

He was excited, talking volubly but, 'Eat. Eat,' begged Mr Srinivasan. Auntie Sanni turned her eyes away.

For the Brownes she had ordered a bottle of white wine; Samuel had it ready in a silver bucket. The flowers on the table were like a bouquet; the head *mali* had sent an underling inland to gather orchids so that even Kuku was satisfied. 'Though, of course, there isn't a florist even in Ghandara,' she had complained. Samuel was eagerly hovering but Blaise Browne came into the dining room alone.

He did not notice the flowers, ignored the white wine and nodded curtly to Samuel. The soup was brought and left to grow cold. It was not until ten minutes later that Auntie Sanni saw him stand up – 'He has good manners,' she said softly to Colonel McIndoe – as the young wife came in, following Mrs Manning. 'Oh dear!' said Auntie Sanni.

The soft brown hair fell forward as the girl bent to look at and touch the flowers. Then she saw the white wine. 'Bumble! You ordered *wine*! How exciting and how sweet of you,' the clear young voice sounded across the room.

'Nothing to do with me. Mary, sit down.'

'Are you cross?' asked Mary.

'Of course I'm cross. Think what it looks like.'

'Looks like?'

'Our first night here, a honeymoon couple, and I have to appear in the dining room alone.'

'You should have come to Mrs Manning.' Mary refused to be upset.

'Sit *down*.'

Lady Fisher looked across the room. 'So that's Rory Scott's Mary.'

'Didn't he call her Merry?' Sir John was looking too. 'I thought she was still at school.'

'Schools,' corrected Lady Fisher. 'I seem to remember there were several – Rory was always moving on so that Mary never settled. No wonder he had trouble. Well, a girl without a mother . . .'

'Yes.' Sir John had seen the tilt of the head beside Blaise, the turned shoulder. 'I can guess she's a handful, a plain little piece.'

'Not when she smiles.' Mary had smiled across at Auntie Sanni. 'Not with those eyes. She has her mother's eyes. Do you remember how Anne's bewitched Rory?'

But Sir John was frowning. 'Surely she's young to be married?'

'She must be . . . let me see . . . eighteen.'

'Still too young. He's old Archie Browne's son, you remember them in Istanbul.'

'Yes. The boy was born there. I remember the fuss. So this is the wonderful Blaise! What a nest of diplomats we are! But, John, you must admit he's very good-looking.'

'So was his mother, in a florid way. Archie's a good chap, if humdrum,' which for Lady Fisher confirmed again what she already knew, that Sir John did not care for Mrs Browne but he was looking again across the room.

'It's what they call a good match,' said Lady Fisher.

'Except that it isn't a match. I can guess that girl isn't ordinary, any more than her father,' by which Lady Fisher knew that Sir John did care for Rory's Mary.

The cultural ladies were looking too. 'Charming, quite charming, though not what you'd call a beauty,' they murmured. 'These English girls have *such* complexions!'

'She looks quite dewy.' Dr Lovat sounded almost dreamy.

'Dewy?'

'As if the dew was still on her,' explained Mrs van den Mar.

'Can't we drink the wine?' Mary was saying, but Samuel had already taken matters in hand. A waiter had removed the cold soup, another slipped hot plates in front of each of them while Samuel proffered a dish from which rose a delectable smell, '*Koftas*, Sahib. Little fish balls of fresh crayfish. Very good. I think Sahib hungry,' he said, deftly serving Blaise, while Ganga filled the wineglasses; the pop when he had opened the wine set off clapping from the other tables. 'From Miss Sanni, best wishes,' said Samuel.

'We should drink to her,' Mary raised her glass,

'and to them all.' Flushed, she stood up and drank to the dining room; Blaise had to follow. A pleased hum answered them. After the *koftas* came partridges, plump, each sitting on its square of toast, with a piquant bread sauce, gravy, fresh vegetables. Blaise began visibly to be appeased. The old butler is right, thought Mary, men are better when they have been fed.

Lady Fisher could have told her that.

At first Olga Manning had watched the Brownes' table with a hint of malicious amusement in her eyes, which changed to a curious sadness. When she had finished – she ate far too quickly and too little – she got up and went out; she went so fast the gauze of her sleeves brushed the backs of chairs and the potted palms. She stopped at the verandah bar, ordered a double whisky and, avoiding any talk with Kuku, took it into the drawing room which was not being used that night as the cultural ladies were going out.

Every year at the outset of his tour, Professor Aaron's group was invited to a reception at the old palace of Konak. 'Not that the Maharajah is there,' Professor Aaron explained. He had stood up to brief the ladies while they still sat at dinner. 'He lives in the South of France now. Here he has to be plain Mr Konak but he keeps his titles abroad. It is his steward who will entertain us.'

The palace, built on a steep slope of the Ghandari Hills, was falling into disrepair, 'But you can still imagine its life.' Professor Aaron tried to conjure it up: 'Though there is a grand staircase, there are ramps between different levels so that the court ladies could be transported in miniature rickshaws. One or two rickshaws are still there. They are inlaid with mother-of-pearl.'

'That sounds utterly romantic,' cried Mrs Glover.

'But we won't be transported in rickshaws.' Mrs

Schlumberger was ready to object. 'Does that mean we'll have to walk? I can't manage uphill.'

'You can always spend a quiet evening here.' Mrs van den Mar stemmed the complaint.

'And there might well be elephants.' Dr Lovat was an experienced traveller.

'True, the gateways were built high to let elephants through,' said Professor Aaron, 'but I'm afraid there are no elephants now.' If the ladies were disappointed they did not show it; they had not come to India to see elephants but Mary, who had been listening, sighed.

'I expect the Raja's private court will be lit for you.' The Professor was still trying to beguile. 'That's where the dancing girls danced for their lord alone.' Mary seemed to hear the strange Indian music, the tinkling of anklet bells. 'The courtyard is so high that at night it is said to be roofed with stars.'

'Oh, I should like to go,' said Mary but, 'Has the palace any architectural interest?' asked Miss Pritt. 'Should we bring our notebooks?'

'Perhaps I wouldn't like to go,' said Mary.

In the big empty drawing room next door, Olga Manning began to play.

'Now what's happening?' asked Sir John.

A young man in flowing white had come hurriedly into the dining room.

'Who's he?' Lady Fisher wondered.

'A boy called Sharma. Coomaraswamy introduced him to me. The Party's district agent.'

'He doesn't look like a district agent,' said Lady Fisher. 'More like a dusky angel.'

'A messenger from the gods,' Sir John suggested. 'But I think he has only come to tell them the Party's coach is ready.'

Dr Coomaraswamy reluctantly put down his knife

35

and fork. Mr Srinivasan took a last mouthful; he was still chewing as he went after the Doctor and Sharma.

In a moment or two, Mr Menzies followed them. 'He must be in politics,' said Lady Fisher.

'Or journalism.' Sir John did not seem quite at ease. 'I can't imagine that a journalist of any prominence would find this campaign of importance. Yet I seem to have heard . . .'

'I don't like middle-aged men who try to look like girls.' Lady Fisher had noted the hair ribbon.

She and Sir John were used to long-haired men. Their own son, Timothy, 'Looks like one of the apostles,' said Sir John.

'But he's young and the beard fits it.' Lady Fisher smiled. 'But this . . .'

'Not very attractive, certainly, and − bold,' was the word that came to Sir John from the way Mr Menzies had given orders to the waiters and spoke across the room to the cultural ladies. He was a short man, barely reaching to Sir John's shoulder yet, 'I can guess he's potent.' Sir John still felt an unease.

'They haven't waited for the trifle.' Samuel was grieved for Dr Coomaraswamy and Mr Srinivasan.

'No, I don't like politics in my dining room,' Auntie Sanni said. She did not like quarrelling either.

Dinner at Patna Hall always ended with dessert, home-made sweets, crystallised fruit, fresh nuts, on especially fine porcelain plates, each with a finger bowl filled with warm water and floating flower petals. 'No one has finger bowls nowadays,' Kuku had said, 'and these are silver. They have to be *cleaned*.'

'Kashmiri silver,' said Samuel. 'Old Master Sahib brought them from Srinagar.' The silver was chased with a design of chenar leaves and iris, lined on the inner side with gilt.

'Of course they must be cleaned and polished,' said Samuel. Generations of polishing had worn them thin but, 'No one in my dining room', said Samuel, 'has a dessert plate without a finger bowl.'

He placed them himself in front of Blaise and Mary. 'How pretty,' said Mary of the finger bowls and Samuel smiled.

'Samuel likes that girl,' Auntie Sanni said to Colonel McIndoe as Mary looked up at the old butler.

'Do you think I could have a few carrots and sugar lumps for my donkey?'

'Of course, Miss Baba.'

Miss Baba had slipped out and Blaise's displeasure was back. He said to Mary, 'Miss Baba! You're not a child. It's not your donkey and you're not going to adopt it,' and, to Samuel, '*Memsahib* doesn't want any carrots,' and then, 'Talking of which, I would rather you wouldn't be so friendly with this Mrs Manning.'

'Why not?'

'There's something about her, Mary. I'm a good judge of character,' said Blaise with satisfaction. 'You must let me know best.'

'Even when I don't think you do?'

'They don't look very happy over there.' Lady Fisher had been watching. 'Rory's an old friend, John, and we knew Archie Browne.'

'Slightly.'

'Slightly or not, go and ask those young people to have coffee with us on the verandah.'

Mary had not wanted to have coffee on the verandah; she wanted to be out in the night but Blaise was flattered at being asked by Sir John Fisher. 'He's really my chief – by remote control,' he had whispered to Mary. Blaise had completely recovered himself and now, as he stood talking, the lights showed off his fair hair. Kuku, her vivid sari showing off the brown plumpness below the tight gold of her bodice, brought his coffee, fluttering her eyelashes as she served him; he took the cup without noticing her and went on talking to Sir John. Blaise was palpably enjoying talking to Sir John — Because he is Sir John, thought Mary, which was captious but she knew it was true. Well, why not? she told herself and, It's you who are cross now. We're both tired. Yet she did not feel tired, it was only . . . I didn't want to spend my first real Indian night in chit-chat.

She was sitting on a low stool beside Lady Fisher who, in courtesy, was asking her about her father — 'It's a long time since we saw Rory' — about England and the wedding in Bombay . . . Just what I don't want to talk about.

If only I could get up and walk away, thought Mary, be back on that other verandah where I can watch those waves coming in roller after roller, sending their wash far up the sand. If I could look over them and see how the sky comes down over the sea to meet the horizon, a great bowl of stars. If I held up my hand against it, all round my fingers would be nothing but air, emptiness. I don't want to say Rory is well — as far as I know; that Bumble and I were married in Bombay's cathedral. I don't want to say I like India. *Like!* When I'm . . . what *is* the right word? Yes, enthralled. Then she looked at Lady Fisher, who had discreetly returned to her embroidery and was listening to her husband and Blaise — or thinking her own thoughts? And what must she be thinking of me? thought Mary uncomfortably. Why, tonight, am I not able . . . ? Oh, I wish something would happen, or somebody come to rescue me.

A sudden hubbub filled the verandah. Dr Coomaraswamy had come back surrounded by some of the young men but, 'Go. Go,' he cried to them. 'Go now. I must think,' and mopping his bald head he came along the verandah giving small moans.

'My dear fellow!' Sir John helped him to a chair. 'Let me get you a drink. Brandy?'

'Iced water. Please. Please.'

'And for me,' Mr Srinivasan was even more dishevelled and distressed, 'if you would be so kind. Water.'

'I'll get it,' said Blaise but Kuku had already gone.

'What has happened?'

'*Catastrophe!*' Dr Coomaraswamy sank into the wicker chair, his head in his hands, while Mr Srinivasan beat his together. 'Catastrophe? Utter catastrophe.'

'What kind of catastrophe?'

'Krishnan . . . Krishnan Bhanj . . .' Dr Coomaraswamy could hardly speak. 'Candidate in the state of Konak for the Root and Flower Party, our Party, our candidate—'

'Was our candidate,' moaned Mr Srinivasan.

'Was?' Sir John was startled. 'Is he dead?'

'No. No.'

'He has withdrawn?'

'No. Oh, no! No. No!'

'Better if he had,' wailed Mr Srinivasan.

'Then?'

'Worse than that,' and Dr Coomaraswamy said in a voice hoarse with shock, '*Krishnan Bhanj has taken a vow of silence.*'

Silence. How lovely, thought Mary as a torrent of talk broke out above her. Auntie Sanni and Colonel McIndoe had joined the group; Kuku came with tumblers of iced water as Dr Coomaraswamy began to tell the tale.

'We were all on the platform. Every influential person. All such important people. I, the chairman of the Root and Flower Party—'

'And Krishnan?' asked Lady Fisher.

'Nat-u-ral-ly. Krishnan – on the platform. I myself was speaking, only to introduce him, you understand – I myself—'

'For long?' asked Lady Fisher.

39

'Oh no, not at all. Perhaps ten minutes.'

'Ten minutes *is* long for an introduction,' said Sir John.

'It was the inaugural speech.' For a moment Dr Coomaraswamy had dignity, then the injury welled up. 'Speaking – on the platform when Krishnan got up and – and—'

'And?'

'He walked out.'

'Well, Indian politicians often do walk out,' said Lady Fisher.

'Yes, Lady Sahib, but he left a note.'

'It was I who picked it up,' Mr Srinivasan moaned again.

'What did it say?'

'It said,' came the unfailing voice of Mr Srinivasan, '"This is enough. I am not speaking tonight. I am not speaking throughout the campaign. I have taken a vow of silence."'

A sound, quickly smothered, came from Sir John, a sound that made Dr Coomaraswamy look at him sharply.

'This Krishnan Bhanj,' Mary, in a low voice, asked Lady Fisher, 'what is he like?'

'Blue-black,' said Kuku derisively.

'Kuku! I know he's dark—' Lady Fisher protested.

'Blue-black,' Kuku insisted. 'Which doesn't suit his name.'

'"Krishnan" comes from the Hindu god Krishna', Lady Fisher explained, 'one of the avators or manifestations of Vishnu, second god of the Hindu Trinity – Brahma the Creator, Vishnu the Preserver and Shiva, Death, who is also Resurrection. Whenever there is trouble on earth Vishnu comes down; at first he was a fish, then an animal, later as a man or god like Krishna, who is usually shown with a blue skin.'

'Blue? A *blue* skin?' asked Mary.

'Pale blue,' said Lady Fisher. 'Krishnan is dark but he

is a man and he can't help his colour. After all, he isn't Krishna. The god is blue because he drank poison in the milk of his wet nurse. She was a demon in disguise but the milk did not harm him, only her. He sucked so fiercely that he emptied her body of all energy and she fell dead. That's what they say.'

'Old folk tales,' said Kuku in contempt.

'They're not exactly folk tales,' and Lady Fisher smiled. 'When Krishna came down on earth, he was, of course, a baby. He had to be abandoned by his royal parents but was found by a cowherd who brought him up, like Perdita in *The Winter's Tale*.'

'William Shakespeare,' said Kuku, proud to know.

'Yes.' Lady Fisher's needle went in and out with a gentle plucking sound that made this, to Mary, fantastic conversation of gods and demons mixed up with cowherds and poison, everyday.

She looked up at Auntie Sanni who had come to sit with them, towering among them; Mary was reminded of a mountain with small towns, villages and farms and their innumerable occupations and preoccupations held safely in its folds. Auntie Sanni obviously loved to hear Lady Fisher talk, and Mary guessed that Auntie Sanni would be indulgent to any belief – as long as it is belief, thought Mary. And why am I so interested? she wondered. Usually I hate being told things, but now she wanted to know more about these strange immortal beings and, 'Go on, please,' she said to Lady Fisher.

'As Krishna grew older he sported', Lady Fisher chose the word carefully, 'with his foster father's *gopis*.'

'*Gopis*?'

'Milkmaids.'

'Sported!' Kuku was indignant. 'Imagine, Mrs Browne, the *gopis* were so much in love with him they longed to be his flute so that his lips would perpetually caress them. Silly girls! Like all men, he was heartless.'

41

'All men?' Lady Fisher laughed. 'Certainly not all men. Take Krishnan Bhanj.'

'Like all men.' Of course! As Lady Fisher said, this Krishnan Bhanj is a man. That thought gave Mary a slight shock and, looking at Kuku, she wondered if perhaps he had 'sported', that exact word, with her. 'You know Mr Bhanj?'

'He was staying here when I first came.' Kuku gave a still indignant little snort. 'He called me Didi – sister. I am not his sister.'

'I'm sure he said that as he would have said Bhai – to a young man.' Lady Fisher defended him. 'Bhai means brother,' she told Mary.

'Exactly,' said Kuku with venom and, I can guess it was you who tried to sport with Krishnan, thought Mary with a sudden astuteness, which was confirmed when Kuku said, 'Krishnan. Krishna. What is the difference? All Krishna did was to play tricks on poor girls.'

'Not always,' said Lady Fisher. 'Remember, there was Radha.'

'Radha?' asked Mary.

'Krishna met his match with Radha in more ways than one. She seemed to be a *gopi* but Radha was a god as well.'

'Goddess. She shone among the *gopis*.' Though she was contemptuous Kuku had seen pictures from the Hindu scriptures. 'Anyway, Krishnan Bhanj may think he is a god but he's not Krishna.'

'That's not what the villagers think.' Mr Menzies had come up the verandah and was standing beside them.

'Krishnan Bhanj was so good, so excellent,' Mr Srinivasan lamented. 'A barrister, he is particularly versed in law, England returned.' Mr Srinivasan's English belonged to the thirties and forties. They talk differently, thought Mary. They don't take short cuts – is not instead of isn't; will not instead of won't; they break

42

up syllables . . . 'Par-tic-u-lar-ly' 'Krishnan also speaks English per-fect-ly,' Mr Srinivasan was going on. 'Also his great advantage to us is that he speaks Tamil as well as Telegu.'

'What advantage is that if he will not speak at all?' Dr Coomaraswamy was in despair.

'Where is Krishnan now?' asked Sir John.

'We do not know. We do not know *anything*.' Once more Mr Srinivasan beat his hands together.

'I, myself,' said Dr Coomaraswamy, 'am going now to look for him. He was at Ghandara where, for the election, as I have told you, he preferred to stay.'

'One little room,' Mr Srinivasan went on, 'a *charpoy*, table and chair, not even a fan when he might have stayed here. He cannot be in his right mind. To go off and leave us in this fixation.'

'We went straight to headquarters. He was not there,' explained Dr Coomaraswamy. 'He left his clothes, his suit, shirt, tie— '

'Even his shoes, his socks!'

'So what is he wearing?'

'I suppose national dress. Maybe only a *lunghi*. It would not be past him, our candidate!' Dr Coomaraswamy cried bitterly. 'What has come over him? Where is he?'

'Have you asked in the village?'

'Nat-u-rally. They are a wall.'

'You mean, they stonewalled?'

'Yes, walls of stone!'

'They knew in the village before you knew.' It was the first time Auntie Sanni had spoken.

'But why should he have come here, except to Patna Hall? What is there for him here in Shantipur?'

With quiet footsteps, the young Sharma came along the verandah, made a graceful *namaskar* to the company and handed the Doctor a note.

'I ab-so-lute-ly do not understand,' Dr Coomaraswamy

cried when he had read it. 'Why? What use?' and he read it aloud. '"Tomorrow, by first dawn, you will get a lorry and in it set up a small *pandal* . . ."'

'What is a *pandal*?' Mary whispered to Lady Fisher.

'A sort of tabernacle. The people make them on festival days for an image of one of the gods. They are usually bamboo, decorated with banana tree stems and garlands of lucky mango leaves and marigolds.'

'"A pandal,"' read Dr Coomaraswamy, '"as for a god. I will sit in it. The people will see me." But this is idiotic!' he cried. 'This is i-di-o-tic.'

'It is brilliant,' said Mr Menzies.

'Surely,' Blaise said to Sir John when the Indians had gone, 'it can't be serious. This Krishnan must be some sort of jumped-up play actor who has taken them all in?'

'On the contrary, Krishnan Bhanj has not only been canvassing for weeks throughout Konak, for the past five years, he has been steadily and culminatively working towards this election in his own way here in Konak and doing untold good, how good we shall not know for perhaps decades. Besides, his father is perhaps the most respected politician in all India, of absolute integrity,' said Sir John. 'I know of no one who would not trust him.'

'And extraordinarily good-looking, with a great presence,' came from Lady Fisher. 'Krishnan is very much his son.'

'Vijay Bhanj has been Ambassador in Washington and has represented India in conferences everywhere from Sri Lanka to Moscow. No young man could have a better background.'

'Partly because', said Lady Fisher, 'his mother, Leila, is a deeply spiritual woman, some of which, I think, is in Krishnan too. She comes from near here, from South India which perhaps has the deepest roots. I love Leila,' and Lady Fisher told Mary, 'When I came out to Delhi, as a new bride, she would not let me be the usual English wife, blind to the country. She taught me Hindi and about Hinduism for which I shall be eternally grateful. I hope, Mary, someone will do the same for you.'

'Sir John laughed. He laughed. I am sure of it.' Dr Coomaraswamy was standing by the window of the first floor room in the party's headquarters at Ghandara. The room, usually used as his office and usually buzzing with activity, was silent; the whole of the two-storey stucco-faced house, important in this town of bazaar shanties, corrugated iron, cheap concrete blocks, was empty. Every helper had been sent far and wide, some to look for Krishnan, some in search of the required lorry.

On the outside, the house verandah and balconies were swathed with muslin draperies in the Root and Flower Party's colours, green, saffron yellow and white: 'Green for hope, saffron for holiness, white for pure intention,' Dr Coomaraswamy liked to explain. Over them hung the party's posters; for weeks the disciples had been putting them up all over the state – it was a point of honour between all parties not to tear down each other's posters. They were pictures with a symbol. 'You must remember most of our people cannot read, so the party symbol is of utmost importance.' Dr Coomaraswamy always emphasised, 'And it must be recognisable instantly.' Krishnan's symbol was of three wise-looking cows lying among flowers; they would be on the voting papers too and instantly identifiable with Krishnan. 'There is', Dr Coomaraswamy said in satisfaction, 'not one man, woman or child who does not know the Krishna story.' At Head-quarters every poster was garlanded with fresh lucky mango leaves; their very freshness seemed a mockery to Dr Coomaraswamy.

He was not even sure now about his inaugural speech. He heard Sir John's voice, 'Ten minutes is long for an

45

introduction.' 'But I like to speak,' said Dr Coomaraswamy piteously to the empty room. 'Also, what I had to say, was it not important?'

'Yes, but it still depends on the way you say it,' Krishnan had cautioned and, 'He knows me,' Dr Coomaraswamy had to admit. Krishnan had also forbidden any expletives: 'No foul words or abuse.'

'But Gopal Rau has denounced you as "cheat", "liar", "hypocrite"; Mrs Retty as "dirty humbug", "ignorant swine"—'

'And in return you will call them "gentleman", "lady", "benefactor", "mother", even, "prince".'

'But those are kindly.'

'It depends on how you say them.' Krishnan had smiled.

'Yes, but,' Dr Coomaraswamy had been sad, 'my words were so beautifully foul!'

He had opened his speech with what he thought was simple directness – and in the current fashion: 'Friends,' and then went on, as Mr Srinivasan told him afterwards, to spoil it by 'people of Konak, men, women and our beloved children: accustomed as I am to public speaking, tonight when I come to open this, the final week, of our Root and Flower Party's campaign for which we owe so much to so many of you, my heart is so full that I can hardly speak . . .'

'Speak. Speak,' hissed Mr Srinivasan who, as always, had been close beside him.

'The few words I have to say to you tonight are of such import, such freshness, newness of approach that they awe me and make my very lips to tremble . . .'

'Don't tremble. Go *on*!' mouthed Mr Srinivasan.

'We shall begin with the root. The root goes on to flower, the flower will bring you fruit, much fruit. For you, for all Konak, perhaps for millions, our new manifesto offers this hope. Men and women, for you, at this very moment, hope is hovering with bright wings . . .'

Dr Coomaraswamy had particularly liked 'bright wings' but Mr Srinivasan was making frantic accelerating gestures and Dr Coomaraswamy had gathered momentum – too much momentum. 'You must think before you speak,' Uma, his wife, had always urged but at speed, 'Friends,' he had cried, 'you are aware that for decades, if not generations, our beloved country, through the corruption, avarice, greed, exploitation of the few in power, has been standing on the edge of the precipice of utter disaster. Let us,' and here he had raised his fist in exaltation as his voice rang out, 'let us take the first step forward.'

Too late he saw Mr Srinivasan collapse; too late knew what he had said but the most bitter mortification of all had been that no one had noticed. They had not been listening, Dr Coomaraswamy thought now in anguish. My words might have been hot air. Perhaps they were hot air but he had not lacked courage; he had continued but then Krishnan had walked out.

Yes, he has made me a laughing stock, Dr Coomaraswamy thought bitterly now of Krishnan: umbrellas, a lorry, a *pandal* as for a god. 'I will sit in it,' Krishnan had said. 'You will not,' Dr Coomaraswamy had vowed but then Sir John had laughed – he, Dr Coomaraswamy, was certain it had been a laugh. Not only that, there were other cryptic things that had been said. 'What did they *mean*?' asked the Doctor.

'Krishnan is bats. Bats,' Mr Srinivasan had been moaning.

'Bats hang upside down, which seems topsy-turvy to us but it's their way.' Sir John had been perfectly grave.

'So he should have been.' Dr Coomaraswamy was momentarily incensed. 'It is no laughing matter. I, myself, have invested two *crores* at least in this campaign . . .' – 'And did I not tell you not to?' Uma had said, over and over again, thought Dr Coomaraswamy wearily.

'And why care so much about Sir John?' Uma had said

that too, also over and over again. 'You are a Doctor of Medicine, MA, MRCS, Edinburgh,' she said this continually. 'Also, I do not care, at all, for Lady Fisher.'

'You mean she does not care for you.' Dr Coomaraswamy had not said that; Uma was formidable, bigger than he. 'Lady Fisher is an inveterate snob,' said Uma but, I believed Sir John and I were friends, Dr Coomaraswamy thought now. He calls me Coomaraswamy, I say, Sir John . . . He winced, remembering the terrible time when he had said, 'Sir Fisher'. 'Solecism! Solecism!' he could have cried aloud to the unresponsive walls of Headquarters.

He had taken off his jacket to ease the tiredness of his shoulders, had let his braces hang down. My God, my belly! thought Dr Coomaraswamy – he could not see his feet and could feel the rolls of fat around his neck and face; to add to his misery he knew sweat was glistening on the baldness of his scalp. I am thoroughly unlovely, no girl would look at me, thought Dr Coomaraswamy.

'Girl? What girl?' Uma seemed to pounce even on his thoughts. 'What is this I hear about a girl?'

'My angel, you know there is no one else but you,' and at once, as if in reality he had said it, there came into Dr Coomaraswamy's mind a vision of Kuku as she had been this night: the sweet scent of her hair, the enticing girl flesh between *choli* and sari – he could have put his hands around her waist – the shadow of the long eyelashes on her cheeks. 'Those eyelashes did not flutter for you,' he told himself cruelly. 'They were for that young Blaise Browne, you old fool.' Still he found he was listening for the soft swish of a sari – Uma wore hers kilted up to show thick ankles and sensible nurse's white canvas shoes, which made her feet look larger than ever, whereas Dr Coomaraswamy could not help having, in his eye, the sight of little feet with slender bones, the nails painted red, delicate sandals held by a thong between the toes. Each time he saw them a quiver of delight had run through Dr Coomaraswamy. No one has ever written a poem to toes, he thought. He had a mind to try, but again, 'Old fool, keep to what is your business,' he told himself and his thoughts returned to the deserted Party, the lost *crores* of rupees – worst, the loss of face. He could have wailed aloud, 'What to do now? What, in heaven or earth, to do?'

It was late, almost on midnight, when Dr Coomaraswamy came back to Patna Hall. The breeze was soft, benign, as he left his taxi and crossed the courtyard. The house slept; the moon had gone. Then, as he came out on the verandah, he saw a figure sitting quietly in a chair.

'At last,' said Sir John.

'You . . . you have been waiting for me?'

'I was getting worried. You look all in. You need a stiff drink.'

'Whisky peg, Srinivasan still calls it,' Dr Coomaraswamy tried to joke.

When they had their glasses, 'Well, have you found him?' asked Sir John.

'Nowhere. Not anywhere.'

'Hari, what are you going to do?'

'I don't know. I *do not* know. John' – Sir John had said Hari – 'John, you tell me.'

'There's only one thing you can do. You haven't time to get another candidate. In any case, Krishnan Bhanj has not withdrawn, so—' Sir John interrupted himself, 'Are you sure it's not nerves? Young candidates often have a case of nerves.'

'Krishnan has no nerves. I wish he had, it might make him more amenable. Nervous? On the contrary . . .'

'Then', said Sir John, 'you can only do as he says.'

'This antic? You mean the lorry, the *pandal* and all? This nonsense?'

'I mean the lorry, the *pandal*, this nonsense – to the

49

letter – and now, Hari, my friend, go to bed and try and get some sleep.'

'Hari. My friend.' It was as if all the sore places had miraculously healed. Tears came into Dr Coomaraswamy's eyes. 'John— ' he began.

'Hallo,' said Sir John, 'who's that?'

He had gone to the verandah rail. Dr Coomaraswamy joined him. Someone was running along the beach, a slim someone in a pale blue dress, hair flying. 'That is Mr Browne's young wife,' said Dr Coomaraswamy, 'and alone.'

'Alone?' Sir John scanned the beach. 'So it seems.'

'She should not be out alone this time of night.'

'She should not,' said Sir John, 'but she is.'

Sunday–Monday:
Midnight Hour

'I should have said no in Bombay.'

Sunday's evening had grown better as it went on; Blaise, unusual for him, had joined the women: Auntie Sanni, Lady Fisher – and me, thought Mary. Kuku had gone to bed. Sir John was talking to Professor Aaron who, having brought his ladies safely home from the palace, had come on to the verandah to say goodnight. 'Professor Webster and I have our lectures ready.' He stretched and yawned. 'Tomorrow we go to see the cave paintings in the hills.'

Mr Menzies had disappeared to do some telephoning. 'Always he is telephoning,' Kuku had said as she watched him go.

Sitting in a chair by Auntie Sanni, Blaise had drawn Mary, on her stool, to lean against his knee. He was listening, not talking, and every now and again he ran his fingers through her hair – he might have been Bumble again. Auntie Sanni's voice was soothing too in its quiet singsong; she was telling Blaise the history of Patna Hall and of her grandfather's estate in Bihar, his factory and indigo fields. Indigo. Indigo: Mary seemed to see acres of a strange plant brilliantly blue – but it's Krishna who is blue, or is it Vishnu? Vishna? Krishu? The names began to merge into a maze. 'Mary, you're half asleep,' said Blaise. 'Come, I'll take you to bed.'

'It's very late, almost midnight.' Lady Fisher folded her embroidery. As Blaise pulled Mary to her feet and

51

steadied her, she bent and kissed Lady Fisher and Auntie Sanni.

Outside in the garden it was magical, the air balmy, the sky a dome of stars. The long flowerbeds were spangled with fireflies. Fireflies and stars, which are which? wondered sleepy Mary, while there was a scent of such sweetness that it made her more sleepy still. Then, at the foot of the steps, they heard the piano. 'She's still playing,' said Mary. It made her uneasy and as she listened, 'Chopin,' she whispered. The nocturne ended; Olga Manning began the little A major prelude with its pleading and, 'I should go and say goodnight to her.' Mary moved towards the steps.

'You should not,' said Blaise and caught her back. 'Don't you see, she's desperate for friendship.'

The music seemed an echo of that; it made Mary say, 'Haven't you ever felt desperate?' but Blaise was in a peaceful mood. 'I'm desperate to go to bed.'

A waiter on late duty came down the steps. 'Memsahib,' he called, and handed Mary a basket of carrots and sugar lumps. 'Samuel say for donkey.'

'Throw them away,' said Blaise but, forgetting Mrs Manning and the playing, Mary had run down the bungalow path. 'How do you call a donkey if you don't know its name?' She tried a whistle. There was an answering whicker and when Blaise caught up with her most of the carrots and sugar were gone. 'I don't believe anyone has been kind to him before,' she told Blaise. 'I'm going to call him Slippers.'

'Call him gumboots, if you like,' Blaise said yawning, 'as long as he stays in the garden and doesn't come on the verandah.'

While Blaise undressed in the bathroom, Mary went out to look at the sea. The thundering of the waves seemed to have a lulling sound now; the breeze, gentle tonight, blew through the room. 'That's why,' Auntie

Sanni had told Blaise when, among other things, he had asked for a mosquito net, 'at Patna Hall we do not need them. We do not have mosquitoes which is a boon.' The big double bed, without a net, had its sheet and light quilt turned back – Patna Hall had thin Indian cotton quilts, 'Not proper blankets or eiderdowns,' Kuku had lamented. Mary's short nightdress had been laid out; she looked at it and felt a sudden distaste.

'Where did you meet that outrageously handsome husband of yours?' Mrs Manning – Olga – had asked.

'In Norway. Rory, my father, has a lodge there, like a chalet above one of the fiords. He likes fishing, when he can.'

'Your father's a diplomat?'

'Yes. Bumble – Blaise was his Second Secretary in Kuala Lumpur. When they came on leave, Rory asked Blaise to Norway to fish. I joined them. I had just left school, my last, thank God.'

'So . . . Blaise is in the service too?'

'Yes,' and now, It has not really dawned on me, thought Mary looking at the nightdress, how important to Blaise his work is yet he jeopardised it, or thought he did, for me. Well, he had been out of England for a year, perhaps he was starved. She knew now that, when in any foreign posting, Blaise would never have considered any of the native girls. And I? thought Mary. I had not been really close to a young man before – she could see that schoolgirl Mary – and I suppose I was feeling emancipated, grown up . . .

There was a little hut where we put overflow guests . . . she had not, of course, told Olga Manning this – never, never anybody, thought Mary. Blaise and I used to go there, mostly at night. Nobody knew. It was fun, thought Mary, with longing. We made love – and it was love. There was only a single bed; once Bumble fell on the floor. He just laughed. It was good. It never seemed

53

wrong, but . . . Mary's nails dug into the flesh of her palms. In these double beds, I can't.

'Merry, are you coming?'

'Don't call me Merry.'

'Does it matter what I call you?' Blaise had come amiably out of the bathroom; he was wearing only a *lunghi* – many young Western men new to India had taken to sleeping in them – it wrapped his loins and stalwart legs. His torso still shone from the ladling of water from the mug; as he bent his knees to look in the looking glass, his hair glistened too. He was young, fresh, powerful, but Mary asked, 'Blaise, in Norway, what made you tell Rory about us and the hut?'

'It was the only honourable thing to do.'

'Wouldn't it have been more honourable to ask me first?'

He ignored that and went on, 'Besides I had to, you weren't like other girls.'

'I was exactly like other girls.'

'Not for me.' For a moment Mary thought it was Bumble speaking, her Bumble, but then, 'Rory was my chief,' Blaise explained. 'In my very first posting which was vital. If I hadn't told him and he had found out, he might have wrecked my career before it really started.'

'I see.' Mary said it slowly and, 'You haven't told me that before.' She swallowed trying to keep down her dismay. Then she blazed, 'Rory wouldn't have done that. Even if he had minded – and I think he did mind – he would never have done that. He's not that sort of man. Don't you know *anything* about people?' and Save me, save me, beat in her every nerve.

An answer came, a clip-clopping and Slippers appeared on the verandah. He gave a whicker when he saw Mary, came confidently through the doorway and began nosing round the chest of drawers, clopped to the bed, nuzzling the pillows. 'He's looking for more carrots and sugar!' Mary's laugh was cut short.

'Get out! Out, you little beast,' yelled the already angry Blaise. 'In our *bedroom*!' and, as the little donkey looked at him in surprise, a shoe came hurtling across the room. Slippers shied in fright, slipping and slithering on the stone floor; hampered by his hoofs, he could not get his balance and half fell across the bed. Blaise took up the other shoe.

'Blaise, don't! Don't!'

'I'm only trying to get him out.'

'You needn't *hurt* him,' but, 'Get off the bed,' Blaise shouted at the donkey. 'Get *off*!'

Slippers righted himself and stood trembling. 'Don't. *Don't!*' wailed Mary again but, holding the shoe by the toe, Blaise advanced on Slippers and beat him with the heel on his rump and sides. Blaise had not meant it but the shoe flew out of his hand and caught the soft nose. 'He's bleeding!' screamed Mary.

Blood had begun to ooze from one nostril; the ears went back as with terrified brays, stumbling over his distorted hoofs, Slippers fled to the verandah. Slipping and sliding again, they heard him crash down the steps. 'He may have broken his legs!' and Mary shouted at Blaise, 'I'll never like you again! Never!' as she ran down the steps. 'I'm going,' she shouted 'and I'm not coming back!'

Slippers had not broken his legs. He was stumbling along the beach. She ran after him.

'Mary, don't be silly. Come back. Come back at once.' Blaise's words floated back to him on the breeze.

Mary ran along the beach past fishing boats drawn up, nets stretched to dry, until she caught up with Slippers. For a while he would not come to her but at last the bruised and bloodied nose touched her hand. Taking off her shoes, holding him by the rope around his neck, she led him into the sea, hoping the water would ease his legs – they must be bruised. With her free hand, she patted him, talking to him; the trembling eased to a quivering. Then she led him back to dry land.

There, her arms round his neck, Mary began to cry, cry as she had never done before. I should have said no in Bombay, gone with Rory to Peru/. . . Peru, London, the North Pole, anywhere. She sobbed against Slippers's rough neck as the donkey stood quietly, holding her weight. I should have been warned, thought Mary. Hadn't Blaise said that very first time when he got up from the ridiculous bed, 'I shall never forgive myself, never. I must see your father at once.' She had only pulled him down, 'Don't you dare,' and kissed him. And there was magic, she insisted now, a sort of magic, in the long Norwegian summer days, hardly any night. Then how had it come to this? She did not know. I suppose in Ootacamund I kept my eyes shut tight. Now they were painfully open and, 'Oh, Rory, Rory, I wish you were here.'

Far out to sea there was a steamer, its lights making a chain of pinprick reflections across the water; the steamer looked as small and lonely in that vastness as Mary felt. She turned to go back but behind the beach was a line of what seemed to be small trees, soft and feathery with, behind them again, taller trees; though Mary did not know it, this was the casuarina and mango grove. As she looked, she saw a glow that flickered. A fire, thought Mary.

Her shoes in her hand, her bare feet making no noise on the sand, she walked up slowly through the fuzzy trees, their feathery branches brushing her face. Vaguely she could see, among them, bushes of what seemed to be scarlet flowers, hibiscus; holding the bell of one of them, she stood at the edge of a clearing among the taller trees.

There was a roof of palm matting stretched between two slender trunks of trees; below it, animal skins, deer

and goat, lay on the sand before a seat or a couch —
or was it a throne? To the side was a big earthenware
pitcher for water, a brass *lota*, a few brass platters and
long-handled spoons — Mary had come out without her
spectacles yet every detail seemed printed on her eyes. A
washing line was stretched, too, between two trees — a
line hung with loincloths and, incongruously, a sweater.
Behind the washing was a pile of brushwood and green
brown stems — could they be sugar cane? wondered Mary.

The fire was in front, a fire of wood; tending it was
a young man, blue-black — Mary felt as if she recognised
him. He was wearing a loincloth with another cloth across
his shoulders. His hair looked oddly white; then, as the fire
flared up, Mary saw his hair was full of ashes. On his face,
two arched eyebrows were drawn in white with, between
them, a white U-shape that Lady Fisher had said was the
sign of the god Vishnu; the lips were scarlet.

He stood up. At that moment, Slippers, who had
followed Mary, gave her such a sudden shove with his
nose that she dropped her shoes.

At the sound, quick as a cat, the young man had
leapt to the couch and was sitting in the lotus position
— legs crossed, each foot up to rest on the opposite knee,
looking exactly, thought Mary, like one of the gods in the
pictures she had seen in the bazaar.

'Come,' a voice called, a mellifluous voice that had
an echo of a flute. 'Come.'

Her arm around the donkey's neck, Mary came. 'Oh,
it's you,' the young man said and got off the throne.

Mary had stepped into the circle of light; there was a
small lantern set on the sand. He picked it up, holding it
to see her. Mary knew her face was tear-stained, her eyes
red from crying, her hair in tangles, her skirt soaked with
salt water from washing Slippers and that she smelled of
donkey. 'Never mind. Please sit down,' he said, as if he

had read her thoughts, and then, not a question but a statement, 'You are from Auntie Sanni's.'

'Yes.'

'Mrs Blaise Browne.'

'Yes.' Mary was reluctant to say it.

'On honeymoon.'

'Yes.'

'Not much honey, I think.' He was holding the lantern closer. 'Too much moon?'

'Yes.' That was like a sob.

'Moons wane,' he said, 'not like ours tonight which will grow bigger. That is propitious. If you start anything new always do it on a waxing moon. Perhaps your husband would say that is superstitious?'

'Yes.'

'It is not superstitious to take notice of seasons, tides, sun and moon. So, you ran away to be with the donkey instead?'

'Yes.'

'If you can only say one word,' he laughed, 'undoubtedly "yes" is better than "no".'

Was he mocking her? No. His voice was tender — and, You could trust him to be tender, she thought, instinctively. She was beginning to unwind from the hard little ball she had made of herself. There was something about the gaiety that was irresistible; she found she was responding. 'They are looking everywhere for you,' she told him.

He laughed. 'Looking far and wide. They will not think of looking close.'

'But why are you talking to me?' she said. 'I thought you had taken a vow of silence.'

'A public vow. This is private. The make-up is public too; underneath it, I assure you, I am a most presentable person.'

More than that, Mary could have said. There was

58

something magnificent about him — a curious word to use for a young man. She found she was looking at him with an again curious minuteness; he was not tall but was so slim he looked taller. She could see, in the firelight, how the muscles moved with rippling ease, almost like a great cat's, under the dark skin — Yes, blue-black, thought Mary. The shoulders were broad, the head well set, his face fine-boned, a straight nose with sensitive nostrils; his eyes were brown not black as with many Indians — they looked light in the darkness of his skin.

'You ask me why — the vow, I mean.' He bent down and scooped a little of the sand and let it trickle through his fingers. 'I think you know', he said, 'what it is to be out of love?'

'Yes.' That was so fervent that they both laughed, happy, easy laughter.

He threw more wood on the fire which leapt up, sending sparks high in the air. Sparks, fireflies, stars. Mary felt dizzy; the sand though, warm and dry, was firm under her as she sat, her wet skirt spread around her; he was opposite, sitting Indian fashion on his heels.

'Your name is Krishnan from Krishna?'

'That is so.'

'Do you play the flute?'

'No, only the fool,' he laughed, then conceded, 'well, I play a little but not as well as Krishna, who could? And your name is?'

'Mary.'

'Mary Browne.' He tried it over.

'Browne with an e,' Mary mocked which she knew was disloyal.

'Then, Mary Browne, how did you come here?'

'Blaise, my husband, was posted to India. I followed him.'

'He wasn't your husband then?'

'No, not until Bombay.'

Blaise had insisted, 'It must be properly arranged.'

'Properly?' She had laughed but to her surprise, Rory, who had always allowed her to do as she wanted – almost, she had to admit, there had been those schools – and who did not care a fig what his world thought about him, took the same view but, 'I . . . I'm not ready to be married yet,' Mary, even in her ardency, had said.

'Exactly what I think,' and Rory had urged, 'Merry, come with me to Peru.' Rory, too, had a new and even more senior posting. 'Then if in two or three years' time you still . . .'

'Two or three years!' the young Mary had cried in anguish, at eighteen that seemed aeons, and, 'So I came,' she said now to Krishnan.

'*Atcha!*' He accepted that with the ambiguous Hindustani word.

There was a sound of crashing: something heavy was coming through the trees. Slippers, who – contributing to the peacefulness – was lying near on the sand, his legs bent under him, his ears still, pricked them and gave a whicker as, behind the shanty shelter, a big hulk appeared. 'An elephant!' cried Mary.

'My elephant,' said Krishnan. 'At least she belongs to the Maharajah but as he is absent she has been lent to me for the campaign.'

'I didn't know there was a Maharajah.'

'His Highness Tirupatha Deva Raja of Konak. He has other titles but not as lovely for instance as, best of all, the Seem of Swat. The Maharajah used to own the state. He had palaces, three forts, an army, foot and horse.'

'And elephants?'

'Yes, especially one elephant, very fierce, the Maharajah kept for trampling people. In those days that was the usual punishment and every now and then the fierce elephant was sent into towns and villages to trample a

60

few peasants and officials to remind them the Maharajah was the Maharajah.'

'That can't be true.'

'I do not always speak the truth,' said Krishnan. 'Who does? But this is true. Now the current Maharajah is plain Mr Konak, the treasury is forfeit, most of the palaces are colleges or hospitals, the forts and armies gone. He has only this one small elephant — she is small because her mother discarded her. She has become a pet.'

'Where is her — is it a *mahout*? — the man who drives her?'

'Drunk, I expect,' said Krishnan. 'She wanders at night.'

'But is she safe?'

'She wouldn't trample a chicken, she's far too wise. The villagers give her sweets.'

'Will she come if you call?'

'If I have sugar cane. Fortunately I have,' and in his fluting voice he called, 'Come, come, Birdie.'

'*Birdie?* That's not a name for an elephant.'

'It is in remembrance,' said Krishnan. 'When I was a little boy I had an English governess, Miss Birdwood. We called her Birdie. She, too, was an orphan.'

'Is that why you speak English so well?'

'Well, I was at school in England, then went to Oxford.'

He let these small details about himself fall into the conversation. Is he showing off? thought Mary. Yes, he is, to me. It made her feel pleasingly important. She tried to see the small dark boy he must have been with the governess, Birdie; he would have had the same brown eyes, probably mischievous, the haughty face. Miss Birdie could not have had an easy time except that, Mary was sure, he was affectionate. At Oxford he must have worn a suit, at least a jersey and trousers, which seemed incredible, and at once, as if she had spoken aloud, Krishnan said, 'I assure you, I was perfectly proper.'

Mary blushed but the elephant had come, standing,

swaying on the other side of the fire from the donkey who stayed in quiet comradeship.

Krishnan had said Birdie was small but to Mary she loomed large. She looked at the width of her back with its grey, wrinkled skin, the ridiculously small tail, the outsize toenails on the big feet, half buried in the sand, and lifted her eyes to the head with its curious dome – again, she was looking in detail. The ears were not as big as the elephants she had seen in Africa. 'Indian elephants are more elegant,' said Krishnan. 'Perhaps because they are used for state occasions and for walking in processions.' Birdie's ears were shapely, mottled pink and brown on the underside. The eyes looked – tiny, Mary thought in surprise, yet elephants' eyes are supposed to have a hundred facets. More surprising were the eyelashes – 'I never knew elephants had eyelashes!'

'Like a film star's,' said Krishnan. The trunk was reaching towards him, its tip lifted to show small pink divisions. A stem of sugar cane came, was accepted whole with leaves; the trunk stuffed it into the mouth with its absurd underlip, came back again while Krishnan crooned words in Telugu. How gentle he is, thought Mary.

'You give her some,' said Krishnan.

'Would she take it from me? Would she?'

'Don't be so doubting, try.'

The trunk came towards Mary, accepted, then suddenly slapped the ground, sending a shower of sand over her. 'Ayyo!' cried Krishnan. 'That's enough. That was play,' he explained. 'She's the only elephant I know who amuses herself. The palace uses her to fetch marketing and firewood. For that she has to go inland, across a river, wide and shallow. To while away the time, she puts her trunk just under the water and blows bubbles but she would much rather walk in processions – they hire her out for weddings,' and he sang:

'With rings on her fingers
[though they would have to be earrings]
And bells on her toes,
She shall have music
Wherever she goes.'

His voice was full and sweet; it filled Mary with
a happiness as light as the bubbles Birdie blew. What
did it matter if they broke and disappeared? 'It seems
so strange,' she said. 'Nursery rhymes and bubbles. To
be at Oxford you have to be clever.'

'Naturally. I got a first.'

'Then politics – and you know about elephants?'

'At the moment I know everything,' said Krishnan.
'My father says when I am older I shall know that I
don't know anything but I haven't reached as far as
that yet.'

'My father says', Mary was not to be outdone, 'that
you should always pretend to know less than you do about
things. With me, that isn't difficult. I don't know anything.
One of my headmistresses wrote in my report, "Mary has
a marvellous capacity for sitting in a class and absorbing
absolutely nothing." But I can speak French and Italian –
servants' French and Italian.'

'You talk to the servants, you won't talk to our
friends,' Rory used to reproach her.

'Your friends,' even as a child, Mary had retorted
that. 'We move about so much, I don't have time to
make any.'

'I don't think', she told Krishnan now, 'I ever had a
friend but the servants stayed with us. They took me to
market. Markets are much more interesting than drawing
rooms. I suppose there have to be drawing rooms.'

'For you, yes,' said Krishnan. 'You see, I know your
father's name: Roderick Frobisher Sinclair Scott.'

'That's not half as grand as it sounds. It's only

63

because in Scotland, if you inherit land, for instance from your mother or grandmother— '

'On the maternal side?'

'Yes, you add her surname to your own. You could end with four but Rory's only a younger son.'

'They are proud old names, yet you would rather be Mary Browne?'

'That's what I thought,' and Mary quickly turned the talk away from herself. 'Sing something again,' she said, 'something Indian.'

He sang in Tamil first, then in English:

'A cradle of *chaudan*
A cord of silk.
Come, little moon bird
I'll rock the cradle,
Rock you to sleep
Sleep.'

'That,' said Krishnan 'is one of the lullabies *ayahs* sing to children when they are in bed.' He stood up. 'Now, before you go to sleep, moonbird, or they send out a search party and raise a sensation, I must take you back.'

'I'll leave you here,' he said when they came near the bungalow. 'I don't want to be shot.'

Mary watched him go. Suddenly he began to dance in and out of the waves, taking long leaps over the stretched-out nets and the prows of boats. Slippers and Birdie had come out of the grove to watch, standing one behind the other at the foot of the dunes; as he turned to join them, he looked along the beach and raised his hand.

Mary raised hers in return.

Monday

'Rory's family couldn't be bettered,' Lady Fisher said in satisfaction. Sir John had told her about seeing Mary on the beach late last night. 'Her mother was a Foljambe, a Devon Foljambe. That ought to be all right.'

'Alicia, you are a constant joy to me.' Sir John in his dressing gown was standing at the window. 'You never change.'

'I see no reason to change.' Lady Fisher was as placid as ever. 'I believe in good breeding – at any level – and it's a comfort to know people's backgrounds . . . it helps one to understand why they behave as they do.'

It was a perfect morning. Early mornings in India are not like mornings anywhere else; they have a purity, 'Perhaps', Sir John often said, 'because they begin with ritual washings and prayer.' In every town and village the people were making their morning ablutions, going down into the rivers or village tanks or pools, standing waist high in the water, pouring it over themselves, lifting their hands in prayer. In Shantipur the villagers did not go into the sea like the fishermen – the waves were too strong – but all were at prayer, purifying themselves.

There were smells: of dew on leaves and grass, of smoke from small fires of dung, of cooking in mustard oil; sudden whiffs of sweetness came from flowers opening in the first sun and, oddly mingling, European smells of toast for the early morning teas being made in the pantry at Patna Hall.

The wind was only a breeze. Along the beach, the waves were almost gentle; black dots of fishing boats were out on a calm sea. 'They must have gone out early,' said Sir John.

Auntie Sanni's doves were calling from the dovecote in the courtyard while parakeets swung and chattered in the jacaranda and acacia trees; monkeys were industriously searching one another for fleas. There was a tumble of bougainvillaea and of morning glory along the walls, their convolvulus-shaped flowers brilliantly blue. As Sir John looked, Hannah came down the upstairs verandah, bringing their morning tea with toast and plantains, small bananas, extra sweet. 'Who could want breakfast after this?' asked Lady Fisher.

'I do,' said Sir John, 'at Patna Hall.'

Hannah, in a clean white sari, her bracelets clinking, put down the tray and made *namaskar*. Lesser guests had their trays brought by the houseboys.

'Thank you, Hannah.' As Lady Fisher poured, she began again where she had left off. 'Anne, Mary's mother, Anne Foljambe remember, would never have countenanced this marriage. Mary should have stayed at that excellent convent in Brussels. She had seemed settled. Do you remember we took her out while we were there?'

'Rory always let her do what she liked.'

'Yes, but to marry so young.'

'Probably couldn't stop her,' said Sir John. 'Pity the young man's not up to her.'

'Most people would say the other way round. He's an only son, there's plenty of money but . . . How does he stand with you, John?'

'Steady, therefore dependable. Completely honest, of course. Excellently briefed – up to a point – but I detect', Sir John winced, 'a certain arrogance, or is it pretentiousness?'

'That's from Mother,' Lady Fisher said at once.

'Yes. Old Archie Browne's a good chap though, invaluable in secondary places where, I can guess, Master Blaise will follow him.'

'Poor Mrs Browne.'

'But, Alicia, that girl! She's quicksilver. I was watching her last night when you were telling the Krishna story, response in every line.'

'Probably too much response.' Lady Fisher sighed. 'Well, she married him, she'll have to conform, though it seems a pity to clip her wings.'

'I don't think she'll let them be clipped,' said Sir John.

Dr Coomaraswamy, in his shirtsleeves, without a tie, his fringe of hair ruffled, was on the telephone. 'Since six a.m. have I been on the telephone,' he told Samuel, who was supervising the tables for breakfast, while Mr Srinivasan frantically looked up numbers. 'Hallo. Hallo.' Another stream of Telegu then the Doctor hung up. 'No contractor has a lorry free. Not one.'

'And what, anyway, are we doing with a lorry?' Mr Srinivasan seemed to beseech heaven.

'Only what we have to do,' said Dr Coomaraswamy – 'Gloomaraswamy', as Krishnan often called him.

'What we have to do? And what will that be?'

Gloomaraswamy lost his temper. 'I only know if this fool antic has to be done at all, it must be done properly.'

'*Pandal*, garlands and all?'

'*Pandal*, garlands, posters, loudspeakers, bloody well all.'

'We cannot do it without a lorry,' said Mr Srinivasan in despair.

'I have a lorry.' Fresh as the morning, his white clothes immaculate, his ringleted hair oiled, came Sharma, once more a messenger for good. 'A beautiful lorry.'

'Who got it?'

'I,' said Sharma. 'Am I not District Agent?'

'Whose is it?'

'Surijlal Chand's.'

'Surijlal's? But he's Opposition.'

'No longer,' said Sharma with his angelic smile. 'No longer.'

'But . . . how?'

'I took him to see Krishnan. Surijlal is a highly religious man. He was up at dawn saying his prayers. Do you know where he is now?'

'How could I know?' said Dr Coomaraswamy crossly. 'I am not Surijlal's keeper.'

'He is taking *darshan*,' said Sharma. '*Darshan* of Krishnan . . . sitting, not saying a word, filled with joy and we have his lorry.'

'But . . . what is it costing?'

'Nothing. He has given it.'

'Surijlal has *given* it? And he a *bania*. I do not believe . . .'

'There it is,' said Sharma, leading them through the hall, and there, by the portico, stood a full-size lorry, almost new and already decorated with tassels, beads and paper flowers.

'But this is excellent.' Mr Srinivasan was hopping up and down in excitement.

'Call everyone!' a recovered Dr Coomaraswamy shouted. 'Srinivasan, go up to Paradise and gather everybody at once. Tell them to hurry.'

Auntie Sanni heard the lorry drive up, then, later, Coomaraswamy's voice shrilly exhorting as the young men came hurrying down the outside staircase with a hubbub of excited voices as orders were shouted from under the portico. The other side of the house was in peace and, as Auntie Sanni on her swing couch was sipping her tea, Hannah, in full clinking, massaged her legs.

'Kuku not up yet?' asked Auntie Sanni. 'She should be.'

'Let her sleep,' said Hannah, 'for all the good she is.'

Mary wanted to sleep too but, 'Wake up,' came Blaise's voice. 'Tea. We're going to have a swim before breakfast.'

Their tray had been set down on the verandah table; rolling over, Mary could see the teapot in its cosy, the pile of toast, bananas, and thought of the bedside Teasmaid of the hotel in Ootacamund and smiled. She was too lazy to get up and lay blinking in the light – Blaise had opened the half doors, sunshine lay on the stone floors and Blaise, holding his cup of tea, was in his bathing shorts. 'Come and swim.' Generously he made no allusion to the night before. 'Come on.'

'No, thank you,' said Mary. She was lying on the far side of the bed, the furthest she had been able to get from him but, by his friendliness, he seemed to have forgotten everything or decided to put it out of his mind – he had been asleep when she came in.

Now, as she lay, she was still filled with the happiness and ease of the grove and, 'Krishnan, Krishnan,' she whispered into the pillow.

'Mary, a good swim . . .'

'No, I don't want to have this buffeted out of me,' but she could not tell that to Blaise and, 'You go,' she said, trying to sound half asleep.

'Right, I will.'

Beyond the partition, Olga Manning had been listening to the news. She clicked the transistor off and, standing in the doorway, looked at the waves. She could not see them though; her eyes were blind with tears. As if she had to prevent them spilling down her cheeks, she clenched her hands hard.

* * *

69

A furious altercation broke out on the beach.

'Sahib wish to swim?' Thambi had come up to Blaise. 'I call Somu.'

'Somu?'

'Lifeguard. Very good young man. He swim with you.'

'For what?'

'At Patna Hall,' said Thambi, 'no guest swim in our sea alone and must wear helmet, Sahib.' He showed the pointed, strong wickerwork cap. 'For break waveforce. Necessary, Sahib.'

'Absolute bull! Don't be silly, man. The sea's perfectly calm.'

'Look calm,' said Thambi, 'but deep, has currents, waves in one minute get too strong. Sahib, please to wait while Somu come.'

'Why should I wait? I swim when and how I want.'

'No, Sahib.' Thambi stood firm. 'It is rule. No guest swim alone. I call Somu.'

'Damned impudent cheek!'

Blaise was back in the bedroom putting on his towelling bathrobe.

'Where are you going?'

'To have this out with Mrs McIndoe.'

'Auntie Sanni?' Mary had been listening, willy-nilly: Blaise had been shouting. 'Blaise,' she tried, 'why not just do as they say? Wouldn't it be more simple? When they see what a strong swimmer you are, of course they'll let you be alone.'

'I won't take this from anyone,' declared Blaise.

Mary had to sympathise. His swimming was the thing of which Blaise was most proud and with reason; she remembered him in Norway and how impressed she and Rory had been. 'Blaise,' she began again but was not surprised to find that he had gone.

'Mr Browne, my grandfather kept the rule and so do I,' said Auntie Sanni. 'Each bather takes a man,

70

sometimes two, and wears the helmet. It is wise.'

'Quite, for most people. I don't want to boast, Mrs McIndoe,' said Blaise, 'but I was chosen for training to swim the English Channel.'

'The English Channel is not the Coromandel coast, Mr Browne.' Auntie Sanni was unimpressed. 'I am sorry to disappoint you but no visitor swims alone from our beach.'

'Then I'll go further up the beach.'

'If you like.' Auntie Sanni's singsong was calm. 'Patna Hall beach is netted and enclosed far out to sea. Elsewhere there are sharks. That is why the fishermen go out four at a time,' and seeing Blaise look like a small boy balked, echoing Mary she coaxed, 'Mr Browne, why not, this first time at any rate, go in with Somu? I expect you swim like a man but he swims like a fish, in-stinc-tive-ly. Try him this morning, Mr Browne, then if he and Thambi think—'

'How kind!' said Blaise, which irony was lost on Auntie Sanni. 'I prefer not to swim at all.'

The lorry could not have been better: like all Surijlal Chand's possessions it was flashy, painted bright yellow, 'For-tun-ate-ly one of our party's colours,' crooned Mr Srinivasan. Green was provided by mango leaf garlands, the white by the background of the posters, of Krishnan's symbolic three cows among stylised flowers.

'It could not be more eyecatching,' Dr Coomaraswamy had to admit both of the lorry and symbol. Two loudspeakers were connected to a battery; in case it failed, there was a megaphone. Dr Coomaraswamy was to stand on the tail of the lorry. 'Yes, I myself must speak all day, since Krishnan . . .'

The *pandal*'s throne seat was raised, 'So everyone can see him,' said Sharma, and was handsomely set off by whole banana trees, their wide long leaves fresh; their stems were swathed in yellow and green. When Krishnan took his seat, naked except for a small loincloth, his skin shining blue-black – Sharma had used plenty of oil – his face painted, the U mark of Vishnu on his forehead, the garlands round his neck – white mogra flowers that had a heady jasmine scent – he looked a veritable god.

He sat in the lotus position. 'You will get cramp,' Mr Srinivasan predicted.

'I never get cramp,' wrote Krishnan. He had a pad and ball pen beside him on which he put down his orders.

Everyone was ready. 'But will the people take it?' the Doctor worried – 'buts' were flying about like vicious small brickbats.

'Surijlal took it,' said Sharma.

With a sense of occasion he had found a conch; as the lorry swept out on the sandy road outside the grove, followed by a small fleet of jeeps, motor bikes and Ambassador cars filled and spilling over with the disciples. 'Ulla, ulla, ullulah.' The conch sounded its holiness as the cortège drove past Patna Hall, then slowly through the village. 'Through all villages we must be slow, then away to Ghandara, slow through the bazaar, then other villages, other towns,' cried Sharma. 'Ulla, ulla, ullulah. Ulla.'

'What shall we do?' asked Blaise after breakfast.

'It was a glorious breakfast,' said Mary. She had eaten papaya, a luscious fruit, large as a melon but golden-fleshed, black-seeded, then kedgeree and, at Samuel's insistence, bacon, sausages – 'At Patna Hall we make our own' – with scrambled eggs, which Auntie Sanni called 'rumble-tumble'. Finally, toast and marmalade, all with large cups of coffee.

'I've never seen you eat like this,' said Blaise.

'I've never eaten like this.'

'Are you sure you've had enough?' he teased as she laid down her napkin. 'Well, what can we do today?'

'I'm too full to do anything,' and not only with

72

breakfast she could have said. 'I'm going to lie on the beach in the sun like a lizard.' These dear little Indian lizards, thought Mary/. . . There was one now, climbing up the dining-room wall – she had heard that if anyone touched their tails, the tails would fall off . . . I don't want anyone to touch me, thought Mary.

Back at the bungalow, she took a towel, spread it on the beach and lay face down, basking.

'I think I'll play golf.' Blaise's bag of clubs was bigger than Mary. 'The brochure says there is a golf course.'

He was soon back, disgruntled. 'Call that a golf course. Absolute con! All on sand! Not even nine holes.'

'Better than nothing.' Mary was half asleep.

'Anyhow I can't play alone.' Blaise sounded lost. 'Sir John won't come out. I tried Menzies but he's at his bloody typewriter. Mary, I'll give you a lesson.'

'No.'

'Merry . . .'

'I can't.' Mary shut her eyes and her ears. 'I can't.'

Blaise was reduced to putting on the flattest sand-green he could find.

Mary lay idly watching the small crabs that scuttled down the beach to meet the highest ripple of each wave; each crab threw up a minute flurry of sand. Crabs, lizards, the elephant Birdie, the sea and the sky seemed to merge and come into one, be 'cosmi', thought Mary. That was a big claim yet true. I am cosmic, she thought, so is a crab or a lizard. If she shut her eyes she seemed to see circles of light that moved, changed and fused. Cosmos, thought Mary, or is the plural 'cosmi'? But 'cosmos' can't have a plural, you silly. She went back to being a lizard and was soon asleep.

Mary was woken by Hannah planting a beach umbrella beside her in the sand. 'Not good, *baba*, to lie in sun too long. You have sunstroke, brain fever. Too hot.' She opened the umbrella. It was true, Mary was too hot and was grateful for the shade. 'And you drink,' commanded Hannah. Besides the umbrella, she had brought a jug of still lemon. 'We make our own lemonade . . . drink, *baba*.'

It was plain that Hannah, Samuel and now Thambi, who had come up too and was smiling down at her, had a conspiracy to look after her but '*baba*', thought Mary sitting up, her arms round her bare knees. *Baba*, child. Yes, I am behaving like a child. She put a lock of hair behind her ear; her hair felt soft, like a child's but, 'You must try to be older,' she told herself sternly. 'You're a married woman. Be generous.' That was a word she had not used before and as Thambi asked, 'Missy swim?' she said, 'I must go and tell my Sahib,' got up and went to look for Blaise.

They swam. 'Sahib strong swimmer,' Thambi said in admiration but Mary noticed the young Somu swimming beside Blaise.

Moses and another fisherman held Mary, diving with her under a towering wave. For a moment she felt her feet standing on a floor of sand – the sea floor? – then they swept her up through the wave; it fell like a weight of thunder on her head but the point of the wicker helmet pierced it and she was up; deftly they turned her, their brown hands strong and quick, then, with them, she was riding in on the crest. On the shore they let her go as, gasping, laughing in exhilaration, the wave trundled her up the beach. 'I've never felt anything like this,' she called to Blaise.

'I must say the bathing *is* marvellous,' he shouted back above the noise of the surf. For the first time at Patna Hall he looked happy . . . as a sandboy, thought Mary – he was covered in sand. 'Let's go in again.'

'Yes,' called Mary. He dived back into a wave, followed at once by Somu while Mary held out her hands to Moses and the fisherman.

Towels round their necks, she and Blaise walked

back to the bungalow, then up to the house for lunch in friendliness.

They played tennis all afternoon.

'Isn't there something very dear about this place?' Mrs Glover asked the other ladies, stretching her feet luxuriously as she sat in the comfortable verandah chair. 'Unlike the other hotels we've stayed at, coming back here in the evening is like coming home.'

The group had spent the day driving out into the hills to see the newly discovered cave paintings; now they were resting on the verandah and, 'Yes,' said Mrs van den Mar in content, 'it is like coming home! Such a welcome.'

'That nice Hannah made me sit down, took off my shoes and massaged my feet,' said Mrs Glover, 'pressing them, pulling out the toes. Exquisite.'

Mrs Schlumberger shuddered. 'I can't stand her bangles, rattle, clink, chink. Anyway, she never came near *me*.'

'I'm not surprised,' but Mrs van den Mar refrained from saying it.

'And my feet are more swollen than Mrs Glover's. There was far, far too much walking.' Mrs Schlumberger glared at Professor Webster.

'But those cave paintings, those colours still there after all these centuries.' Miss Pritt was rapt. 'The old true colours, crimson and brown madder and turmeric, indigo – those violets and greens.'

'They looked very dirty to me.' Mrs Schlumberger was still cross. 'Shabby and old.'

'Old! I should say! Two thousand seven hundred years!' Dr Lovat had been as moved as Miss Pritt.

'Maybe later, second century BC,' Professor Webster had to caution.

'Before Christ! Think of it! And as your eyes get accustomed, the faces seem to speak to you, so expressive, witty and eloquent. Those *apsaras*! The heavenly dancing girls, the verses in their honour scratched on the walls.' Professor Webster had translated them and Dr Lovat quoted: 'The lily-coloured ones. The doe-eyed beauties . . . Mystical!'

'Mystical! Utterly disgusting. Obscene! That multiple sexual intercourse!' Mrs Schlumberger said in outrage. 'How dare Professor Aaron expose us to such things?'

'Multiple intercourse was supposed to be the paradigm of ultimate bliss.' Dr Lovat was deliberately taunting Mrs Schlumberger. 'It's an allegory for the way sex is revered in Indian culture. That's why the girls are enchanting,' and she quoted, 'If the senses are not captivated the lure will not work.'

'Lure! I'm surprised at you, Julia.'

'But did you see those student workers?' Mrs van den Mar skilfully changed the conversation. 'Students cleaning those wonderful murals with acetone. *By order!*'

'Yes,' Professor Webster was wrathful, 'the colours will be ruined. I shall write to the Department of Archaeology.'

But Miss Pritt was not concerned with departments. 'Those paintings seemed to distil all these centuries of art as if they had been five minutes.'

'Centuries in which, by comparison, we have gained nothing, nothing,' said Mrs Glover.

'Something happened to painting,' said Dr Lovat, 'when it came off the walls. With murals and frescoes it was pure.'

'You mean, as soon as it turned into pictures, buying and selling came in and something went out,' said Ellen Webster.

'Joy and, yes, awe, you're right,' said Dr Lovat.

'Just as something happened to men's minds when they built office blocks higher than a spire . . .'

Kuku gave an enormous yawn.

* * *

It was towards dusk when Mary and Blaise were leaving the tennis court that they heard the soft beating of drums and with them a chanting; looking up, Mary saw lights moving, people carrying lit torches. A procession was coming down the hill beyond the village. She could make out men in white – they carried the flares – and, less distinct because of their coloured clothes, women who seemed to be carrying round baskets on their heads heaped, she saw when the torchlight fell on them, with fruit and flowers. The light fell, too, on chests carried on poles laid each side of them and painted scarlet. 'Marriage chests,' said Olga Manning.

She had come out in the late afternoon to watch them play. 'Uninvited,' Blaise had muttered. As soon as they came off the court she had come up to them whereupon he had picked up the racquets and presses and left.

Olga had taken no notice. 'It's for a wedding,' she explained to Mary. 'There must be one near, in some village. This is the bride's dowry being brought down to the bridegroom's house. She must be a hill girl. Poor little thing, probably married to a man she doesn't know,' and Mary, startled, thought, I'm married to a man I don't know. Almost she said it aloud but, as if she had, Olga said with curious passion, 'None of us should marry, unless we love a man so much we would go through hell for him, which we shall probably have to do.'

'Well, Hari, how did it go?' Sir John asked on the verandah that evening.

'It did not go. Not at all. Not at all.' Dr Coomaraswamy again was in despair. 'Everywhere we went Padmina Retty was before us, so skilfully she had arranged it. She is eloquent, so eloquent.' Dr Coomaraswamy had tears in his eyes. 'They tell me one speech lasted over an hour, while Krishnan— '

'A contrast indeed!'

'Everyone was so much astonished,' came Mr Srini-vasan's moan.

'Good,' said Sir John, 'good.'

'What good?' Dr Coomaraswamy had become angry. 'What if they are astonished into inertia? Inertia! I myself spoke and spoke but I am no match for Padmina. They did not listen, only looked.'

'Isn't that what they were supposed to do?' asked Sir John.

Lady Fisher, changed for dinner, came out and sat by Sir John. She was smiling. 'Kuku', she told him quietly, 'asked me if there were really a man's club in London called the Savage.'

'How did she come to hear of it?'

'Apparently Mr Menzies gave it as his London address. I think she had a vision of men in skins, tearing meat with their hands and teeth.'

As if she had fathomed Kuku's dearest longings, Lady Fisher had given her, to Hannah's intense disapproval, a pure silk sari. 'Even sent to Ghandara for it. Sharma bought it,' Hannah told Samuel.

'That was dear of you, Alicia,' Auntie Sanni had said. 'I am most glad.' In consequence Lady Fisher now was Kuku's confidante.

'The Savage Club is real enough.' Sir John was thoughtful. 'I'm not as sure about Menzies.'

'Mr Menzies has been at least half an hour on the telephone,' an indignant Kuku told Auntie Sanni. One of Patna Hall's two telephones was in a kiosk that stood in the hall; the other in Auntie Sanni's office was available only to her and Colonel McIndoe. 'I needed urgently to order a few stores. Twice I came back. He was still there. When I stood to show I was waiting, he shut the door.'

'I expect he had some business to do.' Auntie Sanni was not disturbed.

* * *

The International Association of Art, Technology and Culture was having a lecture that night given by Professor Webster. 'And they have been out in the hills since eight this morning. Where do they get the appetite?' Auntie Sanni marvelled as she marvelled each year. 'Kuku, you must warn Mrs Manning – I'm afraid she can't have the drawing room tonight but tell her that, though the lecture is for the group, anyone who cares to is welcome to come.'

'No, thank you,' was Olga's answer, 'and, Kuku, will you tell Auntie Sanni I have to go to Calcutta in the morning and, please, order a taxi for the station.'

'Another of those mysterious trips,' Kuku told Mary, who had come with Blaise to wait for dinner.

'Why mysterious?'

'She keeps on going, coming back. Why so often? She tells no one.'

'Why should she?'

That to Mary was one of the best things at Patna Hall. Except for Kuku, no one asked that perpetual why? why? why? No one asked you why you wanted to lie alone in the sun, only brought you a beach umbrella and a drink of lemon but Kuku's eyes were bright as a little snake's. 'She travels second class,' said Kuku.

Kuku's spite was partly born of a sense of hopelessness; Blaise was wearing white linen trousers, a primrose-coloured silk shirt, a deeper yellow and grey striped tie. They set off his hair, his fresh tanned skin and his height. 'Not Apollo, Adonis,' murmured Kuku. She could have scratched Mary's eyes out, especially when, as if purposely, Mary stopped at Mrs Manning's table in the dining room and asked her to have coffee with them after dinner.

'Mary, you've forgotten,' came the inevitable from Blaise. 'The Fishers have already asked us. I'm sorry, Mrs Manning,' and after he had steered Mary away, 'I told you to stay clear of her. She's a leech.'

On any other night, when after dinner they came back to the verandah, Mary would have gone defiantly and sat down by Olga but, I must keep Blaise in a good mood tonight, she thought. Then he'll sleep – she had not known she could be so guileful. He must sleep because I'm going to see Krishnan.

Krishnan. Krishnan. All day the thought of him had come back to her. Krishnan – happiness. There was a poem she had learnt at one of those schools, a poem she loved:

'My heart is like a singing bird
whose nest is in a watered shoot' . . .

It had sung in her mind all day. Am I in love? wondered Mary. No, I've been in love. I don't want that again, thank you. This is different, unimaginable, like the waves here that are quite different from anywhere else on earth. Outwardly, on Patna Hall's verandah, the young wife of this eminently suitable young man appeared to be listening to the talk that was going on around her while all the time she only heard 'My heart is like a singing bird . . .' and, 'Soon it will be time,' she told herself. 'Soon.'

It was Sir John who broke up the talk early. Mary had already seen him go quietly down the verandah to Olga Manning – To ask her to join us. Mary was grateful but Olga, though she smiled, shook her head. Soon after she had left and now, 'I must drop in on this lecture,' said Sir John.

'The culture lecture?' Blaise was surprised. 'I thought the group . . .'

'Were a bit comical?' asked Sir John. 'What those who knew no better used to call culture vultures?' Blaise blushed. 'In actuality, they are giving India the compliment of trying to understand her art and civilisation.' Oh, I like Sir John, I like him, thought Mary. 'I think we should

80

honour that and I suggest, Coomaraswamy, you come with me and', said Sir John, 'you might invite Professor Aaron's ladies to come to one of your rallies and see how you run your election. Take them round with you.'

'With things as they are?' cried Dr Coomaraswamy in acute pain. 'Also you have forgotten, Sir John, tonight Padmina Retty's inaugural rally is going on with great display. *She* knows how it should be done. I should have been there already to watch, God help me. So – no lecture for me.'

As he and Mr Srinivasan went, Lady Fisher left her embroidery. 'I'll come, John,' but, 'Miss Sanni, Colonel Sahib, Lady Sahib,' Samuel burst out of the dining room in excitement. 'It is the radio. I have been listening to the radio. Come. Come quickly. They say Padmina Retty's rally in utter discredit.'

The voice was going on. 'Poor Mrs Retty. A huge audience was sitting, many on the grass – the rally is being held in Ghandara's botanical park. Bands had been playing as the decorated platform was filled with dignitaries while, over it, was suspended Padmina Retty's symbol, a giant open umbrella which slowly turned showing the party's name, the People's Shelter Party and the slogan promise: "I will shelter you." Mrs Retty, a commanding figure in a billowing blue and silver sari – blue for promise – standing at the microphone was in full eloquence. Certainly she can hold her audience. "I, Padmina Retty . . ." when suddenly, among the audience one figure after the other stood up, men, women, many women and, yes, children, each holding an umbrella which they opened and held up, ancient umbrellas, stained, tattered, torn, some showing only ribs, some with ribs broken, all palpably useless. As their bearers stood steadily it was more eloquent than words!

'Mrs Retty's own words faltered, in any case they would not have been heard because a ripple of laughter

81

began which spread to a gale, the whole audience laughing in complete glee . . . but under the glee old resentments flared. There were catcalls, shouts – something Mrs Retty had not encountered before. I must add that, prominent among the umbrella holders were young women dressed in green, yellow and white, colours, as we know, of another party. It was fortunate that they were protected by their fellow males because, as could have been predicted, fighting broke out. It could have become a riot but the police were prepared and quelled it swiftly . . .

'Mrs Retty had left the platform. There was, of course, no sign of Krishnan Bhanj.'

Samuel so far forgot himself that he clapped. Hannah clapped too, Lady Fisher clapped with her as did Mary, and even Colonel McIndoe. Mary was laughing with delight until Blaise spoke. 'Wasn't that rather an antic in a serious election?' asked Blaise.

'Yes, you see, our young women had been all over,' Dr Coomaraswamy told later when he and his supporters came back. He was still shaking with laughter. His young men, some of them with black eyes, bruises and cuts, were being tended in Paradise by Mr Srinivasan, Samuel and Hannah. 'Krishnan planned it so well,' the Doctor went on. 'A month ago to Bihar he had sent them. By jeep, car, motorcycle, bullock cart they had travelled among the villages to carry out this trading, new umbrellas for old – what you used to call, I think, in England gamps. It took time to persuade the people – they could not believe a new umbrella for old. It also took time to persuade our Konak people tonight. Did I not tell you, just to stand up and open their old umbrellas, five rupees for each we had to give,' but Dr Coomaraswamy said it happily. 'Once they understood how they enjoyed! Our young men and women started the laughter but almost immediately everyone was laughing of themselves.' Dr Coomaraswamy laughed too.

'Just because I hit the donkey.'

'It's nothing to do with the donkey.'

The sound of the hard young voices came through the partition to Olga Manning.

'You might at least try.' That was Blaise. Then Mary, 'It's no use if you have to try.' The voices rose as, 'No!' shrieked Mary. 'No!' and, 'God,' shouted Blaise, 'anyone would think I was trying to *rape* you. You are my *wife*.'

'Do you think you could desist', Olga Manning's voice came from her side of the bungalow, 'and let me get some sleep?'

A guilty silence. Then, 'I apologise', called Blaise, 'for my wife.'

'Apologise for yourself!' shouted Mary.

'Very well. Goodnight.' Blaise flung himself on the bed. Then, seeing Mary dressing, 'Where are you going?'

'Out, if you don't mind.'

'Go where you like. I don't care a damn,' said Blaise.

Auntie Sanni, as if her thumbs had pricked her, had come out on the top verandah, looked down across the garden to the beach and saw Mary fling out of the bungalow and down the steps to the shore.

'*Ayyo!*' said Auntie Sanni.

'Well, Doctor. What will you do tomorrow?' Sir John, Dr Coomaraswamy with Professor Aaron were having a nightcap on the deserted verandah.

'You should not say, "What will you do?" What can I do? God knows! God knows! Tomorrow Padmina Retty is holding a second rally. There will be thousands—'

'This Krishnan Bhanj,' Professor Aaron ventured to say. 'Have you, forgive me, but have you, shall we say, been mistaken, taken in by his charm – I hear he is charming – and perhaps his position? Vijay Bhanj's son?' and the

Doctor seemed to hear Uma's voice, 'You see, Hari' – Uma was emancipated enough to call her husband firmly by his given name – 'you see how you have been carried away by this Krishnan. It is always the same: if they are beautiful, sweet-mannered, you are over the moon. Isn't it the old call of the flesh?' Uma had said 'flesh' with distaste.

'Krishnan Bhanj is a most gifted politician,' Dr Coomaraswamy said aloud, adding silently to Uma, 'Flesh has nothing to do with it,' and at once had a vision of Kuku. 'Please, please,' he cried silently. 'Please, Kuku, get out of my mind.'

She had glided between the tables at dinner, bending to set glasses down on his.

'We have a wine waiter,' Samuel had growled.

'The Doctor asked me to bring.'

That was true. 'What is that perfume you put on your hair?' It had almost touched him.

'Jasmine.'

'I will send you a bottle.'

'Do. It will be costly.' Was there a touch of malice in that?

He had watched her as she went back to the bar, his fork half-way to his lips. 'A great booby you must have looked,' Uma would have told him but the walk was so smooth, sinuous, the hips undulating. 'Is it my fault our candidate has good looks?' he cried now to invisible Uma, yet he could not rebut Professor Aaron and said bitterly to Sir John, 'The campaign is dead loss. Dead loss.'

A car drew up. Then Mr Menzies came along the verandah.

'Where have you sprung from?'

'Madras.'

'That's a long drive.'

'Yes.' He looked tired but his eyes were alert. 'You've had a bad day,' he said to the Doctor as he poured himself a whisky.

'Desperate. Dead loss!' moaned Dr Coomaraswamy.
'I should cheer up, if I were you,' said Mr Menzies.

Mary had to wait on the beach to let her anger die down – instinctively, I can't bring anger into the grove, she thought – waited, too, in case Blaise had, after all, followed her. There was a sound but it was only Slippers. After his tidbit, he had waited hopefully outside the bungalow; now he had plodded after her until he came close enough for her to pat him and pull his ears.

Suddenly he lifted his nose and brayed. At the same time, Mary heard an excited chattering and laughing. A group of boys was standing round one boy who was holding something; their dark skins, black heads, tattered clothes told Mary they were fisherboys. More excited laughter broke out; above it she heard a piercing shriek, than another, a small animal's shriek, and she started to run, Slippers lumbering after her. 'What have you got there? What are you doing?' She cried it in English, scattering the boys. 'Devils! *Shaitan!*' she screamed, because the boy in the middle held a small grey squirrel, one of the squirrels that abound in India.

They had tied a rag over its head to prevent it biting; it cried and squirmed as they poked it with slivers of pointed bamboo, fine and sharp as skewers. Blood was over the boy's hands. 'Give it to me,' stormed Mary. She snatched the squirrel, rag and all, as, with the flat of her other hand, she hit the boy hard across the face, then slapped the other boys. '*Jao!* Go! *Chelo –* ' the first words she had learnt of Hindustani. '*Chelo . . . Hut jao! Shaitan!*'

But these were fisherboys, not town boys easily quelled. She was one among seven or eight of them, not little boys but ten-, eleven-year-olds. Caught by surprise, at first they had stood dumb; the slaps roused them. With an outbreak of furious voices they closed in round her. Holding the squirrel close, Mary stood as hands and fists came out to hit, scratch, pinch, claw. Then Krishnan was beside her. He did not speak but took the squirrel from her. The frantic squirming stopped instantly and it was still as he raised his hand over the boys, only raised it; as one, they bent, scooped up sand and poured it over his feet, touching them with their heads. 'Kanu,' he said to the ringleader boy. 'Lady,' and unwillingly Kanu did the same to Mary who, as he lifted his head, gently laid her hand on it. He shook it off at once and with the others ran away through the trees.

'Is it badly hurt?'

'We'll see.'

He led the way to the fire. Mary's knees seemed to give way and she sank down on the sand. 'How could they? How could anyone be so cruel?' She hid her face so long that Slippers poked her with his nose.

'Look,' said Krishnan. He was sitting cross-legged on his goatskin throne and on one folded knee was the squirrel, sitting upright. Its wounds showed red in the firelight but it was nibbling a nut held in its small claws, its head cocked on one side, its black eyes brilliant. 'We call squirrels *udata* in Telegu,' he said. 'She has had some milk. Now this little *udata* will get well, thanks to you.'

'Not me. Thanks to you. They would have taken her back. Oh, why must people be so cruel? Even children!'

'Particularly children.' He spoke gently. 'They don't know any better,' and now Mary did not see the evil, pointed sticks but the small heads bent to touch Krishnan's feet.

Her angry trembling ceased. 'What are those marks on her back?' she asked.

'Long long ago,' said Krishnan, 'the young god, Prince Rama – another incarnation of Vishnu – had a beautiful wife, Sita. Indian girls, when they are married, are told to be a "little Sita", she was so perfect. But Sita was stolen

86

by a powerful demon – he had ten heads – who carried her off in his terrible claws to Sri Lanka.

'Rama was in despair as to how he could get her back. How could he take his army across that wide sea? But Hanuman, who is the Monkey God, called all the monkeys of India to build Rama a bridge. Thousands of great powerful apes and strong quick monkeys carried stones, rocks, boulders from the mountains to the shore. Quarries were dug, mighty rocks brought down to the sea, great boulders hewn into blocks. It was such a gigantic task that the very gods of heaven marvelled while Rama himself watched amazed.

'As he watched he saw a great monkey almost trip over a squirrel who was on the beach too. From his height, the monkey looked down a long, long way at the tiny squirrel and saw she had a pebble in her mouth.

' "What are you doing?"

'The little squirrel looked up. "I am helping to build the bridge to Lanka so that Rama may bring back his beloved wife, Sita."

' "Helping to build the bridge!" The monkey burst into a roar of laughter and called all the other monkeys. "Did you hear that? The squirrel says she is helping to build our bridge. Did you ever hear anything so funny in your life?" The others laughed too, then all of them said, "Shoo. We've no time for play and the likes of you."

'But the squirrel would not shoo. Again and again the monkeys picked her up and put her out of the way; she always came back with the pebbles until one of the monkeys grew angry and not only picked her up but flung her hard across the beach. She fell into Rama's hands where he stood.

'Rama held the squirrel close – just as you did – and said to the monkeys, "How dare you despise her? This little squirrel with her pebbles has love in her heart that would move heaven and earth with its power." And, lo!'

said Krishnan dramatically, 'Rama was transformed back into his origin, the great god Vishnu, the Preserver. Vishnu stroked the squirrel's back and as he put her down the monkeys saw, on her grey fur, these white lines that were the marks of the great God's fingers. Since when, Udata, you have those marks on your back, haven't you?'

Mary put out a hand and touched the stripes; the squirrel allowed her. 'It's the same as Christ riding on the donkey,' she said. 'All donkeys have the mark of the cross, even Slippers far away in India. It's the same.'

'All the same.'

'Will she come to me?'

'I'll ask her.'

He talks to her as if he were a squirrel, thought Mary.

'How do you know I wasn't?' Krishnan said with his strange power of following her thoughts. 'I could have been a squirrel, couldn't I?' he asked the squirrel. 'But', he said to Slippers, 'I do not seriously think I could have been a donkey.'

'You're conceited,' said Mary.

'If I am, why not? A peacock struts and spreads his tail because he is a peacock. That would have suited me. Peacocks are sacred in India and I am about to become sacred. I could have been a peacock. That is what we Hindus believe,' and he mocked, 'Don't tread on that cockroach, it might have been your grandfather. Don't tread on a cockroach but let children starve because you have put chalk in flour, given short weight, foreclosed on a peasant's one little field before he has time to pay off the debt.' His eyes blazed with indignation.

'Is that what your Party is about?'

'Of course. Why do you think I'm doing this?'

'I don't know. I only know I like what you are doing.'

'Not always. You couldn't. Remember all is fair in love and war. Politics now are a war, a bitter, greedy war and I have to fight Padmina Retty in every way I can. You don't know, Mary, thank God you have had no need to know, but Indian politics are corrupt, venal as never before. If Padmina Retty's manifesto had been truthful, it would have said: (a) The People's Shelter Party totally believes that, in the state of Konak, one family, the Rettys, should have total rule and that in perpetuity; (b) every member of the People's Shelter Party will give full material and emotional help to its leader in misappropriating funds; (c) the People's Shelter Party will support only those people who believe in hooliganism and slander.'

'That's terribly damning.'

'Not damning enough. The same goes for Gopal Rau, though he has not a chance. I tell you,' said Krishnan, 'no one from a family of integrity would dream of going into politics except a mopus like me. Even a mope, though, knows that no one can get into Parliament without so much wheeling and dealing that it disgusts. Not to mention spending money, floods of money, which is where our Dr Coomaraswamy comes in.'

'That funny old fat man?'

'That funny old fat man is a visionary. No one but a visionary would back me. I do not think', said Krishnan, 'poor Coomaraswamy will get his money back. A candidate can only be elected for five years, but he or she can retrieve his money, even make a fortune, by way of taking bribes, cheating, pulling strings, dispensing patronage, which must be paid for. The people know very well, if a village helps to get a candidate elected, it will be the first to get electricity or a well. If it resists, no electricity, no well. Patronage! I couldn't patronise a bee, yet the dear Doctor has worked with me and my ideals for years.'

'Years?'

'Yes, you don't think I came to this in five minutes? And all the time he has had to put up with a barrage from his terrible wife.' Krishnan mocked again, '"So easilee you are bamboozled, Hari" – Hari is Dr

Coomaraswamy's name.' Krishnan, whose English was smoother, more rounded than most Englishmen's, caught the wife's accent to perfection. '"And you are like a child with sweets so easily parted from your mon-ee." But Uma is right,' said Krishnan. 'I am using Coomaraswamy but that is a good man, Mary. How he has helped us.' Krishnan brooded again. 'The fisherpeople should be all right, but they are, in fact, the very poorest, virtually bonded in debt to the middle men and victims of the powerful fish-market Mafia. Mary,' he asked, 'what do you think the village people most need?'

'Water,' Mary said at once.

'Indeed, yes, and the wells will come faster if they work with us. I will not promise what I cannot do. What else?'

'Trees. Seed.'

'Yes, but not first.' His eyes darkened. 'Outside people coming in, would-do-goods, could plant a million trees – a million million – and change nothing because it would all begin again, but someone who plants ideas, knowledge, respect for our earth', Krishnan was deeply in earnest, '*might* just succeed.' Now his eyes seemed alight.

'Mary, I have been trying to do that for the last five years and I know it works, otherwise I would never have presumed – yes, *presumed* – to be a people's candidate. Let me tell you: I got one villager to let us use his piece of land that was bare – he would have said, of no use. He and his wife and children built mud walls and channels so that we could irrigate from quite far away. Then we came with saplings and seedlings. Now on his scruffy land he has an orchard, with pineapples and tea growing under the trees and enough grass to feed his cow and buffalo.'

'If,' said Krishnan, himself visionary, 'if we can teach one or two villages to feed themselves and their animals, that may spread and save the whole continent. If not,' the light went out of his eyes and he shrugged, 'at least a few less villages have less hungry children.'

'Lady Fisher told me', said Mary, 'that when there is great trouble in the world, Vishnu comes down in one form or another. I wish he would come now.'

'It is a belief,' said Krishnan. 'Some people would call it a delusion but I believe it is a good belief.'

'Love and war,' said Mary. 'Can politics be love?'

'They can, thank God.'

Mary watched his hand stroking the contented squirrel. 'I think you love everyone, everything,' she said.

He laughed. 'That wouldn't be possible.' Then he was serious again. 'It is that I am everyone, everything, just as everything, everyone is me.'

'Even the hateful ones?'

'Particularly the hateful ones because I am very hateful, very often.'

'But I . . . I like people and things – or dislike them – violently.'

'That is because you are thinking of yourself, not them,' which was true. 'See, now,' he said, 'here is a creature' – he says creatures, created things, not animals, thought Mary – 'a creature who does like you. Birdie has brought you a bouquet.'

The little elephant – how can an elephant be little? thought Mary, but Birdie is – held in her trunk a whole stem of plantains, at least thirty small bananas on a stem. 'I think you have stolen that,' Krishnan told her. 'Bad girl!' but he patted her trunk. He broke off the plantains, gave two to Mary, took three for himself, bit off a small end for the squirrel, gave ten to Slippers, the rest back to Birdie. The stem he threw on the fire so that the flames leapt up. They munched in companionship. Mary liked the way Birdie ate, picking up a plantain in her trunk and delicately putting it in her mouth; Udata nibbled; Slippers's bananas went round and round in his mouth – he would keep his the longest.

'This is the last time I can speak with you,' Krishnan

said. 'Tomorrow the vow must be absolute. I shall not know who might be listening.'

He sighed. '*Ayyo!* How my legs ache with all that sitting.'

'I ache too, inside me,' but Mary did not say it. She must not think back over the day, 'But the sea was wonderful,' she said. 'Those waves!'

'The sea. Yes. Let's go and get clean.' He jumped up and held out his hand to Mary.

On the beach he unwound his loin and shoulder cloths, leaving him with only a clout. Mary pulled her dress off over her head.

A pile of fishermen's helmets had been left by a boat. 'Put this on.' He put on his own. 'Don't be afraid,' he said. 'Thambi and I have been swimming here since we were five years old.' He took Mary straight through the waves, far out where he let her go. On the shore, Slippers, Birdie and a dot that was Udata had come out to watch. Mary could hear the thunder of the waves on the beach, here it was still; the water, warm and balmy, was dark blue. They swam, floated.

When Mary was tired, Krishnan came behind her, took her shoulders and let her rest. 'Let's stay here for ever,' she said.

'If only we could.'

Back on the beach, dressed, he and the animals walked her back but, before they reached the bungalow, Mary stopped. 'Don't come any nearer,' she said, 'it might be broken.'

Krishnan did not ask her what 'it' was.

Tuesday

'Would anyone object', Mr Menzies asked the whole dining room at breakfast, 'if, because of the election, we put on the morning news?' Without waiting for an answer he switched on the big verandah radio.

'This is the English Programme of All India Radio. Here is the news.'

The news was always read in Tamil, Telegu and English.

Now the voice, speaking in English, was reading the headlines: 'The drought is beginning to be felt in the Gamjam district. In Sri Kakylam there have been riots . . .' The breakfasters listened with half an ear if they listened at all. 'The bodies of two children, both boys, have been found in a field near the village of Palangaon. The trial, under Mr Justice Rajan, of the Englishman, Colin Armstrong, charged with fraud, embezzlement and trafficking in drugs, is drawing to a close . . . and now, the election in Konak.'

'Aie!' cried Dr Coomaraswamy and silence fell as everybody listened.

'The débâcle that befell Mrs Padmina Retty's People's Shelter Party last night could not help but leave traces this morning. For one thing, the symbol of the umbrella has disappeared. All posters have been hastily torn down and there has been some hand-fighting in the square where these two rival Parties' headquarters face one another. Mrs Retty, as befits a professional and long-accustomed campaigner, is cool and unperturbed. Her headquarters is buzzing with activity while the opposite building is strangely quiet and, except for two secretaries, empty. Again, there is no sign of Krishnan Bhanj.

' "I am not surprised," says Mrs Retty. "After that antic last night" ' – she used the same word as Blaise who smiled in self-congratulation. ' "After that antic, Krishnan dare not face me . . ."

'But', asked the voice on the radio, 'could he outface her? Mrs Retty, it seems, has not heard of a lorry that, since dawn, has been driving through the countryside.'

'I, myself, sent him out,' Dr Coomaraswamy interrupted, he had a ray of hope. 'But' – once again 'buts' were flying like brickbats – 'but was I wise?' he sighed.

'You couldn't have stopped him,' said Sir John.

'Have you seen the morning papers?' asked Mr Menzies.

Patna Hall's Goanese cook, Alfredo, collected them when he went to do the marketing at Ghandara, as he did every morning. In time-honoured fashion, the papers were ironed and then Kuku laid them out on the verandah tables for the guests; Colonel McIndoe's were taken by his bearer to his study. 'Ah! The *Madras Times*. The *Nilgiri Herald. All India Universal.*' Sir John picked up the *Madras Times.* 'It's the leading article.'

'Read it. Read it,' begged Dr Coomaraswamy.

Sir John read: ' "Is it disrespectful to ask if Krishnan Bhanj, candidate for the new Root and Flower Party, has taken his startling vow of silence in response to a direct commandment from the gods – in which case who dare say him 'nay'?" That's a tongue-in-cheek remark if ever I heard one,' said Sir John. ' "Or is this rising young politician playing a wily game of cards? If so, he is playing it well. Mrs Retty was routed last night and without violence, simply by a superior display of that insidious and most deadly of weapons, ridicule, making a story that will be told as long as politics exist. Already a ripple is spreading through Konak, a ripple from town to town, village to village. It may be only curiosity, maybe it is reverence, but one can forecast that soon, Mrs Padmina Retty's audience will have gone elsewhere, waiting for a garlanded lorry that has on it a *pandal* and, in the *pandal*, a young god silently blessing." That', said Sir John, 'was written, I'm sure, by Ajax.'

'Ah!' Dr Coomaraswamy gave a very different sigh.

'Who is Ajax?' asked Mr Srinivasan.

'Probably the best political correspondent in India and the Far East. If he is covering this election, you are in luck but he is best known for his gossip columns which spread on occasions to London and Europe. He is adept at dirt.'

'*Ayyo!*' Dr Coomaraswamy was well pleased.

'Looking to see if anything has been cut?'

Coming out from breakfast, Sir John had found Mr Menzies at one of the verandah tables, studying the article in the *Madras Times* and, as he looked up startled, 'You are, of course, Ajax,' said Sir John.

'I am.' There was something more than self-satisfaction, insolence, in the way Mr Menzies said that. 'And I don't let them cut my stuff. Clever of you to guess,' he told Sir John.

'Not at all. It was quite transparent,' and with a nod Sir John went on down the verandah leaving Mr Menzies slightly taken aback.

It is going to be a lovely empty day, thought Mary. They are all going away.

'I am taking Mrs Manning to the train,' Kuku told Mary. Her eyes were bright with the same brightness, Mary could not help thinking, that had been in the boys' eyes when they were tormenting the squirrel. 'I think she will be meeting someone.'

You want me to ask, 'What sort of someone?' thought Mary. Well, I won't.

Kuku's look said, 'Prig.'

* * *

95

Professor Aaron was taking his group to see the famous Dawn Temple at Gorāghat, fifty miles along the coast.

Sir John, Lady Fisher and Blaise were going too.

'I'd much rather be swimming or playing tennis,' Blaise grumbled as he picked up his packed lunch, binoculars and hat.

'Then why don't you?' asked Mary.

'If Sir John goes, I must.'

'Why?'

'You're always asking why.' Blaise was irritable. 'He's a big noise, that's why.'

'I think he'll know if you're pretending.'

'Pretend what? The Dawn Temple is very fine, even from the point of view of history. It's marvellous how they carried those enormous blocks of stone to build it. It's one of those things one should see.'

'Even if you don't want to? And it isn't only history, it's beauty,' said Mary, 'old, old beauty. Lady Fisher says it faces East and just at dawn, as the sun rises, the whole temple turns gold and rose-coloured.'

'If it makes you so lyrical, why don't you come?' But Mary shook her head. 'I'd like to go there early, early in the morning before dawn, all by myself, not in a coach full of people with cameras and binoculars and notebooks.'

Mary's day turned out not to be empty, not at all: it was filled with Patna Hall. 'Samuel is taking me to the bazaar,' she had told Blaise.

'You mean you would rather go with a servant to see an ordinary squalid bazaar than a splendid excursion like this, with Sir John, Professor Aaron, his group – and me?'

'Much rather,' said Mary.

'I find you utterly incomprehensible.'

'I know you do,' said Mary sadly. 'And I you,' but she did not add that.

Blaise hated all bazaars. 'All those rows of shanty huts and booths, corrugated iron, stucco houses blotched with damp! Even the temples are tawdry. Their silver roofs are made of beaten-out kerosene tins.'

'I think that's clever if you can't afford silver,' said Mary.

'And the *smells*! Cess in the gutters . . . men squatting down to relieve themselves even while you pass. Rancid *ghee* from the cookshops and that horrible mustard oil they cook in. Rotting fruit and meat hung too long and flies, flies, flies. If you walk on the pavements – if they can be called pavements – you tread on phlegm and red betel where people have spat. Ugh! And all those beggars and children with swollen stomachs and sore eyes. Once, perhaps, one could find good things in the bazaar, muslins, pottery, but now it's all machine-made, plastic, ugly. Mary, I hate you to go there. I know there are wonderful things to see in India but there are some things it's better for you not to see.'

'I want to see it whole.'

But Blaise had made up his mind. 'You're not to go,' he said as authoritatively as Rory. 'You're not to go.'

'I'm going,' said Mary.

Auntie Sanni had overheard. 'You're not very kind to that husband of yours,' she said.

'He shouldn't order me about. I'm not his child.'

'Come. Come. He only wants to protect you,' said Auntie Sanni. 'If your husband is a real man, that is in-nate.'

'I don't want to be protected. Don't you see?' Mary was hot-cheeked. 'I've never been anywhere, seen anything . . .'

'Except, as I understand, Italy, Paris, Norway, Brussels . . .'

'I meant India. Besides in those countries Rory always sent me to *school*.' Mary said it as if it were the ultimate betrayal. 'You don't know, Auntie Sanni, what girls' boarding schools are like, so – so little. I was – choked.' Mary could not find the right word. 'There was one,' she had to admit, 'a convent in Brussels which was part of something bigger. The nuns had something else to concern themselves with apart from girls.' She said that word in scorn. 'Even at home, Rory never let me be really free to do things – or thought he didn't. Now Blaise thinks he won't allow me either. Well, he has another think coming.'

'It's early days yet,' said Auntie Sanni.

'I knew you'd say that.'

'I do say it,' Auntie Sanni spoke sternly. 'Mary, child, be careful. You may cause more damage than you mean.'

'I'd like to go to the bazaar every day and do my own shopping,' Mary was to tell Blaise. It was an every day she had not glimpsed before yet perhaps had sensed. Everything Blaise had said of the bazaar was true: the stench, the shanty huts and booths, the flies . . . but the first shop she and Samuel came to was the shop where kites were made and sold costing a few *annas*, kites of thinnest paper, in colours of pink, green, white, red, with a wicker spool to fly them from, wound with a pound of thread. The thread had been run through ground glass so that the boys – Samuel told Mary that kite-fliers were always boys – could challenge other kites, cross strings with them, cut them adrift and proudly tie another bob of paper on their own kite's tail.

The front of the moneychanger and jeweller's shop was barred; he sat behind the bars on a red cushion, quilted with black and white flowers. Though this was South India he was a Marwari from Marwar in Rajasthan, known for businessmen and financiers. He had a small black cap on his head, steel spectacles and many ledgers.

There was nothing in his shop but a safe, a pair of scales and a table a few inches high. In India jewellery is sold by weight, jewellery made of silver threads woven into patterns and flowers. Mary, watching fascinated, saw a man buying a ring – which the Marwari took out of his safe – and paying for it. The moneylender took the money and reckoned it by weighing.

'Miss Baba like something – a nice brooch, nice ring?' asked Samuel but Mary did not want to buy, only watch.

A little black goat came by with twin kids; they butted their mother in vain because her udders were covered by a neat white bag.

'Goat milk very precious,' said Samuel.

There was a bangle shop with most of the bangles made of glass in clear goblin fruit colours of green, blue, amber and red. 'Miss Baba not buy,' Samuel cautioned. 'They break and cut very bad.'

The sari shop had the shimmering colours of heavy silk. 'They expensive,' said Samuel with feeling, remembering Lady Fisher's gift to Kuku: cotton saris like Hannah's had plain borders. Children's dresses with low waists, cut square and flat, like paper-doll dresses, hung outside in the street. The grain shops had grain set out in different colours in black wicker baskets and with them were sold great purple roots and knots of ginger, chillies and spice. There was a stall devoted to selling only drinking coconuts which could be split there and then if the customer wanted. 'Coconut milk very refresh,' said Samuel.

'I'd like to taste them,' said Mary.

'Not in the bazaar,' said Samuel.

A tassel shop had silk tassels in vivid colours of scarlet, brilliant pink or blue, orange, violent yellow, and, 'What are those for?' Mary saw small velvet and gold thread balls.

'For missies to tie on end of pigtail, very pretty.'

To Mary the temple was interesting and, Yes, clever, thought Mary, its outside walls and floors tessellated with broken pieces of china, countless pieces. The temple's gods were two big Western jointed dolls with eyes that opened and shut. They were dressed in gaudy muslin and tinsel and wreathed with paper flowers. 'Priest puts them to bed every night, morning gets them up. Hindu worship,' said Samuel with contempt but Mary saw that in front of them was a low table with offerings of sweets and flowers. A woman came to pray; on the brass tray she put a little powdered sugar and with her thumb she made on it the pattern of the sun for luck.

She looked up at Mary and smiled.

A sound like a murmur began to run through the bazaar: it grew louder and, with it, music and the ululation of a conch blown in jubilation. A lorry was coming down the road, heralded by motorcyclists, carrying between each pair of them long scarves of green, yellow and white. One held aloft on a pole a poster like a banner – the poster of 'The Three Wise Cows', as Mary had begun to call them.

She had seen them last night in the grove when Krishnan had shown a copy to her, three stylised cows, bells hung round their necks – clearly they were cherished – lying at peace among equally stylised flowers and looking out at the people with wise kind eyes. 'Is the script Telegu?' Mary had asked.

'Yes. Telegu script is decorative for posters. It goes oodle, oodle, oodle.' It certainly looked it.

'You speak Telegu?'

'I speak everything,' Krishnan had said. 'As required – Tamil, Telegu, Hindi, English, French, even a little Russian.'

'Don't boast,' Mary had said in pretended severity. Then 'Why did you choose cows?'

'Because they symbolise me,' and, as she had looked

100

puzzled, he had said like Dr Coomaraswamy, 'Symbols are crucially important in an Indian election. Every party has one. You must remember that most of the men and women in Konak cannot read so that written names and slogans mean nothing to them and, when they come to vote, how can they tell which is the candidate they want? Only if the symbol is at once identifiable. You have heard Padmina Retty had an umbrella, signifying "shelter". Well, we put an end to that. Now she has a star, which is not very wise for voters. Our third candidate, Gopal Rau, has a flower . . . so . . . "The star," they'll say, "might be Padmina . . ." yet equally the flower might be Padmina but my cows . . . There is no one,' said Krishnan, 'in towns or villages, near or far, who does not know the story of Krishna, the cowherds who adopted him, the *gopis*, so, as soon as they see my cows, three for prosperity, "Ah!" they will say, "That's Krishnan," and, notice, under the cows there is a flute.'

Now, in the bazaar, Mary heard it.

All the people began to look, pressing nearer. Shopkeepers stood up on their stalls; small boys wriggled through the crowd to the front; other urchins ran to meet the sound. The murmuring was loud now and grew to a shout as the lorry came close and paused. On a throne Krishnan was sitting – How his legs will ache tonight, thought Mary. The blue-black of his skin shone – with sweat? she wondered. Or oil? – against the *pandal*'s bright green leaves that fluttered as the lorry drove. It was the first time Mary had seen Krishnan in daylight and, with a shock, saw, even with the make-up, the Vishnu horseshoe shape in white on his forehead, eyes outlined in black, reddened lips, how beautiful he was. Not handsome or good-looking, beautiful, thought Mary.

Dr Coomaraswamy, sweating and stout, stood on the tailboard of the lorry bellowing through a microphone; when he paused, out of breath, Indian music invisibly played while behind the lorry followed jeeps and cars, one behind the other, overflowing with young men and women who immediately jumped down and came through the crowd to give out small pictures of the god Krishna. Sharma, in his flowing white, stood on the roof of the lorry's cab. A man beside Mary gave a shout, 'Ayyo.' The crowd took it up. 'Ayyo, ayyo-yo. Jai, Krishna. Jai, Krishna.'

Krishnan's eyes looked. Has he seen me? wondered Mary. She hoped he had.

Everyone was shouting now. Dr Coomaraswamy put down his microphone, he could not be heard, but Sharma's conch sounded over the noise. Still Krishnan did not move except to raise his hand, palm towards the people, fingers pointing upwards in benediction, blessing them while he smiled his extraordinary sweet smile.

The lorry passed on, Dr Coomaraswamy talking again through his microphone in a strident torrent of words. The jeeps crowded after and after them, bicycles, bullock carts, the bullocks being urged on, the driver whacking them and twisting their tails so that Mary hid her eyes. 'Miss Baba, better you come home,' Samuel said in her ear.

All that morning, 'It is too early to say,' Dr Coomaraswamy had told himself, 'always you are too optimistic,' as Uma had said over and over again 'Always you are carried away, either despair or huzzahs,' but the Doctor could not help seeing how, as the lorry approached, people stopped at once on the road; men shut their umbrellas in respect – it could be reverence; one or two prostrated themselves in the dust; women bent low as they peeped behind their saris.

'I am not huzzahing.' In his mind, Dr Coomaraswamy was telling Uma that. 'But, my darling, I begin to think . . .'

* * *

102

As Mary came up on the bungalow verandah on her way to wash and change for lunch, she saw Kuku coming out of Olga Manning's rooms. 'Just checking to see everything is clean,' Kuku explained, but there was an elation about her that made Mary pause. As if that showed she was curious, Kuku came closer. 'I was right,' Kuku whispered, 'she has a lover.'

'She's too old,' was Mary's instant young reaction, then remembered what Blaise had said of Olga's desperation and, 'How do you know?' she felt compelled to ask.

'Looking in her drawers, I found gentlemen's handkerchiefs,' said Kuku with relish. 'Not only that, gold cufflinks, a gentleman's gold watch.'

'She is keeping them for someone.' The whole of Mary was drawn together in repellance. 'Why were you looking in someone else's drawers? I have a good mind to tell Auntie Sanni,' she said.

At lunch time Mary found it strange to be in an almost empty dining room. Only she, Colonel McIndoe and Auntie Sanni were there. 'Come over and join us,' called Auntie Sanni.

Mary enjoyed being with them; little was said except of quiet domestic things, which brought a feeling of well-being, of goodwill – towards everyone, thought Mary. It seemed, as with Krishnan, that if Auntie Sanni disliked anyone – Mary had fathomed she had a reserve towards Blaise – she managed to see beyond the dislike. I wish I could, thought Mary, but I can't.

'The stores have come from Spencer's,' Auntie Sanni was telling the Colonel. 'Once a month,' she explained to Mary, 'stores of things one cannot get locally' – Mary was charmed by the way she said 'lo-cal-ly' with a lilt up and down – 'not in the village or Ghandara, come from a big shop in Madras. Samuel has unpacked them. Now Kuku and I must check them, make a list and put them away. Would you like to come and help?'

Mary loved it; the stores seemed to bring an intimacy with Patna Hall that gave her an odd satisfaction. Why should it make her happy to call out to Auntie Sanni, 'Twelve dozen tins of butter'? and, 'I never knew butter could be tinned.'

'Here we can only get ghee,' said Kuku in contempt. 'Butter made with buffalo milk and clarified so it is oily.' She shuddered. 'Horrid!' Twelve dozen tins, that is a gross, thought Mary. The quantities were immense: 'Two hundredweight of brown sugar, white sugar, caster sugar, icing sugar.' Kuku's voice became singsong too as she enumerated: 'Tea, coffee, chocolate. Tinned apricots, prunes.'

Strawberries came from Ootacamund, as did cheeses. Few wines. There was Golconda wine from Hyderabad, liqueurs from Sikkim.

Auntie Sanni checked. Mustafa, the head waiter, Abdul, the next, put sacks, bottles, tins away in cupboards and on shelves. 'Goodness,' said Mary, 'I never dreamed what it takes to run a hotel. Kuku, I would like your job.'

'Like my job?' Kuku was amazed. That anyone should want to work when obviously they did not have to was beyond her. She was particularly out of love with her work at the moment because she knew, when the last tin or bottle had been checked and the store room securely locked, the keys would be given to Samuel. 'I ought to have them,' she said each time; each time Auntie Sanni seemed not to hear.

When at last Mary went down to the bungalow she found that Blaise had come back from the Dawn Temple, plainly anything but exalted. He was asleep on the bed; camera and binoculars had been flung down, he had not taken off his shoes and, even in his sleep, his face was cross, over-pink with sunburn. Mary quietly changed into her swimming things, tiptoed out and was soon laughing and playing in the exhilaration of the waves, Moses and Somu each side of her. When they had finished, Mary beaten by the rollers – 'all over' she would have said – her hair dripping, Somu shyly produced a bracelet of shells threaded on a silk string. Each shell was different: brown speckled ones, pink fingernail-sized ones, almost transparent, brown ones curled into a miniscule horn and fragments of coral, apricot red. She tied the bracelet on while Moses and Thambi applauded. 'I shall keep this for ever,' said Mary, and Somu, when Thambi translated, blushed dark brown with pleasure.

She looked up and saw Blaise, awake now, watching them from the verandah. She waved, showing her arm with the bracelet. 'Look,' she called, 'a present from the sea,' but Blaise had gone into the bedroom.

'You don't want to get familiar with those chaps,' he told Mary when she followed him. 'They might misunderstand.'

'Misunderstand what?'

'I believe that part of the tourist attractions in foreign countries are the, shall we call them, "attentions of the locals"?'

'You mean fucking?'

'That's not a word I would use – and I wish you wouldn't – but yes, it's supposed to be part of the adventure, even for the elderly, or especially the elderly, women.'

'In a group like Professor Aaron's?' Mary did not believe it for a moment. 'Mrs van den Mar. Professor Webster. Dear Mrs Glover. Dr Lovat.' Mary laughed. 'I can't believe it.'

'It wouldn't surprise me,' said Blaise. 'That Miss – is it Pritt?'

'Miss Pritt is in love with India, not Indians.' You spoil

105

things, she wanted to say, then saw that, fortunately now, for her Blaise could not spoil anything. You don't disturb me one iota, thought Mary. These are my friends.

'. . . This is the news.' It was the middle of dinner and Auntie Sanni looked up and frowned but the voice went on. 'The Government has taken measures to bring relief to the effects of the Gamjam drought . . . Tons of grain, rice, fodder and medical supplies are being flown in . . . Troops have been sent in to reinforce police in quelling the outbreak of riots and violence in Sri Kakylam. The two boys found dead in the village of Palangaon have been identified as Pradeep and Bimal, twin sons of Birendranath Hazarika, a local landowner. Police are treating it as a case of murder.'

'In the trial of the Englishman, Colin Armstrong, charged with fraud, embezzlement and trafficking in drugs, Mr Justice Rajan has today begun his summing up and hopes to finish it tomorrow.

'In Konak, the candidate of the fancifully named Root and Flower Party, Mr Krishnan Bhanj, has been touring the state today. It is said that his strange vow of silence is arousing great interest in towns and villages; his symbol of the three wise cows is everywhere, while the people flock to see him.

'"I am not afraid," his chief opponent, Mrs Padmina Retty says. She has a new symbol – the defeated umbrella has disappeared – it is now a star. "My star is rising, not setting," she laughed. "The people of Konak are my people. They look to me. They will not let me lose. I shall win."'

'And she well may.' Dr Coomaraswamy was Gloomaraswamy again. 'She is the mother figure, so potent in India.'

'Mother is very dangerous,' Mr Srinivasan, too, was in gloom. 'We must talk very ser-i-ous-ly to Krishnan.'

* * *

106

Professor Webster's lecture was to begin at nine o'clock.

'Dear, are you coming to join us?' kind Mrs Glover asked Mary.

'I'm afraid I can't. Auntie Sanni is going to introduce me to the cook.'

'The *cook*?' Mrs Glover's expression plainly said, 'A cook, when you could listen to Professor Webster!' while Miss Pritt said gravely, 'My dear, Professor Webster is world famous as a lecturer. It's a privilege to hear her.'

'I – I promised,' Mary stammered, and escaped. She had noticed that Auntie Sanni did not come on the verandah after dinner for coffee. 'No, it's my time then to see Alfredo, our cook. We plan the menus and orders for the next day.'

'I thought Kuku . . .'

'Kuku is not capable,' Auntie Sanni said shortly. 'She thinks she knows better.' It was the nearest thing to condemnation Mary had heard her say. Then she asked, 'But would you like to come sometime and listen?' Now Mary caught her just as she was going, like a ship in full sail, into her office.

Every evening when he had finished cooking, Alfredo from Goa left the kitchen to his underlings; he would come back later to see that it was spotless. He bathed, changed into a clean white tunic and trousers, a black waistcoat with red spots, a silver watch chain and a silver turnip watch far bigger than Dr Coomaraswamy's. In the cookhouse it was kept on a shelf in its case with a steady ticking; in all Alfredo's now ten years at Patna Hall it had never lost time. With his lists he presented himself to Auntie Sanni.

They discussed food as two connoisseurs. For luncheon Alfredo suggested fish kebabs.

'*Fish* kebabs?' Mary was surprised.

'Yes, any kind of firm fish, made into cubes, marinated with ground onion, yoghurt and spices, then threaded on

107

skewers and grilled. Very good,' said Auntie Sanni.

'Then, as some sahibs liking English food,' said Alfredo, 'young roast lamb, new potatoes and *brinjals*.'

Auntie Sanni rejected the *brinjals*. Peas would be better.

'What are *brinjals*?' asked Mary, as she continuously asked 'What are . . . ?'

'Missy taste tomorrow.' Alfredo smiled. Missy, Miss Baba, not even Miss Sahib, none of them calls me Memsahib, thought Mary, a little startled.

Dinner was to be carrot and orange soup – again, something of which she had not heard. 'It is delicious,' and Auntie Sanni laughed seeing her doubtful face. 'Refreshing and light, which it needs to be because we are having tandoori chicken.'

'Tandoori?'

'*Tandoor* means an oven, a large long earthenware pot which is buried in clay and earth – fortunately we have one. We put charcoal inside and when it is red hot the coals are raked out; the chicken, spiced and ready, is put inside and sealed and it cooks with an un-im-ag-in-able taste.' Auntie Sanni sounded almost rhapsodical. 'People try and cook it as a barbecue or on a spit. Of course, it is *not* the same! And we shall finish', she told Alfredo, 'with lemon curd tart . . . as an alternative, peppermint ice-cream.'

'I'm going to have both,' said Mary.

When the menus were settled, to Mary's surprise, Auntie Sanni opened the bag she always carried and counted out notes, notes for a hundred rupees not the usual twenties, tens, fives and ones. 'Do you give Alfredo money every night?'

'Every night,' said Auntie Sanni. 'He has to shop in the bazaar, here and in Ghandara, and must pay cash. In the morning he will give me his account. Then there will be a great argument, eh, Alfredo?' Alfredo smiled and nodded. 'He himself will have bargained and so he has to have his "tea money" — the little extra on everything where he has cheated me, but not too much,' said Auntie Sanni in pretended severity. 'He understands and I understand.'

'How nice!' said Mary.

'Would you like to see the baskets of what he will bring?'

'Oh, I would.'

'You will have to get up early.'

'I will' — again there was that happiness. Is it, Mary asked herself as she went back to the verandah, because all this is something I haven't known anything about, making other people happy and comfortable? Then that was lost as, Soon, somehow, I will see Krishnan again, thought Mary. We might — we might swim, but she could not go until Blaise was asleep and Blaise was playing bridge with the Fishers and Colonel McIndoe, their four heads bent over the green baize of the table Kuku had set up. The cards gleamed in the electric light.

'Two hearts.'

'Three no trumps.'

'Four clubs . . .'

Bridge! thought Mary, while outside the night waited, the waves sounding on the beach, the moon, bigger now, shedding light on sea, sand and on the trees in the grove. Is Krishnan waiting there? wondered Mary.

She knew, of course, he was not waiting for her — no one could be more self-contained — but, 'Krishnan, Krishnan,' all of Mary sent that call out silently over the verandah rails, to the sea, the sky and the grove until, 'What are you looking at?' Blaise asked from the table.

'I was wondering where Slippers was.'

'Mary's like Titania,' said Sir John.

'Titania?' asked Blaise, momentarily puzzled.

'Methinks I am enamoured of an ass!'

'Don't be silly, John.' Lady Fisher spoke with unwonted asperity. 'She's simply sorry for that poor donkey. I do not

109

understand how Auntie Sanni let him get like that.'

'He belonged to the washerman.' Mary had learned that from Hannah. 'He has never been broken. When they tried to make him carry the washing, he kicked and bolted so the washerman let him go wild. By the time Auntie Sanni knew, his hoofs were like that because no one could get near enough to cut them. I shall have them cut one day,' said Mary with certainty.

Lady Fisher looked at her over the cards.

The lecture was over. Professor Aaron and the ladies came out on the verandah – 'For the cool air,' called Mrs Glover – but, seeing the bridge players, they hushed their voices as they collected around the bar for a goodnight drink and soft discussion. Professor Webster came to Auntie Sanni.

'We have finished.'

'And I'm sure successfully.'

'Yes, I'm glad to say.' Professor Webster's cheeks were flushed from her efforts; her eyes shone.

'And what was your subject?'

'After today, at Gorāghat and the Temple, it was about Usas, goddess of the Dawn, one of the Shining Ones, the old nature gods.' Mary was listening: It's these old gods, true gods, I believe in, she thought. 'Usas is the daughter of the sky,' Professor Webster went on, 'sister of night and married to Surya, the sun god. She travels in a chariot drawn by seven cows; its huge wheels are carved in stone, the cows are there too. The temple faces the east so that when the sun rises its first rays touch the cows and they turn rose red. I have slides to show this and there is a path of gold to the sea.'

'Oh!' breathed Mary. 'Oh!'

But Lady Fisher broke the enchantment. 'Dear,' she called to Mary, 'I feel a little chilly. Would you run upstairs and fetch me my wrap? It's on a chair, just a light shawl. Thank you, dear child.'

As, noiselessly, Mary came up the stairs, she saw a small black figure sidling along the corridor towards one of the rooms. It was the boy on the beach, the squirrel boy. What is he doing here? wondered Mary. Next moment the same question came ringing down the corridor. 'Kanu! Why you here?' and a stream of scolding Telegu. It was Hannah, come from turning down the guests' beds for the night. She strode down the corridor, her jewellery clinking, one hand uplifted ready to slap but the boy ducked and escaped down the stairs.

'That boy very bad, little devil. Evil!' and, 'How dared he?' cried Hannah, her nostrils snorting. 'Dare come into Patna Hall at all, then come upstairs. *Upstairs!*'

It was past midnight when Mary got to the grove.

'God, I'm tired,' Blaise had said in the bungalow bedroom.

'I'm not,' said Mary, 'but then I didn't go all that way to the temple. I think, for a little while, I'll go along the beach.' Perhaps she had sounded breathless because Blaise was suddenly alert. 'Out? At this time?'

'Just to stretch my legs.'

He accepted that, perhaps too tired to bother. 'Don't be long,' was all he said.

Slippers came as he always came but as Mary turned from the beach towards the grove, where the fire should have been leaping there was only a dull red glow.

She stepped nearer. The grove was as she had always seen it: the fire, the roof of matting between the trees, the seat with its goatskins, the brass *lota* and pans shining as if someone had cleaned them, the pitcher of water, the line of white washing, the cut sugar cane, all there the same but the grove was empty.

She stood, sick with disappointment, balked. Then there was a sound, light as the wind, and a young man appeared . . . The same young man who came with

111

a message into the dining room our first night, thought Mary. Swiftly he began to mend the fire, kicking the wood together with his bare feet until the branches flamed. He jumped when Mary came into the firelight, then stood holding a branch as if he were brandishing it.

'I think you are . . .?'

'Sharma,' he said, still on guard.

'I am Mary Browne, staying at Patna Hall. Do you speak English?'

'A little.'

'Where is/. . .\Mr Krishnan?'

'Krishnan Bhanj is holding *dhashan* at Ghandara.'

'*Dhashan*?'

'Many peoples coming to see him. He will be there all night.'

'All night?'

'Yes. I must hurry,' said Sharma. 'We get ready for tomorrow.' He paused. 'I think I see you in the bazaar?'

'Yes,' said Mary. 'Yes.'

He was gone. Mary waited but it did not seem as if even Birdie would come; there was no sign of Udata. Perhaps Krishnan had taken the squirrel to Ghandara and Mary had turned to go when she heard voices, light young voices. Another fire was burning beyond the trees, the voices were singing in a gentle contented chant. Followed by Slippers, Mary went to see.

It was the boys, the same boys who had tormented Udata but now were squatting on their heels in a circle, faces illumined by the firelight, black polls bent, their hands busy making garlands, and, at once, Of course, thought Mary, garlands for the lorry. They are helping Krishnan. As she stepped nearer they looked up but without animosity; their eyes, bright in their dark faces, were merry, their hands did not stop and, 'Show me,' said Mary. As if they understood, the smallest handed up a garland. It was made of mango leaves, fresh, pungent and surprisingly heavy.

'*Shabash*!' said Mary, another word she had learned. 'I'll help you,' and she knelt to sit down as they made room for her. She looked round the circle. 'Where's the big boy? Where's Shaitan, Kanu?'

'Kanu?' For a moment they stared at her, then they collapsed into laughter as if she had made a good joke. 'Kanu!' The name went from lip to lip. 'Kanu! Kanu!' they cried. 'Kanu! *Ayyo! Ayyo! Ayyo-yo.*'

Mystified, Mary picked up a garland to see how it was knotted.

'Mary,' came a voice. 'Mary.'

Quickly, still holding the garland, Mary stood up, like a nymph surprised.

'What the hell are you doing?' asked Blaise.

'Why did you come after me?' In the bungalow bedroom Mary turned on Blaise.

'Isn't it reasonable,' asked Blaise who was being extraordinarily patient, 'reasonable for a husband, if his wife goes wandering night after night— '

'Only two nights,' Mary interrupted.

'Three,' said Blaise. 'Tonight's the third.'

'Why? Can't I do what I like?'

'Making garlands with fisherboys as if you were one of them seems a strange thing to like.'

'I happen to be interested in the Root and Flower Party.'

'How can you be?' Blaise asked. 'You haven't been here long enough. Nor do you know anything about India.'

'I knew more about India in five minutes than you would if you stayed five years,' Mary wanted to fling at him. Yet, of course, what he said was true and, What do I know? she thought hopelessly.

'Anyway, I don't want you to be involved with any of this damned masquerade.'

'If it's a masquerade I'm sure it's for a good cause.'

113

'I doubt it and I don't want you to be involved.'

'I would give anything to be involved,' she told him flatly, but had to add, 'I don't see how I can be.' Had Krishnan not said, 'This is the last time I can speak with you.'

In Ghandara after the *dhashan*, 'We must find ourselves a mother figure,' Dr Coomaraswamy told Krishnan.

'Copycat' wrote Krishnan on his pad. For a moment he sat, wrapped in thought, then wrote, 'Not a mother. Allure.'

'*Allure?*'

'Yes. Goddesses. Two goddesses, Lakshmi for good fortune, Radha for love; both young, beautiful.'

'Who?'

'Kuku,' wrote Krishnan. 'Kuku in the most brilliant most vulgar of her saris so that she looks like the *bania*'s glossy catalogue pictures of Lakshmi. Lots of jewellery, you'll have to hire. Auntie Sanni will give her leave, I'm sure. Yes, Kuku for Lakshmi.'

'And Radha?'

Krishnan smiled. 'Little Radha?' and he wrote, 'Mrs Blaise Browne.'

'But she is English! It would not be popular at all if Radha was a Western goddess.'

'Dress her up,' wrote Krishnan.

'We could, and hide her hair. She is sunburned.' Mr Srinivasan liked the idea. 'She could pass for fair wheaten complexion which a goddess should have.'

'But it's impossible,' Dr Coomaraswamy almost spluttered. 'Can't you imagine? Sir John and Lady Fisher, they would never approve. Sir Professor Aaron, the ladies, Hannah, Samuel, and that young man, Mr Blaise!' Dr Coomaraswamy did not like Blaise. 'He's her *husband*. He would never consent.'

But Krishnan wrote, 'Don't ask him. Ask her.'

Wednesday

'Dr Coomaraswamy Sahib coming,' said Thambi.

Thambi, who was alert to everything that happened in Konak to its very borders, was Krishnan's loyal supporter and knew exactly why Dr Coomaraswamy was coming. Blaise and Mary had come out early for a morning swim; Blaise had already gone in, Moses after him. 'Can't I once, even once, swim without these water rats?' Blaise had exploded.

'Sea can change any minute,' Thambi had answered as always, 'Moses knows this sea,' and, 'Wait, Miss Baba,' he said as Dr Coomaraswamy came puffing down the sandy path — Even walking downhill, he gets out of breath, thought Mary. It was not that; Dr Coomaraswamy was agitated.

'Mrs Browne, forgive me for intruding at this early hour. I hope I have not disturbed you.'

'Of course not. I was just going to swim.'

'No. No. Not now. Please not now, Mrs Browne. I have an ex-tra-or-din-ary favour to ask you. Please do not take offence.'

He mopped his forehead. Does he always have to mop? thought Mary as, 'What favour?' she asked.

'One that I myself would never have asked, but Krishnan—'

'Krishnan?' Now Mary was surprised.

'As, at present, Krishnan Bhanj himself will not go into society, you do not know him . . .' Mary did not

115

contradict the Doctor, 'but in India's mysterious way he knows of you . . .'

'The ways of India are even more mysterious than you think,' Mary would have told him, but again did not say it. Instead, 'What does Mr Bhanj want?'

Dr Coomaraswamy cleared his throat – if Mary had not been there he would have spat the phlegm out on the sand. 'It has happened that Mrs Padmina Retty, candidate for the People's Shelter Party, Krishnan's opponent, has come out as the Mother Figure for the state, that is the Mother Goddess. Padmina is a very clever woman, Mrs Browne. Also, in all religions, the "mother" is, ī think, potent but in India you do not know how potent.'

'You mean, like the Virgin Mary?'

'Indian goddesses are not virgin, Mrs Browne, not at all and, so, more potent. We shall have to combat. We, the Root and Flower Party, need for Krishnan a feminine counterpart. Not a mother, that would be copycat.' Dr Coomaraswamy quoted Krishnan with as much satisfaction as if he had thought of this himself. 'We must be different, also challenging. So we shall import goddesses. Mrs Browne, will you come with us on our lorry to be the goddess Radha? *Please*. We so need this allure.'

'I'm not alluring.'

'Indeed you are, but it is the female element that is more important, gentle, supportive, as are the Hindu goddesses.'

'I thought they were fierce.'

'Some, not others. Supportive, also beautiful.'

'I am not beautiful, Dr Coomaraswamy.'

He did not think so either but, 'As Radha you will be. We shall dress you. All the clothes I have ready.'

'What would I have to do?'

'Nothing but sit and smile most graciously. Hold your hand so, Krishnan will show you. You will have a small throne on the lorry. With bamboo and leaves we shall shade you. Please.'

Mary did not waver any more. Go with Krishnan, she thought. Be near him all day. See the villages and little towns and, 'What can I say but "Yes".' She smiled happily on Dr Coomaraswamy. 'Goddesses don't wear spectacles though. Give me a minute to put in my contact lenses and I'll come.'

When she came back Blaise was far out to sea and, 'Tell Sahib I have gone out for the day. I'll see him this evening,' Mary told Thambi.

'Not for all the tea in China,' said Kuku.

'I am not talking about tea, I am talking about cash.'

'How much?' asked Kuku.

'She'll not consent,' Dr Coomaraswamy had told Krishnan.

'She will if you offer enough. Try three hundred rupees.'

Three hundred?'

'Kukus are expensive and we don't want to fail.'

'We shall give you a hundred rupees. *One hundred*,' the Doctor told her now.

Kuku gave a snort. 'How much do Krishnan's girls at Ghandara get?'

'Our young women do it for love.'

'I'm sure they do. Krishnan's *gopis*!'

'Miss Kuku, you may not sneer at our candidate. Three hundred.'

Kuku settled for five — And I, myself, shall extort every *anna* of that, Dr Coomaraswamy had peculiar pleasure in promising himself this. Yet, 'If you had known,' he told Kuku silently, 'I would have given you a thousand rupees, two thousand. For you, I am weakness itself.' Instead, he was able to say, 'You will stand throughout.'

'I shall faint.'

'That will be ten rupees off. You will wear green with

yellow and white or yellow with green and white – Party colours.'

'I will wear yellow and green, India's colours.'

'You will wear what I say,' said Dr Coomaraswamy, 'and you will not ogle Krishnan Bhanj.'

'Ogle? What is ogle?'

'You know very well,' and Kuku laughed.

She did not laugh when the lorry came and she saw Radha.

'Who is that?'

'Don't you know?' Dr Coomaraswamy was delighted but Kuku had seen the grey eyes.

'Mrs *Browne*!' she cried.

'Kindly, Mrs Browne has consented to be the Radha goddess, your companion,' said Dr Coomaraswamy.

'For kindness, not for cash,' Mr Srinivasan put in.

Kuku said at once, 'She is far better dressed than I am.' It was Shyama who had dressed Mary in the gatehouse. The sari was green gauze patterned with gold thread stars, the *choli* gold tissue – Mary was titillated to feel her midriff bare; fortunately, from wearing her bikini, it was sunburnt too. Her hair was hidden by a black silk cap gathered at the back into flowers, a pigtail hanging ended by one of the little velvet and gold thread balls she had seen in the bazaar. Below the cap her forehead had been painted white which made her skin look darker, the white edged with red dots; her arms were painted with patterns too, the soles of her feet and the palms of her hands red. There were strings of white flowers, a gold necklace and bangles. Shyama had outlined Mary's eyes with kohl, painted the lids blue and reddened her lips vividly red. 'She says you must take this make-up with you, to freshen in the heat,' Dr Coomaraswamy had said, and, 'She says to tell you now you are most beautiful.'

Then, by the lorry, 'Far better dressed than I am. I'm not coming,' cried Kuku.

Sharma picked her up and put her in the lorry. 'You have come,' he said.

'Thambi, that was a bad thing to do.' Auntie Sanni had sent for Thambi immediately when, as was inevitable, she heard about the dressing up in the gatehouse. She spoke in English to be more severe. 'Very bad.'

'Bad?' Thambi was astonished. 'It was for the Party.'

'I suppose that was what Krishnan felt,' Auntie Sanni said when she told the Fishers. 'Better you hear this from me than from Samuel or Hannah.'

'All the same, I am surprised at Krishnan,' said Sir John.

'I think Krishnan', said Lady Fisher, 'is not averse to a little play. Think how mischievous the god Krishna was.'

'But Mary must have known this was *not* right,' Sir John was fulminating. 'All those years with Rory . . .'

'She did not know,' said Auntie Sanni, 'because she did not give herself time to think. Nor would I – or you – have done at eighteen.'

The decorated lorry made its way from small town to small town, village to village, a slow way because it was stopped again and again by the crowds. Soon each stop seemed joined to the other by the people along the roads as Sharma blew his conch, drums beat from the jeeps and cars behind with the shrill whine of Indian music and Dr Coomaraswamy bellowing from the microphone. Every time they stopped, a throng pressed forward.

'Where do they all come from?' asked Dr Coomaraswamy.

'I think from everywhere.' Mr Srinivasan was almost cheerful.

It was a reverent crowd. Again men shut the umbrellas that had shielded them from the sun and made *namaskar*; women, usually shy, hiding themselves behind their sari ends, now threw flowers, garlands, jostled forward to touch. 'You *must not shrink*,' Dr Coomaraswamy said angrily to Kuku. 'Stand up or else . . .'

He glanced at Mary who sat so still he thought she was asleep – but no; she bent a little to the crowd, let the women touch her, received the homage, dutifully kept the other hand in blessing. He saw her, now and again, look at Krishnan and Krishnan looked back with that irradiating smile but once Dr Coomaraswamy saw what he could hardly believe: Krishnan gave young Mrs Browne a . . . wink? wondered Dr Coomaraswamy. Could it have been a wink? There was no time to think further. He had to go back to his microphone. 'People of the State of Konak, men and women, friends . . .'

'*Jai* – Krishnan. *Jai* – Krishnan,' and as the crowd swelled the cry grew into a roar.

'Stand up,' he commanded Kuku.

'I want to blow my nose.'

'That will be five rupees off.'

'Out for the day!' On the beach Blaise had been incredulous.

'She say,' Thambi could not help enjoying this – he had heard 'water rats' – 'she say she see you this evening,' and he volunteered, 'She quite safe. Sahib.'

'But where has she gone?'

And Thambi had pleasure in saying, 'On Krishnan Bhanj's lorry.'

'That young Blaise!' Sir John had said in wrath. 'Not a word or, I can guess, a thought as to what is going on between him and Mary, only what people might think.'

Blaise had come up to breakfast but had contained himself until the Fishers had finished. He followed them on to the verandah. 'Gone on this fool lorry. Not a word to me only a message from that far too cocky fellow Thambi,' and, 'Suppose it gets into the papers?' Blaise said in agony.

'Well, it's bound to be on the news. They seem to be following this election step by step. The papers will, of course, copy.'

'I meant the British papers.'

'My dear boy, to the average Britisher, if they know where it is at all, Konak is a little patch, perhaps the size of a postage stamp on the map of India and about as interesting.'

'Not if there's something unusual. This chap Ajax seems to be able to make anything unusual.'

'It is unusual, one can't gainsay that.'

'She is dressed up. They may not know it is Mary.'

'In this blasted country everyone knows everything. 'No.' Blaise set his teeth. 'This time Mary has gone over the edge.'

'Many people are bewitched on their first encounter with India.' Lady Fisher tried to be soothing. 'Bewitched or repelled.'

'I'd far rather she was repelled.'

'Still, if you're wise you'll take no notice.'

'Notice!' Blaise had exploded again. 'She's my *wife*.'

'Blaise have you thought', said Lady Fisher, 'that the effect of this could be the reverse of scandal? If Krishnan Bhanj wins— '

'He can't win, surely?'

'Suppose he does, wouldn't it be a commendation – what Dr Coomaraswamy would call a feather – for a rising young diplomat to have a wife with such understanding of Indian affairs, so percipient that she personally backed this election and went campaigning?'

121

Blaise looked at her dumbfounded, shook his head bewildered and left.

Mr Menzies was again going through the newspapers and Sir John deliberately voiced what he had said to Lady Fisher. 'I'm surprised that a journalist of your reputation should take such an interest in what, after all, is not a big or important election.'

Mr Menzies looked up. 'To me all elections are important.' There was a distinct swagger. 'Not because of the politics. They're not really my game.'

'Game?' asked Sir John. 'In India they are vitally serious.'

'Exactly. That is why, in my case, it's not the politics, it's the politicians at election times. They are so beautifully vulnerable.' Mr Menzies chortled.

'For your filthy column?' Sir John managed to keep his voice pleasant.

'Exactly,' Mr Menzies said with delight.

'So? I don't think you'll find much in the way of titillation in Padmina Retty, or poor old Gopal Rau – or Krishnan Bhanj.'

Sir John added Krishnan deliberately and kept his voice mild.

'We'll see,' said Mr Menzies, highly pleased. 'We'll see.'

'John,' Auntie Sanni called from her swing couch where she had come to sit quietly before going on with the day's round – 'I like to take this time to consider my guests', she had told Mary, 'and their needs.' This morning the needs were troubling her and, 'John, have you time to come and talk a little?'

'All the time in the world.'

'For the first week in years,' said Auntie Sanni, 'I'm troubled, very troubled, about my guests – some of them.'

'Such as?'

'Obviously, Olga Manning.'

'With reason,' said Sir John.

'Someone must help her,' and Auntie Sanni looked at him, the sea-green blue eyes as trustful as a trusting child's. 'You will, John.' It was not a question; it was a fact.

'If I can. I'll try and talk to her when she comes back from Calcutta – if she comes back.'

'She owes me money, so she will.' Auntie Sanni said it with certainty. 'Then there's Kuku.'

'She is meant to be a help not a worry.'

Auntie Sanni smiled. 'I know – and she *is* a help, she works hard but . . .'

'But?'

'When she left St Perpetua's she was sweet. Now she's so knowing. We haven't done her any good, and I foresee pain. She hasn't a chance, and I can't give her one, not of the kind she would thank me for.'

'I hope you're wrong. Who besides? Mary?'

'No. Mary can look after herself.'

'Which is why you like her!'

'She is likeable,' was as far as Auntie Sanni would go. 'No, John, it's the young man, Mr Browne.' Sir John noticed he was still Mr Browne. 'Oh, John, why can't we all be born with wit?' She looked far across the sea, sparkling in the morning, an increasing frown on her face. 'John, I'm afraid. Mary doesn't know, doesn't dream . . . This isn't England or even Europe. It's such a violent place.'

Sir John got up, went to the railing and looked down at the out-bungalow, whistling as he pondered. Suddenly he broke off. 'That young fool!'

Two men in bathing shorts were strolling along the beach. 'He's talking to Menzies,' said Sir John.

'No! Oh, no,' said Auntie Sanni.

123

It was the coconut water that woke Mary out of her trance.

'Where have I been?'

'Only four hours on that damned lorry.' Kuku had collapsed on the sand.

To Mary it had seemed like five minutes. Now the lorry and its following jeeps and cars had pulled off the dust road into a small oasis of trees in the midst of what had seemed to be a desert wasteland without villages. There were no people, only birds: cranes, wading in a stagnant pool, small wild brown birds she recognised as partridges wandering in coteries, mynahs and, of course, crows. Mats were being spread. 'You must rest and eat,' Dr Coomaraswamy told Mary. 'Drink a little, not too much,' and Sharma had sent a boy shinning up a coconut palm – there seemed to be innumerable small boys. Some had ridden on the car roofs or hung on to their backs. Mary tried not to think of the abominable Kanu.

The boy up the palm tree threw the nuts down to the ground where Sharma took the tops off them with a *panga*, splitting each so skilfully that none of the water was lost. 'Drink. You must drink,' Dr Coomaraswamy told Mary again as she sat; she still seemed dazed.

'It has been too much for her,' said Mr Srinivasan but Krishnan took the nut and held it to her lips. Even here he could not speak. 'In India even the trees have ears,' Dr Coomaraswamy would have told her but Krishnan's eyes commanded her; she felt the rough wood of the nut edge, the coolness of the water, as, obediently, she drank.

It was Krishnan, too, who had lifted her down from the lorry; Kuku had had to jump only helped by Sharma's hand. Now she stood up to wring out her sari. 'My God! The sweat. You'll have to get me fresh clothes.'

'They will dry in the sun,' Sharma soothed her.

Mary, oddly enough, was untouched, her sari still fresh, and, never, thought Dr Coomaraswamy, had he seen anything as shining as her grey eyes. He was unused to light eyes; his ideal was for brown eyes, lustrous, deeply lashed — Not like Uma's he thought with a pang of guilt, though Uma, when she was young, had been handsome. Kuku's eyes were black, small and, he had to admit, malicious. Then why am I so much seduced? He did not know but now, 'This blue-grey,' he murmured to Mr Srinivasan, 'we do not have this colour of eyes in India, sometimes violet or green but not this.' Mary Browne's eyes today were like diamonds, he thought, brilliant in a way that alarmed him. Has she fever? and, 'Eat a little,' he urged her. 'See we will bring food to you. Then, on this mat, you must stretch out and sleep!'

Krishnan himself had had to be helped off the lorry; now two of the young men were pummelling him and rubbing his legs. 'He has been im-mo-bile all those hours.' Mr Srinivasan hopped like an agitated bird. 'How can he keep it up?'

Krishnan did say one word. '*Chūp.*' Then, while Mary watched, he clasped his hands behind his neck, using his elbows to support him until he stood on the crown of his head, his feet high in the air, his powerful body erect as a pillar, 'So that the blood can run the other way,' Dr Coomaraswamy explained to Mary, 'which is good for the body — and the brain.'

'I could not have done those hours on the lorry without yoga,' Krishnan told Mary afterwards as he stretched, bent, leapt, ran.

Food was brought on banana leaves for Kuku and Mary to eat in the Indian way with their fingers and apart from the men, 'Usually *after* the men,' Kuku said with acerbity, 'with their left-overs,' but Mary found it restful – no fuss with talk or plates, knives, forks, spoons. The food was hot and good; it had travelled in aluminium pans that fitted together into a carrier, the bottom pan filled with live coals. There were rice, curry, spicy little *koftas* of prawns, *puris*, vegetables but Mary only nibbled. 'I don't want to be disturbed,' she could have said. Soon she lay down and was asleep.

Dr Coomaraswamy had to wake her. It was the first time he had seen an Englishwoman asleep. He looked at the shadow her eyelashes made on her cheeks; the skin below them was . . . like petals, he thought – why did Mary Browne continually make him think of flowers? It's because she's so young, he thought – and pure. He hesitated to touch her.

Kuku laughed as she watched. 'Go on, wake her with a kiss.'

Dr Coomaraswamy was shocked. To him Mary, like Krishnan, was in a different category – she was Blaise Browne's wife but Dr Coomaraswamy felt she belonged to Krishnan, he did not know how or why but he had seen Krishnan not only look at her and give her the especially tender smile he gave to most women and children – 'and to a little goat or a squirrel,' the Doctor had to say – but he, Dr Coomaraswamy, had seen that wink. The wink immediately put her on a level he could not reach.

'Go on, kiss her. You like young women.'

'Kuku, you are most lewd. I shall fine you fifty rupees.'

'We misjudged Menzies,' Blaise told the Fishers at lunch time. 'Thought he was just a journalist who likes to make a mystery. Actually, he's a sympathetic type.'

'Type's the right word for him.' Sir John almost said it but stopped himself, only saying, 'I hope you didn't talk to him about Mary.'

126

'Of course not.' Blaise, Sir John was sure, lived by a code which laid down that one did not talk about one's wife to other men. 'Of course not, at least I hope not,' and Blaise defended himself. 'If I did a little, what's the harm? He's on holiday. Apparently he has a hell of a life in Delhi and in London. It seems that to write a newspaper gossip column means continual parties and pressures from people wanting to get into the news. He's here for quiet. He's taking me to Ghandara this afternoon so we can get a decent round of golf but the course wouldn't be grass, would it?'

'Sand,' said Sir John. 'For grass you would probably have to go to Madras. . . . Pity you couldn't – out of the way,' he wanted to add.

'Why should Mary Browne?' Kuku was asking. 'Why should she sit when I have to stand?'

'I'll stand,' said Mary. 'Let Kuku sit.'

'That is not the plan.'

'She has stood for four hours.'

'So she should at that price.'

'Price?' Mary was puzzled.

'Do you think I would do this for nothing? Or do you call it love?' sneered Kuku.

'I don't call it anything. I just want to do it.'

'For love?' Kuku insisted.

Dr Coomaraswamy intervened. 'It will not be long now,' he soothed. 'As we get towards evening it will be cooler, it will not seem so long.'

'I like it long,' said Mary.

'This seems a roundabout way to get to Ghandara,' Blaise said in the car.

'So it is. I'm sorry. I must have taken the wrong turning. Hallo!' said Mr Menzies. 'Here they are!'

'You promised.' Blaise was furious.

'I'm sorry but how was I to know where they would be?'

Mr Menzies had to stop, the crowds round the lorry were so thick. He opened the sun-roof and stood on the seat. *'Golly!'* he said. Reluctantly, Blaise stood up beside him.

Surrounded by the surging mass of people the lorry looked small, the figures on it even smaller, but Blaise recognised Kuku, then looked from her to the smaller throne and, 'Is that Mary?' he asked dazed.

'Cleverly disguised at any rate,' Mr Menzies comforted him. 'But yes, it undoubtedly is.'

Kuku, Lakshmi, in her green and white patterned gold-edged sari, gold bodice, seemed to melt into the lorry's decorations as did Krishnan, though his blue-blackness could be seen, while Mary, Radha, shone in all the wheaten fairness Mr Srinivasan had hoped.

'Couldn't be more conspicuous,' Blaise agonised. 'And she must be recognised as she's the only Western person there.'

'She wouldn't have been the only one if you had gone with her,' Mr Menzies pointed out.

Blaise stared at him. 'I? With that rabble?'

Mr Menzies gave a soft whistle. 'So you *are* at odds!' He sounded amused. 'I thought you were.'

'Why?' Blaise was cold, trying to fend him off.

'From what I have seen. No one can say I am not interested in my fellow men – and women,' said Mr Menzies sweetly. 'Your wife is so transparently young.'

'You make me sound like a child-stealer. It was she who wanted us to be married.'

'And now she doesn't.'

'Who said so? Good God! We haven't been married a month.'

'That *is* quick.' Unerringly, the insidious drops of poison fell. 'But India does go to people's heads and Mr

128

Krishnan Bhanj knows very well how to make himself – shall we say – attractive?'

'Don't!' Blaise cried out before he could stop himself, then tried to recover. 'I don't think I feel like playing golf. Would you be kind enough to drive me back to the hotel?'

Kuku had seen Blaise at once and began to redrape her sari more gracefully, then waved the peacock fan Sharma had given her to help against the heat.

Dr Coomaraswamy, for a moment released from his megaphone – the microphone had failed – followed her eyes. 'Menzies, young Browne! You will not plume,' he said furiously to Kuku. 'You are here for the crowd. Also put that fan down or you will get nothing at all.'

'It is I who have bought you for today,' he wanted to cry, 'so no tricks.' The plain fact that Kuku liked Blaise inflamed his own longing. The bodice she wore showed the cleavage between her breasts; her sweat had stained the silk under her arms and, where the bodice ended, her midriff glistened with it; he could imagine the glistening between her thighs and delight carried him away. Besides, it was sweet to torment her. What fun, thought Dr Coomaraswamy, if I could whip Kuku. If I could have – is it a *sjambok*? – that long whip that hisses in the air as its lash comes down. He saw himself wielding it, then had to say, as Uma would have, 'And how silly you would look,' and 'Stand up, girl,' he shouted. 'Smile!' It was no use saying, 'I'll fine you,' he knew he never would.

Mary had not seen Blaise, she was too interested; in contrast to the morning when she had been entranced, everything now was vivid. As the lorry drove and stopped – stopped every few minutes, it seemed to her – she had never imagined such crowds or smelled them, the peculiar smell of an Indian crowd: not dirt, Indians are personally clean, but of sweat, the *coconut* oil men and women used on their bodies and hair and an intrinsic spicy yet musty smell of clothes washed too often and seldom properly dried; of the spat phlegm, cess and dust everywhere trodden in and, over it in the lorry, the strong heady scent of crushed flowers and the withering leaves of garlands.

Dark hands reached out to touch her, voices and eyes pleaded; babies, their eyes rimmed with kohl, were held up to see and for her to see and bless. The voices chanted: 'Jai Krishnan.'

'Jai Krishnan.'

'Jai Shri Krishnan.'

'Jai Krishnan Hari.'

Dr Coomaraswamy's voice boomed on through the megaphone with words Mary could not understand. Mr Srinivasan took his place but his voice was reedy after the Doctor's rounded mellifluent tones, 'Which could coax a bee off a flower,' Krishnan used to joke but, as if the bee had stung, It can't coax Kuku, thought Dr Coomaraswamy.

As soon as the megaphone paused, music and songs from the jeeps and cars took over,

'O Krishnakumar, the one who steals butter,
The one with red eyes,
The one who brings bliss,
O Krishna . . .'

sung with drums, cymbals and the sound of the conch, though now, Mary noticed, it was not Sharma who blew it but a disciple called Ravi.

Over it all was Krishnan enthroned, not moving only smiling, holding up that benevolent hand. I don't care what anyone says, thought Mary, there *is* something mystical about this. Perhaps it comes from the people, their faith, yet it is through Krishnan.

130

One outside moment did break through: towards late afternoon she became conscious that a red car, its sun-roof open, had drawn alongside the lorry with – on its back seat – a photographer, his camera pointing through the window, first directly at her, next at Krishnan; then, as the car drew a little away, it took in both of them. The driver was Mr Menzies and standing on the passenger seat beside him was Kanu, his eyeballs, as they rolled in excitement, showing white in his dark face as, with one hand in easy familiarity, he steadied himself on Mr Menzies' shoulder. A moment Mary had put out of her mind came back, giving a feeling of dismay: that early morning, when she came through Patna Hall on the way to the gatehouse and had run up to the top verandah to look down on the beach to see if Blaise was still swimming, there, along the corridor, was Kanu again, sitting cross-legged on the floor outside a door. This time he was dressed in clean white shorts, a yellow shirt – silk, Mary had thought – a red flower jauntily behind his ear. As he gave her a salaam without getting up, which she knew was impertinent, she had seen on his wrist a new watch. The door was Mr Menzies'.

Why should I have minded that? wondered Mary – and why should she, who hated tell-tales, have said to Samuel, who had come – solicitous as always – to see the lorry off, 'Samuel, that boy Kanu is upstairs again.'

'Kanu?' and, '*Ayyo*,' Samuel said with distaste. 'Miss Baba, I will see to it.'

Now as she saw the new watch gleam on the thin dark wrist, Mary did not like it. She did not like the camera either.

'Mrs Browne,' Dr Coomaraswamy whispered to prompt her. With a start of guilt, Mary went back to Krishnan's afternoon.

Offerings were laid at her feet as well as his, flowers thrown in her lap: marigolds, flaunting scarlet cotton-tree

131

flowers, white mogra buds. Coins were thrown too — they hurt like little flints: *annas, pice,* even cowries — those little shells, used as the smallest possible coins; sometimes whole rupees were recklessly thrown from hard-earned savings. Kuku grew angry. '*Ari!* They hurt!' But Mary was touched almost to tears. 'Scoop them up and give them back,' she wanted to say but knew she must only smile and accept.

'How was it?' Sir John asked when at last the lorry drove into Patna Hall to drop off Mary, Kuku and the disciples before taking Krishnan, Dr Coomaraswamy, Mr Srinivasan and the young women back to Ghandara for Krishnan to rest before the evening *dhashan* he would hold that night. Sir John came to meet them, jumping Mary down among the admiring disciples.

'How was it?'

'Exaltation!' said Mary.

'Mary,' Sir John was grave, 'I want to speak to you and so does Alicia.'

'You're angry! You mustn't be. Oh, Sir John, not tonight. Don't be angry tonight when everything's so wonderful.'

'What could I do?' he asked Lady Fisher.

'You must be tired.' Lady Fisher had come into the hall.

'I'm not in the least bit tired,' and suddenly Mary clasped her in a tight hug, gave her a resounding kiss, kissed Sir John then whirled through the hall on to the verandah where she hugged Auntie Sanni, dared to kiss Colonel McIndoe and a few of Professor Aaron's ladies, Mrs van den Mar, Professor Webster, Miss Pritt and Dr Lovat who had come back from a second expedition to the Dawn Temple. She left them slightly startled, met Hannah and threw her arms round her, darted into the dining room to shake Samuel's hands and the waiters', even the stately

132

Ganga's. 'Where's Bumble?' she called. 'Oh, I expect down at the bungalow. I'll call him. It would be nice to play a silly game. Come on,' she called to the disciples. 'Come down to the beach. Give me ten minutes to get out of these beautiful clothes in the gatehouse and we'll show you how to play rounders. Come!'

Released, too, for the moment, the disciples came with whoops of joy. Soon the beach was full of running white figures with Mary's blue shorts and shirt flashing among them.

'She's over-excited,' said Auntie Sanni, watching from the verandah, where Lady Fisher had come out to join her.

'Violently over-excited,' said Lady Fisher. 'Oh dear!'

'It looks rather fun,' said Dr Lovat. 'Let's go down and join in.'

'I'm not talking to you,' Blaise had said.

'I don't want you to talk. We want you to play.' Changed back into her morning clothes, her face and arms clean where Shyama had reluctantly washed off the kohl, henna and colours — 'She say you much more pretty with,' Thambi had told Mary — she had run into the bungalow bedroom to fetch Blaise.

'Play?'

'Yes, with me and the young men, Dr Coomaraswamy's young men, and I guess some of the ladies.'

'And, I suppose, Krishnan Bhanj.' It was meant to be withering — Mr Menzies' insinuations had rankled — but Mary's, 'Oh, Krishnan has gone back to Ghandara,' was so careless that Blaise felt slightly reassured.

'Play what?'

'Rounders.' Mary had cast off her shoes.

'That's a kid's game.'

'All the better.' Already she was outside and showing

133

the disciples how to mark out the round – 'With my golf clubs!' Blaise, who had followed her, was outraged.

'It won't hurt them. They make good posts.'

'You haven't a bat.'

'This'll do.' She had picked up a flat-faced piece of driftwood. 'Anil. Ravi,' she called to two of the disciples whose names she knew, 'Blaise and I will go first to show you.'

Blaise came portentously forward. 'I'll tell you the rules— '

'We don't need rules,' Mary interrupted. 'We've chosen our sides. They'll pick it up as we go. You'll see. Come on. You bowl, I'll bat. See,' she called to the young men and ladies – five of the cultural ladies had come – 'you have to catch the ball to get me out or catch it and throw it to hit me when I'm between posts and I'll be out. Are you ready? Blaise, throw!'

'You're not playing properly.'

'Don't be such a pomp. Throw!'

They were, Blaise had to admit, quick – he had not yet met India's barefoot quicksilver hockey players – and now two more ladies came. 'Can we join, Mr Browne?'

Mollified by their presence, 'Of course,' said Blaise. 'Join the team. I'll be umpire,' and he threw the ball to Anil.

'We don't need an umpire,' called Mary.

Nor did they. 'Out!' shouted Blaise when Ravi fell headlong by a golf club post a moment before he was caught.

'I'm not out, my head is in,' cried Ravi.

'Out.'

'In,' they chorused, laughing.

'Of course, if you're going to cheat . . .'

You do not, Mary sensed, even in her daredevil mood, accuse Indians of cheating: it is like holding explosives to flame and hastily she intervened. 'Of course we're going to cheat. All of us will cheat. It's part of the fun. I'll cheat. You'll cheat.'

'I don't call that fun and I don't cheat.' Blaise stalked off into the bungalow.

Mrs Glover went after him. 'Mr Browne, do play. You make us feel badly.'

'In England we play games properly. We keep the rules.'

'Well, I don't know about properly and rules but this is real fun and what we needed. We've all been at a high pitch of emotion all day.' Reluctantly Blaise came out but only stood watching.

'Letters for you, Doctor.'

'Not now. Not now.' Dr Coomaraswamy said it irritably. 'Not when I have a thousand, thousand worries.' Then he saw that it was Kuku.

There was no one else on the verandah; except for Auntie Sanni and Colonel McIndoe who had gone to the knoll, everyone else was in their room or on the beach. 'It looks a nice romp,' said Dr Coomaraswamy.

'I do not romp,' said Kuku. 'Besides I have work to do.'

'Unfortunately I, too . . .' Dr Coomaraswamy passed his hand over his eyes as if to shut out doings with which he could no longer cope. Then, 'Kuku, where are you going?'

'To bath and change.'

'I myself must bath and change.'

'But first,' said Kuku, 'I should like my five hundred rupees,' and seeing his face grow immediately stern, came closer with what she knew was a winning smile – the smile he had asked for all day – as she murmured, 'You are not going to fine me, are you?'

She had never been as close; he could smell, not her scent, that had faded in the sun, but, far more tantalising again, her warmth, her girl sweat. Her hair dishevelled,

135

almost brushed his temples – she was taller than he. All thought of Uma faded from Dr Coomaraswamy's mind. 'Kuku, first come to my room.'

'Your room?' Kuku laughed. 'Don't be a silly old man.'

'You are so beautiful. I'll give— ' he swallowed, 'I'll give you another five hundred rupees.'

For a moment a glint came into Kuku's eyes; he thought it a promising glint that made him quiver but she looked down to the beach where, among the dark figures, a blond head stood out as the last rays of the sun going down over the sea, touched the blond to gold.

'Not for ten thousand rupees,' said Kuku, her whole face softened, illumined and, when she spoke next, her voice was soft. 'You see, Dr Coomaraswamy, I too am in love.'

It was beginning to be dusk on the beach; they could no longer see the ball; the play, the running ebbed. At the same time the flames of braziers showed on the roof of Patna Hall while lanterns shone along the parapet. Some time before Anil and Ravi had slipped away; now they came back washed and changed. They stood together and Ravi cried, 'You are invited to Paradise. Auntie Sanni has agreed. Tonight is the end of our campaign so the Root and Flower Party invite you to a barbecue, Indian fashion – on the roof. Please, everyone, yes everyone, come. Sir John. Lady Fisher. Professor Aaron. Mrs van den Mar. Professor Webster. Ladies. Mr and Mrs Browne – par-tic-u-lar-ly Mrs Browne – please to accept.'

'What could be better?' It was Mrs van den Mar's voice.

'Well, I must say,' said Mrs Glover, 'that was the best time I've had in months. Who would have thought my old legs could run as fast!'

'Who would have thought', Miss Pritt was aglow, 'that an archaeological tour could have ended in a children's ball game then being invited to a party by those delightful young men?'

'Charmers all of them,' said Dr Lovat.

'Julia! Beware.'

'They're far too busy,' Dr Lovat said calmly, 'and too committed. Later tonight we, too, shall be truly serious.'

'Yes.' Professor Webster spoke to Mrs van den Mar as they walked up to Patna Hall. 'We mustn't be late for the *dhashan*.'

'We shan't. They'll all be needed for it, the young men,' said Mrs van den Mar.

'But which *dhashan*?' Professor Aaron had come to meet them. 'I've just been listening to the radio news and it seems there will be two, so where do we go?'

'To Krishnan Bhanj's *dhashan*.'

'Both are Krishnan's.'

'That can't be. He can't be in two places at once,' Dr Lovat objected.

'It appears he can.'

It had been in that noon break in the oasis that the news had come to Dr Coomaraswamy. One of the disciples had taken the opportunity of listening to the mid-day radio and had run to get the Doctor to come to his jeep in time for the repeat of the news in English. First the headlines, 'Padmina Retty outwits – and out-distances – Krishnan Bhanj . . .' Then, 'On this, the final day of the campaign, dismayed perhaps by Krishnan Bhanj's, shall we say, "divine progress" through Konak's towns and villages, Mrs Retty has gone into space. She has hired an aeroplane and so today, this final day, she has covered far more of Konak than he. "His poor little lorry is slow," says Padmina. "Ignorant puppy, the very crowds impede

137

it! I shall be swift, able to appear in outlying places he cannot hope to reach . . ." '

'Damn Padmina Retty to hell!' swore Dr Coomaraswamy. He rushed to alert Krishnan who was peacefully eating. 'She will go by air. Do we now have to hire a plane?'

'Copycat,' wrote Krishnan again. 'Aeroplane will utterly destroy image so carefully built up,' he wrote and continued eating, crunching the still crisp *dosas* between his white teeth.

'Then what to do?'

Krishnan licked his fingers and wrote, 'Duplicate.'

'Duplicate?'

'Yes, immediately.'

As one who was now part of the campaign, though only like Vishnu's squirrel helping to build the great bridge by bringing pebbles, Dr Coomaraswamy told Mary about this latest move. 'Fort-un-ate-ly, our benefactor Mr Surijlal Chand has an identical lorry, same make, same colour. It is to be decorated i-den-tic-ally – I have detached some of our young men to see to this – same *pandal*, same garlands, colours and posters and Sharma is so like Krishnan that, i-den-tic-al in dress and make-up, few will tell the difference.'

'He's not nearly as dark,' objected Mary.

'All the better. Krishnan should be fair.'

'Nor as big.'

'We shall seat him higher. We shall be touring until the early hours.'

'What happens', asked Mary, 'if they meet or the people see them both?'

'No matter.' Dr Coomaraswamy spoke almost cheerfully as he echoed what Krishnan had written, 'Hindu gods can duplicate themselves, indeed multiply themselves. Did not Krishna become twenty-four Krishnas to please the *gopis*, the milkmaids?'

'My goodness,' said Professor Webster on the path up from the beach. 'How I'd like to go to both *dhashan*s.'

I only want to go to one, thought Mary.

On the knoll, looking down on the empty beach, the blaze of light on the roof, 'I feel there is a tide,' Auntie Sanni said to Colonel McIndoe. 'Listen to the drums.'

When Blaise came up from the bungalow, Patna Hall's big verandah was deserted.

He had avoided Mary, going into the bathroom as she came out of it, staying there until she had gone, coming out changed into slacks, a thin jersey, then strolling along the beach until he was sure she was at the roof barbecue. He had heard the invitation; at the bar there was no one, he poured himself a drink, then another. He could hear sounds of people going up and down the outside stairs, of American voices, Indian voices, laughter; they came down too from the roof. He turned his back.

Fireflies flickered in the garden and down the path. A garden boy came out to switch on the lanterns down the path sending the bats away where before they had flown and swooped almost brushing Blaise's hair. 'Yuk!' he had cried out in horror; they seemed part, to him, of this horrible night. He had another whisky. 'That girl should have been at the bar,' he muttered but Kuku, too, was up on the roof – though treating the barbecue with disdain, making a point of talking to Professor Aaron and the ladies, not to the disciples, except in their role as waiters.

'Why is the dining room closed?' Blaise had finally come in from the bar to find the dining room empty, the tables bare. Only the youngest waiter, Ahmed, was there fetching glasses from a cupboard. 'Why is the dining room closed?'

'No dinner in dining room tonight.' The boy picked up his tray obviously wanting to get away from this inexplicably angry sahib.

'No dinner! In Christ's name, why not? This is supposed to be an hotel.'

'Plenty of dinner.'

To Ahmed's relief, Samuel appeared. 'Plenty but tonight served up on the roof. Miss Sanni's orders. Come, Sahib, I show you the way.'

'No, thanks.'

'Excellent dinner,' crooned Samuel. 'It is our Root and Flower Party's invitation. Miss Sanni say we all accept.'

'Does she?' Blaise sounded dangerous.

'Indian fashion barbecue. Western as well. I and Ahmed cook that. Sahib enjoy it very much.'

A voice interrupted; in the pantry Ahmed had turned on the radio and the voice of the reader in English came through: 'This is All India Radio. Here is the news. The trial of Colin Armstrong closed today. Mr Justice Rajan . . .' A clatter of plates drowned the rest. Then, 'In the state of Konak, the election has entered an impressive stage . . .'

'Turn that damn thing off!' Blaise almost screamed. Samuel was more than perturbed. That a sahib, one of Auntie Sanni's sahibs, should misbehave – Samuel could not bring himself to say 'offend' – seemed unbelievable. Yet not half an hour ago he had had another such encounter, worse, a confrontation he had to admit. He had caught Mr Menzies in the hall as he went out. Mr Menzies had not been invited to the barbecue but did not seem to mind.

'Menzies, Sahib.'

'What is it? I'm in a hurry.' He had been in a hurry all day, the red car whizzing in and out. 'Well?'

'Sahib, that boy Kanu, he may not come into Patna Hall,' and before Mr Menzies could object, 'If Sahib is needing a body servant— '

'Body servant! That's rich.' Mr Menzies was laughing – it sounded to Samuel like demon laughter. 'Ho! Ho!' He clapped Samuel on the shoulder. 'You say more than you know, old man,' but Samuel shook off the hand as if it had been a snake and drew himself up to look Mr Menzies in the face.

'I am knowing' – Samuel deliberately left out the 'sahib' – 'I know very well, which is why I have to speak.'

The laughter ceased. 'And I suppose you will tell your Auntie Sanni?'

'Miss Sanni,' Samuel corrected him. 'I do not tell such to a lady. I am telling *my* Sahib, Colonel McIndoe.'

For a moment Samuel had thought he had disconcerted Mr Menzies. Then Mr Menzies shrugged and went off whistling to his car. Now Samuel's grave eyes took in Blaise's flushed face, over-bright eyes, the smell of whisky and, 'Sahib must eat,' said Samuel. 'If Sahib too tired to come upstairs, I bring some good things down.' He spoke a few quick words to Ahmed. 'Ahmed is laying you a table.'

'Don't bother. I don't want anything.'

'Sahib must eat.'

'Shut up, you,' shouted Blaise and went back to the bar.

'Miss Baba, come down,' Samuel whispered to Mary up on the roof. 'Ask Sahib to come to the barbecue. Missy, come down, please.'

No, thought Mary, please no.

She had been utterly content, sitting in the firelight on a *durrie* by Auntie Sanni. The disciples had provided stools and benches for their older guests; the rest sat on mats or *durries* while a few of the young men, more adventurous, dared to sit on the parapet, their backs to the sixty-foot drop below, while they ate and dangled their legs. Samuel and his staff had carried up china, glasses and cutlery but Mary had been delighted to see there were also banana leaves and the small metal tumblers used for drinking. The disciples, sniffing success, were overflowing with hospitality and affectionate happiness.

'Eat, please eat.'

'Here is drink.'

'Please, Auntie Sanni.'

'Professor.'

'Lady.'

'Lady.'

'Mrs Browne.'

'Call me Mary.'

'Not Mary, Radha. We think you are true goddess, Radha.'

Up on the roof is nearer to the stars, Mary had been thinking. The sky seemed like a spangled bowl meeting the horizon far out to sea and, as she had seen when she had looked over the back parapet, was met by the tall palms and cotton trees of the village with, behind them, the hills, holders of the cave paintings that had so thrilled the ladies. To the east was Auntie Sanni's knoll, to the west, the sand-dunes lit tonight by a chain of shrine lights, though the grove itself was, at the moment, dark and still. On the lit roof, plied by the disciples, she was contentedly eating the delicious food with her fingers.

'Ugh!' said Mrs Schlumberger and, peering, 'What is it?'

'Delectable!' said Dr Lovat.

'But I like to know what I am eating. It smells.'

'Of course. It's spicy.'

'Memsahib rather have western? Hamburger? French fries?' Anil was anxious to please but when he brought them, 'Not on a *leaf*, boy. I'm not a barbarian.'

'I am, I'll eat them,' Mary offered. 'I'm ravenous,' but Anil had spirited up plate, knife, fork, napkin, while Ravi emptied a pyramid of saffron rice on a fresh banana leaf for Mary. Then Samuel was at her elbow.

'Missy. Miss Baba.'

'Oh, all right.' Like Krishnan, Mary licked her fingers, one by one, laughing. She stood up, shook out her skirt — she had changed into a dress for the *dhashan* — and went downstairs.

* * *

142

'A pretty poor show,' said Blaise, 'a hotel not serving dinner.'

'Blaise, don't you see, it's an exceptional night? Everyone has election fever and there's such good food. I've never tasted real Indian food before. Bumble, do come. Everyone's up there, Sir John, Lady Fisher, Professor Aaron and all the ladies. Auntie Sanni— '

'She's *not* your aunt.'

Mary was too happy to quarrel. 'It won't be long. We will all be going on to the *dhashan*. Bumble, why won't you join in?'

'I did try to join in there, down on the beach and a bloody fool you made me look.'

'I'm sorry. I suppose I was excited.'

'If anyone knows how a game should be played,' the whisky was beginning to work on Blaise's resentment, 'how it ought to be played . . .'

'It wasn't an ought sort of game.'

'Then it ought to be.'

'Ought! Ought!' Mary was near to losing her temper. 'Ought is a bully word. Blaise, why? Why do you have to spoil everything?'

'*I* spoil?'

'Yes,' but Mary felt an odd pang of pity. 'Bumble, please. This is an . . . an enchanted night. Look at the fireflies, the stars. Everyone's so happy, so affectionate. Krishnan— '

'Don't talk to me about that black cheat. Don't dare to say his name. Go on,' shouted Blaise, 'go upstairs to him and his like,' and he slapped Mary hard across her face. 'And you can take that with you.'

The sound of the slap seemed to reverberate through Patna Hall. In the pantry Samuel dropped a dish.

For a moment Mary stood still with shock, the red mark spreading on her cheek. Her hand came up to feel it as if she could not believe it. Then she said, in a whisper, 'You won't do that again. I'm going.'

It was late when Sir John went down to the bungalow. He had left Lady Fisher and Auntie Sanni on the verandah. Kuku had gone to bed. Paradise was dark now, its bonfires sunk to embers; along the beach, the noise of the surf was broken by drums beating from the grove where Sir John could see lights, flares, behind the lights of the shrines as he came down the path. The drums quickened; he could hear the high notes of a flute, then chanting, a slow rhythmic chant. Slippers, driven away by the crowd, was standing looking wistfully at the bungalow. He turned to follow Sir John. 'Better not, old fellow,' Sir John told him and with a pat turned him round.

Blaise, it seemed, had had more whisky — the room's own small bar stood open, its whisky bottle three-quarters empty. Samuel, though his legs were tired, his feet sore from climbing up the steep stairs to Paradise, had come bringing a plate of sandwiches and a basket of fruit; they were on the table untouched while Blaise sat staring out to sea, his head on his hands. When Sir John came in he looked up, glowering, 'I wanted to be left alone.'

'So I gathered but I have come', said Sir John, 'to take you to the *dhashan*.'

'The bloody *dhashan*? That's the last thing . . .' The words were slurred.

'I think you should come, for your own sake,' said Sir John and, peremptorily, 'Stand *up*, boy.'

At first Blaise could not walk beside Sir John but wove an unsteady way, veering down almost to the waves, back up the sand; then slowly the cooler air and the breeze revived him. Soon, too, the size of the gathering began to dawn on him; it reached far wider than the grove, overflowing through the dunes and the fluffy casuarina trees and along the beach. Blaise had seen the crowds that afternoon but here were, 'A thousand? Two thousand?' he murmured, dazed.

'More,' said Sir John. 'Far more.'

The music and chanting had stopped for a breathing space and they heard the stirrings, the undertone murmuring of a reverent multitude, men and women packed close sitting on the sand, the women with flowers in the coils of their hair; some men were bareheaded, most had small turbans – the pale cloth shone in the glow of lanterns hung in the trees and on poles, stretching away as far as they could see. Boys were everywhere, some up the trees; girls, small and older, sat with their mothers.

Among them, like vigilantes in white – again Sir John was reminded of angels – the disciples stood sentinel or moved silently offering *chattis* of hot coffee or pepper water, *biris*, fruit or pān – betel nut. Though the people took them, their heads never moved, their gaze was too fixed on where, in a clear space, a fire burned sending up sparks, while behind it, on a high throne heaped with flowers, sat Krishnan, blue-black as usual, his skin shining with oil, his eyes outlined with kohl, his lips vermilion, the white U mark of Vishnu on his forehead. He looked outsize as he smiled gently, tenderly, on his people. Behind was an elephant Sir John had often seen in the village; now it was unattended, content. On Krishnan's knee sat a squirrel, its grey fur ruddy in the firelight, its tail plumed up. As they watched, Krishnan absently gave it a nut; it nibbled, holding the nut in its paws, its beady eyes giving a quick look at the crowds, then trustingly up at Krishnan. 'I must say he is magnificent,' said Sir John.

Blaise stood staring, a little of the implications reaching him at last – until he saw Mary.

The cultural ladies were here and there among the people; most of them had brought camp stools but Mary sat on a deerskin almost at Krishnan's feet. She was stringing a garland as were the boys squatting round her; as she looked down to pick up a flower her hair swung its bell round her face and fell back as she looked up again to thread the flower; her white dress seemed, like the squirrel, to be stained with red light from the fire. As Blaise looked, she held up the garland towards Krishnan.

'Lady Fisher said she was bewitched.' Blaise's voice was far too loud.

'Hush!'

'She's not bewitched. She's besotted. Sotted.'

'That's an ugly word.' Sir John spoke quietly, firmly, hoping to calm him.

'Ugly! Look at *that*!' Blaise shouted the words out. Krishnan had smiled on the flowers. '*It*'s bloody ugly.'

'*Chūp!*' Sir John used the Hindi word and, at the same time, slapped his hand over Blaise's mouth. 'How dare you disturb everyone? What is ugly in this? The fire, flowers, animals – even the monkeys behave – these children and humble people?' Then, by luck, Sir John saw Thambi standing with Moses and beckoned them with a quick jerk of his head. 'Take Browne Sahib back to the bungalow. *Take* him,' ordered Sir John.

'Jai Krishnan. Jai Krishnan,' and as even greater reverence broke through, 'Jai Shri Krishnan,' then, 'Jai Shri Krishnan Hari.'

Chanting. Music. Silence. Silence, chanting, music; even in the silence the piercing yet sweet call of the flute seemed to go on as Krishnan now and again put it to his lips to play. 'I didn't know how well Krishnan played the flute,' Mary murmured to Ravi when he paused beside her.

'He has to play but, then, Krishnan can do anything,' whispered ecstatic Ravi.

Can Sharma? wondered Mary.

The moon rose higher, began to go down so that it hung lower over the sea. In twos and threes, the cultural ladies began unostentatiously to leave; Professor Aaron followed them. Sir John made his way to Mary. 'That's enough, young Mary. This will go on all night.'

'I *should* have liked to go to the other *dhashan* to see Sharma Krishnan,' said Professor Webster who had lingered.

'That will go on all night too.'

'Yes.' Dr Coomaraswamy had joined them. 'Also, I myself have been back and forth every hour. That *dhashan* is at Mudalier, not far from Ghandara on the inland side, exactly the replica of this. The effect is ex-tra-or-din-ary!' His eyes shone. 'Believe me, some of these people will walk the twelve miles to see the duplication.'

'They believe im-pli-cit-ly.' Mr Srinivasan, too, was in euphoria.

'An extremely successful political trick.' Mr Menzies, in his now almost familiar way, had appeared from nowhere.

'Trick!' Mr Srinivasan's voice was shrill from the affront. 'It is to save the people. They must be saved,' the little man said earnestly. 'Krishnan has made no false promises – unlike other candidates – only the truth, simple truth of what he can do with this holy help, what, we pray, he will do.'

'Well! Well! Well!' said Mr Menzies. 'Be as it may, I am going to look at Number Two. Mrs Browne, can I take you?'

Mr Menzies did not ask Professor Webster and Sir John moved closer to Mary but she had instinctively drawn back. In any case, Sharma after Krishnan, no, she thought, and aloud, 'I think I'd rather not.'

'Good girl,' said Sir John. 'I will take you back.'

'Back?' Startled out of her happiness, panic set in. The slap Mary had forgotten seemed to tingle on her cheek. 'I can't go back. I don't know where to go but I can't sleep in the bungalow with Blaise. I can't.'

'Of course you can't.' Sir John put his arm round her. 'Blaise has had enough, too, for tonight. You are to sleep in our dressing room. Auntie Sanni has arranged it. Come.'

Thursday

When the first beginnings of daylight filtered through the dressing room curtains, Mary still had not slept. Too tired? Too excited? Too dismayed? But she did not feel dismayed, even though she knew the dismay was serious, nor was she tired or excited, only awake and waiting. Waiting for what?

Then it came; the sound of a flute played softly. She flung off the sheet, went to the window and looked behind the curtains. Yes, it was Krishnan standing under the window and with him, in the dim light, she saw the big shape of Birdie.

Krishnan wore no make-up, no garlands, only a clean white tunic and loose trousers, his hair brushed back. As he saw her, he put a finger to his lips, hushing her, then beckoned.

Mary had gone to bed in her slip; now she pulled last night's dress on, brushed her hair with one of Sir John's hairbrushes and, taking her sandals, stole out in her bare feet and ran downstairs.

'Krishnan.'

'Ssh! Mary, would you, will you, come with me?'

Krishnan seemed suddenly young and – not unhappy – troubled.

'Come where?'

'To the temple.'

'The Dawn Temple?'

'No, no. There's a little temple. It's so hidden in the

148

hills hardly anyone knows it. I call it mine. I'm going there to make my *puja*.'

'*Puja?*'

'Prayer. Before the voting. I promised my mother.' He took Mary's hand, twining his fingers in hers. 'Perhaps, Mary, thinking of her, I find myself very lonely. Well . . .' For a moment he was proud again, 'I have to be lonely but sometimes everyone needs . . .' It seemed to be difficult for eloquent Krishnan to find words. Then, 'Mary, will you come with me?' and, rapidly, 'Birdie will take us, it's not far into the hills, as she's always coming and going no one will notice us. I won't be long. You'll be back in bed before anyone is up to see you gone. You— '

'Ssh!' said Mary in her turn. 'Of course I'll come.'

Birdie knelt down to let them climb on to the pad Krishnan had fastened on her back; he swung up and reached down a hand to help Mary. 'Lie down behind me,' he whispered as he settled himself on the elephant's neck.

'I thought no one could drive an elephant except its *mahout*,' said Mary as they went along.

'Perhaps in another time I was a *mahout*.'

Mary had ridden elephants before, short rides in a *howdah* but not in this free, ordinary way; she could feel Birdie's great body through the pad, her shoulders moving, her powerful, comfortable, half-rolling half-swaying gait. Birdie had been well trained: if a branch overhung – this roundabout way to the hills led through patches of jungle – to a command from Krishnan, her trunk came up to break it off in case it hit her passengers. When they came to a swamp she tested the ground with a cautious forefoot before she would venture on it. Presently they began to climb; Mary felt a cooler air and, as she lay, lulled by the rhythmical swaying, she went, at last, to sleep.

* * *

149

The temple was inset into the hills, higher hills fold on fold around it so that it looked out across vistas to the sea; it was walled with small bricks made of native earth turned by centuries of sun to dark gold, as was its courtyard floor of smooth, old stone. There was a stoop for water in one wall and a small pillared pavilion in which hung a bell. 'What a funny smell,' whispered Mary. 'What is it?'

'Bats,' said Krishnan, wrinkling his nose. '*Ghee* gone rancid and, I should guess, crushed marigolds.' She could smell their pungency.

Krishnan set the bell lightly ringing; the sound carried over the gulf all around. Behind the pavilion Mary could see an inner temple, empty under its dome though in the centre of the floor, on a low plinth, burnt a fire with a steady flame. 'It never goes out,' Krishnan told her.

She had woken when Birdie stopped and knelt. Krishnan had lifted her down and she had stood, rubbing her eyes awake, blinking at the sunlight while he brought down from Birdie's back the bundle of sugar cane he had brought as feed, untied it and scattered the canes. '*Kachiyundu*,' he told her in Telegu, as she got to her feet. The little eyes blinked as Mary's had, the mottled ears flapped and Birdie did as she was told.

'Come.'

'Why the fire?' asked Mary.

'This temple belongs to another of the old, old elemental gods like Surya, the Sun God, Indra, God of Storm, Thunder and Rain. This is for Agni, God of Fire. We all love Agni because though he is the son of heaven he lives on earth and in all our homes because he warms them and cooks our food. Perhaps that is why I love to come here when I miss home. Agni can never die because he is born each time we make a marriage by rubbing two pieces of dry wood together or strike a flint or match and he, like us, has to be fed.'

150

Krishnan laughed. 'See, I have brought him an offering of *ghee*.'

As Krishnan poured the butter on the fire and the flame shot up, the priest appeared: not old, a young man wearing only a *lunghi*, his hair oiled back and the Brahmin sacred thread, three-stranded across his chest from his shoulder to his waist.

'Krishna-ji,' he greeted Krishnan as an old and revered friend, making *namaskar*. '*Anandum*. Peace.' He gave a deep *salaam* to Mary, then silently opened a slit of a door behind the fire, motioning them to go in.

Mary had taken off her shoes but still she hesitated, looking up at Krishnan. 'You can go in,' he said, 'but, Mary, it is the innermost sanctuary, infinitely holy. It is in all our temples but you have to find it. You will only find it if you come there to take *darshan* which is simply to be with, behold, God, not kneel or pray, only look . . . look . . . and not with cameras and notebooks . . . People who bring those, cut themselves off, they cannot come in. We call it the womb-house because, as only God is there, in it you can, as it were, be born again.'

'Even I, an outsider?' she whispered.

'There are no outsiders here. Go in.'

Mary went in: the little room, windowless, smelled of incense, the oldest symbol of prayer. It was lit by the flickering of the butter-fed fire and on the wall was a painting, very old, thought Mary, painted directly on to the stone, not of a god or goddess but of a sun rising, its rays still showing traces of pigment, red and yellow; below it, storm clouds were dark and swollen with rain falling. At the base, rising to meet them, as if challenging the storm, rose Agni's flames, coloured red with deep yellow. 'Sun – Storm – Fire – Surya – Indra – Agni,' whispered Mary and, as if he would say that too, Krishnan took her hand again. They stood together, looking as he had said she should look, only looking while, behind them, the young priest took a shallow brass bowl with, in it, five *dipas* burning in oil and, quietly chanting his mantra, waved it before the fire, walking round it.

As they came out, he handed the bowl to Krishnan who waved it too, his lips moving, as the light of the small flames shot high up into the dome. Krishnan handed the bowl to Mary and, as she waved the flames, 'O God, Gods, please, for Krishnan,' she urged in a mantra of her own. 'For Krishnan, please.'

It was late when she woke in the dressing room. 'I shan't go to sleep,' she had told Krishnan. 'I can't after this.'

'At least lie down,' he had said and yawned himself. 'I shall sleep now. I haven't for two nights, it hasn't been possible but, you see, for twenty-four hours before voting all parties have to stop campaigning, not a move, not a step, not a speech. Of course, we are all busy behind the scenes getting ready for tomorrow but dear Coomaraswamy will do that. I shall sleep, sleep, sleep and I am not homesick any more. Thank you, Mary.'

Though Patna Hall had been stirring, no one had seen her go and come; undisturbed she had slipped into bed and, before she could tell it all over again in her mind as she had meant to, she was asleep.

Now as she lay in bright sunlight, for a moment she wondered where she was until she saw Sir John's hairbrushes, ivory-backed and crested on the dressing table, his ties hanging over the looking glass. Someone had hung her dress over a chair, put the shoes she had cast off neatly together; they were a reminder that, 'People expect me to do everyday things . . . I shall have to do them,' she told herself. 'To begin with, go down to the bungalow, wash and get into clean clothes.' She could have asked Hannah to bring her things but, 'You'll have to go sometime,' she told herself. 'With luck, Blaise will be asleep.'

'I'm afraid Blaise will have a massive hangover,' Sir John had said but, of course, sometime he'll have to wake. What then? thought Mary. The mark of the slap was still on her cheek, and it had stung more deeply. 'I'll never speak to him again!' she had vowed. Now, 'Don't be childish,' said what seemed to be an older, steadier Mary. Then, 'What am I to do?' she asked and, as if Krishnan had answered, 'You can try being kind.'

Two days ago, she would have been in revolt against that. Why should I be kind when Blaise . . .? But now she seemed to see, in the temple, the little flames in the bowl as Krishnan waved it, sending the light high into the dome. 'I couldn't send it as high as that,' she whispered. 'But, yes, I can try.'

Slowly, she got out of bed.

'Hannah,' said Auntie Sanni when, on the upper verandah, Hannah brought her morning tea. 'I should like you to go down to the bungalow this morning and see if Manning Memsahib's things are ready to be packed.'

'Packed?' Kuku looked up from where, at Auntie Sanni's dictation, she had been writing out the day's menus. 'You think she won't come back?'

'She may not be able to,' and Auntie Sanni went on to Hannah, 'Do any washing that is needed and Kuku, in any case, put flowers in her room.'

'She owes you so much money, she will probably stay away,' said Kuku.

'That is the one thing that may bring her back,' said Auntie Sanni.

'I'll go to the bungalow,' Kuku offered.

'I asked Hannah,' said Auntie Sanni.

Blaise, a long mound in the wide bed, stayed inert while Mary washed and dressed. He was breathing heavily and, He reeks! she wrinkled up her nose in disgust then, unexpectedly, Poor Blaise! She left the shutters wide open for the sea breeze to blow in, salty, cleansing, and went up the path for breakfast; again, she was ravenously hungry.

After it she lingered on Patna Hall's verandah, trying to will herself to go down to the bungalow. If I want to swim, and I do, I must get my things. She had some sugar lumps for Slippers. He's waiting for me but I'll walk along the beach first, she decided, putting off the moment of going back to Blaise.

As, carrying her shoes, she walked, in and out of the ripples of the waves, the water cold on her feet, the sun warm on her neck, How I love this place, thought Mary. It isn't only Krishnan. She lifted her face to the sun, the breeze and shut her eyes, standing to feel the sun through her eyelids but, 'You can't stay here all day with your eyes shut,' she told herself. 'You have to go back. But what can I say?' she asked. 'What can either of us say after that slap?' Then, 'Be patient. Something will come,' and suddenly, That might be a little splinter of Auntie Sanni's wisdom, she conceded smiling.

The fishing boats were coming in; it must have been a good morning because they had been out twice. Mary could hear the men chanting as they pulled in the heavy nets, long lines of them along the beach. As usual, the best of the catch was being taken either to the refrigerated lorry vans drawn up ready or to the drying sheds; the rest was spilled out on the sand for the fisherwomen to take, either to use or to sell in the villages. A little group was standing looking at something on the sand, something boys were racing up to see.

Mary went closer.

'Bumble! Bumble! Wake up. *Please.*'

Mary was calling that from the verandah but Blaise

was already awake, sitting up in bed holding his throbbing head as she came hurtling in. All Mary's serenity was gone: half sobbing, her eyes wide with horror, she begged, 'Blaise, don't ever, *ever* even think of going swimming further along the beach away from our own. Don't, *please*.'

'What *are* you talking about?'

'You've said you would from the beginning. Remember how cross you were with Thambi and Moses but, Blaise, don't. Don't.'

He saw her shorts were soaked and stained red, her legs too, her arms and hands. 'Is that blood?'

'Yes . . . Yes.'

'Come here,' said Blaise. He was still wearing the shirt of the night before, his hair rumpled; he still stank but Mary came. Gently he pulled her nearer, she was shaking. He put his arm round her and took her to the bathroom.

'Please . . . get the blood off my hands.' Her lips were trembling.

He washed her hands over a *gharra*, washed her face, too, and gave her a glass of water. 'Rinse and spit it out,' then he brought her back to the bed. 'What is all this about? Tell me.'

'The catch was on the beach, the part left for the people to take, fish, flapping and slipping, starfish, crabs. There was a baby shark.' Mary began to tremble again. 'Not longer than three, four feet. They had turned it on its back; it was white and hard though it was a baby. When its tail flailed it knocked over a small boy. Its mouth came down almost to its middle, hideous,' she shuddered, 'almost a half hoop with teeth. Cruel teeth. An old woman bent down to look and touched it and it snapped . . . took . . . took off her hand.' Blaise held Mary fast. 'The other women made a great noise but kept back. Thambi came and clubbed it. I had to help

155

him hold the stump in the sea until the men came and took the old woman away. Blaise, promise me you won't swim anywhere, *anywhere* outside our nets.'

'I thought you didn't care what I did.'

'Of course I care.' How could I help caring about that for anyone? but this different Mary did not say that. A new thought had struck her. That night when I swam with Krishnan, there weren't any sharks – or were there?

But Blaise was speaking urgently. 'Mary, let's go away. There's a mid-day train. Let's go now.'

'Now?' She pulled away from him. Sat up. 'Before the election?'

'Damn the election. It's nothing to do with us.'

'It is. It is to do with me,' she said the words slowly. 'I'm bound up in it,' and, more quickly, 'I couldn't possibly go now.'

'Mary, please. Since we came here everything's been wrong.'

She looked at him in amazement. 'For me everything's been right.'

'It's this Krishnan. You're under a spell.' Blaise was choosing his words carefully. 'Mary, you don't realise it but you are. I'm not going to blame you,' he said magnanimously. 'Lots of girls go in at the deep end when they first meet Indians.'

'In at the deep end?' Mary looked at him, incredulous. 'I'm up. Up where I have never been before.'

'He's using you——'

'That's what's so wonderful and I never dreamed until this morning he could need . . .' again she did not say it as, 'Tell me something,' Blaise went on, 'did you go to him or he to you?'

'I didn't go. I . . . came across him. In the grove our first night. The night you drove me out over Slippers. I sat by Krishnan's fire. We talked,' said Mary, half dreaming.

156

'Was that all?'

'That was all.' All! It was everything.

'Did he ask you to come back?'

'No.'

'Who asked you to go on the lorry?'

'Dr Coomaraswamy.'

'Not Krishnan?'

'Krishnan told him to. I asked the young men to play rounders.'

'You went to the *dhashan*.'

'We all went.'

'Did he ask you to?'

'He never asks.' That had been true – until this morning – and Mary had to pause.

Blaise noticed that and, at once, 'Mary, I want a straight answer to a straight question. Tell me the truth.'

'Krishnan doesn't need to ask.' It was the best evasion she could think of. 'People come to him. They give.'

'More fools they.'

'Don't be horrid.'

'I'm not horrid. I'm worried.' Blaise took her firmly by the shoulders and swung her round to look at him. 'Mary, I have to ask you, have you done anything wrong?'

'Wrong?' She was startled. '*Wrong?*' How could it be wrong? Then she looked at Blaise's face, perplexed as it was honest and miserable. 'You mean . . .'

'Yes. You wouldn't be afraid to tell me, would you?' He was still gentle. 'I'd rather know.'

At that moment Mary liked Blaise more than she had liked him since Bombay and, 'If I haven't told you everything,' she said, 'it's only because you wouldn't have understood but I know I haven't done anything – wrong.'

'I believe you,' said Blaise. 'But promise me one thing.'

'What?'

'That you won't go to the grove or near any of them, unless you are asked.'

Mary thought she owed Blaise that and, 'I won't go unless I am asked,' she said resolutely, at once, perversely remembering under her window at dawn the sound of the flute.

There were footsteps on the verandah. Hannah had come to look after Mrs Manning's things.

'Ayah,' called Blaise. 'Ayah.'

Hannah was not used to being called Ayah but came. 'Will you help the little Memsahib? She has had a shock.'

'Thambi told me.' Hannah clicked her tongue when she saw the blood on Mary. 'Come, Baba.'

'If you don't mind I'll sleep some more,' Blaise said when Hannah had gone. 'Mary, I'm sorry about last night.' He had realised his state. 'Then I'll have a swim, from our beach.' He smiled at her but, It won't do, thought Mary as, leaving him, she went up to the house. 'I want a straight answer to a straight question. Tell me the truth.' That rang in her ears but, 'How can you answer when you are only just finding out?' asked Mary. No one had told her of the Indian concept of truth, that it is like water poured into your hand but you can only catch a few drops.

Professor Aaron and the cultural ladies were leaving.

Their coach was drawn up under the portico/which was crowded with luggage while they gathered in the hall; all had their raincoats, cameras, binoculars, shooting sticks, camp stools and satchels of notebooks. 'Far more full than when we came,' they said in satisfaction. Last snapshots were being taken of Auntie Sanni, Kuku, Samuel, Hannah, Thambi; Professor Aaron was counting heads and trying to placate Mrs Schlumberger. 'We should have had a discount for sharing a room and you should tell Mrs

158

McIndoe about the disgrace of the bathrooms,' but, from the others, 'We've had a wonderful, wonderful time,' was said over and over again. 'We never expected anything like this.'

Miss Pritt was almost in tears. Mrs van den Mar had the recipe for mulligatawny soup, Mrs Glover a collection of flowers Hannah had helped her to press. Professor Webster declared she was coming back next year, 'If you will have me, dear Auntie Sanni.'

'And me,' cried Dr Lovat.

Kuku was dazzled, though at first she had been offended, by large tips. 'No. No, nothing. I cannot take this. I cannot possibly take this.'

'Of course you can, my dear, you deserve it.'

Mary appeared panting. In her distress over the shark she had forgotten the ladies were leaving until Hannah reminded her; she had had to run up the path.

A chorus broke out. 'We thought you weren't coming to say goodbye.'

'Of course I was.'

'I should have hated to go without seeing you.'

They gathered round her, gave her their addresses. 'If you come to the States again be sure to let us know,' and, 'We'd love you to stay awhile with us.'

'My apartment's so small,' Mrs Schlumberger hastened to say, 'I can't offer a guest room.'

'I can offer you three,' Mrs Glover laughed, 'any time.' They thanked her for last night. 'It was real fun,' and, 'You're no ordinary girl,' they told her. 'We didn't know English girls could be like you,' and Mrs van den Mar called, 'Say goodbye for us to that lord of creation of yours.'

'Lord of creation?'

'More than a mite dictatorial,' said Mrs van den Mar. 'My dear, you shouldn't let him.'

'And don't *you* get dictatorial,' said Dr Lovat.

When the coach had gone, Patna Hall was extraordinarily quiet. Are the disciples all asleep? wondered Mary, Or are they away working behind the scenes as Krishnan had said? Dr Coomaraswamy and Mr Srinivasan had breakfasted in the bridal suite, though Mr Srinivasan had been out early to Ghandara. He had come back disturbed. 'Hari, do you know who made all the arrangements for Padmina Retty's aeroplane?'

'Who? Not Surijlal?'

'Surijlal is most loyal adherent. It was that Menzies.'

'Mr Menzies! I thought he was on our side.'

'I think he is playing loose and fast. Hari, I fear trouble.'

'There can't be trouble now,' said Dr Coomaraswamy.

Mary did not want to go back to the bungalow and Blaise. Anyway, he's sleeping it off. Then, Shall I swim? But a shudder came. I'd rather swim with him. Sleep in the sun? She had had little sleep yet was filled with a curious energy. What can I do?

'Mary.'

'It is strange,' Auntie Sanni had said to Colonel McIndoe. 'This girl I have never set eyes on before, nor she on me, seems to feel much as I do about Patna Hall,' and did not all the servants call her Missy, Miss Baba? While Christabel, the pet mynah bird, had begun to call 'Mary' in Auntie Sanni's voice.

Colonel McIndoe had patted Auntie Sanni's hand.

Now Auntie Sanni, wearing a huge white apron and drying her hands on a towel came to call Mary. 'Thursday is the day', said Auntie Sanni, 'when we make what Hannah calls "dainties" — desserts and sweets for the week. These cannot be trusted to Alfredo. Always I make them myself.'

'Yourself! Only Hannah, me, two boys and a washer-up

woman to wait on her,' Kuku was to say in an aside to Mary.

'Also, today, we are crystallising cherries. They have been flown in from Kulu in the north where it is almost the cherry season. These are early. I thought you might like to come and help. Would you?'

'Would I!' If a life belt had been thrown to Mary in a choppy sea she could not have caught it more thankfully.

It was, Mary saw at once, a ritual, 'Every Thursday,' as Auntie Sanni had told her. The confectionery pantry, as it was known at Patna Hall, was separate from the kitchen, in fact in the courtyard annexe, next to the linen room, store rooms and near Auntie Sanni's office. The same flowers were there but no cats, goat or kids were allowed; no birds could fly in; doors and windows were screened with fine mesh.

The room had a tiled floor and walls that could be washed; counters were fitted with surfaces of wood that could be scrubbed and on them were slabs of marble of different sizes. Shelves of copper saucepans, moulds – 'Best French ones,' said Auntie Sanni – were in easy reach, all sparklingly clean and polished with ashes, 'Our washer-up women earn their pay.' The calor gas cooker was large, the refrigerator larger, a vast old-fashioned one run on kerosene; its whirring filled the room punctuated by the cooing of Auntie Sanni's doves outside, the only birds bold enough to come near. Monkeys had thieved some handfuls of cherries as they had been carried in but Hannah had scolded them back into the trees.

The cherries from Kulu, in finely woven travelling baskets, were on the floor; two boys, well scrubbed, wearing white shorts and tunics were carefully de-stalking them under Hannah's watchful eyes. 'To stay fresh, cherries must be picked on their stalks,' Auntie Sanni told Mary.

They were carefully de-stoned, too, the boys using small silver picks, the stones thrown into a bucket, while the cherries were put, carefully again in case they bruised, into large bowls. When enough were ready they were taken to Hannah who was stirring hot syrup, heavy with sugar and tinged with rosewater. 'They must not boil or they won't stay firm,' said Auntie Sanni. 'Then, when they're cooled they will be rolled in fine sugar.'

As Hannah worked her bangles clinked. 'It's not hygienic. You ought to take them off,' Kuku told her.

'They will not come off,' said Hannah serenely. 'My hands are grown too big.'

The crystallised cherries were not only for the week but to last the whole year. 'These are the second batch. Hannah is just finishing off the first – it has taken twelve days.'

'Twelve days!' Mary looked with awe at the racks of cherries drying, plump and tender.

'Fresh syrup has to be boiled every day, then poured over the fruit, then they are drained. On the sixth day the fruit is simmered for three or four minutes – this helps to keep the cherries plump; they are left to soak for four more days. Then you carefully take the cherries out, put them on racks to drain, next in a cool oven to dry until they are no longer sticky to handle. Now Hannah will give them the crystallised finish.'

Kuku gave a yawn but Mary, enchanted by this minutiae, watched how skilfully Hannah dipped each cherry in a pan of boiling water, then rolled it in sugar that had been spread on clean paper.

'Come,' said Auntie Sanni, 'I will teach you to make *rasgula*, a Bengali recipe. See, we take two pints of milk, lemons, semolina . . .'

'Semolina?' Mary was surprised.

'Here it is called *sooji* and we shall need green

cardamom seeds for spice.' The spices, dozens of them, were in a special glass-fronted cabinet.

'They are very costly,' said Kuku. Hot and cross, she pushed her hair back with sticky fingers. 'We could buy these sweetmeats far more cheaply in Ghandara. There are good Bengali sweetmeat sellers there.'

'It wouldn't be the same.'

Of course it wouldn't be the same, Mary felt, almost fiercely. This – this is home, what makes a home, which is why I love Patna Hall so much. She remembered what Krishnan had told her that very morning – her secret morning – of Agni who warms our homes and cooks our food and, 'How can you say it would be the same?' she upbraided Kuku.

'Besides, they haven't the good milk,' said more practical Auntie Sanni. Her desserts were made with rich milk from the Jersey cows she had imported. Their faces look like Krishnan's wise cows, Mary had thought. They were kept in Patna Hall's small homestead behind the knoll where, too, was the poultry yard so that eggs were fresh every day, chickens and ducks provided plump for the table instead of the usual Indian scrawny ones. 'Besides,' Auntie Sanni went on, 'bought Indian sweetmeats are too sweet for Western tastes. But don't think we do all Indian,' she said to Mary. 'We have *hereditary* recipes, some, I think, unique. There is a velvet cream that came from my English grandmother, perhaps from her grandmother, rich cream, lemon, a little leaf gelatine, wine . . .'

'In the recipe it should be raisin wine. We have to use Golconda,' Kuku was spiteful, 'and the cream can curdle as you put it in.'

'Only if you are impatient,' said Auntie Sanni.

'Costs a fortune but that doesn't matter,' said Kuku, but Auntie Sanni only said, 'Put on this apron, Mary, and I'll show you.'

The time went more quickly than Mary could have

163

believed, they were so busy. Samuel brought cold cucumber soup – 'Delicious,' she said – rolls and butter, fruit.

Later, 'Why don't you take this into the dining room,' Auntie Sanni said of the latest confection, 'and let them taste what you have made?'

Only Sir John, Lady Fisher and Blaise were in the dining room, sitting together. Blaise had swum then sluiced himself in the bathroom, put on fresh clothes but his face was pinker than usual. His eyes look as if they had been boiled, thought Mary, which was not kind, I must have cooking on the brain, but how can you help what leaps into your mind?

'This is Mrs Beeton's "Pretty Orange Pudding",' she said putting the dish down in front of them. 'Auntie Sanni has one of the earliest editions of the cookbook, eighteen sixty-one. It says, "Take six oranges", though we took sixty to make ten puddings, for dinner tonight. Mrs Beeton calls it, "A pretty dish of oranges, exceedingly ornamental", and isn't it? I made it.'

She was wearing one of Auntie Sanni's capacious aprons, wrapped and kilted around her; her cheeks were flushed, her hair dark with sweat; her spectacles were askew – 'It's too hot for contact lenses,' she had said – she had a dab of powdered sugar on her nose but to Sir John she looked almost pretty; the grey of her eyes lit almost to blue. 'Thank you, hussy,' he said.

'It is a pretty pudding,' said Lady Fisher.

'Mary seems to have been adopted as the child of the house,' said Lady Fisher.

'She isn't a child. She happens to be a married woman.' Blaise was stiff again. 'Something Mrs McIndoe chooses to forget.'

'Auntie Sanni?'

'I prefer to call her Mrs McIndoe. I'm afraid I don't share your high opinion of her.'

'It's not only high,' said Lady Fisher, 'it's loving. We've been coming here for years, haven't we, John, and we know how wise she is.'

'I don't subscribe to that either. In any case, I am taking Mary away tomorrow, a day early.'

'Will she go?' asked Lady Fisher, which Blaise ignored.

'When she is through with this nonsensical cooking, I'll tell her *and* she has promised me not to go near this Krishnan creature again.'

They looked at him, both incredulous. 'Mary promised that?'

'I'm glad to say she did.'

'I'm not glad,' said Lady Fisher and, 'Blaise,' began Sir John, 'Mary is having an experience—'

'Which I don't choose to let her have—'

'You have just said she isn't a child. Don't you see,' Lady Fisher pleaded, 'how Mary longs to be part of something, to be needed, be of help . . .?'

'She can help me. That's what she married me for, didn't she?' He got up, leaving the pudding. 'If you'll excuse me, I'll go and get some more sleep. I still have a bit of a head and, of course, I apologise about last night.'

When he had gone, 'Insufferable young dolt,' said Sir John, but Lady Fisher only said, 'Poor silly boy.'

The confectionery was over by two o'clock. Hot, sticky all over even to her hair, but happy, Mary ran down the path to the bungalow and came quietly into the bedroom, thinking Blaise might be asleep. He was not; looking considerably ruffled, he was writing a letter.

'Who is that to?'

'Mrs McIndoe.'

'Auntie Sanni. Why?'

Instead of answering he looked at her. 'God, you look a mess. You'd better go and wash.'

'Not before you've told me why you are writing to Auntie Sanni.'

'To tell her we are leaving tomorrow.'

'No!'

'Yes.' Blaise held up a hand. 'Please, I don't want a fuss. Besides, what is there to stay for? You've promised to have no more to do with the election.'

'I didn't say that.'

But Blaise had risen. 'I'm taking this up to the house now.'

How dared he? Left in the bedroom Mary felt choked. Without asking or consulting! She walked up and down in helpless anger, then, I'll go for a swim. It was either that or tears.

Thambi came to help her. Somu too but Thambi, as if he sensed something was more than wrong, took Mary himself, Somu swimming alongside, but there was none of the exhilaration and joy of riding in on the waves. Afterwards they brought a beach umbrella as Mary spread her towel and lay down; only then could she give way.

No tears came though, only indignation. Without even consulting. I can't go now, not before the election, yet how can I stay? Blaise has all our money. She could not be sure where Rory was. Peru – or it could be Washington or London.

Then, suddenly, I know, thought Mary, I'll go to Auntie Sanni. She'll find a way. I'll talk to her tonight after she has seen Alfredo.

It was a comfortable thought; the anger ebbed. Mary gave a great yawn and was soon asleep.

When Mary had gone to sleep, the sun had been hot on her legs so that she had been careful to keep her head in the shade of the umbrella. When she woke she was chill.

As she sat up, rubbing her eyes, she saw that the men had left; the foreshore was empty and the sun was going

166

down, its rays sending a path almost to her feet. She could still feel the battering of the waves on her body; they still crashed down but beyond their white crests the sea was calm, deep blue. Then the sun went behind the horizon, the gold lingered and was gone. The heat haze from the water rose in a mist over the waves; by contrast, a chill little wind blew over the sand.

It was twilight, the Indian short twilight, 'cow-dust time' Krishnan had called it, and Mary remembered what she had seen from the train, cattle being driven home, dust rising from their hoofs, patient cows, lumbering oxen and buffaloes while smoke rose from the cooking fires among the huts of the villages. As she looked now at the bunga-low, lights were up on the verandah: Thambi must have switched them on as he went to his gatehouse, as he had the lanterns along the path.

Why is twilight always a melancholy time? wondered Mary. She listened, there was no sound of a drum. Along the beach no small lamps burned before the shrines. Paradise was dark, everything was in abeyance though probably the disciples were in Ghandara or in other countless voting places getting ready for tomorrow. Probably Krishnan too. That's why the grove is dark and the thought dawned poignantly, I shan't see Krishnan again and, in desolation, I suppose I must – *must* go in and dress, have some dinner – though she wanted neither. She got up and picked up her towel. Thambi or Moses would put down the umbrella when they drew out the fencing along the foreshore. As, reluctantly, she walked towards the bungalow, more lights came on in the other half and she saw Thambi putting down luggage, Hannah drawing the curtains. Olga Manning was there.

'You *have* come back,' Mary said in the doorway and before she could stop herself, 'Auntie Sanni and Hannah thought you mightn't.'

167

'There was nowhere else to go.'

At once Mary's own unhappiness dwindled into an ordinary everyday trouble, this was tragic. Olga's usually erect figure was bowed. Still in her travelling clothes she was making no effort to unpack or change but sat at the room's solitary table looking out at the darkening sea. Under the electric light her skin looked bruised; her hair had come undone, its coil was tumbling down her back; her hands were dirty.

'Olga, is there anything I can do?'

'Please, Mary, I can't talk to you now.' The deep voice was a hoarse whisper.

Mary went next door. Blaise was in the bathroom. Fresh whisky had been put in their bar. She measured a large one, added more, took the tumbler round the partition and put it quietly on the table.

'Bless you.'

'Would you like/. . .' Mary ventured, 'like me to get Samuel to send your dinner down here?'

'My dinner!' Olga laughed. 'I don't think I can say "my dinner" any longer but I suppose one must eat while one can,' and seeing Mary's concern, 'No, Mary darling. I shall change and come up as usual.'

For dinner the dining room was full. Dr Coomaraswamy and Mr Srinivasan were eating less hurriedly than usual. 'I have only two speeches to write,' Dr Coomaraswamy had said and Mr Srinivasan, 'A success speech and a loss speech – just in case.' 'Victory! Victory!' Dr Coomaraswamy had let himself write but, 'Victory is not yet,' said cautious Mr Srinivasan.

Auntie Sanni and the Colonel and Mr Menzies were at their accustomed tables. Olga Manning had appeared, groomed, clean, changed, to Mary's relief and had gone unobtrusively to hers, only nodding to Auntie Sanni; Blaise and Mary were dining with the Fishers, 'As it's our last

168

night.' Mary did not contradict him. At least it means I needn't talk to him.

The diners were augmented by a dinner party of men. 'From Ghandara,' Sir John told them. 'Here for some kind of conference.' It seemed to be a festive meeting; there was laughter, even cheers as Kuku, in the beautiful violet-coloured silk sari Lady Fisher had given her, flitted round them. Dr Coomaraswamy kept his eye on his plate as the banter filled the room.

Suddenly it ceased. 'This is All India Radio. Here is the news.' There was absolute attention. 'I expect there'll be something about their meeting,' whispered Blaise as the news began but first was the election.

'In Konak, expectancy is tense on this day before voting as interest mounts in the struggle between the long-established Mrs Padmina Retty and Krishnan Bhanj's new Root and Flower Party. In spite of Mrs Retty's helicopter, all yesterday it was Krishnan Bhanj who drew the crowds. In fact today he has had to hide himself to avoid the charge of illegally campaigning. "He campaigns in spite of himself," said Dr Coomaraswamy, leader of this brilliant concept. Here are a few words from Dr Coomaraswamy himself . . .'

As his words boomed out, Dr Coomaraswamy kept his head bowed while the whole room listened. Samuel had interrupted the serving; he and the waiters stood respectfully still. Only Kuku moved and flaunted. When the voice finished everybody clapped.

The news, though, was not finished: 'Today in Calcutta, Mr Justice Rajan sentenced the Englishman, Colin Armstrong, to twelve years' imprisonment. Mr Armstrong was convicted of fraud, smuggling and trafficking in drugs.'

At an imperative nod from Colonel McIndoe, Samuel switched off the radio. At the same moment Mr Menzies got up and crossed the dining room to Olga Manning's

169

table. 'Good evening, Mrs Armstrong,' he said.

A gasp went from table to table. The whole dinner party had turned to look. Mary sprang up but Blaise pulled her down as Auntie Sanni rose to her massive height. Her dress billowing, she, too, crossed the room. 'Mr Menzies,' she said, 'you will leave my hotel, *now*.'

'Of course you knew he was Ajax?'

'I'm afraid I didn't.' Blaise blushed.

'No? I should have thought those recordings, those articles were unmistakable.'

'Auntie Sanni knew from the beginning,' Lady Fisher had pleasure in saying.

'Then why didn't she turn him out before?'

'He was being very useful,' said Sir John, 'bolstering our election. Auntie Sanni, remember, is a dear friend of the Bhanj family and Menzies could hardly have been more helpful but tonight . . . Swine!' said Sir John.

'After all this distress and unpleasantness,' Blaise said a little later, 'what I feel like is a game of bridge.'

'Sensible idea,' Sir John stopped walking up and down. 'But we haven't a four.'

'Mary,' said Blaise, 'it's time you learnt to play.'

'You know I hate cards.' She was seething with – she sensed unreasonable – anger and indignation. 'If you're uncomfortable about anything, play cards!'

'There is nothing we can do for Mrs Manning,' Sir John told her gently, 'She has gone with Auntie Sanni so she's in good hands.'

That was part of the dismay. There would be no chance now of talking to Auntie Sanni. So I'm trapped, thought Mary, trapped.

'McIndoe might play,' Sir John was saying. 'He sometimes does. I'll ask him.'

The Colonel got up, willingly Mary thought. I expect he, too, wants to put this out of his mind. Kuku brought

170

the card table, fresh packs of cards, score pads and stood by while they sat down, her eyes fixed on Blaise as Lady Fisher dealt.

Mary had thought of asking Sir John to intercede with Blaise; now she remembered vividly how once Lady Fisher had – gently, it was true – remonstrated with her when she, Mary, had gone to the bazaar instead of the Dawn Temple, 'As Blaise so wanted you to do,' and she had retorted, 'I've been doing what Blaise wanted for three whole weeks. Can't I have anything for myself?'

No sympathy, instead, 'Diplomats have to keep a certain position,' Lady Fisher had not said 'prestige'. 'Their wives, in a way, have to be diplomats too, even if it means tremendous self-sacrifice. I did it, your mother did it, so why not you?'

It would be no use talking to either Fisher – and a surge of frustration filled Mary, made worse when, 'Mary,' said Lady Fisher, 'come and talk to us when one of us is dummy.' 'Good God, *no*!' Mary wanted to scream but succeeded in only shaking her head. She stood up and put on Blaise's jacket. 'I think I'll go to bed. I'm chilly and tired.' Yes, go to bed, put her head under the sheet and shut out everything, everyone and never care about anything ever again.

As she stood up on the path, the shadowed garden seemed dark and empty, the lanterns on the path dim. Only the lights on Patna Hall's verandah were bright, shining down on the four heads bent over the green table. Bridge! thought Mary furiously.

A waft of sweetness came to her. Who was it who had once told her that flowers can send you a message? The scent was queen of the night, with its small scented flowers. Carnations? Roses? I know what I can do, thought Mary. I'll pick a bunch of flowers to put in Olga's room, with some more whisky. That will show her at least *someone* cares about her. In the pocket of Blaise's jacket was a small mother-of-pearl-handled penknife; she took it out. Cutting stems along the borders was soothing, laying one flower against another, sniffing the fragrance; the storm in her mind began to lull, and, though she could not exactly remember the words, she began to hum that Hindi lullaby . . .

> 'A cradle of . . .
> A cord of silk . . .
> Come, little moonbird . . .'

When she had cut enough she went, softly singing, down the path. 'All right, Slippers,' she called, 'I'm coming.' She had his sugar and carrots in her handkerchief.

He whickered back.

'Tsst.'

A small boy stepped out of the shadows. Mary knew him; he was one of the boys she had made garlands with. True, he had tormented the squirrel but he was smaller than the others and had attached himself to her, hanging all day yesterday around the lorry. Now he held out a paper to her, thin Indian paper folded. She recognised Krishnan's writing and her heart began to beat quickly as she took the paper to the nearest lantern to read.

'Mary, can you come and help me? I am alone.'

'Krishnan Sahib. Where is Krishnan Sahib?'

The boy pointed along the beach.

He's here! In the grove! A surge of happiness rose in Mary but she looked towards the verandah.

'*Kachiyundu*,' she said to the boy as Krishnan had said at the temple to Birdie, '*kachiyundu*. Wait,' and gestured that she would give him money.

Forsaking Slippers she ran to the bungalow, left his sugar on the chest of drawers, quickly arranged the flowers in a vase, carried them and a glass of whisky

172

to Olga's room then wrote on the back of the paper 'For Blaise. You see I *have* been asked!' In the pocket of his jacket she found some change and, taking a rupee, she hung the jacket on the back of a chair – she was no longer chill. Tingling with warmth, she ran back to the boy. 'Take this,' she gave him the paper, 'take,' she pointed to the lit verandah. 'For Sahib.' She held up the rupee.

The boy's eyes gleamed as he saw it. He nodded, took the rupee and the note and set off up the path. Mary watched him then, 'Stay,' she said to the disappointed Slippers, 'I can't stop now,' and ran to the beach.

She did not see a bigger boy, wearing a yellow shirt, leap out of the bushes and jump on the smaller one, screwing the rupee out of his hand and beating him until he fled.

For a moment the boy in the yellow shirt scrutinised the note, crumpled it and let it drop as he set off after Mary.

The note lay on the side of the path.

Mary did not have to go as far as the grove. From a distance, across the stretch of moonlit sand, she saw what first seemed to be a dark rock in the froth and whiteness of the waves' edges. It can't be a rock, she thought, this beach doesn't have rocks. Then, as she came nearer, she could see a figure standing on it, a dark-skinned figure wearing only a loincloth. As she looked, something like a thick snake came up – A sea monster, thought Mary for a horrified moment, or no, a hose, as a spray of water was sent up into the air then fell, deluging the figure. '*Ayyo!*' came a furious voice. '*Mōsāgadu! Pishācha mu!* Bad girl! Devil!'

It was Krishnan. He saw Mary and came to meet her, streaming with water, his hair in wet streaks.

'I thought you were hidden at Ghandara, or are you your double?'

'In a way, yes. Sharma is there. But come, we are wasting time.'

As he spoke the rock stood up — an elephant, Birdie.

Mary stared. 'What *has* happened to her?'

'You may well ask. Idiots! Idiots!' It was the first time Mary had seen Krishnan angry.

Birdie had been painted — Decorated? thought Mary — her forehead and trunk, her sides and legs bedizened with patterns in yellow, vermilion, indigo, black and white; her ears were patterned as was the length of her trunk. 'Idiots!' cried Krishnan again. 'They have spoiled everything.'

'Spoiled what?' Mary had to ask.

'Tomorrow, election day is crucial — you know that.' She nodded. 'All parties will go each in their procession through Ghandara ending at the town hall; the candidate from Madras, Gopal Rau, of whom no one seems to have heard, Mrs Retty and us. Gopal Rau will not have much, Padmina will have everything, a great *tamasha* — razzmatazz, bands, military, maybe even a tank, loudspeakers. She has a white jeep but probably she'll arrive in her aeroplane.'

'And you?'

'We shall have nothing.'

'*Nothing?*'

'Let Padmina have the blare, we shall be dulcet.' Krishnan lingered on the word; he had recovered himself. 'Fortunately, she has chosen to go first, then poor Rau, so we shall be last which is propitious. The last will be first.' He laughed. 'In front will walk our young men and women, the men all in white, feet bare — they will be making *namaskar* — the girls in our colours, muslin saris, simple, hair coiled with flowers, they will be leading garlanded cows—'

'The *gopis*,' said Mary.

'Exactly. For weeks we have been fattening them and grooming them — the cows not the girls. Then will come children; we have chosen the healthiest, again a little plump. The boys will have garlands and carry paper kites, again in our colours; the little girls will have baskets of flowers to scatter, constantly replenished,' he sounded as if he were Dr Coomaraswamy. 'They will sing. For other music there will be only the conch, drums, a single flute. I think there will be silence to hear it. We must leave room for reverence.

'Then will come my friend the priest from Agni's temple, wearing a saffron robe with his beads, his staff — he is of height but not the height of me. He will lead a sacred bull. Then I shall come, not in regalia or paint as the god Krishna but as I, myself' — and he said, 'I sound like Coomaraswamy — not wearing a best English suit but, like my people, a loincloth, walking in the dust . . . little Udata on my shoulder.'

'If she'll stay.'

'She'll stay. I, not riding on an elephant but humbly leading her, she to be carrying her fodder on her own back.' The fury returned. 'To decorate an elephant takes two, three days and we must wash it off tonight — the *mahout* is too drunk to help. To call the village or fishermen would be publicity, take away surprise. Look, I am scrubbing Birdie's sides, legs and feet with sand and a brick. That is too heavy work for you but could you do her face and ears? I went to the Hall and borrowed scrubbing brushes — but be careful, her ears may flap you.'

'Won't Birdie mind?'

'She adores it, all elephants love their bath and she is accustomed. She does, though, get playful — watch her trunk. When you come to do her trunk stand astride it so that if she lifts it you will only tumble into the wash of the sea, but you will be soaked as I am. Better take off your dress,' and, suddenly formal, he said, 'Mrs Browne, it is most good of you to come.'

'Browne with an e.' Mary felt suddenly impish.

175

'Browne with an e,' said Krishnan and laughed again. 'Oh, how I like you, Mary. I like you very much. See, my temper has gone.' Suddenly, too, he leapt and danced across the beach, did handstands, then, 'That's enough. Come to work.'

'Is Mary with you?' Blaise was standing at Olga Manning's door.

The game of bridge had petered out as soon as Auntie Sanni came out alone on the verandah. Colonel McIndoe immediately laid down his cards with an apology, got up, went with her to the swing couch and sat down beside her. Sir John and Lady Fisher followed them, leaving Blaise at the table; he shuffled the cards, put them into neat packs, stood a moment looking over to the now moonlit beach. Then, 'I had better go down to Mary,' he said, and to Auntie Sanni, he began, 'I know I booked for a week but . . .'

'You will not be charged for the extra day.' Auntie Sanni cut him short.

'Well, goodnight.'

Talking in low tones, their faces grave, they hardly noticed him go.

At the bungalow steps Slippers was patiently waiting, he was missing Mary and, 'Where is my ritual of carrots and sugar?' he was patently saying. He whickered at Blaise who only said, 'Shoo,' then waved his arms, advancing so threateningly that the little donkey shied away.

'Merry, where are you?'

No answer.

'Mary.'

The room was empty, the shutters wide open, the bathroom empty too; the bedsheets were folded back, his *lunghi* and Mary's short nightdress laid out in Hannah's way.

'Is Mary with you?'

176

Olga Manning came to her door. She was wearing a faded kimono, her hair hanging down her back; even Blaise noticed the tiredness of her face and was moved to say, 'Rotten about your husband.'

She flared. 'It isn't rotten. It never was. Colin did not do that. He was framed.' She put her hand to her throat as if it choked her to speak. 'Better not talk about it. No, I haven't seen Mary.'

'Didn't she come to the bungalow?'

'Not that I know of,' and Olga offered, 'She goes to the grove.'

'I know but they're all at Ghandara.'

'Krishnan Bhanj isn't. I met him in the hotel garden as I came down.'

'Krishnan Bhanj?'

'Yes,' and innocently Olga said, 'Perhaps she has gone to see him.'

It was Blaise's turn to flare. 'Then she has broken her promise.' He stopped and his own innate honesty made him say, 'Yet I'm sure Mary wouldn't do that.' Then the seeds Mr Menzies had sown began to grow. 'Or would she? It seems she will do anything,' and bitterness burst out. 'We haven't been married a month. You'd think she could be faithful for just a month, and with an *Indian*. All right,' he shouted. 'All right!'

He strode across the verandah on to the beach.

'Phew!' Krishnan stood up, wiping the sweat and salt water off his face with his hand. 'There seems to be a mighty lot of elephant.'

The paint had lodged in the cracks of the coarse grained scaly skin. 'They must have put oil in the tempera,' said Krishnan. Both he and Mary were stained with the yellow, vermilion and blue; the black had got under Mary's nails; only the white came off in flakes.

'I should have thought the fisherboys would have loved

177

to help.' She rested: after a fierce bout of scrubbing her arms ached.

'They would but they would have talked.'

'How did you get rid of them?'

'Told them to go.' His look seemed to say, 'How else?'

'It's odd,' Mary put back a wet strand of her hair, staining it red, 'when you tell someone to do something, they obey and want to do it.' She was thinking aloud. 'When Blaise tells them, they don't – and won't. Why?'

'Because Blaise Sahib is Blaise Sahib and Krishnan is Krishnan. There is no other explanation. There never is,' said Krishnan.

A voice came from the beach. 'Mary. Mary. Where are you? Come back at once.'

Blaise!

He came bearing down on them, with a splat of wood – the piece of flotsam they had used in rounders last night – in his hand. 'Mary!' The shout was so loud that Birdie surged to her feet. Blaise stopped and gaped. 'What in hell are you doing?'

'As you see, giving an elephant a bath,' Krishnan said equably.

'Giving an elephant a bath? What tomfoolery is this?'

'It is anything but tomfoolery. For reasons I have no time to explain, it is imperative she is bathed,' and, '*Ūrakundu*,' Krishnan ordered Birdie, '*ūrakundu* – Lie down.'

'In any case I was not speaking to you,' said angry Blaise. 'I have come to fetch my wife. Do you hear?'

'Then you are speaking to me.'

'Yes.'

'Ask her if she wants to go,' Krishnan said between scouring – Birdie was recumbent again. 'Better stand back if you, too, don't want to be soaked.'

'Mary, *will* you come?'

'I can't. An elephant has two ears, and I have only finished one.'

Blaise turned on Krishnan. 'I also came to have this out with you. Come on.' He brandished the splat of wood.

'My dear man, I'm far too busy to fight with you just now,' said Krishnan. 'Why not forget it, get a brick — there's a pile over there — and help us?'

The hand holding the wood dropped as if Blaise were bemused. Mary again felt that pang of pity. 'Yes, Bumble, be a sport' — she knew that word would appeal to him. 'Join in. There's nothing to be cross about.'

'Nothing to be cross about! I'm not a fool. Do you think I don't know what's been going on?' Astonished they stood up though Krishnan kept a quiescent hand on Birdie. 'Look at you,' screamed Blaise, 'both half naked and soon you'll be more naked from what I hear. I'm not going to have it,' and he advanced on Mary with his splat.

'Don't do that,' Krishnan warned him. 'You won't want to have done that.'

'Out of my way,' and Blaise came on.

With one leap Krishnan was off Birdie, caught Blaise and, with a twist, sent him spinning down on to his back on the sand; next moment Krishnan had lifted him and set him on his feet. 'Go back to the Hall,' Krishnan said sternly. 'Mary will doubtless come when we are finished.'

'We! You impertinent bastard.'

'I am not impertinent and I am not a bastard and I don t want to have to knock you down again,' said Krishnan. 'Please go so that we can get on with the work — the little elephant is getting tired and hungry.'

'I'm not one of your sycophants', ranted Blaise, 'to do what I'm told. Do you think I don't know all about you pseudo Krishnas? We have them in England too. You with your young girls and boys, your slaves.'

Krishnan took no notice but worked on with his brick.

'Mary!' It was a bellow now. 'I'll give you one more

179

chance. Come now or don't come at all. Which? *Which?*'
Mary did not answer; she, too, went on scrubbing, this
time on Birdie's second ear.

For a moment Blaise stood irresolute in his anger,
then before turning, he spat.

'*Blaise* spat!' Mary sat back on her heels amazed.

'Being an Indian I can spit further than you,' Krishnan
called after him. 'Naturally. We have had centuries of
practice.'

Even Krishnan did not see a small yellow-clad figure
come out from behind the nearest casuarina tree and take
itself quickly to the road where a red car was waiting.

Blaise heard the noise before he came into the bedroom,
heavy hoofs clopping about on stone. Seeing him gone,
Slippers had dared to come into the bedroom, seeking the
sugar he thought was his due. He had knocked over the
photograph of Blaise's mother that stood on the dressing
table, breaking the glass; nuzzled brushes, combs, creams
and lotions off on to the floor and now, having found
on the chest of drawers the sugar Mary had left, was
munching contentedly when Blaise switched on the light.
At the sight of him, Slippers gave the equivalent of a
donkey scream, a bray.

'What are you doing here, you little brute?' and, seeing
the devastation, all Blaise's thwarted anger broke. 'Take
that and that,' the splat of wood came down again and
again. '*Chelo. Jao.* Go. Go. *Hut jao.* Go at once. *Chelo.
Chelo.* Hurry up.' But Slippers could not go. In panic,
slithering on the floor, trying to get away, he had penned
himself behind the bed. The little donkey's ears were laid
back, his eyes rolled but he could not move. '*Hut jao!*'
There was a sudden stench: a flux of liquid dung spattered
on to the floor. 'Christ! Phewgh!' screamed Blaise.

'He couldn't help it.' Olga Manning had come in.

180

'You drove him behind the bed. Here, help me push it and let him out,' and, to the miserable donkey, 'Here, boy, gently, boy. Come. Come.' Trembling, guided by her hand, Slippers back-clopped out and fled. They heard him slipping on the verandah then crash down the steps.

'You deserved that,' Olga said to Blaise. 'I'm glad he did it. Just because you can't juggernaut over your very nice wife, you take it out on an animal. You big bully.'

'Go away and mind your own business!' Blaise exploded. 'A dirty business it is from what I hear, dirty, no matter what you say. Go!'

'With pleasure,' said Olga. 'You can clear up the mess.'

Kuku answered the house telephone — she had an extension in her room. 'What? *What?* My God, how disgusting! I am coming down. Go on to the verandah and we shall come. I am bringing the sweeper women, hot water, disinfectants.'

The explosions had done good and Blaise was calmer now. 'I'm sorry to have disturbed you.'

'You didn't disturb me in the least,' but Kuku was in a thin wrapper dressing gown; the two sweepers, roused from sleep for the second time that day, were grumbling under their breaths.

'I'm afraid I did disturb you but donkey shit is no joke.'

'Certainly it is not. I shall speak firmly to Miss Sanni in the morning. As for disturbing, that is what I am here for. Now, while the women are finishing, let me straighten the bed.'

As she bent forward, the dark hair brushed the side of the bed where Blaise's *lunghi* was laid; as she carefully smoothed it, her wrapper swung open showing the rounded brown body, the perfect small breasts, rose-tipped nipples. Modestly Kuku caught the wrapper together, glanced up at Blaise and laughed.

Blaise had not looked, really looked, at Kuku before, taking her almost as part of the hotel furniture and not far removed from Samuel and Hannah though he had thought her saris a little flaunting. 'Showing off,' he would have said.

Now he was struck with her beauty, provocative beauty: the small roguish face set in the mane of black hair, eyes brilliant — and knowing — below expressive eyebrows and, when she looked down, as she met his gaze, he saw the long lashes that had so entranced Dr Coomaraswamy. Kuku's mouth was slightly pouted, she had a small tip-tilted nose, small pretty teeth. When she stood up, supple in every movement, and tightened the wrapper round her, Blaise could see through it even to the fuzz of hair between her thighs; it was dark brown not black; at once he felt an answering movement in himself. 'I suppose I've been starved,' he almost said aloud, pitying himself.

'Now that the sweepers have gone, let me get you a drink.' With her gliding undulating walk, Kuku went to the small bar. 'You were so-o distressed,' she crooned.

'Well, donkey shit on your bedroom floor.' Blaise tried to be normal.

'Disgusting!' She brought him the glass. 'I have put ice in it.'

'You deserve one.'

Kuku's eyes shone but, 'Auntie Sanni doesn't let me drink.'

'Just for me,' said Blaise and she poured a small one.

'And give me another,' he said.

She brought it. Now she was so close he could smell her scent and sweat, as the Doctor had done; as he took the glass her fingers touched his; he let them tighten.

'Kuku is a beautiful name.'

She shrugged. 'One gets tired of it. "Kuku do this.

182

Kuku do that." Day in, day out. I am an orphan, you know. I cannot do what I want.'

'What do you want, Kuku?'

She looked up at him. 'You,' breathed Kuku. The worship in her eyes was balm to his soreness. 'I have loved you from the first moment I saw you,' she whispered. 'These people are all blind. They do not know what you are.' This was balm too. 'Your little silly Mary thinks she has found a god in that Krishnan. I know when I have found mine.'

The two heads, black and gold were together on one pillow; the sheet, thrown back, showed brown and pale legs closely entwined. Kuku's hand again and again caressed while his played with a strand of her hair. 'Kiss me, a long, long kiss,' and, 'Love me again,' pleaded Kuku.

'No more.' Blaise was sleepy.

'One more.' She bit him on the ear, raising a spot of blood. 'I'm a tiger.' A shrill squeal of laughter.

'You're a mosquito.' Another shriek as he rolled over on her again.

'No! No!' squealed Kuku.

'You asked for it . . .'

'Well. Well. Well.' Once again it was Olga Manning. 'You'd think', she mocked, 'he could be faithful for one month – and with an Indian.'

An outraged shriek came from Kuku as, startled, she snatched her wrapper and ran to the bathroom. Blaise, caught mid-way in the act, looked up as dampness spread round him.

'I'm sorry I interrupted you', Olga was contemptuous, 'but I couldn't think what the noise was. Well,' she said again, 'you've done it now.'

'Have I? Did I?' He sounded dazed. Then, as he looked round the room, the floor still wet where the sweepers had washed it, his clothes flung down on it, and smelled disinfectant mingled with the jasmine scent on his pillow, realisation came back, realisation and disgust. 'To hell with all women,' shouted Blaise. He caught up a towel, pushed past Olga in the doorway and out on to the beach.

'That was the last I saw of him,' Olga Armstrong was to say.

It was beginning to be dawn, the sky paling over the sea as Krishnan at last led a clean and shining Birdie out of the waves; not a speck of paint was left on her as she stood, flapping her ears to dry them, lifting her trunk in happiness to spray herself again. 'She did not like the paint either,' said Krishnan as he took her up the beach. 'Now she must have a good feed. I have sugar cane, *gram* and *jaggery* balls which she loves.' Mary followed them wringing the water out of her slip. She was so tired she staggered.

'For us I will make some tea. You must take off your wet things. Here, dry yourself with this.' He threw her a towel.

As Birdie contentedly ate, breaking up the cane with her foot and trunk, picking up the balls and stuffing them into her mouth, Krishnan put the remains of the fire together, poking it with a stick, throwing on pieces of wood. He had lit a small methylated stove, incongruous in that setting, but soon a pan of water was boiling and he threw in tea leaves. Mary, unaccountably shivering, was glad of the fire, even more glad when Krishnan handed her a bowl of strong sweet tea. She had pulled on her dress, hung her slip and briefs on a bush to dry.

'A little rice?'

She shook her head. 'I had dinner.'

'More than I had.' The rice had been left cold. Krishnan warmed it, mixed it with dried fish, and soon was scooping it up with his fingers. Again she saw how white and even his teeth were.

'I think,' he said, 'it would be better if you did not go back to your husband tonight.'

'I don't think I could.'

'The question is, what to do with you? All Patna Hall will be asleep and we don't want to cause a stir. If I made you comfortable, here in the grove, would you be afraid?'

'I'm too tired to be afraid.'

'True. You're half asleep,' but, 'Where will you be?' she asked, all at once awake.

'Udata and I have to ride Birdie to Ghandara. I dare not trust Birdie to her *mahout* and his people. They might try to paint her all over again.' He laughed.

'Krishnan, are you ever tired?'

'Not when I cannot be.' He got up. 'Here is a clean *lunghi*. Sleep in that.'

He arranged a bed for her on the deerskins, taking quilts and pillows from the throne. Mary lay down, the *lunghi* round her. Krishnan tucked its end in, Indian fashion. 'Your hair will dry. Sleep.'

But, 'Krishnan, what about Blaise?' she asked. 'Is it my fault? Why is there all this trouble?' and Krishnan answered as he had answered before, 'Because you are you and Blaise is Blaise. The two don't mix.'

'Then what am I to do? How can we live together?'

'You will get older,' said Krishnan. 'So will he. I don't think he can change but you will learn how to live with him – and not mix – as many wives do, the wise ones. Indian women, I think, are particularly wise in this: they know how not to mix yet never let their husbands guess it.'

'Must I?' asked Mary.

His hand closed over hers; she could have stayed with that warm clasp for ever.

'There are destinies,' Krishnan said. 'Yours and mine. But don't think of that tonight. Go to sleep.'

He took his hand away, touched her hair and left. She heard him call to Birdie, then a rustling as they went through the trees.

Friday

Mary was woken by the parakeets. A pair was quarrelling in a tree overhead, their bright green flashing between the dark-leaved mango branches, their red beaks chattering as they made their raucous cries. Perhaps they're husband and wife, thought Mary smiling – Blaise and me – then ceased to smile as she remembered the angry words on the beach. Krishnan did his best, even when he had to interfere. Mary thought Blaise would really have hit her; He slapped me before. She shut her eyes trying to keep thoughts of Blaise out of the way. This is Krishnan's day, his vital day. She thought of him riding Birdie away last night, through the dark – with Udata, of course; Birdie would be docile. Docile, dulcet, there was a sweetness about those words; with Krishnan everything, everyone became docile – even me, thought Mary and, Yes, I must go back.

When she sat up she found she had been showered with scarlet petals, the *simile* trees were dropping their cotton flowers. In one week they are going over, thought Mary and realisation came to her – Today we go away too. She could not believe it, the very thought brought such a feeling of emptiness that she hurriedly put it out of her mind. 'Don't think about it yet,' she told herself. Instead, 'Today is the election.'

Krishnan will win, thought Mary. He couldn't not, yet the sceptical voices intervened: 'Of all the way-out notions.' 'The man's mad!' 'Masquerading as a god.' Krishnan himself had told her, 'It will be tricky.' Mary picked up a cotton flower that had fallen without breaking and began to pick off the petals. 'He will win. He won't. He will. He won't.' Yet knowing, as the scarlet petals fell over her feet, they would end, 'He will.'

'But I', she whispered, 'have to go back to Blaise.'

'Must I?' she had asked Krishnan.

'I think you must.'

If I can, thought Mary. I . . . I have to get over myself first. I can. She picked up another flower. 'You can. You can't. You can.' Mary sat looking at the sepals of the flower, bare now that the brilliantly coloured petals had gone all but one. She pulled it. 'You can't,' it said.

'The elephant was decorated especially and at great cost for the pomp,' pleaded Dr Coomaraswamy.

'I had told you, *ordered* you.' The campaign was over. Krishnan could speak. 'There will be no pomp.'

A bitter scene was going on in the Ghandara headquarters between Krishnan and Dr Coomaraswamy.

'You have undone the elephant,' the Doctor almost screamed. 'After such work! Such cost!'

'Against express orders.' When Krishnan was cool, it meant he was angry.

'*I* am the director of this campaign,' Dr Coomaraswamy blustered.

'He is the director,' Mr Srinivasan echoed.

'And I am the campaign.'

'True. True,' said Mr Srinivasan, 'but—'

'There is no but. Everything is to be carried out exactly as I said.'

'Krishnan, think. I beg you to think. This is *the* day. The crucial day.'

'Then this is all the more crucial.'

'Surely it is time for a little display? True, you have brought the people out marvellously . . .'

'Most marvellously,' piped faithful Srinivasan.

'They will be disappointed.'

'Far more disappointed if I renege.'

'Renege?'

'Destroy my image, which is what you would have me do. *Stupidity!*' cried Krishnan.

'I do not like stupidity.' Dr Coomaraswamy drew himself up.

'Then don't be it. Can't you *see*?' asked Krishnan.

'I see that Padmina Retty will come with a great splash, aeroplane, bands, decorations – maybe *decorated* elephants – horses, parade.'

'Yes, and you will ask her, demand of her, to tell you, in public, then and there, what it cost. You will say to the crowd, "Ask your Mother Padmina what it cost" – "Mother" will be mockery. "Ask her what it cost and who will pay." Krishnan stood up, his eyes flashing. ' "Who pays? Not your mother. Not any Retty. Oh, no! Then who? You," ' stormed Krishnan. ' "You, the people. Ask her how many of the *pice* you have been allowed to earn with your toil, your poor tools, have gone into her pocket. Or the pockets of her aides who talk to you so sweetly. Oh, yes! They hold out a hand to you, sweetly, sweetly, while the other hand is robbing you." '

'Then ask, "What is the cost of Krishnan Bhanj? Nothing. He asks nothing. Not one *pice* do you have to pay. He himself takes nothing. His followers take nothing. He gives and so people give gladly to him. Brothers and sisters, give him your votes." That is what you will say,' said Krishnan.

'But . . . I have already ordered two bands.'

'Then you can pay them yourself or tell them to go away.'

'I have hired horses. Already they are caparisoned.'

'Then uncaparison them.'

'Boy and girl scouts.'

'Boy and girl scouts I don't mind.'

'He doesn't mind boy and girl scouts.' Mr Srinivasan was thankful.

'Yes, that is a good idea — but — scouts? *Are* there any in Konak?'

'In truth, no,' and Dr Coomaraswamy had to admit, 'I have had to buy uniforms.'

'The children can keep the uniforms. They will be delighted but wear them they will not, *will not*,' repeated Krishnan severely, 'for the procession. If anything is not in truth, then no. This political campaign, unlike all other political campaigns, must be in truth. Absolute truth. Nothing else will I have.'

'Then it will be disaster.'

'Then it will be success.'

Mary sang as she went along the shore. Singing! I oughtn't to be singing. I have to make peace, at least a sort of peace, with Blaise. I'll try — though it seems unlikely, thought Mary. Yet still she sang:

> 'Early one morning,
> Just as the sun was rising,
> I heard a pretty maiden in the valley below:
> Oh, never leave me,
> Oh, don't deceive me.
> How could you use a poor maiden so?'

She laughed as she picked up a piece of seaweed with her toes and cast it back into the sea.

There were no boats on the shore; the fishermen must have gone out early; it was, as well, too early for people to come down to the beach. The dawn was rosy — she thought of Usas the Dawn Goddess, daughter of the sky, sister of night. There was a pink light over the sea, pale tender pink, giving no inkling of the heat that was to come. Yes, it will be hot, thought Mary, hard for the people who have to walk in the processions.

She would have liked to have gone up to the Hall to see if she could find Hannah and ask her for some earlier-than-normal early tea but first she had to make herself respectable. I need a bath. The stains of colour would be difficult to wash off. I wonder if it's too early to ring the house for hot water. I could telephone quietly so as not to wake Blaise. I must look an apparition. I need to wash my hair too.

Her bare feet made no sound on the verandah; the shutters were open; a half door swung in the sea breeze. Mary stepped inside and stood puzzled.

There was no one in the room; the bed was oddly rumpled, its pillows cast aside. There was, too, an odd smell; strong disinfectant but with it, or under it, a stink, thought Mary, wrinkling up her nose . . . something that reminded her of the smell that hung about stables.

Coming further in, she saw Blaise's clothes lying in a crumpled heap at the foot of the bed. Perhaps he had wanted a swim to cool himself off after the quarrel . . . but his bathing trunks, put to dry, still hung on the verandah rail.

Did he change to go up to the Hall? But why change? He didn't get wet. Was he so angry that he had determined to leave Patna Hall at once and gone up to order a taxi? She looked through his clothes; they were all there. He wouldn't have gone up to the Hall naked. Besides, wouldn't he have packed? She couldn't imagine Blaise leaving his possessions behind. Then where is he? wondered Mary.

She looked at the partition. Shall I ask Olga? But there was no sound from her rooms. She looked so tired and unhappy last night she should sleep, and Mary quietly went out. 'Blaise, Blaise,' she called along the beach. 'Blaise.' The sound came back to her from emptiness.

190

It was then that she heard a whickering, not a pleased sound but a whickering of distress: Slippers came out of the bushes and with him the stench she had smelled in the bedroom but stronger. He was limping, worse than limping, lurching as he tried to move; one foot was dragging and Mary saw the fetlock was swollen, the pitiable hoof was on its side. Slippers was shaking in violent spasms. His sides were smeared with dung and there were marks on his neck – Blaise with the heel of his shoe again! Mary, too, was shaking but with fury. He had hit Slippers on the eyes as well: one was swollen and bleeding; there was blood on his nose. 'Horrible,' cried Mary aloud. 'Horrible! Blaise must have found you in the bedroom again,' she cried to Slippers. 'Oh, why did you go in?' and then she knew. 'You were looking for your sugar because I forgot to give it to you. It's *I* who am horrible.' She buried her face in Slippers's furry neck. 'He drove you off the verandah too quickly and you have broken your poor foot. Stay there,' Mary ordered him. 'Don't try to move. Stay.'

She tore up the path; the house was silent, shuttered. How odd! People come for the sea breezes and sleep with their shutters closed, but at the gatehouse she found Thambi, squatting on his haunches, beginning to blow up a small fire for the lazy Shyama.

'Thambi! Thambi!'

Thambi rose to his feet at this frantic apparition.

'Thambi – Slippers – donkey – hurt, very hurt. Get vet. Vet-er-in-a-rian animal doctor. Animal hurt. Doctor. Quick.'

Thambi, always intelligent, understood. 'Animal hurt,' but doctor seemed to him strange. Donkeys, to Thambi, were neither here nor there, a means of transport, bearers of burdens. He, Samuel and Hannah had often deplored Auntie Sanni's keeping of Slippers. The donkey did not matter but Mary's distress did. 'I come,' said Thambi. 'First I call Miss Sanni.'

191

'The vet. The vet,' Mary was still saying it hysterically as she stood by Slippers.

'There is no use for the vet,' and Auntie Sanni said words in Telegu to Thambi who ran to the house.

Auntie Sanni's nightclothes looked no different from her dresses; she had come down the path billowing and calm. Gently she spoke to Slippers, touching the bloody marks on his head and eye, only her mouth had tightened, the sea-green of her eyes grown dark. Gently she had felt down his leg to the broken fetlock and had shaken her head. 'The bone is fragmented. See, bits are through the skin. He has made it worse by dragging it. Besides the hoof is too heavy for it to mend. Poor donkey,' she said. 'Why wouldn't you let us . . . ?' Then to Mary, 'Colonel McIndoe will come.'

'Colonel McIndoe!'

'He is firm and quick,' said Auntie Sanni. 'Mary, go inside.'

White to the lips, Mary said, 'I'm not a child, Auntie Sanni, I'll stay.'

The shot rang out to the hills and echoed back. 'Better go to Mr Browne,' Auntie Sanni told Mary. 'This will startle him.'

Mary stood up from where she had knelt by Slippers, stretched prone now on the sand. Her tears had fallen on his fur.

'No more pain,' said Auntie Sanni. 'No more blows. Poor little donkey.'

'Just because I forgot his sugar.' Then, 'Blaise!' Recollection came flooding back. 'Auntie Sanni, Blaise isn't there. He isn't — anywhere.'

Quietly, methodically, Auntie Sanni went through the room, questioning Mary as quietly. 'If he had come up to the Hall, I should have known – our nightwatchman would have called me and,' Auntie Sanni sniffed, 'Mary, someone else has been in this room.'

'Who?'

Auntie Sanni did not answer that. Instead, 'You are sure he has taken nothing?'

'Nothing,' and, out on the beach again, Mary said, 'He must have gone swimming but what – ' she felt as if she asked the sky, the sea itself, 'what's the harm in that? Blaise is a strong, strong swimmer.'

'Miss Baba, look,' and Mary saw what she had not noticed before, the long mesh screen with its barbed top and hinges was still stretched between its iron posts across the Patna Hall beach. 'Is not open,' said Thambi – he had not unlocked it. 'Ten foot high,' said Thambi. 'No sahib, even athlete, get over that.'

'Then . . . ?' Mary looked with rising horror along the beach. 'No. Oh, no!'

'I think yes,' said Thambi. Scanning the wash of the waves, he saw something, darted along the sand, lifted a small object, white, limp and brought it to them. It was an hotel towel.

'*Ayyo!*'

'*Ayyo! Ay-ayyo!*' Thambi cried in horror. '*Ay-yo-ma!*'

Up in their room, the Fishers heard the shot. Sir John put on his dressing gown and went out on the upper verandah to look. 'As far as I can see,' he called back to Lady Fisher, 'something has happened to the donkey. Colonel McIndoe is there.'

'The Colonel? Then it's serious.'

'Yes. The poor beast is down.'

'Mary will be upset. Poor child.'

Then came running footsteps, a voice, 'Sir John! Sir John!'

It was a Mary they had not seen before, her dress limp,

stained with odd colours as was she, colour-stains from Birdie's paint and blood – that had been from Slippers's eye. Her feet were bare, her hair stiff with dried salt, her face tear-stained, the eyes wide with panic.

'The poor donkey's been put down,' Sir John began but, 'Worse – than Slippers.' Mary was out of breath. 'Worse.'

'What is worse?'

'Blaise,' stammered Mary. 'Blaise. He went for a swim.'

'Is that all?' their looks seemed to say when a sound like another shot but a muffled shot came from over their heads. The next moment, across the verandah, they saw a shower of coloured stars descending over the sea. 'A rocket,' said Sir John.

Next moment came another, then another. 'It's Patna Hall's own alarm signal,' said Sir John. 'Thambi is letting rockets off from the roof to alert the fishing boats, maybe the coastguards.'

'Great God in heaven!' said Lady Fisher.

Out on the verandah, carrying the Fishers' morning tea tray, Hannah heard the rockets. As if in echo of Lady Fisher, putting the tray carefully down on a table, Hannah knelt, made the sign of the cross and she, too, whispered, 'God in heaven. Merciful God. Mother of God. Blessed Virgin.'

Kuku was woken by the shot.

From the window she saw the gathering on the beach and drew a sharp breath. Like Sir John, 'Colonel McIndoe is there,' she whispered. 'My God!'

She dressed as fast as she could but her fingers were trembling so much that she could hardly knot her sari; when she tried to brush out her hair, she dropped the brush. Managing to slip through the house without being seen by any of the servants she ran, not down the path but by a side track through the bushes to the bungalow,

194

coming round its far end. No one was near as she knocked on Olga Manning's door.

'Olga. Olga. Please may I come in? It's Kuku.'

There was no answer.

'Olga, I *must* come in.' The door was not locked. Kuku pushed it open.

Drugged by tiredness and the whisky Mary and Auntie Sanni had given her, Olga had slept through the shot, the voices, the rockets. Now Kuku shook her awake. 'Olga, *please*. Try and wake. It is *urgent*. Olga.'

Slowly, struggling through waves of weariness and heaviness, Olga sat up. 'It's morning.' She blinked at the light.

'Of course it's morning. Olga.'

'Who . . . who is it?'

'Kuku. Kuku.'

'What d'you want?'

'Promise,' cried Kuku, 'promise you won't tell.'

'Tell what?'

'What you saw last night.'

'Last night?'

'Yes. Blaise — Mr Browne — and me. Please, Olga. They're all out there now. They can't find Blaise and Mary is making a great fuss. Nobody knows but you. It all depends on you. Auntie Sanni would send me away.'

'I don't think she would.' Olga Manning was struggling to be awake, to remember. 'Not Auntie Sanni.'

'She might. Hannah, Samuel, they'll sneer. Always they have hated me. Olga, I was virgin. I am not a girl like that. Blaise was the first and I love him. Olga, don't injure him or me. Give me your word. Promise you won't tell.'

'I promise I won't tell. In any case, it's not my concern, nothing to do with me. Now go away and let me sleep.'

* * *

195

'I can't drink brandy before breakfast.' Mary said it with a tremulous laugh. 'I can't.'

'You are going to,' said Lady Fisher.

'I not understand English memsahibs,' Thambi had told Auntie Sanni. 'Miss Baba, she cry for donkey, no tear for husband.'

Mary was too appalled to cry. 'I told Blaise about the baby shark,' she had said that over and over again. 'I told him. I thought he had listened but he was so angry. Why was he so angry? I don't understand. I don't. I don't. I don't.'

'Mary, tell me something,' said Lady Fisher. She had not attempted to hold Mary close as she would have liked to do or try to comfort her. 'She would have cast me off,' she told Sir John.

'Tell me something,' she said again to Mary, 'did you promise Blaise you would not see Krishnan Bhanj again? Did you?'

That arrested the frenzy. Mary looked at Lady Fisher in astonishment. 'I didn't. I wouldn't have. I promised Blaise I wouldn't go near any of them – unless I was asked.'

'You were asked?'

'Of course. Krishnan asked me. I left you playing bridge. I hated you for playing bridge when poor Olga . . .'

'Yes, yes, but go on,' said Lady Fisher.

'There was a boy waiting on the path. He had a note, a piece of paper really, from Krishnan.' Mary's voice trembled. 'It asked me to come and help him in the grove.'

'But he was at Ghandara.'

'He wasn't. He was with the elephant.'

'*Elephant?*'

'Yes. We had to wash the paint off Birdie. It was *imperative*.' In her distraction Mary quoted Krishnan to Lady Fisher's bewilderment.

196

'I don't understand a word you are saying.'

'No I don't suppose you do, nobody does but it's true. There's to be no grand decorations in Krishnan's procession so we had to wash the paint off the elephant. Krishnan couldn't do it all so he asked me to help him and I went. I don't care if you don't believe me, but first I made the boy wait and wrote a note on the back of the paper – so Blaise knew where I was. The boy took it.'

'No note came.'

'I gave the boy a rupee.'

'No note came . . .' but light broke on Mary. 'I see! Blaise thought I had broken my word. *That*'s why he was so angry but I did send the note, I did.'

'Yes, you did.'

Sir John had come on to the verandah. 'I found this on the path.' He had undone the crumpled ball of paper, wet and limp but decipherable. 'For Blaise,' read out Sir John, and, ' "You see, I have been asked." '

'Yes.' There was a slithering sound. To her surprise Mary slumped to the floor.

'But what are they *doing*?' That was Mary's first frantic question.

She had come round to find herself lying on her dressing-room bed with Hannah mopping her face with cold water, pouring more over her hands while Lady Fisher held her. Impatiently Mary shook her head but Hannah persisted. 'Baba, lie still. In a moment better,' and, strangely, Mary let her. Hannah dried her face and hands, sat her up and Sir John held the glass of brandy to her lips. 'Not a word until you've drunk this . . .'

Then, 'Something. We must do *something* – at least *try*,' begged Mary.

'Look,' said Sir John and took her to the verandah rail.

The fishing boats had come back but not to the beach. Thambi and Moses had taken Patna Hall's own motorboat out, '. . . and a battering they got as they went through the waves,' said Sir John. Now the other boats had closed in to make a flotilla; through Sir John's binoculars Mary could see Thambi conferring. Then, as the gazers on the verandah watched, the flotilla broke up, the boats going in different directions.

A few minutes later, a speedboat from the coastguard station came into sight and soon was circling round them. 'I should be on that,' Mary cried. 'Sir John, I ought to be looking. I must go out. I will.'

'You would only be a hindrance,' said Sir John. 'You must trust them, Mary. No one knows this coast better than these men. If anyone can find Blaise they will.'

'And if they can't?' Mary stared across the sea. 'Give him back. Oh, please, give him back,' she was pleading.

'Mary, *baba*. Come with Hannah. You must change that dress, wash, eat. Many sahibs will be needing you,' but, 'Leave me alone,' cried Mary. 'Just for one minute, leave me alone.' She tore herself from Hannah and ran down into the hall.

'Let her go,' said Sir John. 'Samuel and I will see she doesn't go down to the beach. Let her go.' He followed her downstairs.

'Sanni, is there any chance?' Sir John asked as Auntie Sanni came to join him.

'If there were, the fishing boats would have picked him up long ago – they went out first at midnight. The coastguards say there has been no other boat near.' Auntie Sanni seemed heavier than ever.

'Blaise was a strong swimmer.'

'Even so, our strongest young men don't go out alone into this sea, John, it is infested. If they find him,' said Auntie Sanni, 'God knows what they will find.'

* * *

198

'Mrs Browne.'

Mary spun round. She had gone into the hall. No one was there and holding on to the reception desk she had been trying to still her turmoil. Now she saw that a familiar small red car was drawn up under the portico.

'Mr Menzies!' Mary recoiled. 'I don't want to talk to you.'

'But you will,' Mr Menzies smiled. 'I have come to bring you good news of your friend Krishnan Bhanj. He is your friend, isn't he?'

'I . . . I have been working for his party.' Mary's instinct told her to be cautious.

'Very laudable,' said Mr Menzies. 'So you will be very glad. Voting began at dawn this morning. Konak is usually politically apathetic. Krishnan has roused it. I have never seen such a turnout. In my opinion Padmina Retty might as well pack up and go home.'

'You mean Krishnan might win?' Mary, off her guard, came nearer. 'He will win?'

'I believe overwhelmingly. There! At least that has made you happy,' and Mary felt she had to say, 'Thank you for coming to tell me.'

'And now you tell me,' said Mr Menzies. 'Mrs Browne, when did you last see your husband?'

Mary flinched but firmly shut her lips and turned to go.

'You won't tell me? I have just been to see Mrs Armstrong. She won't tell me either. Pity. You ladies are making a mistake. If you won't tell me, I shall have to make it up or rely on other people – as perhaps I have done already – perhaps someone who doesn't like you so well. They are apt to distort. So am I.' Mr Menzies laughed but he was serious. 'Of course, this *isn't* gossip, in which I specialise, yet it soon could be. You wouldn't want this catastrophe— '

'It isn't catastrophe— '

'Yet,' he finished for her. 'You wouldn't want it

turned into sensationalism, would you? Wouldn't it be better to talk to me? When did you last see your husband?'

'He was – playing bridge.'

'And where were you? That is the question, isn't it?'

Mary, unfailingly transparent, was looking round the hall this way and that, trying to escape but Mr Menzies came nearer.

'Mrs Browne, tell me. I think your father is a well-to-do man, isn't he? Very well to do.'

'Rory?' Mary could not think what Rory had to do with this. 'I ... suppose so.'

'And the parents of poor Blaise ... more than well to do. Wealthy?'

'Why are you asking me these questions?'

'Well, you see,' said Mr Menzies, 'I know what happened later that night on the beach.'

For a moment Mary looked at him wide-eyed, then she followed his glance to the portico and the red car and saw the now familiar curly black head, though the yellow shirt had been changed for a red one and, 'I see,' said Mary. 'Kanu!'

'Kanu is an excellent small informer – and helps me in more ways than one.'

You really are repulsive, thought Mary, with your horrible ribbon scruff hair and crab pink face and horrid plumpness.

'Still there are ways', he was saying, 'of keeping things out of the papers.'

'Certainly there are.' Sir John had appeared in the Hall. 'Ways and means you probably have not taken into account but, Menzies,' said Sir John, 'Miss Sanni ordered you out of her hotel. Will you go or shall I have you put out?'

'I have a reason to be here, Sir John.'

'I am sure you have. In fact, I know you had a hand

in this mischief, if tragedy or near tragedy can be called that. I hope it will rest on your conscience.'

'My conscience is perfectly at ease, thank you, Sir John. I am a newsman and news is news.'

'Not all news. We have a police injunction.'

'Injunction!'

'The police insist that nothing is released until the full facts are known. They are thinking of our Office and of Mr Browne's family — which is more than you have done — also of Patna Hall which you will leave at once and take your scurrility with you.'

'Sir John, did you say, "the police"?'

He had brought Mary back to the verandah, holding her, trying to stop her quivering. 'You and Hannah are the only people she would let touch her,' Lady Fisher was to say and soon, 'Sir John,' Mary managed to whisper, 'did you say the police?'

'It has to be the police, Mary. Chief Inspector Anand has sent a message — he cannot leave Ghandara while the voting is on, he hasn't that many men though he has sent to Madras. He asks that you, Mrs Manning — I mean Mrs Armstrong — and Kuku will come to him.'

'Olga and Kuku?' Mary was puzzled.

'Also Thambi and the sweeper women who cleaned up the mess in the bungalow last night.'

'Slippers's mess?'

'Yes, he fouled the floor.'

'*That* was the smell and Blaise hit him, hit him with the heel of his shoe like he did before and it's all my fault. Oh, I can't bear it. I can't bear it.' She was shuddering from head to foot.

Sir John held her but Auntie Sanni had come out. 'Stand up,' said Auntie Sanni to Mary. 'We have Kuku in hysterics. That's enough. Go and get yourself ready and be of help.'

201

'Oh, Aunt Sanni,' Lady Fisher demurred but it acted like a charm. Mary stood erect, tossed back her hair, tried to give them a smile and obeyed.

'That is my girl,' said Auntie Sanni.

Krishnan had told Mary that election days in India were joyous events but she had not known it would be like this. 'It's a *mela* – a fair,' said Sir John. All along the roads on the way to Ghandara, men, women and children, in what they had as best clothes, had come on foot, singing. 'All over Konak they have been out since dawn,' said Sir John. They came, too, in bullock carts, the bullocks garlanded, the carts decorated with flowers and scraps of bright cloth. Lorries wearing jewellery and tassels swept by, while cars and jeeps, sent by the parties to ferry voters, had drapes in party colours, the blue of Padmina Retty, red for Gopal Rau, green, yellow, and white for Krishnan Bhanj. Bicycles were decorated too, as were the rickshaws; some of the rickshaws had loudspeakers.

The square by Ghandara's town hall was packed and, as in every town in the State, entertainers had come: men who danced on stilts, conjurors, puppet theatres – those whose puppets told the story of the God Krishna were especially popular, as were his storytellers. There were sweetmeat sellers; rival teahouses were free, paid for by their parties. 'One bowl of tea or coffee with one biscuit only,' Dr Coomaraswamy had specified, 'and that will cost me a *lakh* of rupees.' Toysellers came through the crowds carrying poles wound in straw, stuck with paper windmills in bright colours, paper dolls, long paper whistles which made piercing squeals.

Coming from a side road, hooting as they inched through the crammed roads, the Patna Hall cars had to wait while the processions passed. Gopal Rau had decided not to process at all which, under the circumstances, was wise but they saw the tail end of Padmina

202

Retty's display: mounted soldiers in full dress, their lances fluttering pennants; foot soldiers wearing the dress of the Maharajah's late army. Behind them Padmina rode, not in her famous white jeep but in the blue *howdah* of a decorated elephant much larger than Birdie. 'They must have had to send away for that one,' said Sir John. All round her marched her men in brocaded *achkans*, gauze turbans or English suits; her women helpers in glittering saris carried peacock feather fans. Behind them came brass bands blaring Indian and English music, new tunes and old favourites, the 'Dambuster's March' and 'Colonel Bogey', while overhead circled her aeroplane, pulling a banner, bright blue with a star. The rear was brought up by horsemen and boys running almost between their hoofs.

It was impressive. 'Very well done,' said Sir John.

'Horrendously well done,' Dr Coomaraswamy had said.

Then came a silence, all the more striking after the fanfare and tantara that had gone before, until an old and reverend priest with a white beard and saffron robe appeared on a white horse without saddle or bridle. The priest held up his hand for quiet. Even the rickshaws hushed as the ululation of a conch sounded and Krishnan's procession came into sight.

It was exactly as he had said with, after the deafening bands, that soft undulating ululation introducing the drums beating to keep time with the seductive melody of a flute piercing through the crowds – 'Yes, dulcet,' murmured Mary. Then came the disciples, young vigorous men barefoot in spotless white, their hair flowing, their hands held in *namaskar*.

Behind them, on a lorry, bare and plain, Dr Coomaraswamy spoke through a microphone. 'I cannot walk and speak,' he had told Krishnan. 'I am too aged. Besides, on the ground no one will hear me.'

'All the better,' said Sharma, the irrepressible.

When the Doctor paused to draw breath, the young men sang.

Then came a space in which another priest, young – 'From Agni's temple,' Mary whispered – dressed in saffron, led a huge sacred bull, the cap on its hump worked in beads, its neck garlanded. It placidly chewed its cud as it walked, veering from side to side when the crowd offered it tidbits.

Next walked the children, healthy pretty boys and girls. They drew 'ahs' and 'aies' from the people as the little girls scattered flower petals while the boys carried their kites and garlands. They too sang, their voices shrill:

> 'Lord Krishna, Lord of All,
> We put you in your cradle.
> We bind you with a chain of gold,
> Your hands are red with henna.
> We gave you milk, we gave you kisses.
> Little Lord Krishna.'

Last came Krishnan, magnificently tall, his skin oiled so that once again it shone but with its own darkness, still almost blue-black – Perhaps Krishna blue is intrinsic, thought Mary, and even in her misery that strange happiness swelled. He wore only a loincloth; the squirrel was on his shoulder as he led Birdie on a saffron-coloured rope, the elephant shining too with cleanliness, her trunk every now and then touching Krishnan. He did not look at the crowd, only straight forward as waves of reverence and, yes, love, thought Mary, came on all sides and a murmured, 'Jai Krishnan. Jai Krishnan,' then 'Jai Shri Krishnan. Jai Shri Krishnan Hari.' It swelled louder and louder as the crowd took it up. Behind him, which drew delighted laughter, three of the most good-looking girl disciples led the three cows of the Root and Flower symbol.

204

For a moment Mary forgot the terrible present. 'Jai Krishnan,' she breathed. 'Jai Shri Krishnan.'

The crowds had surged around the bull so that the procession had to halt while the young men ran to persuade the people to move back. 'No police. No force,' Krishnan had laid down so that it took a little time. Meanwhile, the lorry was on a level with the first Patna Hall car which held Sir John and, in the back seat, Mary, Olga and Kuku – Thambi and the sweepers were behind. Dr Coomaraswamy, who was not sweltering in a suit – he had to wear national dress: 'Though I am not habituated' – saw that Kuku, nearest the window was weeping.

Weeping! Immediately Dr Coomaraswamy was transported into a dream ... 'Uma, here is a girl in trouble' – he did not know what trouble but never mind – 'Let us take her into our home and befriend her. Always she has been treated as a nobody – we will set her on her feet. You, Uma, will teach her in your wonderful ways. I . . .' He did not know quite what he would do but he saw a grateful Kuku, sweet, emollient, 'I am so grateful, so grateful,' and he would say, paternalistically, of course, 'Kuku, come here.' At that the dream broke. 'For what', Uma would, of course, ask, 'are you befriending this girl? Tell me the truth.' Dr Coomaraswamy had to admit he knew another truth. 'I too am in love.' He saw Kuku's face illumined, softened as she had said that and he knew, no matter what her grief, there was no place in it for him. It was as well that the lorry was able to move a few paces. The cars succeeded in getting by and Kuku was borne away, as far as Dr Coomaraswamy was concerned, for ever.

The police station, undecorated, was a sturdier building than the town hall, made, too, of stucco. 'It will be cool,' Olga said thankfully.

Two policemen stood on the steps in regulation khaki shorts, tunics, puttees, boots and red-banded turbans; brass shone on their belt buckles and shoulder straps. 'Chief Inspector Anand keeps his men in trim,' Sir John approved.

The Chief Inspector came out to meet them: a plump, dapper little man, his uniform, too, was impeccable. He had a moustache so fine it looked as if it had been pencilled in dandy fashion but his eyes were kind as he took them into a waiting room, apologising for bringing them out in the heat.

'May I see you first, Mrs Armstrong, since you were the last person to see Mr Browne . . .' He did not add, 'alive.'

Olga Manning Armstrong did not lie; she simply told the truth but not the whole truth, giving her testimony with a quiet steadfastness that impressed the Chief Inspector.

'Well, I am used to courts,' she told Mary afterwards.

'Mr Browne came to your door.'

'Yes, to ask if I had seen Mary, his wife.'

'And you had not?'

'No. I was going to bed.'

'It must be painful for you', said sympathetic Chief Inspector Anand, 'to have me question you just now when there is so much tragedy but you can be of utmost help. What made you, Mrs Armstrong, go in later?'

'He, Mr Browne, was hurting the donkey – of course, I didn't know then how badly it was hurt but I heard the blows. I couldn't stand that.'

'He was angry?'

'Very. Then I heard Kuku – Miss Vikram. She had come down with the sweepers.'

'And later?'

'I thought I had better look in to see if there was anything I could do – really for Mary's sake.'

206

'She was not there?'

'No. I didn't do any good. Mr Browne pushed past me and rushed out.'

'Why do you think he rushed out?'

'He did not like what I said.'

'About the donkey?'

Olga bowed her head.

'You did not see him again?'

'How could I? I went back to bed.'

'Thank you, Mrs Armstrong.'

To Kuku lies were second nature but she did not dare to tell them now. 'Mr Browne telephoned the house. You answered?'

'Nat-u-rally. I am hotel manager.' Kuku did not say it with pride, she was terrified. 'I called two of our women sweepers. We cleaned up the room. It was – disgusting. Blaise – Mr Browne – was right to be angry. He was right,' pleaded Kuku.

'When the sweepers had gone?'

'I tidied the room. The donkey had smashed a photograph – glass . . .'

'Then?'

'I went back.' There had been only an infinitesimal pause.

'You did not see Mr Browne go out?'

'No. I had gone myself,' said Kuku with truth.

'Thank you, Miss Vikram.'

'Do I have to tell the Inspector everything?' Mary asked Sir John, still shuddering.

'Strictly speaking, you don't have to tell him anything. It is simply that we and they are trying to find out what has happened to Blaise. We must find out so that it will help if you tell them what is relevant.'

'That I was with Krishnan?'

207

'It is relevant. I'll be with you, Mary. Tell the Chief Inspector openly how you helped Krishnan with the elephant, how, from the time you came to Konak, you have helped with the Party's plans, made friends with all of them, believed in them,' but the Chief Inspector was to ask, 'Your husband, did he share in this belief?'

'No.'

'Do you know why?'

Mary was too honest to prevaricate. 'He did not like me having anything away from him.'

'Ah!' said the Chief Inspector. 'Perhaps last night he came after you?'

'Yes.'

'Has he done that before?'

'Yes,' and, 'I know what you mean,' flashed Mary, 'but he saw nothing because there was nothing to see.'

'Last night? To be fair, Mrs Browne, most men would not be pleased to find their wife, a newly married wife, Mrs Browne, out on the beach at night with someone who was to him . . .' the Chief Inspector did not say 'outsider', instead he said, 'a stranger,' and he asked, 'Was there a quarrel?'

'Not a quarrel. We were only teasing him. I wish we hadn't.'

Chief Inspector Anand was acute. 'Because your husband did not understand you were only teasing?'

'Yes,' and Mary had to say, 'I'm afraid he took it seriously.'

'Seriously enough to make him take his own life?'

'Take his own life?' The aghast astonishment was genuine. '*Blaise*,' and involuntarily it came out, 'Blaise would never have done that. I was the one who was always wrong.'

'Yet he must have gone deliberately into that dangerous sea.'

'He was angry, too angry to think what he was doing.

208

Oh, don't you see?' cried Mary. 'He was angry with us. He went back to the bungalow and found Slippers – the donkey. That was my fault. I had forgotten the sugar.' Tears came into her eyes. 'Slippers made that mess. It must have made Blaise furious. I'm sure he didn't know what he was doing. He probably felt filthied. He was always very particular. I'm sure he just wanted to get clean.' Into her mind came Krishnan saying, 'The sea washes everything away,' and suddenly, 'Don't. Don't,' cried Mary. 'Don't ask me any more.'

There was the sound of a motor scooter, the Indian put-putti. A policeman came into the room and whispered to the Chief Inspector. 'Excuse me for a moment, Mrs Browne, Sir John.'

They heard a murmured colloquy but not the words. Then quick orders. Sir John got up. The Chief Inspector came back and with him a middle-aged policewoman, the first Mary had seen. I didn't know India had them, she thought. This one wore, Mary was always to remember, khaki trousers, tunic and cap like the Chief Inspector's, with a red border. She moved quietly to stand behind Mary's chair.

Chief Inspector Anand cleared his throat. 'A messenger has just come from the beach at Shantipur. Mrs Browne, I do not want to distress you but I must ask you, do you recognise this ring?'

A heavy gold ring with a crest, a stag's head and a motto, *Loyauté et vérité*. 'Yes,' Mary said with stiff lips. 'It's his. It is – his signet ring. He always wears it on his left hand.'

'Mrs Browne, a fisherman found it. Diving, he saw on the sea bed a small shine of gold. It was on . . . on . . .' The Inspector hesitated to go on. The policewoman moved to Mary. 'On – a finger, Mrs Browne.'

'Only a finger?' Mary whispered.

'I'm afraid it is only a finger. The – the shark must

209

have dropped it. Maybe there were two sharks and they had a fight. That can happen . . .'

'I told him about the baby shark!' Mary screamed it so loudly that the policewoman put her hands on the quivering shoulders. Mary shook her off. 'I told him. I begged him. He wouldn't listen. I told him.' She suddenly stood up. 'I think I'm going to be sick.'

They had been a long time at the police station. Mary had vomited until she thought she had brought up the dregs of her being. The Chief Inspector had wanted to call a doctor but 'She'll be better after this,' said Olga, whom Sir John had called in; strong and capable, she had held Mary steadily, not sympathising but encouraging her. When at last they drove back through the town it was in the afternoon sun; the processions had long ended, the crowd was milling round the town hall though voting was still going on, the queues, seemingly endless, moving step by step towards the polling booths.

Voters made their cross or mark opposite the symbol, many of the women holding a baby on their hip while a toddler clutched their sari, but all eyes were alight with interest and awe.

Krishnan, though, was standing alone on the town-hall steps. 'Good!' Sir John could not help saying, 'Good!'

Mary opened her eyes and looked.

Krishnan was no longer wearing his loincloth; he was dressed like the disciples, all in white, but stood head and shoulders above them as they gathered jubilantly round him. He stood making *namaskar* over and over again to the crowd. There was no sign of Padmina Retty.

'Is he winning?' asked Mary.

'Counting will go on all through the night,' said Sir John, 'but it looks as if he has already won.'

Of course he doesn't know, thought Mary. How

could he? As she thought that, Krishnan looked up.

He saw the car, the police — Chief Inspector Anand had given them outriders. Krishnan looked, a long look. Then he bent and whispered to Sharma who ran down the steps, wriggled and squeezed his way through the mass of people. He could not get to the cars but reached a police outrider.

'Get me a car,' ordered Krishnan.

'A car? Why a car? You can't go anywhere now,' cried Dr Coomaraswamy.

'I must. I shall be back as soon as I can.'

'But, *Krishnan*! How can you go? Look at the multitude. You cannot leave them.'

'I must. You must talk to them until I come back.'

'That will not satisfy them. Krishnan, wouldn't someone else do? Sharma . . .'

'No one else will do.' Krishnan was violent. 'I have a debt to pay. Sharma, get me a car — or better, a motorbike and a helmet and gloves to disguise me.'

As evening came on a hush lay over Patna Hall, a tense hush. Hannah, Samuel and the servants did their work quietly with shocked faces, Hannah's lips moving constantly in prayer. Kuku was prostrate in her room. 'Why should she take on so?' Hannah said to Samuel. 'We go on with our work, why cannot she? What was Browne Sahib to her?' asked Hannah indignantly, 'While little Memsahib, poor little Memsahib . . .'

For the second time Hannah had helped Mary to clean herself. Auntie Sanni had moved her out of the bungalow into the room next to the Fishers. There Hannah had put her almost bodily into bed. Mary had gone into a deep sleep with Lady Fisher watchful in the next room. 'Eighteen and a widow,' she had said in grief.

Olga Manning — it was still difficult for Patna Hall

to think of her as Olga Armstrong – had tactfully gone down to the bungalow. 'Do you mind being there alone?' asked Sir John.

'I think I am past minding anything.'

Now Sir John was on the telephone trying to get calls through to England and New York. 'Mary,' he had said, 'you must tell Rory.'

'Rory? What is this to do with Rory?' her look seemed to say. 'Rory may be in New York, Washington, Peru.'

'It's quite easy to telephone any of them.'

'I know. At school I used to have to call all kinds of places but if I did, what could he do?'

'Look after you,' but Sir John refrained from saying it. 'And Blaise's people. His poor mother . . .'

'Mrs Browne? Yes,' said Mary. 'I know I must speak to Mrs Browne.'

'Perhaps tomorrow,' said Sir John. 'For now, better let me.'

'If you would.'

The telephone system at Konak was antiquated. 'It takes time to get through,' Auntie Sanni always told her guests. 'You need to have patience,' and now, 'Kuku should have got through for you.' For the first time that day Auntie Sanni was exasperated.

The beach was empty now. All the fishing boats had come back, the coastguard speedboat had gone. There was no more they could do. Thambi had let them go and sorrowfully made his way back to the gatehouse where, for once, Shyama had made him an evening meal. 'Is my fault,' he had said miserably again and again. 'I am guard.'

'Not all night as well as all day.' Auntie Sanni had tried to comfort him. 'Besides, Browne Sahib was headstrong.'

The villagers, too, had gone back to the village –

those who had not gone to Ghandara to vote or had come back. A drum was beating but mournfully, though, as usual, smoke from the cooking fires had begun to go up. 'Life has to go on,' said Auntie Sanni.

At Patna Hall the cookhouse was already lit; Samuel, in the dining room, was beginning his ritual. 'They must have dinner,' though who would come he did not know. Not, of course, Dr Coomaraswamy or Mr Srinivasan – Samuel had not thought it respectful to switch on the news. Not, he was glad to think, Mr Menzies. Mrs Manning, perhaps. Sir John and Lady Fisher. Miss Sanni, Colonel Sahib – that evening the Hall was closed to outsiders. 'Attend to the bar,' he told Ganga, 'that good-for-nothing will not come down.'

Auntie Sanni herself had bathed and changed; Colonel McIndoe had dressed and, as usual walking together, they went up to the knoll where they sat on the bench. Every now and then Colonel McIndoe's hand patted Auntie Sanni's knee.

'It looks all just the same,' she said at last. Patna Hall and its domain, its private beach where the net was up and locked; today no one had wanted to go swimming. The palm trees in the village stirred quietly in the breeze, the hills behind were darkening; the grove was still darker. 'But I think they will light the lamps at the shrines tonight,' said Auntie Sanni. There was a little break in her voice; Colonel McIndoe patted her knee.

Suddenly she stiffened, stood up, shading her eyes from the rays of the setting sun as she looked.

'Aie!' said Auntie Sanni. 'Aie! Look, Colonel. Look.'

A lone figure was coming down the beach. Straining her eyes, Auntie Sanni saw the height and size, its blue-blackness.

'Krishnan,' she whispered. 'It's Krishnan.'

As they watched he dived into the sea.

* * *

213

'Mary. Mary, dear. You must wake up.' Lady Fisher, usually so gentle, was shaking her firmly. Mary sat up, dazed. 'Here, put on your dress.' Hannah had put one ready and Lady Fisher brought it. 'Wash your face.' She led Mary to the washbasin, splashed cold water, dried her, brushed her hair. 'You're needed downstairs.'

Lady Fisher was grave, portentous. She took Mary's hand. 'You know, dear, that Blaise is dead.'

'Worse than dead.' The shudder came back.

'No,' said Lady Fisher, 'Krishnan has brought him.'

'*Krishnan?*'

'Yes, brought his body,' and, as Mary did not move, 'It's not frightening, Mary. It's touching. Come and see.'

It was in the courtyard. There was no sign of Krishnan – Of course, he has to be at Ghandara, thought Mary. The servants had respectfully kept out of the way but Samuel and Hannah, as privileged, moved to stand protectively by her.

Thambi, Moses and Somu were with a circle of fishermen and villagers. They had made a bier. 'It was the only way they could carry him,' said Sir John who stood beside it as it lay where they had put it down on the courtyard ground. It was a simple Indian bier of bamboo poles, laced together like a hammock with coconut fibre string, a bier the fishermen would have used for themselves though – as probably they would not have done for themselves – it was garlanded with leaves and flowers, hibiscus, marigolds, a tribute to Auntie Sanni: Blaise had been her guest.

His body was covered with a clean white sheet but Indian fashion his head, left bare, rested on the flowers. His hair had dried and looked strangely fair against their brilliance; his eyes were shut as if he were asleep. The healthy sunburn of his skin had gone: it had a blue tinge as did the lips; there were dark bruises, too, but the face was peaceful. Blaise was handsome even in death.

'He was a wonderful swimmer,' said Sir John. 'Instinctively he must have dived deep down and the currents wedged him between two rocks. There are caves down there but it's a miracle the sharks left him and that Krishnan found him.'

'Krishnan is his father's and mother's son,' said Lady Fisher. 'He risked his life going into that sea.'

'He always does,' Mary said it almost absently. 'He and Thambi have been swimming there since they were little boys. I've been in that sea with him.'

'With Krishnan?' Sir John and Lady Fisher looked at one another.

'With him it was quite safe,' explained Mary. 'He knows the currents and crevices and the sharks don't touch him but Blaise . . .' Shudders shook her again.

'He went in without a helmet,' said Sir John. 'They were all locked up. Thambi thinks he would have been at least half stunned by the waves – mercifully.'

There was the sound of frantic cries. Kuku rushed into the courtyard, her sari dragging, her hair half over her eyes. She cast herself down by the bier, tears flooding as she pulled the cloth back to kiss Blaise's feet. When she saw them mangled, her shrieks filled the courtyard.

'Kuku! Stop that.'

'What are you doing here?'

'How dare you interfere?'

'You should show more respect.'

Hannah, Samuel, even Sir John were trying to drag her away. 'Come away at once,' Lady Fisher commanded but Kuku took no notice, only clung.

'I loved him. You never did,' she flung at Mary. 'I loved him.'

'Mary, don't speak to her.'

Kuku crouched over the bier, her sobbing went on. 'I loved him.'

'I'm glad you did,' said Mary and put her hand on

Kuku's shoulder. 'I'm glad.' She looked at the others. 'Help her, please, please,' and Auntie Sanni came, lifted Kuku gently and led her away.

Mary bent down, touched the flowers, not Blaise. She stood up and, 'Thank you,' she said to the men. 'It's beautiful.' As Thambi translated, she made them a *namaskar*.

They, too, turned away.

'Bumble,' Mary whispered as she stood looking down at the bier. 'Blaise. The sad thing is', she whispered, 'that you would so much rather have had a proper coffin. I'm sorry. I'm sorry.'

Saturday

Blaise was buried early in the morning next day. 'There is nothing else to be done in this heat,' Sir John had said on the telephone to Mr and Mrs Browne. 'Even if you flew out tonight, you couldn't be in time.'

It was so early that, as Mary had seen the morning before — Only yesterday, she thought — the waves breaking on the beach were pink, the sands rosy, too, in the first light. Auntie Sanni had suggested that the burial should be in Patna Hall's own small private cemetery set behind the knoll and securely walled against jackals and roving animals. In its centre was a gūl-mohr tree, now in blossom, a riot of orange and yellow. 'My grandfather, grandmother, father and mother are all buried here,' said Auntie Sanni, 'as Colonel McIndoe and I shall be in our turn.' She did not mention a little grave, with an even smaller cross that had only a name, 'Mary McIndoe', the daughter who had lived only one day. 'We will put Blaise here,' Auntie Sanni had said to this second Mary. 'They can move him later if they like.'

Auntie Sanni did not say 'you'. It was as if she knew that, in her mind, Mary had handed Blaise back to the Brownes.

Overnight he had lain in the chapel Samuel and Hannah had hastily improvised. They knew what had to be done. A coffin was produced — 'It was to have been mine,' said Auntie Sanni. 'The Colonel and I have always kept ours handy. Coffins do not exist in Shantipur, not even in Ghandara.'

217

It was put on trestles in the centre of the room, a wreath laid on it – Hannah would have liked a cross; candles in tall candlesticks were lit on each side to burn all night; there were cushions to kneel on and, 'I'll watch with you,' Hannah told Mary.

'Watch whom?' said Mary's puzzled look.

'I shall watch,' said Kuku who had stolen in to look.

'That Miss Sanni will never allow.'

'Kuku shall do as she likes,' Mary was firm, 'but if it had been me . . .' she looked at the candles, the shut room, 'I should have liked to be burned on my bier on the beach.'

Kuku was shocked. 'English people do not do such things.'

'Shelley did,' said Mary.

'Shelley?'

'But he was a poet,' Mary went on, 'Blaise wasn't.'

No Episcopalian priest was near enough. 'He would have had to come from Madras.' There was a priest at Ghandara, Father Sebastian Gonzalives was chaplain at the convent but, 'Roman Catholic,' said Sir John. 'Better not. The Brownes might not like it.'

'Why do religions have to have edges?' asked Mary.

Surprisingly, Colonel McIndoe, not Sir John, read the burial service and led the prayers. All Patna Hall's staff was there except Kuku: 'I couldn't bear it. I couldn't,' she had wept. Olga Armstrong, as she was beginning to be called, was beside the Fishers. The servants stood in a circle, Christian, Muslim, Hindu, every one of them from Samuel down to the sweepers including the two women who had cleaned up Slippers's ordure but, as untouchables, they had to stand apart, especially from the gardeners who were Brahmins – More edges, thought Mary.

I suppose Slippers has been taken away. Do they have knackers in India? She shivered. I wonder, she thought dizzily, if he and Blaise will ever meet – would it

218

be in heaven? The next world? Another world? Or would it be in what, I think, they call limbo? And what would they say to one another? You're supposed to forgive and the thought struck her, How surprised Blaise will be to find a donkey in heaven. To me, it wouldn't be heaven without them. She came back to the funeral and listened as Colonel McIndoe's voice, modulated and clear went on, '. . .We therefore commit his body to the ground, dust to dust/. . .' But here it shouldn't be dust, she thought, it should be sand. If it had been the sea – this time she did not shudder.

Of his bones are coral made,
Those are pearls which were his eyes . . .

That would be right for Krishnan. Krishnan had had to go back, after all, thought Mary, there is still an election. She looked up at the spreading gūl-mohr tree; Blaise would have liked an apple tree or a rose bush. The sound of the waves was too loud now. He was stunned by the waves – mercifully. 'Oh, God, stun me,' prayed Mary.

'Mary. Mary, dear. They want you to sprinkle a little earth on the coffin. You have to be the first.' All of them sprinkled, the servants *salaam*ing when they had done it. Samuel and Hannah made the sign of the cross. Then the grave was closed.

'Kuku, you will get up im-med-iat-ely.' It was after the funeral breakfast which Samuel, to fit the occasion, had served at one large table, a breakfast even more lavish than usual though nobody ate more than a little. Kuku had still not appeared. 'Now, get up. Dress yourself properly and come and do what you are here to do.' Auntie Sanni was stern.

'I can't.'

'There is much work. Everyone is leaving after lunch. Sir

219

John will want his account, also Dr Coomaraswamy. That will be large because of all the young people in Paradise. Let the Brownes' bill rest. I expect Mr Browne Senior will settle that.'

'The Brownes' bill? Blaise's! How can you be so heartless?'

'We are running an hotel. The accounts must be done. We must go through the register and allot rooms. Other guests will be arriving.'

'Other guests.' Kuku sat up. 'Haven't you any *feeling*?' she demanded. 'If not any respect? Out of respect, surely, we should close for tonight.'

'And inconvenience and disappoint several people who are coming, maybe have already left home, hoping for a little rest and peace? I will give you half an hour,' but in the doorway Auntie Sanni stopped and said more kindly, 'It is time to stop crying, Kuku. I have been running this hotel for fifty years. In that time, of course, all kinds of things have happened, small things, big ones, bad and good, happy and tragic, but Patna Hall has never closed,' said Auntie Sanni.

'Mary, would you like me to help you pack?' asked Olga.

'Pack?' It had obviously not occurred to Mary.

'Yes. Say if you would rather I didn't but today is Saturday, change-over day. Hannah is too busy to do it for you. I don't know if your room in the bungalow is let or not but in any case I thought packing might be painful for you, especially Blaise's things, and being in the bungalow alone.'

'I don't want to be in the bungalow at all.'

'These things have to be done.' Olga was kind. 'If you let me help you, it can be very quick.' As Mary still did not answer, 'I assume you will be going away like the rest of us.'

'You?' asked Mary.

'Yes. I can't trespass on Auntie Sanni's kindness any longer.'

'Where will you go?'

Olga shrugged. 'Somewhere, probably in Calcutta. I have been offered work – of a sort.'

'I was going to tell Blaise I would stay on here with Auntie Sanni without him,' said Mary. 'Now that I'm without him, I can't stay.'

Samuel had not thought it respectful to put on the radio during the funeral breakfast so that Dr Coomaraswamy and Mr Srinivasan had to follow the news in the papers.

'Krishnan Bhanj triumphs in Konak.' 'A landslide victory for Krishnan Bhanj.' 'Though counting is still going on, Krishnan Bhanj and the Root and Flower Party already have a majority of some hundred and forty thousand votes over the other candidates, a near record for any candidate in elections anywhere in India.' Dr Coomaraswamy, marvelled 'A hundred and forty thousand plus! Even the great Aditya family landowners have forsaken Gopal Rau and come over to Krishnan.'

'Mrs Padmina Retty, eighty-nine thousand.'

'Gopal Rau, fifty.'

Every fresh paragraph was balm to Dr Coomaraswamy – Uma cannot say now I should not meddle in politics.

There were, of course, other headlines. 'Young English diplomat drowned . . .'

Dr Coomaraswamy hastily folded the papers.

Though he and Mr Srinivasan had been up all night they had come from Ghandara for the funeral. 'When we have so much to do,' complained Mr Srinivasan.

'It is only seemly. We have been, after all, staying in the same hotel, Mrs Browne has taken part in the campaign. Above all, Sir John Fisher would expect it. In any case we have to leave. There is packing up, accounts to settle – I must leave you to do that and we must prepare for this afternoon. We are holding a victory celebration,' he had told Sir John. 'But before anything else,' he said to Mr Srinivasan now, 'we must pay condolence respects to Mrs Browne.'

'Is she able?' asked Mr Srinivasan.

'Probably she will be lying down but still . . .'

'When my daughter had the measles,' Mr Srinivasan was filled with concern, 'we caused her to lie on a mat on the floor, a mat woven of grasses and dampened for coolness – to cool the fever,' he explained. 'Also, we surrounded her with fresh neem leaves. Neem is so very soothing.'

'Mrs Browne has no fever,' but, Dr Coomaraswamy was distressed, 'She is so young to be widowed. I do not know what to say.'

To put off the moment, they lingered on the verandah and leafed through the papers again until, at last, 'Speak from the heart,' suggested Mr Srinivasan, 'then you cannot be wrong,' but Dr Coomaraswamy's heart was elsewhere.

He had not lingered only from embarrassment; in spite of all resolutions he had been waiting, hoping – A last glimpse, he told himself, though to Sir John, 'I, myself, must go straight to Delhi and make my report,' he had said, 'also see Krishnan's father. I expect he and Mrs Bhanj will come here. Then I must return to my neglected work and, of course, to my beloved wife, Uma,' but, as he said it, the heart Mr Srinivasan had spoken of felt like lead. He saw his clinic – he had been so proud of it – with its spacious grounds, its chalets, communal lounges and dining room, the big medical building, and it all seemed sterile; even the corridors were sterile, everything arranged according to Uma. Outside the clinic windows would be neat gravel walks, no vista of green lawns, white sands, blue sea, colours of flowers; no blooms of jasmine to put in someone's hair. There would not be the teasing voice,

222

the laughter, even if the laughter, the teasing were not for him.

'It's getting late,' Mr Srinivasan reminded him and Dr Coomaraswamy was forced to ask Samuel, 'Where is the little Memsahib?'

'She helping Miss Sanni with the accountings.'

That shocked both the Doctor and Mr Srinivasan.

'Surely she should be weeping?'

'A widow should weep.'

'She is in the office,' Samuel assured them.

Mary had never seen Auntie Sanni as pressed – Come to that, I have never seen her pressed at all. Now she was busy in her office, busy at reception, in the linen and store rooms.

Olga had been right: the packing had not taken long, the luggage was soon ready, Mary's separate from Blaise's, '. . . which will go to England if his father and mother want it.' Mary looked at the golf clubs in their heavy bag, the tennis rackets in their presses, the camera, and turned away. His watch had gone; the signet ring she had put in the pocket of her shorts. Then, going to find Auntie Sanni in the office, seeing her desk littered with papers, account sheets, stacks of small signed chits on different spikes, 'Can I help?' asked Mary. 'I'm quite good at accounts.'

'That's more than I am.' Auntie Sanni laid down her pen. 'Kuku says we should have a computer but who of us knows how to work one? There is a calculator but I don't know how to use that either,' she sounded in near despair, 'and there are all the flowers to do. I cannot arrange flowers.'

'Where is Kuku?'

'Lachrymosing.' Mary had not heard Auntie Sanni be as cross.

'If that one takes on so much over what is nothing

223

to do with her,' Hannah with two houseboys, their arms full of folded sheets, pillow cases and towels had brought the key of the linen room to Auntie Sanni, 'what she do', demanded Hannah, 'when she have real sorrow?'

'Perhaps it is real sorrow,' said Mary.

'Pah!' Hannah sounded as if she spat.

'If you really could do these accounts,' Auntie Sanni wavered, 'but it doesn't seem fitting.'

'It is. It is,' urged Mary. 'I should be better with something to do. *Please.*'

'Well, then. Here are the account forms. You see they are divided – hotel accommodation and board, telephone, laundry, drinks – each room has its chits. You check them and enclose them with the account. For Dr Coomaraswamy there is another account for the young people in Paradise, they only had half board and then,' Auntie Sanni said of what evidently defeated her, 'you have to add them all up to a total.'

'I think I can do that.'

'You enclose them neatly in an envelope, *sealed*,' Auntie Sanni specified. 'Kuku wanted to add ten per cent for service charge but no, we would not do that. Guests give or not give as they choose.'

It was peaceful working in the office; the doves' cooing seemed gently healing. The stack of envelopes – sealed, thought Mary with a smile for Auntie Sanni – grew steadily. By noon she had almost finished. 'Perhaps I can do the flowers as well?'

When Sir John had seen Mary come up to the Hall and go in to Auntie Sanni, he went down to the bungalow. Olga, dressed to travel, was sitting on the little verandah. 'May I join you for a moment?'

'Of course.'

'Mrs Armstrong, Olga, would it be an intrusion if I asked you what you are planning to do?'

'I must do what I can.'

'Alone in Calcutta?'

'Well, I don't see people now or expect them to see me. I shall have to earn, of course, some kind of living. Colin, naturally, has had no salary these past two years. There is a clinic I worked for in Calcutta, a poor one, not like Dr Coomaraswamy's,' she smiled, 'in the slums. They will take me back and provide a room but, at the moment, we're penniless.'

'Then I suggest you let me give you this.'

Startled, she said, 'Oh, no!'

'Oh, yes! Alicia and I have worried about you.'

'Worried about *me*?'

'Is that so unusual?'

'Most unusual, I have found . . .' She could not go on.

'Then . . .' and Sir John put a folder on the table.

'What is it?'

'An air ticket to London – London's a good starting ground – and a little wherewithal to help while you find your feet. We, Alicia and I, want you to take it. Will you?'

She was silent, looking at the folder, struggling, then, 'I can't find any words,' she said.

'It doesn't need words. Take it.'

'Colin would tell me to accept.'

'Well, then?'

'I can't, Sir John.' The eyes lifted to his were full of tears. 'There are no thanks good enough, grateful enough to you and Lady Fisher but I can't. I must stay as close to him as I can.'

'For twelve years?'

'It may not be twelve years. He may get remission but, if need be, for ever.'

'They will only let you see him once a month.'

'I shall still see him once a month.'

Sir John put his hand on hers. 'And I thought . . .'

he said, 'I thought I knew something about loyalty and love.'

'It makes one do silly things, doesn't it? Like staying in abominable Calcutta. Never mind.' With a smile, she gave the folder back to him. He had not seen her smile before; it transformed the ravaged face and lit her eyes to a luminous brown. 'Please don't feel badly. One day, even if it's not for twelve years, I may come and ask you for other air tickets — for two.'

'I go to my beloved wife.' Dr Coomaraswamy had repeated that when he had made his farewell speeches, flowery to Auntie Sanni, more flowery to Mary, 'My beloved wife,' but could not stop himself saying, 'Miss Kuku, I think, is not appearing . . . No?' asked wistful Dr Coomaraswamy.

'Our Doctor,' said Auntie Sanni when Mr Srinivasan had escorted him away, 'our dear Doctor, fancies Kuku. I say "fancies" because he will never get as much as a glance from her, poor man. His wife is a gorgon. Yes. Poor man.' Auntie Sanni sighed.

Poor Kuku, Mary wanted to say but instead, 'Auntie Sanni, may I go up and see her?'

Auntie Sanni gave Mary a long and penetrating look. 'I'm sure you will be kind,' she said.

'Kuku?' Mary knocked again.

'Kuku?'

'Go away. I don't want any of you to come in,' cried a hysterical voice.

'I'm not "any of you",' said Mary and pushed — the door had no lock.

Kuku was lying on the bed as dishevelled as when Mary had last seen her at the foot of the bier. Her sari was half off and rumpled, her face so swollen with tiredness and crying that she looked almost ugly. Has she watched all night? wondered Mary, who had not gone near the chapel but stayed, watching, in her room.

'And of them all,' snarled Kuku, 'the last person I want is you.'

'I know.'

'Then why force yourself on me? What do you want?'

'To give you this.'

Mary took the signet ring out of her pocket and held it out. 'It was his.'

'His?'

'Yes. Didn't you notice? He always wore it on the little finger of his left hand.'

'The finger that the shark . . .'

'Yes.' Mary hurried on. 'Look. This is his crest, a stag's head. He was proud of that.'

'Most people not having a crest?' Kuku whispered.

'Exactly.'

Kuku seemed stunned by wonder. She held the ring close, turning it, turning it; her own little finger traced the stag head. 'He should have been proud. His ring – and you want me to have it.'

'Yes. I think you should.'

'What do the words mean?'

'They're French. Loyalty and truth. You should have it. You were more loyal than I and you loved him.'

Kuku was driven to be honest. 'Mary, he didn't love me. He . . .' she brought herself to say it, 'for him, I didn't exist . . . until the end.'

'That doesn't matter. You loved him.' Mary closed Kuku's fingers over the ring.

'Mees.' As Mary came out of Kuku's room, an apparition startled her, as did the urgent voice. 'Mees.'

Kanu, in his haste to reach her, was scrambling on all fours to the door opening on to what had been Mr Menzies' room. His red shirt was as rumpled as Kuku's

227

sari had been; his face, too, was swollen with tears. He has been hiding under the bed, thought Mary. Behind him, the room was empty, clean, swept, dusted, the bed freshly made up; towels, drinking water, flowers, ready for an incoming guest.

'Kanu. If Hannah— '

'Hannah!' He spat, got up on his knees, entreating Mary.

'Menzies, Menzies Sahib. Mees. Please.'

'Menzies Sahib has left hotel. Gone.' Mary tried to free herself but the small black hands held her.

'Gone car,' sobbed Kanu, 'no take Kanu. "Get out car. Get *out!*" he mimicked Mr Menzies. '"Out!"' Then sobs overtook him. 'No take Kanu. No take.' Terrible sobs. Kanu was suddenly a small boy woefully bereft. A gabble of Telegu followed – Mary guessed he was saying, 'Where is he?' and, 'I don't know where. Not know.' She shook her head. 'Ghandara? Madras? I don't know.'

'Kanu go too. Please. Mees.'

Mary shook her head again. 'Kanu, I can't help.'

They heard Hannah's bangles, her tread: with a cry of despair, Kanu vanished down the stairs.

'*Chota* Memsahib' Mary had been promoted: 'Little Memsahib.' It was Samuel. 'The telephone. Master's father and mother. They wish speak with you.'

'Oh, no.' Mary visibly shrank.

'They waiting,' Samuel said severely.

The line was not good but Mary could hear the grief and concern in their voices – they were speaking on party lines – 'Dear, dear Mary. Are you better? Sir John said . . .'

'Much better now.'

'He says you are being very brave. Poor little girl.'

Mary winced. 'Not brave. Not little girl.'

'Can't hear. Never mind. Just to tell you we are

228

bringing darling Blaise home from that horrible place.'

'*Horrible* place?' From the open telephone kiosk Mary could catch a glimpse of the garden, gūl-mohr trees and pink and white acacias, parakeets flying in them. She could hear Auntie Sanni's doves and, distantly, the sound of the waves, feel the sea breeze, warm, scented. She tried to come back to the telephone. 'Take Blaise?'

The voices seemed to go on in a meaningless babble. 'I don't understand,' said Mary.

'Never mind. We don't want to distress you, dear child, Sir John will explain,' and, 'Mary, darling,' came Mrs Browne's voice, 'the moment you are home, you must come straight to us.'

'Home?' asked Mary, bewildered.

'Yes, Archie has been trying to get in touch with Rory.'

'I don't know exactly where Rory is,' said Mary.

'Your own father?' — faint disapproval.

'I often don't know where he is.'

'Can't hear. Never mind, get Sir John. Don't worry. We'll take care of you.'

I can take care of myself — but this new and learning-to-be-more-gracious Mary did not say it, only, 'Thank you . . . thank . . .' Unexpected sobs overtook her. Sir John quietly put her out of the way.

'They said, "Take Blaise home." '

'They mean back to England.'

'How?' The telephone call, its jerk into reality, had amazed Mary.

'A special coffin is made, then they fly him home by air.'

'You mean dig him up and bury him again?'

'Dear Mary! I hope you didn't say that to his mother?'

'That's what it is, isn't it?'

Like Mrs Browne, Lady Fisher wanted to be tender. 'Don't distress yourself,' she said. 'It will all be seen to. You needn't know anything about it,' but, 'I think it's the best thing,' said Mary, 'Blaise never liked it here. I think it's what he would have wanted.' Her face lit. 'And it means I can come back here to Auntie Sanni. She says I can come whenever I like.'

'Mary,' Lady Fisher knew she had to be practical, 'you're leaving here with us, of course, coming to Delhi?'

'Delhi?'

'John,' called Lady Fisher, 'John.'

'You'll stay with us in Delhi, won't you?' Sir John used tact. 'At least until we get in touch with Rory. If he's in New York I'm sure he'll fly over to fetch you.'

Come straight to us. You're leaving here with us. Fly over to fetch you. 'No,' said Mary. 'Thank you both and everyone, especially you,' she said to Lady Fisher, 'and Sir John for all you've done but I'm going by myself.'

'Where?'

'To Calcutta. That's the worst place, isn't it? I want the worst. To Calcutta like Olga.'

'To do what?'

'To try and do what Krishnan has taught me.'

There was a silence then, 'Mary,' said Lady Fisher, 'you seem to have known Krishnan Bhanj well, far more well than we thought.'

'It *was* well.' Mary smiled, a happy confident smile. 'Dear Lady Fisher, don't worry. I'll find work in a hostel, a poor people's or children's home.'

'Mary, you don't have to. There'll be plenty of money.'

'I do have to. I need to do something difficult, dreadful. Don't you see I have to try and ... and make up.'

'Expiate,' said Sir John and touched her cheek but, 'Isn't that a little exaggerated?' asked Lady Fisher.

'No it's *not*. Olga understands. She'll help me.'

'How can she, in her situation?'

'That makes her the very person.'

'At least try and tell us this: what did Krishnan teach you?'

'To love,' said Mary simply.

Again the Fishers looked at one another in some consternation.

'Mary, do you know what you are saying?'

'For the first time I do.'

'You and Krishnan Bhanj!'

'Not just Krishnan.' Mary's eyes were dreamy. 'Everyone. Anyone.'

'Mary!' For a moment they were shocked, but afterwards 'We ought to have trusted her,' Lady Fisher said to Sir John. 'Besides, we knew that Krishnan as a true Hindu would not in any way traduce another man's wife. While Mary . . .'

'It's not what you think.' Mary had said that at once. 'It's . . . it's that . . .' she had picked up a shell from one of the bowls of shells kept on the verandah tables. And suddenly she found words – I only had thoughts, could never say them – but now, 'Most of us, almost all of us,' said this newly eloquent Mary, 'are shut in a shell and because it's so filled with ourselves, there's no room to let anyone or anything in, nothing outside ourselves when, if we only knew, there's the whole of . . . well everything . . .'

'Creation?' suggested Sir John.

'Yes. We don't know it but we are part of everyone, everything.' Mary saw Krishnan's hand stroking Udata's grey squirrel back, saw her stripes from Vishnu's hand. 'It's all there only we're too shut in our shell to see it or feel it. Krishnan opened my shell and let me out. It's perfectly logical because', she held the shell to her ear and listened, 'it's only in an empty shell,' said Mary, 'that you hear the sound of the sea.'

'All the same,' Lady Fisher told Sir John with certainty when Mary had gone, 'it's Krishnan that girl really loves.'

* * *

231

'Mrs Browne, please to excuse me', it was a flustered Mr Srinivasan, 'but I have looked in reception and there is no one there. Not Miss Kuku. Not Miss Sanni. It is the last thing I have to do and urgent as I have to go to Ghandara for the parade. You were in the office, Mrs Browne. Can you help me?'

'If I can,' and 'If you will come to reception.' Mary followed him and, 'What is it you have to do?'

'Book a room, a permanent room, for Mr Krishnan Bhanj.'

'Here? At Patna Hall?'

'Where else?' asked Mr Srinivasan. 'He will have to come so often to his constituency. Not like other members, he will be continually among his people, working with them,' and seeing her startled face, he said again, 'Where else? Always he has been coming here, first as a little boy with father and mother.'

'Of course,' said Mary slowly, 'that's when he made friends with Thambi.'

'He will need to be much at Konak. He must be with his constituents.'

The words were like small hammers driving reality in. 'Here, not in the grove?'

'The grove, I think, is over.'

When Mr Srinivasan had gone and she had made a note for Auntie Sanni and entered the booking in the register, 'Mr Krishnan Bhanj, MP', which looked strange, almost foreign, Mary put her elbows on the cool teak wood of the reception counter, her hands over her ears to shut out the sound of the sea, her eyes closed to keep out the sunshine outside. 'Understand,' said Mary to Mary, 'Krishnan will come and you will not be here. It is probable you will never see Krishnan again.'

'Then you are not looking,' said a voice.

Mary's eyes seemed to fly open, her hands to fall. It was Krishnan's uncanny way of knowing her thoughts

232

but who was this elegant young man standing in the hall, tall, exceedingly good-looking, exceedingly dark? He wore a well-cut European suit of fine linen, a shirt of palest blue that set off his good looks, a public-school tie – Harrow? wondered Mary – pale socks and polished shoes; his hair was cut and brushed back. 'Ready for the victory parade,' said Krishnan.

Then he came closer. 'Mary, I am sorry. Deeply, deeply sorry. I wish I hadn't taunted Blaise,' said Krishnan.

'So do I. We both did.'

'We are birds of one feather.'

'We always have been,' said Mary and, unsteadily, 'Except . . . Krishnan, I can't forgive Blaise for Slippers. The rest I can manage but that . . .'

'It is still raw,' said Krishnan. 'Still sore.'

'But for us, it's over.' 'Over' seemed a desolate word.

'Not at all,' said Krishnan. 'When something is over, something else begins. Therefore' – Krishnan still kept some tags of old-fashioned English – 'we shall see one another again.'

'I don't think so. I shall be, I hope, working in a slum in Calcutta. You will be in Delhi in Parliament. Don't they call it the Round House?'

'The Monkey House,' said Krishnan. 'I am still not there yet. Also, I may not stay there just as you may not stay in your slum. Perhaps one day, when we are old, Auntie Sanni might ask us to run Patna Hall for her. That would be fun.'

'Yes,' said Mary fervently.

'And, Mary, I should very much like you to meet my father and mother. And now,' said Krishnan, 'let's go and have a drink.'

Mary came round the reception desk counter. 'I have never known you drink anything but coconut water and that out of a coconut shell.'

'Monkeys can change their ways,' said Krishnan.

233

'Krishnan. Sir John. Krishnan. Sir John.' The frantic voice reached the drawing room where they were all gathered; a sudden squall of rain had driven them from the verandah where Kuku, dressed and groomed, only her face still marked with tearstains, her eyelids red, had been serving coffee after luncheon – a special luncheon that Samuel had been allowed to plan as if to show that Patna Hall was still Patna Hall, 'no matter what,' as Auntie Sanni said. The luncheon had included mulligatawny soup.

It was also a farewell to which the drawing room lent a certain stateliness. Everyone was ready to go; the luggage was in the cars. When Kuku finished serving, she began taking round the visitors' book for signing when Dr Coomaraswamy, his bald head and coat shoulders wet with rain, came in panting, Mr Srinivasan at his heels. 'Sir John! Sir John!'

'Doctor! What is it?'

'It is that –' Dr Coomaraswamy almost choked, 'it is that in two hours we should be holding the victory parade, ju-bi-lant-ly. We were— ' Dr Coomaraswamy really did choke.

'We were dry and home,' Mr Srinivasan helped him. 'Krishnan has won by a hundred and sixty-nine thousand votes, far over Padmina Retty. A record! A hundred and sixty-nine thousand.'

'I myself was so jubilant. Now look at this. *Look* at this!' Dr Coomaraswamy had a typewritten sheet in his hand. 'Scandal!' cried Dr Coomaraswamy in an extreme of horror. 'We cannot have scandal now.'

'But we have,' cried Mr Srinivasan.

'No Member of Parliament can afford scandal. Oh, why didn't you tell me, Krishnan? You could have confided. We could have prevented. Sir John, you have influence in London, more influence here but even you, I think, cannot avert this.'

'But it must be stopped.' Mr Srinivasan was wringing his hands.

'Stopped! It must be blown sky high but who is to blow it? How can we block this?'

'You can't.'

Mr Menzies, as cool as Dr Coomaraswamy was hot, sauntered into the room. 'Coomaraswamy is right,' he said, 'not even you, Sir John, can stop it. The injunction is over. This is public news now. News.'

'What news?' Krishnan stood up.

'Ah! The successful candidate, God Krishnan!' Mr Menzies made a mock bow.

'Tell us what news.' Krishnan was unperturbed.

'I suggest you read it,' said Mr Menzies. 'Read it aloud. As the Doctor seems upset, for which he has every reason as you shall hear – perhaps you, Sir John?'

Sir John took the sheets with disdain. ' "The gods amuse themselves," ' he read aloud. 'Indeed they do! Who was the dressed-up girl who travelled Konak with Krishnan Bhanj on his lorry? Was she Radha the goddess, conveniently come to life, or was she, in fact, the young bride of Mr Blaise Browne who has so mysteriously drowned? What was Mrs Browne doing alone with Krishnan in the grove at Shantipur where he had made his ashram? An ashram for two?

' "Is it surprising that there was a midnight quarrel on the sands? A quarrel that ended in Mr Browne's being knocked down after which a certain lady did not come back to her hotel all night, the night on which Mr Browne took an unaccountable swim in a sea he knew to be dangerous, so dangerous he might not come back. One has to ask, 'Did he want to come back?'

' "Krishnan Bhanj has won his election in a landslide of triumph. Could it not turn into an avalanche to bury him?

' "Krishnan Bhanj took the vow of silence we have

235

heard so much about; it would seem he took no vow of anything else. How ironic if his – shall we call it appetite? – and his temper, will silence him for ever." '

The appalled stillness was broken by a shriek of joy. 'Menzies Sahib! Menzies Sahib!' A scurry of small feet and into the drawing room hurtled Kanu in his red shirt, his face bright with happiness as he flung himself on Mr Menzies. 'Sahib back. Come back for Kanu. Sahib! Sahib!'

'Well,' said Krishnan, 'your little spy.'

Kanu clung to Mr Menzies, the curly head rubbing against him, his face upturned in rapture. 'Sahib. Kanu's Sahib.'

'*Chūp!* Get out!' Mr Menzies wrenched the thin arms away. There was a slap, a piteous cry. 'Haven't I told you? Go!'

He was holding Kanu by the back of his shirt, shaking him, when Auntie Sanni spoke. 'Let that boy go. How dare you hurt a child in my drawing room?' She said a few words in Telegu to Kanu as he stood whimpering and cowering, then clapped her hands.

Samuel appeared as if by magic – 'Or not magic,' Krishnan murmured to Mary, 'he has been listening.'

'Samuel take Kanu away,' Auntie Sanni said in English. 'Keep him. Don't let him out of your sight and send for his father and mother. We shall be needing them.'

When Samuel had taken Kanu, 'That boy', said Mr Menzies in bravado, 'has been pestering me all this week.'

'So you pestered him with silk shirts, a watch, car rides, sweets,' said Krishnan. 'Or should we say paid him?'

'Krishnan, please,' Dr Coomaraswamy interrupted in misery, 'the boy is not important—'

'He is very important,' said Auntie Sanni.

'But, Miss Sanni, time is running fast. Can we not return to our business?'

'Certainly,' said Mr Menzies.

Sir John came back to the paper. 'I take it,' he said with disdain, 'this will go out tonight?'

'To every Indian newspaper. It is my own, shall we say, scoop? It will be on the evening news, radio and television. It may make the evening papers. London will follow suit, press and all the media, unless . . . ' said Mr Menzies.

'Unless?'

'It is always possible to buy things,' said Mr Menzies to the air.

'He is asking' — Dr Coomaraswamy could hardly bring himself to say it — 'asking eighty *lakhs* of rupees.'

'Five hundred thousand pounds,' moaned Mr Srinivasan.

'Almost a *crore*.'

'You are lucky it isn't a *crore*,' said Mr Menzies.

'Eighty *lakhs* is not possible. I have not got it. The Party has not got it. All that I have is already staked in this election.'

'Pity,' said Mr Menzies. 'Would the Brownes not help since they would be, shall we say, distressed?' Mr Menzies was smooth. 'They, I think, have plenty stashed away — or your father, Mrs Browne? The redoubtable Rory, Roderick Frobisher Sinclair Scott,' he mocked.

'Blackmail is, may I remind you,' Sir John had even more disdain, 'a criminal offence.'

'So it is. The trouble with blackmail', Mr Menzies seated himself on the arm of one of Auntie Sanni's sofas and lit a cigarette, 'is that to prove it all the allegations have to come out, be made public and you wouldn't want that, would you?' He turned to Krishnan. 'Or you, Mr Bhanj. Your parents are very wealthy. What is this worth to them and you?'

'Nothing,' said Krishnan. 'To them or to me. Publish your filth.' He looked at his watch. 'In precisely one hour I

237

shall be facing my people. I shall face them and – Sir John, would you give me that paper – I shall read to them, but in their own language, yes, over the loudspeakers, what Sir John has just read to us here. Every word,' said Krishnan. 'Then I shall ask them what I am to do with my victory – forfeit it or use it to serve them? The Root and Flower Party is founded on the people, for the people. It is for them to decide but not one *anna* will you get from any Bhanj.'

'And Delhi?' asked Mr Menzies. 'What will they think in Delhi?'

'What they think in Konak.' Krishnan was steady. 'My father is there.'

'And London? I think I can say I am certain of London. They will be extremely interested in . . . shall we call it the personal side?'

'London is very far away,' quavered Mr Srinivasan.

'Not for the Brownes,' said Lady Fisher.

'Not for Blaise.' Mary, who had sat proudly up after Krishnan's words, hid her face in her hands.

There was a movement. Auntie Sanni, majestically massive among them, held up her hand, then said what they had all heard her say many times, 'That is enough.'

'You must all have wondered', said Auntie Sanni, 'what Mr Menzies was doing here at Patna Hall. Now we know – almost in full. As Ajax, a clever journalist, it seemed he was attracted to Konak by the scent of an unusual story, Krishnan's vow of silence, but he found more. In elections there is usually something more, which can be very rewarding in a different way. That is perhaps why Mr Menzies is so assiduous in attending them.

'I am not concerned with politics,' said Auntie Sanni. 'They pass but some things do not pass. Though I wish Krishnan Bhanj's Party well, this attempted blackmail is not so important.' Dr Coomaraswamy gave an indignant gasp. 'What is of utmost concern is the damage you, Mr

238

Menzies, have done or are trying to do to other people's lives: to a rising politician who has dedicated his life to his cause; to a young woman who, no matter how you make it seem, is innocent. Worse, a young man on whom your insinuations worked to such a pitch that it ended in his death.'

'You can't accuse me of that.'

'In part.' Auntie Sanni did not falter. 'And, perhaps worst of all, a child. Kanu may not seem of much importance to any of you as Dr Coomaraswamy has said, but he is significant, very significant.

'I must remind you, Mr Menzies, that under Indian law, homosexuality, even with consenting adults, is a criminal offence. Seduction of a child is an even worse offence and Kanu is only ten.'

'What has he been telling you?' Mr Menzies' tongue came out to moisten his lips which seemed to have gone dry; his pink was now a curious grey. 'What?'

'Nothing as yet but he will. As you heard, Samuel has sent for his father and mother. Also we can call Chief Inspector Anand.'

'The police!'

'Yes.' Colonel McIndoe got up and stood by Auntie Sanni's chair. 'We shall give you one chance, Menzies. You will not only leave this hotel, you will leave the state of Konak today. I and two of Dr Coomaraswamy's aides — if you will allow them, Doctor — will have much pleasure in escorting you to Madras, Delhi, Calcutta, wherever you prefer to go, but the moment you publish one word of your allegations we shall inform the police — as you said of London, they will be much interested in the personal side.'

Mr Menzies looked at him with hate.

'Well?' said Colonel McIndoe. 'Yes or no?'

'Why do you ask me? You know I have to say yes.'

'Very well, we'll go now. We'll arrange about your

239

car. My wife will take care of Kanu. Doctor, please call your young men.'

'Not yet.' Krishnan, too, was up. 'I have a few things to settle with Mr Menzies.' He took Mr Menzies by the coat collar almost lifting him off his feet and, as Mr Menzies cried out, 'I'm not going to hit you,' said Krishnan. 'Unfortunately, you are as much protected by the law as we innocents are. I shall not leave a mark on you, I promise. It will be a little wrestling match, except that I do not think you are a match for me.'

'No. No.' Mr Menzies' cry was almost a shriek but Krishnan only said, 'Come outside.'

'Congratulations on your victory, Doctor, and to you, Mr Srinivasan,' Auntie Sanni was saying as she stood making farewells. 'I don't suppose we shall see you again for a time. Let us hope Konak will not need another election for some years.'

'Miss Sanni, madam, Colonel McIndoe,' Dr Coomaraswamy cleared his throat, 'we can never express our gratitude. This momentous victory . . .'

'Most momentous,' said Mr Srinivasan.

'is entirely owing . . .'

'Don't let him make a speech,' Sir John whispered in her ear. 'We shall miss our train,' and, 'Goodbye, dear Doctor,' Auntie Sanni said firmly, 'Goodbye, Mr Srinivasan. You must leave, I know, for Ghandara. Your victory parade,' and she went on to the Fishers. 'John. Alicia. Next year and I hope more peacefully.'

Kuku had drawn Mary aside. 'Will you tell Miss Sanni you have given me the ring? They will think I stole it else.'

'Kuku, they would never—'

'Hannah and Samuel would,' and Mary had to admit she could hear their voices, 'Give poor young master's ring to that good-for-nothing girl.'

'I'll tell her.'

Kuku gave Mary a kiss.

'Mary, come to us and Patna Hall whenever you can and bring Olga.'

'I shall. I . . . can't begin to say thank you.'

'Then don't. You will be my girl always.'

'Always.'

Mary had been down to the beach to say goodbye to Thambi, Moses and especially Somu. They were gathering up the helmets to clean them, shaking out the umbrellas, raking over the sand, getting ready for the incoming guests. The umbrellas, like the sand, were wet from the rain.

They came to greet her. Mary had brought Blaise's splendid pair of binoculars to give to Thambi who took them with deep respect. 'Memsahib come back soon,' said Thambi. 'Memsahib not be afraid. Sahib, he rest now.'

'They are taking him to England,' Thambi inclined his dignified head – the ways of Westerners were unfathomable to him – 'but Memsahib stay India.'

'I hope so.' Yet Mary could not help a sense of a knell sounding in her: The scarlet cotton flowers are dropping. Well, all flowers lose their petals, the brilliance fades. Slippers has gone. Udata and Birdie will come looking for Krishnan. It is over, thought Mary, then stopped. Hadn't Krishnan said, 'When something is over, something else begins'?

At the same moment, 'Look,' said Thambi.

Over the sea, still dark from the storm, far out away from waves made angry by wind and rain, their crests a strange grey as they crashed on the shore, was a rainbow, a perfect rainbow, its arc in all its colours, meeting the sea on either side. 'Indradhanassu.' Thambi gave its Telegu name. 'Is bow of Indra.' Indra, God of Storm and Mary remembered the painting in the hill temple: he sets his bow to show that every storm has an end.

* * *

'Mr and Mrs Prendergast,' Kuku read from the register.

'Number one,' said Hannah.

'They are old friends,' explained Auntie Sanni.

'The Right Honourable Viscount Normington and Viscountess Normington,' Kuku read with relish.

'They have booked the bridal suite. Their servant can go in Paradise.'

'Mr and Mrs Arjit Roy and three children.'

'They will have the whole bungalow.' Kuku gave a little gasp; if Auntie Sanni and Hannah heard they made no sign.

'Mr and Mrs Banerjee . . .'

'Two hundred *and fifty* sheets this week. Five hundred pillowcases,' shouted the *vanna* in the linen room. 'Worse than last week. It is *too* much.'

'It was because of the election.' Hannah tried to soothe him. 'The election is over. This week will be more peaceful. There will not be so many. Come, brother,' she crooned. 'Take them and wash them.'

'Wash them yourself.' The *vanna* left them on the floor.

All the clamour had died away. Everything was . . . 'normal,' said Auntie Sanni. The fishing boats had gone out, come back; the catch was on the shore. The grove was silent, the village went about its daily chores. The *mahout* had taken Birdie back to the palace. A small grey squirrel, plump now and agile, played in the trees. 'I wish you could have had a more peaceful time,' she had told the Fishers as they said goodbye.

'Oddly enough, no matter what happens, here there is peace,' said Lady Fisher.

'Yes,' said Auntie Sanni. 'Sometimes there is upset, this week a deep upset, but slowly . . .' she dropped into her singsong voice, 'it is like the sea, the waves — they beat in such thunder, the wash surges up the beach but cannot help spreading into ripples. Then they ebb. Everything goes with them, in a short while there is not even a mark left on the sand. No. There may be a little mark,' conceded Auntie Sanni.

Epilogue

January

Dear Mr and Mrs Browne,

[wrote Auntie Sanni who still kept her careful school-girl script – she remembered the 'e'.]

I am writing to you at the request of Miss Kuku Vikram recently in my employ. She has gone now to better herself at an hotel in Bombay. She wishes me to tell you that a little boy was born to her here at Patna Hall on Christmas Eve, the son of your late son, Mr Blaise Browne. There is no mistaking; the resemblance is extraordinary. The child is fair, with his father's blue eyes and shows promise of the same . . .[Auntie Sanni was not sure how to spell physique so wrote] physic. A lovely healthy child. He has been baptised as Blaise.

Kuku, who is now only twenty-one, is unable to support him, she is an orphan and has to make her way. She will make no claim on him if you will take him as your own. He is presently at Patna Hall with me.

I await your instructions.

Yours truly,

Sanita McIndoe
Proprietress

Underneath she wrote 'Auntie Sanni'.

244

Glossary

NB Telegin words are spelt phonetically.

achkan	tunic coat, high-collared and buttoned as worn by Nehru
almirah	wardrobe
anna	small coinage equivalent to a penny but sixteen to the rupee
apsara	celestial dancing girls dedicated to the gods
Ari!	'Oh!' but stronger. Frequently a remonstrance
Atcha	agreed, good
ayah	children's nurse or female servant in the service of women
Ayyo!	as for *Ari* (Telegu)
bania	merchant, money-lender, shopkeeper
biri	type of cigarette made from raw dried leaves
brinjals	egg plant/aubergine
charpoy	simple Indian bed with wooden frame and legs laced across with string, usually coconut string
chatti	earthenware bowl; for a tea chatti, small – and smashed when it has been drunk from
Chelo	Get going. Go!
choli	tight-fitting bodice
Chūp	Hush. Shut up
crore	100,000,000 rupees. Ten million. Ten lakhs
darshan	an audience, as for a king or holyman, but also, for the person attending, gaining grace by the simple act of 'beholding', looking without speaking or trying to make any sort of contact – certainly not taking photographs
dipa	small earthenware lamp, heart-shaped with a little wick floating in oil

245

dosa	pancake, sometimes stuffed, made from slightly fermented gram flour
durbar	state or court formal reception
durrie	cotton, woven, striped rug or carpet
gharra	large earthenware vessel
ghee	clarified butter
gopi	milkmaid
gram	grain
Hut jao	Go at once. Swiftly [but stronger]
jaggery	a kind of molasses but thicker, almost like fudge
Jai!	(pronounced Jy) Hail!
Jao!	Go!
Kachiyundu	Wait (Telegu)
kofta	ball of minced fish or meat
lakh	100,000 rupees
lota	small pot, usually of brass
lunghi	sarong
mali	gardener
namaskar	a greeting made with the hands held together as in prayer
pandal	a form of awning, usually connected with a religious feast day or a wedding. Can be made of silk or cotton, brightly coloured, or leaves such as banana leaves on their stems
panga	a long blunt-ended blade with one sharp side
pice	a quarter of an anna
punkah	overhead fan, now usually electric-bladed
puri	deep-fried small round of puffy flat bread, sometimes stuffed
Shabash	Fine. Good. Well done
shaitan	devil
simile	cotton trees
tamasha	a great show; something done lavishly
vanna	washerman (Telegu)

SUMMER DIARY

The Herbogowan

'When the lotus comes it is time to go.' That is what we say in Kashmir. June, July and August are high summer and the famous vale grows intolerably sultry. Though the Pir Panjals that ring it still bear, on some mornings, streaks of fresh snow, a heat haze hangs over the lakes and even the swift Jhelum seems to run sluggishly. The earth is dry, the green dusty; the last of the nomad clans, the bakriwars or goat people, have passed through with their flocks and herds of buffalo on their way to summer in the mountain valleys; we too begin to think of tantalizing coolness and green; of the smell of firs in the sun and tumbling streams of icy water; of sheets of clover and alpine flowers, while here in Srinagar on the Dal Lake the great pink lotus beds open, each with an extraordinary suddenness in the heat, to float and rock among leaves so flat and thick that a baby could lie on them. The lotus are in flower. It is time to go.

Go where? Each year it is the same question. Never for us to the accepted hill stations of Pahalgham or fashionable Gulmarg with its houses – of logs and shingles, it is true, but houses all the same – houses and hotels, shops and clubs, golf, polo and tennis. Always for us it is to camp in one of the high valleys. Sonamarg, perhaps, or Nil Nag, the Blue Lake; or in the Liddar; camping where there is only a village of a few huts, a serai for caravans, possibly a post depot, but for the rest an empty valley, forests, peaks and, every year, a trek. This year we decided to drive, by way of the Manasbal lake to Baltal, now head of the motor road, and trek over the Herbogowan, a pass of 1,400 feet, to the valley of the Liddar. This is one of the most ordinary treks in Kashmir and renowned for its beauty, but being high it is one of the more lonely ones and in the five days we took to do it, until we came down into the comparative civilization of Aru, we saw no one but the bakriwars, the nomad goat people, a few villagers and, once, a caravan. The tents and furnishings for our permanent summer camp were to meet us in the Liddar valley at the end of the trek.

'We' were myself, my daughter Paula, who had broken off her pony-stud training to come out to India for a few months, and her cousin Simon, a Cambridge undergraduate who was here for the long vacation. There was also Sol, the most experienced and intrepid of my Pekingese; he was also the ugliest; in fact the ugliest Pekingese I have ever met, being liver-coloured – a colour not recognized by the Kennel Club – with a ruff that was cream-coloured and stuck straight up, oddly stiff where it should have fallen in soft, rich feathering; his final disgrace was that his nose was brown; but Sol was cheerfully unaware of his hideousness, he was sure he was everyone's friend and certainly no Pekingese, in our family's long line of Pekingese, had ever been more beloved. His only luggage was a walnut that he had treasured for a year and would play with for hours, particularly if he could get a human to do a little team-work with him.

As we meant to travel lightly and quickly, we decided to take only one servant, Subhan, the owner of our houseboat, who was also a cook-guide. Most visitors to Kashmir take a house-boat for their stay in Srinagar – for it is a water city – and this year, though I was long familiar with houseboat owners and their ways, we had rented Subhan's *Hoopoe* for the season.

Subhan had disliked me on sight; I sympathized. Coming to Kashmir, says the proverb, is like putting one's head into an exquisitely beautiful hornets' nest and what houseboat owner would want to have as his tenant someone who had been quite often stung before? But we had taken the *Hoopoe* and we had to make the best of one another. Subhan's best could be very good indeed; he was a wily old Kashmiri and he looked a patriarch, indeed he had a big and needy family in the cooking boat behind the *Hoopoe*; his beard was dyed with henna, though I am sure he had never been to Mecca, and he was plausible with forty or fifty seasons of letting houseboats behind him. When he was outraged, for instance when I told him mildly and firmly that eggs could not cost fifty annas a dozen, or that I should like an account for the fifteen rupees I had given him yesterday, he would take off his turban – it came off in one piece like an intricately folded meringue – and cast it on the floor at my feet. Allah would be his witness, he would cry, if any memsahib had ever insulted him like this. The first time I was impressed; for a Mahommedan to take off his head-covering is momentous, but soon I knew that in the end he would always pick it up and put it on again, while we would settle amicably for a total somewhere between his figure and mine.

So we took Subhan and, in spite of his more expensive suggestions, very little camp luggage: two tents for us, a cook tent in which Subhan and the pony men would sleep; three camp beds for us and a roll each of blankets – the men would sleep, as they always slept, on the ground and Sol on the end of my bed; a folding chair each and one folding table; a leather-covered basin between us and a small canvas bath. There were also two kiltas – wicker-lidded baskets covered in leather that held cooking pots, vegetables and enough stores, for we should find nothing, after we left the road, but milk, some eggs, perhaps chickens and honey. Subhan had a try to persuade me not to come. The pass was very high, he said. He was sure I should break down and, 'Don't come, Memsahib,' he begged. 'It will be much more fun without you.'

'I don't mind. I am coming.' I said.

We left by lorry in the early morning in the middle of June. The vale of Kashmir is a land of rice, fruit and honey; the foothills up to the mountains are cut and terraced with rice fields in jigsaw patterns edged with small mud walls or dykes. That morning the rice was still young, only a few inches high, and showed the water between its roots, reflecting the blue of the sky. Every village we passed had its walled garden of fruit; in some they were picking the apricots and men with flat baskets, covered against the sun with leaves, were carrying the fruit into Srinagar.

We passed the big golden-orange mosque of Hazrat Bal and the fort, red-walled on its hill, and drove across the vale and past the bridge at Gangabal, with its little lake, so deep that, the legend tells, a man spun rope for ten years, weighted it and dropped it in and it did not reach the bottom.

The Manasbal lake is larger and further away; the road skirted the dried-up foothills and, on the burnt dun colour of their slopes, the crops showed brilliantly: rice, wheat and ripe oats, blue-flowered flax plentifully mixed with poppies, while, along the road itself, were the vineyards that give the small green Kashmiri grapes. We drove on and on until we turned so steeply into a gap in the hill that it seemed we were driving into the sky itself; the car seemed to hang in the air for a moment and then point downwards and there below us was Manasbal, the lake with its famous kingfisher-blue water, its shores rising in cliffs of cream-rose earth planted with mulberry, poplar and willow trees. Across the lake the Pir Panjal mountains cut off the sky, their crests reflected white in the far water. The near shore with its gentle bank was shaded with chenars, the giant trees, like plane trees, planted long ago by the Moghul Emperors, Abhar and Shah Jehan. In among the tree-reflections in the blue water, lotuses were in bud.

The road grew wilder after we left Manasbal and had turned into the gorges of the River Sinde, which has rapids all the way so that it runs a peculiar milky blue, broken with spray and falls. As we began to climb, the mountains came down closer to the river on each side and now the trees were spruce and fir, showing here and there a glade of green. We passed Kharghil bridge, where the river widens into pools, good for trout, and a valley of pebbles. It was here that we had our fishing camp when I was a child; then it was three days' march from the vale by pony caravan; now the road goes far past it and past the

252

villages of Khanghan and Gunde, where we used to spend the night in small wooden rest houses. There were other lesser villages along the road, each with their small orchard of fruit and almond and walnut trees, hedges of wild roses, children in short robes and round caps – boys and girls alike – chickens and goats.

We met caravans of pack ponies and clans of bakriwars making their way up the valley. The women pulled their dogs off the road as we passed, big and furry dogs not unlike huskies and very fierce. I had to hold Sol to stop him jumping from the car. To me these nomads are romantic, especially their clothes. The women have thin striped trousers, draped and full, and black tunics fluted so that they swing as they walk, embroidered down the front with white buttons. They wear a small round cap in deep blue or scarlet, tilted forward, and over it a black veil stencilled in magenta or yellow or scarlet. All of them have silver jewellery, with chains and scarlet beads, and many carry a baby in a sling. They sound colourful but are unspeakably filthy. Nearly every group of them stopped us and asked me for medicines for stomach and sores, and one poor woman for what I thought must be a tumour. They were miserable while the men were clean, extraordinarily strong and handsome; the men looked biblical with their long coats and turbans; like the Kashmiris, each of them carried a shawl, folded as a plaid on their shoulders, but they carried nothing else – the women were for that – and they had staves and sandal shoes, thonged with turned-up toes, while the women, of course, were barefoot. Their children wore caps embroidered and trimmed with beads, with a flap hanging down behind like an elongated sunbonnet to keep away the flies and sun.

We met people every day of the march with their ponies, buffaloes and goats, or on their summer-grazing pastures.

We met Kashmiri villagers too, coming down, carrying silkworms to Srinagar, and once we were held up by a caravan of those endearing but slow-moving beasts, zobos, cross between a cow and bull yak, black and almost square and heavy, driven by Ladakhis. All the while, each side of the road, the gorge grew narrower and narrower while the slate and pumice-coloured mountains seemed to grow taller. We passed our first glacier, ice right down to the river; until I came to Kashmir I had always imagined glaciers to shine with snow and green-blue ice, but this, like most Kashmiri ones I have seen, was brown and dirty, littered with debris and fallen trees.

Now the villages grew fewer, only an occasional huddle of dark wooden shacks in the solitude of the mountains, with no fruit trees or roses, nothing near but the river and a few fields, still bare and rough, perhaps some sheep grazing, a straggle of chickens and hobbled pony or two.

'What do the people do here in the winter?' Simon asked Subhan.

'What is there to do? Sit in the house and wait for the spring,' and spring does not come here until June. After a moment Subhan added, 'But there is a trouble: ponies, chickens, sheep, children, eat all winter.'

We left the dark gorges and climbed up and up, into the sun, until we came into the long valley of our old camping ground, Sonamarg.

Marg in Kashmiri means 'a meadow'; Sonamarg is the Meadow of Flowers, and it is as beautiful as it sounds. On every side of it, the mountains come down, their peaks ribbed with snow and glaciers; but there is no feeling of narrowness for the valley is wide and rolls for miles with undulations of grass, rocks, fir trees, and hidden pockets grassed with clover, forget-me-nots and geums. Its sounds are quiet except for the streams. It has a village with a serai and post office and from it the road to Baltal now follows the river to the foot of the Zoji-La pass into Leh or Little Tibet. We drove quickly through where once we used to wander and laze. There were only two villages in all the nine miles, rough Ladakhi villages of a few huts. The winter snow-bridges were still standing in the river, but the valley and the slopes of the mountains were already pastoral with flocks and the calls of the herdsmen came down to us.

254

Simon and Paula wanted to explore a Ladakhi village so we stopped the car and walked up a bridle path through the fields. The village was in the gully of a mountain stream and, unlike the Kashmiri villages or nomad camps, the houses were not of wood but stone, flat-roofed like forts, with narrow slits of windows and wooden lattices. The people lived on the first floor because of the snow and, like Kashmiris, penned their cattle below. The lanes between the houses were running with filth and calves, hens and chickens were wandering loose. We were invited into one house and climbed into it by a ladder of branches; its room was a blackened hole, the beams scorched to charcoal. There was a cooking fire of stones in the centre, a hole in the roof for the smoke, some iron pots and a bed of stenching sheepskins. We came out very quickly.

The people were plump and healthy, mongolian-faced with pink cheeks; the men wore robes of grey-cream homespun wool, caps or velvet hats and were surprisingly clean and handsome, but the women looked degraded and unattractive, their clothes black cotton trousers, tunics and a curious cap with a long neck piece. They had some rough jewellery and each had a brass keyring and a brass spoon hanging from a chain on the breast. If a Ladakhi woman has a sheepskin and a basket on her back, she is married, and we asked to see a baby in a bag but there were none; this custom, of which I had been told, must be dying out − if it ever existed; the baby is alleged to be put into a bag with sheep dung and entrails and tied up to the neck to keep it warm, only being taken out once or twice a month. It seems too horrible to be true.

We bought eggs, a keyring and spoons. Simon wanted to buy some of the homespun but they had only narrow strips.

He asked Subhan what these people ate. 'Atah flour made into chapattis, and makhai,' which is Indian corn.

'No vegetables?'

'No, only shalgam,' a kind of turnip.

'But the summer climate is so beautiful,' Simon argued, 'They could grow potatoes, green vegetables, corn.' Subhan shrugged and said that besides the Indian corn only a black coarse grain was grown for horses.

We went back to the car and soon the road ended, running out beside a low line of wooden houses and a serai, with a guest house on the other side of the river. It was Baltal, the motor-head and we saw our ponies waiting for us, five baggage ponies and two riding ones, Bulbul and Lallah – all ponies in Kashmir seem to be called Bulbul or else Lallah after the flaunting red Kashmiri tulip. With them was Jobara, headman of his village, caretaker of the Sonamarg rest house, and for long years our ponyman and friend, and beside him was his son, Amar, who had known Paula and Simon as children and was remarkable for his aquamarine blue eyes that, with his pale brown skin and his black curly hair, made him look as I have always imagined the young Joseph to look. There was also another ponyman and an old bearded coolie for fetching and cutting wood.

We made our camp above the river and, while the ponymen put up the tents, the coolie gathered wood, Subhan fried chicken and potatoes on the clay stove Jobhara had built ready for us, he and Amar came and talked, telling us all the news of their village and ponies since last year.

We put our table by the campfire built in the circle of our tents of whole logs and branches laid across one another loosely so that the fire was fanned gently by the evening wind. After dinner we watched the sun, which had left us long ago and was now slowly leaving the mountains, turning their rock purple and then blue and rose, then snow pink and gold. We listened to the river and the steady sound of the ponies grazing and sniffed a new scent added to the good one of wood smoke, a scent that was pungent and always nostalgic for it brings back my childhood – the smell of the hookah passing from one of the men to another as they sat on their heels outside the cook tent; the gentle sound of the water bubbling in the pipe bowl made an accompaniment to the noisier river.

We saw the quarter moon go down over the mountains opposite. As soon as the moon had gone the stars grew enormous; if we walked away from the fire we could see the mountain snow-crests shining in their light.

Jobara came later to talk over plans for tomorrow. He sat companionably down on his heels beside us and spoke in his usual quiet way, but he wanted us to change our plans and go up the Zoji-La towards Leh. June was early, he thought, for the Herbowagan. 'But Subhan said . . .' I began.

'Subhan!' Jobara did not say any more but it was enough. I knew his opinion of the Srinagage boatmen – and I knew that he knew that, from the moment we had decided to come and, as a matter of course, engaged Jobara, Subhan had never ceased to tell us what a rogue Jobara was, how he overcharged for ponies, coolies, milk, eggs, everything, how much better he, Subhan, would have arranged . . . Kashmiris are arch-backbiters and Subhan was only being true to his kind, but in all the time I had known him I had never heard Jobara say as much as he had tonight.

'But we *must* go over the Herbogawan,' said Simon, 'it's the only chance we have,' and in the end Jobara agreed we should. 'But it will not be comfortable,' and he warned us we must make an early start.

I was glad. 'I want to see the sunrise,' I said.

'I will show it to you,' said Jobara with his usual courtesy.

When he had gone I made hot rum and milk – being Mahommedan he could not have shared it. As I moved between the tent and the fire I felt the wind ice-cold on my cheek, but we all had a warm sleepiness after so long a day and there was only a moment in bed to look out and see the stars and hear the river before we were asleep.

What I always remember most about mornings in Himalayan camps is the dew, the intense silver greenness of it on the grass, and the chill. As the sun slowly came down the mountains to reach the valley, we crept out of our tents to the fire that Subhan had kicked together again and tried to stop ourselves shivering, drink our tea and eat the tough camp toast. Sol refused to get up until the bed was taken down under him. The ponies were being driven in and camp was struck behind us as slowly the sun came nearer and warmed the air, taking the cold from it but leaving it fresh and clear. The mountains had fresh snow, every fir was stainlessly clean and when, leaving the basin for Simon to shave in, Paula and I went to wash in the stream it was like crystal and the flowers by the rocks were shining with dew. We left camp at a quarter-past eight, Sol, now wide awake and warm, circling and skimming the grass.

Sonamarg is 9,000 feet, Baltal 11,500 feet, and the ascent out of these high valleys is always literally breathtaking. As we rode or walked we were rising up the height of the mountains, meeting their snow, and the valley dropped away until it looked like a valley in the background of an Italian primitive, curiously complete and small, with the pastoral green of the glades, the fir-tree forests, the pale colour of the silver birches, and the limpid blue windings, clear like a ribbon, of the river; and then the track turned, the range was spread out around us, and we saw it opened out in all its size.

I feel I have not made enough impression of the height of these mountains. My mind has dwelt too much in the valleys and on their smaller, pocket-like alpine valleys, invitingly green in the immensity of the mountains, an immensity of huge clefts forested with fir and spruce and birch until one gets above tree level, when they are rock-veined with glaciers; above, higher still, and overhanging the track so high that they are even out of eagles' reach, are cliffs and pinnacles of rock in all colours of slate and pumice, grey, purple, dun, rose, perpetually streaked with snow. There are always eagles flying below these pinnacles and to look up to them one has to bend one's neck far, far back.

As we climbed it grew quieter and quieter, 'because we have left the streams behind,' said Paula. We came to a belt of flowers, some of them almost over in the valley below. We passed a silver-birch wood, its floor covered with small hill iris, and slanted queer staircases of rock and frozen streams that made miniature glaciers. The ponies plodded up, their small

258

hooves sending stones rattling down and sometimes, from a rock or a pile of stones, a marmot, those queer little red-brown animals with round heads and eyes like a happy puppy's, sat up on their haunches and scolded us. Each time Sol gave chase and had to be retrieved from a wilderness of stones.

We lunched by the way and all afternoon climbed higher and higher. It became more comfortable to walk than to ride, though our calves ached and our breath seemed to clot in our chests. We longed to stop but Jobara still led us up and up.

We crossed a large glacier, which is always troublesome at this season; the snow is not quite hard on top and gives at every step. The ponies walked fearfully; sometimes the path was on the edge of a crevasse, ominously blue, and in parts the snow was soft enough to sink through. To our surprise we met a small caravan coming down, a Hindu merchant, his wife, a ponyman and three ponies. Where had they come from? What were they doing? Though we greeted one another, we never knew. The merchant walked but his wife sat perched on a pack pony; wearing a blue robe like a kirtle edged with scarlet, of the graceful kind that Kashmir Hindu women wear and with a white cuff, she looked like a Virgin in a primitive Italian *Flight into Egypt* except that she also wore gaiters and sand shoes.

Soon after four o'clock we began to climb down to the small lake of Her Nag, where we were to camp. It was a merciful relief to walk downhill and Sol began to circle and bark in his usual way. Her Nag already had a big encampment of buffalo and goat people, come back to the cluster of log huts in the rich grass that was their summer pasturage. The unmistakable acrid smell of dung and wood smoke filled the air but the little valley was exquisite with a long waterfall, falling sheer from the rock onto the glacier above us and looking, not like a waterfall, but a plume of mist. The glacier clefts showed a true ice-blue, the air was filled with the bleating of goats and the whole valley was spread with flowers: primulas, geums, gentians, columbines, forget-me-nots and white anemones.

When we stopped, waiting while the packs were taken off

259

and the tents unrolled, we realized how cold it was and Jobara came to us. 'Put on your coats at once,' he commanded. Long ago I learned that it is always wise to do what Jobara says.

Soon after we left camp next morning we met a flock of goats coming down where we were climbing up. They were not being driven as sheep are but were running independently, quite fearless as they bounded from rock to rock; they were kingly goats, standing as high as a young bullock calf, with coats like silk, beards that looked as if they were combed and fierce yellow eyes. Sol decided he would keep close to us; once long ago he had tried an encounter with a goat and still had a horn scar on his shoulder. A goat boy came up and asked us if we would like a drink of milk, offering it in a wooden bowl. When we had drunk a little for politeness, he and his companion sat down on a rock and drank turn about from the same bowl. One of them had a crimson turban, the other a rose-coloured skullcap of the kind Jobara wears.

Now we had to come down to the long valley below the pass itself. The descent was down one of the natural stone staircases, spiral and hewn by ice from the rock. It was so steep, so winding, that the ponies had to be brought down one by one, two men to a pony, holding it head and tail. Even climbing down on our own was slippery; our legs shook, our ankles ached, while our ears thrummed as the wind rushed up the narrow cleft way; but we did not have it to ourselves for we met a bakriwar clan coming up, the rocks echoing with their shouts and whistles.

The elders had come up first and we had met them sitting in comfort at the top drinking tea from a samowar – the big Kashmiri teapot, elaborately chased and scrolled, that has charcoal in a hot pipe inside it, keeping the water bubbling, and that brews the Kashmiri kawa or pink salt tea. At the elders' feet foals were lying, carefully carried up first, and the hookah went round as the younger men, and the women ceaselessly toiling, brought up the flocks and herds. The goats came by themselves but sheep had to be carried, the ponies steadied as ours had been by mane and tail, while the buffaloes were literally shouldered up. Jobara said eleven men could carry one of these unwieldy great black beasts but I was puzzled to know how their horns would pass through some of the narrower clefts.

A young blood of a herdsman, driving his ponies, let me look at the baby tied on his back in a blanket. I knew it must be an especial child as nomad babies are always left to the women; I pulled down the blanket to see and it smiled at me over the folds. It had a red cap trimmed with cowries, dark eyes and a skin more like a peach than any baby I had seen. We met two little girls in embroidered caps, pretty children with the same great dark eyes as the baby; as goat children always do, they asked for money. Then a woman came up with a newborn child. She wanted aspirin, which I gave her, but only two tablets or she might have taken them all at once; Jobara made her show us how she had bound the baby's feet and legs with strips of cloth into a tight papoose shape for travelling. The clan does not stop if a baby is born on the march; an old woman stays to help with the birth and, after an hour or two, she and the mother catch up.

After we had left the cleft we met someone still more behind: a boy driving two goats and a kid each with a broken leg laced into a network of twigs so that the hurt limb was held still. Limping and bleating, they travelled very slowly; every now and then the boy picked up the kid and carried it but it was plainly too heavy for him. He had another, smaller kid in the front of his coat. We gave him two cigarettes – his face lit up when he saw them though he could not have been more than twelve. I kept looking back over my shoulder to see his forlorn little party getting smaller in the distance. I hope he caught up with the clan before the last of the flocks were taken up the staircase and that there would be men – or women – waiting to carry up his charges.

Our way led down across an ice field but when we reached the valley floor there was grass, with wide streams running across it from the melting snow; they reflected the sky and the marshes between them were covered with alpine flowers, flat carpets of blossom as if my beloved Kirman carpets had come to life; there were small magenta primulas, celandines, gentians, anemones, growing among patches of blue water and white snow. We were almost too tired to enjoy them, terribly tired, partly because of the altitude. One pack pony fell on its knees and had to be whipped up, I stumbled as I walked and at the end, to reach our camping place, the only place protected enough if the wind should rise, we had to cross a deep ice stream. That meant the men would have wet clothes tonight – none of them had a change – and there was no fuel to build a campfire, only a little wood carried by the old coolie for the cooking stove and juniper bushes that burn at once; fortunately the long coats that all the men wore were of the rough country tweed that is pure wool and each of them carried the inseparable companion of every Kashmiri man – the women are not as lucky – the big soft shawl that they wear folded on one shoulder like a plaid.

We camped above the stream and below a curious mountain, quite different from any of the others we had seen; it had not slate or granite colours but was entirely white as if it had been blown violently together of packed snow; perhaps it had, as it had wind-swirl patterns on it.

The ponies grazed on what they could find up the mountain; we had no milk and there was no village at which to buy eggs but we thankfully ate Subhan's stew – even though we suspected it was kid, not lamb, as he said. It was marvellously hot and so was the tea – we laced it with rum.

Sol had walked nearly all the way, only occasionally accepting a ride on a pack pony; he had come down the stairway on his own four paws and crossed the glaciers by himself, yet when he came in he asked at once for his walnut and played with it until dinnertime.

It was so cold that we went to bed at seven, but not to sleep. All night birds like seagulls flew below the mountain, making seagull noises. 'They can't be seagulls,' said Paula, 'We must be dreaming.' We never discovered what they were.

We had to leave our valley of primulas very early if we were to get over the pass in a day. I was sorry for there was something different and enchanted about this valley and its white mountain; perhaps it was the reified air that gave it its peculiar enhancement, a rare snow-iced air which made each pleat of the snow mountain, the patches of snow and grass, the streams, flat and blue to the sky, and the scattered colourings of the flowers, stand out with an extraordinary clearness.

We rode and walked slowly along, our shadows making long shapes in the early sun, the ponies sluggish because of their poor night's grazing. Paula was distressed about this; 'You should carry hay for them,' she told Jobara.

'Where should I get hay?' he asked. 'They have to take what they find, as I do.'

We began to climb again, and again it was over ice, ice fields, ice slopes, frozen rocks. We looked down on a lake, deep blue with small icebergs floating in it; they would float all summer, Jobara said, even when the lake shores had thawed. They were thawing now; already, where the sun caught the slopes, patches of grass showed, flowered with gentian. Every now and then we came to a difficult place of rock or ice and again the ponies had to be manhandled across them. Sol rushed about looking for marmots but there were none here.

We reached the ascent of the pass itself that looked like a bite – a small one – taken out of the mountain high above us and above a sheer flank of snow. Here we could only climb by criss-crossing, countless times across the snow, leaving a network of tracks. It was exhausting work. Sol had to give up; his legs sank in like pegs so that he could not lift them, and the snow balled on his fringes and between his pads. Sol hated to be carried – he thought it undignified – but he would have been tipped off his pony as it floundered and struggled and in the end he had to submit; but the only person allowed to carry him was myself and I had not realized till then how much a little dog can weigh; he seemed to send me down deeper at every step and I thanked goodness we had brought our alpenstocks. The sun was hot now and beat on our backs as we toiled in a line from left to right, waited and got our breaths, and crossed back only a fraction higher, it seemed to me, from right to left, looking like ants on that great white expanse. We grew tireder and hungrier; 'I told you it would not be comfortable,' said Jobara; and it was long past lunchtime before we came out in the curiously undramatic hollow that was the pass head and where the wind blew as if it were in a tunnel. We were ready to drop down there, even in the wind, but 'We musn't rest here,' said Jobara urgently and went forward again. It was then that we saw what we had to go down; below us was a drop of two hundred feet, rock with only a tiny serrated path, which seemed to me almost perpendicular. It looked impossible for men, let alone horses, but as we stood there once more some of the goat people were coming up; the elders leading the way and behind them the women, who tumbled their babies and the netted cooking pots they carried on their heads down beside the path, before they went down again to help the men. 'Where they can go, you can,' said Jobara.

Our ponies were unloaded and Jobara led the first, Lallah, to a glacier at the side, coaxing, pushing, pulling, with Amar at her tail. Lallah was an experienced old mare and she sat down and, on her haunches, slid the first twenty yards or so, held and swung by the men. I could not look; it seemed every moment she must crash down onto the ice below but presently Simon called me and there she was, standing far below on her own four legs, safe, unhurt and cropping the tufts of grass that had broken through by the path. Amar came up and he and the ponyman started off with Bulbul, while, exhorted by Subhan and clinging and sliding, Simon, Paula, Sol and I started down the path that Jobara was keeping clear of goat people. For their sakes we could not delay. 'Come on,' said Simon. I had no hands for Sol; he yelped and put his front legs stiff and, with a surprised expression on his face, slid, fell sideways and scrambled, straightened up and held with all his toes to the rock. Then, seeing we had gone down further, he gave another little yelp and came on down. When he reached the bottom his claws were bleeding. I had torn the knee of my trousers, and we had all scraped the skin on our hands; our legs trembled like the ponies' but there was a wonderful feeling of satisfaction. 'I told you you could do it,' said Jobara.

It was four o'clock when we had our lunch, there, at the foot of the rock. Sol sank into sleep the instant we stopped.

After lunch we went wearily on down until we left the ice and came to rocks and streams and fir trees again. Once more the marmots were with us, to Sol's delight. One came so near that we could see its markings, not unlike the markings of a respectably coloured orange-sable Pekingese; it turned itself upon its haunches to scream at us after we had passed, holding its paws in front of it like any little animal begging.

This patch of country reminded me of the country of Andrew Lang's 'The Princess and the Goblins': the rocks and rushing streams, the celandines and anemones and primulas, and the strange shapes of the trees twisted by the snow.

We came in to camp in Narpa, in a glade with the river falling into rifts of streams to the north; above the streams the ring of mountains opened to show one vast snow peak looming up into the sky. Here there were more goat people encamped, in caves or huts that were hardly distinguishable from the forest trees, built of the same russet brown logs and roofed with earth and branches that were still green.

Subhan had gone ahead to make camp as we were so tired but we had to make him move it because, to save himself trouble, he had pitched it among the herdsmen and the buffalo tethers, with all their flies and smells. In a rage he abused one of the herd boys, who had come to sell us milk. The boy, who was almost a young man and very dignified, answered back and Subhan hit him with a stick on the arm. Jobara brought the boy to me, his elbow swollen and hurt. Subhan created a great noise and said the boy had hit him first but he was a gentle, ignorant creature and I did not believe it. I doctored him as best I could with hot fomentations and put his arm in a sling, and asked him to come down with us to Sonamarg, where I would send him in by car to the hospital; but the evening was spoilt by the loud voices and dislike. This is the end of Subhan for me.

But peace came back; in the late evening we, and Sol, walked up a little stream by the camp and found what I had never seen before, white primulas. Buffaloes were being driven down from the mountain, and from the encampment, now on the opposite side of the stream from us, the women brought the calves out onto the bank; they held them as the calves lowed and at once the mothers came running down to be milked; but I cannot like buffaloes; even the calves were ungainly and hideous. After each woman had milked, she loosed the calf, but one was ousted by a child that drank straight from the udder.

A huge fire tonight and, at last, a hot bath. As I lay in bed, the sparks from the fire seemed to go up to the stars and behind them faintly glimmered the snow peak.

The bakriwar pony bells kept me awake and I lay for what seemed hours watching the snows in the starlight that grew brighter as the fire burned down. I only fell asleep towards dawn and could not be roused when Subhan called us, so that we left camp late. The herd boy came with us, keeping close to me away from Subhan, and did not speak a word. I had a feeling he was badly hurt, perhaps the arm broken, but there was nothing to be done except take him down with us and send him on to the hospital at Srinagar. He kept his arm in his shirt, not in the sling I had given him, and had his shawl folded round him. He was shivering with pain but showed us the way as we went through the forests and crossed streams by rough log bridges. Here there were thousands of yellow violets and white clover, the whole air was scented with violet scents and honey.

I stopped to rest, sitting on a log by the track, and a bakriwar girl came up to me. She spoke but I could not understand. She

266

took my hand and held it and laughed, comparing it with her own, which was dark for a bakriwar, with such hard palms that my hand seemed soft, almost boneless, in hers. Then she let it go, laughed again and made a beautiful little gesture of goodbye. I had not known one of these women as friendly or as cheerful. All the people looked at Sol far more than at us and we kept a sharp eye on him in case he might be snatched up and taken away.

We went on, by the streams and over them, stepping over roots of trees, passing glades, each a little *marg* of green where there were usually buffaloes and their herdsmen and a bakriwar hut. Each *marg* had its stream, its rocks and firs.

It was a short march and soon after one o'clock we came to Aru and camped on the slope of the hill, on an island covered with clover, with a stream on each side. In front of us the hill rolled down, glade and meadow, until it opened into the valley of Aru at the foot of the mountains, a wide *marg* with, as always, streams and a wooden rest house near a small untidy wooden village and, on the mountain facing us, forests of fir topped with snow crests and threaded with waterfalls. It was warmer here, there were no glaciers and the valley was as quiet as Sonamarg, with once again only the sound of the streams and the neighings and nickerings of ponies, for it was full of mares with their foals. It was not as open a valley, not as rolling as Sonamarg, and more civilized. I counted three other camps, but the tops of the mountains in the sun had a blue I had not seen before; it was almost bluebell.

In the afternoon we went down to the village, which was wretchedly poor, its wood and earth houses meagre and shaped like boxes, with one room for the cattle below and another for the whole family above. The people close the animals in for the winter and the steam of the midden rises up and heats the room above. Only the largest house had windows and a verandah, on which men were drinking tea out of bowls; a woman carried a winnowing basket down the steps and a man outside a shop was spinning, but there seemed no other working life. Four shops all sold the same things: salt, a little grain, cloth, cigarettes, the country soap that looks like old cheese, white buttons that bakriwar women buy to trim their clothes, and, hanging from the ceilings, bundles of brightly coloured threads in colours of saffron, green, red and white, for making mens' caps and the coloured braid, like pyjama cords, with which they hold their loose trousers up. Goats wandered down the village street; a tailor had a shop with some white calico and an ancient sewing machine, but he was not sewing; in fact all the men were sitting or standing about with nothing to do. 'Is this a very poor village?' asked Simon.

'These men are land-holders,' said Jobara, as if to say, 'Then they must be poor.'

I woke very early that morning at Aru and watched the sun come down the mountains, turning the snow to even more colours that I had seen it turn before: first to violet, then pink, then gold, then yellow-cream, then white while, all the time, the rocks held that curious bluebell blue. Waking like this and looking down into the vale of Aru with the dew shining on the uplands, I had to use words that were half-forgotten and sounded affected: vale; uplands; pastoral; but these valleys are pastoral, not at all in the French sense but in a Chinese pastoral way. We got up early and after breakfast broke camp and took the way to Lidderwat.

It was a long day walking and riding, through pine woods now, and over rough grass like the downs in England, or on a hot dusty road that had openings among the trees that showed us the Liddar river, not milkily blue like the Sinde but a brown and rushing river. We passed more bakriwar clans on the move and were struck, as I have always been struck, by the type of face so many of the older women have, piercing and hawklike, thin and gaunt with misery. They are not really old but have led hard, often cruelly suffering lives, toiling for their men, bearing children on the march, carrying all the heavy gear; the great nets of iron cooking pots, firewood, sick animals, dragging their big dogs, and usually with a heavy baby in their slings.

The children are lovely, their hair bleached almost gold, often ivory-skinned and pink-cheeked. As soon as they saw us they scampered up to ask for money and tried to sell us crystals, water-polished in the streams. We passed three boys hiding together under a rock and laughing; in the shadow of the rock we could see hardly anything but their teeth and eyes shining. How virile and hardy these people looked after the inertness of the Kashmiri peasants in the village.

At Lidderwat were more wild ponies and foals, few flowers except clover, but that filled the small, enclosed, rather hot valley with such a smell of honey that it was almost stupefying. There were the same buffaloes and herdsmen, huts and firs and a motor road leading to Pahalgham. We watched a tribe of monkeys and Sol fell off his pony with excitement. He was surprised and resentful but not hurt. Then we took a short cut up to our last camping place, passing through a flock of sheep; the first big flock we had seen since we started.

There had been a theft at Pahalgham and the police were chasing the bakriwars up the valley. Our hurt boy abruptly disappeared. 'You see,' said Subhan, but I think he was simply frightened of the police. It was too peaceful to argue, even with Subhan. Opposite our camp was a stream that ran from the snowline to the river, winding in white threads down the mountain, disappearing into the forest and coming out into waterfalls. It seemed to hedge us round for our last night.

It was our last night. I walked away from the camp to see it so that I should remember it: the small white tents in the light of the young moon, the fir forest and the snow peak behind it. One big star above the snow, and the moonlight and firelight shining in the stream.

If you loved this book, then you might also like . . .

THE GREENGAGE SUMMER

By Rumer Godden

*On and off, all that hot French August, we made
ourselves ill from eating the greengages . . .*

The faded elegance of Les Oeillets, with its bullet-scarred
staircase and serene garden bounded by high walls; Eliot,
the charming Englishman who became the children's
guardian while their mother lay ill in hospital; sophisticated
Mademoiselle Zizi, hotel patronne, and Eliot's devoted
lover; sixteen-year-old Joss, the oldest Grey girl, suddenly,
achingly beautiful. And the Marne river flowing silent and
slow beyond them all . . .

They would merge together in a gold-green summer
of discovery, until the fruit rotted on the trees and cold
seeped into their bones . . .

The Greengage Summer is Rumer Godden's tense, evoca-
tive portrait of love and deceit in the Champagne country
of the Marne – which became a memorable film starring
Kenneth More and Susannah York. In the preface, Rumer
Godden explains how it came to be written.

If you loved this book, then you might also like ...

THE PEACOCK SPRING

By Rumer Godden

*Not a usual marker, but a feather, a tip feather
from a peacock's train, lucently blue and green ...*

Una and her younger sister Hal have been abruptly summoned to live in New Delhi by their diplomat father Sir
Edward Gwithiam. From the first meeting with their new
tutor and companion, the beautiful Eurasian Alix Lamont,
Una senses a hidden motive to their presence. But through
the pain of the months to come, the poetry and logic of India
do not leave Una untouched. And it begins with a feather, a
promise of something genuine and precious ...

In *The Peacock Spring* Rumer Godden evokes the magic
of the India she knew so well – and all the bitter sweetness
of loyalty and love. In the preface she explains how this
timeless novel came to be written.

extracts reading groups
competitions books new events
discounts extracts
competitions extracts discounts reading groups
books new events
new books
events extracts books
extracts new titles reading groups
interviews events new
discounts events books
new books events interviews new books
events new reading groups
discounts extracts discounts books

www.panmacmillan.com

extracts events reading groups
competitions books extracts new

Susanna Gregory was a police officer in Leeds before taking up an academic career. She has served as an environmental consultant, worked seventeen field seasons in the polar regions, and has taught comparative anatomy and biological anthropology.

She is the creator of the Matthew Bartholomew series of mysteries set in medieval Cambridge and the Thomas Chaloner adventures in Restoration London, and now lives in Wales with her husband, who is also a writer.

Also by Susanna Gregory

The Matthew Bartholomew series

A Plague on Both Your Houses
An Unholy Alliance
A Bone of Contention
A Deadly Brew
A Wicked Deed
A Masterly Murder
An Order for Death
A Summer of Discontent
A Killer in Winter
The Hand of Justice
The Mark of a Murderer
The Tarnished Chalice
To Kill or Cure
The Devil's Disciples
A Vein of Deceit
The Killer of Pilgrims
Mystery in the Minster
Murder by the Book
The Lost Abbot
Death of a Scholar
A Poisonous Plot
A Grave Concern
The Habit of Murder
The Sanctuary Murders

The Thomas Chaloner Series

A Conspiracy of Violence
Blood on the Strand
The Butcher of Smithfield
The Westminster Poisoner
A Murder on London Bridge
The Body in the Thames
The Piccadilly Plot
Death in St James's Park
Murder on High Holborn
The Cheapside Corpse
The Chelsea Strangler
The Executioner of St Paul's
Intrigue in Covent Garden

SUSANNA GREGORY

The Clerkenwell Affair

sphere

SPHERE

First published in Great Britain in 2020 by Sphere

1 3 5 7 9 10 8 6 4 2

Copyright © Susanna Gregory 2020

The moral right of the author has been asserted.

All characters and events in this publication, other than those
clearly in the public domain, are fictitious and any resemblance
to real persons, living or dead, is purely coincidental.

All rights reserved. No part of this publication may be reproduced,
stored in a retrieval system, or transmitted, in any form or by any means,
without the prior permission in writing of the publisher, nor
be otherwise circulated in any form of binding or cover other than that
in which it is published and without a similar condition including
this condition being imposed on the subsequent purchaser.

A CIP catalogue record for this book is available from the British Library.

ISBN 978-0-7515-6273-6

Typeset in ITC New Baskerville by Palimpsest Book Productions Ltd,
Falkirk, Stirlingshire
Printed and bound in Great Britain by Clays Ltd, Elcograf S.p.A.

Papers used by Sphere are from well-managed forests
and other responsible sources.

MIX
Paper from
responsible sources
FSC
www.fsc.org
FSC® C104740

NORTHAMPTONSHIRE LIBRARIES & INFORMATION SERVICES	
00401200926	
Askews & Holts	
NC	

For my lovely 'new' family:
Pat and Martin
Juliette and Hugh
and
Jess and Steve

Prologue

Thomas Chiffinch was in an awkward position. He held two important Court posts – Keeper of the Closet and Keeper of the Jewels – and had a reputation for efficiency, refinement and discretion. Unfortunately, the same could not be said of his brother Will, who was one of the worst offenders for shaping the Court's current reputation as a place of debauchery, corruption and greed.

Chiffinch wished Will would behave with more decorum. He might be loved by the King and His Majesty's dissolute friends, but the rest of the country hated him, and there was growing anger at the brazen squandering of public money on courtesans and lavish feasts. Indeed, the King's popularity was at its lowest ebb since he had been restored to his throne six years earlier, and Will's ability to organise spectacularly decadent revels played no small part in this.

Back in January, some Londoners had capitalised on the ill-feeling generated by the moral bankruptcy of courtiers like Will, and had engineered an uprising. Their

1

efforts had come to nothing in the end, but the King stubbornly refused to heed the lesson and rein his favourites in, so resentment continued to fester. The plague had not helped. It had killed the poor in their tens of thousands while the King's response had been to show a clean pair of heels, fetching up in Oxford, where he had continued to frolic as though nothing was wrong. He had come home when the danger was over, but London grieved for its dead, and his merry excesses at White Hall rubbed salt into an open wound.

Chiffinch sat in his sumptuous palace apartments and mulled the problem over. The people were nearing the end of their tether, and the last time a king had made himself this unpopular, he had been executed. Chiffinch was a loyal servant of the Crown, and was not about to stand by and do nothing while a second Charles went about losing his head.

He sighed. Unfortunately, Will and his silly friends – the most flamboyant of whom called themselves the Cockpit Club – were not the only reason why the King was despised by his subjects. His leading ministers did nothing to ease the situation either. They declared war on the Dutch, introduced oppressive taxes, and devised laws to suppress religious freedom. And as for the Earl of Clarendon, his sale of Dunkirk to the French at a ridiculously low price had given rise to the popular belief that he had allowed himself to be bribed. Now the man could not step outside his house without someone howling abuse at him.

Then there was the Duchess of Newcastle, who shocked and unsettled Londoners with her unorthodox behaviour. Her very presence in their city was a source of dissent – some relished her odd ideas, while others found them horrifying. Not only did she hold controversial political and religious opinions, but she questioned the natural order of things. For example, she itched to join the Royal Society, despite the fact that membership was restricted to men, and she wrote books under her own name, instead of having the decorum to use a male pseudonym.

Her antics went against all that was decent, and Chiffinch was terrified of what might happen if she remained unchecked. What if other women followed her example, and brayed *their* opinions to all and sundry? What if she demanded a seat on the Privy Council, on the grounds that she was more intelligent than the current male incumbents? She was, of course, but that was beside the point. And what if she went to the House of Lords and insisted on having a say? Such eventualities would fly against all that was right, just and proper.

Clearly, something had to be done to save the King from his own Court – from the wild licentiousness of Will and the Cockpit Club, from prim old Clarendon with his penchant for bribes, and from the Duchess with her alarming opinions. Chiffinch frowned. But what?

Then the answer came to him, and his once-handsome face broke into a broad grin. He would save his country from anarchy yet! There would be bad feeling and dismay, but it would only be temporary, and the King would thank him for it eventually, while the general populace would rejoice to see their grievances addressed. Still smiling, Chiffinch began to write a letter.

Chapter 1

'Mr Chiffinch cannot be dead, sir,' said Thomas Chaloner, struggling for patience. He disliked the way Court gossip spread like wildfire, growing more ridiculous with every whispered telling. 'I saw him walking around not two hours ago.'

'It was very sudden, apparently,' replied the Earl of Clarendon, a short, fat, fussy man who wore a great yellow wig and shoes with uncomfortable block-heels to make himself taller. 'But I assure you, he is no longer in the world of the living.'

He tried to hide his pleasure in the news, although it was plain for all to see. Chaloner did not blame him: Chiffinch hated the Earl, and who would not be relieved to learn that an implacable enemy was no longer in a position to plot against him?

'Everyone thought it was the plague at first,' the Earl went on. 'But then Timothy Clarke arrived and said that Chiffinch died of an abscess – he called it an impostume – in the breast.'

Chaloner raised his eyebrows. Clarke was Physician to the Household, so perhaps the tale *was* true – a medic would know what he was talking about. Or would he? Some of Clarke's colleagues had been rather scathing about his professional abilities in the past. Moreover, if Chiffinch had been suffering from something serious enough to kill him, would he really have been sauntering about a short time before?

The Earl saw Chaloner's bemused expression and misread it. 'Perhaps you are thinking of the wrong Chiffinch. The one who died today is the *older* of the two brothers: Thomas, Keeper of the Closet and Keeper of the Jewels.'

'I know,' said Chaloner shortly. True, he was not as familiar with White Hall as he might have been, because the Earl kept sending him away on missions and errands, but he was not entirely uninformed. He certainly knew the people who meant his employer harm. His official title was Gentleman Usher, but his real remit was to protect the Earl from men such as Chiffinch and others like him.

'As opposed to *Will* Chiffinch, the Pimp-Master General,' the Earl went on, sniggering as he used the title conferred on the younger brother by a contemptuous general public.

'Yes, sir,' said Chaloner, wondering if the Earl would be quite so amused if he knew that, far from being mortified, Will considered the title a great compliment and revelled in it.

'The matter will have to be investigated, of course,' the Earl went on. 'We must ascertain that it really was an impostume that carried Chiffinch off. He was not very popular, you know.'

6

Chaloner reviewed his own impressions of the man – a stiff, humourless, proud individual with a firm belief in his own rectitude. Unusually for a King's favourite, Chiffinch was reasonably ethical and genuinely cultured. He was also a devoted Royalist, and had recently expressed concern over the fact that the King was not as well liked as he had been when he had first been restored to his throne.

'Investigated by whom?' he asked, then saw the calculating gleam in his employer's eyes and raised a warning hand. 'It cannot be me, sir. His family will object to any attempt by us to meddle in their affairs, and you may open yourself up to harm if you—'

'I am Lord Chancellor of England,' interrupted the Earl haughtily. 'I have the authority to appoint whomsoever I please to explore a case of foul play among the King's friends.'

'There is nothing to suggest foul play, sir,' objected Chaloner, loath to dabble in such murky waters. And not just for himself – if Chiffinch *had* been murdered, it was sheer madness for his sworn enemy to appoint the investigator. 'A physician has deemed the death natural—'

'But you just told me that Chiffinch was walking around two hours ago,' countered the Earl. '*You* wonder how a man can be alive one minute and dead the next. I can see it in your face.'

Chaloner was suspicious, but that was beside the point. 'Then I will tell Clarke to look at the body again in order to—'

'No, you will arrange for a second opinion,' interrupted the Earl firmly. 'Ask Surgeon Wiseman to examine the corpse at his earliest convenience.'

It was a good idea. Wiseman was not only Chaloner's

friend, but a man who could be trusted to find the truth. He would almost certainly provide a more credible explanation than the one Clarke had offered – an apoplexy or a seizure, perhaps, which might well have carried the victim off in a flash.

'Until Wiseman has given his verdict,' the Earl went on, 'you can determine what happened between the time you saw Chiffinch alive, and the time he dropped dead from "natural causes".'

The way he sneered the last two words made it perfectly clear that he expected the surgeon to declare Chiffinch's end suspicious. Chaloner opened his mouth to repeat that it was not a good idea to interfere, but the Earl overrode him.

'Of course, you will have to hurry if we are to have answers before Chiffinch is laid to rest. He will be buried in Westminster Abbey on Tuesday, just four days hence.'

Chaloner blinked his astonishment. 'Arrangements have been made already? That is fast!'

'Very fast,' agreed the Earl. 'Indeed, one might say *suspiciously* fast.' Then he relented. 'Of course, it may be because the dean is away, so cannot object to such a vile creature being laid to rest in his domain. The family aims to present him with a fait accompli.'

Chaloner remained astounded. 'All this has already been decided, even though Chiffinch was alive two hours ago?'

'It has, so when you compile your list of murder suspects, make sure you put the family at the top. It would suit me very well if you prove that one of them killed him.'

Chaloner was sure it would, as discrediting the Chiffinches would deal a hefty blow to those who had united against him. Of course, he would not have nearly so many detractors if he refrained from scolding the King and his followers like errant schoolboys. Chaloner tried one last time to dissuade the Earl from a course of action that might prove disastrous.

'Even if Chiffinch did die at the hand of another – which I cannot believe he did – it is a mistake for you to get involved. It is better to stay aloof from the entire affair.'

'I disagree. It will show those who hold me in low esteem that I am cognisant of their welfare – that I am an ethical Lord Chancellor, who wants justice for all, even the fools and worthless debauchees who mean me harm. However, you do not have long to discover the truth: *Royal Oak* sails on Easter Sunday, and I want you on her when she goes.'

Since entering the Earl's employ, Chaloner had spent more time away than at home. Indeed, he had only returned from Scotland the previous day – the Earl was a great supporter of the northern bishops, and had sent Chaloner to spy on the Presbyterians who were making life difficult for them. These missions were frustrating, exhausting and prevented him from putting down roots, so he was beginning to resent them. And yet, he thought wryly, the ocean would be a good place to be if he did stir up a hornets' nest by prying into Chiffinch's death.

'What do you want me to do on *Royal Oak*, sir?' he asked curiously.

'Find the sailor who stole a lot of saltpetre while she was moored at Tower Wharf last month. The navy is short of funds, and cannot afford to lose its supplies to light-fingered tars.'

'No,' said Chaloner, although as the navy had decided

9

not to pay its seamen's wages, he did not blame them for finding other ways to feed their families. 'But saltpetre is used to make gunpowder. Surely it is more important to find the buyer than the thieves?'

'Williamson is doing that as we speak – the trail has taken him to Dover. However *Royal Oak*'s crew is currently on leave, which means he cannot question them about the thieves. Ergo, you will sail on her at Easter and do it.'

He referred to Joseph Williamson, the Spymaster General, who was responsible for matters pertaining to national security. Chaloner neither liked nor trusted Williamson, and was pleased to learn he was seventy miles away, thus eliminating the possibility of a chance encounter in London.

'There will be another great sea-battle when our fleet meets the Dutch,' mused the Earl, when Chaloner made no reply. 'The intelligence you gathered in the United Provinces last year told us that they have built newer, heavier ships, so let us hope you are not blown to pieces while you are gone.'

He did not mean it. Despite Chaloner proving his loyalty on any number of occasions, the Earl was unable to forget that he had not only fought on the 'wrong' side during the civil wars, but had been one of Cromwell's spies into the bargain. Not for the first time, Chaloner wished he could leave the Earl to his enemies, but it was not easy for former Parliamentarian intelligencers to find employment, and he knew he was lucky to have a job at all. He had no choice but to do what the Earl ordered, no matter how asinine, pointless or dangerous.

As Lord Chancellor, the Earl had been allocated a suite of rooms in the Palace of White Hall, but because he suffered from gout and was often immobile, he had taken to working from his home, Clarendon House, instead. This was a glorious new mansion on the semi-rural lane called Piccadilly, although his staff were currently unimpressed with the place, as a sharp downpour the previous morning had flooded the library. His entire household – other than Chaloner – had spent the last twenty-four hours struggling to contain the damage.

Still feeling that probing Chiffinch's death was a mistake, Chaloner left Clarendon House and walked towards White Hall, where the hapless courtier had breathed his last. It was a beautiful day, and warm for the time of year. The hedges along the side of the road were white and pink with blossom, while the scent of new growth was in the air. He inhaled deeply, savouring the heady aroma of fresh leaves. The air did not stay sweet for long though, as a sudden breeze brought a whiff from the city – the stench of ten thousand coal fires, the stink of the laystalls, and the distinctive tang of its tanneries, mills, slaughterhouses and foundries.

Despite London's drawbacks, Chaloner was glad to be back, especially now the plague was in abeyance. Only twenty-six fever deaths had been noted in the previous week's Mortality Bill, compared to seven thousand when it was at its peak. He had lived through some of it in January, when he had investigated a plot centred around Covent Garden, although the Earl had dispatched him to Scotland the moment that matter was resolved.

On his way south again, Chaloner had planned to spend a few days with his family in Buckinghamshire, but an urgent message from the Earl begged him to ride to London with all possible speed. He had made the journey in record time, cognisant of the fact that his

11

employer was never far from disaster. He had arrived the previous afternoon, saddle-sore and anxious, only to learn that there was no emergency, and the Earl could not even recall why the summons had been sent.

Chaloner resented not seeing the family he loved. His clan was a large one, even by the standards of the day. His grandfather had married twice, siring eleven children with his first wife and seven with the second. Most of these aunts and uncles had produced prodigious broods of their own, which meant Chaloner had enough kinsmen to populate a small village. The wars had scattered them, so there were some cousins he had never met, but he was fond of the ones he knew, while his siblings meant the world to him.

He had been blessed with an idyllic childhood, and all his memories were happy right up to the day when one uncle – another Thomas Chaloner – had dragged him off to join Cromwell's New Model Army. Nothing had been the same since, and he felt as though he had spent his entire adult existence leaping from one precarious situation to another, in constant danger and with nowhere to call home. Even his two marriages – both brought to untimely ends by plague – had been unsatisfactory, and at thirty-six years of age, he felt weary and jaded. His brothers and sisters were a much-needed rock in the unsteady, shifting sea of his life.

But dwelling on the matter was doing no good, so he turned his mind to the task the Earl had set him. He began by reviewing what he knew about the dead man, which was not much. Chiffinch was a favourite of the King, and one of his duties had been to buy art for the royal palaces. This he had done extremely well, showing himself to be a man of taste and refinement.

Chaloner thought about his own encounter with Chiffinch earlier that morning. He been strolling down King Street, aiming to break his fast in the Sun tavern in Westminster, when Chiffinch had scuttled out through White Hall's main gate. It had been just as the abbey bells chimed six o'clock. Although Chiffinch disliked the Earl and his household, good manners had compelled him to stop and exchange polite greetings with Chaloner. Then he had shared a bit of gossip about the Duchess of Newcastle, who had evidently gone to the theatre wearing an inappropriate costume. The plump Chiffinch had been flushed and a little breathless, so it was entirely possible that unaccustomed exertion had given him a fatal seizure.

Chaloner would have to find out why Chiffinch had been up at such an hour – whether he had risen early or had not yet been to bed. He suspected it would be the latter: Chiffinch did not indulge in the same wild revelries as his despicable brother, but no successful or ambitious courtier slept while his King was awake and might dispense lucrative favours.

He walked on, enjoying the spirited bustle of the city, although it was still nowhere near as lively as it had been before the plague. Even so, most of the weeds that had grown up between the cobbles around Charing Cross had been trampled away by the returning wheels, feet and hoofs, and although some houses remained boarded up, most showed signs of being inhabited again.

Yet the city was not the cheerful place it had been eighteen months ago. No one had forgotten the fact that the King and his favourites had fled to safety, leaving London to fend for itself, and folk were less willing to overlook their profligate ways now the Court was back. Indeed, most were of the opinion that they were better off without His Majesty and his cronies, especially as there was great resentment over the draconian new taxes levied to fund the royal household.

Moreover, the year was 1666, and it had escaped no one's notice that the combination of three sixes was inauspicious. Soothsayers were predicting a calamity that would make the plague pale by comparison. Worse yet, Good Friday – the day of Jesus's crucifixion – would fall on Friday the thirteenth, a detail that had sent the gloom-merchants into a frenzy. How could something terrible not befall London on such an unlucky date?

As he walked, Chaloner heard people talking about it in low, worried voices. Personally, he thought the chances were that Good Friday would pass without incident. Of course, then the city would be full of anticlimax and disappointment, which would bring its own problems.

'I saw it myself last Sunday,' breathed a laundress. 'A cloud, shaped like Satan himself, hovering over Clerkenwell. His forked tail was perfectly clear.'

'Clerkenwell,' whispered her companion darkly. 'There are tales about Clerkenwell. Courtiers have mansions there, so of course it will be full of wickedness.'

'And do not forget that the new cemetery is nearby,' the laundress went on. 'The Church has agreed not to consecrate it, so that Quakers and other dubious sects can use it to bury their dead. If you ask me, that is a sure way to attract demons and other denizens of hell.'

'Then they will make their presence known on Good Friday,' predicted the friend, pursing her lips. 'And God help us all.'

The Palace of White Hall was vast, boasting more than two thousand rooms. It straggled between the River

14

Thames and St James's Park, with King Street running through the middle of it. The word 'palace' was a misnomer, as there was no main house, and it comprised a random collection of buildings that had been raised as and when they had been needed, resulting in a peculiar mismatch of styles and sizes. A maze of alleys with unexpected dead-ends, dog-leg turns and crooked yards connected them all, and it had taken Chaloner weeks to learn his way around properly.

The only part that was truly grand was the Banqueting House, a handsome edifice designed by Inigo Jones with a ceiling by Rubens. The rest comprised apartments for the King, his Queen and various princes, nobles and bureaucrats, along with government and Treasury offices, accommodation for servants and retainers, a chapel, and an array of kitchens, laundries, storerooms and stables. Most of these lay to the east of King Street, while to the west were the tennis courts and the cockpit.

Once through the Great Gate, Chaloner paused to look around. He was in a vast cobbled yard, with the Banqueting House on one side and ranges of offices on the others. There was a large fountain in the middle, working for the first time in months. Some wag had been at the statue of Eros in its centre, which now wore a yellow wig, block-heeled shoes and a Lord Chancellor's gown. Servants stood around it, laughing.

Chaloner's first task was to find Surgeon Wiseman and ask him to examine Chiffinch's body. After all, there would be no need to launch a murder inquiry if the courtier had died of natural causes. Unfortunately, he learned that the Queen was ill, and Wiseman had vowed not to leave her side until he had seen some improvement. Chaloner scribbled a note, begging his help for an hour,

15

and paid a page to deliver it. Moments later, the page returned with Wiseman's reply. It was not polite, and accused Chaloner of being callous for putting the needs of the dead above the those of the living. It ended with the curt suggestion that he ask again tomorrow.

With an irritable sigh, Chaloner supposed he would have to start asking questions without the surgeon's verdict, and was just deciding where to begin when he heard someone call his name from the shadows. It was a man who would have been invisible but for his bright white falling band – the square of cloth that covered his chest like a bib; otherwise, he was dressed entirely in black, a colour that suited his sinister demeanour. His name was John Swaddell, and he was one of the deadliest, most disturbing people Chaloner had ever met.

Swaddell worked for Spymaster Williamson, officially as a clerk, although it was common knowledge that he was really an assassin. He was frighteningly good at his work, and Chaloner was always unnerved by the ruthless efficiency with which he dispatched those deemed to be enemies of the state.

He had performed a peculiar blood-mingling ritual the first time he and Chaloner had been ordered to work together, which he claimed had forged an unbreakable bond between them. Chaloner was uncomfortable associating with such a lethal individual, but allies were rare at Court, and not to be lightly dismissed. So, although Swaddell was not a friend, he was at least on Chaloner's side.

'You are back,' said Swaddell, with a grin that was meant to be friendly but that Chaloner thought was unsettling. 'Did you find your annoying Presbyterians? And neutralise them?'

16

'I warned them about the dangers of fomenting unrest and advised negotiation instead,' replied Chaloner, to make the point that *he* was not in the habit of dispensing his own brand of justice. 'What are you doing here? Something for Williamson?'

'He is in Dover, investigating the theft of some saltpetre from *Royal Oak*. My remit is to lurk in the city and report anything untoward. But it is dull work, and I miss his company.'

'You do?' blurted Chaloner, astonished that anyone should say such a thing about Williamson, who was sly, secretive and unlikeable. Then he supposed that Swaddell was much of an ilk, so the pair would have a lot in common.

Swaddell smiled again, revealing small, pointed teeth and a very red tongue. 'I shall miss him less now that you are home. We must adjourn to a coffee house, so you can tell me about your adventures in more detail.'

'Later,' promised Chaloner, planning to avoid it. 'I have work to do first.'

'I suppose your Earl wants you to look into what happened to Chiffinch,' surmised Swaddell. 'I confess I was astonished to learn he was dead. He seemed hale enough yesterday.'

'Have you heard any rumours or whispers about him?'

Swaddell grimaced. 'People tend to stop talking once they see me listening to their conversations. However, I can tell you that he spent most of last night in the Shield Gallery.'

Chaloner was grateful for the information, as it told him where to start his enquiries. 'Were you there, too?'

A bitter expression suffused Swaddell's face. 'Unlike you, I am no gentleman usher – I was not allowed in. But I know Chiffinch was there, because I overheard his

17

brother Will tell one of their friends as much. Unfortunately, that is all I heard him say, because he spotted me in the shadows and moved away.'

'Pity,' said Chaloner, although he would have done likewise if he had seen an assassin eavesdropping on him, even if the conversation had been entirely innocent.

'However, I do know that Will requested an audience with the King within minutes of learning about his brother's death,' Swaddell went on. 'Apparently, Will accepted the royal condolences, then asked if he might inherit all Chiffinch's titles and duties. The King agreed and invested him on the spot.'

'That is interesting,' mused Chaloner, wondering if the Earl was right to suspect foul play among the dead man's kin after all.

'Not really,' sighed Swaddell. 'Will could have waited a decent interval, but then he would have lost out, because someone else would have rushed to the King and begged to be Chiffinch's successor. White Hall is for the bold and greedy, not the respectfully reticent.'

'How has London been these last few weeks?' asked Chaloner, moving to another subject, as it was one on which he trusted Swaddell's opinion more than anyone else's. 'When I was last home, we only just managed to stop malcontents from blowing half of it up.'

Swaddell lowered his voice. 'I thought the King and his friends might have moderated their revels, given that their bad behaviour was what precipitated that crisis in the first place, but if anything, they are worse. Have you heard of the Cockpit Club?'

Chaloner shook his head. 'What is it?'

'A gaggle of idle, wildly hedonistic courtiers who have declared themselves bored with life at White Hall and

18

who have elected to pursue more "interesting" forms of entertainment, most of which are distasteful and some of which are illegal. Their sole remit is to have fun, and they care nothing for anyone or anything else.'

'Then perhaps someone should tell the King to curb their excesses before they provoke yet another attempt to remove him from power.'

'Your Earl tried, but he refused to listen. Apparently, His Majesty feels that doing what his subjects ask will encourage them to make more demands of him in the future.'

Then he was a fool, thought Chaloner, and if he followed his father to the executioner's block, he had no one to blame but himself. All he hoped was that good men would not die trying to quell the trouble that his arrogance and stupidity might spark. But these were private thoughts, and not ones to be shared with a man in the pay of the Spymaster General.

'Unfortunately,' Swaddell went on, 'when they heard what Clarendon had done, the Cockpit Club declared all-out war on him.'

Chaloner groaned: the Earl had enough enemies already, and did not need more. 'Who is in this society?' he asked, supposing he would have to monitor them as well as all the others.

Swaddell recited thirty or so names, which included the Court's most dissipated rakes. Some were heirs to titles and fortunes, kicking their heels while they waited for their sires to die. Others were penniless aristocrats bent on securing sinecures. Their de facto leader was one Colonel Widdrington, whose family had somehow contrived to hang on to its money during the civil wars and the upheavals that had followed. Widdrington and

19

his wife Bess oozed wealth, superiority and entitlement. Chaloner had always found them unpleasant.

'So these men see my Earl as their enemy,' he sighed, when Swaddell had finished.

'Not just him but his entire household, so take extra care while you are here. I doubt they will risk a physical encounter with you, but they are vengeful, vindictive and petty. And selfish, given that they consider their pleasures more important than the King's standing with his people. They are not good friends to him, no matter what he thinks.'

Chaloner nodded his thanks to Swaddell and went on his way, glad to step out of the shadows and into the bright morning sunshine.

The day had turned hot, with the sun blazing down from a clear blue sky. Usually, fair weather was greeted with delight by Londoners, as persistent rain turned their city's streets into rivers of stinking mud. That year, however, they were inclined to see it as an evil omen, as it had been a long, hot, dry spell that had presaged the plague the previous year.

To avoid arriving in the Shield Gallery drenched in sweat, Chaloner walked slowly across the Great Court, aware of Swaddell's beady black eyes tracking him as he went. He reached the fountain, then wished he had taken another route when he saw who had taken up station on its shady side. Fifteen or so courtiers, all of whom Swaddell had just identified as Cockpit Club members perched on its edge or paddled in its shallows. Some moved to intercept him.

Each was dressed in the height of fashion and moved with the flouncing mince that such people thought showed breeding and refinement. They slathered themselves with face-paints, and the men occasionally donned women's clothing, although Chaloner had never understood why. He could only assume it was something they had picked up in France.

In the vanguard was Colonel Widdrington, whom Swaddell had just identified as their leader. He was a tall, impossibly handsome man with thick brown hair and laughing eyes. By contrast, his wife Bess was plain enough to be ugly, with a snub nose, bad skin and a pugnacious chin. They had married not for love, but because it had been demanded of them by their families. Bess was openly delighted at having landed such a beautiful spouse, but Widdrington felt cheated, and it was common knowledge that he would divorce her if he could. Unfortunately for him, a lot of money was invested in the alliance, so he was stuck with her.

'It is the Lord Chancellor's creature,' Widdrington drawled. 'What errand are you on, Chaloner? Finding him shoes that do not make him waddle like a pregnant sow?'

His cronies guffawed obligingly, Bess the loudest of all.

'You must make sure they are sturdy, to support his great weight,' she put in, casting a sidelong glance at her pretty husband to ensure he noticed her elaborating on his jest.

Widdrington yawned, flapping a lace handkerchief in front of his mouth. 'God, I am bored! If we do not do something interesting soon, I shall turn into stone, like Eros here. Oh, it is not Eros, it is the Lord Chancellor! Do you see, Chaloner? It is your employer who stands so chubby and proud above us.'

21

'Goodness!' exclaimed Chaloner. 'I thought it was the Duke of York. *He* certainly thinks so, because I heard him complain to his brother the King about it not ten minutes ago.'

It was a lie, but he had the satisfaction of seeing the Cockpit Club monkeys scramble to remove the offending items before there was trouble.

'It is far too hot out here,' Widdrington declared, once the statue had been stripped of its incriminating vestments. 'So let us go to the Shield Gallery, to see the place where Chiffinch spent his last night.'

Bess gave a squeal of appreciation, although the others looked taken aback. The suggestion was in poor taste, even by Court standards.

'An excellent notion!' Bess cried. 'Perhaps *Will* Chiffinch will be there. Then he can tell us what revels he has planned to honour his brother's memory.'

They set off at once, walking with the exaggerated strut of people who thought a great deal of themselves. Chaloner watched in distaste, hoping the King would come to his senses and bring them to heel before their antics did him harm. And if they did? Why should Chaloner defend a regime that he had never wanted, and which had proved itself to be just as corrupt and useless as the one he had fought so hard to overthrow? Then he remembered that his employer was part of that regime, and hoped he would not soon be faced with some difficult choices.

There was no point going to the Shield Gallery if the Cockpit Club men were there, as they would make it impossible for Chaloner to ask questions – either by looming over him and intimidating anyone he tried to

22

talk to, or by driving witnesses away by dint of their objectionable presence. Instead, he went to the kitchens, where he filched a freshly baked knot-biscuit and a cup of cool ale.

When he had finished, he decided to sit in the chapel for half an hour, sure Widdrington and his cronies would have gone to find other 'entertainment' by the time he emerged. But he had not taken many steps before he met two more men whom Swaddell had named as Cockpit Club members. These were not, the assassin had claimed, part of the charmed inner circle, but individuals who lurked on the fringes, hoping to profit from their association with rich and powerful men.

One was Captain Edward Rolt, who was related to Cromwell, but was determined to be seen as a Royalist; his name was a byword for duplicitous sycophancy. The other was eighteen-year-old George Legg, whose father was Master of Armouries, a post he would eventually inherit; until then, his time was his own.

'Have you heard the latest?' Legg asked, all goggling excitement. 'About the Duchess?'

'Which one?' asked Chaloner, aware of at least six who regularly inspired gossip.

'Newcastle, of course,' replied Legg impatiently. 'She has recently arrived from her country estates, and the whole city itches to see her.'

'Really? Why?'

'Because of her reputation,' explained Rolt. 'She is a singular lady. For example, she believes that women are equal to men.' He laughed at this outlandish notion.

'She cannot really think that,' countered Legg with youthful disdain. 'It is just a way to make herself the centre of attention. She is very vain.'

'She does like to be noticed,' sniggered Rolt. 'Did you hear what she did when she went to watch *The Humorous Lovers* at the theatre? She wore an antique costume in the classical style, which was cut so low that it revealed her scarlet-trimmed nipples.'

Chiffinch had remarked on this particular incident when he and Chaloner had exchanged greetings earlier that morning. He had been disapproving, on the grounds that noblewomen strutting about in that sort of attire reflected badly on the King.

'I was there,' giggled Legg. 'It caused quite a stir. Apparently, she designed the ensemble herself. I could not take my eyes off her, so I have no idea if the play was any good.'

'It was a serious error of judgement on her part,' declared Rolt. 'She aimed to present herself as a heroic woman of antiquity – bold, strong and romantic. Instead, everyone thinks she is a common strumpet.'

'Other courtiers don that style of dress,' said Chaloner, feeling it was unfair to castigate one woman for what the rest did on a daily basis. 'The King's mistress, for a start.'

'Yes,' acknowledged Legg. 'But *they* do it here in the palace, whereas the Duchess displayed herself for any commoner to see. It was unedifying. Besides, she is forty-three. Ugh! It was like being faced with my mother's naked breasts.'

'Why could you not take your eyes off them, then?' asked Chaloner tartly, and watched the young man blush and flail around for an explanation.

'Rolt has lost a button,' Legg blurted, changing the subject so abruptly that Chaloner could not help but smile. 'Have you seen it?'

'Strangely enough, no. Shall we set the palace guard to hunt for it?'

Rolt regarded Chaloner coolly. 'I do not usually care about trifles, but that belonged to my father – one of a set that I like to wear on my favourite long-coat. But we should not keep you, Chaloner. I am sure you have something important to do – like preventing your Earl from destroying himself with his scolding tongue.'

'Yes, he is his own worst enemy,' agreed Legg pompously. 'You should advise him to be nicer to people, because there are rumours that the devil will visit London on Good Friday, and Satan will certainly snatch the souls of men who sit in judgement of their peers.'

Personally, Chaloner thought there were far blacker souls available at White Hall than the Earl's, and that if Lucifer did drop in, he would be spoiled for choice.

White Hall's chapel was an underused, plain building near the pantries. Chaloner stepped into its cool interior, glad to be on his own for a moment. Inside, it was silent and musty. At first, he assumed it was empty, but then he saw someone sitting at the back. It was the Earl's new clerk, John Barker, a tall, gangling man who always looked shabby, despite his fine clothes: he never managed a close shave, his fingers were invariably inky, and his long hair had a natural tendency to greasiness. But he was efficient and reliable, and the Earl liked him.

'I saw you talking to Legg and Captain Rolt just now,' Barker said admonishingly. 'You do know they are part of a vicious cabal that has sworn to see our employer's head on a block, do you not? And they do not mean figuratively – they actually aim to see him executed.'

'Yes,' acknowledged Chaloner. 'I suspect they do.'

'That Cockpit Club is an abomination,' Barker went on hotly. 'The old King would never have countenanced their vile antics. He would have driven the lot of them out in disgrace.'

Without being asked, Barker told Chaloner how the club had come by its name: because its members used White Hall's cockpit as their headquarters. Then he embarked on a brief history of the building, which had originally been intended for bird fights, but when blood-sports had fallen out of favour under the first Stuart kings, it had been converted into a theatre. The current King preferred his plays in the Banqueting House or on Drury Lane, so the cockpit had lain unloved and forgotten until Widdrington had given it a new lease of life. Barker finished his lecture with an angry question.

'Did you hear what they did there last week?'

'No,' said Chaloner cautiously. 'What?'

'Horse fighting!' Barker pursed his lips in disgust. 'They tethered a mare to a pole in the centre of the arena, then brought in two stallions. The males went wild, flailing at each other with hoofs and necks until the weaker one was killed.'

'Killed?' Chaloner was astonished, as horses were expensive. 'No one stopped the contest sooner?'

'Large sums of money were involved, and the losing animal belonged to Rolt, who dared not end the spectacle while his friends were enjoying it – not when he thinks his future depends on winning their good graces.'

Chaloner grimaced his revulsion. He deplored blood-sports and had been glad when Cromwell had banned them. Technically, they were illegal still, but the government made no effort to enforce the laws prohibiting them.

'News came today that the Queen's mother is dead,'

26

said Barker, moving to another subject, 'but as Her Majesty remains ill after losing the latest child she was carrying, it has been decided to keep the news from her.'

'Is that wise?' asked Chaloner, sure it was not. 'Someone is bound to let it slip, which would be a cruel way for her to find out.'

'Surgeon Wiseman advocated honesty, too, but Dr Clarke the physician argued against him and won, which is no mean feat if you have ever met Wiseman.' Barker blushed. 'But of course you have – you are his lodger. I mean no disrespect, but . . . well . . . Wiseman is . . .'

Chaloner had not liked Wiseman at first either, considering him arrogant, opinionated and rude. Their association might have ended there and then, but the surgeon had decided that Chaloner was worthy of his company and the two had eventually become friends. Wiseman also rented Chaloner the top floor of his Covent Garden mansion for a very reasonable price.

Embarrassed by his faux pas, Barker changed the subject again. 'Now it is spring and the ocean is calm we shall have a resurgence of hostilities with the Dutch. They are still smarting after our victory at the Battle of Lowestoft last year, and want revenge.'

'They will have it,' predicted Chaloner soberly. 'While our ministers lounged and frolicked all winter, the Dutch forged anti-England alliances with France, Spain, Denmark *and* Brandenburg. They also built themselves heavier ships.'

'So we will lose the next sea-battle?' asked Barker worriedly.

Chaloner nodded, supposing he would be there to witness it if he was on *Royal Oak*. 'The hawks on the Privy Council are wrong to predict victory.'

'Perhaps they will come to their senses next week.'

Chaloner frowned. 'Why? What happens then?'

'Good Friday falling on the thirteenth day of the month, in a year containing three sixes. Everyone knows that something terrible will occur, and *I* think it will result in all our ministers abandoning their wicked ways and treading a straighter, more ethical path.'

Chaloner snorted his scepticism. 'Then I am afraid you will be disappointed.'

'Perhaps.' Barker grimaced. 'But I live in hope.'

The Shield Gallery was not a gallery at all, but a long room with views across the river. It had changed since Chaloner had been there last. Then it had been an unwelcoming place, cold, cheerless and hung with drab shields that had been won in jousting tournaments decades before. Now it was cosy, with rugs on the floor, paintings on the walls, and curtains – a new fashion from France – hanging in the windows. There were also small tables and comfortable chairs, provided for those who enjoyed card and board games.

That day it was busy, with courtiers standing in huddles, all speaking in low whispers. Sharp-eyed glances were being directed towards one particular table, leading Chaloner to surmise that it was where Chiffinch had spent his last night.

He examined it, although he was not sure what he expected to find. It was no different from the others, although oily stains on the cloth showed where something had been spilled. He bent to sniff it, and detected a fishy odour. There was nothing else, so he looked around for someone who might be willing to talk to him. The Cockpit Club had already been and gone, as he had predicted, but there were plenty more who disliked the Earl, and there was no point in approaching those.

His eye lit on Sir Alan Brodrick. Although a notorious debauchee, Brodrick was also the Earl's favourite cousin – the Earl steadfastly refused to believe ill of him, and was determined to secure him a good post in government. Fortunately for the country, he had not succeeded, as Brodrick was wholly incapable of holding a responsible position. His only redeeming feature, as far as Chaloner was concerned, was that he loved good music.

Music was Chaloner's greatest delight, and there was little he liked more than playing his viol. As a child, he had longed to be a professional musician, but his father had deemed it an unsuitable occupation for gentlemen. Chaloner often suspected that his sire would have changed his mind if he could have looked into the future, and seen that the alternative was being hired as a henchman for an unpopular Royalist.

'Ah, Chaloner,' said Brodrick as the spy approached; he indicated the man who was standing with him. 'Have you met Baron Lucas? He is the Duchess of Newcastle's brother.'

Lucas was in his sixties, with long grey hair and a soldierly bearing. There were multicoloured stains on his coat, suggesting that he liked to dabble in alchemy. Such pastimes were popular among the wealthy, and those who were good at it were invited to share their findings with the Royal Society – the group of men who began to meet soon after the Restoration with the aim of promoting scientific knowledge.

'I suppose my cousin has told you to find out what happened to poor old Chiffinch,' said Brodrick, after

29

Chaloner and Lucas had exchanged bows. 'We are all shocked to learn of his death – he was in fine form in here last night.'

'I played a game with him myself,' growled Lucas. 'Backgammon. I lost, and it cost me ten guineas. He smirked horribly as I counted them out.'

'Did he win against anyone else?' asked Chaloner, cognisant of the fact that no one liked a gloat, and courtiers were quick to take offence. Perhaps the Earl was right to suggest that something untoward had befallen Chiffinch.

Brodrick nodded. 'Just about everyone he played – other than the King, of course. His Majesty excels at backgammon, as he excels in all things.'

'Yes,' said Chaloner flatly, aware that only the mad or the reckless defeated a monarch. It was entirely possible that His Majesty was a perfectly gracious loser, but no one had ever been brave enough to find out. 'Who else did Chiffinch play?'

'His brother Will,' began Brodrick, obligingly, 'followed by Timothy Clarke, the physician who examined his body so sensitively today, and Clarke's wife Fanny—'

'You speak as if you like them,' interrupted Lucas, scowling. 'But Clarke is an ass and Fanny is the dullest woman alive. Talking to her is about as interesting as conversing with a bucket, and her idea of high excitement is choosing a needle with which to sew.'

'True,' acknowledged Brodrick. 'Although she did me a good turn when I brought my daughter to Court. That rogue Rolt took an unseemly interest, but Fanny saw him off before there was any trouble. It was kind of her. My daughter did not appreciate it, though, besotted as she was . . .'

30

'You say Clarke examined Chiffinch "sensitively",' said Chaloner. 'So how did he discover the impostume in his breast?'

'By feeling about with gentle hands,' explained Brodrick. 'Although Clarke has been wrong before, and I have never heard of anyone else dying from such a thing. Shall I continue with my list of those who lost to Chiffinch at backgammon last night?' He did so without waiting for a reply. 'Widdrington and his wife Bess—'

'Along with two dozen other rogues from the Cockpit Club,' put in Lucas. 'Did you know they have all enrolled in the Artillery Company – the military unit that will defend London when the Dutch invade?'

Brodrick shuddered. 'I hope the rest of us will not be expected to do likewise. I am not much of a warrior.'

'Nor are they,' spat Lucas contemptuously. 'I would not have them in any regiment of mine.' He turned an appraising eye on Chaloner. 'I might consider you, though.'

'Thank you,' said Chaloner, and turned the subject back to the dead man. 'What did Chiffinch think of the Cockpit Club?'

'He could not abide them,' replied Brodrick promptly. 'Of course, he also hated my cousin the Earl.'

'And my sister the Duchess of Newcastle,' added Lucas. 'He considered one too prim and the other too radical. You could not win with him and I cannot say I liked the fellow.'

'So is that a complete list of everyone he played last night?' pressed Chaloner.

'Well,' hedged Brodrick and glanced at Lucas. 'Yes, except for . . .'

'You can say it, Brodrick,' said Lucas briskly. 'Except for my sister, her husband and her stepson. She won handily, but the other two lost. She is a clever lass.'

'How did Chiffinch seem to you last night?' asked Chaloner. 'Did he complain about feeling unwell?'

'No, which is why his demise is so unsettling,' replied Lucas soberly. 'He seemed to be in excellent health and spirits. Nothing wrong whatsoever.'

'I agree,' said Brodrick. 'The only other thing I can tell you about last night is that he and his brother Will did not part on the best of terms. I recall a dispute over a fifty-pound wager.'

'They quarrelled?' asked Chaloner keenly.

'There was an exchange of words, although I did not pay much attention, and I left not long afterwards – immediately after watching the Duchess defeat Chiffinch – because Lucas invited me to Newcastle House to see his laboratory.'

'I did,' said Lucas, and scowled. 'Although you only accepted because you expected to see lead turned to gold, even though I explained that it is beyond the ability of any man.'

'The Duke came with us,' said Brodrick, ignoring the rebuke. 'But the Duchess and her stepson remained. She wanted to defeat Chiffinch again, while he hoped to see her soundly trounced. He does not like his father's second wife very much. Families, eh?'

Eventually, Brodrick and Lucas wandered away, leaving Chaloner to run through the names they had given him in his mind, supposing he would have to speak to them all if he wanted a full account of Chiffinch's last night. Well, not the King, of course, and probably not the Newcastles either, given that royals and nobles

32

tended not to appreciate being interrogated like criminals. That left the Cockpit Club, the Clarkes and the dead man's family.

He decided to start with the family.

Although Chaloner did not really believe that Will would hurt his brother, he knew the Earl would expect him to speak to the man anyway. In the interests of diplomacy, he decided to disguise the true purpose of his visit by offering his condolences. Of course, Will was not stupid, so Chaloner was going to have to tread with considerable care.

Fortunately, Chaloner had one ally. Will's wife Barbara was a kindly, motherly soul who had befriended him when he had first arrived in White Hall. She had not wanted to marry Will, but her wealthy family had seen the advantages of the connection, so she had had no choice. She accepted her fate stoically, rarely condemning her husband's excesses, but not encouraging them either.

Chaloner had never been to their home, although he knew it was on St Martin's Lane. He also knew that the Pimp-Master General was never there, preferring to sleep in a chamber near the King, lest His Majesty should suddenly find himself in need of a prostitute. Thus Barbara had the house to herself most of the time, which suited them both. Chaloner decided to speak to her first, to see what she had to say about the untimely death of her brother-in-law.

He walked there briskly, taking the longer route across Scotland Yard to avoid Widdrington and his Cockpit Club cronies, who had taken up station by the fountain again. He knocked on Barbara's door, which was answered by a maid who wore a black sash over her apron to denote mourning. She informed him that everyone was at the palace.

'My master is moving into his brother's old quarters,' she explained, 'and my mistress is there to make sure he does not appear too gleeful about it.'

Chaloner smothered a smile, sure Barbara would be mortified if she knew her servants were making that sort of remark to visitors, although he imagined it was true. Will had secured his brother's posts with unseemly haste, so why not seize his White Hall apartments, too?

He retraced his footsteps, and saw the Great Gate was now ringed by a group of yelling people. Such protests were becoming increasingly frequent as the King continued his slide into disfavour. The complaints were myriad, but mostly about tax – the newly imposed ones to pay for the Dutch war and the Royal Household, the recent levy on coal that the poor could not pay, and a butlerage on wine that everyone resented because they felt it went towards funding the Court's debaucheries.

The demonstration that day was unusual, as all the protesters were female. Some looked to be the kin of wealthy merchants, while others were obviously paupers. Indeed, it appeared that some were prostitutes, if the painted faces and low-cut bodices were anything to judge by. Their leader was a striking woman with long red hair and vivid green eyes. The proud way she carried herself suggested that, while not rich, she was certainly not humble.

Anticipating that no one would listen to them, they had taken the precaution of writing their grievances on wooden placards that they waved. Intelligently, their slogans were short, which meant passers-by could not avoid reading them:

SCHOOLS FOR WOMEN.

NO TO HEARTH TAX.

LEARNING FOR ALL.

BANN COK FITES.

He felt a certain sympathy with them all, although the last was closest to his heart. It was being touted by a slack-jawed child whose clothes were dusted in feathers, telling him that she was probably a chicken-keeper in some wealthy household. He liked birds, and failed to understand how people could find pleasure in watching them injure each other.

When various petitioners had first started to take up station outside the palace gates, the guards had responded by moving them on, but demonstrations were now so frequent that this was impractical. Thus an alternative strategy had been devised: closing the affected gate and advising courtiers to use another one. Deprived of relevant ears, it was not usually long before the protesters gave up and drifted away.

Unfortunately, Widdrington and his Cockpit Club friends heard the rumpus and came to investigate. They shoved past the guards, and emerged on King Street. Delighted to be presented with a target for their grievances, the women regaled them with a torrent of noisy abuse. The Cockpit Club bristled with indignation, although Bess prudently scuttled back inside.

Rolt hastened to urge the rest of them to do likewise. As a man determined to win favour from anyone with influence, the slippery captain was in a quandary: he could not afford to be involved in a skirmish, which would besmirch his reputation with the more respectable elements at White Hall, but nor could he abandon his

35

silly friends. Ergo, his only option was to defuse the situation before it did him any harm.

'Please come away,' he begged. 'They are all women.'

'So what?' demanded Widdrington hotly. 'Or do they frighten you?'

Rolt forced a smile. 'Of course not. But it would be demeaning to trounce the fairer sex.'

'It would be fun,' countered a thin, unhealthy-looking courtier named George Ashley, who was a notoriously heavy drinker even by White Hall standards. 'I am game for a spat.'

'How about I trounce you instead?' said Rolt, and gave him a playful shove before dancing away, brandishing an imaginary sword. 'We shall leave these lasses to the guards, because there is no sport in sparring with common folk.'

The courtiers might have withdrawn at that point, as most of them had already lost interest, but Ashley had other ideas. He pushed Rolt away and lurched towards the demonstrators.

'You have no business here,' he slurred belligerently. 'Clear off.'

He lashed out with a wild sweep of his arm. It was a clumsy blow, and anyone should have been able to avoid it. Unfortunately, the chicken girl was slow to duck, and although his hand barely grazed her shoulder, she lost her balance and fell. She burst into tears, and the Cockpit Club brayed derisive laughter.

'Stand up, Molly,' ordered the red-haired woman briskly. 'Do not give these scum the satisfaction of thinking that they have hurt you.'

Ashley stopped cackling and went red-faced with anger. 'This person called us scum. Did you hear that, gentlemen?'

'*Gentlemen?*' The redhead turned to her own supporters. 'They consider themselves gentlemen. Have you ever heard anything more ludicrous?'

It was the women's turn to laugh, which they did long and hard. By now, the commotion had attracted passers-by, who were quick to side with the protesters.

'You dare insult me?' demanded Ashley, trembling with drunken rage. '*I* am a Yeoman of the Larder. I will teach you a lesson, you filthy whore. Come here and—'

'Whore, am I?' snarled the woman, affronted. 'Well, for your information, I have a perfectly respectable occupation. Moreover, I pay my rent and I buy my own food. Can you say the same? No! You are a leech, whose life serves no useful purpose.'

'We should go, Sarah,' said one of her companions haughtily. 'Why waste time bandying words with these asses? They can no more understand what it is to be decent than they can fly to the moon.'

Widdrington gaped his astonishment when he recognised the woman who had spoken. 'Eliza Topp? What are *you* doing in such low company? I cannot imagine your mistress will approve. The Duchess of Newcastle may be a lunatic, but she would never countenance her staff encouraging sedition among the stinking masses.'

'Stinking?' echoed Sarah in disbelief. 'You accuse us of *stinking?*'

Chaloner was not sure what happened next, but suddenly half the Cockpit Club had swords in their hands, while Sarah began swinging her placard about like a battleaxe. A fight was in progress, and he was in the middle of it.

Chapter 2

Chaloner jerked backwards to avoid the placard that was aimed at his head, a move that placed him directly in the path of a wild swipe from the drunken Ashley's rapier. He twisted sideways in the nick of time, then retreated to a safe distance, where he watched the fracas in distaste, feeling both sides were at fault for their short fuses and goading of the opposition.

Fortunately, everyone involved was an indifferent warrior. The courtiers' swords stabbed and swished, but so ineptly that the protesters were easily able to avoid them, and Chaloner found himself thinking that the Artillery Company would be better off without them in the event of a Dutch invasion. Captain Rolt was the only one with any skill, and he did no more than defend himself, staying in the shadows in the hope that no one who mattered would notice his involvement.

The women were not much better, as their placards were too flimsy for walloping and disintegrated the moment they struck home. The exception was Sarah, who had contrived to turn hers into a savagely pointed spear. She wielded it with a ruthless efficiency.

Meanwhile, Molly the chicken girl wept her terror. She had dropped her board and was crouched on the ground, hands over her head as she was buffeted this way and that by milling feet. Unwilling to see her hurt, Chaloner braved the mêlée to haul her out.

'That nasty man *pushed* me!' she sobbed, once she was safe. 'I am going to tell my Duchess and she will chop off his head. Eliza and me, we work for her, see. *I* am her best poultry-keeper.'

'Are you?' asked Chaloner absently, his attention on the skirmish.

'I have chickens, ducks and geese,' Molly chattered on. 'I live in Newcastle House, and the Duchess is very kind to me. Newcastle House is in Clerkenwell, you know.'

Chaloner did not know, but was more interested in watching the whirlwind of red hair and lance that was Sarah, wanting to laugh at the way the Cockpit Club men scattered before her.

'Enough!' came a furious roar from the gate. 'What is wrong with you all?'

It was Baron Lucas, the Duchess's brother, hands on his hips and a scowl on his face. His voice was loud enough to still the skirmishers, although by this time, both sides were aware that a stalemate had been reached. Neither faction was able to advance or willing to retreat, so most were only too glad to end what had become a futile exercise.

'Wine,' announced Widdrington, turning his back on the demonstrators to express his contempt for them. 'To wash away the stench of these harlots.'

'Harlots?' screeched Sarah, bristling with new outrage. She was prevented from racing forward to attack him by her friend Eliza Topp, although not without difficulty.

'I am going to tell your Duchess about you,' slurred Ashley, pointing an accusing finger at Eliza. 'She will not want a rabble-rouser in her retinue and she will—'

'Come, Ashley,' interrupted Rolt hastily, grabbing his arm to tug him away before his intemperate tongue could reignite the trouble. 'We have things to do elsewhere.'

'Such as what?' jeered Sarah, still incensed. 'Watching a cockfight? Gorging on syllabub while the city starves? Thinking of new ways to tax us?'

'Such as running the country,' retorted Ashley as he turned to follow his companions, a claim that drew genuine laughter from all those who heard it, including his own side.

'Go on, slink off,' howled Sarah, trying to struggle free. 'Skulk away like whipped curs. You do not even have the courage to stay and listen to our grievances. Cowards!'

But the Cockpit Club had lost interest in the spat, which was fortunate, as further interaction between them and the women was unlikely to be productive. They sauntered away, shoving each other playfully and laughing at some remark made by Rolt.

The excitement over, the spectators began to disperse. The women inspected each other for cuts and bruises, after which Sarah made a short but passionate speech about their rights as Londoners. Her words made them stand a little taller. Confidence restored, they marched away singing a popular song that listed the King's many flaws. People were arrested for less, but the guards prudently elected to overlook it. Eventually, only two were left: the child Molly, who still held Chaloner's hand, and Eliza Topp, who came to collect her.

'I saw what you did, sir,' said Eliza, ruffling the girl's hair affectionately. 'I would have helped Molly myself, but I was too busy protecting Sarah. One of those courtiers would have stabbed her in the back if I had not been there to stop them.'

She was in her mid forties, still beautiful, even though the flush of youth was gone. She wore a peculiar turban on her head, and her dress was made of some heavy material that looked Middle Eastern. Chaloner could only suppose that she had learned her unique fashion sense from the controversial Duchess in whose household she was apparently employed.

'I doubt any of them could have slipped past *her* defences,' said Chaloner drily. 'She is more warrior than the lot of them put together.'

'True,' acknowledged Eliza with a smile, and after she had asked his name and position at Court, described her own. 'My husband is the Duke of Newcastle's steward, and I am the Duchess's companion. She and I grew up together, and she considers me more friend than servant. I owe her everything.'

'I do not suppose you accompanied her to the Shield Gallery last night, did you?' he asked, aiming to see if she had witnessed her mistress playing backgammon with Chiffinch.

'No, I stayed home,' Eliza replied, 'although she did mention today that she was the only one – other than the King – to defeat him. My lady is very clever, and more than a match for any man. Have you met her?'

'Not yet.'

'Well, she has promised to visit the Queen on her sickbed later today. You may see her then, and if you do, you are in for an unforgettable experience.'

Chaloner was beginning to appreciate that this might well be true.

*

As Keeper of the Closet, Chiffinch had been allocated a suite of rooms adjoining the King's. It comprised a parlour with a bay window that overlooked the river, and two smaller L-shaped chambers for sleeping and working; all were linked by a handsome wood-panelled hallway. The apartment was accessed from stairs that led from a tiny but pretty courtyard, and was clearly among the most desirable lodgings in the palace.

Chaloner knocked on the door, and was pleased when it was answered by Barbara rather than her husband. She wore a russet-coloured gown that she would have to change soon, as the current mourning fashion was to dress entirely in black; even buckles and jewels were hidden, lest one should emit an unseemly glitter. Her tense expression softened when she saw Chaloner.

'It has been a trying morning,' she confided unhappily, ushering him into the hall. 'I dare not go home to don more suitable attire lest Will . . . well, you know how it is.'

Chaloner did. She and her husband might not be close, but she was fond of him, and would try to prevent him from doing something that would later cause him problems.

'How is he?' he asked.

Barbara grimaced. 'He has already arranged for his brother to be buried in Westminster Abbey on Tuesday. Now he is here, tossing out things he does not want to keep, and poring over those he does. I am trying my best to persuade him to show more decorum, for appearance's sake, but with scant success.'

'The two of them did not get along?' fished Chaloner.

Barbara shrugged. 'He will grieve later, I am sure, but in White Hall if you do not move at an indecent lick, someone else beats you to it.'

At that moment, Chaloner heard the chapel bell strike one o'clock, which meant Will had achieved an impressive amount in the few hours since his sibling had died.

'Is it true that he will inherit Chiffinch's titles and privileges, as well as these rooms?'

Barbara nodded. 'The agreement is already signed and sealed. Poor Thomas never had sons, so it was a straightforward matter to put to the King.'

'Will did well to persuade him to act so quickly,' mused Chaloner. 'His Majesty is not a man for speedy decisions, so he must hold Will in very high esteem.'

'He does love his Pimp-Master General,' said Barbara, acidly for her. 'I suppose I am glad that Will is the one who will profit from our loss, but Thomas's death was so sudden that I fear tongues will wag unless we make some pretence at sorrow.'

'Were you in the Shield Gallery last night?'

'Yes, but I went home early, so all I can tell you is that Thomas and Will played two games of backgammon, both of which Will lost. The first I heard about Thomas being dead was when my maid broke the news to me at about eight o'clock this morning.'

'I have been told that Will and Chiffinch quarrelled.'

'It would not surprise me. They argued all the time, mostly over the fact that Thomas thought Will's pimping brought the Court into disrepute.' Barbara looked Chaloner in the eye. 'I do hope you are not planning to investigate the matter. It would be most unwise.'

'You mean it may harm Will?'

Barbara made an impatient sound. '*He* has nothing to hide. I meant for you and your Earl. If you have been listening to malicious and unfounded tittle-tattle about foul play, then stop. Thomas died of natural causes. It

43

is very sad, but these things happen, and if you meddle, you will anger a lot of important people.'

'You seem very certain that Chiffinch's death was natural.'

'I *am* certain. Dr Clarke diagnosed an impostume, and there is no reason to doubt him. Now, shall I take you to see Will? I am sure he will appreciate your sympathy.'

Chaloner followed Barbara along the hall. Trained to notice such things, he spotted several holes bored in the panelling, allowing the resident to monitor what was going on in the King's chambers next door. These would no doubt prove invaluable to Will, for deciding which prostitutes would best suit His Majesty's particular mood. Then Barbara opened the door to the parlour, which boasted some of the finest artwork Chaloner had ever seen. Clearly, Chiffinch had kept the best for himself when he had been assigned the task of furnishing White Hall.

'What do *you* want?' demanded Will when he saw Chaloner, and scowled at his wife. 'Why did you let him in? You know we do not like each other.'

Although two years younger than his brother, Will looked older, as night after night of carousing had taken their toll. He had removed his wig for comfort, revealing his grey-stubbled pate, and his clothes, although fine, were stained with wine and spilled food from the evening before. His eyes were bloodshot, and he had an impressive paunch.

'I came to express my condolences,' began Chaloner, 'and to—'

'If you are here to say that Clarendon is sorry my brother is dead, you can save your breath,' interrupted Will shortly. 'Because I know he is not.'

'Please, dear,' said Barbara, laying a soothing hand on his arm. 'Tom only came to—'

'I know why he came.' Will's sour expression made him look like an elderly and peevish schoolboy, and Chaloner eyed him in distaste, wondering why the King favoured such people. 'He aims to investigate me for murder.'

'He does not,' said Barbara firmly. 'I have already told him that—'

'I know what people are saying,' snapped Will. 'They saw me argue with Thomas after he defeated me at the gaming table, and they think I dispatched him in a fit of pique. Your Earl will certainly believe such tales, and will claim it is his duty, as Lord Chancellor, to order an inquiry. Am I right?'

'No,' lied Chaloner. 'There is no talk of murder at Clarendon House.'

Will sniffed. 'Well, for your information, I did not see Thomas again after we parted in anger. That was at two o'clock in the morning, and I know for a fact that he played others after me – Physician Clarke and his wife, Widdrington and his Cockpit Club friends, the Duchess of Newcastle and her stepson . . .'

'I understand you lost fifty pounds to your brother,' said Chaloner. 'It is a lot of money.'

It was a veritable fortune, near eight times what a labourer would earn in a year, and far more than Chaloner would ever bet on a game of chance.

Will sneered. 'Not to me. Besides, Thomas would never have made me pay, although as I then won the same amount from the Duchess of Newcastle, he could have had it if he wanted.'

'*You* defeated her, but your brother could not?' asked Chaloner doubtfully.

45

Will huffed his indignation. 'I am not his second in everything, you know. And I happen to be very good at lanterloo, which is what I played with her. But that is by-the-by. The point is that I had no reason to harm my brother, so any tales to the contrary are malicious slander, and if I learn that your Earl is behind them, I will sue him for every penny he owns.'

'He is not a gossip,' said Chaloner, although this was a brazen falsehood, as the Earl loved derogatory chatter about his enemies. 'And even if he were, he is not acquainted with the kind of people who would regale him with it.'

'True,' conceded Will. 'His friends are mostly prudish dullards, who have no place in a lively court. My brother hated him. Did you know that? He hated anyone who brought White Hall into disrepute, because he felt it damaged the King's standing with his subjects.'

'So he hated you as well?' asked Chaloner, thinking that Will's antics were more harmful to His Majesty than almost everyone else's combined.

'He loved me,' said Will firmly. 'But he was not very keen on my Cockpit Club friends. Or the Duchess of Newcastle, whom he considered the most dangerous person in the country.'

Chaloner was astonished, feeling there were far better candidates for that role. 'All I know about her is that she dresses spectacularly for the theatre.'

Will laughed with genuine amusement. 'It was quite a sight, and the King said later that he could scarce believe his eyes – he kept rubbing them, to see if they deceived him. However, it was not her clothes but her ideas that really alarmed my brother: she thinks women are as clever as men, an eccentric notion that will turn the world upside down if it is encouraged.'

46

'Yes, because there are dozens of White Hall ladies who are *vastly* superior to him in intellect,' sniffed Barbara. 'And he was terrified of them. Yet Will loved him, despite his shortcomings. Tell him, Will, dear.'

'I did,' said Will obligingly. 'And I rushed to claim his titles and possessions purely to ensure they pass to a *worthy* successor. I did not act out of personal greed or ambition.'

'Of course not,' said Chaloner flatly.

'Yet I do not believe he died of natural causes.' Will raised his hand when Barbara began to object. 'I know you disagree, Babs, but I have been thinking about it, and I am sure I am right. My brother made a lot of enemies by telling folk that their behaviour shamed the King, and I think one of them murdered him.'

'I see,' said Chaloner, while Barbara pursed her lips irritably. 'Do you have any particular suspects in mind?'

'I do,' replied Will. 'The man behind this vicious crime will be his most *deadly* enemy.'

'Not the Duchess?' asked Chaloner warily.

'Of course not. I refer to the one with the blackest heart of all – the Earl of Clarendon.'

'I told you it was a mistake to poke about in Thomas's death,' said Barbara crossly, as she showed Chaloner to the door a few minutes later. 'It was *your* reckless questions that prompted Will to accuse the Earl. Before you came, he was inclined to think the culprit was one of the Cockpit Club. It is your own fault that he settled for your employer instead.'

'Why the Cockpit Club?' asked Chaloner, unruffled. 'I thought Will was a member.'

'He is, but that does not mean he likes them. White Hall is a snakepit, and no friendship or alliance can be relied upon for long.' Barbara sighed. 'You had better warn the Earl to be on his guard, because once Will has a notion in his head, it is very difficult to disabuse him of it.'

'But you will try?'

'Yes, although I doubt he will listen. Of course, if Will *does* start a rumour that the Earl ordered Thomas dispatched, you know who will be charged with doing his bidding.'

'Who?' asked Chaloner stupidly.

'You – the cherished spy who has performed all manner of feats to thwart his enemies.'

'I am not cherished,' said Chaloner, startled. 'Most of the time, the Earl can barely stand to be in the same room as me. I am useful, but that is all.'

'He values you more than you think,' countered Barbara, 'but he does not want you to know it, lest you demand a pay rise – he is a terrible miser. And fingers *will* point at you if he is accused of ordering Thomas's death, because even you must admit that you are sinister.'

Chaloner blinked his disbelief. 'Sinister? *Me?*'

Barbara began to count points on her fingers. 'You wear clothes that mean no one notices you until you are in their midst; you creep up on people when they least expect it; you disappear for weeks on end on business that you then refuse to discuss; and you have dark skills acquired during the wars and in the service of Cromwell's Spymaster. Of course you are sinister!'

Chaloner was horrified to learn what was being said about him, having assumed that no one gave him a second thought. Moreover, it was a shock to learn that his efforts to be unobtrusive seemed to have had the opposite effect. He sincerely hoped that people did not believe that he was to the Earl what Swaddell was to Williamson.

Barbara saw his consternation and patted his arm. 'It has its advantages, dear. It means few will risk taking you on in a fight. However, it does render you vulnerable to a different kind of assault – namely, charges of dispatching your master's enemies. Thomas *did* die of natural causes, but we all know how hard it will be to extinguish rumours to the contrary, once they have taken hold.'

'And it will be difficult to prove my innocence, given that I may have been the last to see him alive,' said Chaloner gloomily. 'I met him in King Street at six o'clock this morning – he gossiped to me about what the Duchess of Newcastle had worn to the theatre. Then he wandered off towards the tennis courts, while I went to the Sun tavern.'

'Not the tennis courts,' said Barbara. 'The *cockpit*. At least, that is where his body was found, exactly an hour after you say you parted from him. I cannot imagine why he went there, as it must have been deserted at that time of the day.'

Chaloner stared at her. He knew Chiffinch had died in White Hall, but he had assumed it was at home. 'Chiffinch breathed his last in a place where no one goes except Widdrington and his monkeys?'

Barbara wagged a cautionary finger. 'He breathed his last in a place that is never locked, and that is open to anyone. Do not confer on it a significance it does not have.'

'Was the cockpit in use last night?'

'I believe there was a bird fight at some point, although it would have been over long before six o'clock in the morning.'

'Have you been to the cockpit lately?' Chaloner had

49

seen a play there once, but all he could remember was that it had been rather dark and smelled of urine.

'Not since it was commandeered by Widdrington's horde. I do not like them much, and I wish Will would not carouse with them. But to return to Thomas's death, you must have your alibi ready, should anyone make an accusation. I cannot imagine the Sun was busy at that time in the morning. With luck, the landlord will remember you.'

Chaloner shook his head, as he had sat in the shadows and eaten alone, but then he reconsidered. If Barbara thought him sinister, then perhaps the taverner did as well, and would be able to confirm that he had indeed been breaking his fast when Chiffinch had died. Regardless, he hoped that Wiseman would end the speculation when he examined the body. Then no further probing would be necessary and the whole matter could be quietly forgotten.

Barbara sighed. 'People will tell you that Thomas was in good health, so had no reason to drop down dead, but the truth is that he was in his sixty-seventh year and he ate too much, drank too much, and was too fat. He also complained of pains in his chest.'

'From the impostume that Clarke found?'

'Perhaps, although that is a question for a surgeon to answer.'

'Wiseman will do it,' Chaloner told her. 'As soon as the Queen is on the mend.'

'Then you will not have answers today,' said Barbara with the authority of one who knew. 'And perhaps not tomorrow either, unless she rallies overnight, poor lady. The premature end of another pregnancy has all but crushed her.'

Chaloner thanked her for her help and took his leave,

50

after which he went straight to the Queen's apartments and wrote a second message to Wiseman, asking him to recommend another surgeon because the matter of Chiffinch could not wait. The reply came via a footman who had been ordered to repeat it verbatim. The fellow stood stiffly to attention, and recited the words in a mono-tone to a spot on the wall above Chaloner's head.

'"Hire another *medicus* at your peril, as none of my colleagues can be trusted to find the truth. I will oblige you at the earliest opportunity, so wait for a man who knows his business or risk the consequences."'

'I did not ask for a full-blown anatomy,' muttered Chaloner irritably. 'A quick examination would have sufficed.'

The footman shrugged and reverted to his normal voice. 'The examination might take a moment, but what of the travelling to and from the Westminster charnel house? It will take Mr Wiseman away from Her Majesty for far too long.' Then he looked around thoughtfully. 'Unless you arrange for the corpse to be brought here . . .'

Chaloner was horrified by the notion. 'I do not think that would be a good idea – on so many different levels!'

Although inclined to think that Barbara had exaggerated when she had told him that he cut an eerie figure, Chaloner nevertheless took more notice of the people he passed as he returned to the Shield Gallery. Was it his imagination, or did they eye him with a combination of unease and curiosity? And if so, was it because they considered him an unsettling presence with an unsavoury past, or because Will was not the only one who thought the Earl might be responsible for the sudden demise of one of his greatest detractors?

Regardless, he decided that the best way to combat

any unpleasant rumours was to conduct his investigation openly, so if anyone did point an accusing finger, he would be able to claim that he would hardly be trying to solve a murder he had committed himself.

His mind made up, he marched to the Shield Gallery, making sure to stay in the sunlight and tipping his hat back so it did not shade his face. It felt contrived, forcing him to wonder if he really had grown too used to living in the shadows. He ran up the stairs, careful to step in the middle of each one – he usually kept to the edges, which were less likely to creak – and threw open the door at the top. It cracked against the wall, causing everyone to turn towards him.

'The Earl of Clarendon, Lord Chancellor of England, is saddened and shocked by the sudden demise of Mr Thomas Chiffinch,' he announced. 'Dr Clarke has determined the cause of death as an impostume in the breast, but the Earl wishes to be certain, so he has ordered an official inquiry. He expects everyone to cooperate.'

'Does he indeed?' murmured the Duke of Buckingham. He was another of the Earl's enemies, and so was the woman who stood at his side – Lady Castlemaine, the King's mistress. 'What does he want us to do? Confess to the murder?'

'He was murdered?' pounced Chaloner. 'How do you know?'

Lady Castlemaine laughed languorously. 'You should watch what you say, Bucks, or the Earl's spy will hang you with your own words. But we have nothing to hide, so let the man do his duty. Come, start with me.'

She undulated towards him. She had donned a very flimsy gown, so it was difficult for Chaloner to concentrate when he asked his questions, and he was acutely aware of her smirking at him all the while. He was relieved when Buckingham sauntered over to join them, and he was able to look somewhere other than at her perfectly proportioned body.

He spent the rest of the afternoon and evening talking to everyone who had been in the Shield Gallery the previous night, along with a lot of people who had not but who admitted to seeing the dead man at other times during the day. As he had anticipated, he learned nothing to suggest that anyone had done Chiffinch harm. Eventually, as the sun began to set, he gave up, and went to stand by a window to think.

Until Barbara had shattered his illusions, Chaloner had prided himself on his ability to blend into the background. Indeed, it was a talent that had allowed him to survive ten years of espionage, which was a long time in such a treacherous profession. He had brown hair, currently covered by a wig, clear grey eyes, and pleasant but unremarkable features. He was neither tall nor short, fat nor thin, and was as comfortable in slums as he was at Court.

But as he stood looking over the grubby ooze of the River Thames, he asked himself whether the skills that had kept him alive in the past might be his downfall in the present and future. It was not a comfortable thought, and he found himself wishing that Cromwell had not died, and that he was still an intelligencer in Holland. It had been perilous work, but at least he had been at ease with it.

Not long after, he bumped into Brodrick again. The Earl's cousin was with three strangers, and Chaloner could tell they had recently arrived in the city because their clothes were newly tailored. Brodrick introduced

53

them with suspicious eagerness, then claimed pressing business elsewhere, scuttling away fast enough to verge on the impolite. It did not take Chaloner long to understand why he had been so keen to escape: the trio were trying company.

Their leader was Viscount Mansfield, the Duke of Newcastle's son and heir from his first marriage. He was small, fair and delicate, with a long nose, pale eyes and a wig that was too showy for the occasion. As his stepmother was forty-three, she had to be less than a decade his senior, and it quickly became apparent that he hated her.

The other two were the Duke's chief stewards: Francis Topp managed the family seat at Welbeck, while Andrew Clayton had charge of the West Country estates. The pair could not have been more different. Topp was short with white hair and an excruciatingly obsequious manner; Clayton was younger, tall and dark, with the hungry air of a man with ambitions.

For a while, Chaloner had no choice but to stand and feign interest while Mansfield made catty remarks about anything that caught his splenetic eye – the dreary artwork, Buckingham's old-fashioned boots, Lady Castlemaine's fading beauty. Topp gushed agreement with every spiteful observation, while Clayton was a dark, brooding presence on Mansfield's other side. Chaloner determined to have words with Brodrick later.

'I met your wife earlier,' he told Topp, the moment he could insert a word into the malicious tirade. 'Outside the Great Gate.'

He chose to mention Eliza because he thought the venomous Viscount would be unlikely to make snide remarks about his retainer's wife – at least, not while Topp was present – and he was keen to put an end to the disagreeable diatribe. Unfortunately, the subject sparked a quarrel between the two stewards.

Topp groaned. 'Oh, Your Honour, *please* do not say she joined those foolish women in their protest! I urged her to stay home, but she is a lady of independent spirit.'

'Only because you allow her to be,' said Clayton, smugly gloating. 'Mine would never venture out once I forbade her. It is a question of establishing who is in charge.'

'*I* am in charge,' averred Topp between gritted teeth. 'However, that does not mean I am a petty tyrant, afraid of a woman who is my intellectual equal.'

'Pah!' sneered Clayton. 'You are a weakling, too frightened to show Eliza her place. Intellect has nothing to do with it.'

'Eliza has fallen under my stepmother's evil spell, Topp,' said Mansfield, all supercilious disdain. 'And has been corrupted with indecent ideas.'

'Please do not speak ill of the Duchess, Your Worshipfulness,' begged Topp unhappily. 'You know I adore her more than any woman alive, save my wife. I live to serve her.'

'Perhaps you should spend less time grovelling and more time controlling Eliza,' put in Clayton with a smirk. 'Then your wife might think twice about fraternising with rebellious commoners, all demanding education for girls and other such nonsense.'

'Eliza does *not* fraternise with commoners,' objected Topp, fixing him with a haughty glance. 'She is a *lady*, not some lowly farmer's lass.'

Judging by the way the blood drained from Clayton's face, this was a low blow. 'At least my Harriet does not embarrass the Duke by brawling in the street,' he retorted tightly.

'My father *would* be mortified if a member of his household was involved in a public spat,' Mansfield informed Topp. 'So, for your sake, I hope Eliza has an explanation.'

Topp began a blustering defence, while Clayton and Mansfield expressed their opinions of his claims with disbelieving snorts and exaggerated drops of the jaw. Chaloner listened in astonishment, amazed that the two stewards should bicker in public – and that the Viscount should join in.

'The Duchess is having a soirée next week,' said Clayton to Chaloner, when Topp's agitated monologue eventually petered out. 'She has charged me with organising the music, and Brodrick said you might advise me. I was thinking of hiring a troupe of flageolet players.'

'Flageolets!' jeered Topp, still livid and looking to retaliate. 'Any fool knows those are for taverns. The Duchess would be mortified if you brought those to Newcastle House. What a peasant you are, Clayton!'

'A consort of violas da gamba might be more appropriate,' put in Chaloner quickly before there was another spat.

'Brodrick thought you would suggest that,' said Clayton, pointedly ignoring Topp's remark. 'He also told me that you own no small talent yourself.'

'Hire him, then,' ordered Mansfield, and looked the spy up and down critically. 'But no drab clothes, if you please. The soirée will be next Wednesday at Newcastle House. Do you know the place?'

'It is in Clerkenwell, Your Worship,' put in Topp helpfully. 'A beautiful spot for a glorious mansion, although no building is too good for our Duke and his Duchess, of course.'

'Are they musicians themselves?' asked Chaloner,

wondering if he had ever met anyone who was more shamelessly servile than Topp.

'*She* is not,' replied Mansfield at once. 'She spent her youth with her nose in a book, and neglected to practise, so she is rubbish.' He sniffed his contempt. 'Of course, all that reading has given her a false sense of her own worth, because now she feels compelled to bray her opinions to all the world. She thinks we should be fascinated by them.'

'We *are* fascinated by them,' averred Topp loyally. 'Her *Philosophical and Physical Opinions* is in its second edition, while *The World's Olio* and *Nature's Pictures* sold more copies than any other book last year.'

'Only because the plague drove all right-thinking people out of the city, leaving only lunatics and radicals to frequent bookshops,' retorted Mansfield. 'And what is an olio anyway?'

'A spicy soup, Your Significance,' supplied Topp obligingly. 'Very tasty.'

'More like a porridge of scraps,' scoffed Clayton. 'Paupers' fare, in other words.'

As the trio seemed to delight in being recklessly indiscreet, Chaloner mentioned the sudden death of Chiffinch, hoping they would gossip about that, too.

'He was younger than my father,' sighed Mansfield, evidently a man who saw everything in terms of himself. 'God knows what will happen when *he* dies. His new wife will see me beggared.'

'She will not, Your Magnificence,' said Topp stoutly. 'She is not interested in money.'

'Perhaps not,' said Clayton slyly. 'But she is interested in the things money can buy – books, microscopes, telescopes, costly scientific instruments . . .'

57

Mansfield sneered. 'She thinks she will be invited to join the Royal Society – that those learned gentlemen will forget she is female and admit her to their august gatherings. Can you credit the woman? She aims to destroy the proper order of things with her vanity.'

Struggling for patience, Chaloner brought the subject back to Chiffinch, and eventually managed to ascertain that the two stewards had watched Mansfield lose two games of backgammon to him.

'He cheated,' declared Mansfield petulantly. 'I am better at it than my stepmother, so it is impossible that she should have succeeded where I failed.'

'Were you angry about that?' fished Chaloner.

'Furious,' spat Mansfield. 'I wanted a third game, so that Clayton could watch more carefully for sleights of hand, but Chiffinch refused. He gloated that he had taken enough of my money, and did not need any more of it.'

'When did you last see him?'

'At four o'clock, when he stood to leave – I heard the clocks chime the hour as he did so. By then I was tired, but not sleepy, so I went to watch the river for a while. Water always soothes me when my mind is uneasy.'

'Did you go there alone?'

'There would be no point in doing it if someone was with me yammering,' retorted Mansfield unpleasantly. 'So, yes, I was alone. And then I went home, arriving at perhaps seven or eight o'clock. In time for breakfast anyway.'

More questions revealed that Clayton and Topp had left some time before Mansfield, and had alibis in each other, as they had travelled back to Clerkenwell together. They had then sat in the kitchen with other members

58

of the Duke's household until dawn, neither willing to go to bed first, lest the other one said nasty things about him behind his back.

Eventually, Chaloner made his escape, thinking that if Wiseman did discover that Chiffinch had not died a natural death, then Viscount Mansfield's petty malice would put him at the very top of the list of suspects for his murder.

The Shield Gallery grew increasingly hot, as more courtiers crammed themselves inside to see what entertainments had been arranged to honour the dead man. It stank, too, as people perspired in their elegant clothes, and the reek of body odour mingled with an eye-watering combination of perfumes.

The air rang with self-important voices, every one of which had an opinion about Chiffinch. To die of natural causes was far too mundane, so Chaloner was not at all surprised to hear that tales of murder were rather more popular. When he eventually tired of the ghoulish speculation and aimed for the door, he was aware of people watching him. Was it because he was suspected of dispatching Chiffinch on the Earl's orders, because they feared the investigation he had announced, or because he was starting to attract the same kind of nervous interest as Swaddell?

He went to the Spares Gallery, technically a repository for superfluous artwork, but which also served as an informal common room for senior officials. A small pantry was usually stocked with food and wine, and there were comfortable chairs for relaxing. Chaloner drank a cup of ale, savouring the peace of the place after the clamour and press of the noisy courtiers upstairs. He was not alone for long though, as the door opened and Brodrick walked in. The Earl's cousin helped himself to a large goblet of wine, drained it in a single swallow, then poured another.

'I have a bone to pick with you,' began Chaloner coolly.

Brodrick grinned, unrepentant. 'I was stuck with Mansfield for the best part of an hour, so it was high time someone else took a turn. Did he ask you to perform in Newcastle House next week? If so, I shall inveigle an invitation myself. Good music is in short supply these days, as people are still afraid to hire professional players lest they have the plague.'

'The plague is almost gone,' said Chaloner. 'Only twenty-six deaths last week.'

'Which is nine *more* than the seventeen at the end of March,' countered Brodrick, evidently one of those who studied the official figures assiduously when they were released each Thursday. 'So it is still here, as far as I am concerned. And who knows? Perhaps *that* is the dreadful thing that will happen next Friday – a second wave of it. Of course, if so, it will be over by Easter Day.'

Chaloner frowned. 'How did you reach that conclusion?'

'Because that is what the soothsayers predict: a terrible calamity on Good Friday, followed by great rejoicing on Easter Sunday. But you look morose, Chaloner. Are you having trouble with the Chiffinch affair? I did recommend that my cousin keep his nose out of it, but he refused to listen.'

Chaloner regarded him coolly. 'I wish you had made your case more forcefully.'

'I did my best, but I had a terrible headache this morning, and it was hard to string two words together.'

Brodrick grinned again. 'Last night was a lot of fun. I do not play backgammon, but there were plenty of card games on the go – maw, lanterloo, quinze. . .'

'But you left early to go to Newcastle House,' recalled Chaloner.

'At roughly half past three, which shows how drunk I was, because I am not remotely interested in laboratories. Incidentally, I asked a few questions on your behalf today – fellows who will talk to me, but not to you. They say Chiffinch left the Shield Gallery at four o'clock precisely, and they were under the impression that he was off to do some work.'

'Where? In his apartments?'

'They thought so, but I have been unable to find anyone who can say with certainty. The next time he was seen was almost two hours later, when he walked across the Great Court with members of the Cockpit Club – Widdrington and a few others.'

'Really?' asked Chaloner, thinking immediately of frantic attempts to avoid debts incurred by losses at backgammon. 'Was their conversation amiable?'

'My friends could not tell, so you will have to ask Widdrington's cabal yourself. That will not be pleasant! And an hour later, at seven, the corpse was found. Naturally, I went to see it when the alarm was raised.'

'How?' asked Chaloner. 'You were in Newcastle House.'

Brodrick waved a dismissive hand. 'Oh, I had escaped Lucas's smelly pots and bubbling cauldrons by then. I heard the commotion, and my curiosity was piqued, so I went to see what was happening. Do not look so disapproving, Chaloner. Only a fool does not keep abreast of happenings in the place where he intends to flourish.'

'And your friends are certain of all these times?

Chiffinch left the Shield Gallery at four, disappeared for two hours, and was last seen walking across the Great Court just before six?'

'And found dead in the cockpit at seven,' finished Brodrick. 'Yes, quite sure.'

Which meant, Chaloner thought uneasily, that he himself probably *had* been the last person to see Chiffinch alive, as the courtier had been alone by the time he was in King Street.

'What was he doing in the cockpit?' he asked. 'Have you heard any suggestions?'

'There was a bird fight, but it had been over for hours by then. Try asking Fanny Clarke – you know her; she is married to the Physician of the Household. It was she who discovered the body. Of course, you have to wonder what *she* was doing there at such an hour, too.'

'Where does she live?' Chaloner set down his cup and stood.

Brodrick laughed. 'You cannot interrogate her now, man! It is late, and she, being a respectable lady, will be asleep in bed. You will have to wait until tomorrow. But if Chiffinch does transpire to have been murdered, I hope one of the Cockpit Club is the culprit. It will discredit the whole cabal, which will please my cousin. They mean him serious harm.'

'What can you tell me about them?'

'That Widdrington is a mean-spirited elitist who cares for nothing except his pleasures. That his wife Bess is an ugly, spiteful harpy, who aims to win her husband's love by aping his vileness. That Ashley is a drunkard and—'

'Not so loud!' warned Chaloner, aware that Brodrick's voice had risen in its passion.

'That Captain Rolt is a sycophant, who is all things

62

to all men. And that the rest are detestable dullards with no redeeming qualities.'

'So they are destined for top posts in government then,' said Chaloner drily.

'Fortune always favours the unworthy,' agreed Brodrick bitterly. 'Or rather, the King does. But the whole vile coven is united by its hatred of my cousin, and they do not want him disgraced – they want him executed. It is deadly stuff, Chaloner.'

'Then perhaps you should persuade him to leave London and live quietly in the country. There is only so much I can do to protect him against this level of malice.'

'I have tried, believe me, but he will not listen. Incidentally, Widdrington has organised a cockfight for tonight – it will be starting as we speak. You should go and watch these rogues in their natural habitat, as you will learn more about them there than from listening to me.'

Chaloner baulked – he detested bloodsports. But then he supposed that Brodrick had a point, and if the Cockpit Club really did mean his Earl harm, then it was his duty to learn as much as he could about them, so as to be ready to fight them off.

The Cockpit was a square building lined with steeply pitched rows of benches and a central, circular arena. It was very luxuriously appointed, with ornate mouldings on the walls and a glass turret that allowed light to flood in during the day. At night, it was lit with torches, which flickered and smoked, lending the place a rather insalubrious atmosphere.

Cockfights were noisy occasions, especially ones in White Hall. There were agitated crows from birds awaiting their turn in the ring, but most of the racket came from the courtly spectators, who cheered, booed, hissed and howled. Chaloner climbed the stairs to the stalls, wrinkling his nose at the stench of overheated people, spilled wine and chicken droppings.

He reached the top tier and surveyed the scene below. The benches were packed with important, wealthy and influential people – the Cockpit Club had invited Members of Parliament, Treasury officials, half the Privy Council, several prominent churchmen and a lot of high-ranking lawyers. Although they were predominantly men, there were some ladies present, most notably Bess Widdrington, Lady Castlemaine and a bevy of *filles de joie* from the infamous 'gentleman's club' in Hercules' Pillars Alley – the establishment that was owned and run by Wiseman's lover.

A fight was in progress, with a big white cockerel launching itself at a smaller blue-black one. There was something peculiar about their heads, and Chaloner saw that their combs and wattles had been sliced off, to prevent opposing birds from fastening on to them. Neither had been fitted with metal spurs, as they would have been in Spain, although their natural ones were still sharp enough to cause serious injury.

Chaloner looked around again, thinking it was here that Chiffinch had died. Had the courtier breathed his last down in the arena or on one of the benches? And why had he visited the place at such an hour? For a meeting perhaps? Chaloner wished he had come sooner, as any clues would be long gone by now.

He took up station in a shadowy corner and studied the people he still wanted to question – unless the Earl came to his senses and ordered him to leave the matter

64

well alone. Or better yet, Wiseman pronounced Chiffinch's death natural and ended the speculation.

About twenty members of the Cockpit Club were there. They included the rich and arrogant Colonel Widdrington, the wife he did not love, the poor but ambitious Captain Rolt, and the drunken Ashley. Viscount Mansfield was there, too, trying to look jolly, but clearly ill at ease in such boisterous company. Young Legg was fast asleep, leading Chaloner to wonder if he was old enough to handle the late nights that his cronies kept.

Bess Widdrington screeched abuse at the black cockerel when it limped away in defeat, suggesting she had lost a lot of money. Her husband sidled away from her with a moue of distaste. When the exhausted birds had been whisked away, two more were produced. Widdrington presided over the betting, and Chaloner noticed that while Rolt was very free with advice regarding which combatant to back, he kept his own purse securely in his pocket.

At that point, a Cockpit Club member, whom Chaloner knew was named Thomas Cobbe, stood up. Like Rolt, Cobbe was a penniless nobody, but he elected to win his peers' notice by being outrageous – that night he wore a scarlet suit with pink lace. With careless aplomb, he placed a wager so huge that a stunned silence descended over the entire gathering.

'Are you sure?' breathed Widdrington, shocked. 'On the *brown* one?'

'It reminds me of my grandfather,' drawled Cobbe, revelling in the attention, 'and with his sainted soul smiling down on me, how can I lose?'

When Widdrington laughed and the others clapped their appreciation, Mansfield bet an identical sum on the opposing bird.

'It looks like my stepmother,' he quipped, 'and that woman wins at everything.'

He grinned, expecting people to applaud his wit, too, but no one did because it lacked originality. Then Cobbe's chicken won, earning him enthusiastic cheers, whereas Mansfield received nothing but a smile of sympathy from Rolt, who never missed an opportunity to curry favour with a nobleman. Mansfield might be a member of the Cockpit Club, thought Chaloner, but he was not really one of them.

Eventually, there was a break in the 'entertainment', while servants came to sprinkle the bloodied arena with fresh sand. Desultory conversation broke out, so Chaloner eased closer to the Cockpit Club contingent to eavesdrop.

'Perhaps I should have betted on the outcome of the skirmish between you lot and Eliza Topp's whores,' said Mansfield sulkily, still smarting after his defeat. 'The one you had outside the palace gates today.'

'If you had been with us, we would have won handily,' declared Cobbe, draping an elegant arm around the Viscount's narrow shoulders. The others guffawed, although Mansfield blinked uncertainly, not sure what to make of the remark.

'Those women should have been at home, cooking and cleaning for their menfolk,' declared Bess, glancing at Widdrington in the expectation that he would agree. 'It is a woman's duty to support her husband in all things, not prance about screeching rebellious slogans.'

'Is that why you are here tonight, Bess?' slurred Ashley. 'To support Widdrington? You did not come to win a few pennies on the birds?'

'To serve him is my sacred duty as a wife,' retorted Bess loftily, and would have added more, but Widdrington

66

had started talking to Mansfield, and was not listening to her. She flushed with disappointment and fell silent.

At that moment, young Legg woke himself up with an undignified snort. Embarrassed, he blurted the first thing that entered his mind.

'Did you find your button, Rolt? The one you lost here last night?'

'You have been looking for a *button*?' Cobbe's voice dripped laconic astonishment. 'Is it made of diamonds then? Or has it been blessed by the Archbishop of Canterbury?'

The captain forced a smile. 'Its value is sentimental – it belonged to my father. Obviously, I would not demean myself hunting for it otherwise.'

'Speaking of fathers, Chiffinch is not much mourned by his daughter,' piped Legg, refreshed by his nap and ready to make up for lost time by providing some gossip. 'He thought her only use was to marry someone who could benefit him, but she believes she is worth more.'

'Then she is mistaken,' declared Ashley, all tipsy indignation. 'Women were put on Earth to be useful to *men*. I do not want females making decisions for themselves – it would result in anarchy! Incidentally, did you know that Chiffinch died right in the centre of our arena?'

'How do you know?' asked Cobbe curiously.

'Because Fanny Clarke – the physician's wife – told me,' replied Ashley. 'Although I cannot imagine what *she* was doing in here at such an hour.'

'The same is true of Chiffinch himself,' said Widdrington, willing to rejoin the discussion now that Bess had left it. 'This building is ours – the place where we have fun. I hope he did not come with the intention of sabotage.'

'Well, if he did, he died before he could do anything,'
shrugged Cobbe. 'Nothing has happened to us, and all
is well with the world.'

He performed an elegant twirl that made his coat-tails
fly, revealing their beautiful pink silk lining. There were
murmurs of admiration from anyone with an eye for
fashion. Unfortunately, it was looking at Cobbe that
caused Bess to spot Chaloner in the shadows beyond.
Her square, homely face broke into a scowl that turned
it uglier than ever.

'Why are *you* here?' she demanded in a voice that was
shrill with indignation. 'I do not recall members of
Clarendon House being invited.'

The Cockpit Club surged to their feet as one, and hands
dropped to the hilts of rapiers. Chaloner was not unduly
concerned about a fight, having seen their martial abilities
outside the palace earlier that day. Even so, he was loath
for everyone to think he had come to spy, so he flailed
around for an excuse to explain why he was there.

'I came to say that you owe Chiffinch money,' he
blustered. 'The debts incurred at the tables last night did
not die with him, and the family still expect you to pay.'

It was not a complete lie, as he was sure Will would
be delighted to be handed some free cash, while there
were laws governing the settling of posthumous financial
obligations.

'Do they?' gulped Rolt in dismay. 'That is damned
unfortunate!'

It was impossible to eavesdrop once he had been exposed,
so Chaloner decided to go home. Perhaps the Queen
would have rallied, releasing Wiseman from his bedside
vigil, and the surgeon could be persuaded to examine

Chiffinch at once. But he had taken no more than two or three steps towards the door when someone stalked through it, barring his way.

The Duchess of Newcastle was immediately identifiable by her eccentric appearance. She wore a riding coat with breeches and bucket-topped boots, and she carried a brace of pistols, although they were only wooden replicas. Black face-patches had been stuck over the smattering of pimples around her mouth, and she had adopted a feminine hairstyle with curls forming a fringe across her forehead.

She was accompanied by Eliza Topp and twenty pages, each of whom was dressed in identical white satin longcoats. There was not really enough room for them all, resulting in a noisy commotion as they tried to cram themselves inside anyway.

Mansfield scowled his outrage that his stepmother should foist herself on what he considered to be his territory, and he made a point of standing to leave in a huff. No one noticed, because all eyes were on her.

'I have long wanted to see this place,' she declared, looking around appraisingly. 'But it is disappointing. I thought it would be bigger – and not so full of smelly people.'

It was hardly a remark to win friends, and there was an offended silence. Then she gave a disdainful sniff before turning to walk out. Her retinue followed close on her heels, so when she stopped suddenly, they all ploughed unceremoniously into the back of each other.

'I almost forgot,' she announced loudly, 'is Edward Chaloner here? Or was it *William* Chaloner? Everyone I meet these days is an Edward or a William or a John. It is difficult to keep them all straight.'

69

She cackled, amused by her observation, although Rolt was the only one who laughed with her. He desisted hurriedly when he realised it was doing him no favours, and hastened to deflect any hostile attention away from himself.

'Here is *Thomas* Chaloner, Your Grace,' he said, jabbing a finger at the spy. 'Will he do?'

'He will have to,' drawled Widdrington slyly. 'Because the only other Chaloner of our acquaintance was the regicide. He is dead, thank God, but this fellow is his nephew.'

Chaloner wished the floor would open and swallow him up. It was bad enough belonging to a family of dedicated Parliamentarians, but far worse to have had an uncle who had signed the old King's death warrant. The older Thomas Chaloner had died shortly after the Restoration, but the Royalists had not forgiven his crime and never would. Chaloner glanced around quickly, looking for another exit to use, should the situation turn even more awkward.

To his surprise, Eliza Topp came to his defence, which he supposed was in return for him rescuing Molly the chicken girl earlier that day.

'You cannot visit the sins of the fathers on their children,' she said firmly. 'We are all responsible for ourselves, and it is on our own lives that we shall be judged.'

'I disagree,' countered Widdrington, his eyes cold and hard. 'I will *never* forget the role the Chaloners played in the old King's murder. They are—'

'I deplore cruelty to animals,' interrupted the Duchess, pointing to where a servant was ready with the next pair of cockerels. 'And anyone who disagrees with me is a fool.'

'I beg to differ, ma'am,' countered Widdrington shortly. 'It is a—'

'Just because they cannot speak does not mean they have no feelings,' the Duchess blared on. 'Cromwell was right to ban bloodsports.'

A murmur of shock rippled through the gathering, not just for her condemnation of something they happened to enjoy, but that she should express approval of the hated Cromwell. Widdrington opened his mouth to argue, but the words died in his throat when she fingered the handguns in her belt. He was evidently unaware that they were incapable of doing him harm.

'I have had enough fun for one night anyway,' he declared, indicating that the servant was to take the birds away. 'And finishing our revels early is a sign of respect for poor Chiffinch. We grieve deeply for him after all.'

'Do you?' asked the Duchess, with what seemed to be genuine bemusement. 'Because he considered *you* to be a worthless idler and a bad influence on the King. If it had been you who had died, he would be dancing for joy.'

Widdrington gaped at her. 'I hardly think—'

'Of course, he did not like me either,' she went on blithely. 'Although I fail to understand why. I am no vile, bird-torturing debauchee.'

'Chiffinch did not approve of anyone,' said Cobbe soothingly, evidently aiming to defuse the situation before there was trouble. 'He could not help it – it was in his nature.'

'He was a scoundrel,' stated the Duchess haughtily. 'With dreadful taste in poetry.'

At that point, Widdrington decided he had had enough of her, and led his entourage away without another word. Everyone else waited to see what the eccentric Duchess

71

would do next. She gazed around with an imperious eye, then strode towards Chaloner.

'Surgeon Wiseman mentioned you when his path crossed mine at the Queen's bedside an hour ago,' she said, peering at him as she might some exotic insect.

'How is Her Majesty?' asked Chaloner, not liking the notion that his friend talked about him, especially to the likes of the Duchess.

'Recovering, thank the good Lord, although Wiseman says he will not leave her until tomorrow afternoon at the earliest, just to be sure. However, he told me that he aims to be at the Westminster Charnel House at three o'clock to inspect Chiffinch, and that he expects you to be there. I shall accompany you.'

Chaloner blinked. The examination of a courtier's body was hardly something to be conducted in front of an audience, and he was sure Wiseman would never allow it.

'It will not be—' he began.

The Duchess cut across him. 'Wiseman believes that Chiffinch was unlawfully killed, so I *insist* on watching him work. I have never seen a murder victim dissected before. Well, I have never seen anyone dissected before, if you want the truth. However, I predict it will be very interesting from a scientific viewpoint.'

Chaloner stared at her, sure she must have misunderstood. 'How can Wiseman have reached that conclusion? He has been nowhere near the body – not if he has been at the Queen's bedside all day.'

The Duchess shrugged. 'All I can say is that he seemed very certain that he would unveil a case of foul play tomorrow. We shall both have to wait for his explanation.'

72

Chapter 3

Unfortunately for Chaloner, Wiseman remained with the Queen all night, and refused to step outside, even for a moment, to explain why he had decided that Chiffinch's death had not been a natural one. Chaloner loitered until the small hours, hoping the surgeon might spare him a few minutes, but eventually gave up and went home.

He woke at six o'clock the following morning, roused by the clatter of the market that was establishing itself in the piazza outside. He glanced out of the window to see bakers and grocers setting out their wares on make-shift stalls. The fresh bread, pies and vegetables were quickly snapped up by servants from the nearby houses, who were glad to be spared the trek to the larger markets around Smithfield and Leadenhall.

He turned his back on the bustle and looked at the place he now called home. It comprised a sparsely furnished parlour, a bedchamber, and a tiny pantry for foodstuffs, although it rarely held more than a jug of wine and some cheese. It was considerably cleaner and neater than the rest of Wiseman's domain, because Chaloner did his own housework – the surgeon's footman, whose duties included dusting and sweeping, was an indifferent domestic and Wiseman did not care enough to make a fuss about it.

Chaloner washed and shaved, then donned a blue long-coat and matching breeches that one of his sisters had made for him. It was a brighter shade than he normally favoured, and he wondered if it might help dispel the image of Swaddell-like menace he seemed to have acquired.

Wiseman's lazy servants were making the most of their employer's absence by having a lie-in, so Chaloner was obliged to make his own breakfast. He ate a piece of bread, then collected a bowl of grain and went to the henhouse. He opened the pop-hole, and stood back so the feathered residents could flow out into the early morning sunshine. He had acquired five chickens the previous winter, but had bought more because they reminded him of his happy childhood in Buckinghamshire, where his duties had included care of the family poultry. He had always liked birds, and found much that was comforting and restful in hen-keeping.

He collected the eggs, then scattered the grain. Suddenly, there was a commotion, and several birds screeched their alarm. He looked around to see what had startled them and glimpsed a flicker of movement near the gate. The gate had a faulty latch, and a ginger cat had contrived to slip through it. Chaloner began to herd the animal out, and was doing well until his largest chicken, Ada, darted forward in a flurry of angry wings and claws. Terrified, the cat shot through the gate like a cannonball.

'Was that a *fox*?'

Chaloner turned to see the question had come from Wiseman's cook, who was rubbing his eyes with his one

74

remaining hand – all the servants were missing body parts, but Chaloner could never bring himself to ask whether the surgeon was responsible.

'A cat,' he explained. 'Will you hire a smith to mend the latch? Leaving it broken is an invitation to burglars.'

'No, it was a *fox* and Ada saw it off,' breathed the cook. 'I saw it with my own eyes.'

Before Chaloner could tell him he was mistaken, the cook had raced away to tell the groom and the footman. Chaloner could have followed and attempted to put him right, but he knew from experience that he was unlikely to succeed. All Wiseman's retainers were men of unbending convictions, and once their minds were made up, nothing could change them. Instead, he sat on a bench to enjoy the contented chatter of hens while he planned his day.

His most important task was to meet Wiseman at the charnel house at three o'clock, where he would learn the truth about Chiffinch's premature demise. He hoped it would be without the Duchess looming over his shoulder. In the meantime, he decided to assume that Wiseman was right about Chiffinch being murdered, which meant he should start hunting seriously for the killer. After all, the best way to protect himself and the Earl from damaging accusations would be to produce the real culprit.

The first thing to do was speak to Timothy and Fanny Clarke, both of whom had played Chiffinch at backgammon and lost. Chaloner also needed to know why one had diagnosed an impostume, and why the other had been in the cockpit at such a peculiar hour.

Next, he would turn his attention to the others Chiffinch had defeated. He ran through a list of them in his mind. The Duke of Newcastle and Baron Lucas could be eliminated as suspects, because they had gone home with Brodrick while the victim was still alive. The Duchess had won the backgammon, so Chaloner was inclined to cross her off the list, too. That left Mansfield, her malcontent stepson, who thought Chiffinch must have cheated.

Also on the list was Will, who had gained so much from his brother's death and who had quarrelled with him. His name was followed by various members of the Cockpit Club, who also may have felt that the older courtier had been less than honest – which would certainly matter to them if large sums of money had been wagered.

But before he interviewed suspects, he had two other matters to attend. First, he should report to the Earl, and second, he wanted to visit his old friend John Thurloe in Lincoln's Inn, to see what advice he might have to give on exploring the death of an important courtier.

He stood, brushed himself down, and set off for Piccadilly.

It was another glorious day, although he heard many muttered concerns about five days without a drop of rain. A drought had preceded the devastating plague the previous year, and Londoners were naturally afraid that history was about to repeat itself. Chaloner revelled in the sunshine, though, and once he was striding along Piccadilly, he breathed in deeply, savouring the scent of clean air from the fields that lay to the north.

As he walked, he looked at the houses that were sprouting up on what had recently been farmland. The Earl was not alone in wanting to live away from the city's noxious airs, so several areas were being turned from meadows to suburban sprawl. These included Clerkenwell and Hatton Garden, as well as Piccadilly.

He reached Clarendon House to see that anti-Earl slogans had been daubed on the surrounding walls during the night, most pertaining to the unpopular sale of Dunkirk. They would be washed off later, but were always back within a few hours, no matter how many guards were hired to prevent it. Chaloner suspected the sentries sympathised with the protesters, something that would never be remedied as long as their employer treated them like dirt.

He nodded a greeting to the soldier on the gate, then walked up the gravelled drive. As a gentlemen usher, he could have used the grand front door, but instead he walked to the back. He entered via the kitchens, which were a chaos of noise and steam as the cook and his assistants prepared to feed the Earl, his family, and their army of staff and officials – more than a hundred people in all. It was a major undertaking, so Chaloner was surprised when they stopped working to exchange pleas-antries with him. All smiled and some even bowed.

Bemused by the unusually friendly reception, he moved on to the formal rooms beyond – the domain of the Earl and his more senior retainers. The first person he met was Barker the clerk, who eyed him approvingly.

'You are very handsomely dressed today, Tom. Are you meeting a lady? I am glad. It has been ten months since Hannah died, so it is time you found yourself a replacement. Besides, no one should board with Wiseman for too long, as his company must be very tiresome.'

Chaloner was astonished that the clerk should offer

77

such intimate advice to a man he barely knew, especially as Hannah's death remained painful to him, despite the passage of time, and he was far from ready for a 'replacement'.

'My other coat seemed a little drab,' he said, aiming to keep the conversation brief if Barker was going to be personal.

'More than "a little",' said Barker bluntly. 'But if you want to attract the lasses, a pretty outfit is a good place to start. I can introduce you to some suitable candidates if you want. I have several nieces you might like. All are young, intelligent and polite. Of course, none have a dowry worth speaking of, but I do not believe you to be a pecuniary man.'

'I shall not marry again,' vowed Chaloner firmly, aiming to stop Barker from doing something both of them might regret. 'Twice is enough.'

'I am on my fourth,' confided Barker, and winked. 'Rich old widows, who are the easiest way to supplement one's income. But never mind that. I have some good news for you. Have you heard the rumour that Chiffinch was dispatched on the orders of our Earl?'

Chaloner nodded. 'Why is that good news?'

'Because I have witnesses who will swear that you are not the one who carried out the order.'

'You do?' asked Chaloner warily.

'I went to the Sun tavern to break my fast this morning, and all the talk was about the murder. Then Colonel Widdrington – the fellow who heads the Cockpit Club – piped up to bray that the Earl told *you* to do it, but the landlord and his regulars remember you. They swore that you were in the Sun from six o'clock until half-past seven, thus proving your innocence.'

Chaloner frowned his mystification. 'Why would they remember me?'

'Because you unnerved them and they were glad when you left.' Barker looked apologetic. 'It is your own fault, Tom. You insist on wearing anonymous clothes and you scowl a lot. Moreover, it is obvious from the way you move that you are an old soldier. You cannot help it, I suppose. It is what the wars made of us.'

Chaloner was grateful for the Sun's patrons' testimony, but was not sure it helped. The truth was that he had entered the tavern a few minutes *after* six o'clock, so would have had ample time to follow Chiffinch to the cockpit and kill him before going to eat his breakfast.

'You are safe from accusations,' finished Barker when Chaloner made no reply. 'But the rest of us are not, and nor is our Earl, so please find the culprit as quick as you can. Until then, you are the only member of Clarendon House who cannot be blamed.'

'So that was why the kitchen staff went out of their way to greet me this morning,' mused Chaloner. 'It was not friendliness or civility, but brazen self-interest.'

'So?' shrugged Barker. 'What is wrong with that?'

Clarendon House had been designed for show, and was not a pleasant place to live. It was full of marble, and its large function rooms were impractical for a middle-aged couple with children who had mainly flown the nest. The most obvious example of this was the chamber known as My Lord's Lobby, a vast, chilly mausoleum that the Earl used as an office. Even on warm days, it was cold, despite the fire burning in the hearth.

The Earl was huddled close to the blaze, his gouty

79

foot on a stool in front of him. There were black smudges under his eyes – he had slept badly.

'Have you heard?' he whispered as Chaloner walked in. 'There are tales that I ordered Chiffinch's murder, and aim to disguise the fact by setting you to investigate.'

Chaloner felt like saying 'I told you so', but prudently held his tongue.

'The only way to prove them wrong is by exposing the real culprit,' the Earl went on shakily. 'Today, before the gossip does me serious harm. Who are your suspects?'

'None I am ready to list, sir,' said Chaloner, afraid that if he did, the Earl would bandy the names about in an effort to silence the whispers about himself, which would likely land him in more trouble than ever. 'Although I have several leads to follow.'

'Then do it quickly,' urged the Earl, ashen-faced. 'Barker tells me that *you* have an alibi, but what about the rest of us? When you became unavailable as a scapegoat, people started to murmur that my cousin was responsible.'

'*Brodrick?*' Chaloner started to laugh, amazed that anyone should think the Earl's lazy, dissipated kinsman capable of anything as energetic as murder.

'Yes, Brodrick,' said the Earl, fixing him with a baleful eye. 'He is the only member of my staff – other than you – who was not rescuing books from my flooded library. My enemies were quick to pounce on the fact. Of course, I imagine they will accuse us all in time, regardless of whether we can prove our whereabouts when the crime occurred.'

'Probably,' agreed Chaloner.

The Earl winced at his bluntness. 'I received an urgent dispatch from Spymaster Williamson in Dover earlier. *He*

80

wants the matter resolved before there is trouble, too, and suggests pooling our resources. He has detailed his man Swaddell to investigate, and recommends a joint inquiry to expedite matters.'

'You want me to work with Swaddell?' asked Chaloner uneasily, aware that such an alliance would convince even more people that he and the assassin were of an ilk. His reputation might never recover!

'I do. Of course, if you had done your job and resolved the matter yesterday, we would not be in this terrible position today.'

Chaloner itched to suggest that *he* should try solving a murder in a couple of hours if he thought it was so easy, but opted to maintain a dignified silence instead. It stretched out until the Earl spoke again.

'My plan misfired,' he said bitterly. 'When I ordered you to investigate, it was to cast shadows over *Chiffinch's* reputation, not my own. You should have warned me.'

'That is why you asked me to look into his death?' asked Chaloner, startled. 'You told me it was because you wanted your enemies to think you care about their welfare.'

The Earl released a derisive snort. 'What I care about is seeing them all banished to some rural backwater where they can do me no more harm – a place where they can reflect on their evil deeds before they are judged by God.'

'I see,' said Chaloner, who had scant faith in divine justice. In his experience, unless he organised it himself, it tended not to happen, allowing the undeserving to prosper and leaving their hapless victims to make the best of it.

'So you must work fast,' the Earl went on. 'It is in

your own interests to do as I say, because no one else will hire a man with your dubious past, and if I fall from grace, you will tumble with me.'

Chaloner did not need to be reminded. 'I will do my best.'

'I want more than that, Chaloner. This time, I think we might need a miracle.'

Chaloner was in a sullen frame of mind as he left My Lord's Lobby. He resented having Swaddell foisted on him, not just because he preferred working alone, but because he did not want to be associated with the Spymaster's favourite assassin. Then he brightened. The Earl had not specified *when* he and Swaddell should start collaborating, so he decided to begin without him. Perhaps he would solve the case before their paths crossed, and they would both be spared the experience.

He met Brodrick by the front door. The Earl's cousin was pale and there were shadows under his eyes, which Chaloner attributed to being up at a time when he would normally be in bed. Maliciously, he wondered how Brodrick would fare if people really did think that he had dispatched Chiffinch. It would certainly put a dent in his social life, as no one would invite a suspected killer to their homes, and the Earl was not noted for scintillating entertainment.

'I know you will do your best for me, Chaloner,' Brodrick said miserably. 'But please hurry. I do not want to be beheaded or whatever it is they do to murderers these days.'

'They are usually hanged,' supplied Chaloner, a piece of information that made Brodrick blanch. 'But you can help yourself by staying out of the public eye. Either remain here quietly, or better yet, leave the city altogether. Out of sight, out of mind.'

'I considered that, but Barker told me that if I disappear, folk will assume that I have fled the scene of my crime. He advises me to be my normal self and pretend that nothing is wrong. But I do not know if I can do it, Chaloner. I am not very good at dissembling.'

And the likes of Widdrington would make mincemeat of such an easy target, thought Chaloner, sorry for him. 'Then perhaps you should pretend to have the plague. That will keep visitors away and the forty-day quarantine will allow everyone to forget about you.'

'It is tempting, believe me. Court is not what it was, and I dislike the "entertainments" offered by the Cockpit Club. Barker told me that after they left White Hall last night, they went to the Bear Garden in Southwark and spent the rest of the night watching dogs getting killed. I do not mind the occasional dab of blood, but that is sickening.'

Chaloner fully agreed.

As Chaloner left Clarendon House, he saw the unmistakable figure of Swaddell hurrying along Piccadilly towards him. Hoping his new blue suit would render him unrecognisable, Chaloner turned in the opposite direction, then cut across the building site that was St James's Fields. He glanced behind and heaved a sigh of relief when Swaddell continued towards Clarendon House. He had escaped – for now, at least.

He trotted on until he reached St James's Park, and rather than waste time convincing the guard that he did indeed have right of access – it was a royal park, so the general public were not allowed inside – he scaled the back wall and walked through a small copse until he met the footpath that ran east.

Although trees and shrubs were bursting into life, the aviaries were empty and no water-fowl graced the banks of the man-made lake known as the Canal. Those birds rash enough to overwinter there had long since been snared and eaten by people struggling to stave off starvation – there had been a dearth of food because farmers had refused to trade with plague-ravaged London. A solitary mallard preened on an empty patch of mud, but it flew off when Chaloner approached. He wondered how long it would be before the wildlife recovered.

As one of the park gates exited near the cockpit, Chaloner decided to stop there and look at the place where Chiffinch had died while the building was empty. He did not expect to find or learn anything useful, but it was something he felt he should do.

He arrived to discover that the Cockpit Club had not been content with the carnage at the Bear Garden, and had returned to resume the cockfighting that the Duchess had interrupted. The games had finished at dawn, but a hardy few had lingered to finish off the remains of the wine. These included the outrageous Cobbe and Will Chiffinch, who were just lurching out through the door. Will was drunk, and Cobbe was struggling to hold him upright.

'You missed a good night, Chaloner,' slurred Will, a greeting that suggested he was too inebriated to remember the accusations levelled the day before.

'So did your brother,' retorted Chaloner pointedly.

'Thomas did not like cockfighting,' said Will, the barb missing its mark completely. 'He preferred backgammon. He was a bit stupid in that respect.'

'*Is* it stupid to prefer an intellectual challenge over watching two birds claw each other to death?' asked Chaloner coolly.

'Yes, I think so,' replied Will, after a moment of serious consideration. 'But perhaps you prefer bull-baiting?' He smirked. 'Or are dancing fleas and slug-racing more to your taste?'

'Wit-spotting,' retorted Chaloner, and when Will frowned his incomprehension, he elaborated. 'You put two courtiers in a room and bet on the first one to say something intelligent. Sadly, the match usually ends in a draw, with neither participant able to oblige.'

Will was far too drunk to appreciate what Chaloner was saying, which was probably just as well. He frowned his bemusement for a moment, then spoke in a pensive voice.

'Yet the bear-baiting bothered me. Black Ursus was supposed to be invib . . . invis . . . *invincible*, but one little dog saw him in his grave. Nothing can be taken for granted these days. Small hounds kill great big bears, while my whores claim they have purer souls than their customers. Our world is turning upside down yet again.'

Just then, Bess Widdrington emerged from the cockpit. Captain Rolt was behind her, struggling to support a crony named James Tooley, a hulking young man whose elegant clothes could not disguise the fact that he looked like an ape: he had a backward-sloping forehead, thick lips and peculiarly elongated arms There was no sign of Bess's husband, and her face fell when she realised that he had selfishly taken their carriage, leaving her stranded. Then her eye lit on Will, who was also wealthy enough to keep his own coach and four.

'Of course you may borrow Will's conveyance,' gushed Rolt, anticipating her need, and hastening to spare her the ignominy of admitting that she had been abandoned by the man she loved. 'Now he has taken up residence in his brother's old quarters, it will take but a moment to drop him off. Then his driver will take you anywhere you would like to go.'

'I am not sure I want to ride with him while he is in that state,' said Bess, eyeing Will in distaste. 'He might be sick over me.'

'I will not allow that to happen,' said Rolt gallantly. 'You can trust me.'

'Well, hold him upright, then,' ordered Bess, after considering her options and deciding they were painfully limited. 'Then Cobbe can run and tell Will's driver that we are waiting.'

Chaloner watched in amusement as Cobbe shoved the listing Will at Rolt, who then had two drunken friends to support. While the captain struggled under their combined weight, Cobbe sauntered away, clearly having no intention of 'running' anywhere. To pass the time Bess regaled Rolt with gossip, pointedly ignoring Chaloner as a person of no consequence.

'Did you hear about the devil visiting the Red Bull tavern in Clerkenwell the other night?' she asked. 'Apparently, he just strolled in and ordered a drink.'

'Did he pay for it?' asked Rolt, snatching at Will as he reeled sideways. He shot Chaloner a pleading glance for help, which the spy ignored.

'I cannot tell you that,' replied Bess, 'but Satan appearing so brazenly is a warning for the evil that will befall the city on Good Friday.'

'The Red Bull,' mused Rolt thoughtfully. 'A place you

86

know well, of course. I followed you and Fanny Clarke there a few days ago, all the way from White Hall.'

'You did what?' demanded Bess indignantly.

'You were in disguise, so my interest was piqued,' explained Rolt, fighting to prevent Tooley from sliding out of his grasp. 'However, while it started out as fun on my part, I was worried when you entered Clerkenwell. Some of that area is not very safe for respectable ladies, so I watched you very closely, lest you needed my assistance.'

'You are mistaken,' said Bess coldly. 'First, I have never donned a disguise in my life. Second, if I did embark on some wild venture, I would certainly not do it with Fanny Clarke, who is too staid for japes. And third, I would *never* visit the Red Bull – it is a brothel.'

'We are going to a brothel?' slurred Will. 'Excellent! Lead on.'

He lurched away from Rolt, lost his balance and collapsed in a heap. He giggled foolishly for a moment, then closed his eyes and began to snore.

'I suppose it must have been someone else I saw then,' said Rolt, propping Tooley against a wall, and wiping his sweaty brow on his sleeve. 'Because you are right about Fanny being too staid for japes. She is the dullest woman I have ever met.'

Bess's eyebrows shot up. 'But you think *I* visit brothels?'

Rolt was appalled that he had offended a lady who might do him future favours, even if it had been inadvertently. 'You mistake me, ma'am,' he gushed. 'The Red Bull must have stopped being a brothel and become respectable. Indeed, I imagine it is now . . .'

His flustered apology was interrupted by Cobbe, who arrived with Will's carriage.

'Did I just hear you call the Red Bull a brothel?' he asked, jumping down next to them. 'Because it is actually a common kind of theatre. The Duke of Newcastle's latest play – *The Humorous Lovers* – was performed there recently.'

'Was it?' asked Bess in distaste. 'I saw it in the rather more salubrious surroundings of Drury Lane.' Her ugly features twisted into a malicious smirk. 'As did the Duchess of Newcastle, who was virtually topless. It was embarrassing in a woman of her age.'

'And Fanny Clarke flounced out in protest,' recalled Cobbe, laughing. 'You should not associate with her, Bess. She is a bore, always telling us what we should and should not do.'

'She is all right,' shrugged Bess. 'And she is only thinking of the King. She worries about anything that might damage his reputation as an upright, virtuous man.'

Chaloner struggled not to smirk – or to point out that the King had never been considered upright and virtuous, even by his most blinkered admirers.

'Well, the only good things *I* can say about Fanny is that first, she is an excellent judge of lemons, and second . . .' Cobbe trailed off, leaving everyone to surmise that the lemons were it.

'Lemons?' slurred Tooley, coming to and joining the conversation. 'They are nice squeezed over shellfish, but they are difficult to come by at this time of year. I am an expert on them, though, because I am a Yeoman of the Larder. Indeed, it is . . .'

He faltered, too drunk to pin down the thought that had sprung into his mind. After a moment, he closed his eyes and began to slide down the wall, forcing Rolt to catch him before he landed on Will. Bess flounced towards the carriage, climbed in and banged on the ceiling to tell the driver to go. Rolt gaped as it rattled away.

'I did not mean her to make off with it on her own! How are we going to get this pair home now? Tooley is heavy.'

'Poor old Bess,' said Cobbe softly. 'She aims to win her husband's love by being as decadent as he is, yet she also craves the respect of prissy old birds like Fanny Clarke. She thinks she can have both, but will end up with neither.'

'Is this why I came to London?' muttered Rolt, as he heaved the semi-conscious Tooley upright. 'To haul drunks around?'

Cobbe made no effort to help. 'Perhaps this is how you lost your button, Rolt – it was ripped off while you lugged insensible friends to their beds.'

Rolt scowled. 'That damned button! I wish I had never mentioned the thing. Is either of you going to help me, by the way, or am I to struggle with this great oaf alone?'

'He is all yours,' said Cobbe cheerfully. 'I have Will to see home. Or would you rather he learned that not only did you give away his private carriage, but you left him to sleep off his excesses in the dirt?'

Fuming, Rolt staggered away with his burden. Since they were alone – the somnolent Will did not count – Chaloner took the opportunity to ask Cobbe some questions.

'Were you in White Hall the night Chiffinch died?' he began.

Cobbe shook his head. 'I was in Chelsea all last week, and only returned yesterday morning. I can provide witnesses, should you doubt my word as a gentleman.'

Chaloner tended to doubt anyone who expected him

to believe that gentlemen never lied, but he had better suspects to pursue than Cobbe, so he decided not to ask for the witnesses' names just yet.

'Have you heard any rumours that might explain what happened to Chiffinch? Other than the ones that claim my Earl killed him, which we both know is a nonsense.'

'It is a nonsense,' agreed Cobbe, much to Chaloner's surprise. 'Clarendon would never murder his enemies, although I imagine he is sorely tempted on occasion. However, the only rumours I heard have nothing to do with Chiffinch, but are about the Duchess of Newcastle. Have you met her simpering steward Topp? I cannot abide that man. He is so greasily servile that it is difficult to take him seriously. Do you think he and the Duchess are lovers?'

'What?' blurted Chaloner, startled.

Cobbe winked as he podded Will awake with his foot. 'Well, who can blame him? She is a remarkable lady, and if you do not believe it, ask her.'

It did not take many minutes in the cockpit for Chaloner to see he was wasting his time. Too many feet had trampled in and out since Chiffinch had died. He did learn that it would be a good place to kill, though. It was tucked away in a remote corner of the palace, so any cries for help from the victim were unlikely to be heard by anyone else if the cockpit was empty.

Aware that more time had passed than he had intended, Chaloner took a hackney carriage to Lincoln's Inn, flagging one down just outside the Holbein Gate. There followed a hair-raising journey as the driver demonstrated his intimate knowledge of shortcuts, some of which were barely wide enough for his coach and that

Chaloner would never have attempted at such high speeds. While he drove, the man regaled his fare with gossip.

'I am going to Ratcliff on Thursday,' he bellowed, struggling to make himself heard over the furious clatter of his wheels. 'To avoid the terrible calamity that will hit London the following day. After all, how can disaster *not* strike the city, when Good Friday falls on the thirteenth day of the month in the year with three sixes in it?'

'How indeed?' gulped Chaloner, as the man twisted around for an answer. He breathed his relief when the fellow turned his attention back to the road.

'Mother Broughton has ideas about what form the crisis will take,' the driver went on. 'Have you heard of her? She is the famous seer who lives in Clerkenwell. All her prophecies come to pass. Every one of them.'

'What does she think will happen?' asked Chaloner, then held on tight as they took a corner so fast that the right-hand wheels lifted off the ground.

'That Good Friday will see a lot of weeping and gnashing of teeth, and that a great darkness will cover the city. It will not lift until Easter Day.'

'Goodness,' murmured Chaloner. 'And this seer hails from Clerkenwell?'

'Near Newcastle House, home of that peculiar Duchess. Mother Broughton can often be found in its local taverns of an evening.'

'Drinking?' asked Chaloner pointedly, but they had just reached the Temple Bar, where the Strand met Fleet Street and all traffic was obliged to pass through a very narrow entrance. There was a queue, forcing the driver to haul on his reins to prevent his horse from ploughing into the back of the vehicle in front.

The near-collision precipitated a lot of bad-tempered swearing, during which Chaloner's driver somehow contrived to hurtle through the gate ahead of everyone in front of him, and there was another stomach-wrenching lurch as he took a sharp left into Chancery Lane. Chaloner clambered out unsteadily and paid. Then the driver was off again, belting along as if the devil was on his tail, scattering everything and anyone who went before him. Chaloner pitied his hapless horse.

Lincoln's Inn was one of the four legal foundations that licensed lawyers, and owned not only several ranges of buildings along Chancery Lane, but also the large open space to its west called Lincoln's Inn Fields, an area worth a fortune, given the current demand for more houses. The Inn itself was encircled by walls that granted its residents privacy and security, and encompassed a chapel, a splendid hall, living quarters for its 'benchers', and extensive gardens.

The youthful porter recognised Chaloner from previous visits. He waved him inside, and exhorted him to enjoy the next six days, as they might be his last. London's wicked, he informed Chaloner soberly, would not make it to Easter. Then he promised to pray for Chaloner's soul, the implication being that he considered himself one of the godly few who would survive, whereas the spy stood no chance whatsoever. Normally, Chaloner would have laughed, but he was still smarting from the news that he was sinister.

The man he was going to see lived in Dial Court, although Chaloner knew his friend would be walking in the grounds at that hour of the day. He hurried there at once, barely noticing the bright green of new growth

92

in the trees, or that the Inn's gardeners would soon have to do something about the weeds sprouting up in the rose beds.

John Thurloe had been powerful during the Commonwealth. He had been Cromwell's Spymaster General and sole Secretary of State, and it was often said that the Lord Protector could not have clung to power for as long as he had, if it had not been for his brilliant first minister. Chaloner did not know if it was true, but there was no question that Thurloe was one of a kind. He was slightly built, and resisted the current fashion for wigs, although there was more lace at his throat and cuffs than he had worn when the Puritans were in power. The most remarkable thing about him were his large blue eyes, which gave the appearance of soulful innocence, although he had a core of steel that had seen more than one would-be traitor sent to the gallows.

'Tom!' he cried in delight. 'I heard you had returned from Scotland, although I am horrified that you took so little time before immersing yourself in trouble.'

Despite the fact that he no longer had dozens of intelligencers reporting to him every day, a number of old agents still kept Thurloe up to date with events, and he was far better informed than the current Spymaster. Thus Chaloner was not surprised that he already knew about the investigation into Chiffinch's death. He gave him a brief account of what he had learned about it, including Wiseman's contention that he was murdered.

'Chiffinch was a man of rigid opinions,' mused Thurloe. 'And devoted to the King. He deplored anything that he felt damaged His Majesty or the reputation of his Court.'

'Such as the Cockpit Club,' surmised Chaloner.

Thurloe nodded. 'He hated the way its antics made White Hall the subject of gossip and disgust. Its members objected to his censure, so if he *was* murdered, you should certainly look among them for the culprit, and that includes his silly brother. However, his disapproval was not restricted to debauchees. He was very outspoken about the Duchess of Newcastle as well.'

'He certainly complained to me about the costume she wore to the theatre.'

'He also deplored her radical ideas, which he felt threatened the established order of things – the books written under her own name, her belief that women are as clever as men, her controversial views on religion. He hated your Earl, too, for selling Dunkirk and for being so prudish that people mock him.'

'And he was the perfect courtier, I suppose,' said Chaloner acidly. 'Neither too prim nor too licentious, and all his opinions were a credit to his King.'

'Naturally,' said Thurloe. 'It is very possible that he plotted to remove anyone he considered to be a danger or a nuisance, so any list of suspects must include Newcastle House and your Earl's household, not just the Cockpit Club.'

'There are rumours that the Earl ordered his death, and until Barker proved otherwise, there were whispers that I obliged him.' Chaloner hesitated for a moment, then blurted, 'Do you consider me sinister?'

'Of course! Why do you think I recruited you to work for me?'

Chaloner was not very pleased to hear this. 'So I am of an ilk with Swaddell?'

'To a degree. But do not look so dismayed. It is part

94

of what has kept you alive all these years – and part of what stands between your Earl and the scaffold. He would be dead by now if his enemies were not afraid of what you might do if they contrive to see him beheaded.'

Although Chaloner usually respected Thurloe's opinion, he was sure the ex-Spymaster was wrong about this. 'They barely know I exist.'

'Oh, they know,' averred Thurloe. 'But your friends appreciate your good heart, and there is nothing wrong with being considered strong and resourceful by your enemies. Besides, why does it matter what folk at White Hall think? Most are beneath our contempt.'

Chaloner regarded him in surprise. Thurloe rarely voiced an opinion about the current regime, given that to do so might see him arrested for treason. Chaloner was touched by his friend's trust, but also alarmed, revealing as it did that the Court's antics were trying even Thurloe's dogged patience.

'I can tell you that no one at Clarendon House killed Chiffinch,' Chaloner said, tactfully changing the subject. 'First, they were too busy with a flood in the Earl's library to sneak off and murder anyone; and second, none of them are capable of doing it without being caught.'

'Your word is good enough for me, but I doubt the Earl's enemies will accept it.'

'No,' sighed Chaloner. 'I have to speak to Timothy and Fanny Clarke when I leave here: he claims Chiffinch died of natural causes and she found the body. Do you happen to know where they live?'

'They have taken up residence in the mansion your grandfather built, and that your Uncle James inherited: Chaloner Court in Clerkenwell.'

Chaloner winced. He was unfortunate in having not one but two kinsmen associated with the regime that had executed the old King. Uncle Thomas was the one everyone remembered, because he had signed the death warrant and was a flamboyant supporter of Cromwell. But there was also Uncle James, who had spent much of the Commonwealth governing the Isle of Man. Both had been condemned as traitors at the Restoration, and all their goods – including Chaloner Court – were confiscated. Chaloner had barely known James, recalling him only as a quiet man with a passionate devotion to 'godly religion'. Both were now dead, but their ghosts kept returning to haunt him.

'Is it still standing?' he asked. 'I thought it would have been demolished by now.'

'Clarke bought it for a very reasonable price,' replied Thurloe, 'but he lives in fear that His Majesty will pardon the regicides and return all property to their heirs.'

'There is no danger of that,' said Chaloner ruefully. 'The King will never forgive them.'

'No,' agreed Thurloe. 'He will not, but Clarke is uneasy even so, especially as James's widow lives in very reduced circumstances on the Isle of Man. James's son – a vicar – has a small income from a country parish, but his daughters are wholly unprovided for.'

'How do you know?' asked Chaloner. He had not been aware of their predicament, although he was not surprised by it: his own branch of the family was struggling under a massive burden of penalties, and they had had nothing to do with the old King's death.

'Because James's son wrote to me recently, and asked if anything could be done to get some of his father's holdings back. I advised him to be grateful for what he

96

had, and not to draw attention to himself with requests that will never be granted.'

'Goodness!' muttered Chaloner in alarm. 'Will he listen to you?'

'I believe so. But we digress. The point is that you will have to go to Chaloner Court if you want to speak to Clarke and his wife. While you are there, will you take a moment to look around Clerkenwell and assess it for me?'

'Why? Because it is where the Duchess of Newcastle lives with her revolutionary ideas? Because a Satan-shaped cloud was spotted there last week? Because it has a tavern called the Red Bull, where its landlord served Lucifer a drink? Or because a seer named Mother Broughton resides there?'

'All these reasons,' replied Thurloe. 'Something unsavoury is brewing in the area – something that should be stopped before it does any harm.'

But Chaloner felt that if Thurloe could voice dissatisfaction with White Hall, then so could he. 'And what if the "something unsavoury" only harms the current regime? God knows, I do not want another civil war, but our country is being dealt a poor hand by these Royalists. They make no pretence at justice and decency, and all the promises they made when they returned to power have been broken.'

Thurloe regarded him lugubriously. 'Perhaps so, but please dispel any hopes of another glorious revolution, Thomas. We have no Cromwell to lead us, so it would fail, and we have seen enough turmoil for a while. See what you can learn in Clerkenwell, and report back to me.'

Chaloner said that he would.

Chapter 4

It was not far from Chancery Lane to Clerkenwell – just up to Holborn, through Hatton Garden, and across the bridge that spanned the reeking Fleet River.

Chaloner enjoyed the walk, although reminders of the plague were everywhere. He saw a number of houses with fading red crosses on the doors, marking where the sickness had been identified within. Some had been reoccupied and the owners had not yet scoured the marks off, but others remained empty and boarded over. A few had notices nailed to them, saying they were subject to legal proceedings as rival heirs competed over the spoils from the dead.

Much of Clerkenwell was a very desirable place to live. It was close enough to the city to be convenient, but still retained a spacious, slightly rural air. It boasted a number of impressive mansions, not least of which was the Charterhouse, once a religious foundation, now a school set in extensive gardens. Further to the east were the wide open spaces of the Artillery Ground and Bunhill Fields, the latter of which had recently been set aside for use as a cemetery.

The centre of Clerkenwell was its green, an expanse of grass bordered by handsome houses on all four sides, although the ones at the western end trailed off into hovels and slums. As in Covent Garden, the prospect of easy sales to wealthy residents had encouraged a small market to develop. His eye was caught by a handcart piled high with shellfish. Or rather, by the woman who was selling them, as it was Sarah, the woman with the flaming red hair who had led the protest outside White Hall the previous day. He was amused to note that she even managed to make that innocuous activity appear radical, and the manner in which she yelled her prices was more challenging than informational.

Dominating the north side of the green was Newcastle House. This was a perfectly symmetrical H-plan building, with quarters for the Duke on one side and the Duchess on the other. In between were the grand reception rooms where the couple entertained guests.

Diagonally opposite Newcastle House was a mansion that was simultaneously familiar and different. Chaloner Court was a blocky house with a forest of Tudor chimneys. In his youth it had been soot-stained and forbidding, but its current owners had lavished so much money on it that it was now bright, clean and boasted gaily painted window shutters. Chaloner had expected to experience a flood of memories when he saw it, but all he could think was that the slate slabs used to retile the roof looked a little too heavy for the house's foundations.

'I thought I might catch you here,' came a low voice from behind him. Chaloner spun around in alarm to see Swaddell standing at his shoulder. 'Although I expected you sooner. I have been waiting for over an hour.'

'Have you?' Chaloner cursed himself for not anticipating that the assassin might try to hunt him down. Worse,
he had been so preoccupied with looking at Chaloner
Court that he had failed to pay attention to his surroundings, which was an unforgivable lapse in his line of work.

'We are to explore the Chiffinch affair together,'
explained Swaddell, brushing invisible dust from his spotless black long-coat. 'Did the Earl not mention it? He
promised he would.'

'I did not know where to find you,' lied Chaloner.
'How did you know I would be here?'

'By reasoning that you would want to speak to the
person who discovered Chiffinch's body. Discreet enquiries revealed that you did not do it yesterday.'

Swaddell smiled, revealing his sharp little teeth and
red tongue. Chaloner was irked that the assassin had
read him so easily. How was he going to convince
everyone that they were different if Swaddell knew him
well enough to predict his movements?

'We have had reports of something dangerous brewing
in this area,' Swaddell went on, looking around him.
'Although none of our spies have been specific. They just
say that there are worrisome rumblings.'

'Probably because of a local seer who has predicted a
dreadful calamity for Good Friday,' said Chaloner. 'Her
name is Mother Broughton. Perhaps you should set
someone to watch her, as it would not be the first time
that a prophet cheats to make sure a "foretelling" comes
true.'

'Unfortunately, all our spies are busy. Dutch-loving
traitors supply the enemy with information about our
ships and defences, and Williamson says rousting them
out must take precedence.'

'Can he not hire more men?' asked Chaloner, exasperated. 'There is no point preserving our shores from foreign invaders if there is rebellion at home.'

'Money,' explained Swaddell tersely. 'We do not have any, and our politicians refuse to allocate more. And they should, because it is not only Mother Broughton who warns of imminent disaster. It was predicted in the tailed star that blazed across the sky last winter, along with the plague, eclipses of the Moon, the position of Saturn in relation to the Sun . . .'

'Superstition and coincidence,' interrupted Chaloner dismissively.

'And the date,' finished Swaddell. 'How can there *not* be trouble when Good Friday falls on the thirteenth day of the month, in a year containing three sixes? Of course there will be a calamity of monumental proportion.'

His words sent a shiver down Chaloner's spine, despite the warmth of the day. To take his mind off it, he looked at the shellfish-seller, admiring her slender figure and the defiant angle of her head. She wore a shawl over her hair, although one red tendril escaped to curl at the side of her face. Her apron was white and her clothes spotless, even though hers was not the cleanest of trades. She stood with her hands on her hips, scowling at passers-by so that he wondered how she expected to win any customers.

'She is splendid, is she not?' Swaddell's low voice cut into his ruminations. 'Sarah Shawe is a person of interest to the intelligence services, because she has opinions.'

'Opinions about what?' asked Chaloner, irked that Swaddell had caught him ogling.

'Women,' replied Swaddell darkly, 'and what she considers to be their rights. For example, she thinks they should be able to divorce men who prove to be unsatisfactory. Can you imagine anything more disturbing? Half the men in the country would find themselves solo if women were allowed to decide what is best for themselves.'

'Would that be such a bad thing?' asked Chaloner provocatively.

'Not for them, but it would be a disaster for us. Well, not for me, as I would never give a lady cause to get rid of me. Should I ever win myself a female companion, I would do all I could to ensure she thought she was the luckiest woman alive.'

'Good luck with that,' said Chaloner, sure Swaddell would never be in a position to put his plan into force, as no woman would be stupid enough to let him get anywhere near her. 'But I do not see why Sarah's opinions should unsettle the intelligence services.'

'She also believes that women are as intelligent as men, that they should be paid the same as their male counterparts, and that the country would be better governed by a Privy Council of ladies. She considers men too violent and rash, and says that if females were in charge, we would have fewer wars, less corruption, and a kinder, more ethical society.'

'She might be right,' said Chaloner. 'And an all-female Privy Council cannot possibly be worse than the one we have already.'

'Do not let anyone else hear you say that, Tom,' advised Swaddell, glancing around uneasily. 'It is radical stuff. But your subversive thoughts are safe with me, because we are blood brothers, tied by an unbreakable bond of loyalty.'

'Right,' said Chaloner uncomfortably, and changed

the subject. 'I am told that Chiffinch disliked the Cockpit Club, the Duchess of Newcastle and my Earl, and that he may have gone beyond angry words to actual plots against them. Have you heard anything about this?'

Swaddell shook his head. 'He *was* vocal in his disdain for people he disliked. I heard him grumbling myself. However, I doubt he did anything more than rail against them.'

'We should bear it in mind anyway,' said Chaloner. 'Perhaps you should return to White Hall and make enquiries there, while I speak to the Clarkes.'

'No, we should stick together,' countered Swaddell. 'However, first, we must pool all the information we have, which will allow us to work more efficiently. Come to Myddleton's Coffee House with me. We shall do it there.'

Coffee houses were where men – never women – went to discuss religion, politics and other contentious subjects over a dish of the beverage that had been unknown a few years before, but that was now very popular. The government considered them sources of sedition, and longed to close them down, although that would likely ignite the very trouble it aimed to avoid. In theory, anyone was welcome to speak his mind in a coffee house, be he an earl or a scullion. In practice, some establishments catered to the wealthy elite, while others were for ordinary folk.

Myddleton's was one of the latter. It was a shabby building near where the elegant homes around Clerkenwell Green gave way to the hovels that lined the Fleet River. It had benches that had been polished to a bright sheen by the rumps of pontificating customers, and tables that were ring-stained from spillages.

Coffee-house etiquette was that arriving patrons sat next to whoever was already there, but Swaddell chose an empty table in the window. His dark, menacing presence was such that no one objected to him breaking the rules. Myddleton scurried forward with a long-spouted jug, filled two dishes with an aromatic brown sludge, and retreated to his regulars, where they conferred in low voices about the two disquieting strangers in their domain.

Swaddell sipped his coffee, gave a nod of appreciation, and began to talk about Chiffinch. He knew little that Chaloner had not already learned, other than the fact that the courtier had been outspokenly critical of a number of people at Court, not just the Cockpit Club, the Duchess and the Earl. All had earned his enmity for doing or saying something that he felt reflected badly on the King.

Reluctantly, as it went against his nature to share information, Chaloner outlined what he had found out. Then he recited his preliminary list of suspects and confided his hope that Wiseman would provide a definitive explanation that afternoon in the charnel house for the courtier's sudden death.

'So the Duchess wants to see Chiffinch anatomised,' mused Swaddell, when Chaloner had finished. 'And she is on your roll of people who may have done him harm.'

'I did not include her at first, on the grounds that she defeated Chiffinch at backgammon, so had no cause to resent him. However, now we know that he openly condemned her eccentricities, she is certainly a suspect. However, even if she is innocent, I will not allow her to watch him dissected, even if it is only for scientific curiosity. It would not be right.'

Swaddell chuckled. 'If you do succeed in keeping her out, you will be inundated with demands from people wanting to know how you did it. She is not a woman easily dissuaded from a particular course of action once she has set her mind to it.'

Before either could add more, there was a commotion outside as a flock of people marched on to the green. At their head was a large person who carried herself with great authority. She wore a sugarloaf hat of the kind that had once been popular with Puritans, but a velvet doublet and skirt of a style that was currently favoured by Royalists. There was a plain white apron around her waist, and her hands were big, red and competent.

'I suspect this horde has just come from the Red Bull,' muttered Swaddell, watching through narrowed eyes. 'Once a theatre, then a brothel, now a place where malcontents gather.'

When the procession reached the centre of the green, the woman waited while two men hurried forward with a wooden box. They set it down and helped her to stand on it. When she was up, she folded her arms and looked around imperiously. Immediately, her followers fell silent.

'I have had another vision,' she declared in such a loud voice that she was perfectly audible from inside the coffee house, especially as the other customers had stopped muttering about Chaloner and Swaddell, and had opened the door to listen to her.

'Mother Broughton, I presume,' murmured Chaloner.

'It must be,' Swaddell whispered back, 'and we should take heed of what she is about to announce, because you are right to say that some seers are not above making sure their predictions come true – and I do not like the

105

sound of the wailing, gnashing of teeth and darkness that she claims will afflict London on Good Friday.'

'The dead will walk on Tuesday,' declared Mother Broughton in sepulchral tones, which caused a frisson of fear to ripple through her listeners, the ranks of which were rapidly swelling with folk who lived around the green. Among them were Eliza Topp and Molly the chicken girl from Newcastle House. Sarah Shawe had abandoned her wares and also stood nearby.

'What dead?' called someone uneasily. 'Not plague victims?'

'If they lived godly lives, those will rest in peace,' replied Mother Broughton grandly. 'But if they were evil, they will rise to move amongst us, clad in long black cloaks to hide their mouldering bones. In their hands, they will hold red lights – not lamps to illuminate their way, but the vessels that contain their tainted souls.'

'Crikey!' breathed Myddleton, turning to regard his customers with frightened eyes. 'I do not like the sound of that!'

'The first sighting will be in Bunhill,' Mother Broughton boomed on, 'where too many Quakers and Baptists are being buried. The second will be in Westminster Abbey.'

'I have an uncle interred in Westminster Abbey,' Swaddell told Chaloner conversationally. 'It will be interesting to meet him again.'

Chaloner regarded him askance, but then his attention was caught by a remark from Eliza Topp, who was speaking anxiously from the back of the crowd.

'But if only the *wicked* dead will have their eternal rest disturbed, we shall we inundated with nasty people: wife-beaters, religious fanatics, bullies, thieves, killers, courtiers—'

106

'Courtiers!' spat Sarah in disgust. 'Scoundrels to a man! God forbid that they should make an honest living. Or engage in something that might tax their intellects, like devising ways to end this stupid Dutch war or to help the downtrodden poor.'

'You cannot tax something you do not have,' put in Eliza, an assessment that drew a snigger of appreciation from the crowd.

'The government taxes *us* on what we do not have all the time,' countered Sarah. 'They take our hard-earned wages to support a palace that is full of expensive, worthless toadies.'

'Goodness!' muttered Chaloner, wondering if she would be so frank if she knew the Spymaster's favourite assassin was listening. 'She is bold.'

'She is,' agreed Swaddell worriedly. 'Our informants are right to say that something worrisome is bubbling in Clerkenwell. The whole area is ripe for insurrection, and Sarah Shawe will be at the heart of it.'

'But the dead will not stay among us,' Mother Broughton went on, eager to reclaim the attention. 'They will return to the soil. Then I predict that three things will come to pass.'

'Why are there always *three* things with seers?' muttered Swaddell. 'Never two or four?'

'Just be thankful she did not say thirteen,' quipped Chaloner, 'or we would be here all day.'

'The first will be on Maundy Thursday,' Mother Broughton announced. 'Five days hence. There will be a death, which will cause much sorrow.'

'Of course there will,' spat Swaddell. 'We live in the biggest city in the world. Someone will also die today, Sunday, Monday, Tuesday, Wednesday and Friday.'

107

'Who?' called Eliza, alarmed. 'Did you see that in your vision?'

'Naturally,' replied Mother Broughton loftily. 'It will be an important messenger – someone who carries vital news and makes it public. A diplomat, perhaps.'

'George Downing is due home next week,' gulped Swaddell. 'Our ambassador in the United Provinces. We are expecting him to bring detailed intelligence on the enemy, and there will be much sorrow if *he* dies, because we are desperate for the military advantages his report will provide. I had better send word for him to be on his guard.'

Chaloner would not be sorry if Downing met an untimely end. The man was selfish, duplicitous, greedy and unreliable, and it was largely because of him that England had declared war on the Dutch in the first place.

'The second will be on Good Friday,' Mother Broughton went on, and dropped her voice to make her next words full of dark foreboding, 'which falls on the thirteenth day of the month in the year sixteen sixty-six.'

'She is a charlatan,' scoffed Chaloner, as the crowd exchanged fearful glances. 'How can people not see through these clumsy theatrics?'

'There will be a rain of fire, which will destroy the wicked,' Mother Broughton informed everyone confidently. 'It will be followed by a darkness that will cover the entire city. I have already told you that there will be wailing and gnashing of teeth on Good Friday. This is why.'

'Her predictions are vague enough to mean anything, yet contain enough detail to make them seem convincing,' observed Chaloner contemptuously. 'She is crafty.'

'Yes, damn her,' muttered Swaddell. 'Which means

my colleagues must squander precious time keeping an eye on her. What is wrong with the woman? Can she not see that we should be concentrating on the Dutch, not wasting our time on the likes of her?'

'The third thing I foresaw will happen on Easter Sunday,' Mother Broughton finished. 'And it is this: the wicked will be gone and the righteous will take their places. There will be such happiness that even the Sun will dance for joy.'

'That will be a sight, Tom,' said Swaddell, as the seer was helped off her box to tumultuous applause. 'Let us hope you and I will be in a position to appreciate it.'

As Swaddell was worried by the notion that Ambassador Downing might be assassinated, he asked Chaloner to wait an hour before tackling the Clarkes, while he mingled with the crowd to see if he could learn anything else of use. Chaloner agreed, as all the window shutters at Chaloner Court were closed, suggesting the Clarkes were still abed. Moreover, the delay provided an opportunity for him to survey Newcastle House without Swaddell at his side.

There was nothing much to see at the front of the ducal residence, so he did a circuit around the outside. The grounds were extensive and surrounded by high walls. On one side was a large gate leading to the stables, which were a glorious creation of honey-coloured stone, set prettily around a cobbled yard. Chaloner recalled that horses were the Duke's passion, and that they were said to live in greater luxury than most Londoners.

The gate was open, so Chaloner stepped through it, aiming to strike up a conversation with one of the many grooms, after which he hoped he would have a clearer picture of the Duchess and her husband. He was just deciding which lad to waylay when four men emerged from one of the stalls. He recognised two. The first was Baron Lucas, the Duchess's curmudgeonly brother. The second was Andrew Clayton, the younger and more sullen of the Duke's two stewards.

'I do not understand why it failed to work,' Lucas was grumbling angrily. 'You must have done something wrong.'

'I followed your instructions to the letter,' countered Clayton, and indicated the other two men with a curt wave of his hand. 'If you do not believe me, ask Booth and Liddell here.'

'They are your lickspittles,' said Lucas, regarding them with haughty disdain. 'Ergo, they will say whatever you want me to hear. Their testimony means nothing.'

'You insult two good men,' objected Clayton, incensed. 'Booth is vicar of St Quentin's near Nottingham, while Liddell is a respected horse-trader. Their integrity is beyond question.'

'Humph!' spat Lucas, before turning and stamping away.

Chaloner thought the Baron was right to be sceptical, as neither Booth nor Liddell looked trustworthy. The cleric was small, shabby and devious-eyed, while the horse-trader positively oozed guile. In the hope that their spat with Lucas might dispose them to indiscreet gossip, Chaloner strolled up to them.

'Baron Lucas is a difficult man,' he began, all friendly sympathy. 'Nothing seems to please him, so it cannot be easy to work in Newcastle House.'

'He is a fool,' growled Clayton, recognising Chaloner from White Hall and greeting him with a bow. 'He

110

bought a bay horse last month, but the Duke said her coat is too dark. Instead of accepting the fact, Lucas thinks to lighten her colour by feeding her white food.'

'He is in the Royal Society,' put in Vicar Booth, making it sound sinister, 'and is of the opinion that anything can be achieved through science, even changing the hue of a horse's fur.'

'Hair,' corrected Liddell. 'The poor beast has been eating bleached oats ever since.'

'Why did you agree to do it?' asked Chaloner, feeling they should have refused for the horse's sake.

'Because if we had not, his grumbles would have driven his sister – the Duchess – to buy him another,' explained Clayton. 'And that would be unfair on Viscount Mansfield. She spends money like water, but it is not hers to waste – it is Mansfield's inheritance. The poor man will have nothing left if she is permitted to squander it as she pleases.'

'I see,' said Chaloner, recalling from the encounter in White Hall that Clayton was firmly Mansfield's man. 'Are the Duke's finances so precarious then?'

If they were, he thought, glancing around at the beautiful stables, then he should not be splashing out on fancy new accommodations for his equine friends.

'He still has massive debts from the wars,' explained Clayton. 'Mansfield wants his father to pay them off, so the estate will be in credit when the old man dies.'

'It is all Steward Topp's fault,' sniffed Vicar Booth. 'He encourages the Duchess to spend money on things she does not need, just to hurt poor Mansfield.'

'Well, Topp does hail from merchant stock,' said Clayton cattily. 'So what do you expect? I imagine he siphons off a percentage of all her purchases for himself.

The man is a rogue, and I fail to understand why she trusts him.'

'She trusts him because he is married to Eliza,' growled Liddell. 'And Eliza is her closest and most valued friend. I liked Eliza until she came to London, but living here has turned her opinionated.'

'She listens too much to Sarah Shawe,' put in Clayton, pursing his lips, 'who thinks women should have the same rights as men. She should not be permitted to say such things in public. It is dangerous, and a direct challenge to God's authority.'

'Of course, Sarah Shawe is not nearly as bad an influence on Eliza as the Duchess is,' gossiped Booth. '*She* should be in Bedlam. I read her books, and I was appalled. They are the rantings of a lunatic, and should never have been published.'

'I read one of them, too,' said Liddell. 'It was mostly gibberish to me, but I did understand that she wants the world turned upside down again, this time by having women at the top and us men at the bottom.'

'I do not suppose you have heard her mention Thomas Chiffinch, have you?' asked Chaloner, the moment he could insert a question into their venomous tirades.

'Only to remark that she disliked him,' replied Clayton. 'Well, of course she did! He told his friends that it is wrong for women to publish books for public consumption. She was livid.'

'Was she?' fished Chaloner.

'Oh, yes! I imagine she is delighted that he is no longer in a position to insult her.'

'She is not the only one,' said Booth. 'Mansfield is sure that Chiffinch cheated him of fifty pounds when they played backgammon on Thursday night, and he hates parting with money. And who can blame him when the Duke keeps him on such a meagre allowance?'

'Then why did he risk fifty pounds of it on a bet?' asked Chaloner pointedly.

'Because of the Duchess,' explained Clayton. 'She won against Chiffinch, and Mansfield is a better player than her. He assumed he would emerge victorious, with a tidy sum to supplement his income. Poor Mansfield. She injures him at every turn.'

They returned to the subject of the overly dark horse at that point, so Chaloner took his leave, his mind full of questions. Would a middle-aged Duchess really dispatch a man who disparaged her? Or would her feeble stepson kill a cheat? Suddenly, he was glad Swaddell would be working with him. The assassin could share the blame if they found answers that might not be to the authorities' liking.

By the time Chaloner returned to the green, Swaddell had finished his eavesdropping, but before either could tell the other what he had learned, Newcastle House's front door opened, and a number of people filed out. All began to walk towards a waiting coach. The Duke was in the lead, but went to examine the horses first. Behind him were the Duchess and her stepson Mansfield, quarrelling, while the obsequious Topp scurried at their heels.

She stretched out a hand to touch Mansfield's arm, an attempt at affection that he killed dead by knocking it away. The expression of contempt on his face made her bristle. In revenge, she shouted something to her husband, who turned and laughed. Fuming, Mansfield shoved past her, jumped into the coach and ordered the

113

driver to take him to White Hall immediately. Clearly, if this command was followed, his father and stepmother would be left without transport. The driver glanced nervously at the Duke.

'Go, you damned fool!' Mansfield screeched. 'Or look for another post.'

The Duke rolled his eyes and nodded at the driver, who flicked his reins to urge the horses into a trot. The Duchess murmured something to Topp, who hurried off towards the stables. The steward returned a few moments later with Liddell and two prancing stallions. With a whoop of joy, the Duke dashed towards them, and there followed a lot of serious discussion as he contemplated which one to ride. The Duchess watched with an indulgent smile.

'He has an affliction,' Swaddell explained to Chaloner. 'An uncontrolled trembling in his limbs. His physicians have forbidden riding, which is a cruel blow to a man born in the saddle. The Duchess has made him very happy by allowing him to ignore their strictures for once.'

'Then let us hope he does not topple off,' said Chaloner. 'Or Mansfield will accuse her of trying to kill him.'

'Of course, Mansfield did himself no favours by hogging the family coach,' Swaddell went on. 'His father is unlikely to forget such selfishness, and the Duchess certainly will not.'

Eventually, the Duke made his selection, climbed into the saddle and showed off with a series of fancy manoeuvres. His lady cooed and clapped appreciatively, causing him to flush with pleasure. Then, with Liddell on the second horse, he cantered away, yelling over his shoulder that the spare coach would not be long, and that he would wait for her at the other end.

114

As the spare carriage did not materialise immediately, Chaloner took the opportunity to go and pay his respects to the Duchess, aiming to dissuade her from visiting the charnel house later – assuming she had not seen sense and reconsidered already, of course. She was talking to Eliza Topp, who had come to keep her company while she waited. As he approached, he heard they were talking about the Red Bull tavern.

'Eliza has established a school there,' the Duchess informed Chaloner, although he had not asked. Indeed, he had not even had time to bow or utter even the briefest of greetings. 'For intelligent ladies.'

Eliza smiled, and took her arm in a gesture of easy familiarity, which showed they really were friends rather than mistress and servant. 'And the Duchess is generous with money for books. Perhaps you would care to visit, Mr Chaloner, and see our good work for yourself. Come tomorrow. You are sure to learn a great deal, as all our students have very keen minds.'

Before Chaloner could respond, there came a wail of anguish. A woman was walking past carrying a cloth-covered basket over her arm. Hot on her heels was Molly. Sobbing in distress, the chicken girl tried to grab the basket, to which the woman responded by kicking at her. Chaloner went to intervene before the child was hurt. Unwilling to do battle with someone who might kick back, the woman backed off, although she did not relinquish the basket. She tried to stalk off with it, but was forced to stop when the Duchess herself barred her way.

'I have warned you before,' the Duchess said coldly. 'Molly is simple, and responds to kindness, not abuse, so why are you—'

'Dutch Jane has *stolen* Audrey, lady,' wept Molly,

distraught as she pointed an accusing finger. 'My best chicken. She is going to sell her and keep all the money for herself.'

'I am not!' declared Dutch Jane indignantly. 'The little half-wit is mistaken, as usual.'

An avian cluck from inside the basket made a liar of her. Molly lunged and pulled off the cloth. Underneath sat a pretty brown hen, which the girl retrieved to cuddle protectively.

'She put it there herself, to get me into trouble,' declared Dutch Jane defiantly.

The Duchess regarded her in distaste. 'Molly is incapable of implementing such a sly scheme. Nor would she risk harming one of her birds.'

Dutch Jane shrugged carelessly. 'Then you explain how it got there.'

The Duchess blinked her astonishment at the impudent response, but then her expression hardened. 'You are dismissed from my service with immediate effect.'

Dutch Jane was not expecting this, and her jaw dropped. 'But—'

'I do not tolerate thieves and liars,' the Duchess went on crisply. 'Or disobedience. I issued an express order that none of our poultry were to be harmed until I have ascertained whether they are capable of intelligent thought.'

'They are, lady,' Molly assured her. 'They are all very clever. Not like Dutch Jane, who thinks I will not notice if she filches one of them.'

'Yes, Molly,' said Eliza kindly. 'Now take Audrey back to her friends.'

Molly scurried away, leaving Dutch Jane standing with her fists clenched and her face as black as thunder. Eliza

116

clearly thought the woman represented a danger to the Duchess, because she stepped forward protectively.

'You cannot dismiss me,' snarled Dutch Jane. 'You brought me to this country, so you are morally obliged to look after me. You cannot expect me to find my own way home.'

'You should have thought of that before stealing birds and ignoring orders,' retorted the Duchess, unmoved. 'Now, be gone before I have you thrown in gaol. Hah! Here is our transport. Eliza, your husband is a treasure. I shall see *you* at three o'clock.'

The last remark was addressed to Chaloner, and was accompanied by a meaningful wink.

'You have an appointment with him, Your Loveliness?' asked Topp, overhearing. 'Then you cannot keep it. You promised to spend all afternoon with the Queen.'

'She will not miss me for an hour,' averred the Duchess. 'And my assignation with him is a matter of great scientific import. I shall include any discoveries in the next edition of my *Philosophical and Physical Opinions.*'

'That would distress the dead man's family,' said Chaloner quickly. 'So stay with the Queen today, Your Grace, and I will see that Wiseman writes you a full report of his—'

'No,' interrupted the Duchess, in a tone that told him further argument would be futile. 'I *will* watch the surgeon at work. Topp, assist me into the carriage.'

Topp hastened to oblige, then handed Eliza in beside her. He scrambled in last, although not before shooting Chaloner a sympathetic glance – the kind that suggested he was used to his mistress making up her own mind and then not being budged from it.

'She is insane,' spat Dutch Jane furiously, as the carriage rattled away. 'No low deed is beneath her, despite her pretensions to being a great lady. And what does she expect us to eat if we are no longer allowed to slaughter chickens?'

'Try bread and cheese,' suggested Chaloner. 'But what will you do now you are dismissed? Return to the United Provinces?'

'That is none of your business,' snapped Dutch Jane unpleasantly. 'However, I can tell you one thing for sure: I am not going anywhere until I get revenge for this outrage. The Duchess will regret treating *me* like scum.'

Chaloner hoped the Duchess's staff would be on their guard.

The bells in nearby St James's Church were ringing for the noonday service by the time Chaloner and Swaddell arrived at the Clarkes' house. They walked up its short drive, through a neatly manicured garden that was unrecognisable as the tangled wilderness Chaloner remembered from his youth. The door was opened by a liveried maid, who ushered them inside and asked them to wait while she went to see if her employers were receiving visitors.

'So this is your ancestral home,' said Swaddell, looking around enviously. 'You must have been devastated when you lost it at the Restoration.'

'Not at all,' said Chaloner firmly, unwilling for Swaddell to report *that* to Williamson. 'First, it was never owned by my branch of the family, and second, it has been years since I was last here – so many years that virtually none of it is familiar.'

It was the truth: the house was so different that it might have been another building. Gone were the dark wooden panels, and in their place were fresh white walls.

118

The heavy oak stairs had been removed to make way for an elegant French creation, while the rough flagstone floors had been replaced with modern tiles. Absently, Chaloner noticed that several of the tiles were already chipped, while the plaster was flaking in one or two places – the Clarkes had replaced substance with style, and although the improvements looked pretty, they were inferior and would not survive the test of time.

The maid reappeared and indicated that they were to follow her to a reception room at the rear of the house. This was a handsome chamber with windows that overlooked the main garden. Chaloner was bemused to note that all the original portraits still adorned the walls, but the identifying plaques at the bottom had been amended, so that his ancestors were now those of the new owners. He smothered a smile, wondering what his stuffy old grandfather would have thought about being passed off as 'Sir Ignatius Clarke'.

The physician was sitting at a table in the window, pretending to read a medical tome. He was a nondescript man with mousy features, who had attempted to render himself more interesting by donning glorious clothes and an impressive wig. It had not worked, and he looked as though he had been at someone else's wardrobe, as well as someone else's forebears.

'Mr Swaddell from the office of the Spymaster General, and Mr Chaloner, Gentleman Usher to the Lord Chancellor,' announced the maid, before backing out and closing the door behind her. The way she intoned the introductions suggested that she was impressed by their credentials, although the blood drained from her master's face.

'Chaloner?' he gulped. 'With the Spymaster's assassin?

119

Please! I have done nothing wrong! I bought this house perfectly legally. You cannot demand it back!'

'I know,' Chaloner assured him hastily. 'My family has no claim on it now.' He flailed around for a compliment, to put him at ease. 'You have made it very attractive.'

Clarke relaxed slightly. 'Thank you. We spent a fortune on repairs, especially the roof. It leaked horribly, but the new one keeps us lovely and dry.'

'I should like to live in a house like this,' said Swaddell wistfully. 'Perhaps my future wife will provide me with one.'

'You are betrothed?' asked Clarke politely.

'Not yet,' replied Swaddell. 'But I am always on the lookout for suitable candidates, so if you happen to know any, send them my way.'

Clarke was patently horrified by the notion of Swaddell on the marriage market, so Chaloner tried to change the subject before they were thrown out.

'We are here to talk about—' he began.

'You aim to question my decision regarding the Queen,' interrupted Clarke, eyes narrowing angrily. 'But it is *right* to keep her mother's death a secret. She is fragile after yet another failed pregnancy, and it would be cruel to heap more misery upon her. Besides, it is not for the Lord Chancellor and Williamson to meddle in medical matters.'

'We shall tell them you said so,' drawled Swaddell, much to the physician's alarm, while Chaloner was tempted to point out that the Queen was likely to hear the news anyway, given White Hall's propensity for loose-tongued gossip, and in a way that would cause her a lot more pain than if broken gently. But it really was none of his business, and time was passing.

120

'We want to ask you about Chiffinch, not the Queen,' he said briskly. 'I understand you inspected the body.'

Clarke nodded as he struggled to regain his composure. 'Yesterday morning. I was in the Shield Gallery, handing out remedies for overindulgence, when I heard that Chiffinch was in need of medical attention. I ran to the cockpit, and arrived to see a large number of people already there. None had dared go near him, though. They were afraid of the plague.'

'Chiffinch was alive and well an hour earlier,' said Swaddell. 'Surely they know the disease does not strike that quickly?'

Chaloner doubted they were aware of any such thing, given that they had all raced to safer pastures at the first mention of buboes.

'Of course it can,' countered Clarke, thus proving that he had been one of them, despite the fact that, as a *medicus*, he should have been better informed. 'However, Chiffinch died of an impostume in the breast. I felt it under my fingers as I examined his corpse. He must have known it was there, but he neglected to seek my help, so it killed him.'

'What kind of—' began Swaddell, but Clarke cut across him.

'When I finished my inspection, I sent one of the onlookers to carry the news to the King, and arranged for the body to be removed to the charnel house. Then I returned to my duties in the Shield Gallery.'

'You played backgammon with Chiffinch the night before he died,' said Chaloner. 'How did he seem then?'

Panic showed in Clarke's face as it dawned on him that this question had no good answer. If he admitted that he had failed to spot a serious ailment hours before

121

it killed a man, he would appear incompetent, but if he declared that Chiffinch was fit and well, it would make his diagnosis of a deadly impostume unlikely.

'He was a politician,' he said eventually, 'and thus a skilled dissembler. He could convince anyone of anything, so, naturally, he was careful to conceal symptoms that might have aroused my professional attention.'

'He deliberately withheld evidence of ill health?' Swaddell's voice dripped disbelief. 'Why would he do such a thing?'

Clarke shrugged uncomfortably. 'Perhaps he did not want to be forcibly retired, so that a younger, fitter man could be appointed in his place. And he was right to be uneasy, because that is exactly what *did* happen, within minutes of me declaring him dead.'

'Are you suggesting that we arrest Will for bringing about his brother's death?' asked Swaddell keenly.

Clarke eyed him with dislike. 'You twist my words. I do *not* accuse Will. He is a good man, who loved his sibling dearly.'

'Can you tell us anything about Chiffinch's last evening?' asked Chaloner, after a short silence, during which all three men reflected on the fact that Will was as far from being 'a good man' as it was possible to be, and that he probably had not loved his brother either. 'For example, did you witness any quarrels or hot words?'

'No, but all my attention was on Baron Lucas – a florid man of a certain age who might soon require medical expertise. I am always looking for new clients . . . I mean, people to help.'

Chaloner moved to another subject. 'We have been told that your wife found the body. What was she doing in the cockpit at seven o'clock in the morning?'

Clarke regarded him coolly. 'That is her business and none of yours. However, I hope you do not intend to pester her for answers. You will leave her be, if you are gentlemen.'

'Chaloner is a gentleman,' said Swaddell with one of his crocodilian smiles. 'But I am not, so *I* have no objection to pestering women. Where is she?'

'I refuse to say,' declared Clarke stoutly. 'It is my duty to protect her.'

Swaddell took a menacing step towards him. 'Then perhaps I shall pester you instead.'

'In that case,' gulped Clarke, 'she will be in the orangery. Follow me.'

There had not been an orangery when the previous owners had been in residence, and Chaloner was not sure there should be one now. It looked odd, tacked on to the rear of the house, like a very long lean-to with a plethora of windows. Access was via a door from another reception room, although judging by the way the lintel sagged, the builders had chosen to punch through a load-bearing wall. He eased under it quickly, wondering how long it would be before the Clarkes experienced structural problems with their so-called improvements.

Inside, the orangery was crammed with exotic plants in pots. The large windows allowed the light to flood in, while the air was moist, and filled with the aroma of lemons. Chaloner recalled the outrageous Cobbe declaring Fanny to be an excellent judge of the fruit, and if she grew them, that was likely to be true. He thought he heard the chunter of chickens from deeper in the foliage, but told himself that this was unlikely.

Fanny Clarke was fast asleep in the sunshine when

they arrived, slumped on a bench with her mouth hanging open. She wore a blue silk mantua – a kind of dressing-gown – and her hair fell loose down her back, brown and plentiful. Some embroidery sat neglected in her lap.

When she did not wake at once, her husband poked her. Her initial confusion turned to horror when she saw she had visitors, and she immediately began to berate him for showing them in while she was improperly attired. Clarke interrupted her curtly.

'They want to know why you were in the cockpit yesterday morning,' he said, glaring at her. 'I told you to stay away from the place, and you should have listened to me. Now you have landed yourself in trouble. Tell them why you were there.'

Fanny blushed and her hands began to tremble. 'I would rather not say.'

'You must,' said Swaddell sternly. 'Or we shall conclude that *you* killed Chiffinch.'

Fanny gaped her shock. 'That is a terrible thing to say! Why would I do him harm? Besides, no one killed him. He died of an impostume. Ask Timothy.'

'His death *was* natural,' said Clarke between gritted teeth. 'As I have already told you.'

'So why were you in the cockpit?' demanded Swaddell, ignoring Clarke and concentrating on Fanny so intently that she looked frightened. Chaloner felt sorry for her.

'If I say, you will think me deranged,' she whispered wretchedly. 'Worse, you will tell everyone and I shall be a laughing stock. My reputation as a respectable lady . . .'

'Better that than the alternative,' said Swaddell menacingly. 'Which is that we arrest you for refusing to cooperate with an official inquiry.'

124

'For God's sake, Fanny,' snapped Clarke, 'just tell them. And in future, perhaps you will accept that your husband knows best when he forbids you to do something.'

Fanny hung her head. 'I went to see if there were any injured birds to rescue,' she mumbled uncomfortably, 'from the fighting the night before. Their keepers do not bother with the damaged ones, you see. They just leave them to suffer.'

As if on cue, a cockerel strutted out from among the potted foliage. It was limping, missing an eye, and wore a bandage around its middle. It gave the humans an appraising look, before disappearing back to its tropical foraging grounds.

'She brings them to me for medical care,' explained Clarke with a long-suffering sigh. 'I succeed with some, but others are beyond even my superior skills. She is upset when they die, but I am a physician, not a bird-healer. A very good *royal* physician.'

Wiseman also bragged about his abilities, leading Chaloner to wonder if instruction in brazen boasting was included in the medical curriculum, perhaps to disguise the fact that most practitioners had no idea what they were doing.

'I hate cockfighting,' said Fanny with a small spurt of defiance. 'It is disgusting and so are the people who enjoy it. If I were a man, I would campaign to see it stopped.'

Chaloner felt himself warm to her. 'Do you visit the cockpit after every fight?'

She winced. 'Unfortunately, there are too many of them, and I can only go when my Court duties allow.'

'She sews for the Queen,' put in Clarke, pride in his voice as he indicated the embroidery in her lap. 'As you can see, no one else can make such beautiful stitches.

And it is, of course, a far more genteel pastime than rescuing wounded birds.'

He shot her a pointed look, but she did not see it, because a different cockerel had appeared through the leaves, and was pecking at her feet in the hope of treats.

'You were in the Shield Gallery the night that Chiffinch died,' said Chaloner, watching her feed the bird raisins, an expensive import from Spain that most Londoners would never taste. 'And you played backgammon with him. How did he seem to you at the time?'

'She cannot answer that,' said Clarke at once. 'She is not a physician.'

'We do not want a medical opinion,' said Swaddell, eyeing Clarke with such venom that the man took an involuntary step back. 'We want her observations.'

Fanny considered the question carefully. 'Well, he spent most of our game denigrating the Duchess of Newcastle. He disliked her intensely – her dangerous views on religion, politics and philosophy, her outrageous clothes, her outlandish behaviour. If she ever heard half of what he said about her, she would never appear in decent society again.'

'Did you speak to him after that exchange?' asked Chaloner.

'Yes, when he came to demand five pounds from me, which he claimed I owed for losing to him.' Fanny gave a brief smile of satisfaction. 'But I disapprove of gambling and would never stake money on the outcome of a game. He swore and argued, but eventually conceded that I was in the right.'

'So he was angry with you?'

'A little, but he had the last word, because he was able to inform me that he had already wrested twenty pounds from my husband, who *had* agreed to wager with him.' She gave Clarke an arch stare.

'I had no choice,' said Clarke defensively. 'I cannot take a moral stance on gambling, because I rely on men like Chiffinch for business. It would be foolish to alienate them by denouncing what they love. Besides, the King enjoys betting, and if he likes it, then so must I.'

'His Majesty likes breaking his marriage vows with harlots as well,' retorted Fanny acidly. 'But I sincerely hope you do not intend to follow *that* example.'

'Of course not,' gulped Clarke. 'Harlots indeed!'

Fanny gave him another cool glance, then picked up her sewing. Her rapidly flying needle revealed so much skill that Chaloner was momentarily mesmerised by it.

'I dislike the immorality that abounds at Court,' she confided as she worked. 'I fear it will lead to trouble. The only courtier with decent principles is the Earl of Clarendon.'

Much good it did him, thought Chaloner caustically, given that it rendered him no more popular with Londoners than the debauched monkeys of the Cockpit Club.

'Were there any further exchanges between you and Chiffinch that night?' he asked.

'No, and I spent the rest of the evening with Lucy Bodvil and Mary Robartes, discussing how we would rather be at home in bed. None of us enjoy these riotous late nights.'

Chaloner knew Lucy Bodvil and Mary Robartes would not. They were the staid, middle-aged wives of ambitious officials, who were obliged to accompany their spouses to courtly functions but who usually found some quiet corner where they sewed and talked. They were an exception to the rule that all courtiers were dedicated hedonists with no redeeming qualities. Behind his wife's back, Clarke grimaced his disdain for such uninteresting company.

'They are your friends?' asked Chaloner.

Fanny nodded. 'There are half a dozen of us who deplore drinking and gambling; we always seek each other out on occasions like the one on Thursday.' She went on to name four or five other worthy matrons, all of whom tended to be mocked for their lack of conversation and devotion to the mundane. 'Then yesterday morning, I rose early and went to the chapel for my morning devotions Afterwards, I hurried to the cockpit to see about the birds.'

'Alone?' asked Chaloner.

Fanny winced. 'Yes, unfortunately. My friends do not share my fondness for poultry.'

'Nor does your husband,' put in Clarke pointedly.

'I thought the cockpit was empty,' continued Fanny, 'but then I saw someone lying in the middle of the arena. It was Mr Chiffinch. I was so shocked that I forgot my errand of mercy and fled. On my way out, I collided with Captain Rolt, who had come to look for a lost button. He bade me sit down and take some deep breaths while he went inside to look for himself. Moments later, he dashed out and ordered a passing servant to fetch a *medicus*.'

'Did he indeed?' mused Chaloner. 'He did not mention any of this to us.'

Which was curious, as Rolt loved recognition and would have gained a lot of it by declaring that he had taken control of the situation when Fanny had emerged in a fluster. Had *he* killed Chiffinch, then realised a button had been torn off in the struggle, so had gone back to retrieve it before it incriminated him? Or was his silence that of a gentleman aiming to protect a lady from being mocked for panicking at the sight of a corpse? Regardless, Chaloner decided to speak to Rolt again at the first opportunity.

'Before you bolted, did you notice if Chiffinch was breathing?' he asked.

Fanny shook her head. 'It was obvious that he was dead.' She shuddered. 'It was a terrible thing . . . A man I had seen alive a few hours before, suddenly all cold and still and . . .'

'You can rescue injured birds, but corpses unnerve you?' asked Swaddell sceptically.

Fanny's expression was bleak. '*Human* corpses do. And Mr Chiffinch . . . well, he . . . he made a *noise*. My husband says escaping air . . .'

'Corpses release some awful sounds,' explained Clarke with an amused smirk. 'Fanny understands that now, but she did not at the time. Hence her alarm.'

Perhaps Rolt *had* been sparing her blushes then, thought Chaloner, because this was certainly a tale that would be repeated with relish by White Hall's prurient inhabitants. As she was looking mortified, he moved to another matter.

'Rolt tells me that you and Bess Widdrington went to the Red Bull the other day. It—'

'Did you, Fanny?' interrupted Clarke, startled. 'I wish you had not.'

'Captain Rolt is mistaken,' said Fanny firmly. 'It would be most improper for me to visit a common tavern. But if you want someone who does not care about such things, talk to the Duchess of Newcastle. *She* would have no qualms about frequenting that sort of establishment. Indeed, last week, she expressed a wish to watch the Cockpit Club at their revels.' She shuddered again.

'Well, she got her wish last night,' said Chaloner. 'She appeared with her retinue.'

Fanny looked astonished, then thoughtful, and Chaloner could almost see her mind at work. Clearly, the Duchess appearing at the murder scene was suspicious in her eyes.

'Perhaps your Earl should teach the woman how to behave,' said Clarke, pursing his lips. 'She is a menace to decent society with her peculiar opinions. For example, she told me that women should abandon their homes to work like men; that they should endeavour to be as vain, ambitious and greedy as men; and that telling lies is good, because it sparks debate.'

'I have had enough of revolutionary ideas,' said Fanny tiredly. 'We have suffered far too many of them over the last thirty years, and all I want now is a country that is stable, safe and decent, where everyone knows his or her place.'

'Quite,' said Clarke tersely. 'Which is *not* in the cockpit looking for injured cockerels.'

'Yes, dear,' said Fanny, contrite.

They had taken longer in Clerkenwell than Chaloner had anticipated, and he saw he was going to be late for his appointment at the charnel house. He hurried to John Street, where there were usually hackney carriages for hire. Swaddell fell in at his side.

'I did not take to the Clarkes,' the assassin declared. 'He is a pompous fool with an inflated sense of his own worth, while she is a prim bore with inflexible ideas.'

130

'True, but Fanny has one thing in her favour,' said Chaloner. 'She saves injured birds.'

'I suppose,' conceded Swaddell. 'Now, tell me what you make of the tale Captain Rolt told us – that Fanny and Bess Widdrington visited the Red Bull together. I cannot see that pair being comfortable in each other's company: one is a rake, the other is a dullard.'

'They have both denied it, so I am not sure what to believe. We will ask Rolt about it again when we next see him, although I doubt it is relevant to Chiffinch's death.'

'If it is, I shall prise the truth out of him. I shall just threaten to slit his throat unless he cooperates.' Swaddell saw Chaloner's expression of distaste and hastened to defend himself. 'I am not saying that I *will* slit his throat, but most folk confess if they believe it is a possibility.'

'You can try, but Rolt earned his captaincy by taking part in battles, unlike most courtiers. He may not be so easily intimidated.'

'He will,' averred Swaddell confidently. 'I shall do it now in fact, when I shall also demand to know why he did not mention being at the cockpit when Fanny hurtled out. It is suspicious that he neglected to mention the central role he played in the incident.'

'I agree. There is something distasteful about him. Brodrick said he is all things to all men, and it was an astute observation. With him, I always have the feeling that he is waiting to see which way the wind blows before committing himself to anything.'

Swaddell's eyes narrowed. 'His association with Widdrington has already cost him a horse, so he will be looking to make good on his losses. I do not trust him an inch. But what about you, Tom? Where are you going in such haste?'

'To the charnel house, to learn once and for all if Chiffinch was murdered. Wiseman expects the answer to be yes, but I have been unable to corner him to ask why.'

Swaddell looked more interested than was nice. 'Perhaps I should do that. You can corner Rolt instead.'

It was tempting, but Wiseman would never countenance such an arrangement because he disliked Swaddell and would baulk at being in his company. Reluctantly, Chaloner decided he had no choice but to endure the ordeal himself.

Chapter 5

The Westminster Charnel House had once been an unprepossessing place, situated at the end of a narrow alley and sandwiched between a coal-merchant's warehouse and a granary. The plague had changed all that, as its owner, Mr Kersey, had grown fabulously rich by accepting property that no one else dared touch.

He had bought the granary and converted it into a museum for all the artefacts he had collected from the dead over the years. More recently, he had purchased the warehouse, too, which he had demolished and replaced with a pretty cobbled yard, complete with ornamental trees and tethering for horses – his charnel house was a popular attraction for London's wealthy elite, who paid a fortune to go in and look around.

The main building had two elegant rooms at the front. The smaller one was an office, where Kersey recorded all the 'guests' who passed through his hands. The larger one was a parlour where he received grieving friends and relations; Chaloner had always been impressed that the same gentle courtesy was extended to paupers and nobles alike. Behind these was the mortuary proper, a long, low-ceilinged chamber crammed with wooden tables. Each body was respectfully covered with a clean grey blanket.

Kersey was a neat, dapper little man, always impeccably dressed. There was gold thread in his handsome mauve long-coat, while French lace frothed at his throat and wrists. He was plumper than the last time Chaloner had met him, and his cheeks were pink with rude health and vitality. Business was good.

'I am glad to see you home,' he said warmly, gripping Chaloner's hand. 'Although I hope you will not be crushing any more rebellions. The one in January promised to teach our cowardly rulers a lesson, and I was sorry when you thwarted it.'

Uncomfortably, Chaloner recalled that Kersey was one of those who had been particularly outraged by the fact that the King and his Court had fled the moment the plague had started to take hold in London. He could not imagine what the charnel house had been like when the disease was at its peak, so did not blame Kersey for resenting the fact that his city had been so selfishly abandoned by those whose duty it was to protect it.

'I have visitors at the moment,' the charnel-house keeper went on, and grimaced his distaste. 'Courtiers. I despise them all, but I like the colour of their gold, so I avenge myself on their spinelessness during the plague by charging them a fortune for guided tours.'

Chaloner glanced past him into the parlour, and saw he had been taking a glass of wine – which he knew from experience would be of excellent quality – with three men from the Cockpit Club: Colonel Widdrington, the drunken Ashley and the massive, apelike Tooley. He started to back away, having no wish to exchange words with them, but they had seen him.

'Have you come to view the corpse?' called Widdrington, yawning as he stood. 'Good luck with that! This fellow refuses to let us anywhere near it.'

'Which is unfair,' growled Ashley, who had to be helped to his feet by Tooley, suggesting he had swallowed more of Kersey's wine than was polite. 'We offered him good money.'

'And it is not as if we are ghouls,' put in Tooley indignantly. 'We came because we want to join the Royal Society, and assessing cadavers will show us to be men with enquiring minds.'

'I am sure the Royal Society will be delighted to enrol such dedicated students,' said Kersey smoothly, although Chaloner heard the disdain behind the words. 'But as I have already explained, Mr Chiffinch's family has requested privacy.'

'So what?' demanded Widdrington petulantly. 'I shall not mind people admiring *my* corpse when the time comes, so why let them keep Chiffinch to themselves? It is hardly reasonable.'

'We always accede to the family's wishes,' said Kersey, although Chaloner did not know how he kept his calm with the man. 'I am afraid my hands are tied.'

'Perhaps Will dispatched his brother,' slurred Ashley slyly, 'and he aims to conceal his guilt by preventing anyone from seeing his victim's body. After all, he did leap into his shoes with unseemly haste, before the rest of us could even *consider* doing it ourselves.'

'I would not have minded one of those posts,' sighed Tooley, although Chaloner suspected that even the King, no great judge of character, would have had reservations about appointing *him* as Keeper of the Jewels. 'And if Will *is* a killer, perhaps we should be more picky about who we enrol in the Cockpit Club from now on. For example, Rolt is not really our kind of fellow. He—'

'We should leave,' interrupted Widdrington with a bored yawn. 'The King promised to come to our wrestling tournament tonight, so we had better ensure that everything is ready.'

'Just one question before you go,' said Chaloner. 'You were seen walking across the Great Court with Chiffinch shortly before he died. How did that come about?'

'It is none of your damned business!' declared Tooley angrily. 'How dare you try to quiz us like common criminals. You have no right!'

Widdrington raised a soft, white hand. 'Steady now, Tooley. We have nothing to hide, and we do not want the Earl's rat to go away thinking we are responsible for giving Chiffinch his impostume. I say we let him ask his questions.'

Chaloner took him at his word, and launched into an interrogation that had Tooley and Ashley huffing their outrage at its sharp, discourteous tone, although Widdrington stubbornly declined to be ruffled.

'Why were you with Chiffinch in the Great Court just before he died?' he asked again.

'Our paths crossed,' shrugged Widdrington. 'By accident, not design. We kept company with him until he trotted through the gate towards King Street, and we went to the Banqueting House.'

'What did you talk about? The money you owed for losing to him at backgammon?'

Widdrington smiled pleasantly. 'Yes, he did mention our debts. We promised to settle them, and schedules for payment have since been negotiated with his next of kin.'

'What else did you discuss?'

136

Widdrington's grin did not waver. 'The weather, the King's new horse, the fact that a mutual friend is about to give birth, even though she has not seen her husband in a year.'

'How did Chiffinch seem to you?'

'As he always was,' put in Tooley sourly. 'Smug, boring and quick to give his opinions.'

'His opinions about what?'

'All the people he deplored,' replied Tooley. 'Radicals, prudes, pacifists, women who want schools for girls, Puritan divines, female writers, merrymakers – even though his own brother is the biggest merrymaker of all.'

'He and Will were on bad terms?'

'We would not know,' said Widdrington. 'We rarely saw them together, and when we did, it was Will whose company we preferred.'

'Where were you when news came that Chiffinch was dead?'

'Still in the Banqueting House. We shall stage one of Lord Rochester's plays there soon, and we were discussing the scenery. When we heard what had happened, we hurried to the cockpit to see if we could be of assistance.'

'Our motives were honourable, not ghoulish,' put in Ashley unconvincingly.

'What did you see when you arrived?'

'Chiffinch lying on the floor, surrounded by spectators,' replied Widdrington. 'Although none stood too close, lest he had died of the plague. Then Clarke arrived, diagnosed an impostume, and arranged for the corpse to be brought here.'

Chaloner was learning nothing he did not already know, and had the distinct sense that Widdrington was

137

laughing at his efforts to catch him out in a lie or an inconsistency.

'You may go,' he said, aiming to annoy the man with a summary dismissal. 'Naturally, I shall be verifying your claims with your wives and friends.'

Widdrington laughed. 'I doubt Bess will give you the time of day, but you are welcome to try. Poor Bess! She tries so hard to fit in at Court, but the task is entirely beyond her. I shall send her to the country soon, where she will be much happier.'

'I rather think she is happy here,' said Chaloner, not surprised that Widdrington wanted to be rid of her, but sure he would never have the courage to do it. 'With you.'

Widdrington smirked. 'No woman knows what is best for her, which is why we have marriage – so she will have a man to look after her interests.'

Chaloner found himself imagining what most females of his acquaintance would say to this remark, and suspected it would be nothing polite.

'Besides,' put in Tooley, 'it is unseemly for Bess to trail at his heels all day. Some of our activities are more suitable for men than for ladies.'

The way he leered made Chaloner suspect they were suitable for neither sex.

When the three courtiers had gone, Kersey invited Chaloner to wait for Wiseman in his office, where he provided not only a goblet of his fine wine, but a plate of pastries. Chaloner was hungry, and devoured the lot while the charnel-house keeper regaled him with his own news and gossip, none of which was pertinent to Chiffinch. It was now well past three o'clock, and as the

138

Duchess had not put in an appearance, he dared hope that she had had second thoughts.

'Wiseman is late,' he said, wishing the surgeon would hurry up so he could leave.

'Good,' said Kersey. 'It was been too long since you and I had a decent natter.'

'I suppose so,' said Chaloner, although there were places he would far rather do it than the charnel house.

'Widdrington and his ghouls are not the first I have sent off empty-handed,' said Kersey with a satisfied grin. 'Dozens of courtiers have come, and it has given me great pleasure to refuse them all – although only *after* they have paid an exorbitant entry fee, naturally.'

'Why does Chiffinch's family want him kept from prying eyes?' asked Chaloner.

'The instruction came from his sister-in-law Barbara,' replied Kersey. 'She is that most rare of specimens – an honourable courtier. She said that Chiffinch was a proud, private man, who would not have wanted to be paraded as a spectacle.'

'Does this mean that Wiseman will be unable to perform?' asked Chaloner worriedly.

'As Surgeon to the Person, he has the right to examine anyone he chooses, whether the family agree or not,' said Kersey. 'Barbara was indignant when I told her, as she is sure Clarke's diagnosis is correct and rejects Wiseman's cries of foul play.'

'Then let us hope she is right,' said Chaloner. 'Incidentally, the Duchess of Newcastle expressed a desire to watch Wiseman at work. Will you repel her, too?'

'I shall. However, I am willing to make an exception for you, as you come in search of the truth, not to amass grisly tales with which to entertain a lot of idle fools.'

139

Just then, they heard the rattle of wheels outside. Chaloner glanced out of the window, and his heart sank when he recognised the coach. It was the Duchess, arriving fashionably late in the arrogant expectation that Wiseman would not have dared start without her. Steward Topp jumped out first. He helped his wife and the Duchess to alight, escorted them to the door, then darted back to the coach. He climbed in and drew the curtains, making it clear that this was the full extent of *his* participation in the unpalatable venture.

Kersey went to escort them into his parlour. The Duchess held out her hand for Chaloner to kiss, then ignored him, inspecting the room with an interest that bordered on the invasive. Eliza stood anxiously by the door, leaving Chaloner to surmise that it would take very little for her to dash out and join her husband. Loyalty to one's employer and friend had its limits.

'So this is where all the plague victims were brought,' mused the Duchess, a remark that did nothing to soothe Eliza's obviously raddled nerves. 'You must have been very busy.'

'We handled but a fraction,' replied Kersey soberly. 'Most went straight into the pits.'

'How many died, in your opinion?' asked the Duchess. 'I have heard wildly divergent estimates, although I know the official figure stands at sixty-eight thousand.'

'Unfortunately, the old women hired to determine causes of death were easily bribed and often wrong,' explained the charnel-house keeper. 'Then there were those who declined to notify the authorities at all, like Quakers, Anabaptists and Jews. All told, I suspect the toll was nearer a hundred thousand – one in every three souls who lived in the city and its environs.'

140

'Shocking,' breathed the Duchess. 'I am glad I was safely in the country.'

Kersey's mouth tightened into a hard, straight line at this bald admission of self-interest, so Chaloner hastened to change the subject. He liked Kersey, and did not want him in trouble for speaking his mind to someone powerful enough to harm him. Eliza helped by mentioning that Newcastle House had just been completely refurbished, which allowed the Duchess to brag about a special glass ceiling she had designed, so that its hall and ballroom were now flooded with natural light.

'Unfortunately, it is difficult to clean and has started to leak,' she admitted ruefully. 'It was also *very* expensive to install. But I am proud of it, even so.'

When she told them what it had cost, Chaloner struggled not to gape, although Kersey, a wealthy man himself, was unmoved. However, the gleam of malice in her prominent blue eyes led Chaloner to suspect that at least some of her delight in the venture derived from the fact that such a massive outlay would have sent her stepson into paroxysms of impotent rage.

'I am afraid you have had a wasted journey, ma'am,' said Kersey, when the subject of transparent ceilings had been exhausted. 'Mr Chiffinch is not available for inspection. However, I can show you some other corpses, if you are interested.'

'I am,' declared the Duchess. 'So I shall view them while we wait for Mr Wiseman to appear. Then I will watch his examination of Chiffinch – I have made up my mind to do it, which means no one can stop me. Is that wine on the cabinet? Good. You may pour me a glass, and when I have had it, we shall begin the tour.'

Wrong-footed by her supreme self-confidence, Kersey

141

did as he was told, and while he busied himself with his beautiful crystal goblets, the Duchess sat on the bench recently vacated by Widdrington. Chaloner was becoming worried, wondering why Wiseman had failed to appear. Had the Queen taken a turn for the worse?

'No,' replied the Duchess, when he asked the question aloud. 'She is on the mend, although she might have a relapse unless we finish here soon. I promised to read to her from one of my books, and she will be getting desperately impatient with the delay.'

She was not the only one, and Chaloner chafed at the passing time. He was on the verge of going to do something more useful when the Duchess began to talk about the morning when Chiffinch's body was discovered.

'I was nowhere near White Hall when the alarm was raised,' she said, 'so I missed viewing the body then. I only heard about it hours later, when my stepson came to tell me.'

'When did you arrive home exactly?' asked Chaloner, keeping his voice casual, so she would not guess he was trying to establish if she had an alibi.

Unfortunately, her sharp gaze revealed that she knew exactly what he was doing, although she did not seem to take umbrage. 'I cannot recall specifically when I left the palace, but I travelled in a hackney carriage. I had never been inside one before, and I was in the mood for an adventure. However, I shall not do it again, because it stank of onions.'

'You rode a hackney on your own?' breathed Eliza, aghast. 'My Lady! You should not have taken such a risk. London is full of undesirable characters—'

'Pah!' interrupted the Duchess. 'I was perfectly safe. The driver was a charming fellow, and did not mind at all when I remunerated him with a gold ring instead of coins. I did not have any money with me, you see, and I could not be bothered to go in the house to fetch some.'

Chaloner was sure the man had been delighted, given that it sounded as though he been seriously overpaid. 'Who greeted you when you rolled up?'

'No one,' replied the Duchess. 'They were all still abed. Is that not so, Eliza?'

'Yes,' replied Eliza, who had gulped her claret down in a single swallow and looked as though she wished she was somewhere else; she smiled gratefully when Kersey poured her a refill. 'You later said that you let yourself in, then curled up with *Paradise Lost*.'

'By John Milton, who is our neighbour,' nodded the Duchess. 'Although he is completely blind now, and his circumstances are very reduced. I tried to visit him on Thursday evening, but he was out. I waited an age in his parlour before I gave up and went to White Hall instead.'

Eliza blinked. 'Was someone else with you, My Lady? It was not me, because I was in Newcastle House all day, sorting through your old clothes.'

'I need no chaperone for Milton,' averred the Duchess. 'He is a poet.'

'Did you like Chiffinch?' fished Chaloner, feeling they were ranging too far from what he wanted to know.

'Not particularly. When I defeated him at back-gammon, he pouted like a spoiled brat. He reminded me of Mansfield, who also cannot accept the fact that I am cleverer than him.'

'Were you aware that Chiffinch disapproved of your . . .' Chaloner faltered, suspecting that while she was happy using pejorative words to describe other people's views, she would be rather less tolerant if the same rule was applied to hers.

Eliza came to his rescue. 'Your philosophical and intellectual opinions.'

The Duchess sniffed. 'Yes, but he was a dim-witted, self-satisfied hypocrite, who had no time for anyone's views but his own. Yet I bear him no ill will, especially now he is dead. But where *is* Wiseman? I thought he said three o'clock.'

'Perhaps you should go back to the palace,' suggested Chaloner hopefully. 'Wiseman might be delayed for ages yet.'

The Duchess grimaced. 'Unfortunately, the opportunity to watch a vicious critic dissected does not come along every day, and I shall never forgive myself if I miss it. In the interim, Mr Kersey can show me his best corpses.'

For the next hour, Chaloner trailed after the Duchess, Eliza and Kersey, viewing all manner of 'interesting' cases, while time ticked past relentlessly. Fortunately, nothing too gruesome was in residence, the bloodiest being a man who had died from a blow to the head the previous Wednesday.

'It damaged his brain irreparably,' explained Kersey. 'But he still managed to stagger to the River Fleet, where he died. Wiseman says he was as good as dead as soon as he was struck, but his limbs continued to function anyway. It must have been an eerie sight.'

The thought of it was too much for Eliza, who raced out with her hand over her mouth. Chaloner followed, partly to see if she needed help, but mostly because she was not the only one who needed some fresh air.

'There is no need for you to miss the rest of that . . . unusual tour, Mr Chaloner,' she said unsteadily, wiping her mouth with the back of her hand. 'I shall sit with my husband in the coach until Her Grace comes out.'

'I do not mind missing it, believe me,' said Chaloner fervently. 'I have seen enough death and violence in my life.'

He had not intended to make such an intimate confession, and was surprised at himself, although Eliza gave his arm a sympathetic squeeze. 'Have you decided whether to accept my invitation to the Red Bull tomorrow? I should like you to meet our talented pupils.'

'I will come if I can.'

'Good. Hopefully, you will be so impressed that you will donate some money for books and the like. We are always short of funds, although the Duchess is generous. And who knows? Maybe you will learn something. We women have much to say that is worth hearing.'

'I know,' said Chaloner, aiming to stem the tirade he sensed was coming. 'It is—'

'Do you?' interrupted Eliza, her eyes bright with the strength of her convictions. 'Then when did you last listen to one, and I mean *really* listen? Moreover, I know what you were thinking in there – that my Duchess is a lunatic who should be locked in Bedlam.'

'I thought nothing of the kind,' he objected.

She regarded him intently, then relented with an apologetic smile. 'Perhaps I misspoke. However, you do consider my lady to be an oddity. I could tell by the way you looked at her.'

'Well, she *is* an oddity,' retorted Chaloner, thinking Eliza should be used to it, given that everyone else thought the same. 'But that does not mean she is mad.'

'I will lend you some of her books, and when you read them, you will see that she is a great visionary,' Eliza went on with some passion. 'Her brother, Baron Lucas, agrees, and *he* is a member of the Royal Society.'

Chaloner was not sure that being in the Royal Society proved anything. So was the Duke of York, set to become King James II unless the Queen provided an heir, and he had never had a rational thought in his life.

Once Chaloner had deposited Eliza in the coach, he returned to the tour. The Duchess had finished looking at bodies, and was in the museum. The vast pair of drawers that had enjoyed pride of place for years had been relegated to an antechamber, and the star attraction was now Kersey's huge collection of false teeth. Lying on a table nearby was an eclectic assortment of objects waiting to be catalogued – some oddly shaped shillings, letters and a book.

'All these belonged to the man who walked around while he was effectively dead,' Kersey explained, and smiled. 'However, I doubt his kin will come to claim them.'

'Why not?' asked the Duchess, agog.

It was Chaloner who answered. 'Because of the coins. Some of the silver has been clipped from their edges, and that is a capital crime. To claim them will risk being implicated, and the government takes a dim view of people who devalue the national currency.'

The Duchess poked the money with a plump forefinger, then picked up the book. 'Coin-clipping was not the rogue's only capital crime,' she declared, her voice suddenly harsh with anger. 'The wretch has been through this tome and made some very unpleasant annotations.'

'I was not aware that defacing—' began Kersey, bemused.

'It is one of mine,' interrupted the Duchess coldly. '*The World's Olio*. And his inane scribbles show him to have been a man of very limited intellect. Regardless, I hope you do not intend to put this on display, Mr Kersey. It insults me.'

'It will never see the light of day again,' promised Kersey diplomatically. 'And you must forgive me for leaving it out. I have had scant time to assess—'

'Do the letters reveal the rogue's identity?' asked the Duchess, making a grab for them. 'If so, I shall visit his kin, and put them right about his asinine remarks.' Then she frowned. 'I cannot make head nor tail of them, and none are signed. Are they in code? And what is this symbol that looks like a broken wheel? What does it mean?'

'I do not know,' replied Kersey. 'However, I shall send them to the Spymaster when I have a spare moment. I suspect our dead friend was embroiled in some very dark business, which is probably why he met his untimely end.'

Wiseman arrived eventually, so Chaloner went outside to meet him. Unrepentantly, the surgeon explained that his lateness was due to an emergency with the courtier who would soon give birth to the child she had claimed to have carried for the past twelve months. He already knew that the Duchess aimed to watch him at work, and was delighted that his expertise was about to be witnessed by a high-ranking noblewoman.

'Perhaps you are, but you cannot allow it,' said Chaloner, while Kersey nodded fervently at his side. 'First, it would not be seemly, and second, she might

147

march up to Chiffinch's family and tell them what she has done. It will distress them and cause trouble for you.'

'Nonsense,' argued Wiseman. 'I am Surgeon to the Person, and who I invite to admire my skills are for me to decide. Not Chiffinch's family and not you either.'

Wiseman possessed an impressive physique to go with his larger-than-life personality. He was tall and muscular, and kept himself fit by lifting heavy stones each morning. He always dressed entirely in red, right down to his boots, and as his own auburn locks had started to lose their lustre, he had bought a massive wig made from fiery ginger hair. He was in one of his belligerent moods, almost certainly because staying with the Queen had deprived him of sleep. It meant he would be trying company until he had rested.

'You have not seen the body, so why are you so sure that Chiffinch was murdered?' Chaloner asked. 'Clarke thought it was natural causes.'

'And *that* is why,' replied Wiseman loftily. 'Clarke is an ass, and any diagnosis he makes is bound to be wrong. Ergo, I took the opposing view.'

Chaloner regarded him askance. 'You had me hunting a killer on that basis alone?'

Wiseman gave a superior smile. 'Along with some clever deductions that I shall explain after I have examined the body. Now, I shall partake of a small cup of wine and then begin.'

'How is the Queen?' asked Chaloner, knowing there was no point in urging him to hurry, so following him into the parlour where the Duchess was idly flicking through the ledger where Kersey wrote the names of all his guests.

Wiseman's expression softened. 'Past the worst, thank

148

God. Now she must rest, to allow her body to mend. Fortunately, that is no problem, because the poor lady sleeps all the time.'

'If you have finished drinking, Mr Wiseman, let us begin,' said the Duchess, speaking almost before the surgeon had taken his first sip. 'Time waits for no woman, and I have been here too long already. The Queen will be missing me.'

'She will not,' averred Wiseman, nettled. 'Indeed, she barely notices *me* keeping vigil at her bedside because she is so deeply asleep. But you are right in that time passes. Come.'

He led the way to the mortuary, the Duchess sweeping along imperiously at his heels. Eliza and Chaloner followed more reluctantly. They arrived to find that Kersey's assistant had prepared Chiffinch for the ordeal – clothes removed, surgical implements set out, and a bucket of clean water set ready to sluice away any mess. Wiseman donned a leather apron, warned everyone to stand well back, and began. Chaloner kept his eyes fixed on the dead man's face so he would not have to see what was happening further down, thinking that the Keeper of Jewels looked smaller, older and more insignificant now he was stripped of his worldly finery.

While Wiseman worked, the Duchess kept up a non-stop monologue about her plans to write a play featuring surgeons. To his credit, Wiseman did not allow it to distract him, and his replies were little more than grunts as he concentrated on the task at hand.

Chaloner was not squeamish, having seen more of death, battle and violence than most men, but there was something about the cold act of dissection that repelled him deeply. He glanced away, and saw the Duchess staring fixedly at a spot on the wall above Wiseman's head. He realised then that the self-serving chatter was her way of dealing with what was happening in front of her – that she was appalled, but did not know how to escape without losing face.

'Shall we go now, Your Grace?' he asked gently. 'Wiseman has almost finished.'

'Yes, I think I have seen enough,' said the Duchess, struggling for insouciance. 'I expected the art of anatomy would be . . . well, an art. Not all this hacking and yanking.'

'Hacking and yanking?' echoed Wiseman, looking up, affronted. 'I assure you, madam, that my dissections entail great finesse, and you will find me a far more elegant operator than all the other butchers in my profession.'

'What did you find?' asked Chaloner quickly, before there was a spat.

Wiseman straightened from the gore that had once been a living, breathing person. 'That I was right to claim Clarke was mistaken. Of course, it was not easy to discover the truth, and no other surgeon would have found it, but there *is* evidence of foul play. This man was murdered – by the most ingenious means I have ever encountered.'

Wiseman would say no more until he had sewn his subject back together and dabbled his fingers in a bucket of water. It immediately turned red, as did the cloth on which he then dried his hands. Kersey pursed his lips at the stains, although Chaloner thought he should have known better than to provide a white towel for the purpose. Then, with blood still encrusting his fingernails, Wiseman led the way back to Kersey's parlour.

They arrived to find Eliza and Topp there, having

150

grown tired of sitting in the carriage. Eliza hastened to see the Duchess comfortably seated, while Topp and Kersey fussed around her with cushions and wine.

'I did warn you, Your Loveliness,' said Topp, all paternal concern. 'I witnessed an anatomy myself when we were in Holland, and I have been unable to eat sausages ever since.'

'I never liked sausages anyway,' said the Duchess, and gave a wan smile. 'But I am glad I came, as I now have plenty of material for my play. I shall call it *The Bloody Barber.*'

'An excellent title, Your Grace,' gushed Topp, although Wiseman looked ready to argue.

Chaloner wanted the Duchess to leave, so that Wiseman could tell him what he had learned about Chiffinch in confidence. Unfortunately, she had other ideas. She indicated that Topp and Eliza were to sit next to her, and ordered Wiseman to begin his report. The surgeon took a sip of claret, then began to pontificate. He loved showing off.

'When I first heard that Chiffinch was alive and well at six o'clock, but dead by seven,' he began, 'I assumed an apoplexy or a seizure had carried him off. He was, after all, old, fat and unhealthy. However, I changed my mind the moment I heard Clarke burbling about impostumes. He is a buffoon, and how he was appointed Physician Royal, I shall never know.'

'So there was no impostume?' asked Chaloner, before he could embark on a diatribe.

'Chiffinch was wearing this locket,' said Wiseman, tossing it on the table; it contained a miniature portrait of one of the King's ex-mistresses, suggesting a degree of hypocrisy when Chiffinch had condemned others for breaking their marriage vows. 'And it was this that Clarke's questing fingers detected – that he mistook for an abscess. As I said, the man is an ass, who should not be trusted to tend Chaloner's chickens, let alone the King.'

'Are you suggesting that chickens deserve an ass to oversee their welfare?' asked the Duchess coolly. 'They are intelligent beings. As intelligent as us, in fact, although they lack the means to communicate their political and philosophical ideas.'

'Chaloner's hens are not intelligent,' quipped Wiseman. 'When I stopped off at home on the way here, my servants told me that one of them challenged a fox this morning, which was hardly sensible.'

Chaloner shot him an unpleasant look. Covent Garden was not 'on the way' to Westminster from White Hall, and he resented the surgeon taking detours while he himself had been left kicking his heels.

The Duchess sniffed. 'As you would not have bothered to mention the incident if the fox had won, I deduce that the hen did, so my point is proven: this bird saw a problem, assessed it critically, and devised a solution based on logic. Ergo, she *is* intelligent.'

'Chiffinch,' prompted Chaloner, before the discussion could range any further into the bizarre. 'You were telling us how he was murdered.'

'No,' corrected Wiseman pedantically. 'I was explaining how I knew that Clarke was wrong before I had proof of it in the locket that the fool mistook for an abscess. In short, there would have been specific symptoms if Clarke's diagnosis had been correct. I reflected on all my recent encounters with Chiffinch, and concluded that there were no such signs.'

152

'Very well,' said Chaloner. 'But it is a big leap from suspecting that Clarke made a mistake to saying that Chiffinch was unlawfully killed.'

'Yes,' acknowledged Wiseman. 'But by then, I was in possession of a second piece of information – one I had from Captain Rolt.'

'Which was?' prompted Chaloner impatiently when Wiseman paused for dramatic effect.

'That Chiffinch ate nothing all night except a large plate of oysters, which he had ordered in specially and that he did not share with anyone else. They were delivered to him at around midnight, and he swallowed them in fits and starts, until the last one slid down his throat at four o'clock, just before he took his leave.'

Irritably, Chaloner struggled to understand what the surgeon was saying. 'So he died from a surfeit? Or because one of these shellfish was bad?'

Wiseman shot him an arch glance. 'If that had been the case, there would have been vomiting and pain, and we all would have known about his discomfort.'

Chaloner controlled his exasperation with difficulty, although Wiseman was revelling in his role of shrewd detective. The Duchess was spellbound by his analysis, while Topp, Eliza and even Kersey hung on his every world.

'So what, then?' Chaloner demanded. 'Poison?'

'Yes, and the way it was administered was very clever. The killer must have known not only that his victim was a glutton for this particular dish, but also that he never chewed them.'

Using his hand, Wiseman mimicked someone tipping a shell and propelling a hapless crustacean straight down his throat.

'How do you know how he ate?' asked Chaloner, bemused. 'You were not there.'

'Because all twenty-four oysters were still whole – or virtually so – inside his stomach,' explained Wiseman. 'Unfortunately for him, each had been implanted with a little capsule of poison. Most of these pods are still intact, but a couple had ruptured, which was why he died. Death was inevitable with two or three doses, but with twenty-four . . .'

Chaloner glanced at the Duchess. *She* would be familiar with Chiffinch's eating habits, given that they met at Court. Moreover, the oysters must have been poisoned *before* they were delivered to him at midnight, as he would have noticed someone meddling with them once they were in his possession. And he recalled that the Duchess's alibi for that particular time was waiting – alone – in the parlour of a poet she had never met.

But surely she could not be so macabre as to want to see her victim anatomised? Or had she foisted herself on the procedure in the hope of preventing Wiseman from finding out what she had done? Or was she just an innocent but very peculiar lady with odd notions of what was acceptable behaviour?

'So I was right to predict foul play,' finished Wiseman with great satisfaction. 'And I was right to inform you of my suspicions before I had examined the corpse, so you could begin your hunt for the killer at once. I imagine it has given you an edge.'

'Not as much as if you had told me all this yesterday,' said Chaloner ungraciously.

'I considered the Queen's health more important,' said Wiseman loftily. 'Besides, my word alone should have been enough. Surely you trust my remarkable abilities by now? You have relied on them often enough in the past.'

'What was the poison?' asked Chaloner, declining to pander to his vanity.

'One containing henbane, probably. But do not expect to find the killer by tracing the apothecary who made it. Anyone with a modicum of medical knowledge could have thrown the ingredients together, and none are difficult to acquire.'

'But if Chiffinch ate the oysters between midnight and four o'clock, why was he still walking around – seemingly well – at six?' asked Chaloner, thinking about the man who had gossiped so disapprovingly to him about the Duchess and her preferred theatre-wear.

'The capsules are made of a substance that takes time to dissolve,' explained Wiseman, 'allowing the culprit to be well away from his victim when the toxin is released. Once that happened, death would have been fairly quick – less than an hour.'

'So who prepared the capsules?' asked Chaloner. 'From what you say, you have never encountered such a thing before, so the maker should not be too difficult to identify.'

'It is the *idea* that is clever, not the capsules themselves. Anyone could fashion them from the intestines of a rabbit and some weak glue.'

Chaloner considered the information, thoughts tumbling. How had the killer managed to insert the capsules into the oysters? And when? Clearly, a visit to White Hall's kitchens was required as a matter of urgency. He decided to go as soon as he left the charnel house.

'If I were investigating this crime,' said the Duchess,

155

'I would start by looking at those people he defeated at backgammon on the night he died. I won, of course, so I am exonerated.'

'No one would suspect you anyway, Your Sweetness,' Topp assured her. 'Everyone knows you are good, gentle and kind, even if your reading has taught you a lot about toxins.'

'Knowing and using are hardly the same,' said Eliza, shooting her husband a sharp look.

The Duchess stood to leave, thanking Wiseman for indulging her scientific curiosity. Then she swept out, Eliza at her side and Topp scurrying at their heels.

'Eliza is the more intelligent of those two women,' remarked Wiseman, when they had gone. 'I detect a sharp mind behind that modest façade, whereas the Duchess is not as clever as she thinks she is.'

'Should I include Eliza on my list of suspects then?' asked Chaloner. 'You did say the killer was ingenious.'

'I did, but I doubt Eliza is the guilty party. She cannot have known Chiffinch well, if at all. You would do better to concentrate your enquiries on Will, who has inherited some very lucrative posts and some lovely accommodation. Incidentally, there are visitors waiting for you at home. Two pretty young ladies.'

'For me? Are you sure?'

Wiseman nodded. 'I asked what they wanted, but they refused to say. I recommend you race home and find out what they want before they give up on you and leave. It would be a pity to miss them.'

'I will,' said Chaloner. 'But not before I have visited White Hall's kitchens to find out how Chiffinch's food came to be poisoned.'

*

The kitchens were less impressive than might have been expected for a palace with hundreds of residents needing to be fed. They comprised a sprawl of buildings, many of which were very inconveniently placed. Thus the bakery was some distance from the cellars where the flour was kept, while the buttery was nowhere near where the milk was delivered each day.

The kitchens were busy, as a veritable army of cooks, their assistants, scullions and children scurried about preparing the feast that would be served to the King and his Court later. When that was done, more food would be needed for the dozens of courtiers, footmen, maids and underlings who had served it and cleaned up afterwards. The rooms were hot, steamy, noisy and full of delicious smells.

The Master Cook was William Austen, a plump, red-faced man who looked as though he tasted each of his culinary creations personally before allowing them to be served. He gaped in horror when Chaloner explained what had happened to Chiffinch's oysters.

'But I have prepared thousands of them for him over the years, and nothing like this has ever happened before. Are you certain? There is no mistake?'

'None,' replied Chaloner. 'Did anyone other than Chiffinch eat oysters on Thursday?'

'No – most courtiers consider them vulgar, because they are so plentiful in season that paupers gorge on them. No White Hall resident wants to eat beggars' fare.'

'But Chiffinch did not mind?'

'He was unusual in that respect. He ate them live, with a sprinkling of lemon and salt.'

'Who supplies them to you?'

'The fish market in Lower Thames Street, where we

buy all our seafood. We have been using them for years, and I trust them implicitly. We were a little late ordering Chiffinch's repast that day, because his request slipped my mind until late afternoon. They did not arrive until about six in the evening.'

'What happened to them then?'

Austen wrung his chubby hands, frightened and defensive in equal measure. 'Like all perishable goods, they went directly to the larder, which is underground and thus cool. Oysters always go into a bucket of cold water, which keeps them fresh until they are needed.'

'Who has access to the larder?'

Austen indicated the labouring throng around them. 'Anyone who needs the ingredients that are stored in it. There are guards, who are meant to prevent theft, but their task is nigh on impossible, given that so many of us are in and out all day and night.'

'I see,' said Chaloner, realising with resignation that identifying the poisoner by tracking the oysters from the fish market to Chiffinch's plate would likely be hopeless. He persisted anyway. 'So what happened to them once they were in the bucket?'

'They remained there until just before midnight, when I sent one of the kitchen boys to fetch them. When they arrived, I arranged them on a platter, and added the lemon juice and salt. Then a page took them to Mr Chiffinch.'

'He did not want them sooner?'

'No – he had dined with the King at seven, so was not peckish again until later.'

The page was summoned, but all he could add was that he had taken the oysters straight to the Shield Gallery, and that Chiffinch had devoured five or six at once. The rest he had eaten at intervals through the night, with the last couple disappearing just before four o'clock, when he had retired to his apartments.

Chaloner was thoughtful. 'So the oysters were left unattended from six o'clock, when they arrived at the palace, until just before midnight?'

Austen nodded. 'Yes, so if Wiseman is right, these poisoned capsules must have been inserted between those two times. The responsibility lies with the larder, not the kitchens.'

'How do you know the toxin was not there when you bought them from the market?'

'Because we always rinse them thoroughly before putting them in the bucket of water. Anything nasty would have been washed out then.'

'Fair enough,' said Chaloner. 'Do you have any thoughts about the murder?'

'Only that the intended victim was definitely Chiffinch. It was common knowledge that he always had oysters when he spent the evening in the Shield Gallery.'

He took Chaloner to the larder, which comprised a series of cool cellars with thick walls, designed to keep perishable foodstuffs fresh. There Chaloner learned that although the door was always guarded, Austen was right to say that security was very lax. The sentries tended to admit anyone claiming to be on kitchen business, because the palace cooks were notoriously irascible and reacted with fury if their underlings failed to bring them what they wanted. Worse, some guards were rumoured to let anyone inside for a few pennies.

'No wonder it costs so much to keep White Hall in victuals,' said Chaloner, disgusted. 'Half of London can come in and load up.'

'Yes,' agreed Austen. 'So is there anything you would like, since you are here?'

Chaloner was so appalled by the dismal security that he marched straight to the guards' quarters and announced that their ineptitude and corruption might have allowed the killer to poison the King and his entire Court. His censure fell on deaf ears, and he was curtly informed that they did not need an old Parliamentarian to teach them how to do their jobs. He continued to argue, but gave up in disgust when they returned to their card game, clearly with no intention of listening to anything he had to say.

To take his mind off their criminal complacency, he turned his mind to the 'pretty young ladies' who had called on him at home. He wondered if they were still there, or if they had despaired of him ever returning and had left. He walked a little more quickly, but had only reached the end of King Street when he was inter- cepted by Swaddell. He grimaced. Was the assassin stalking him? He seemed to be everywhere.

'I could not find Rolt,' explained Swaddell. 'But it is evening now, so I imagine he will be preparing for another night of fun in the cockpit. Shall we go there together?'

But Chaloner had had enough for one day. 'I must return home. Wiseman says there are some ladies waiting to see me.'

Swaddell looked interested. 'In that case, I shall come to hear what they have to say. Perhaps they know who killed Chiffinch. And while we walk, you can describe what happened in the charnel house – and why you then went to White Hall.'

Chaloner did not mind telling him what Wiseman had

discovered, or about the shoddy practices among the palace guards, but he was not about to take the assassin home with him. Thus, while he spoke, most of his mind was devising ways to escape without causing offence.

'Chiffinch was better than most of the King's favourites,' mused Swaddell, when Chaloner had finished. 'He was not particularly underhand, all the bribes he took were modest, and he furnished White Hall with some lovely paintings.'

'Is that what will go on his epitaph?' asked Chaloner, amused. 'Not especially dishonest, only moderately corrupt, and had good taste in art?'

'I can think of worse – such as that he cheated at backgammon and was a judgemental hypocrite.' Swaddell cleared his throat. 'I have a list of suspects. Do you want to hear it?'

'Very well.'

'At the top are his brother and the Cockpit Club, all of whom he despised for being dissipated, which he felt damaged His Majesty's reputation. All bitterly resented his criticism.'

'Resented it enough to kill him?'

Swaddell shrugged. 'Perhaps, although I would have thought they would do it with political intrigue rather than murder, but . . .'

'The Cockpit Club has about thirty members. Are they all on your list?'

Swaddell nodded. 'But some names are higher up it than others. Such as Colonel Widdrington, because he is in charge; the outrageous Cobbe, because he loves to shock and Chiffinch's death has certainly done that—'

'Cobbe was not in London when Chiffinch died, and he says he has alibis to prove it.'

Swaddell continued as if he had not spoken. 'Captain Rolt, because he was first on the scene, using the pretext of a lost button; young Legg, because he is desperate to make an impression among his older, more urbane cronies; Ashley, because he is a drunk; and Tooley, because he is a mindless lout.'

'I see,' said Chaloner. 'Anyone else?'

'Yes – Dr Clarke. He is not in the Cockpit Club, although I think he would like to be. He is on my list for insisting that Chiffinch died of an impostume when he did not. I wonder what he will say once the truth emerges. It will reveal him either as incompetent or a liar, neither of which will do his reputation any good. Now tell me who you want to include.'

'The same people as you. However, two more Cockpit Club members deserve a specific mention: Bess Widdrington, because Chiffinch hated the husband she loves; and Viscount Mansfield, because he is weak, jealous and spiteful. I would also include his stepmother the Duchess of Newcastle, and Fanny Clarke.'

'I understand why you include the Duchess – it is hardly normal to want to see someone you know anatomised – but why Fanny?'

'Because Rolt did not find Chiffinch's body. *She* did.'

'Very well,' acknowledged Swaddell. 'Anyone else?'

Chaloner nodded. 'White Hall is a dangerous place, where ambition runs fierce, hot and deep. Any courtier with power will accrue enemies, so we shall have to identify all those that Chiffinch has made since he was appointed six years ago.'

'That will include your Earl,' warned Swaddell, then eyed him appraisingly. '*You* did not dispatch Chiffinch, did you? I will understand if you did – an order is an

162

order – but it would be awkward if I uncover proof that sees you in trouble.'

Chaloner regarded him askance. 'I would never poison anyone!'

'Nor would I,' agreed Swaddell earnestly. 'There is always a danger of killing the wrong target. A blade is much more reliable.' He removed one from his belt. 'This is Florentine steel, very expensive. There is nothing quite like it for slitting a throat. Would you like me to procure one for you?'

'No, thank you,' said Chaloner firmly, feeling the discussion was sliding into very dark waters. 'I am not an assassin, and the Earl would never ask such a thing of me.'

Unfortunately, the same could not be said of other nobles and courtiers, and Chaloner realised with a sense of despair that he would also have to find out which of Chiffinch's enemies were the kind of people to hire others to do their dirty work. That would not be easy.

'I must see what these ladies want,' he said tiredly, 'so will you go back to White Hall and look for Rolt?'

Swaddell shook his head. 'I should see these women, too. Perhaps they are the two who fought each other earlier – Dutch Jane and Chicken Molly. Maybe they have intelligence for us about our suspects at Newcastle House.'

Chaloner blinked. 'How on Earth did you reach that conclusion? And even if you are right, why would they visit me? They cannot possibly know where I live.'

'It would be easy enough to find out, and Dutch Jane has some experience in matters of espionage. She is a spy.'

'One of yours?'

'One of the enemy's. The clue is in the name, Tom – *Dutch* Jane. She tells the United Provinces' ambassador things she has learned from snooping about in Newcastle House.'

'What ambassador?' asked Chaloner. 'Michiel van Goch went home in January, when his government decided there was no hope of peace.'

'He is back, much against his will,' replied Swaddell. 'Ambassador Downing spies for us in The Hague, and the Hollanders realised that recalling van Goch had put them at a disadvantage. So they ordered him to return, and Dutch Jane is one of his informants.'

'You let her remain at large?'

Swaddell smiled superiorly. 'We use her: we write letters to the Duke about our war plans and ships, which we know she will see. All are false.'

'So she betrays her employers. Why? For money?'

Swaddell smirked. 'She thinks van Goch arranges for cash to be deposited with a goldsmith in Antwerp, but he "forgets", so her account is empty. Such is the lot of the spy – an unsavoury profession begets unsavoury liaisons. Present company excepted, of course.'

'She will find out soon. The Duchess has dismissed her, so she will be going home.'

'We heard,' said Swaddell, and grinned again. 'Dutch Jane will be livid when she finds out she has been working for free all these years.'

As it happened, Chaloner and Swaddell bumped into Rolt on King Street. The captain was walking from the direction of the cockpit. At first glance, his clothes appeared to be the height of fashion, but a closer inspection showed that the elbows in his coat were worn, while his shirt was made of rougher linen than courtiers usually favoured. Chaloner wondered if his failure to secure a Court sinecure meant he was getting desperate, and had dispatched a critic in order to improve his chances.

'We understand that you found Chiffinch's body,' he said, launching into an interrogation with a brusqueness that made his victim start in surprise.

'Then you understand wrong,' said Rolt indignantly. 'Fanny Clarke found the body. I just happened to be passing when she came reeling out, wailing for help.'

'Passing the cockpit?' echoed Swaddell incredulously. 'At seven o'clock in the morning?'

'I was searching for my lost button,' replied Rolt irritably. 'As I have already explained. I expected the place to be empty, so it seemed a good time to hunt.'

'Is that what you have been doing this evening?' probed Swaddell. 'Having another look for it? You must really want to locate the thing.'

Rolt shrugged. 'It belonged to my father and I am a sentimental fool. And yes, I thought I would have one final ferret about before the wrestling tonight. But I could not find it, so I must put it out of my mind.'

'Why did you not mention that you played such an important role in the discovery of Chiffinch's body?' demanded Chaloner. 'Helping Fanny Clarke to recover, going to inspect him for yourself, sending a servant for a *medicus*. All very heroic.'

Rolt shrugged again. 'All I did was sit her down and make sure she had not mistaken what she claimed to have seen. My actions were hardly worth alluding to. Besides, at the time, we thought he might have the plague, and I did not want to be shut away for forty days.'

'Chiffinch despised the Cockpit Club,' said Swaddell.

165

'He thought your wild carousing would harm the King. Indeed, I learned today that he aimed to see your cabal disbanded. What do you say to that?'

'He did advise us to moderate our behaviour,' acknowledged Rolt, 'but he could never have crushed us. We have too many powerful members and the support of the King.'

'Did you see him eating the night before he died?' asked Chaloner.

Rolt nodded. 'I have already told Surgeon Wiseman all this. Chiffinch had a plate of oysters, which arrived around midnight. He scoffed the lot over the course of the evening, and left at around four, saying he had business to attend to. I assumed he went to his rooms, so I was surprised when Fanny said he was in the cockpit.'

'On a different note,' said Swaddell, before Chaloner could press him further, 'Fanny and Bess deny going to the Red Bull. Are you sure it was them?'

'Fairly sure. But of course they deny it – the place is frequented by whores and rebels.'

Did this mean Eliza was educating prostitutes and insurgents with the Duchess's money? Chaloner supposed he would have to accept her invitation and find out. He bade Rolt good night, then hurried on to Covent Garden, Swaddell sticking to his heels like glue.

The parlour that Wiseman used for entertaining was eye-catching. It had been decorated by his lover, Temperance North, who ran a brothel off Fleet Street, and reflected her tastes as well as his own. There were scarlet-frilled curtains, comfortable chairs, and shelves along the walls that displayed his favourite anatomical specimens. He believed his grisly collection would be

166

conversation pieces for visitors, although there were very few of these, as Chaloner and Temperance were his only friends.

'My goodness!' breathed Swaddell, looking around in distaste. 'No wonder you were reluctant to bring me home. It is a chamber of horrors!'

Standing in the middle of the room, obviously uneasy and full of trepidation, were two young women. Both were pretty, with fair curls and grey eyes, and although their clothes were of good quality, they were unfashionable and much mended. The elder of the pair was politely demure, but the younger had a very mischievous grin.

'May I help you?' asked Chaloner, beginning to be suspicious. Wiseman and Temperance thought he should remarry, and were always suggesting 'suitable' candidates. Had they encouraged these women to visit, in the hope that one would take his fancy?

'Which of you is Thomas Chaloner?' asked the elder, her eyes flicking between him and Swaddell. 'Or are you just colleagues of the man who was here earlier? We thought he was the devil when he exploded in on us, dressed all in red and leering like a pirate.'

'Wiseman has that effect on people,' acknowledged Chaloner, aware of Swaddell chortling under his breath. 'But he is no demon. Just Surgeon to the Person.'

'What person?' asked the younger woman, intrigued. 'Yours?'

'The King's,' explained Chaloner, supposing the title would sound peculiar to those unfamiliar with it. 'Wiseman tends His Majesty and the Court.'

'Is he married?' she asked keenly.

Chaloner blinked, taken aback. Wiseman's wife had been incurably insane for years, but had fallen prey to

167

the plague the previous year, despite the surgeon's best efforts to keep her safe. Everyone who had met her thought her death was a blessed relief from the tormented hell of her ruined mind, although Wiseman disagreed and felt he had failed her. Chaloner admired the fact that his friend had never given up on her, and had consistently put her welfare above his own convenience and happiness.

'Not any more,' he replied, deciding not to mention Temperance until he knew more about who was asking. 'Why do you want to know?'

'Never mind,' replied the girl, and smiled in a way that was vaguely predatory. 'I am sure there are others who will suit our needs. Preferably ones who are younger and more handsome. Rich is important, obviously, but it should not be our only consideration.'

Chaloner looked from one to the other, and saw there was something familiar about their eyes: they were the same shade of grey as his father's. And his own, for that matter.

'Do I know you?' he asked curiously.

'We have never met,' replied the older with quiet dignity, 'but you will have heard of us. We are your cousins, Ursula and Veriana, daughters of your Uncle James.'

Chaloner was aware of an uncomfortable feeling growing in the pit of his stomach. He was usually pleased to meet other members of his enormous clan, but he sensed trouble would follow if he began to associate with the progeny of Uncle James – the fervent Parliamentarian, whose wife and children had remained on the Isle of Man after the Restoration, shunning all contact with the rest of the family.

'*James* Chaloner?' asked Swaddell, his usually flat black

eyes bright with interest. 'Is that the fellow who was arrested for supporting Cromwell's rogue government? Word is that he deliberately swallowed poison when he was in prison, to avoid being tried for treason.'

Veriana, the older girl, glared at him. 'That is a lie put about by spiteful Royalists who were disappointed because he passed away before they had finished hounding him. Our father departed this life because he caught a sickness in their horrible gaol.'

'It must have been difficult for you,' said Chaloner hastily, before she could quarrel with a man who might report the discussion to the Spymaster. 'But why are you here? I hope it is nothing to do with reclaiming Chaloner Court from its current owners.'

'Unfortunately, our lawyers say the government's seizure of that house cannot be challenged,' said Veriana bitterly. 'It is lost to us for ever, along with everything else we once owned. They even took Ursula's dolls.'

'Although I do not play with those any more,' put in Ursula hastily. 'I am eighteen now, and too old for such nonsense. Indeed, I am ready for a husband, which is why we are here.'

'You are to be married?' asked Chaloner politely. 'Congratulations.'

'Thank you,' said Veriana briskly. 'But your felicitations are premature, because first, you must find us suitable partners.'

'*I* must?' blurted Chaloner, startled. 'I hardly think—'

'Our family is destitute,' interrupted Veriana. 'Our mother survives by mending shirts, and our brother Edmund is an impoverished country parson. Ergo, Ursula and I must make good marriages. Ones that will restore the family fortune.'

169

'I appreciate that,' said Chaloner. 'But I cannot—'

'You are a courtier with important connections,' cut in Veriana. 'And our mother wants you to use them on our behalf.'

'I am sure she does,' said Chaloner coolly, 'but it is out of the question.'

'But if you refuse,' cried Ursula, distraught, 'we shall be condemned to wed tenant farmers with no prospects, and our branch of the family will be doomed to penury for ever. *Everything* depends on you.'

'So no pressure, Tom,' muttered Swaddell, smirking his amusement.

'But I have no idea how to go about organising such matters,' objected Chaloner, sure it would be a lot harder than it sounded, given that some matches were rumoured to be years in the making. 'You will be better off applying to—'

'So who will you choose for me?' asked Ursula eagerly. 'Rich *and* handsome, remember. And preferably young.'

Veriana shot her a warning glance. 'Rich will suffice. We are prepared to sacrifice our happiness for family honour, so you are free to choose whomsoever you please. Neither of us will question your decisions.'

'Even so, I cannot help,' said Chaloner firmly. 'Our name is not one people are willing to associate with these days. You should go home and—'

'There is nothing for us at home,' blurted Ursula, tears starting in her eyes. 'All the eligible rich men are taken. You are our only hope.'

'I will help,' offered Swaddell, and smiled, revealing his sharp little teeth and red tongue. Chaloner saw both women take a step back, unsettled. 'Do not worry about a thing.'

Ursula and Veriana were not the only ones unnerved by this offer. So was Chaloner, who did not want Swaddell's assistance in such a personal matter. Indeed, he did not want the task at all, so it was with considerable misgiving that he even agreed to let the girls stay the night. Before they could thank him, he warned them that they would be on the first coach home in the morning, although it would not be with spouses in tow. He was powerless to do anything about that.

'I will see *you* tomorrow,' he told Swaddell curtly when the assassin started to accompany them upstairs. 'White Hall kitchens at noon, where we will see if we can learn any more about how these oysters came to be poisoned. Someone must have seen something useful.'

Swaddell did not look convinced, and Chaloner did not blame him, suspecting they had gone as far as they could go with that particular line of enquiry.

'Good evening, then, ladies,' said the assassin, effecting a bow that was all thin black legs and sharp elbows. 'And welcome to our fine city. You will like it here, I promise.'

When he left, he was humming and there was a definite spring in his step.

Chaloner inspected and rejected several bedrooms before he found one that met his approval, which essentially meant one that was not filled with alarming medical specimens or piles of risqué spare clothing from Temperance's brothel. It was, however, thick with cobwebs, although the women were too well-mannered – or too desperate – to complain.

'We will unpack tomorrow,' said Ursula, plumping herself down on the bed and then coughing as dust billowed around her. 'Although you must buy us some

171

new clothes, or people at Court will think that we are fortune hunters.'

Well, you are, thought Chaloner, aware that her words showed she had no intention of being sent home the next day.

'We will pay you back,' promised Veriana. 'Once we have rich husbands.'

'It is not the money,' said Chaloner, although equipping two young ladies for White Hall would use up funds he had set aside for his own family. 'It is that I do not know how to begin.'

Ursula smiled rather wolfishly. 'Oh, do not worry about that. All you need do is introduce us to any wealthy man in need of a wife, and we will manage the rest.'

She and Veriana went to the window, and began to scrub away the grime so they could look out, chatting excitedly as they peered down at the piazza below. Watching them, Chaloner tried to think of anyone he knew who was in the market for a spouse. There were two ancient clerks at the Treasury, although he doubted his cousins would be thrilled by those. Then there were several single Cockpit Club men – Cobbe, Legg, Ashley and Tooley, for example – but they would do nothing to restore family honour, and would never agree to allying themselves with a family of Parliamentarians anyway.

Just when he was beginning to despair, two names popped into his mind. First, there was his friend Will Leybourn, the mathematician–surveyor; he was a good man who earned a respectable wage. And second was Captain Salathiel Lester, currently at sea fighting the Dutch.

He decided to write to them as soon as he had caught Chiffinch's killer.

Chapter 6

The next day was Palm Sunday, and as registers were kept of those attending church – anyone who stayed away was suspected of that most heinous of crimes, religious dissension – Chaloner had no choice but to put in an appearance at St Paul's, Covent Garden. However, the service was not until mid-morning, and as he had risen shortly after three o'clock, woken by a churning unease about his cousins, he had plenty of time to pursue the matter of Chiffinch's murder first.

He donned his grey long-coat and breeches, but recalling what the Earl's clerk had said about his dowdy clothes making him sinister, he tied a blue ribbon around his hat. Then he crept down the stairs and left via the back door. He could hardly call on witnesses or ask questions about Chiffinch's death at such an ungodly hour, so he took a hackney carriage to the Red Bull in Clerkenwell, to determine what manner of place it was – if it was still open to revellers or respectably closed.

It was not a pleasant night, with rain hissing down in sheets. The roads were already muddy rivers, and one or two drenched early-risers tried to hail his carriage as it rattled past, keen to share his ride. The driver ignored them, for which Chaloner was grateful, as he wanted to be alone with his thoughts and concerns.

The Red Bull was a timber-framed tavern on John Street, east of the green. It had a number of spacious public rooms, and a large courtyard. It had once been a famous theatre, but had since been surpassed by the richer, bigger, purpose-built playhouses in Drury Lane. It was closed, but Chaloner picked the lock on a side door, and spent half an hour exploring. When he had finished, he could state with certainty that it was not a brothel, and that Eliza's school had a large number of pupils, judging by the great piles of books stacked in every corner.

He slipped away when women began to arrive for pre-dawn classes, all heavy-eyed from lack of sleep, but determined to study before their daily rounds. Then he prowled the surrounding area, fulfilling his promise to Thurloe to monitor it for signs of trouble.

There was certainly an atmosphere. Resentment still festered that the King had abandoned Londoners to the plague, then strolled back in the expectation that everyone would be pleased to see him. Worse, there was a consensus that his immorality had brought the disaster down on them in the first place, so anti-monarchist sentiment was rife. But there was also hope, inspired by Mother Broughton's prophecies, that the city was heading for a brighter, kinder, fairer future. Chaloner wondered what would happen when Easter Day arrived and folk woke up to find that nothing had changed.

He wandered deeper into the overcrowded slums between Smithfield and the Fleet River, an area that never slept, and heard the seer's name on many lips.

Most talked about her predictions concerning the dead rising from their graves, and there was a widespread belief that it would be wise to avoid cemeteries for the next few days. Alehouses were abuzz with activity – workers fortifying themselves for the day ahead, or revellers still enjoying the night before. Cheers and angry squawks from one told him that courtiers were not the only ones who liked cockfighting.

He was about to leave when he saw someone slinking along so furtively that he could not help but stop to watch. The man wore a hooded cloak, and kept glancing behind him, to see if he was being followed. He was so intent on staying invisible that he did not watch where he was going, and stumbled in a pothole. The curse that followed was in a voice Chaloner knew.

'Barker?' he called, watching the Earl's clerk jump in alarm. 'What are you doing here?'

'I might ask you the same thing,' retorted Barker sharply. 'It is not nice to jump out on people in the dark. Did no one ever tell you that?'

'I am on the Earl's business,' replied Chaloner, honestly enough.

Barker peered at him. 'You mean Chiffinch's murder? His killer lives *here*?'

'I am following a number of leads,' replied Chaloner, not about to be specific lest Barker told the Earl, who was notoriously indiscreet. 'But speaking of Chiffinch, what can you tell me about him? I barely knew the man, and would value your opinion.'

Barker pondered. 'Well, he loved the King, and deplored anything that might hurt him or his reputation – which included the antics of his brother, the Cockpit Club, the Duchess of Newcastle, and, on occasion, our

175

Earl. He was fairly honest, and neither prim nor debauched.'

Chaloner knew all this. 'Have you heard anything about him moving from grumbles to actual plots against those he had taken against?'

'Not specifically, but he was a courtier, so I would not be surprised if he had. I would say his death is good news for our Earl, but enemies are like sewage leaking into a cellar – you scoop away one foul bucket, but more oozes in to take its place.'

'True,' agreed Chaloner, and changed the subject. 'So why are you here at such an hour?'

'My mother lives in John Street, and the only time I can visit her is when the Earl is asleep. When he is awake, his demands on me are constant.'

'I am sure they are,' said Chaloner. 'But your mother died last summer.'

'She got better,' replied Barker shortly. 'But I must return to Clarendon House before the Earl misses me. Nice hat-ribbon, by the way. The lasses will love it.'

He shot away, leaving Chaloner to watch him uneasily. Why was the clerk lying about his reason for being in Clerkenwell? Did he have a lover, and wanted to keep her existence from his latest elderly wife? Or had he been there for a darker reason, perhaps relating to whatever trouble was brewing in the area? After all, it was not just Londoners who deplored White Hall's excesses – so did many palace servants, who were exposed to them on a daily basis. It was entirely possible that Barker was one of these, and Chaloner saw he would have to be alert for rebellious rumblings in Clarendon House if he wanted to keep his employer safe.

*

176

On his way home, Chaloner passed the Duke and Duchess of Newcastle's residence. All the upstairs windows were shuttered, but lamps blazed in the stables. He went to find out why, and discovered a rumpus concerning a colicky mare. Clayton, the sullen steward, was walking the ailing animal around the yard, while the Duke shouted anxious advice. His voice was loud, and had woken the other servants, who had come to watch. They included Clayton's two disagreeable friends – Liddell the horse-trader and Vicar Booth. Chaloner went to talk to them.

'These nags have better accommodations than I do,' said Booth, glowering around with open envy. 'And the Duke prefers that mare to his own son. Poor Mansfield would be better loved if he had pointed ears and a tail.'

'So would we,' growled Liddell, while Chaloner marvelled anew at their indiscreet grumbles. 'Although I am glad he is taking such pains to save Henrietta Florence. She is a fabulous beast, and it would be a crying shame to lose her.'

'Your "fabulous beast" sympathises with criminals,' retorted Booth darkly. 'A thief stole my purse last Wednesday, and I chased him into her stall. She would not let me get near him – every time I tried, she feinted at me. The rogue escaped in the end, thanks to her antics.'

'Was it a very full purse?' asked Liddell sympathetically.

'No, but I cannot afford to lose a penny, given my recent misfortunes.' Booth elaborated for Chaloner's benefit. 'My church, St Quentin's, was struck by lightning and caught fire. The year of three sixes is certainly unlucky for me, because that disaster came hot on the heels of a flood in my house and my father being struck down with a palsy.'

177

'I have had some vile luck myself,' sighed Liddell unhappily. 'My stables were damaged in a storm and I lost a foal to fever. Then there is the rent I pay the Duke. It used to be a fair sum, but the Duchess said it was too low and insisted on doubling it. It was unkindly done.'

'She does not care about tenants and servants,' averred Booth bitterly. 'Just about her books and how many copies she can sell. Did you hear what she did to Dutch Jane? Cast out without a penny? And her a foreigner in a strange land! I cannot say I liked Dutch Jane, but that was just plain cruel.'

'It is Topp's fault for always telling the Duchess that she is the best philosopher and playwright in the world,' put in Liddell acidly. 'She believes him and now thinks that whatever drivel oozes from her pen will rival that of Plato and Aristotle.'

At that point, Clayton called for Liddell to take over walking the sick horse. Once the steward had handed over the bridle, he came to stand with Chaloner and Booth, wiping his sweaty face with his sleeve.

'I think we are winning the battle,' he reported, although Booth was not very interested. 'Poor Henrietta Florence. She *will* bolt her food.'

'Liddell and I were talking about Topp,' Booth told him. 'And how he encourages the Duchess to write, even though she is not very good at it.'

'Topp!' spat Clayton. 'Always telling people what they most want to hear. And I am sure he steals from the mistress he claims to adore. Did you hear about the silver ship-shaped brooch that went missing? I am sure *he* took it. He does not really love her – just her money.'

'Eliza loves her, though,' conceded Booth, albeit reluctantly. 'They are more like sisters than mistress and

178

servant.' Then his spiteful little face hardened. 'I cannot abide Eliza or her silly ideas about teaching women their rights. What rights? I tell my wife to sit at home and give me heirs, which is all she should expect from life.'

But Clayton was already thinking about something else. 'There were ghosts abroad in Bunhill cemetery last night. Did you hear?'

'No, but I am not surprised,' replied Booth. 'Mother Broughton predicted it. She said the dead would rise from their graves: Bunhill first, then Westminster Abbey.'

Chaloner started to ask for details, but more people had poured into the yard to see what was going on, and there were now so many that he was jostled away from the gossiping pair. One of the new arrivals was Molly, who gave him a shy smile. Then she was almost knocked from her feet as Viscount Mansfield bulled roughly past her. She was saved from a tumble by Baron Lucas, who was walking behind the younger man.

'Have a care, boy!' he bawled. 'Only oafs ride rough-shod over their servants.'

Mansfield whipped around to regard his step-uncle challengingly. 'Tell that to your sister, who dismissed Dutch Jane over some trivial nonsense. I was shocked by her callousness.'

Lucas opened his mouth to reply, but at that moment, the Duke released a great whoop of joy, jabbing an excited finger at a steaming pile of horse dung. Henrietta Florence was on the mend. Everyone surged forward to express their delight. Mansfield was first, but his good wishes were so obviously insincere that his father only inclined his head in polite acknowledgement. Then others crowded

179

around and the Duke's face split into a grin as he accepted their more genuine felicitations.

'Be a man,' Chaloner heard Lucas inform the resentful Viscount. 'If you want him to love you, do something to deserve it.'

'I should not have to,' snapped Mansfield petulantly. 'He should take me as I am. Why should I have to fight for what should be freely given?'

Chaloner did not want to be caught listening to that sort of conversation, and slipped away before either of them noticed him.

As dawn was still only a yellow smear of promise in the night sky, Chaloner decided to go to Bunhill cemetery, to find out exactly what had happened there the previous night. It had nothing to do with Chiffinch, but Thurloe would appreciate a report, given his concerns about the area.

He walked briskly, aware of smoke belching from chimneys as thousands of Londoners heated water for washing, cleaning and cooking. Church bells tolled all over the city, advertising the first of their Sunday services, a bright sound over the deeper rumble of the many feet, hoofs and wheels on cobbles. He hurried past the Charterhouse with its towering walls, then skirted the Artillery Ground, where musketeers drilled, reminding all who saw them that England was currently at war.

Beyond the Artillery Ground was Bunhill Fields, part of which had been set aside for a burial ground during the plague, when the city graveyards began to overflow. The disease had relinquished its hold before any pits could be dug there, but a man named Mr Tyndal had

180

paid for the designated area to be enclosed by walls anyway, anticipating that there would always be a demand for graves, and that money could be made from it.

Chaloner arrived to find Tyndal supervising a funeral. The mourners wore the kind of clothes that revealed them to be nonconformists, for whom the Bunhill cemetery was perfect – most of it was unconsecrated, so Quakers, Baptists and their ilk could use it without compromising their religious beliefs. All carried lanterns, indicating that the deceased had been a person of substance – lamp fuel was expensive, so burying someone in the dark was a public statement of wealth.

Tyndal was a thin, cadaverous individual with long bony limbs, who was forever wringing his oversized hands. He twisted and rubbed them obsequiously until the last mourner had filed past him through the gate, then heaved a sigh of relief.

'Thank God that is over! Mr Bagshaw was meant to be buried at midnight, but *things* were seen, so we had to delay until they had gone. His family expressed an immediate desire to take him somewhere else, so I had to bribe them to stay with a hefty discount.'

Chaloner introduced himself as an envoy of the Lord Chancellor, then said, '"Things"?'

'The walking dead,' elaborated Tyndal hoarsely. 'Of course, we knew they were coming, because Mother Broughton mentioned it. Is that not so, boys?'

The last question was aimed at four men who stood nearby, all larger, younger versions of himself. In the gloom of approaching dawn, they looked vaguely eerie, and Chaloner had noticed a number of the departing funeral party shoot them wary glances as they passed.

181

'Did you see these mobile corpses yourselves?' Chaloner asked. 'Or did someone just tell you about them?'

'Oh, we saw them,' replied Tyndal grimly. 'At first, we thought they were grave-robbers. Surgeons pay handsomely for fresh specimens, you see, and some are not too picky about where they come from.'

'So what did you see exactly?'

'Well,' began Tyndal, 'we were over by the wood, trimming the turf around Edward Bagshaw's new-dug grave . . . Have you heard of him? He was a famous Puritan divine.'

'Of course.' Chaloner struggled for patience. 'But you were by the wood and you saw . . .'

'The dead,' replied Tyndal in an unsteady voice. 'They wore long black cloaks to conceal their mouldering bones, and they carried their red-glowing souls in little pots.'

'It is true,' put in the biggest son. 'I did not believe Mother Broughton's prophecy before last night. You cannot afford to be superstitious in our line of work, so I usually treat such claims with a healthy scepticism. But now I have seen those terrible figures . . .'

'We fled,' finished Tyndal. 'As fast as our legs could carry us.'

'How do you know it was not a prank?' asked Chaloner, thinking it sounded ludicrous enough to be risible. 'Or one of Mother Broughton's disciples, aiming to add credence to her prophecies by ensuring that one "came true"?'

'Because we know a cadaver when we see one,' replied Tyndal firmly. 'I ran straight to the nearest church and begged the vicar to come and recite some dead-banishing prayers. Only when he pronounced our cemetery safe again did we allow the Bagshaw ceremony to proceed.'

182

Chaloner asked exactly where the 'dead' had been seen, and went to investigate. None of the Tyndals offered to accompany him.

The cemetery was enormous, but as it had only been operational for a few months, it was mostly devoid of graves. The rest was undulating pasture broken by an occasional scrap of woodland. The 'dead' had been spotted inside the largest copse, near the westernmost wall. Chaloner explored it carefully, and found a rope that someone had used to scale the wall, along with footprints in the mud at the bottom. As he had thought, there had been no walking corpses – just people using Bunhill for reasons of their own.

The only other thing of interest was something that was almost invisible in the long grass, evidently having been dropped by mistake. It was a bonnet of an unusual style. He had seen it, or one very similar, on Dutch Jane. He picked it up and saw that a brooch had been pinned to the inside, to keep it out of sight. It was silver and in the shape of a ship. He recalled that Clayton had mentioned something of the kind going missing from Newcastle House and had accused Topp of stealing it. Clearly, the surly steward owed his rival an apology.

As his route home took him past Newcastle House, Chaloner stopped to return the brooch and ask if anyone knew why Dutch Jane had been in Bunhill the previous evening, possibly pretending to be a walking corpse. He entered the yard, and saw Topp and Eliza there, watching servants wash the coach that would take the Duke and Duchess to church later.

'They intend to ride there?' asked Chaloner, startled.

'But the church abuts their house. Surely it would be quicker to walk?'

Eliza shot him a mock-stern look. 'Walk? Perish the thought!'

'Besides, I would sooner carry my beloved Duchess on my back than let her sully her feet in London's filth,' declared Topp stoutly, then reconsidered. 'Although she may be a little too heavy for me these days.'

'If such heroics are necessary, we shall ask Clayton to do it,' said Eliza acidly. 'He is good at lugging hefty burdens about – far more so than the delicate business of estate management.'

'True,' agreed Topp, and smiled at Chaloner, revealing cracked yellow teeth. 'I am pleased you offered to bow your viol for us on Wednesday, Your Honour. It will be much nicer than the flageolets he had intended to hire.'

Chaloner had 'offered' nothing of the kind, and had no intention of playing in Newcastle House, sure he would be too busy. He flailed around for an excuse to decline.

'I am afraid my cousins arrived unexpectedly last night, so I am needed at home.'

He did not bother to say that the girls would be gone long before Wednesday.

'Bring them, Your Worship,' gushed Topp. 'The Duchess will not mind, especially if they can sing or play an instrument.'

'Although she will think more of them if they have some *useful* skills,' put in Eliza. 'Like reading and knowing their own minds. Any ape can bow a jig.'

'But not any ape can make it sound pleasant,' retorted Chaloner, thinking the remark revealed her as a barbarian.

'Men use music to keep women in their place,' announced Eliza pompously, 'by forcing them to practise,

184

so they have no time for more worthy pursuits. I thank God daily for my own dear husband. *He* is not afraid of clever ladies.'

Chaloner glanced at Topp, and decided it was not progressive thinking that prompted the man to grant Eliza her freedom, but fear of what she might do to him if he stood in her way.

'So bring these cousins, Your Honour,' said the steward, speaking to bring an end to the sparring. 'They will be most welcome.'

Chaloner declined again, but Topp was insistent, claiming first that the Duchess would be disappointed to lose a decent violist, and then that she would want to meet two talented young ladies. The second point prompted Chaloner to reflect that he did not know if the girls *had* any talents, and if they did, whether they were socially acceptable ones. What if they took after him, and had an aptitude for spying or swordplay?

'You are kind,' he said briskly, 'but I do not—'

'Good, it is settled then, Your Nobleness,' said Topp. 'There is no need to bring your own viol, because we have hired a set. The Duchess cannot abide instruments that do not match, and says that the look of them is much more important than the way they sound.'

'Does she indeed?' murmured Chaloner, thinking the occasion was sounding worse and worse. He hastened to ask his questions so that he could leave before he was bludgeoned into something else against his will. 'Clayton mentioned a missing brooch earlier—'

'The silver ship,' interrupted Topp wearily. 'He thinks I took it, but I never did. Why would I would steal from the mistress I love? And why would I risk losing a nice job with a large salary and free accommodation?'

Chaloner rummaged in his pocket. 'Is this it?'

Topp snatched it from him. 'Where did you find it? *Please* tell me that Clayton sold it to you. I should love to see him disgraced.'

'It was pinned inside this.' Chaloner presented the hat.

Eliza frowned. 'That is Dutch Jane's cap. Are you saying *she* stole the Duchess's jewellery? I suppose she might have done. She *was* caught red-handed with a pilfered hen.'

'Have you seen her since she was dismissed?'

'No, but I cannot say I miss her,' replied Eliza. 'She had developed a nasty habit of listening at keyholes and pawing through personal documents. She never did it when we lived in Holland, but the moment we arrived in England . . . I wondered if she was a spy, to be frank.'

Topp scoffed. 'My lady is only interested in academic pursuits, while my Duke is only concerned with horses. I cannot see the enemy learning anything of value from them.'

'So Dutch Jane has not been back, begging to be reinstated?' asked Chaloner.

'Just once, Your Brilliance,' said Topp. 'But she was more indignant than contrite, so I gave her some money and sent her on her way.'

'Enough for her to buy passage home?'

'No, but more than she deserved – and more than the Duchess would have wanted me to give. My lady was furious with her, because her antics hurt Molly, who is a simple child. Moreover, the Duchess had decreed that all our poultry were under her personal protection, so the theft of a chicken was a deliberate affront to her authority.'

186

'Why all these questions?' asked Eliza curiously. 'And why do you have Jane's bonnet?'

'I found it in Bunhill cemetery. Do you know why she might have been there?'

Eliza raised her eyebrows in astonishment. 'I cannot see her – or anyone from Newcastle House – frequenting such a place. She would have been afraid of meeting its walking corpses.'

'And those *have* been out and about,' put in Topp. 'Our milkmaid told us this morning. Apparently, cloaked skeletons were seen carrying their bloodied souls in glowing cauldrons.'

'Pranksters,' said Chaloner dismissively. 'Or cronies of Mother Broughton, who want everyone to think her predictions are coming true. Dutch Jane was probably one of them, given that her hat was found where these so-called bodies were seen.'

'You are wrong,' stated Eliza firmly. 'First, Dutch Jane would never pretend to be a corpse – she is far too dour for japes, not to mention far too superstitious. And second, Mother Broughton is a great seer whose prophecies are always accurate. Have you met her?'

'No,' acknowledged Chaloner. 'But she is—'

'Then come with me now. I shall introduce you, and you can judge her for yourself.'

Chaloner followed Eliza to the maze of alleys between Clerkenwell Green and the Fleet River, where Mother Broughton occupied a small, mean cottage at the end of a row. Eliza rapped on the door, which was answered by a woman whom she introduced as Joan Cole the tobacco-seller. Joan smiled at her, but regarded Chaloner with such rank suspicion that he supposed his attempt to

187

render himself less sinister with a gay hat ribbon had not been entirely successful.

The house was tiny, comprising a downstairs parlour and an attic for sleeping. The floor was of beaten earth, yet was very respectably furnished: new stools around a handsome table, a gleaming set of copper pots hanging over the hearth, and some clean, bright cushions. They all looked like recent acquisitions, so he supposed they were gifts from admirers.

Mother Broughton sat in a throne-like chair by the fire, smoking her pipe. The room was hot to the point of stifling, and Chaloner, whose clothes were still damp from poking around the cemetery, began to steam. Predictably, the seer was offended when Eliza told her that there was some doubt over the authenticity of Bunhill's ambling cadavers.

'I am a genuine soothsayer; I have no need for deceit,' she snapped. 'My prophecies *will* come true, so I do not need anyone to help them along. Perhaps Dutch Jane went to the cemetery to *watch* the walking corpses, and fled when she saw they were real, dropping her bonnet in the process.'

Eliza looked doubtful. 'I do not see her visiting a cemetery in the dark.'

Mother Broughton sniffed. 'I do. She is a nasty piece, and took against me after I foretold that she would come to a bad end – one entailing a vat of milk and a sausage.'

'Goodness!' muttered Chaloner, trying to envisage how that could possibly come about. Then he thought about the rest of Mother Broughton's testimony. If she and Dutch Jane had fallen out, then it was unlikely that Jane would go to Bunhill and put on a show on her behalf,

188

so what *had* she been doing in a place that must have been eerie at night, especially for someone who Eliza said was superstitious?

'Do you know where I might find her?' he asked.

The women shook their heads. 'But I will ask around,' offered Eliza. 'And if I track her down, I will say that you will pay for her time. Greed will bring her running to your door.'

'Then do it quickly,' advised Mother Broughton. 'I told you: her days are numbered.'

'I heard your predictions for the coming week,' said Chaloner, supposing he had better learn more about them for Thurloe's benefit. 'Walking corpses in Westminster on Tuesday, the death of a messenger on Thursday, and weeping and wailing on Good Friday, along with a covering of darkness.'

'It will all come to pass, just as I say,' declared Mother Broughton comfortably. 'However, you left out the best bit – the joy of Easter Day, when all sin and evil will be wiped away, leaving the righteous in charge. I shall be one of them, of course, and I am looking forward to having a bit of power.'

'I am sure you are,' said Chaloner. 'So what happens to the rest of us?'

'The wicked will die, but do not worry, because you will not be among them. I predict that you will leave London and devote your life to cheese.'

Chaloner blinked, wrong-footed. 'To *cheese*?'

Mother Broughton smiled enigmatically. 'You will see.'

Outside, a bell began to chime the hour, and Eliza cocked her head. 'I must go. My lady will be waiting for me to accompany her to church. Now, do not forget,

189

Mr Chaloner – the Red Bull tonight. Your eyes will be opened in ways that you cannot possibly imagine.'

Chaloner was not sure he liked the sound of that.

As there were no coaches travelling west that day, Chaloner took his cousins to the Palm Sunday service in the Covent Garden church, although he doubted the wisdom of this decision when Wiseman accompanied them, and it transpired that Ursula had a provocatively swaying gait of which any prostitute would be proud. Thus it appeared as though he and the surgeon had secured themselves a couple of harlots.

'They are my cousins,' he informed a smirking Dr Clarke, knowing exactly what the Court physician was thinking.

'Of course they are,' replied Clarke with a man-of-the-world wink. 'I have a "cousin", too. Her frolicking company is always a delightful change from my dull old wife.'

'How can you frolic with a cousin, yet have a wife as well?' asked Veriana guilelessly.

'Lord!' muttered Chaloner, while Wiseman smothered a snort of laughter.

'I take it you are new to London, my dear,' said Clarke with an indulgent leer. 'So allow me to explain. Men are—'

'Why are you here, Clarke?' interrupted Chaloner hastily, not about to stand by while a courtier corrupted his cousins, although he suspected that the younger but more world-wise Ursula would learn nothing she did not already know. 'What is wrong with your own parish church in Clerkenwell?'

Clarke pulled a disagreeable face. 'Its services never

start on time, because the vicar is obliged to wait for the Newcastles, who turn up when the fancy takes them. I cannot afford to waste hours sitting around doing nothing. I am a busy man.'

'I see,' said Chaloner, wondering if other parishioners thought the same, and if so, whether it was yet another grievance that Londoners could bring against the nobility.

'Besides, this is a better place to meet new patients,' Clarke went on. 'In Clerkenwell, too many mansions have their own chapels, whereas most rich Covent Garden folk worship here.'

'They do,' agreed Wiseman. 'Why do you think I bought a house on the piazza? Incidentally, did you hear that I examined Chiffinch yesterday and revealed you to be a fool of the first order?'

Clarke scowled. 'You had no right! It shows a lack of professional courtesy.'

'He discovered the truth about Chiffinch's death,' countered Chaloner, before Wiseman could respond with something more forceful. 'Namely that he did not die of an impostume, but was murdered. Your diagnosis would have allowed a killer to go free.'

Clarke eyed him coolly. 'I suppose you think that *I* did something to harm him, then gave a verdict of natural causes to conceal my crime. But you are wrong. I liked Chiffinch. Indeed, he was one of my wealthiest – and thus most valued – clients. Believe me, he was worth far more to me alive than dead, and his demise is a serious financial blow.'

He turned and stalked away before Chaloner could ask him any more.

'I pity his wife,' declared Ursula, watching him go. 'She married an arse.'

191

'That sort of language will not encourage respectable suitors,' warned Chaloner, although he was aware that the rebuke made him sound like a stuffy old matron.

Ursula winked roguishly. 'Then I will have to settle for the other sort. As we said yesterday, it does not really matter, as long as they are rich.'

'Of course it matters,' said Chaloner primly. 'Your mother would not condone you marrying . . .'

'An arse?' asked Ursula innocently when he faltered.

Wiseman roared with laughter.

As it was Palm Sunday, the service was longer than usual, and the vicar, for reasons known only to himself, delivered a rambling homily on the perils of home-brewing, which was irrelevant to most of his congregation, who either had servants to do it for them or could afford to buy from reputable dealers. Veriana sat with her eyes closed, so that Chaloner wondered if she was asleep, while Ursula flirted with two young men in the pew behind. As the vicar droned, Chaloner pondered what the girls had asked him to do.

He began by reflecting on family obligations, trying to guess what his father's position would have been. He kept coming back to the same conclusion: that his cousins had lost everything through no fault of their own, and that it would be unkind to send them home with nothing. He imagined his own sisters in the same predicament, and the sorrow and anger *he* would feel if a kinsman refused to help them.

Of course, the favour they wanted was no small order. It would not be easy to secure wealthy spouses, because no matter how charming, intelligent and pretty they were, they were still the penniless offspring of a man

192

named as a traitor, and no Royalist would consider them a good match. Again, he considered Leybourn and Lester, but neither was in London, and he had a feeling that unless he acted quickly, the girls would take matters into their own hands – which might be disastrous if Ursula's behaviour that morning was anything to go by.

He had asked Wiseman's opinion the previous night, but the surgeon's solution was to set them to work for Temperance, on the grounds that her high-class courtesans were showered with money from besotted customers. Unfortunately, Chaloner doubted his family would approve of him apprenticing his cousins to a house of ill repute, no matter how fabulous the financial returns.

The more he reflected, the more he realised he was massively ill-equipped to handle such a matter. First, he had no idea how to go about it, although he did know that arranged marriages were complex and took weeks, months and sometimes years before mutually satisfactory agreements were hammered out. Second, he was too busy to chaperone two young women, and it was obvious that Ursula in particular should not be allowed out alone. And third, he was unpopular at Court – not only did people remember his past and consider him sinister, but he worked for an earl who tottered nearer to disaster with every passing day. No one would want an alliance with him or his relatives.

Then, with a flash of inspiration, he remembered Thurloe, a man to whom family meant everything. The ex-Spymaster had arranged good marriages for his own kin, and there was no one whose advice Chaloner respected more. The ex-Spymaster might even know some suitable bachelors. Relieved to see light at the end of the tunnel, Chaloner turned his attention back to the dangers of home-fermentation.

The moment the vicar intoned the final grace, Chaloner stood to leave. Usually, he was among the first out through the door, but his cousins had other ideas, and decided to use the opportunity to their advantage. Murmuring that the more people they met, the easier it would be to achieve their objective, they smiled at and curtsied to anyone who glanced in their direction. When Chaloner looked around for Wiseman, aiming to beg his help in prising them away, he saw the surgeon had been cornered by an angry Fanny Clarke.

'You should have been more circumspect,' she was informing him tightly.

'Circumspect?' echoed Wiseman indignantly. 'I reported the facts, madam. It is not in my nature to cover up the ineptitude of incompetent colleagues.'

'My Timothy is not incompetent!' cried Fanny, distressed. 'And while I appreciate that you had to make your findings known, did you *have* to do it in a way that hurt him so?'

Chaloner backed away, unwilling to be drawn into their spat. Then he heard a sibilant voice behind him, and turned to see Swaddell.

'There you are, Tom,' beamed the assassin. 'I have been looking for you.'

'Why?' asked Chaloner uneasily. 'Has something else happened at White Hall?'

'No,' replied Swaddell, and Chaloner saw with alarm that his beady black eyes were fixed unblinkingly on Ursula. 'Although I did go back there after we parted last night, in the hope of cornering one or two suspects.

194

But most were at a private gathering in the King's apartments, to which I was not invited.'

Chaloner blinked his surprise. 'His Majesty held a party so soon after the death of one of his favourites?'

'Yes, and a good time was had by all, judging by the racket they made. It led me to question whether Chiffinch was as popular as his so-called friends claim.'

'It is something to bear in mind. So why are you here? I thought we had agreed to meet in the White Hall kitchens at noon, to ask about the oysters.'

'We did,' replied Swaddell, still gazing at Ursula. 'But you already followed that trail and it took you nowhere. Besides, I felt obliged to come and warn you about the palace – it is not a safe place for you to be at the moment because of the ill-feeling towards your Earl.'

'I know,' said Chaloner drily. 'He has not been popular for some time.'

This was an understatement.

'But it is much worse now that everyone knows Chiffinch was murdered,' said Swaddell, and looked at Chaloner for the first time. 'People really do suspect him of ordering the death.'

'Then tell them he had nothing to do with it. Not only would he never resort to such tactics, but his entire household was struggling to save his library from a flood when Chiffinch's oysters were poisoned. Well, other than Brodrick, but anyone who thinks *him* capable of clever plots is seriously deluded.'

'I will try, but folk believe what suits them, not what is true. Regardless, there is an *atmosphere* in White Hall. I did not want you strolling into it without due warning.'

'Thank you, but you could have sent a message. You did not need to come in person.'

'It was no trouble,' said Swaddell airily, his eyes back on Ursula. 'Besides, I am not averse to attending my devotions occasionally, and this is a nice place to do it.'

'What about your own church?' Chaloner realised he had no idea where Swaddell was currently living.

'The last time I went, there happened to be a clap of thunder, a flash of lightning, and a gust of wind that blew out all the candles. The vicar had the temerity to suggest that it was God objecting to my presence.'

Swaddell's vicar was not the only one who was uncomfortable with the assassin being in a holy place. Some of the Covent Garden congregation had formed a knot by the altar, as if for safety, while those nearest the door had already scuttled through it.

Sincerely hoping that Swaddell's appearance had not permanently ruined his standing with his neighbours, Chaloner hastened to draw his cousins outside. He paused to ensure that the parish clerk had recorded his name in the attendance register, although he had a feeling that everyone would remember that particular visit anyway, then led the way at a rapid clip across the piazza, aiming to be out of sight as quickly as possible. He was irked but not surprised when Swaddell followed, offering Ursula his arm. She took it, and Chaloner supposed he would have to advise her to be more particular.

When they arrived home, they discovered that Wiseman's servants had been busy, and had produced a fairly normal meal – the surgeon had peculiar dietary theories, and had trained his people to produce all manner of 'delicacies' that rational folk would never allow past their lips. However, the presence of two young ladies had prompted them to do something special, so Chaloner, his cousins

196

and Swaddell were presented with fresh bread, eggs from Chaloner's chickens, and a venison pastry. For Wiseman, there was boiled cabbage and raw liver, which he maintained strengthened the blood and improved virility.

'Then I shall share them with you,' declared Swaddell, after listening to the surgeon pontificate on the matter. 'There is nothing wrong with improving virility, as you never know when it might come in handy.' He beamed at Ursula, who grinned back.

Chaloner had not expected Swaddell to dine with them, but the assassin had declared himself available, and Ursula's come-hither smile had seen him shoot through the front door like an arrow. Wiseman had not been very pleased, loath for his reputation at Court to be tarnished by dint of him entertaining state-sanctioned killers in his home.

'You do not consider yourself virile enough already?' the surgeon asked, making no effort to disguise his antipathy. 'Perhaps Williamson should recruit another assassin then.'

'I am not an assassin,' objected Swaddell sharply, although the dangerous gleam in his eye belied the claim. 'I am a clerk. His *favourite* clerk, which means I own the respect and admiration of many people.'

'Do you?' breathed Ursula, patently fascinated by him.

'No!' cried Chaloner, suddenly recalling with awful, heart-stopping clarity that Swaddell had expressed a desire for a wife, and here were two young women in want of husbands. Everyone looked askance at him, so he hastened to conceal his consternation before Swaddell guessed what had caused it. 'I mean, of course you are well regarded, but—'

'You should take Ursula and Veriana to the soirée in Newcastle House on Wednesday,' said Wiseman, coming

197

to his rescue by changing the subject. '*I* shall be at Temperance's club, of course, but as you tell me that place is not good enough for your superior kin, I shall not extend an invitation for them to accompany me there.'

'God help me!' muttered Chaloner, realising he would have to see Thurloe before either Wiseman saw his cousins enrolled as prostitutes or one accepted an offer of marriage from Swaddell.

'Oh, please let us go to Newcastle House, Thomas,' begged Ursula. 'I can sing and Veriana plays the viol.'

'We shall all go together,' determined Swaddell happily. 'You two can entertain the ducal couple, while Tom and I conduct some important business.'

'What important business?' asked Veriana keenly. 'Our marriages?'

'Matters pertaining to the security of a nation,' replied Swaddell grandly and not very truthfully. 'We are influential men, you know.'

'Are you?' gushed Ursula, simpering in a way that made Swaddell beam back rather inanely. 'I thought you must be. You have that air about you.'

At that point, Chaloner saw he could not wait to talk to Thurloe – he had to act now. 'I have given the matter some serious thought,' he said briskly. 'And I have decided upon two good suitors for you. You can go home to the Isle of Man tomorrow, while I begin negotiations on your behalf. Their names are Salathiel Lester and Will Leybourn.'

'Lester is a fine man,' said Wiseman, 'although as a sea-captain in wartime, his chances of survival are slim. However, you should not consider Leybourn. He is too . . . second-hand.'

'What do you mean?' asked Chaloner, offended on his friend's behalf.

'I mean he has tried many times for a happy alliance, and every one of them has failed,' explained Wiseman. 'The common factor in all these romantic disasters is Leybourn himself.'

'That is unfair,' objected Chaloner. 'It is hardly his fault that circumstances have conspired against him.'

'He is not rich either,' put in Swaddell smugly. 'Surveyors are badly paid and their prospects are poor. You should widen the search to include other men. Clerks, for example.'

'I agree,' said Veriana. 'So we shall go to Newcastle House and—'

'No,' interrupted Chaloner sharply. 'I have no intention of going there myself. And if I change my mind, I shall be working and thus too busy for escort duties.'

'Do not let that trouble you, Tom,' said Swaddell smoothly. 'I can mind the ladies, while you see to . . . the vital issues that have been entrusted to us.'

'It is settled then,' said Veriana, pleased, and Chaloner saw he had been outmanoeuvred on all fronts. 'But do not fear that we might disgrace you, Thomas. Ursula and I are accomplished musicians.'

'Then show me,' said Chaloner, partly to see if they were telling the truth, but more because it had been a while since he had had time to play, and if he ever needed the peace his viol could bring, it was that day.

He was pleasantly surprised to discover that they had not exaggerated their skills. Veriana was a solid violist, while Ursula was a sweet, clear soprano. He played duets with one and sang with the other, and although he knew he should be thinking about Chiffinch, he was enjoying himself too much to stop. The only negative was that Swaddell declined to leave.

'I do not relax very often,' the assassin confided, 'but I find your cousins' company a delight. Besides, there is no point going to White Hall today, because the Cockpit Club has organised some fox-tossing in the Privy Garden. Decent people will have gone home, while the rest will be too interested in the resulting blood and gore to talk to us.'

Chaloner grimaced his distaste. Fox-tossing entailed driving the animals across canvas slings that people would then haul on, to see who could flip the hapless creatures highest into the air. Injury was inevitable and death frequent.

'You disapprove?' asked Swaddell, seeing his reaction. 'But foxes kill chickens, and given your affection for birds . . .'

'That does not mean I want to see them tortured,' retorted Chaloner shortly.

'I dislike any sport involving cruelty to animals,' said Swaddell, a confidence that surprised Chaloner, given the assassin's fondness for bloodshed. 'I always sense their longing to be somewhere else, which is how I feel, most of the time.'

Chaloner softened. The admission did not mean he wanted the assassin to marry one of his cousins, but it had certainly rendered him a little more human in his eyes. Perhaps it would not be such a trial to work with him after all, he thought.

Chapter 7

At six o'clock, Veriana and Ursula declared themselves too tired to perform more, although Chaloner could have continued longer. He set down his bow with considerable reluctance, and woke Swaddell, who had fallen asleep on Wiseman's velvet-upholstered 'Knole' sofa. This was a fashionable but acutely uncomfortable piece of furniture, so nodding off on it revealed just how bored he had been. The assassin left soon after, promising to take the ladies for a walk in St James's Park as soon as his duties allowed.

'What a charming man,' declared Ursula, when she returned from seeing him to the door. 'Much nicer than that terrifying surgeon.'

Chaloner saw he would have to supervise her closely, given that she was obviously not a very good judge of character. He asked the footman to bring cake and watered wine, ignoring Veriana's claim that she preferred French brandy, ate quickly, then set off towards Lincoln's Inn. He needed to tell Thurloe about his foray to Clerkenwell, not to mention begging his advice regarding his cousins, and after that, he decided to accept Eliza's invitation to the Red Bull, in the expectation that it would allow him to make casual enquiries about what was brewing in the area. He felt simultaneously energised and relaxed from his musical interlude, and his head was full of melodies by his favourite composers.

He reached Lincoln's Inn, and was told that Thurloe was in his Dial Court chambers. The yard was named for the scientific instrument that graced its middle, although this had been broken and no longer worked properly. It did not matter much, though, as the device was so complicated that no one knew how to use it anyway.

Chaloner climbed the stairs to Chamber XIII and knocked, but there was no answer. He was just wondering where his friend might have gone when he heard his name called. He stifled a sigh of annoyance when he saw Thurloe's fellow bencher, William Prynne, approaching.

Prynne was a pamphleteer, who penned poisonous discourses on anything that drew his disapproval. Most things did, so Londoners were regularly regaled with diatribes on the wrongs of long hair, women's fashion, maypoles, dancing, bishops and politics to name but a few of his bugbears. He had been outrageously vocal in his criticism of the government, and had lost his ears for calling the old Queen a whore. Then the King, in an inspired and uncharacteristic act of genius, had appointed him Keeper of Records. Flattered, Prynne had become an instant Royalist.

'Have you heard?' he began, delighted to find someone to rant at. 'A thousand robins descended on Clerkenwell last week. It means the area will soon suffer a terrible calamity.'

202

'Did Mother Broughton tell you that?' asked Chaloner warily.

'Mother Broughton!' spat Prynne. 'She is a woman, and I put no store in what *they* have to say. No, this information comes from *me*. I saw the birds myself.'

Chaloner raised his eyebrows. 'If there were that many birds in one place, why has no one else reported it?'

'Because they were only seen by the godly and pure in heart,' replied Prynne loftily. 'Obviously, I was the only one who met the criteria.'

'A *thousand* robins? How did you count them all?'

'Well, it was only six, if you are going to be pedantic, but the point is that I sensed great evil there, especially around the Red Bull. That place encourages women in the dreadful and epidemical vanities of our age – like reading and writing.'

Chaloner blinked. 'Those are not vanities! Indeed, you make your living from them.'

Prynne waved a dismissive hand. 'Yes, but I am a man. It is different.'

'Is it, indeed?' muttered Chaloner, half amused and half repelled by the man's bigotry.

'Clerkenwell is a pit of abomination,' declared Prynne. 'It heaves with mischievous sinners, heretics, idolaters, harlots, blasphemers, mahometans, heathens, unbelievers and other miscreants that by their words and acts dare to pour scorn upon the holy gospel of Jesus Christ. I have seen them cavorting in the Red Bull, that notorious hub of filth and debauchery.'

'You have been inside it?'

'Of course not! It is a playhouse, and they stand on the broad, beaten, pleasant road that leads to hell. I watched from a distance, and I witnessed the wicked flocking there for capering wantonness, incontinency and profanity. Every one of them aims to turn the world upside down – to set women over men, the wicked over the just, and promote vice over decency.'

'I do not suppose you noticed Bess Widdrington or Fanny Clarke among the throng, did you? Captain Rolt claims to have followed them there, but they deny it.'

'Fanny Clarke would never enter such a place,' declared Prynne, 'and even that foolish Bess would know better than to step over its idolatrous and epidemical threshold.'

'Oh,' said Chaloner. 'Then—'

'Unless they were led astray by their husbands, of course. Clarke has a vile and iniquitous soul, while Widdrington has no soul at all. Neither should be allowed near His Majesty. Did you hear what they did on this most holy of Sabbaths? The filthy and pestilential entertainment they staged?'

'The fox-tossing?'

'Yes! On Palm Sunday! Widdrington's creature Tooley – the gross, hulking one who looks like an ape – won the game by hurling one fox so high that it is said to have seen Lambeth before it crashed to its death.'

'Perhaps you should write a pamphlet about it,' suggested Chaloner, thinking it was high time that Prynne's vicious pen did something worthwhile.

Prynne smirked. 'There is no need, because vengeance has already been visited upon Tooley – he died shortly afterwards. His demise is blamed on a fever, but I know it was God.'

'Tooley is dead?' asked Chaloner, startled. 'Are you sure?'

Prynne nodded with great satisfaction. 'I shall pray for

his soul, although not even the petitions of a godly man like myself can save *him* from eternal damnation. But speaking of godly men, are you here to see Mr Thurloe?'

Prynne admired Thurloe and was always trying to win his favour. Chaloner was glad of it, as Prynne would make a vexatious enemy with his penchant for libellous diatribes.

'He is in the chapel,' Prynne went on. 'It is Palm Sunday, so of course that saintly soul will be at his devotions. I have been at mine all day . . . well, other than the times I went to White Hall, Clerkenwell, Bunhill Fields, the Tower, and my coffee house.'

'Your knees must ache with all that kneeling.'

Chaloner's sarcasm was lost on Prynne. 'They do, so I must fortify myself with medicinal claret. I deplore strong drink as a vice of Satan, but on occasions such as this, it cannot be avoided.'

Lincoln's Inn's chapel was a pretty building with large windows that allowed sunlight to flood in. At night it was quietly serene, lit by lamps that turned its pale stone to dark gold. It stood above an open undercroft, where the benchers were buried when they died. Thurloe had expressed a desire to lie there one day, although the prospect of a world without the ex-Spymaster was one that Chaloner refused to contemplate.

'There you are at last,' said Thurloe, as Chaloner came to sit on the pew next to him. 'I expected you sooner than this.'

'You did?' asked Chaloner warily. 'Why?'

'Because two of James Chaloner's daughters arrived in the city yesterday, which caused no mean stir among those who still consider him a hero. I informed them

205

that your cousins did not come to lead a new rebellion, but I would have liked confirmation of it before now.'

Chaloner bowed an apology, but was not about to confess that the delay had been because he had been enjoying himself with music. 'Mischief was not their reason for coming. However, they do resent their father's treatment by vengeful Royalists, and grudges are easily tapped by the unscrupulous.'

'They are,' agreed Thurloe. 'So you must find something to keep them busy while they are here. A courtship, perhaps.'

'I am glad you suggested that. Do you know anyone who wants a wife? They say it does not matter if he is old and ugly, but he must be rich.'

Thurloe laughed. 'I am afraid respectable men with large fortunes are in short supply these days. Is that why they came? I should have guessed.'

Chaloner scrubbed his face with his hands. 'What am I to do? They will refuse to leave as long as they are single, and I cannot think of any suitable candidates. I thought Lester and Leybourn might do, but Wiseman raised some concerns about them both . . .'

'I love Leybourn dearly, but I would not want him as a husband for any kinswoman of mine. He is fickle in his affections, and there would be a constant danger that he would tire of her and fix his gaze on someone else.'

'And Lester?'

'He has chosen too dangerous an occupation. War will resume now that winter is over, and ships will batter each other until one side concedes defeat. Lester cannot provide for a wife if he is dead.'

Chaloner was silent. Of all his friends, he liked Lester the most, because he was honest, decent and lacked the

206

eccentricities of the others. He hated the thought of him killed in a senseless conflict that should never have been started in the first place.

'I suppose there is always Kersey,' he said after a while. 'He is wealthy.'

Thurloe laughed a second time. 'He is married already, not to one lady, but to two. He spends Mondays, Wednesdays and Fridays with the first; Tuesdays, Thursdays and Saturdays with the second; and he takes Sundays off.'

Chaloner gaped at him. 'Kersey is a bigamist?'

Thurloe nodded. 'And may be willing to take both your cousins off your hands, too, but I would not recommend it.'

Chaloner was astounded. He had always known that there was more to the quiet, dapper little charnel-house keeper than met the eye – he had once virtually confessed to killing his predecessor, for a start – but he could not see him as an alluring lothario. Then he reconsidered: Kersey was rich, and that was all that mattered, according to Ursula and Veriana.

Thurloe read his thoughts. 'Do not judge your cousins too harshly. Life is harder for gentlewomen than men. You thought you were in a difficult position after the Restoration, but you could work, and now you are a valued member of a noble household.'

'Hardly valued,' muttered Chaloner.

'But Veriana and Ursula's only hope is to make decent marriages. I appreciate that you are busy with Chiffinch's killer, but the lives and happiness of two people are at stake here. You must find the time to do what is right.'

'Yes,' conceded Chaloner. 'Will you help me?'

'Of course. However, first, you must find them more suitable lodgings. They cannot live with you and Wiseman for more than a few days, or people will talk and their reputations will be tarnished. Until you have them respectably housed, you must provide a chaperone. Do you know any virtuous ladies who might oblige?'

'Barbara Chiffinch,' suggested Chaloner. 'She would do it.'

Thurloe raised his eyebrows. 'Taking them to the Pimp-Master General's home is hardly wise, Thomas. Think of someone else.'

But Chaloner shook his head helplessly. There was no one.

'Then you had better acquire some new friends – fast,' advised Thurloe. 'In the interim, I recommend making them your wards, which will give you the legal authority to negotiate marriages on their behalf. I can draw up the document in my chambers now, if you like. And as we walk there, you can tell me all you have learned since we last met.'

The Inn was silent as Chaloner and Thurloe strolled towards Dial Court, its tall walls muting the sounds from outside. Chaloner breathed in deeply, relishing the scent of soil dampened by spring rain, and the sense of ancient solidity from the venerable buildings.

'The peace is deceptive,' said Thurloe, as they crunched along the gravel paths. 'While the city sleeps, a serpent stirs in Clerkenwell.'

'You sound like Mother Broughton. She believes that something terrible will happen on Good Friday, but that anyone who survives until Easter Day will enjoy a glorious Utopia with her and all the other righteous souls. I was taken to meet her this morning.'

'Tell me about her,' ordered Thurloe.

Chaloner obliged, then described what had happened with Bunhill's 'walking corpses', finishing with, 'I do not know if Dutch Jane was involved or just an innocent bystander. Regardless, the dead were *not* up and about – unless they need ropes to climb over walls.'

'So have you discovered any more about what is brewing in the area?'

'Not really, although I plan to visit Eliza's school in the Red Bull when I leave here. Perhaps I will learn something useful there.'

'Then be careful, because the courtier who died this afternoon – Tooley – is rumoured to have caught his fatal fever in that particular tavern.'

'Prynne thinks it was divine punishment for him winning the fox-tossing contest.'

'Fox-tossing?' Thurloe grimaced his revulsion. 'Oh, for a military dictatorship again! Cromwell would not have countenanced such disgusting pastimes.'

'Tooley's death is so untimely that I want Wiseman to look at him. Of course, if it does transpire that he died by sly means, I am not sure what I can do about it. It is not for me to explore the murder of everyone who hated the Earl.'

'It will be if Tooley was poisoned, like Chiffinch,' Thurloe pointed out. 'But tell me about your investigation so far.'

Chaloner did, aware as he spoke that his findings were disgracefully meagre. Then they reached Chamber XIII, where Thurloe sat at his table to draw up the promised contract. Before he began, he reached inside his coat and withdrew a sheet of paper.

'While I work, read this. You can tell me your thoughts when I have finished.'

Chaloner sat by the fire and unfolded the page. It was an anonymous letter addressed to the Duke of Newcastle. The sender began by declaring that he was sorry to cause such a fine, honourable man pain, but His Grace was likely to lose his good name unless he took his wife in hand. It went on to claim that the Duchess was having an affair with Steward Topp.

Chaloner studied the letter carefully. The handwriting was inconsistent, suggesting that the writer had tried to disguise it, although he was only partially successful, as he had failed to change the way he styled his letter *f*s. These were so distinctive that it would be easy to match them to samples taken from suspects. Moreover, Chaloner was sure he had seen them before, although he could not recall where, no matter how hard he tried.

'An unpleasant piece of malice,' he said eventually, when Thurloe set down his pen and scattered sand on the document he had just completed. 'But why do you have it? Was it intercepted by your spies?'

'I have no spies, Thomas,' said Thurloe mildly. 'I have friends who send me news. However, this letter has nothing to do with them. The Duke gave it to me himself.'

'Did he?' asked Chaloner, surprised. 'Why?'

'Because he wants me to find out who sent it. He approached Prynne first. He thought *he* might recognise the handwriting, given that he sees so many different documents in his capacity as Keeper of Records. But Prynne could not help, so he brought the Duke to me. I agreed to look into the matter, because the Duchess once did me a great kindness and I am in her debt.'

Chaloner waited for an explanation, but none came, and he knew better than to pry. 'Does the Duke believe this claim about his wife and Topp?'

'He does not, and is outraged by it. He assures me that the Duchess is more interested in books than amours, and that if she did have an affair, it would not be with Topp.'

'What is wrong with Topp, other than being oily, old and unattractive?'

'First, she loves her Duke, who is a poet, equestrian, war hero and fellow intellectual, whereas Topp is a former coal merchant. And second, when the Duke is away or indisposed, the Duchess always shares her bedchamber with Eliza. Ergo, an illicit liaison would be impossible, because the Duchess is never alone.'

'So the Duke wants to prosecute the writer of this letter for libel? That is why he wants you to hunt the culprit down?'

Thurloe nodded. 'The Bishop-mark shows that it was mailed in Grantham, so I shall go there tomorrow, to see if the postmaster remembers who sent it.'

'Is there any connection between Grantham and the Newcastles?

'None whatsoever, which tells me that the sender thought he was being clever by choosing it. However, he has miscalculated, because the postmaster will not see many missives addressed to nobles, and he will almost certainly recall who handed it to him. I am confident of a good description, after which I may require your help in apprehending the culprit.'

Chaloner inclined his head. 'It should not be difficult to identify him. I already know several people who dislike the Duchess, starting with her stepson.'

'Poor Mansfield does not have the courage to launch such a scheme – he would be too frightened of being caught and losing the last vestiges of his father's affection.

211

But perhaps you will keep your eyes and ears open as you go about your business. Any clues will be gratefully received, and in return, I shall think about husbands for your cousins.'

It was not far from Chancery Lane to the Red Bull, although Chaloner was aware of a very peculiar atmosphere as he crossed the Fleet River and entered Clerkenwell. Some folk walked with a bounce in their step, while others skulked furtively. He supposed Mother Broughton's prophecies were responsible, and people's responses to them depended on whether they considered themselves godly or sinful.

He was just approaching John Street when he saw the Earl's clerk scuttling along. Barker started to duck down an alley when he recognised Chaloner, but thought better of it when he realised he had been spotted. With obvious reluctance, he came to talk.

'I have just delivered letters to Newcastle House,' he gabbled, although his eyes were furtive and Chaloner knew he was lying; for a start, he had been coming from entirely the wrong direction. 'Now I am on my way back to Piccadilly.'

Chaloner regarded him appraisingly. 'Have you been in the Red Bull?'

Barker stared at him. 'Of course not! Bess Widdrington says that is where Tooley caught the fever that carried him to his grave.'

'His death is odd,' mused Chaloner. 'I heard he won the fox-tossing contest, but if he was well enough for that – and I imagine it was strenuous – how can he have been dying?'

'These sicknesses strike very fast, as I am sure you know.'

212

'Not that fast,' averred Chaloner. 'But Wiseman will find the truth. I will ask him to examine Tooley tomorrow.'

'Very wise,' said Barker, and bowed. 'Now, if you will excuse me, I must return to Clarendon House.'

He hurried away, and Chaloner continued towards the Red Bull. He arrived to find all its window shutters closed, and two men minding the door, ready to repel undesirables. It did not take a genius to guess that something illicit was going on within, and he wondered if it was wise for him to enter openly – that it might be better to pick the lock on the side door again and slip in unnoticed. But the sentries had seen him, and it would look suspicious to walk away now.

He took a deep breath and approached them, a little surprised when the guardsmen transpired to be guardswomen. One was the beefy tobacco-seller from Mother Broughton's house – he recalled her being introduced as Joan Cole.

'Name?' she demanded. 'I know we met before, but I cannot remember what you called yourself. Our seer gets so many visitors, see.'

He told her, and she ran a thick forefinger down a visitor list that she tugged from her pocket. Chaloner was evidently on it, because she opened the door and indicated that he was to enter. He did, then gazed around in astonishment.

The main room had been rendered warm and welcoming, with clean rushes on the floor and a fire in the hearth. Its atmosphere was quietly civilised, with none of the rowdy bawling that usually characterised taverns when they were full. And the Red Bull *was* full – there was scarcely room to move between the packed tables. Eliza hurried to greet him.

213

'I did not think you would come,' she exclaimed, smiling. 'You seemed very unenthusiastic when I invited you, but I am glad your curiosity won out.'

Chaloner was still scanning his surroundings. Most of the tavern's clientele were women, but there was also a smattering of men. These included some of Clerkenwell's literati – poor blind John Milton, once the darling of the Puritans but now living in quiet poverty; Dr Goddard, whose cure-all drops were world-famous; Erasmus Smith, the wealthy Parliamentarian, who had founded an educational trust to prevent Royalists from prying too deeply into his financial affairs; and Izaak Walton, author of *The Compleat Angler*.

There were other familiar faces, too. Gruff Baron Lucas was talking to red-haired Sarah Shawe, both wearing the earnest expressions of people engrossed in intense intellectual debate – Chaloner overheard enough to tell him that it was regarding some element of combustion developed by the Royal Society. Dr Clarke sat nearby, ogling Sarah, and Chaloner was sure he would be punched if she noticed.

'Walk around,' invited Eliza with a gracious wave of her hand. 'Or join any group.'

Chaloner took her at her word and began to reconnoitre. Some women were learning to read, supervised by a few of the merchant-class protesters he had seen outside White Hall a few days earlier. Molly the chicken girl was there, frowning in concentration as she struggled to write her name. Others were more advanced, and debated philosophy and science – the Duchess's books were piled on every table, and each copy was very well thumbed.

Eventually, he reached Lucas, Sarah and Clarke. The

two debaters did not notice him, but the physician greeted him with a wary grin.

'Do not tell the wife, eh?' he said, treating Chaloner to one of his man-of-the-world winks. 'Fanny does not approve of this place. She thinks it is a brothel.'

'Then tell her that it is not. She may even like to come herself, as there is clearly a need for more teachers.'

'She would refuse because she thinks educating women is cruel. She is cognisant of the fact that no amount of learning will turn them into physicians, bankers or bishops, so all it does is make them discontented.'

'Do you agree with her?'

Clarke lowered his voice. 'I do, actually. These lasses want to better themselves, but what good will it do? They will still be whores, milkmaids and laundresses, taking orders from men.'

'So why are you here, if not to help them?'

'Because Fanny is a dull old hen, and I prefer more lively company on occasion.' Clarke nudged Chaloner in the ribs and nodded at Sarah. 'Like her. I would not mind giving *her* a complete medical examination!'

Chaloner changed the subject before Clarke could see his distaste, not just for lusting after women who had gone to the Red Bull to escape that sort of thing, but for being ready to cheat on his wife. Perhaps Fanny was a 'dull old hen', but that was a poor excuse for betraying her.

'I understand Tooley died today,' he said. 'Were you in White Hall when it happened?'

Clarke nodded. 'I was the one who diagnosed his cause of death as a fever. However, do not ask Wiseman for a second opinion if you have any affection for him. It has since occurred to me that it might have been the plague.'

215

'I heard a rumour that he was infected here. Is it—'

'Here?' gulped Clarke in alarm. 'Lord! No one told me *that*!'

He leapt up and bolted for the door, slamming it behind him so hard that the window shutters rattled and several people jumped to their feet in alarm.

'Did I hear you say that Tooley caught some sickness here, Chaloner?' growled Lucas, tearing himself away from Sarah with obvious reluctance. 'Because he did not. If that ape had tried to come in, I would have torn his head off. There is no room for his sort in the Red Bull. It is for *civilised* company.'

'So I see,' said Chaloner, and looked around. 'But where is your sister? I understand she has been generous in her support for this venture.'

'She has,' said Lucas, 'but she is conscious of being married to a duke and declines to mix with what she calls "common society". But *I* do not care about all that nonsense. I would rather debate philosophy with a clever beggar than a stupid fox-tossing nobleman.'

Eliza came to join them at that point, and explained that the Duchess herself had chosen the subject for that evening's debate, which was: *There is little difference between man and beast, but what ambition and glory makes.* Animal intelligence was, Eliza explained, something about which her mistress felt very strongly.

'She will include it in the novel she is writing,' she elaborated, eyes shining with pride. 'Which is a story about a perfect society – one that contains only women.'

'Then it will be a very short-lived perfect society,' quipped Chaloner, 'if there are no men to help provide future generations.'

'She does not address that sort of issue.' Eliza sounded

216

shocked. 'She is too genteel to raise vulgar matters like procreation.'

'Your pupils are not,' said Chaloner, aware that the table nearest to them had embarked on a very ribald detour, which had the participants howling with coarse laughter.

'Sarah!' snapped Eliza crossly. 'Your seamstresses need you to keep them on track.'

Sarah obliged, although she was obviously sorry to abandon her intellectual sparring partner. Lucas was just as disappointed, and when she had gone, he informed Chaloner that her mind was far superior to most of those in the Royal Society. Chaloner was inclined to believe him, given that its membership included the King and the Duke of York.

As Sarah passed Eliza, their fingers touched briefly, and the glance they exchanged told him that their relationship was rather more than just two friends who shared common interests. He hoped they were discreet, as the Duchess would not appreciate her staff being at the centre of a scandal, especially if the contents of the anonymous letter ever became public. It would be said that Topp had leapt into the Duchess's bed because his wife preferred women.

Then someone pulled on Chaloner's sleeve, and he looked down to see Molly.

'Come to see Mother Broughton,' she piped. 'I am sure she will want you to admire her.'

She led Chaloner to the hearth, where the seer smoked her pipe and repeated her predictions to anyone who would listen. The women she had cornered slithered away with relief when Molly arrived with fresh prey.

'You came to my house earlier,' said Mother Broughton,

yeing Chaloner closely. 'Although I cannot recall your name. I get so many visitors, see, all wanting my wise words.'

'You told me I had a future in cheese.'

'Ah, I remember now. But I have had another vision since then – of the Fleet River running red with blood. This will happen on Maundy Thursday, and is just one of the terrible things that will come to pass in our fine city before a just, gentle new kingdom is ushered in.'

Chaloner suspected it ran with blood every day, given the number of slaughterhouses along its banks. 'London is the only place these things will happen?'

'Oh, yes! No other city boasts so many wicked sinners.'

Eventually, Eliza brought the evening to a close by thanking everyone for coming. The participants took their leave, laughing and joking until they reached the door. Then they raised their hoods or covered their faces with scarves, and slipped away into the night. Chaloner understood their reluctance to be recognised when he stepped outside and saw that a group of men had gathered there to hurl abuse. They were masked as well, and anonymity made them bold in spouting their opinions.

'Not again!' muttered John Milton, tilting his head to hear what his ruined eyes could not see. 'Have they nothing better to do?'

'They are frightened of us,' declared Sarah with great satisfaction. 'Afraid that if we continue to gain strength by meeting, we will rock their comfortable existences.'

'Or they just want to cause mischief,' countered Chaloner, noting that although the protesters wore shabby cloaks, they had neglected to change their footwear, where silver buckles shone like beacons. Moreover, he recognised mother funded.

'Go away,' Mother Broughton ordered him when she emerged. 'You stupid oaf.'

'Stupid?' echoed Mansfield indignantly. 'It is *you* who is stupid, madam!'

'Hold me up, Eliza,' cried Sarah, pretending to swoon. 'I am so dazzled by this fellow's wit that I might faint at its sheer acerbity.'

'Its sheer what?' asked Mansfield suspiciously.

'She is calling you an ass,' translated Lucas, who had trailed out on Mother Broughton's heels. 'Which you are. And a cowardly one into the bargain — too timorous to show your face.'

'Ignore them, Baron,' said Eliza haughtily. 'They are beneath our contempt. And as the Duchess always says, a better future will come if we bide our time.'

'Yes, it will come on Sunday,' put in Mother Broughton confidentially. 'It is all foretold.'

'I hope it will take longer than that,' countered Lucas. 'I would love to see things improve, but rapid change is dangerous. That is why the Commonwealth failed: it was imposed too fast, and people baulked.'

the air. It sa[...]
and cracked into th[...]
arrowed as she scanne[...]
er fingers went to her belt, [...]
knife.

[...]d Eliza. 'The Duchess said she [...]ding if there is any hint of impro[...]e here. Take no notice of them. They [...]n it.'

[...]ou!' roared Baron Lucas suddenly, stabbing an [...]nger towards Mansfield. 'Yes, I am talking to *you* [...]he stinking weasel holding the handful of mud. Call yourself a man, lobbing missiles at defenceless women? Come here, you snivelling little rat, and fight *me*!'

Mansfield took to his heels when Lucas drew his sword, and his three companions were quick to follow. The Baron then proceeded to bawl such apposite insults that Chaloner suspected that he, too, had seen beneath the disguises, and knew exactly who was on the sharp end of his tongue.

'Now go home, all of you,' ordered Eliza, standing with her hands on her hips to glower at the remaining protesters. 'You have made your point.'

Unnerved by Mansfield's flight and unwilling to risk a tongue-lashing from Lucas, the men began to melt away. Chaloner set off after the one who had thrown the rock. *He* had seen the guilty arm go back, even if no one else had noticed. The culprit saw him following and ran, zigzagging through alleys and yards in a desperate attempt to throw him off.

The pair of them hurtled by the Charterhouse, at which point Chaloner lost his quarry. He stood still, listening intently, then heard footsteps. He set off after them, past Red Cross Street and the silent Artillery Ground. Then he glimpsed a shadow climbing over the cemetery wall. He raced towards it and managed to grab the hem of a cloak as its owner ascended.

'*Godverdamme!*' swore the shadow, and the material snapped out of his hand.

Chaloner scrambled over the wall, too, now in possession of two pieces of information: the culprit's native tongue was Dutch, and 'he' was a she. He made a guess at her identity.

'Jane, please stop!' he called in her own language. 'I only want to talk.'

He reached the ground on the other side, but Dutch Jane had disappeared. Then he saw a shadow by the grave of the Puritan divine who had recently been buried. He set off towards it, stumbling over ground that was uneven with molehills and rabbit holes. Red lights bobbed ahead. Jane had company. The dagger Chaloner always carried in his sleeve slipped into his hand.

'Wait!' he called again. 'I only want to—'

He ducked instinctively at a flicker of movement, and thus avoided the hacking blow aimed at his head by someone with a rapier. He drew his own sword, and engaged in a fast and furious exchange of blows before others came running to his assailant's aid.

'Stop!' hissed Jane, just when Chaloner thought he was going to meet an ignominious end at the hands of people whose faces he could not see. 'Tyndal is coming. Run! Quickly!'

The swordsmen promptly broke off the fight and the red lights danced away. Chaloner tried to follow, but the night was pitch black, and it was impossible to see where he was going. Suddenly, the ground disappeared beneath

221

his feet. He fell and landed with a jarring thump – he had plunged into an open grave. Pain speared through the leg that had been injured at the Battle of Naseby and had never fully healed. As he put out his hands to push himself to his feet, he felt a face, cold and dead. He jerked them back in revulsion.

Then the grave was filled with light, and silhouettes appeared above him. It was Tyndal and his four sons, all carrying lanterns.

'What are you doing down there?' he asked. 'That is the hole we dug for the courtier who died today – Mr Tooley. His own vicar refused to take him, because he was a fever case.'

Chaloner glared crossly up at him. 'You should have covered the hole with planks, not left it wide open for people to fall down.'

'The only ones at risk of that are trespassers,' said Tyndal tartly. 'And they get what they deserve. Is your friend all right, by the way? He is very pale.'

The lamps illuminated the dead face that Chaloner had felt. He recognised it with a shock It was the Cockpit Club member who was always drunk.

'Ashley!'

Chapter 8

Monday dawned bright and sunny, although Chaloner felt sluggish and heavy-eyed after his fraught and very late night at the Red Bull and Bunhill cemetery. When a vigorous wash in cold water and a spell in the garden with his hens did not refresh him, he decided the only remedy was a dish of coffee.

Although his years as an intelligencer had taught him that it was unwise to have regular haunts, he set off for the Rainbow on Fleet Street anyway, feeling the need for something familiar and constant. Home did not count, not with Veriana and Ursula rearranging all his furniture to suit themselves. He had nearly broken his neck the previous night, flopping exhaustedly on to his bed in the dark, only to discover it was no longer where he had left it.

He walked briskly, trying to clear his muddy wits for the day that lay ahead. The streets shone wetly from recent rain, and steam rose in places, while all the potholes were full of mucky water. They were a serious hazard to pedestrians, who risked either being deluged by the carts that splashed through them, or of coming to grief in one that was deeper than it looked.

The city was awake, but sombre, and the churches he passed were busy. Holy Week – the days between Palm Sunday and Easter Day – was a quiet period for the faithful, a time of fasting, reflection and prayer.

The Rainbow was near Temple Bar, and did a roaring trade with those who needed something to calm their nerves after battling through it. Not many months ago, the coffee house had been closed with the plague, and Chaloner feared that its regulars had died. But all had survived, and he opened the door to see the same old faces sitting around the same worn table, amid the familiar reek of tobacco smoke and burned beans. As usual, they were discussing the latest government newsbook – now called *The London Gazette* – hot off the presses that day.

'What news?' called Farr, the owner, in the traditional coffee house greeting. He wore an apron that had once been white, but that was now brown and greasy from the smoke that curled from his stinking beans. 'Oh, it is you, Chaloner. Where have you been these last few weeks?'

'That is a fine welcome for an old friend,' chided Rector Thompson, coming to take Chaloner's hand in a genuine expression of friendship; no one else moved. 'We are pleased to see you home. So what is new at White Hall these days?'

'Do not look to him for information,' said Farr sourly. 'He never has anything interesting to report, even though he has access to the most intimate Court secrets. He must walk around with his eyes closed and his hands clapped over his ears.'

'I might be tempted to do the same,' averred Thompson prudishly. 'White Hall is no place for a decent man, and I admire his fortitude in working there.'

224

This was why Chaloner liked the Rainbow. Accusations might be levelled, but no one was ever obliged to defend himself, as everyone else wanted to do the talking.

'I agree with Farr,' said Stedman, the youthful printer. 'Chaloner is the least observant man I have ever met. If I spent *my* days at the palace, I would have a wealth of fascinating snippets to share.'

'Perhaps he does not have time for that sort of thing,' said Thompson, watching Farr pour Chaloner a dish of his famous viscous brown sludge. 'He may have duties and responsibilities.'

'In *White Hall?*' demanded Farr incredulously. 'A place where no one ever does anything except have fun?'

'Other than the King,' put in Stedman, who was a passionate Royalist, and would hear no word spoken against His Majesty. This had once extended to his Court as well, but the past three or four years had taught him prudence in this respect.

'Have you heard the latest news from Clerkenwell?' asked Farr, changing the subject to one he liked better. 'Corpses with red souls were seen in the cemetery for a second night running, and the man who witnessed the phenomenon was so terrified that he toppled into an open grave, stone dead.'

Chaloner marvelled at the speed with which garbled versions of the truth could spread through the city. It had only been a few hours since he had chased Dutch Jane and found Ashley's body, but already people had put their own slant on events.

'Speaking of mysterious happenings, there are reports of a hen killing a fox in Covent Garden,' said Stedman. 'All are signs that our world order is wobbling once again.'

'I disagree,' said Thompson. 'It is Holy Week. Hens killing a fox is a symbol of Easter.'

'You equate Jesus with a fox?' asked Farr, bemused. 'I cannot see it myself, but . . . Hah! Here comes Speed from the bookshop. Perhaps *he* will have something interesting to share.'

Speed's contribution was to embark on a detailed analysis of Mother Broughton's prophecies, leaving Chaloner to wonder if there was anyone in the city capable of telling the truth without twisting it to suit himself. According to Speed, the glorious event promised for Easter Sunday would be a relaxing of the Sabbath trading laws, so that shop owners like him could open whenever they pleased.

'That is not my idea of a glorious new order,' said Thompson doubtfully. 'I was hoping for something a little more religious.'

'Well, I suppose you would,' said Speed disdainfully. 'You are a clergyman.'

Chaloner arrived back in Covent Garden just as the sun was chasing the last of the night's shadows away. Aware that he would have to go to White Hall that day, he donned his best coat and breeches, then raided Wiseman's wardrobe for some accessories to liven them up – a pair of crimson gloves and a cherry-red band around his hat.

'Very smart,' said Wiseman approvingly. 'Although an all-red ensemble would have been better.'

'Have you heard that two members of the Cockpit Club died yesterday?' asked Chaloner. 'James Tooley and George Ashley.'

Wiseman nodded. 'But if you want me to look at them, it will have to wait until this afternoon. I must bleed the

Queen this morning. Some stupid oaf let slip that her mother is dead, and the shock has played havoc with her humours.'

'It was Clarke's idea to keep the news from her,' recalled Chaloner. 'You argued for her to be told, so it could be done gently.'

Wiseman grimaced. 'I knew some loose-tongued fool would blurt it out in a way that would prove harmful, and I was right. Clarke is as useless at dealing with the living as he is at assessing the dead. Do not believe anything he says about Tooley and Ashley. I will provide you with an *informed* opinion this afternoon.'

Before he left the house, Chaloner went to check on his cousins, and was appalled to find them in the parlour with Swaddell. He glared at the footman for allowing the assassin in, but the man only glared back, silently telling him that repelling such a deadly invader went well beyond his job description.

'There you are, Tom,' the assassin said, and when he turned to smile a greeting, his usually pallid face was flushed; having two unattached females hanging on his every word was much to his liking. 'Do not worry about being late. Your cousins have entertained me royally.'

'Late?' echoed Chaloner indignantly. 'It is nowhere near noon, and my home is not White Hall's kitchens – which is where we agreed to meet last night.'

Swaddell's smile became rather less amiable. 'Yes, but we cannot afford to lose a minute now there are *three* courtiers crying out for justice. Besides, I went to the larder this morning and made my own enquiries. There was nothing to learn that you have not already uncovered.'

'This morning?' asked Ursula, wide-eyed. 'You must

227

have started work very early, Mr Swaddell. The city is fortunate to have such a dedicated servant.'

Chaloner glanced sharply at her, suspecting mockery, which would be rash to practise on Swaddell, but she seemed sincere. Swaddell preened, flattered.

'Did you hear anything about Tooley and Ashley while you were in White Hall?' Chaloner asked, disliking the way Swaddell and Ursula were looking at each other.

'Apparently, both were well at the fox-tossing yesterday,' replied Swaddell, not tearing his eyes from the object of his fancy, 'and they celebrated Tooley's win with a drinking contest. He perished of a fever an hour or so after the party broke up. Wild with grief, Ashley went to sit by his tomb in Bunhill, but he died of fright when he encountered the walking corpses. At least, that is the tale on everyone's lips.'

Chaloner raised his eyebrows. 'But Tooley has no tomb – he has not been buried yet. And who goes to mourn at an empty grave?'

'Quite,' said Swaddell. 'It is suspicious, is it not? I had hoped Wiseman would examine both bodies at once, but he says we must wait until he has tended the Queen.'

Chaloner was about to suggest that he and Swaddell left, when the footman arrived with platters of food. The cook had gone to considerable trouble, and the eggs, smoked pork and fresh bread smelled delicious. Suddenly hungry, he decided to stay and break his fast. So did Swaddell, who proceeded to ignore Chaloner entirely while he regaled the young women with descriptions of the exotic goods that could be bought from the city's many markets.

'Oranges?' breathed Ursula. 'I have never tasted one of those.'

'I eat them most days,' said Swaddell casually, the sophisticated man-of-the-world. 'I shall bring you one later. With your guardian's permission, of course.'

Chaloner supposed the girls had mentioned the recently signed deed making them his wards, and was glad. It would make his task easier when he told the assassin that he was not in the running to marry either of them. To change the subject, he told Swaddell what had happened at the Red Bull the previous night. Ursula gave a shrill squeal of excitement.

'Please take us there, Thomas! *We* could teach these ladies to read, and we could learn a lot from listening to erudite men like John Milton, Baron Lucas and Izaak Walton.'

But Chaloner recalled what Thurloe had said about the anticipation generated by the arrival of two of James Chaloner's brood, and was not about to compound Clerkenwell's problems by introducing two people who might act as magnets for would-be revolutionaries.

'I am afraid you must stay here until I find a suitable chaperone,' he said.

Both cousins regarded him with a distinct lack of affection, but it could not be helped.

'Have you borrowed some of Mr Wiseman's things in the hope of making yourself look more courtly?' asked Ursula sulkily. 'Because if so, it has not really worked.'

'It might do for a gathering of Parliamentarians,' put in Veriana cuttingly, while Swaddell sniggered into his napkin, 'but Royalists will consider you gauche.'

Before he could object, they began fussing around him, exchanging the gloves in his belt for a lace handkerchief, and adorning his hat with a sprig of flowers instead of the band. By the time they had finished, even he was forced to admit that the result did look less contrived.

The moment they were outside, Swaddell began to bombard Chaloner with questions about the girls and their family. Loath to arm him with anything that might be used to snag their affections, Chaloner turned the discussion back to Chiffinch, Tooley and Ashley, making the point that they should do all they could to prevent a fourth death. Swaddell frowned.

'You think there will be another?'

Chaloner shrugged. 'It is impossible to know until Wiseman tells us how Tooley and Ashley died. If they were poisoned – and the suddenness of their departures suggests it is a distinct possibility – we need to find out why. And what links them to Chiffinch.'

Swaddell moved to another subject. 'I am still not clear about Dutch Jane's role last night. You say she was among the protesters outside the Red Bull, but why would she throw her lot in with them?'

'Probably because its school is funded by the Duchess who dismissed her. What better way to retaliate than by provoking a violent scene outside it? She threw the first stone, turning a vocal protest into one where blood might have been spilled.'

'Especially as you say the Cockpit Club men were there with swords,' mused Swaddell. 'We must ask them why they went.'

'We know why: the rumour is that Tooley caught a fever there, so I imagine they went for revenge. Fortunately, they lacked the courage to act. Mansfield tried to follow Dutch Jane's stone with a handful of mud, but he slunk off when Baron Lucas challenged him.'

'So why did Dutch Jane flee to the cemetery? Do you think she is connected to these so-called walking corpses?'

'Well, she knew exactly where to climb over the wall, which suggests she has done it before. We will have to track her down and ask.'

'Very well, but . . .' Swaddell stopped walking in confusion when Chaloner turned west. 'Where are you going? White Hall is this way.'

'I should visit Clarendon House first, to report to the Earl.'

'Oh, I nearly forgot.' Swaddell's expression was suddenly sheepish. 'His clerk gave me a message for you: the Earl wants you to report to him at once.'

Chaloner increased his pace. 'Then I will go to Clarendon House, while you speak to the Cockpit Club about Tooley and Ashley.'

'No,' said Swaddell, skipping a few steps to keep up with him. 'We were ordered to work side by side, so that is what we are going to do. I will wait outside while you are with Clarendon, after which we shall tackle these courtiers *together*.'

Chaloner nodded agreement, but determined to ditch the assassin at the first opportunity. As far as he was concerned, the less they were seen in each other's company, the better. They walked in silence for a while, then Swaddell remarked that he had secured an invitation to the Duchess's soirée on Wednesday.

'Did Williamson's office arrange it for you?' asked Chaloner curiously.

'The Bishop of Winchester did. He mentioned that he was going, so I asked him to take me as his guest. He said he would be delighted.'

'Did he?' Chaloner was astonished. Bishop Morley

was a friend of the Earl, an intelligent, shrewd, ethical man who was unlikely to associate with killers. 'Why?'

'Because he owes me a favour. When one's trade is rooting out treachery, one makes many acquaintances among the wealthy and powerful, as I am sure you have discovered yourself.'

'Unfortunately, most of the wealthy and powerful I meet tend to end up as enemies,' said Chaloner ruefully.

Swaddell changed the subject. 'Can your cousins cook?' he asked casually.

'I have no idea, but I had better find out, as their suitors will want to know.'

'What suitors?' demanded Swaddell, narrowing his eyes.

Chaloner smiled enigmatically. 'Negotiations are at an early stage, but they will be completed soon, even so.'

Swaddell blew out his cheeks in a sigh. 'Then I must stake my claim before you parcel them off to someone inappropriate.'

Chaloner was about to inform the assassin that *he* was inappropriate when it occurred to him that there was no need to offend such a deadly individual. No woman in her right mind would accept romantic overtures from the assassin, and while Veriana and Ursula might enjoy his company when no one else was available, they would never consider him a serious contender for marriage.

Relieved, he increased his stride towards Clarendon House.

Chaloner's reception was cooler than it had been the last time he had visited, and Brodrick explained why: the Cockpit Club had openly accused the Earl's staff of causing Chiffinch's death. Ergo, Chaloner's failure to

232

solve the case meant that no one from Clarendon House dared step outside, lest they were on the receiving end of any unpleasantness.

'We are under attack from all sides,' said Brodrick unhappily. 'I popped my head into the Shield Gallery this morning, and the Cockpit Club men accused me of murder. I have never been so frightened in my life. They clustered around me with their hands on their swords, and I was lucky the King intervened, or I would not be standing here now.'

'Then stay home,' suggested Chaloner. 'If you do not go out, no one can bully you.'

'I shall,' vowed Brodrick. 'Except for Wednesday, when I will attend the Duchess of Newcastle's soirée. She will not invite the Cockpit Club, so I shall be safe there.'

'How do you know she will not invite them?' asked Chaloner, thinking that if bishops and assassins were being included, then God only knew who else might be on her guest list.

'Because she clashed with them over yesterday's fox-tossing. She wrote letters to every courtier in the palace, claiming that decent folk would shun such monstrous cruelty. The Cockpit Club men were livid, because it meant the King decided not to go. He does not usually heed such things, but that lunatic Duchess apparently unsettled him with her forceful opinions.'

Chaloner went on his way, and saw Barker in the hall. The clerk tried to slip away without being seen, but Chaloner caught up with him and grabbed his arm.

'Why were you really in Clerkenwell last night?' he demanded. 'I know it was not delivering letters to Newcastle House.'

Barker glared at him. 'I suppose you base your charge

233

on the fact that I was walking in the wrong direction. Well, for your information, I *did* take a bundle of missives to the Duke, but I stopped off on the way back to visit my mother.'

'Your dead mother?'

Barker scowled. 'I told you: she is alive. However, the Earl ordered me to hurry home, so I am naturally reluctant for him to find out that I disobeyed him. It is a pity Ma needs me, because I would never venture into such a dangerous area otherwise.'

'It is not dangerous! The Duchess of Newcastle lives there.'

'So do a lot of radicals and Puritan poets,' said Barker. 'It is no place for respectable men, so I advise you to keep your distance. You will be much safer if you do.'

He walked away, leaving Chaloner staring after him, not sure what to think. Were the clerk's parting words a friendly warning or a threat?

A few minutes later, Chaloner knocked on the door to My Lord's Lobby. His employer looked pale and tired, and the hope that filled his eyes when Chaloner first walked in faded once he had heard his report.

'But it has been *days* since Chiffinch died,' he whispered, 'and accusations and insinuations grow by the hour. They have reached the point where I dare not show my face anywhere. Nor do my staff. You *must* find the killer. Our future – our lives – depend on it.'

'I will do my best,' promised Chaloner, although the Earl did not seem much comforted. 'Incidentally, did you send Barker to Newcastle House with letters last night?'

'I might have done. Why?'

'Because it may help me understand what is happening

in Clerkenwell,' hedged Chaloner, unwilling to elaborate until he had more information. Barker might have been telling some version of the truth, and he did not want to cost an innocent man his livelihood.

'I do not care about Clerkenwell,' snapped the Earl. 'I care about White Hall – about being accused of killing debauchees.'

'They may be connected, sir. Some of my suspects live in Clerkenwell; Tooley is alleged to have caught a fatal fever there; he will be buried in its cemetery; and Ashley's body was in Tooley's grave. So *did* you send letters to Newcastle House?'

'I cannot recall, but Barker will know, as I always use him to take them. He is the only servant I trust not to go about his own business on the way home.'

'I see,' said Chaloner. 'But why do you communicate with the Duke so often? I thought he no longer concerned himself with affairs of state.'

'I am advising him on a legal matter pertaining to his estate. All I can tell you is that he wants to provide for his wife after his death – to prevent his son from leaving her penniless.'

'What is your impression of Viscount Mansfield, sir?'

The Earl regarded him narrowly. 'I hope you are not about to claim that *he* is involved in these murders. The Duke would be devastated.'

'I did warn you that exploring Chiffinch's demise might lead to uncomfortable truths.' Chaloner realised that this sounded insolent, so he asked his question again before the Earl could berate him for it. 'Is there anything about Mansfield that I should know?'

'Well, the Duke considers him a disappointment. He is a weak nonentity, but he is also greedy, and blanches every time the Duke opens his purse. And he hates his stepmother. Poor Mansfield would have been happier born as an ordinary man, because inheriting a dukedom is quite beyond him. But none of us can choose our kin.'

'No,' sighed Chaloner wryly.

The Earl smiled suddenly. 'Speaking of kin, Wiseman tells me that you have two young cousins wanting husbands. You are honoured to be entrusted with so important a task, and it is an opportunity to secure alliances that will benefit yourself.'

Chaloner struggled not to show distaste at the notion that he would be so selfish as to use other people's happiness for personal gain. 'I hardly know where to begin,' he replied ambiguously.

'By finding suitable lodgings, because you cannot keep them in Covent Garden with you and Wiseman. It is vaguely indecent. Bring them here: my wife will look after them.'

It was a generous offer, and living in the home of a staunchly Royalist family would help with the small matter of Veriana and Ursula's father being charged with treason. Of course, Chaloner would definitely have to ensure that the Earl was not then accused of murder.

'Thank you, sir.'

'Well, I cannot send you away on *Royal Oak* next Sunday if you have women to look after,' said the Earl, thus revealing that it was not kindness that had prompted him to intervene, but self-interest. 'My wife is away until Easter, so someone else must mind them until then. I suggest Fanny Clarke, the physician's wife.'

'Do you?' asked Chaloner, surprised. 'Why?'

'Because she is modest, respectable and *very* dull – a woman you want your cousins to emulate. It will be easier

236

to secure good matches if they are malleable, demure and stupid. After all, no man wants a wife who is too clever.'

Chaloner laughed, then realised the Earl was serious. 'But surely he will appreciate one who can manage his household and provide intelligent conversation of an evening?'

'His servants can provide one and his friends the other,' replied the Earl. 'Besides, the Duke of Newcastle married a lady with spirit, and look at how *she* is regarded in decent society. Take it from me, Chaloner, Fanny Clarke is the woman you need until my wife can take your cousins. Of course, even she can be unorthodox. Yesterday, she tried to stop the fox-tossing.'

'But she did not succeed, and nor did the Duchess. It went ahead anyway.'

'It did, much to White Hall's lasting shame. It attracted a very large audience, although not all onlookers were approving. It was a pity Cobbe's ploy was unsuccessful.'

Chaloner frowned. 'What ploy?'

'He let the foxes out of their cages. He claims it was an accident, but he is intelligent, and understood that such a spectacle might turn Londoners against us. Unfortunately, the foxes failed to find their way out of the palace, and so they were rounded up again.'

'Pity,' said Chaloner. 'For the foxes and for White Hall.'

He emerged from Clarendon House to see Swaddell sitting on a horse trough outside the gate. The assassin seemed uncharacteristically happy, chewing on a blade of grass and humming. Chaloner hoped it was not because he saw the prospect of a bride on the horizon.

'I have just learned that the whole Court is in St

237

James's Park,' Swaddell said, standing and indicating that Chaloner should walk there with him. 'As it is a nice day, Bess Widdrington has organised some dog-races. Her husband is none too pleased, apparently, as he would rather she stayed at home, doing wifely things.'

'Who told you that?' asked Chaloner, falling in at his side.

'Captain Rolt. He lives in Kensington, so he walks along Piccadilly most days. He stopped to chat when he saw me.'

'He was on foot?' asked Chaloner, thinking this was a low mode of transport for a man who aimed to make an impression and win himself a lucrative post.

'He lost his horse in a fight, as you know, and says he has not had time to buy another. I wonder why he lives in Kensington. It is full of hovels and farmyards. He also mentioned that Widdrington aims to send Bess to Ireland soon, because she is becoming an embarrassment.'

'Why Ireland? Does his family have connections there?'

'No, he chose it so she will be separated from him by a wide, very rough stretch of water.'

Chaloner let the tittle-tattle wash over him as they entered the park, enjoying the pretty day with its soft spring light. Birds sang, and the air was full of the scent of blossom and clean, fresh earth. Then he saw the crowds near the Canal, and thought the entire palace must have turned out. A big black wig at the heart of the throng explained why it was busy: the King had chosen to attend, and where he went, his sycophants followed.

The dogs were being raced down one side of the lake, but they did not understand what they were supposed to do, so instead of running in a straight line, they trotted where they pleased, stopping to sniff and cock their legs along the way. Widdrington led the derisive laughter, while Bess's face was a mask of dismay.

'This will cost her money,' murmured Swaddell. 'Fortunes are wagered at these events, but no one will bet on this debacle, which means she will not recoup her expenses. Worse, it was organised to impress Widdrington, but he mocks her the loudest. And now the King has tired of the commotion and is leaving early.'

Sure enough, His Majesty was preparing to go. His senior courtiers rallied around him, although some of the younger ones held back, loath to exchange fresh air for a stuffy gallery. The Cockpit Club men were among the latter, watching Bess vent her disappointment by beating a dog with a stick. It yelped and bit her, which made her husband cackle anew. Cobbe, even more outrageous than usual in lime-green silk, hastened to rescue it.

Meanwhile, the ambitious Rolt was trying to decide whether it would be more advantageous to follow the King who did not know him, or stay with the 'friends' who did. In the end, he compromised by choosing a spot near the end of the Canal, which the King would have to pass on his way back to the palace, but that was close enough to the Cockpit Club men to ensure he was included in any plans they might make for later.

'Widdrington's rabble do not seem unduly disturbed by the deaths of two of their number,' remarked Swaddell. 'Shall we ask them why?'

He and Chaloner walked towards them. Most reeked of wine, suggesting that the morning's races were a continuation of the previous night's entertainment.

239

Young Legg had been sick down himself, which meant that no one wanted to stand too close, while the rest looked seedy and stained. Rolt was alone in being freshly shaved and clean.

'Here comes the Earl's assassin and the Spymaster's creature,' drawled Widdrington. 'Do you see this pair, Pamphlin? One of them dispatched Chiffinch, then accused us of the crime.'

The man he addressed was a thin, spotty courtier whom Chaloner had seen with the Cockpit Club before. He was dressed almost as decadently as Cobbe, and had affected an insouciant pose that entailed leaning on Mansfield's shoulder. The Viscount was trying not to mind, although it was obvious that he was uncomfortable with the familiarity.

'You are lucky Tooley is dead,' said Bess to Chaloner and Swaddell, her face an ugly mask of frustration, bitterness and spite. 'He was big and strong, and would not have tolerated your loathsome presence here today.'

'No,' agreed Mansfield, eager to play his part. 'Nor would Ashley.'

'We can see you are grieving,' said Chaloner, looking pointedly at the makeshift racecourse, 'so we shall be brief. What—'

'Stop right there,' ordered Pamphlin sharply. 'We do not answer to you.'

'Oh, I think you can make an exception, just this once,' said Swaddell with such soft menace that the courtier blanched. 'So tell us about the deaths of your two friends.'

'What do you want to know?' asked Widdrington, also unsettled by the assassin, but struggling not to show it. 'I can tell you that we will miss them. They were lively company.'

240

'Begin with Tooley,' instructed Chaloner. 'Did he seem unwell yesterday?'

'He was in fine fettle when he celebrated his win at the fox-tossing,' shrugged Widdrington. 'We had a drinking game after, and he won that, too.'

'And Ashley? When did you last see him?'

'Just after Tooley died,' supplied Widdrington. 'He was distraught, and said he was going to pray over the body.'

'Then why was he in Bunhill?' pounced Swaddell. 'Tooley was – and still is – lying in the chapel at White Hall.'

'Perhaps he craved peace for his devotions,' suggested Pamphlin slyly. 'And the chapel was busy yesterday because it was Palm Sunday. Ashley was a devout man, who needed tranquillity for his holy contemplations.'

The others sniggered at this claim.

'I thought Ashley and Tooley were your friends,' said Chaloner, shaking his head in incomprehension. 'Why do you make light of their deaths?'

'They would not want us to be miserable on their account,' averred Widdrington carelessly. 'The Cockpit Club is about having fun and living for today. Our only rules are that we do not dwell on what happened yesterday and we do not fear what might happen tomorrow.'

'Well, perhaps you should,' retorted Chaloner, 'because I doubt the sudden deaths of two healthy young men are natural.'

With a dismissive sneer, Widdrington swaggered away. The others followed, but Chaloner did not try to stop them, knowing he would have no answers as long as they were in a pack and too drunk to know when to be sensible. Eventually, the only ones left were Rolt, still nodding and smiling at anyone important who happened past him,

241

and Cobbe, who was playing with the dog he had rescued.

'Perhaps one of those two will be more helpful,' said Swaddell. 'Shall we find out?'

With no audience to entertain with shocking remarks and mincing manners, Cobbe was just an ordinary young man in outlandish clothes. He smiled warily as Chaloner and Swaddell approached and stood hastily, dog forgotten.

'I heard you tried to free some foxes yesterday,' began Chaloner.

'I cannot abide the things,' declared Cobbe with a shudder that convinced no one. 'Unfortunately, they declined to leave, so were killed anyway. But never mind them. I have information for you, Swaddell. Did you know I took refuge in the United Provinces when Cromwell was in power? I have always been a Royalist.'

He shot Chaloner the kind of glance that suggested he did not approve of men who flopped from side to side as occasion demanded.

'Did you like it?' asked Chaloner, declining to be baited.

'Not particularly, although it did allow me to learn Hollandish, so when I heard the Dutch ambassador chatting to his minions in White Hall the other night, I understood every word they spoke. They had no idea, of course, and blathered on obliviously.'

'What did they say?' asked Swaddell keenly.

'That they use the Bunhill cemetery to meet their spies. And that they have devised a simple system of communication, which entails lamps and red cloths. The light is kept white if all is well, but will glow scarlet if there is reason to be cautious.'

'Hah!' exclaimed Swaddell. 'Mother Broughton must have seen these lanterns and decided to include them in her prophecy. Corpses carrying tainted souls indeed!'

'They also mentioned the name of an informant: Janneke.'

'Which is Dutch for Jane,' mused Chaloner. 'So now we know why she ran to Bunhill when I chased her. It is a place where she thought she might get some help.'

'Keep this information to yourself, Cobbe,' Swaddell ordered. 'Then we can place our own people in the cemetery and catch these traitors red-handed.'

'Anything for King and country,' said Cobbe, and yawned exaggeratedly. 'And when you have them under lock and key, I shall be a hero.'

'Unlike last night then,' retorted Chaloner. 'When you and your friends tried to intimidate unarmed women outside the Red Bull. Why did you do it? For Tooley, because someone told you that he caught his fatal fever there?'

'Well, he did,' declared Rolt, overhearing and coming to join them. 'Bess said so.'

'Oh, then it must be true,' said Swaddell flatly. 'She would *never* twist the truth in the hope of winning her husband's good graces.'

Rolt regarded him with dislike. 'Do you mean to investigate his demise as well as Chiffinch's? And Ashley's, too?'

'If they do, we had better provide alibis, Rolt,' said Cobbe with a pleasant grin.

Rolt scowled, but answered anyway. 'We were with our Cockpit Club friends all day.'

'*Most* of the day,' corrected Cobbe. 'We all had personal errands to run on occasion, and there is not a

243

man among us who did not slip out for an hour or two.'
He smiled again at Chaloner and Swaddell. 'I imagine
the same is true of you two.'

'Actually,' countered Swaddell, 'I can prove my whereabouts for every moment.'

Chaloner doubted it was true, but was not about to
challenge him in front of two men who might be killers
themselves – and he was suspicious of both of them.
Rolt was ruthless enough to commit murder if he thought
it would further his ambitions, while Cobbe was an
enigma, whom Chaloner did not understand at all.

'Then perhaps we should narrow the field by establishing exactly when Ashley and Tooley died,' he said.
'Begin with Tooley.'

'Between six and seven o'clock last night,' replied
Cobbe promptly. 'In other words, between the end of
the drinking game and the time when his servant found
his body.'

By Chaloner's reckoning, he and Swaddell had only
his cousins as witnesses to their whereabouts at that time,
and no one was likely to believe the testimony of two
country girls who would lose everything if their guardian
was arrested for murder.

'What about Ashley?' he asked. 'When did he die?'

'All I can tell you about him is that he was alive just
after ten o'clock,' replied Cobbe. 'I know, because I heard
the Clerkenwell church clock chime the hour, and we
parted company a few moments afterwards. His body
was found at some point during the night.'

'Was he with you when you made a nuisance of yourselves outside the Red Bull?' asked Swaddell, although
Chaloner knew he was not – he had been dead by then,
lying at the bottom of Tooley's empty grave.

Rolt raised his hands defensively. '*I* did not go there to make trouble – it was not me who threw the stone. And we all left when Baron Lucas ordered us away.'

'You have not answered my question,' said Swaddell sharply. 'Was Ashley with you?'

'No, he was not,' replied Cobbe. 'He had already disappeared on business of his own. He did not tell us where he was going or what his errand entailed. He just left.'

'Perhaps he went to sell information to the Dutch,' suggested Chaloner.

Cobbe blinked in genuine shock. 'Ashley? Never! He may have been a drunk, but he was a patriotic one.'

Rolt grinned wolfishly. 'So where were you two when Ashley was killed?'

Swaddell smiled back, although it was not a nice expression. 'With the Bishop of Winchester. Then Tom went to the Red Bull – its patrons will confirm it.'

Swaddell's claim was so outlandish that Cobbe and Rolt exchanged a glance of disbelief, and Chaloner silently cursed him. It was simply *asking* to be accused of the crime.

'I see,' said Cobbe keenly. 'And the Bishop will corroborate this tale, will he?'

'Of course!' Swaddell sounded genuinely indignant. 'It is the truth.'

'Do *you* have any idea who killed Tooley and Ashley?' asked Chaloner, eager to move away from the subject of alibis before Swaddell's wild claims landed them in trouble. 'We all know they *were* murdered – that the tales of fever and grief are a nonsense.'

'Well, my first choice of culprits was you two,' replied Cobbe. 'But if you have a Bishop to vouch for you, I

245

shall give you the benefit of the doubt. Now, I have been more than generous with information, so how about some reciprocation? Who do you suspect?'

'Other than you?' asked Swaddell archly. 'A number of your fellow Cockpit Club friends, several courtiers, a servant or two. Why do you want to know?'

Cobbe flapped his handkerchief. 'Oh, just idle curiosity.'

'I neither like nor trust him,' muttered Swaddell as Cobbe minced away, Rolt fawning at his heels. 'There is something very dangerous beneath that smooth exterior.'

Coming from the assassin, this was damning indeed.

Chapter 9

As he felt national security was at risk, Swaddell insisted on travelling to Bunhill at once, to assess the danger posed by the traitors. Chaloner agreed to accompany him, thinking the journey would give him time to think about what they had learned in the park, although it did not take him many moments in the swaying hackney to conclude that it had actually been very little. They had approximate times of death for Ashley and Tooley, but Cobbe had made it clear that any of the Cockpit Club could have slipped away to commit murder, and the lack of grief displayed by the entire pack was suspicious to say the least.

'You should not have used Bishop Morley as an alibi,' he told Swaddell, wishing he had not been ordered to work with the man. 'Prelates do not lie, and we will be in trouble if anyone asks him about his movements last night.'

Swaddell looked hurt. 'But I *was* with Bishop Morley – we took a glass of wine together. You know he has a house in Clerkenwell, do you not?'

'I know he has one in Southwark,' said Chaloner tartly.

'It is called Winchester Palace, and has been the London residence of his ecclesiastical predecessors for centuries.'

'Well, he does not like it, so he bought another,' flashed Swaddell, equally curt. 'It is just down the green from Newcastle House. I thought you would have noticed, given that it has a cross on the roof and stained-glass windows.'

Chaloner supposed he was telling the truth, as it was something that could easily be checked. However, he simply could not imagine Morley and Swaddell enjoying a cosy evening together, and was sure that Swaddell was exaggerating the intimacy of the association.

'Even so,' he continued, 'Morley will not say that *I* was with him last night.'

'He will if I ask. I told you: he owes me a favour.'

Chaloner regarded him uneasily. 'You mean you will blackmail him into lying?'

'He would do it willingly,' said Swaddell, affronted. 'And you should be thanking me, not insulting me. If this is how you treat your friends, I am surprised you have any.'

They rode in silence the rest of the way and reached the cemetery during a downpour. Swaddell told the driver to wait, and they hurried through the deluge, calling for Tyndal. There was a guardhouse by the gates, and Tyndal and his sons were crammed inside it, waiting for the rain to stop. They invited their visitors to join them, which made for a very tight squeeze.

'Those walking corpses will see us beggared,' said Tyndal glumly. 'No one wants their loved ones buried in a place where they might get up and leave.'

'Well, you will have work tonight,' said Swaddell, 'because you are going to help us catch a coven of traitors. It will prove beyond doubt that your "walking

248

corpses" are nothing of the kind, and you will have served your country into the bargain.'

Needless to say, the Tyndals were not very keen on tackling potentially dangerous spies, but Swaddell fixed them with a glower, which had them promising to do whatever he asked. While he issued a stream of instructions, Chaloner walked to the wood where he had found Dutch Jane's bonnet. In the middle of it was an ancient oak with a hole in its trunk. He would never have used it as a 'drop' – a place to exchange secret communiqués – because it was far too obvious. Thus he was astonished when he slipped his hand inside it and found a letter.

It was a report in Dutch, and Jane had even signed it, presumably to ensure that she was paid. It contained a lot of trivial chatter: the Queen's illness, Chiffinch's untimely end, and the Bishop of London being booked to preach in White Hall on Easter Sunday. Then there was some idle gossip: the King had a new mistress, and the Royal Society wanted to expel Baron Lucas before he offended *all* its less-gifted members by calling them stupid.

Captain Rolt merited a paragraph of his own, as it transpired that he was the son of a Puritan divine who had disowned him for becoming a Royalist. There was an account of him losing the only valuable thing he owned – the horse killed during the fight in the cockpit – concluding with the recommendation that he be offered the traitor's shilling, because he was in such desperate straits that he would almost certainly accept it.

Jane also wrote that Rolt intended to blackmail Bess Widdrington for visiting a Clerkenwell tavern without her husband's permission, although how she had discovered this was beyond Chaloner. He could only assume she had overheard Rolt telling someone else. Regardless, it suggested that the captain had been telling the truth, while Bess had lied.

The final paragraph was about Mother Broughton's prophecies, which Jane claimed would definitely come true: Good Friday would see a rain of holy fire, which would set Clerkenwell ablaze and wreak vengeance on the wicked. She ended by informing her reader that she aimed to be gone before that happened, lest she was among the casualties.

Swaddell approached at that point, and read the report with a dismissive sneer. 'Ambassador van Goch will be disappointed with this! She had a lot more to convey when we fed her misinformation via the Duke. The enemy will not care about tittle-tattle, while Mother Broughton's ramblings are irrelevant.'

Chaloner was about to return to the waiting hackney when he spotted something white in the grass. Curious, he went to investigate, and found himself staring at a familiar face, although one that was pale and waxy in death, eyes gazing sightlessly up at the clouds.

It was Dutch Jane, and her throat had been cut. He examined her quickly, recalling Mother Broughton's prediction about sausages and vats of milk, but there was no evidence of either.

He glanced at Swaddell. 'Throat-cutting is your favourite method of execution.'

Swaddell was deeply offended. 'My incisions are works of art, Tom, whereas this is pure butchery. I would *never* make such a mess.'

It did not escape Chaloner's notice that Swaddell was more indignant at being accused of an untidy assassination than he was of being considered guilty of murder.

*

While Swaddell went to inform Tyndal that he had a customer for his funerary services, Chaloner had the uncomfortable sense that events were beginning to spiral out of control, but he understood virtually nothing of what was going on. Who had killed Jane? Someone who knew she was a spy – the execution of a traitor? Or one of her countrymen, for leading a pursuer to Bunhill, forcing them to fight and then flee?

He leaned against the cemetery wall, thinking that he was no further forward with finding Chiffinch's killer than he had been when he had started his enquiries three days ago. Worse, he now had two more victims to investigate – three, if he included Dutch Jane – so he sincerely hoped Wiseman would tell him something useful when he examined Ashley and Tooley. He recalled the Earl's fear and the unease of his staff, with no one daring to go out lest it occasioned an accusation. Chaloner needed to solve the case soon, or irreparable harm was going to be done to Clarendon House.

Eventually, Swaddell finished making arrangements with Tyndal, and he and Chaloner climbed into the waiting hackney, where the driver began to regale them with what he knew about Bunhill's walking dead. He claimed to have seen them with his own eyes, their red souls glowing like hot embers. At first, Chaloner assumed he had seen the Dutch spies, but when he reported decaying legs, arms and jaws, along with trailing grave clothes, it became obvious that the testimony was pure fabrication.

Although Chaloner itched to race to White Hall and beg Wiseman to inspect Tooley and Ashley at once, Swaddell wanted to stop at Newcastle House first, and ask about Dutch Jane.

'Her death is a serious blow to the intelligence services,'

he sighed, 'because now it will be impossible to lay hold of her accomplices. I had planned to use her as bait to trap them.'

'You go to Newcastle House,' suggested Chaloner. 'I will visit White Hall and—'

'We will stick together,' interrupted Swaddell firmly. 'Here we are. Ready?'

He marched up to Newcastle House's front door and hammered imperiously. It was answered by a liveried butler, who took one look at his grim face and stood aside for him to enter. Chaloner followed reluctantly. It was the first time he had been inside, and he was surprised to find the hall unusually bright. He glanced up and saw the high ceiling was made of glass, which allowed daylight to flood in.

'The Duchess mentioned her transparent roof,' he recalled.

'It is a nice idea, but it leaks,' said the butler, and indicated several strategically placed buckets. 'Worse, the rain pools on the glass above, which encourages seagulls to come and paddle. You should see the mess they make.'

At that moment, a maid arrived to report that the Duke and Duchess were still abed, but would be ready to receive visitors in an hour.

'An hour?' echoed Chaloner in agitation. 'We must come back later.'

'Nonsense,' said the butler soothingly. 'Mr Clayton, one of the Duke's stewards, does a lovely tour of our unusual roof for a very reasonable price. The views are lovely. When you are up there, the time will just fly past.'

That was what Chaloner was afraid of.

*

252

The sullen steward appeared with impressive speed, delighted to make a little money on the side. Chaloner deplored the wasted time, but Swaddell was eager to see a part of the house that was normally off-limits to visitors.

The moment the fee was in his pocket, Clayton led them to a servants' staircase, the entrance of which was discreetly concealed behind a statue of a horse. They began to climb, past the grand reception rooms on the ground floor, then the bedchambers and finally the attics in the wings. Eventually, they reached a small, low door that opened on to the roof. He stepped through it, then ducked as wings flapped around his head.

'Damned seagulls,' he snapped, picking feathers from his coat. 'They attack me every time I come up here. I shall have to start bringing a musket.'

Because the house was in the shape of a stubby H – a fat arm at either end with a longer, lower block joining them together – the roof was in three sections, too. There was a 'pyramid hip' over each of the two wings, while the middle part of the roof was flat, with knee-high balustrades running along both edges – one overlooking the street at the front, and the other overlooking the garden at the back. The central section had originally been tiled, but these had been removed – other than a wide 'walkway' immediately outside the door – and replaced with panes of glass, so as to illuminate the hall and the ballroom below. There were dozens of panels, each one in a lead frame. Unfortunately, lead was not very rigid, so the whole structure had started to sag.

The problem had been resolved by installing a massive iron brace, which spanned the flat part of the roof from right to left, dividing it neatly in half. It was impossible to see over its top, so Chaloner could only assume that the

253

far side was a mirror image of the one on which he stood. The warped frames had then been fastened to the brace with smaller supports. Even so, some bits remained lower than others, and as there was no mechanism to let water drain away, it meant that every time it rained, the Newcastles had a series of ponds on their roof.

'Ugly, is it not?' said Clayton with superior disdain. 'She should have given up when the lead startled to buckle, as anyone with half a brain could see that a glass roof will never work.'

'But it *has* worked,' countered Swaddell. 'The hall below is lovely and light, and I imagine the ballroom is, too.'

'Oh, they are light,' sneered Clayton. 'But you may as well have no roof at all in inclement weather, because the ceiling leaks. Surely you noticed the buckets, set ready to catch drips? Worse, there is no way to clean the inside of the glass, so in a few years, it will be coated in soot from the lamps. Then our hall and ballroom will be as dark as ever.'

'Why does the glass not crack under the weight of the water?' asked Swaddell, gripping Chaloner's arm for balance while he tested the depth of one pool with his foot. He withdrew it quickly when it transpired to be higher than his boot.

'Baron Lucas devised a way to strengthen the panes,' explained Clayton, 'although his experiments cost a fortune, and poor Viscount Mansfield's inheritance was used for the whole process. The Royal Society got fat on his tests though, damn them.'

'The central brace is unattractive,' mused Chaloner, eyeing it critically; it comprised a wall of iron plates that stood taller than the height of two men. 'Yet I did not notice it when I looked at the house from the street.'

254

Clayton sniffed. 'You will now you know it is here. It spoils the look of the place in my opinion. Moreover, the wretched thing is so tall that I cannot climb over it.'

Chaloner regarded him askance. 'Why would you want to do that?'

'The gulls,' explained Clayton between gritted teeth. 'They love it up here, but as soon as I chase them off this side, they fly to the other. That means I have to run all the way down the stairs to the ground floor, then all the way up the opposite stairs – at which point the damned things fly back over here again.'

Chaloner could tell from the noise that the birds had indeed landed on the other side of the structure, and supposed that shooing them off would present a challenge.

'The views are nice, though,' said Swaddell appreciatively. 'It would be a fine place to bring a young lady for an unusual jaunt.'

'Not my cousins,' said Chaloner, knowing exactly what he was thinking. 'It is starting to rain again. Can we go now?'

Back in the hall, the butler was waiting to say the ducal pair was still unavailable, but Eliza Topp was in the ballroom and wanted to see them. Chaloner started to object, loath to waste more time, but the man was insistent. They followed him across the hall and through a huge pair of gilded doors, where Chaloner stopped to gaze around in awe. The ballroom was huge, and no expense had been spared on its renovation – so recent that it still reeked of paint and freshly oiled wood. He began to understand why Mansfield was worried that his father might have no money left to bequeath him.

Eliza was by one of the great windows, red-eyed and

clutching a sodden handkerchief. Perched next to her, looking out of place but defiant, was Sarah Shawe.

'My husband,' whispered Eliza. 'Have you seen him?'

Chaloner frowned. 'No, why?'

Sarah took her friend's hand and chafed it comfortingly as she replied. 'He went out last night and did not return. Eliza is worried that something bad has happened to him.'

'He has enemies, you see,' elaborated Eliza shakily. 'Clayton is jealous of the trust the Duke and Duchess place in him, and is always trying to besmirch his good name. And a few days ago, Clayton's horrible friends arrived in the city . . .'

'Liddell the horse-trader and Vicar Booth,' put in Sarah. 'Both are rogues, and we are concerned that Clayton has tired of trying to harm Topp with words and insinuations, and has resorted to actual violence.'

Chaloner thought about the anonymous letter that the Duke had asked Thurloe to investigate – the one accusing the Duchess of having an affair with Topp. Had Clayton sent it, not so much to hurt her as to destroy his enemy? But if so, Clayton would hardly have dispatched his victim before the letter had had a chance to work its mischief.

'Do you have any evidence that Clayton might hurt Topp?' he asked. 'I accept that he and Topp dislike each other, but colleague rivalry does not usually result in physical harm.'

'No,' admitted Eliza, tears coursing down her cheeks. 'But my husband has never disappeared like this before. He knows I worry . . .'

'Were you up on the roof with Clayton just now?' asked Sarah. 'You cannot make out much from down

256

here, with all that thick glass and water, but we thought we saw shadows. Did he mention Topp at all?'

'No,' replied Swaddell. 'But—'

'Then that *proves* he has done something untoward,' declared Sarah. 'Normally, he cannot utter two words without maligning Topp. His silence is suspicious.'

'Not necessarily,' said Chaloner, thinking that Clayton had not had time to talk about Topp, because he had been too busy disparaging the Duchess and her ceiling.

'Perhaps Topp found out about you,' said Swaddell to Sarah. 'No husband wants to share his wife with someone else, and it is clear that he has a challenger for Eliza's affections.'

'He knows my friendship with Sarah does not threaten my love for him,' said Eliza firmly. 'He is my husband – he will always be first in my heart. Him and my Duchess.'

This was clearly news to Sarah, and hurt flashed in her eyes, although it was quickly masked. She forced a smile. 'Besides, if he had gone on a journey, he would have taken his travelling bag with him, but Eliza tells me it is still here.'

'I shall ask my people to keep an eye out for him,' promised Swaddell. 'But I am afraid we are here to bring you other sad news. Dutch Jane is dead.'

Eliza gaped as he outlined what they had learned about the Duchess's former maid, then began to weep afresh, although Sarah's expression hardened.

'*I* am not sorry. She tormented poor little Molly, tried to disrupt our school, and now we learn she was a traitor, too. Well, as far as I am concerned, she got what she deserved.'

Eliza was kinder. 'She was lonely. We should have tried harder to befriend her.'

257

'But I did not want to befriend her,' objected Sarah. 'Of course, we should not be surprised by the news – Mother Broughton foretold it.'

'She also foretold that it would involve sausages and a vat of milk,' said Chaloner wryly. 'Neither of which were in evidence around the body.'

'Sausages would have been,' countered Sarah. 'Dutch Jane loved them, and always had one secreted somewhere on her person.'

'Then seeing one in her future was not very impressive, was it?' said Chaloner. 'Your so-called soothsayer just took some commonly known fact and included it in—'

'You say there was no sausage with Jane's body?' interrupted Sarah, and raised a triumphant finger. 'Then *that* is its relevance! She *always* had one with her, but on the night of her death, she did not. It was the unusual *absence* of a sausage that Mother Broughton foretold.'

'You are twisting the facts to suit—'

'I am proving that Mother Broughton is a genuine prophet,' argued Sarah. 'And nasty old Jane should have listened to her. It is a good thing I have an alibi for the woman's murder, or those with suspicious minds might think I did it.'

'What alibi?' asked Swaddell, showing his thoughts had indeed run in that direction, while Chaloner resolved not to mention the vat of milk again, sure Sarah would find a way to 'prove' one of those featured in Dutch Jane's demise, too, and he did not have time to listen to more nonsense.

'I was with Joan Cole and a dozen others pickling cockles all last night. Then I came here at dawn, when Eliza sent for me. And do not accuse her of the crime either, because she read with the Duchess until sunrise, then raced around this place searching for Topp.'

258

Eliza blushed uncomfortably. 'They do not think we hurt Jane, Sarah. And I am sorry she is dead. I hoped she would get another post in the city. She makes . . . *made* lovely marchpanes.'

Sarah turned to Chaloner and Swaddell with a sneer. 'So there is a summary of Dutch Jane's character for you: spiteful, cruel and ignorant, but a virtuoso with sweetmeats.'

When the butler appeared to announce that the Duchess was on her way at last, Swaddell intensified his efforts to prise more information about Dutch Jane from Eliza and Sarah before the great lady arrived, but Chaloner could tell he was wasting his time. Eliza was too distressed about her missing husband, while Sarah was disinclined to be helpful. Eventually, the Duchess swept in. Chaloner had the sangfroid to bow in order to mask his consternation, but Swaddell just stood and gaped.

The Duchess had donned the costume she was alleged to have worn to the theatre. It was bright blue, and the neckline plunged well below her ample bosom, which had been daubed thickly with red and white powder. The ensemble was completed with a pair of heavy riding boots and what appeared to be a bishop's mitre. Chaloner supposed she had designed it herself, as no dressmaker would have dared.

'My God!' he heard Sarah breathe. 'I thought the rumours about her wardrobe were exaggerated, but there *is* such an outfit.'

'Eliza, my poor friend,' said the Duchess gently, and opened her arms. 'I am sure Topp will return soon. Come, let me comfort you.'

Eliza ran to her mistress and sobbed against her

259

shoulder. Sarah watched for a moment with jealous eyes, then marched out. She did not bother to acknowledge the Duchess, but if the noblewoman noticed, she gave no indication. She patted the distraught Eliza on the back, murmuring that she had summoned Clayton, and aimed to ask him if he knew where Topp had gone. Then she addressed Chaloner, who was careful to keep his eyes fixed on her face.

'I know you asked for an audience with the Duke, but he is getting ready to visit White Hall with my stepson. They could not go there yesterday, because some vile rogue organised cruel games involving foxes. They remained here, in protest against such disgusting sport.'

'They were here all day, Your Grace?' asked Chaloner, thinking that if so, then neither could have killed Tooley, who was dead by seven o'clock.

'Until eight, when my stepson went out for "important business", although I doubt it was anything of the kind. The boy likes to think that all he does is of great significance, but . . .'

She ended with a disdainful sniff, while Chaloner recalled that Mansfield had been outside the Red Bull with the Cockpit Club by nine. His stepmother was right to be suspicious of his self-aggrandising claims, as his 'business' had been the cowardly attack on Eliza's school – one that had faltered under her brother's withering dressing-down.

'Were you with them, Your Grace?' asked Chaloner innocently, thinking he might as well make sure he could eliminate her, too, although he could think of no reason why she would want to dispatch the worthless rogues of the Cockpit Club.

'For some of the time,' replied the Duchess airily. 'But

I had an errand in the early evening. I returned here at eight, which is how I am able to state with certainty when my stepson left – our paths crossed just as the clocks were striking the hour.'

'What errand?' fished Chaloner, but it was a question too far.

'One of a *personal* nature,' she replied, and before the spy could ask more, she sat Eliza on a bench and strode to the window, where she proceeded to treat the gardeners to a fine view of her frontage. Once her back was to him, Swaddell was able to regain his composure.

'So the Duke and Mansfield are in the clear for whatever happened to Tooley,' he murmured to Chaloner. 'The Duchess, on the other hand . . .'

Chaloner fretted impatiently while Swaddell furnished her broad back with an account of Dutch Jane's demise. He was eager to leave, and was sorry he had agreed to the detour. Then Clayton arrived, obviously irked at being summoned by the Duchess he despised. He had brought Booth and Liddell, perhaps with the intention of intimidating her by force of numbers.

'You wanted to see me?' he asked, insolence not only in his brusque tone, but also by his neglecting to address her properly.

'Topp appears to be missing,' replied the Duchess, still gazing out of the window. 'Have you done him any harm?'

'No, I have not!' declared Clayton, wrong-footed by the blunt question. 'I have not seen him since he proved to be so useless during the crisis with poor Henrietta Florence yesterday. If it had not been for me, the Duke would have lost a valuable animal.'

Eliza leapt to her husband's defence. 'Francis's skills

261

lie in other areas,' she said sharply. 'But do you swear, by all you hold holy, that you have not seen him since then?'

'I do,' said Clayton, and his expression turned sly. 'Perhaps he has absconded. I do not know why everyone trusts him with—'

The Duchess whipped around to face him, and the sight of her bare breasts caused the words to freeze in his throat. Liddell gulped his astonishment, while Vicar Booth gave a low whimper of horror and scuttled out of the ballroom as fast as his spindly legs would carry him.

'Topp's loyalty is incontestable,' she declared icily. 'Although I am yet to be convinced of yours. I found more irregularities in your accounts yesterday, so I hope you have a credible explanation. If not, I shall urge my husband to dismiss you.'

'You cannot oust me!' cried Clayton, panic jolting him from his shock at her costume. 'I am His Grace's most dedicated servant, whereas Topp is all slippery manners and ineptitude. You cannot keep him in preference to me.'

'I can if I want to,' flashed the Duchess, and came to stare intently at him. He attempted to meet her eyes, but her presence at such close quarters was too disconcerting, and his gaze dropped to the floor.

'I swear,' he mumbled. 'I have not seen Topp. I do not know where he is.'

The Duchess glared at him a while longer, then returned to the window. 'I suppose I believe you. However, if it transpires that you are lying, I shall have you executed for treason.'

Clayton was unsettled by the threat, even if it was one

she could never carry out within the bounds of the law.
'I *am* telling the truth!'

'Good,' said the Duchess, then turned to address
Chaloner and Swaddell. 'Have either of you two heard
about a certain letter sent anonymously to my husband?'

'What letter is this?' asked Clayton, although the question
had not been aimed at him. 'And why would this pair—'

'I am not supposed to say,' interrupted the Duchess
curtly. 'He swore me to secrecy.'

Not very effectively, thought Chaloner, if she was going
to ask questions about it of anyone who happened past.
Then it occurred to him that she suspected Clayton of
sending the missive, and this was her way of seeing if
she could force a confession from him.

'If it is something that can harm the Duke, then you
must tell me,' said Clayton sternly. 'He trusts me to look
to his interests and—'

'A better man than you is exploring the matter,' interrupted the Duchess. 'One who is assiduous and crafty,
and who will leave no stone unturned. He will find the
truth. But if you cannot help us with Topp, Clayton, you
may go. I have no further use for you at the moment.'

Enraged by the curt dismissal, but not in a position
to do much about it, Clayton turned and stalked out.
Liddell followed.

'Now, let us discuss Dutch Jane,' said the Duchess
when they had gone. 'I suppose you want us to pay for
her funeral, but the answer is no. She is not deserving
of our charity.'

'I think we must,' said Eliza tiredly. 'Or we shall lay
ourselves open to accusations of unkindness. Besides, she
was not really bad. Just dishonest, greedy, disloyal and
cruel.'

Humour glinted in the Duchess's eyes. 'Small failings, I am sure. But my mind is made up. I will not pay, and nor will you, Eliza. I forbid it. Jane read all my husband's letters and told the Dutch what was in them. We are under no obligation to bury a traitor.'

Swaddell regarded her in astonishment. 'You knew?'

'Of course I knew.' The Duchess smiled superiorly. 'I provided all manner of additional snippets for her to blab, each one carefully designed to mislead and confound. Why do you think we won the Battle of Lowestoft? It was all because of me.'

Chaloner had been at that particular skirmish, and felt that at least some of the credit belonged to the brave seamen who had risked their lives to fight it, but he held his tongue.

'So why did you dismiss her then?' demanded Swaddell, exasperated. 'It was inconvenient for the intelligence services to lose such a valuable tool.'

'Because her paymasters were beginning to distrust her reports, so her value was diminishing,' replied the Duchess. 'Besides, she disobeyed an express order about my poultry and she was unkind to little Molly. I do not tolerate defiance or deliberate cruelty.'

'I do not suppose you know who killed her, do you?' asked Swaddell.

'The Dutch, of course. They did not want to spend money on buying her passage home, but nor did they want her roaming around London blabbing about what she had done. Her fate was sealed the moment she agreed to play the spy.'

By the time Chaloner and Swaddell emerged from Newcastle House, their hackney driver had tired of waiting and had disappeared. They hired another on Holborn, with a lively horse that galloped most of the way to White Hall, so that when they arrived, Chaloner felt as though every bone in his body was thrumming from the jolts they had received. He settled the bill, and then heard someone call his name. It was Kersey, hailing him from a private coach – a new one that was all shiny black paint and gold trimmings. He sat next to a woman who was young, buxom and wore the best clothes money could buy.

'My wife,' said Kersey, patting her knee with a fond smile.

Chaloner felt like asking which one, but the charnel-house keeper's domestic arrangements were none of his business. 'It is not often we see you outside your domain,' he said conversationally. 'Where are you going?'

'To Newcastle House,' replied Kersey. 'A body was delivered to me an hour ago, drowned in the Thames, and items in its pockets reveal it to be one Francis Topp. I did hear he was missing, and now it seems he is found. Here. See for yourselves.'

He handed over a bundle of soggy papers – receipts and other mundane documents that bore Topp's signature. There was also a letter to Eliza, begging her forgiveness for leaving her a widow, but stating that it was best for all concerned: if he was in his grave, no one could accuse him of behaving improperly towards the Duchess, and the malicious lies about their alleged affair would fade away. He then assured her that he loved her very much, and asked her to explain his death to their employers.

'Topp and the Duchess?' breathed Swaddell. 'Lovers? I do not believe it!'

265

'Nor did the Duke,' said Chaloner. 'He would have stood by Topp, so there was no need for him to dispatch himself.' He glanced at Kersey. 'Are you sure it was suicide? He was not killed by someone else?'

'It was definitely suicide. However, the stench of ale on the body suggests that Topp's capacity for clear thinking was almost certainly impaired.'

'He was a fool then,' declared Swaddell. 'He should have stayed to prove his innocence.'

'Such allegations are easy to make, but difficult to dispel,' Chaloner said quietly. 'Maybe he knew he would never be free of them.'

'But what about the Duchess?' asked Swaddell indignantly. 'His self-murder makes it look as though they *did* have an affair, but he would rather die than be forced to admit it. He has done her a serious disservice by tossing himself in the river.'

Kersey tapped the letter with a beautifully manicured fingernail. 'This suggests he was trying to act in his employers' best interests. Maybe he *was* a little in love with his Duchess.'

'Of course, there is another explanation for his despair,' said Swaddell. 'Namely that his wife had taken a lover in the form of Sarah Shawe.'

'I shall never understand why folk find that so upsetting,' said Kersey, shaking his head in incomprehension. 'It is quite possible to love more than one person at a time.'

Well, a bigamist should know, thought Chaloner.

Chapter 10

Chaloner felt acutely uncomfortable as he walked through White Hall later that day. It was partly because he was with Swaddell, and the assassin was chatting away as if they were old friends, but mostly because it quickly became apparent that many courtiers believed the Earl was responsible for the recent spate of murders. People he barely knew eyed him warily as he passed, then began to whisper to each other the moment he was out of earshot. All in all, he was glad when they reached the chapel, although he baulked when Wiseman emerged, hands stained with blood.

'Poison,' the surgeon declared. 'In both men. I knew Clarke could not be trusted to give a reliable verdict and I was right. It was the same henbane-based toxin that killed Chiffinch, although delivered boldly this time, not hidden in capsules.'

'In oysters?' asked Chaloner.

'Probably in wine,' replied Wiseman. 'Both corpses reeked of it. They must have gulped it down very fast, or they would have noticed something amiss with the taste.'

'I imagine Tooley swallowed his at the drinking contest

that followed the fox-tossing,' surmised Chaloner. 'That would have entailed gulping, almost certainly by a man who was already drunk.'

'And Ashley?' asked Swaddell.

'He was a sot – the killer could have plied *him* with wine at any time and he would have accepted it. However, I suspect it happened at Bunhill, as I cannot see anyone lugging a body around for no obvious purpose.'

'And where better than that cemetery to commit such a crime?' mused Swaddell. 'Big, dark, isolated and devoid of witnesses – Tyndal and his lads cannot possibly monitor all of it.'

'There was soil under Ashley's fingernails,' put in Wiseman. 'In my professional opinion, the poisoner gave him the tainted wine, then shoved him into a grave when it began to take effect. Drunk and dying, Ashley tried to claw his way out, but failed.'

Chaloner winced at the image. 'How long before the poison took effect? If it was instantly, all we have to do is find out who gave Tooley his last drink.'

'Unfortunately, it is not that simple,' said Wiseman, and adopted the pompous tone he used on his students. 'There is no way to tell how much of the substance Tooley imbibed, which means I cannot say with certainty when the symptoms began. It may have been in his last cup, but it may equally well have been in his first.'

'The drinking contest was in a tavern,' said Swaddell, 'which was poorly lit and crowded. It was not a private affair for Cockpit Club men only. Ergo, the culprit might be anyone.'

'Not Baron Lucas,' averred Wiseman. 'He was with me then, having his bunions filed.'

'Is there anything else you can tell us?' Chaloner

asked, feeling that Wiseman's testimony so far posed more questions than answers.

'Only that you must hurry to get to the bottom of the matter,' replied Wiseman. 'These rumours about the Earl being responsible are dangerous, because his enemies now circle like bees around a wounded hippopotamus.'

And with that, he strode away, muttering about prescribing a tonic for the King, who had also enjoyed the drinking competition and had woken with a headache. Chaloner supposed they should be grateful that it was not His Majesty who had downed the poison.

He went into the chapel and stared down at the two bodies, wondering who had wanted them – and Chiffinch – dead. He reviewed his original list of suspects.

First, the Cockpit Club. He was sure Widdrington would stoop to poison, and so would Bess. Then there was the fickle but ruthless Captain Rolt, conveniently to hand when Chiffinch's body had been found, and Cobbe with his clever mind and contrived manners. There were others, too, such as young Legg, eager to impress his new and influential friends, and the spotty Richard Pamphlin, a silly fop with too much time on his hands.

Next was Will, who had gained so much from his brother's death. Had Tooley and Ashley helped him with the oysters, but as neither could be trusted to keep quiet, Will had decided to get rid of them, too? Chaloner knew for a fact that there was a hard core of ambition under the Pimp-Master General's dissipated exterior.

Then there were the people from Newcastle House, although most of those had now been exonerated. The Duke and his son had been at home when Tooley had died, while Lucas had an alibi in Wiseman. That left the Duchess, although Chaloner could not see her lurking in a dark cemetery with a flask of toxic wine. And if she had, not even Ashley would have accepted a drink under such circumstances.

Finally, there were Timothy and Fanny Clarke, although Chaloner knew of no reason why Fanny would kill three courtiers, while Clarke lacked the intelligence for so sly a crime. Yet the physician had tried to pass off all three deaths as natural, and as a medical man, he would know better than most how to kill with poison. So would a medical man's wife.

Of course, given that Tooley and Ashley had been poisoned in public places, the list now had to be expanded to include the entire population of London. Was the culprit a servant, perhaps one who had been shabbily treated by those particular men? Or someone who deplored the ruling elite and aimed to pick them off one by one? Chaloner grimaced as he realised that the possibilities were endless.

'There is only one way forward that I can see,' he said to Swaddell, who was standing silently at his side, respecting his need to gather his thoughts. 'We must return to the oysters – try to ascertain exactly who slipped into the larder and tampered with them.'

'But we have both tried that already,' objected Swaddell in exasperation. 'And learned that security is so appallingly lax that virtually anyone could have done it.'

'Do you have a better idea?' asked Chaloner.

Swaddell admitted that he did not.

As they left the chapel, they met Legg, who was carrying a massive bunch of flowers. Without being asked, the young man explained that they were for Ashley and Tooley.

'A nice gift might help me if these prophecies of walking corpses come true,' he elaborated. 'I do not want my dead friends vexed with me for not paying their mortal remains proper respect. They were bigger than me, you see.'

'Very prudent,' drawled Swaddell. 'But since you are here, tell us what duties Tooley and Ashley performed at Court – other than engaging in the kind of behaviour that might see the King toppled from his throne.'

'Not much,' replied Legg. 'That is why such posts are popular – it is money for nothing. They were Yeomen of the Larder, so all they had to do was hang around that place for a couple of hours each week and chat to the staff.'

'When was the last time they performed this arduous task?'

Legg considered. 'Well, Tooley worked on Thursday, which I know because he was late coming to the Shield Gallery that evening. I am not sure about Ashley.'

'Thursday,' mused Swaddell. 'That was when Chiffinch's oysters were poisoned – he ate them in the small hours of Friday morning. Is Tooley our culprit then?'

'Not unless he then went out and poisoned himself,' said Chaloner. 'However, it is time we had another word with the larder guards. Are you coming?'

The assassin was not very keen, but followed Chaloner anyway. Unfortunately, they arrived only to be informed that all four guards who had been on duty that night were now on furlough, so were not available for questioning. The clerk who supplied the information – his name was Abraham Hubbert – added that all had left the city to visit their families.

271

'How convenient,' said Chaloner, regarding him through narrowed eyes. 'Almost as if someone arranged for them to be out of the way.'

'You see plots where there are none,' said Hubbert, shoving a ledger at him. 'Our rotas are arranged weeks in advance. Look for yourself. You can see that nothing has been changed.'

'Then perhaps *you* can explain how Chiffinch's oysters came to be poisoned in your domain,' said Chaloner coldly. 'And then two of your Yeomen murdered within days.'

Hubbert swallowed hard. 'I cannot – I rarely leave this office, and it is the Yeomen of the Larder who supervise the guards . . .'

'Then how do you explain all the pilfering that takes place here?' demanded Swaddell, growing angry by their lack of progress, so lashing out at the man. 'You are the larder's clerk: you, of all people, must be aware of how much goes missing.'

Hubbert's expression was a combination of fear and defiance. 'What pilfering? I assure you that everything is in order. You cannot prove such a vile accusation.'

'*We* cannot,' acknowledged Chaloner. 'But Spymaster Williamson will. We shall report our suspicions to him, and he will examine all your accounts.'

He turned on his heel and stalked out, leaving Hubbert white-faced with terror.

'Williamson will refuse to do it,' said Swaddell in a low voice as he hurried after him. 'He is too busy with the Dutch war. Besides, he is in Dover.'

'I know,' sighed Chaloner, then grinned. 'But the threat gave Hubbert a good fright, and perhaps it will serve to turn the place honest, if only for a little while.'

'So now what?' asked Swaddell, disheartened.

'Back to the kitchens, I suppose,' sighed Chaloner. 'Perhaps the Master Cook will have remembered something new to help us.'

As usual, the palace kitchens were frantically busy, and the portly William Austen was harried. He swallowed hard when he saw Chaloner and Swaddell, resentful of the interruption when he had so much to do and alarmed that he was to be interrogated again.

'I have already told you all I know about the night that Chiffinch died,' he gulped, looking from one to the other with uneasy eyes. 'And I thought we had agreed that any blame for what happened to the oysters lies with the larder, not the kitchens.'

'It does,' said Swaddell. 'But we wondered if anything else has occurred to you in the interim. After all, I am sure you want to help us in any way you can.'

The look that accompanied these words was so full of venomous warning that the hapless Austen immediately gave the matter some serious thought.

'Well, you have already questioned the page who took the oysters from here to the Shield Gallery. The only other thing I can suggest is that you speak to the boy who fetched them from the fish market.'

The 'boy' transpired to be one Millicent Lantravant, a girl of eleven or twelve, who Austen said was stronger, more efficient and a faster learner than any of her male counterparts.

'It was four o'clock by the time Mr Austen realised that he had forgotten to order the oysters,' she piped, delighted to be the centre of attention. 'So he sent me to Lower Thames Street to buy some at once. But it was so late in the day that our usual traders had sold out.'

Austen regarded her in alarm. 'You did not mention this to me.'

'Because there was no need,' she replied with a proud toss of her head. 'I solved the problem myself. I was standing there, wondering what to do, when the Duchess of Newcastle happened past. She told me to try the oyster-seller on Clerkenwell Green.'

'Not Sarah Shawe?' asked Chaloner, startled.

Millicent nodded, and his mind raced with questions. Did this mean Sarah was the culprit? But how could she be? It was unlikely that she had happened to have poisoned capsules to hand when an opportunity arose to sell her wares to a servant from White Hall. And why would she want to harm Chiffinch anyway – a man she was unlikely to have met?

'Why did a duchess deign to talk to a child?' he asked, not sure what to think, although Austen's horror at the revelations made it clear that *he* had known nothing of what Millicent had done. 'Were you in your palace livery? Is that why?'

Millicent nodded sheepishly. 'And because I was crying. The boys would have taunted me about coming back empty-handed, you see, so I was upset. They are jealous of me, because Mr Austen says I am better than them, and they would love to see me in disgrace.'

'So you went to Clerkenwell. What then?'

'I found the oyster-seller on the green, just where the Duchess said she would be. When the woman saw my uniform, she tried to charge me a fortune, so I told her a lie about White Hall looking for a regular purveyor of shellfish. She dropped the price when she thought we might become one of her regular customers.'

274

Austen goggled at her. 'My word, child! You have some gall.'

Millicent preened. 'Then I hurried back here, and put them in a bucket of water in the larder, just like we always do. I fetched them just before midnight, when Mr Austen sent for them, and I watched him give them a light sprinkling of lemon and salt.'

'Lemon,' mused Chaloner, recalling that Tooley had claimed to be an expert on the fruit, on the basis of him being a Yeoman of the Larder. 'Are they in season now?'

'Mr Austen grows them in his hothouse,' explained Millicent. 'Shall I take you there?'

'Another time, perhaps. Is there anything else you can tell us?'

Millicent considered. 'When I took the oysters to the larder, someone watched me – a woman, whose face was covered by a scarf. I remember, because the day was mild, so she had no need to wrap herself up so.'

'How can you be sure it was a woman if you did not see her face?'

'Because I can tell the difference,' replied Millicent confidently. 'Of course, the larder is always being watched by people who want to get inside. It contains lots of lovely things, see – sugar, butter, raisins, fruit from Spain . . .'

'What else did you notice about . . . her?'

'That she had very nice shoes – black ones with silver buckles.'

'What of her clothes? Were they the kind worn by servants or courtiers?'

'Servants, although her shoes were of fine quality. I suppose a generous mistress *could* have given them to her, but she looked comfortable in them, as if they had been made for her.'

'But you do not know her name?'

'No, but Michael Mushey might. He was on guard duty that evening and he knows everyone. Ask him.'

'Unfortunately, he is on furlough and has left the city.'

Millicent's expression was scornful. 'Mushey will not have gone anywhere. The other three guards might, but he will still be here.'

'You seem very sure,' said Chaloner warily.

'I *am* sure. He will never leave White Hall, because he wants to be rich, and would be too worried about missing an opportunity. He is only a sentry, but he makes friends with important people, because he has a high opinion of himself.'

'What important people?' asked Swaddell, astonished by her candour.

'Well, he liked to drink with the Yeomen of the Larder, including the two who died.'

'Tooley and Ashley,' put in Austen helpfully. 'And Millicent is right – Mushey does think himself a cut above his fellows. Perhaps he can throw light on what happened to the oysters, although you will have to treat what he says with caution. The man is a born trickster.'

Chaloner thanked them for their help, and walked outside, glad to leave the steam, noise and chaos of the kitchens.

'I wish we had spoken to her days ago,' said Swaddell. 'She probably saw the killer, disguised and waiting for a chance to slip inside the larder. And her opinion of Mushey the guard seems uncannily astute. The only question is: can we trust the testimony of a child?'

'I think we can,' said Chaloner. 'I wonder if the woman outside the larder was the same one who told Millicent to buy the oysters in Clerkenwell. After all, if the Duchess

276

had not intervened, Millicent would have returned to White Hall empty-handed, and Chiffinch would never have eaten the capsules of poison.'

'He would not have eaten them *that night*,' corrected Swaddell. 'I rather suspect they would have been fed to him eventually, given the trouble someone took to make the things. Shall we pay a visit to Mushey now?'

All the palace guards lived in a large building over-looking Scotland Yard, so Chaloner and Swaddell began to walk there at once. They were just passing the larder offices again when Swaddell stopped and pointed to a staircase.

'Tooley's quarters are up there. Perhaps we should spend a moment looking around them. Who knows? It is where he died, so perhaps his killer left some clues.'

'He did not leave any with Ashley,' muttered Chaloner ruefully. 'I spent an age exploring the cemetery, but there was nothing to find.'

Tooley's chambers were surprisingly neat and tidy, other than the bed, which was a tangle of blankets, suggesting that he had flopped there and writhed in his final moments. It quickly became apparent that Chaloner and Swaddell were not the first to have visited, because there was a suspicious absence of anything valuable.

Then Tooley's manservant appeared, and said he had found his master at seven o'clock the previous evening, not long after he had heard thumps coming from the bedchamber. Such sounds were not unusual, as Tooley had been a heavy man with a lumbering tread, and the servant had only thought to check on him when things had gone oddly quiet.

277

'I saw at once that something was wrong, so I ran for help,' he went on. 'Dr Clarke came, and said he died of a fever. Fearing the plague, I kept my distance. His friends were not worried, though. They came and took his best things – said he would have wanted it.'

'Which friends?' asked Chaloner.

'Colonel Widdrington, his wife and Mr Pamphlin. But it was a lie, because Mr Tooley would *not* have wanted it. He told me that his sister was his only heir.'

Chaloner was disgusted, feeling it was one thing for the Cockpit Club not to grieve for a fellow member, but another altogether to race to his quarters and steal his possessions.

'We will have a word with that cabal again later,' he told Swaddell. 'About raiding Tooley's quarters *and* the drinking game that saw him dead. One of them must have seen the killer tamper with the wine. Or perhaps these three did it together, and they are all guilty.'

'If so, we will find out,' said Swaddell, 'because one will break and betray his fellows.'

They left Tooley's chambers and hurried across Scotland Yard. On their way, they met Clarke and Fanny, who were coming from the opposite direction. The couple were quarrelling.

'It is horrible,' declared Fanny, angry and tearful. 'Bess should not have done it. You demean yourself by being there.'

'I have no choice,' the physician snapped back defensively. 'How else can I win more wealthy clients? Besides, it will be fun, and I have never—' He stopped speaking abruptly when he realised Chaloner and Swaddell were listening.

278

'Two more of your verdicts were overturned today,' Swaddell informed him icily. 'Tooley did not die of a fever and Ashley did not die of grief.'

'*Hush!*' hissed Clarke, glancing around to make sure no one else had heard. 'And for your information, I never gave an opinion about Ashley, while Tooley *did* die of a fever. You cannot trust Wiseman. He is a mere barber–surgeon, whereas I am a university-trained physician.'

'Where were you on Sunday evening?' asked Chaloner. 'Between six and seven o'clock, and then between nine o'clock and midnight?'

Clarke glowered at him. 'That is none of your business. And you had better not be accusing me of these deaths. I *like* the Cockpit Club men. Indeed, I am on my way to join them now. Being with them is much nicer than being at home.'

He shot Fanny an unpleasant look and stalked away. Chaloner was about to follow and quiz him further when Swaddell homed in on Fanny like a vulture.

'We know you and Bess visited the Red Bull together,' the assassin began, 'so why did you lie about it?'

Chaloner grimaced his impatience. The women's excursion to a tavern was not relevant to the murders, so why was Swaddell wasting their time with it? Or was he just tired of dishonesty, and aimed to take someone to task for it because he could?

'Captain Rolt should not have gossiped,' said Fanny bitterly. 'He is no gentleman.'

'I shall take that as a confession,' said Swaddell. 'So why did you deny going there?'

'Because you asked me in front of my husband,' replied Fanny defiantly, 'and I did not want him to know that I . . . He frequents it himself, you see, and Captain Rolt

279

said it is a. . .' she lowered her voice prudishly, 'a house of ill repute. I had to know the truth.'

'You could not have sent someone else to find out?' demanded Swaddell.

Fanny regarded him askance. 'You mean ask a friend or a servant to determine whether my husband uses ladies of the night?'

She had a point: it would make her a laughing stock, and her sewing circle friends would likely shun her for it. She would become like Barbara Chiffinch – a decent woman struggling to make the best of life married to a disreputable rake. Clarke, on the other hand, would rise in the estimation of his fellow debauchees.

'You need not have worried,' Swaddell told her. 'The Red Bull is not a brothel.'

'No,' acknowledged Fanny. 'However, it *is* frequented by prostitutes – the unhappy ladies who think that learning to read, write and philosophise will raise them from the gutter.'

'You do not approve of women trying to better themselves?' asked Chaloner.

'Of course, but only in *suitable* subjects. Needlework is best. It is very important to be able to judge the quality of pins, cloth and thread, and then to learn how and when to apply specific stitches.'

Her mood lifted as she warmed to her theme, although her voice remained a monotonous drone, and Chaloner understood why so many people described her as 'dull'.

'Reading and writing could be useful to these women,' he said, cutting across a detailed exposition of the virtues of running backstitch.

'Wrong!' she flashed angrily. 'It will only encourage

discontent. They will expect an improvement in their lot after their hard work, but they will never get it.'

'They might,' argued Chaloner. 'It will qualify them for better posts.'

'Which they will never win,' said Fanny, exasperated.

'That is my point. These posts will go to the same people who always get them – folk from the *respectable* classes. Your educated prostitutes will resent it and there will be trouble. And I do not want more upheaval and chaos. I want everything to be safe and stable again.'

'Easy for you to say,' muttered Swaddell. 'You are wealthy, born into a comfortable life. The Red Bull women should not be held back by—'

'Much as I would love everyone to live in nice houses and do rewarding jobs, it will never happen,' interrupted Fanny, shortly and with passion. 'Our world is unjust, and it is cruel to raise the hopes of these women.'

'So what did you do at the Red Bull?' asked Chaloner, unwilling to waste time by debating social ethics with her. 'Stand outside and spy?'

Fanny grimaced. 'I suppose you could describe it so. There was a crack in the window shutter, so we took it in turns to peep through.'

'I cannot see you and Bess Widdrington having much in common,' remarked Swaddell. 'Why choose to go with her?'

'You mean because I am uninteresting and she is full of fun?' asked Fanny archly. 'Well, for your information, there is one thing upon which we both agree: that our country cannot endure more upheaval. We are tired of it.'

'Then why does she encourage the Cockpit Club's asinine antics?' asked Chaloner. 'She must see that they are turning the people against the King.'

Fanny winced. 'Unfortunately, she sees that as the only way to win her husband's affections. She adores him, and wants him to feel the same way about her.'

And Fanny was fond of Clarke, so that was something else the two women shared – being cursed with spouses who did not love them back. Sensing it was a sensitive subject, Chaloner brought the discussion back to the Red Bull by asking what she had overheard there.

'Baron Lucas giving a talk about some experiment involving the weather,' she replied. 'After which Mother Broughton announced that all London's wicked will die by Easter Sunday.' A pained expression suffused her face.

'I doubt you will be one of them,' said Swaddell, although it did not sound like a compliment, and Chaloner saw he had taken a dislike to this prim woman and her officious determination to prevent the advancement of her sex.

'Perhaps not, but what about Timothy? He thinks that joining the Cockpit Club will enhance his standing at Court, and will not listen when I say it may do him harm.'

'He has the right of it,' said Swaddell. 'The King prefers sinners to saints, so they are the ones who prosper in White Hall.'

'It is not Timothy's prosperity that concerns me,' said Fanny unhappily. 'It is his *soul.* I do not want him corrupted, but look at him now – racing off to watch goose-pulling!'

'What is goose-pulling?' asked Swaddell.

Fanny's eyes filled with tears. 'Riding horses at a teth-ered bird to see who can yank its head off. Have you ever heard anything more vile? Perhaps *this* is why there will be a great calamity on Good Friday – we torture God's creatures in the name of sport.'

'Will you try to stop it?' asked Chaloner. 'Like you did the fox-tossing?'

Fanny looked away. 'But I failed with that, and now everyone laughs at me.'

'Not everyone,' said Chaloner quietly. 'I applaud what you did. So, I imagine, does the Duchess of Newcastle. She also champions animals.'

Fanny sniffed. 'Your approval is acceptable to me, but hers is not. She is a lunatic, and I do not want my name associated with hers in any way. From now on, I shall confine my palace activities to sewing with Lucy Bodvil and Mary Robartes. They are *decent* company. But speaking of decent company, your Earl tells me that you have cousins staying with you.'

Chaloner nodded. 'Until Easter, when Lady Clarendon will take them.'

Fanny nodded approvingly. 'There is no better person to teach them courtly manners. Until then, he has asked me to entertain them for a few hours each day. He is uneasy with the notion of them having no other company but you and Wiseman.'

Chaloner was indignant. 'What does he think we will do? Teach them spying and dissection?'

'I doubt you will manage that before Easter,' said Fanny, a twinkle in her eye. 'But he has their interests at heart, so bring them to me if you like. I shall ensure their needlework is up to scratch, as you will never find them husbands if they cannot ply a needle or a lucet.'

Chaloner's first instinct was to decline, but the worst anyone could say about Fanny was that she was boring, which, as the Earl had pointed out, was no bad thing in a chaperone. Besides, releasing Veriana and Ursula into her care would put them out of Swaddell's reach, and that was no small consideration.

He was in the process of accepting her offer when Bess Widdrington strutted past on the arm of the spotty Pamphlin. She immediately began to brag about the goose-pulling contest that she had organised.

'But it is cruel, Bess,' objected Fanny, distressed. 'You must cancel it. Besides, Londoners will object to such "sport" in Holy Week.'

'Who cares what they think?' shrugged Bess, and gave a smirk of satisfaction. 'My husband is excited by it, and that is all that matters as far as I am concerned.'

Seeing she would not be convinced, Fanny nodded towards Chaloner and Swaddell. 'They know we were at the Red Bull, Bess. Captain Rolt told them.'

Bess's eyes flashed dangerously as she glared at Chaloner and Swaddell. 'Fanny and I were *right* to investigate the place. It is a hotbed of insurrection, which you two would know if you were any good at your jobs.'

'Women learning to read?' asked Chaloner. 'That is hardly revolutionary.'

'Oh, yes, it is! How do you think rebellions begin? By educating the masses! It is dangerous to let them think for themselves, as then they imagine that they have rights.'

'I agree,' said Pamphlin languidly, scratching one of his pimples. 'We should keep women where they belong, under the thumbs of men who know what is best for them. Current company excepted, of course. Noblewomen are different from the rabble.'

'Other than the Duchess of Newcastle,' spat Bess. 'She shames her husband with her eccentric capers, and he should take her in hand before her example encourages others.'

284

'I hardly think—' began Chaloner.

'But as for the Red Bull,' Bess forged on, 'because no one else had the sense to end what is happening there, *I* took charge of the situation.'

'What did you do?' asked Swaddell, while Chaloner regarded her uneasily.

'I sent the Cockpit Club to teach those harlots a lesson. Unfortunately, Baron Lucas drove my boys off.' Bess sneered. 'Well, he is the Duchess of Newcastle's brother, so what do you expect? They are as deranged as each other. Did you know that she wrote letters to dozens of courtiers, telling them to boycott our fox-tossing? How dare she!'

'She was right, Bess,' said Fanny quietly. 'It was very cruel and rather coarse.'

'It was *amusing*,' countered Bess, and turned her ire on Chaloner and Swaddell again. 'But why are you two here, pestering your betters? You should be off rounding up whores and others whose lives do not matter.'

'Bess!' cried Fanny, shocked. 'It is hardly—'

'And if *you* had any sense of decorum, you would not be talking to them,' snapped Bess, eyeing her frostily. 'They are beneath you in every way.'

She flounced away, dragging Pamphlin with her.

'Does she ever visit your house?' asked Chaloner, thinking that if the answer was yes, his cousins would go nowhere near it.

'No,' replied Fanny, understanding exactly why he had asked. 'We are acquaintances, not friends, although I shall take steps to avoid her unless she learns some better manners.'

Before Chaloner and Swaddell could resume their journey to Mushey's room, they were distracted by a

285

commotion. A few people were hurrying towards it, but more were walking in the opposite direction, muttering disapprovingly.

'The goose-pulling is revolting enough to repel even White Hall's jaded tastes,' said Swaddell, watching them go.

'It will not be its grisly nature that horrifies them,' predicted Chaloner, 'but the fact that it is popular in Holland. Bess has seriously miscalculated by foisting it on White Hall.'

'Then we should make sure it does not lead to trouble,' said Swaddell. 'Come on.'

Reluctantly, Chaloner trailed after him to the Privy Garden. This was a pleasant area of grass and trees, bordered on three sides by buildings and on the fourth by a wall that separated it from King Street. A wide gravelled path ran down the centre, and they saw a wooden structure had been assembled at one end of it – two upright posts connected by a crossbar. A goose was tied by its feet to the middle of the crossbar, and a servant was in the process of slathering grease over its head and neck, to render it slippery and therefore more of a challenge to hold.

Members of the Cockpit Club watched in gleeful anticipation, although only half a dozen of them had elected to take part in the exercise. These included Widdrington and Pamphlin, and grooms waited nearby with their horses.

'Pamphlin is a Page of the Presence,' remarked Swaddell, eyeing the pimpled courtier with distaste. 'A page – at his age! If I were him, I would be too ashamed to prance about attracting attention.'

A number of spectators had also gathered, but the atmosphere among them was tense. One or two bawled

286

for the fun to start, but a much bigger faction led by Bishop Morley – the man Swaddell claimed as a friend – called for an end to it. The censure only exhilarated Bess, who delighted in the role of flamboyant rebel. She raised her hands and a reluctant silence fell.

'The object of the game,' she announced in a voice that was shrill with excitement, 'is for the competitors to ride full pelt at the goose and grab its head as they pass. The winner is the one who rips it off. Now place your bets. I shall start by wagering five guineas on my husband.'

Widdrington ignored her adoring look as he mounted up. Struggling to conceal her hurt, Bess took a handkerchief and allowed it to flutter to the ground, the signal for him to begin. A murmur of relief rippled through Morley's party when the rider misjudged the distance and veered away too soon. Pamphlin was next, but came no closer to success than Widdrington.

'This is disgraceful,' declared the Duke of Buckingham, who stood with his hands on his hips and an expression of contempt on his dissipated features.

'The King is furious,' agreed Lady Castlemaine. 'Goose-pulling is popular with Dutchmen, and he does not want Londoners thinking his Court apes their filthy habits. Someone should tell Bess that she has done him great harm with this caper.'

'As long as her husband enjoys himself, she will not care,' predicted Buckingham. 'But we should not linger here, lest the King assumes we condone it.'

When they and their coterie had gone, there was a lull in the proceedings while the competitors clustered around the bird to discuss strategies for laying hold of something that was slippery and that struggled. Chaloner walked towards them, Swaddell at his heels.

'Not you two again,' snapped Widdrington irritably. 'Can a man not even pull the head off a goose without being bombarded with impertinent questions?'

'Your friends Ashley and Tooley were poisoned last night,' said Chaloner, repelled enough by them and their antics to engage in a frontal assault. 'Which one of you did it?'

Widdrington laughed, so his cronies did, too. 'If you expect us to remember anything about last night, you are as mad as the Duchess of Newcastle! I still have an aching head from the amount of wine we sank.'

'A killer sat in your midst, yet none of you are worried,' said Chaloner coldly. 'That means one of two things: that you are either too stupid to appreciate the danger you are in, or that you know more about the murders than you are willing to admit.'

Widdrington regarded him with dislike. 'Watch your tongue or I will—'

'Perhaps you can explain why you looted Tooley's room with such indecent haste, too,' Chaloner forged on. 'Surely, such behaviour should be beneath your dignity?'

'Do not single us out for censure,' objected Pamphlin angrily. 'Will Chiffinch ransacked his brother's quarters within an hour. We waited six.'

'We visited Ashley's lair, too,' said Widdrington, and smirked. 'I got a lovely wig-comb. Do you want to see it?'

'Why are you willing to engage in this vile display?' asked Chaloner, glancing at the goose and hating to see its terror. 'It will only encourage Bess to organise more of the same.'

Widdrington declined to reply, leaving Chaloner to

surmise that he *wanted* her to be in trouble, so that no one would object when he packed her off to Ireland. Before he could ask more, she called the competitors to order. They trotted back to the starting point, and Chaloner looked at the goose again. It was a pretty white creature with coal black eyes, and he fancied it was regarding him pleadingly.

Then Bess's handkerchief fluttered to the ground, and Widdrington kicked his horse into a trot. Bishop Morley leapt into its path, and stood with his arms folded and his face pale but determined. Widdrington only just managed to veer away.

'Move!' he bellowed angrily. 'I will not swerve a second time.'

Morley opened his mouth to reply, but was stopped by a sudden babble of voices. The Duchess of Newcastle had arrived with her usual enormous entourage. She was clad in what appeared to be her husband's nightgown and a massive cavalier-style hat, although her servants were more conventionally attired in matching suits of blue satin.

'I disapprove of bloodsport,' she announced importantly. 'It is nasty.'

She marched towards Morley and stood at his side, striking a rather bizarre pose, like a sailor gazing out to sea. Nothing else happened for a moment, then there was a rush as others hurried to join her. Chaloner was touched that so many people should unite to save a bird until he noticed that the King was watching from a window, and as His Majesty had expressed disapproval of the event, everyone wanted to be seen helping to disrupt it.

Dismayed, Bess screeched at them to mind their own

business, but Widdrington had seen the dark expression on the King's face and opted for a tactical retreat. His friends hastened after him. While she watched them disappear, Chaloner cut the goose free, not caring that it smeared grease over his coat. He was just wondering what to do with it when someone tugged his sleeve. It was Molly the chicken girl. She gave him a shy smile and held out her arms.

'I will take her to your house. Where do you live?'

Chaloner told her and she hurried away, the bird hidden inside her cloak.

'That was reckless,' admonished Swaddell. 'She works for the Duchess, who heads our list of murder suspects – well, mine at least – by virtue of her peculiar alibi for when Chiffinch's oysters were poisoned. Alone in blind John Milton's parlour indeed!'

Chapter 11

It was evening by the time Chaloner and Swaddell finally knocked on Michael Mushey's door. There was no reply, and unwilling to waste time, Chaloner picked the lock. They entered a room that was dark because the window shutters were closed, but Chaloner did not need Swaddell to fling them open to tell him what natural light would reveal.

'Dead,' he said, staring down at the body on the bed. 'Is it Mushey?'

'Yes,' replied Swaddell, and scowled. 'We should not have gone to the Privy Garden. Then we might have reached him before the killer did.'

'He has been dead for hours,' said Chaloner. 'Probably since last night. It suggests that he knew exactly who poisoned Chiffinch's oysters – the person *he* allowed inside for a few coins.'

'Was he poisoned, too?'

'We will ask Wiseman, but I imagine so.' Chaloner picked up the half-empty wine jug that sat on the table, and sniffed it. 'He can test this, too, as I suspect it will contain the toxin.'

'Should we discount the Duchess as a suspect then?' asked Swaddell. 'I cannot see her entering a servant's bedchamber to ply him with drink.'

'She has minions who will do anything for her.'

'Does she, now that Topp is dead? Or do you think Eliza did it? Of course, it may have been the Duchess demanding this particular favour that led Topp to drown himself – it was one duty he felt he could not perform for her.'

'Having met Topp, I think he would have found a way to do it if she asked – assassins can be hired by those who do not want to stain their own hands. Just ask Williamson.'

Swaddell ignored the barb. 'Yet I have the sense that all four deaths – Chiffinch, Ashley, Tooley and now Mushey – have their roots in the Cockpit Club. Tooley and Ashley were members, and the kitchen girl claims that Mushey was their friend . . .'

'And Chiffinch?' asked Chaloner. 'He was not a member or a crony.'

'No,' acknowledged Swaddell. 'But he was poisoned, like the others, so we must be looking at a single killer.'

Chaloner was about to reply when a sound made him glance towards the door. He had a fleeting glimpse of two engraved metal tubes before he dived at Swaddell, sending the assassin crashing to the floor. Two sharp cracks followed as the twin pistols discharged.

Swaddell lay still, eyes closed, and Chaloner lost valuable moments searching for a wound before concluding that the assassin was just knocked senseless by the fall. He dashed outside, but there was no sign of their would-be killer, and no indication as to which way he had gone. He did his best, racing down alleys and across courtyards, but the task was hopeless. Defeated, he returned to Mushey's room.

The shots had attracted attention, and people were clustered around the door, demanding explanations. Swaddell had recovered his senses, and was questioning them about the man who had lived there. No one admitted to knowing anything useful, although Mushey's nearest neighbour – a cook named Stephen Bacon – had heard Mushey singing drunkenly at about two in the morning. He had stopped soon afterwards.

'I was glad, because he was keeping me awake,' Bacon gulped. 'But now I realise he went quiet because he was dying, not because he was asleep . . .'

'Was he singing alone or with company?' asked Swaddell.

'Alone.' Bacon grimaced. 'He was paid to guard the larder, but he let anyone in for a price. The stuff that disappeared from that place! He should have been arrested, but the courtiers in charge were getting their cut . . .'

'Which courtiers?'

'Tooley and Ashley mostly. It is a pity they will never answer to their treachery – and it *is* treachery to cheat the King out of his food.'

Chaloner wrote a note to Wiseman, asking him to examine Mushey and the wine as soon as possible, and asked Bacon to deliver it. Then he arranged for the body to be taken to the chapel. Meanwhile, Swaddell explored the room, and discovered a large sum of money hidden under a floorboard, suggesting that Mushey had grown rich by allowing folk to steal the King's victuals. The assassin wrapped it in a handkerchief and handed it to the chaplain, who was among the onlookers, with an order that it was to be given to the poor.

'Do not eye me askance, Tom,' he said huffily. 'You

293

think that because Williamson views such windfalls as perks of the job, I will follow his example. Well, for your information, I happen to be a very honest man.'

He fingered the dagger at his side, reminding Chaloner that while Swaddell might be averse to theft, he was very much attached to the slitting of throats.

'So, we know one thing for certain,' said Chaloner. 'We would not have been shot at if we posed no risk. Someone is worried that we are on the right track.'

'You think the poisoner and the shooter are one and the same?'

'Well, the poisoner is the one who will most want us to stop prying, so yes. Regardless, we can surmise that the culprit is wealthy, because handguns are expensive.'

'Then perhaps we should look harder at the Duchess.' Swaddell grimaced. 'Williamson will not be very pleased with that solution.'

Nor would the Earl, thought Chaloner.

White Hall was no place to review the possibility that one of the country's highest ranking noblewomen might be a murderer, so Chaloner suggested a nearby tavern. Swaddell argued that Covent Garden would be better, as it would exclude the possibility of eavesdroppers. The gleam in his eye revealed that it was not fear of being overheard that led him to suggest it, but the prospect of seeing Veriana and Ursula.

'It must be nearly ten o'clock,' said Chaloner, determined to prevent it. 'Far too late to disturb Wiseman's household.'

Swaddell grimaced. 'I suppose we had better go to my house then. It is just around the corner, and I have a blood pudding that we can eat while we talk.'

Chaloner was disinclined to step into the assassin's lair, especially to consume something that contained blood, but he could think of no way to refuse without causing offence. He dragged his feet all the way down King Street. Eventually, Swaddell turned into a short but respectable lane called Dean's Yard.

His cottage had a sturdy door and heavy window shutters – natural precautions for a man in his profession. Inside, all was a bleakly functional, with a parlour and a kitchen below, and two sleeping chambers above. The furniture was basic – items that could be abandoned without a backwards glance should their owner ever be obliged to leave at short notice. Everything was neat and clean, though, and an effort had been made to render it more homely with some brightly coloured cushions.

'My mother made those,' said Swaddell, seeing Chaloner look at them. 'I shall take you to meet her soon. It is an honour I have not even afforded Williamson or Bishop Morley.'

'Crikey!' gulped Chaloner, not sure whether to be flattered or alarmed.

He was glad when the blood pudding slipped Swaddell's mind and he was offered a cup of wine instead. Then the assassin got down to business.

'The killer planned Chiffinch's demise very carefully,' he began. 'The capsules were prepared in advance by someone who knew exactly how the victim would consume the oysters – whole, without chewing. The culprit was also sure that no one else would want one.'

Chaloner took up the tale. 'The plan almost came to nothing when the Master Cook forgot to buy them, and it was fortunate that the Duchess was on hand to tell the

295

kitchen girl where else they might be purchased. So, was it coincidence that she suggested going to Sarah Shawe, or was she ensuring that all her preparations were not in vain?'

Swaddell was thoughtful. 'Even if the oysters had been bought from the usual supplier, the killer would still have needed to bribe her way inside the larder, then insert the capsules into the shellfish. It must have been a painstaking process, because it had to deceive the Master Cook and the man who ate them.'

'Was the culprit the woman who Millicent saw waiting outside? The one who kept her face hidden, but who wore fine shoes with her servant's garb, which is an elementary mistake in our trade. People don disguises, then realise they cannot walk or run in unfamiliar footwear, so they keep their own, expecting no one to notice.'

'I think we can conclude that this loitering lady was up to no good. Of course, she may just have been waiting to steal some food. Bacon did say that it happens a lot, and the money I found suggests that Mushey made a princely living from looking the other way.'

'But if the Duchess *is* our culprit, why did she want Chiffinch dead? He criticised her, but so do lots of people. And while we mooted the possibility that he plotted against her, there is nothing to suggest that he actually did anything.'

'Perhaps we shall learn something at her soirée. While she is busy with her other guests, one of us will slip away and search her rooms. But what shall we do in the interim? I confess I am out of ideas.'

'Chiffinch's funeral is at midnight,' said Chaloner. 'We should be there – perhaps the killer will be, too. And tomorrow we will try to learn more about the four victims. Perhaps we will uncover something that links them to her, and we can confront her with the evidence.'

'Very well,' said Swaddell, and glanced at the hour candle. 'Before we pay our last respects to Chiffinch, there is just enough time for a nice piece of blood pudding.'

An enormous crowd assembled in Westminster Abbey to watch Thomas Chiffinch interred in the south transept that night. Although the ceremony was due to begin at twelve o'clock, word came that the King had pressing business, so there would be a delay. Having heard a terrific rumpus emanating from the Banqueting House earlier, Chaloner suspected that the 'pressing business' involved wine and a ribald play. There was nothing for it but to wait, although the mourners' patience began to evaporate as time ticked past.

Bored, Chaloner slipped away to prowl darker parts of the abbey, while Swaddell moved among the mourners in the hope of overhearing incriminating conversations. Kings and queens slept on their marble beds, and every crook and cranny was filled with memorials to the great and the good. Chaloner found the place where Oliver Cromwell had rested before his bones were dug up and dangled from a scaffold. As he looked at it, he heard a scraping sound above his head and glanced up in alarm. There was nothing to see, so he supposed a bird was roosting there. Then he recalled that Mother Broughton had predicted walking corpses in the abbey for Tuesday – and it was Tuesday now, as the bell had just chimed one o'clock.

Eventually, the King and his favourites arrived, most unsteady on their feet. The organ thundered out an incongruously jaunty fugue, and Chaloner abandoned his wanderings to return to the nave, looking around to see else who had turned out.

The Earl was there with an enormous contingent from Clarendon House, evidently feeling there was safety in numbers, although Chaloner thought he would have been wiser to stay at home. The Chiffinch family was nearby, so he went to speak to them, although Barbara was the only one who deigned to acknowledge him. She looked old and tired: her brother-in-law's death, coupled with the strain of keeping Will under control, were taking their toll.

'I thought you would have had a solution by now,' she said, rather accusingly. 'It cannot be that difficult – it is not as if Thomas had lots of enemies wanting him dead.'

'He had more than you might think.' Chaloner looked pointedly at Will, who was dabbing his eyes with a satin handkerchief, although there were no tears to dry.

'My husband is not the culprit,' said Barbara firmly, and winced. 'We lead mostly separate lives, as you know, and as I was unable to vouch for his whereabouts at the salient time, I made some enquiries for my own peace of mind.'

'And?' asked Chaloner.

'He was in Chelsea all last week, procuring new prostitutes for the King. He did not return until late on Thursday night, so he had no time to poison his brother's oysters. Upwards of a dozen women will confirm it.'

'Then why did he not tell me this when I asked?' demanded Chaloner, exasperated.

'To see the Earl's investigation founder, I suppose.'

'But I am looking for his brother's killer. Surely that is more important than scoring petty points over an enemy?'

'He thinks he will have a solution from the inquiry he has commissioned himself. I told him that yours is more likely to succeed, but he does not share my faith in you.'

'Who did he hire?'

'The outrageous Cobbe, so if you see *him* acting suspiciously, that is why. Cobbe was with Will in Chelsea when the killer struck, which is why Will chose him as an investigator: Cobbe is the one man in White Hall whose innocence is beyond question.'

Chaloner realised he should have guessed this when Cobbe had been able to say exactly when Ashley and Tooley had died – his precise replies revealed more than a passing interest in the affair. He had also eavesdropped on private conversations in White Hall, as evidenced by the one he had overheard between Ambassador van Goch and his minions.

'Does he have a list of suspects?' he asked.

'Yes, but I imagine it is the same as yours: Dr Clarke, who lied about the cause of death; the Duchess of Newcastle, who should be in Bedlam; and various members of the Cockpit Club, particularly Captain Rolt, who found the body.'

'Fanny Clarke found the body. Rolt was second on the scene.'

'But Fanny was with the Queen all day on Thursday, so had no opportunity to tamper with oysters. Nor did she have a reason to kill Thomas, as her acquaintance with him was no more than a passing one.'

'So which of these suspects do you favour?'

'Someone in the Cockpit Club,' replied Barbara at once. 'Because Cobbe found some letters proving that Thomas had been in the process of discrediting the entire cabal. Once they had been banished in disgrace, Cobbe thinks Thomas would then have turned his attention to others he disliked – such as your Earl and the Duchess.'

'I wish you had told me this sooner,' said Chaloner irritably. 'It would have been helpful.'

'I have only just found out myself – a few minutes ago, when I overheard Cobbe reporting his findings to Will. So if you have any more questions, ask them, not me.'

Chaloner decided he would, at the first opportunity.

The rite that saw Chiffinch laid to rest might have been beautiful had it not been attended by courtiers, who muttered, shuffled and fidgeted like badly behaved children. The Cockpit Club were the worst offenders. Widdrington could not stop yawning, while Bess whispered and giggled animatedly to Pamphlin, clearly hoping to make her husband jealous. It did not work, and if anything, Widdrington looked relieved that she had found someone else to fawn over.

Chaloner wanted to corner Cobbe at once, but the man had contrived to sit between Rolt and young Legg, making him difficult to reach without attracting attention. Clarke lounged nearby, while Fanny knelt with her head bowed, although she did glance up from time to time to ensure that her piety was noticed by those whose opinions she valued.

The deputation from Newcastle House included everyone from the Duke down to Molly. The Duchess wore a long, black cloak, breeches and a wide-brimmed hat that made her look like a Puritan divine. She had brought a book, which she evidently found a lot more interesting than the ceremony, because she did not look up from it once. She attracted a lot of attention. Some was plain curiosity for a famous eccentric, but more was contemptuous, and one whispered conversation mocked her vanity – her expectation that everyone would want to buy her books.

Eliza sat at her side, pale, drawn and full of grief for her husband. The Duchess did not notice her distress, so it was left to Molly to comfort her. Baron Lucas stood next to Mansfield until he saw some of his Royal Society friends, at which point he went to inform them – loudly – that they were mistaken in their theories pertaining to the density of the air in Tenerife.

'Gentlemen, please!' snapped the Duke of York, glaring over at them. 'I am all for scientific enquiry, but this is a funeral, and some of us are trying to sleep.'

Chagrined, the learned gentlemen slunk away, other than Lucas, who looked around for someone else to corner. His eye lit on Chaloner.

'Have you heard about Topp?' he asked in a whisper. 'Steward Clayton was right to question his character, because it transpires that he stole three hundred pounds before drowning himself in a fit of remorse.'

Chaloner raised his eyebrows. 'I knew about his suicide, but not the money. Was it found with his body?'

'The corpse was discovered by river urchins, so what do you think? But Topp's guilt is unequivocal: he was a rogue, and that is all there is to it. Poor Eliza is devastated, of course.'

Chaloner looked across at her white, strained face, and his heart went out to her. The Duchess remained oblivious to her agonies, though, and was still engrossed in her reading.

'Have you heard the rumours that say your sister killed Chiffinch?' Chaloner asked, somewhat baldly.

Lucas snorted his derision. 'Some folk will bray anything to hurt a clever woman, but they are drooling idiots who could not find their arses in the dark. You should set no store by their asinine claims, especially if the accusations come from that worthless Mansfield.'

Hearing his name, the Viscount came to see what was being said about him.

'I suppose you are discussing the fact that I was right about Topp,' he said smugly. 'He is a filthy thief – and my stepmother's lover into the bargain.'

Lucas clipped him smartly around the ear. 'My sister has no lover, you loathsome little maggot. And even if she had decided to experiment with an amour, it would not have been with Topp, who was old enough to be her father.'

'The *Duke* is old enough to be her father,' flashed Mansfield, hand to his ear; he was careful to stay out of Lucas's reach as he went on sneeringly, 'She has always favoured Topp and Eliza over her own family.'

'Yes – Topp *and Eliza*,' said Lucas between gritted teeth. 'The beloved friend she would never betray. You are a fool, boy.'

'We should dismiss Eliza,' sniffed Mansfield sulkily. 'She was obviously Topp's accomplice, and everyone knows that criminals stick together.'

'If you refer to that letter you found,' said Lucas dangerously, 'you had better shut your mouth before I clout your other ear.'

'What letter?' asked Chaloner.

'The one informing my stepmother that Chiffinch was plotting against her,' replied Mansfield, stepping away, lest the Baron made good on his threat. 'The one that *proves* she had a motive for wanting him dead.'

302

'Chiffinch could have plotted all he liked, but he could never have hurt my sister,' declared Lucas stoutly. 'She has done nothing wrong. Now, I wonder what grubby little worm sent that poisonous piece of nonsense.'

'It was not me,' declared Mansfield indignantly, and pretended not to hear Lucas's disbelieving snort as he turned to Chaloner. 'You will interrogate her if you have any sense, before she turns her murderous attentions on anyone else. You have been warned.'

'Ignore him,' ordered Lucas, as Mansfield strutted away. 'The boy is an idiot.'

'May I see the letter?' asked Chaloner.

'I burned it. Chiffinch was *not* plotting against her, and my sister would never hurt a fly, let alone a person.'

Chaloner thought he should be the judge of that.

The ceremony drew to a close eventually, and Chiffinch's coffin was lowered into its allotted space. The moment it settled, there was a loud crash, followed by an explosion of dust – a carving had dropped off one of the nearby monuments. The dead man was forgotten as everyone hurried to see what had happened.

The fault lay with William Camden, author and antiquary, whose memorial arch included not only a marble bust of himself, but several carvings of grinning Death. One of these had toppled off its moorings. Suspicious scratches revealed that it had not fallen naturally, but even so, Chaloner guessed exactly what was coming next.

'Mother Broughton!' exclaimed someone, although it was too dark to see who. 'She predicted that Death would walk in Westminster Abbey on Tuesday, and so it has!'

The tale was taken up by a hundred voices, and

303

Chaloner knew that by dawn, all London would believe that the second of the seer's prophecies had come true. He tried to determine who was responsible for the hoax, but it was hopeless. There were too many people, all of whom wore hats or veils, and it was dark. Seeing faces was impossible.

When the last of them had filed out, he went to stand by the grave of the man whose murder he was trying to solve. There was no memorial stone yet, but someone had written out what would later be carved, and had pasted it on the nearest wall. Chaloner translated the Latin in his mind:

Here lies Thomas Chiffinch, from his tenderest years a faithful servant, in good fortune and bad, to His Most Serene Majesty Charles II, and thence appointed Comptroller to the Royal Excise, a man of notable honesty and probity. Died 8th April 1666.

As far as Chaloner was aware, the only true words were the first four and the last four.

Chapter 12

It was almost too late to go to bed by the time Chaloner arrived home, but he tried to sleep anyway, and managed two hours before he was wakened by the gathering daylight and the racket from the market in the piazza outside. He donned clean clothes and went to let his hens out, startled when a goose emerged with them – he had forgotten that Molly had delivered it to his house. It had been carefully degreased, revealing snowy white feathers and a pretty face. How anyone could want to tear its head off was beyond his understanding.

He sat for a moment, enjoying the birds' contented chatter, then set off for the gentleman's club in Hercules' Pillars Alley. It had served him well in the past as a source of useful information, so perhaps its bubbling, vivacious ladies would oblige him now – and he was so desperate for answers that he was willing to look for them anywhere.

The club was owned by Temperance North, Wiseman's paramour. She had once been a demure Puritan maid, and Chaloner was not the only one who had been astounded by the speed and extent of her transformation into a wealthy businesswoman. She had never been slim, but unlimited access to fine food and wine had turned her portly. Unfortunately, none of her friends dared tell her that the dresses she liked to wear were unsuitable for the fuller figure.

Although most of the city was just waking, Temperance was about to go to bed: a contingent of courtiers had visited her once the ceremony in Westminster Abbey was over, so she had been busy. She was in the cosy parlour she used as an office, bagging up the night's takings – such a great pile that Chaloner wondered if Wiseman was right to say that Veriana and Ursula would earn more as courtesans than they ever would from respectable marriages. Temperance seemed to read his mind, and her smile turned mischievous.

'Are you here about your cousins? Bring them to me. I will teach them the ways of the world and find them rich husbands at the same time.'

'Unfortunately, none of your customers are the sort of match my family will want me to make for them,' he said wryly. 'Besides, most are already married.'

'True, so what will you do? Ask some pompous dullard – such as Lucy Bodvil, Mary Robartes or Fanny Clarke – to find the sort of bore you aim to foist on these hapless girls?'

'We shall see,' replied Chaloner vaguely.

'I met Veriana and Ursula in Covent Garden yesterday. They are vivacious young women with a sense of fun. You cannot turn them into prim little dolls, their spirits crushed by the burden of respectability. You should let them *live*.'

Chaloner agreed, but thought there were better ways to do it than by enrolling them in a brothel. Prudently, he changed the subject.

'Did you attend Thomas Chiffinch's funeral last night? I did not see you.'

'I was at the back. I saw the statue of Death come crashing down, though, fulfilling Mother Broughton's prophecy. Before I could escape, I was cornered by Fanny Clarke, who urged me to close the club. She thinks it is evil, and believes I will perish on Good Friday.'

'She threatened you?'

'On the contrary, she was genuinely concerned for my safety, and wants me to repent before it is too late. But what is wicked about making men happy? Indeed, we provide a valuable service, as London is much better being ruled by cheerful men than miserable ones.'

Chaloner was disinclined to argue. 'Have you met the Duchess of Newcastle?'

'Not yet, although she has invited us to her house next month. Do not look so startled! We are often hired to enliven elite gatherings, because we are good at breaking the ice.'

Even if the Duchess did want her soirées to go with a bang, Chaloner was sure she would not knowingly recruit *filles de joie* to do it. It was someone's idea of a joke.

'Who recommended you?' he asked.

'Dr Clarke, who is one of our regulars. He is her near neighbour.'

'He is on my list of suspects for killing Chiffinch,' said Chaloner without thinking.

Temperance gaped. 'Do not be ridiculous, Tom! There is no harm in him. All he wants is a little fun, which he cannot have as long as his tedious little wife is there to drone on about needlework, decency and other such nonsense.'

'Yes,' said Chaloner ambiguously, and returned to the matter in hand. 'So have you heard any rumours about Chiffinch? I know you believe all courtiers are as gentle as lambs, but someone killed him.'

'The only tales to come to me are ones that claim you did it,' replied Temperance tartly. 'However, if you want my opinion, the culprit will be someone in the Cockpit Club. I admire high spirits, but theirs are a little *too* selfishly exuberant. To be frank, Widdrington and Bess frighten me. They are so cold and ruthless . . .'

'Cold and ruthless enough to kill a man who criticised them?' asked Chaloner, thinking that if Temperance considered them too hedonistic, they were probably beyond redemption.

She nodded. 'Their club is based on the principle that nothing matters except enjoyment, so they do not care who they hurt in order to get it. They are dangerous, because their antics damage the King, although they refuse to acknowledge it, especially their elite inner circle.'

'Their elite inner circle,' echoed Chaloner, and began to list them. 'Widdrington, Bess, Pamphlin . . . who else?'

'I am not sure. However, it is not Legg who is too young, or Captain Rolt who is too poor.' Temperance was thoughtful. 'And yet White Hall is unpopular for abandoning the city to the plague, so perhaps Widdrington and his friends are innocent, and some disenchanted Londoner killed Chiffinch.'

'Chiffinch died because someone poisoned his oysters – someone who knew that he liked them *and* that he swallowed them whole. Only courtiers have access to that information.'

'Do they?' asked Temperance quietly. 'I knew it and

so do my staff. He dined on them here, and I imagine he ate them in taverns across the city, too.'

With disgust and a crushing sense of defeat, Chaloner saw his list of suspects expand from a handful into thousands.

The discussion had lowered Chaloner's spirits, as it underlined just how far he was from answers. He was also fuzzy-brained from lack of sleep, so he stopped at the Rainbow in the hope that a dish of Farr's best would sharpen his wits.

'What news?' called Farr, but his expression hardened when he saw it was Chaloner. 'Oh, it is you. I am not sure I should serve you, given that your Earl has been killing courtiers. You should leave him and work for someone decent.'

'Unfortunately, decency is in short supply at White Hall,' said Rector Thompson sagely. 'And I do not believe Clarendon dispatched Chiffinch anyway.'

'No, not if the deadly oysters came from Clerkenwell,' put in Stedman. 'He would never go there, because it is where the Duchess of Newcastle lives. She is quite mad, and who wants to risk running into a lunatic?'

'Were these oysters from Sarah Shawe?' asked Farr curiously. 'I buy from her myself. It is a long way to go, but she makes the journey worthwhile. She is a striking lass.'

'She is,' agreed Stedman. 'Although Speed the book-seller told me that she publishes seditious pamphlets, so I would keep your distance if I were you.'

'Seditious pamphlets?' asked Chaloner, sipping the coffee and trying not to wince at the bitter taste. Thompson pushed a plate of sugar towards him, but

Chaloner shook his head. He never took it, as a silent but useless protest against the abuse of plantation slaves.

'About women being equal to men, animals having feelings, and whores being more respectable than courtiers,' elaborated Stedman. 'Perhaps she got these wild notions from the Duchess of Newcastle, who is also determined to turn the world upside down again.'

'Then she is succeeding,' sighed Thompson. 'Because the world *is* turning upside down. We have tiny dogs killing bears, a hen slaughtering packs of foxes, geese unseating men from their saddles, while a thousand robins have united to drive people from a church.'

'Goodness!' breathed Chaloner, amazed by how fast fact had been lost to fiction.

'If all that has happened already, imagine what it will be like on Good Friday – the thirteenth day of the month in sixteen sixty-six,' said Stedman darkly. 'Perhaps we should leave the city while we can.'

'Women should not be allowed to say whatever they please,' said Farr, off on a tangent. 'There is a reason why they are banned from coffee houses.'

'What reason?' asked Chaloner archly. 'That they might spout views that are narrow-minded, hypocritical, uninformed or stupid?'

Rector Thompson laughed, although the barb missed its mark with everyone else. After a moment, Farr took up the reins of the discussion again.

'I blame her husband, personally. The Duke should tell her that we do not want to buy her peculiar ramblings, and he should toss them on the fire, where they belong.'

'My wife bought *Philosophical Opinions*,' said Thompson. 'She enjoyed it, so I read it myself. It contained many interesting snippets, which I have used as a basis for sermons.'

'Then it is a good thing none of us ever listen to you,' said Farr, 'because I do not want to be tainted by the ravings of a madwoman, thank you very much. Of course, the Duchess is not nearly as objectionable as that Cockpit Club. One member – the spotty fellow – was riding so fast this morning that he knocked me down.'

'Pamphlin?' asked Chaloner keenly. 'Was he drunk?'

'No, he was in a hurry. His horse was loaded with saddlebags, and I was under the impression that he was making an escape. Regardless, he should have stopped to see if I was injured, but he cantered off without so much as a backward glance.'

'He is a Yeoman of the Larder, you know,' said Stedman. 'One of the best sinecures in White Hall, as you get the pick of all the surplus delicacies. Dates, figs, marchpanes, pies . . .'

Chaloner frowned, recalling what Swaddell had told him about Pamphlin. 'He is a Page of the Presence, not a Yeoman of the Larder.'

'He *was* a page,' said Stedman. 'But he was promoted a couple of weeks ago, which I know because he told me when we were ringing the bells at the cathedral together.'

Chaloner grimaced, realising that he had been remiss to accept information without question. And now it transpired that a third member of the Cockpit Club been in a position to join Ashley, Tooley and Mushey in depriving the King of his victuals.

'How many Yeomen of the Larder are there?' he asked, aware even as he spoke that the question revealed a disgraceful lack of knowledge about the place where he worked.

'Three,' replied Stedman. 'Although the other two have died recently, so His Majesty will be looking for more. Perhaps he will consider me for the honour.'

He laughed and the others joined in, leaving Chaloner to suppose he would have to track Pamphlin down and find out what had prompted his sudden flight. Was he fleeing the scene of his crime – not just murder but stealing from the larder? Or was he just afraid that he might join his two fellow yeomen and Mushey in their graves?

'Speaking of the Duchess,' said Farr, 'I heard that her steward stole three hundred pounds from her, then drowned himself in a fit of remorse.'

'You should know better than to believe gossip, Farr,' said Thompson pompously, 'because Topp is no more drowned than you are. I spoke to him not an hour ago.'

'You did?' asked Chaloner, startled. 'Where?'

'In my church,' replied the rector. 'I confess he gave me a fright, what with all these rumours about walking corpses, but he had only come in to shelter from the rain.'

'Did you speak to him?'

'Yes, once I had satisfied myself that he was no cadaver. He denied being Topp at first, but relented when I reminded him that he and I have been acquainted for years. To be frank, I suspect he started this tale of suicide himself.'

'To make sure no one looks for him,' surmised Chaloner. 'Or the money he is said to have stolen. Still, it is a cruel thing to have done to his wife. She grieves for him.'

'It is unkind,' agreed Thompson. 'And I said so, which is probably why he stormed off in a huff. No one likes to hear that he is a selfish rogue.'

Chaloner was thoughtful. He had never considered

Topp as a suspect for Chiffinch's murder, but perhaps he should have done in light of what he had just been told. Topp knew his way around White Hall, and it would not be difficult to don women's clothing and lurk outside the larder, waiting to bribe his way inside. But why would he want Chiffinch dead? Because he really did love his Duchess, and he had heard that Chiffinch was plotting against her? And had he then poisoned Tooley, Ashley and Mushey to cover his tracks?

Chaloner decided to visit Newcastle House at once, to see what more could be learned about the steward and the money he was alleged to have stolen – money that had been suspiciously missing from 'his' corpse. Then he would track down Pamphlin, and find out what had prompted him to flee, especially if it pertained to his post as Yeoman of the Larder and three dead colleagues.

It was still early when Chaloner returned to Covent Garden, aiming to ask Wiseman if he had examined Mushey and the wine. The surgeon had already gone to White Hall, but had left a note detailing his findings. Chaloner was not surprised to learn that the wine had indeed contained the same henbane-based potion that had killed Chiffinch, Ashley and Tooley, or that drinking some of it had ended Mushey's life.

As soon as he had finished reading the message, he sent for a hackney and took Veriana and Ursula to Chaloner Court. They were excited by the prospect of visiting a house that had once belonged to their father, but when they arrived, they were disappointed, finding it wholly unfamiliar to them.

'I remember it being dark and rather gloomy,' said Ursula, as they waited in the hall for a servant to

313

announce them to Fanny. 'With a roof that leaked and mould on the walls. Now there is a new roof, and the walls are beautifully clean.'

'They might be clean, but they are no longer straight,' countered Veriana, less easily impressed. 'The new roof has caused them to bow, and the plaster is flaking off.'

'Well, I like it more now,' declared Ursula. 'Do the Clarkes have sons? I could live here very happily.'

The maid returned at that point, and indicated that they were to follow her to where Fanny was waiting. As they walked through the door into the stylish but impractical orangery, Veriana pointed at the crack in the lintel.

'This place is all style and no substance,' she whispered to Chaloner with smug superiority. 'It was a better house when *we* owned it.'

They weaved through the potted trees to where Fanny sat on her favourite bench. Two of her rescued cockerels were with her, and appeared to have made themselves very much at home. She came to greet the cousins with a sweet smile of welcome.

'We shall spend the day darning my husband's old stockings, so we can give them to the poor,' she informed them. 'And later, I shall send for my milliner to see about new hats. Those will not do – you need something in brown or grey.'

As his cousins' current headwear was pink, blue and festooned with ribbons, Chaloner was not surprised when this news was not greeted with enthusiasm. Ursula contrived to accompany him to the door when he left.

'You cannot leave us here,' she hissed. 'She wants to turn us into younger versions of herself. How can we attract interesting men if we are forced to become drab little ducklings?'

314

'It is only for a few days,' he whispered back. 'And it is good of Fanny to take the trouble. Then you can go to Lady Clarendon.'

Ursula groaned. 'She will be even worse. We shall end up married to vicars!'

'Would that be so bad?'

'Not if they are rich,' conceded Ursula, then pouted again. 'But we had hoped to have some fun first, which does *not* mean sewing with boring old ladies. It is not fair!'

Chaloner could see her point: he would not appreciate being parcelled off to mend stockings either. Unfortunately, none of them had a choice if they wanted to secure the kind of matches that would save her family from fiscal oblivion.

'Just do it,' he said tiredly, 'and then, if Fanny has no objections, I will take you to Newcastle House with me tomorrow.'

Ursula gave a whoop of delight, and stood on tiptoe to kiss his cheek before scampering away to tell her sister. He smiled, shaking his head, then pushed his domestic travails from his mind, wondering instead how Eliza would react to learning that she was not a widow.

He left Chaloner Court and began to walk across the green to Newcastle House. It started to rain when he was halfway over, forcing him to break into a run. He knocked on the door, which was opened by the butler, who had one of his mistress's books clapped to his head to protect it from the leaking ceiling.

'I would not mind if it was just water,' he confided crossly. 'But those seagulls are up there, and their mess is all mixed up in it. I do not want *that* in my lovely new wig.'

He disappeared to tell Eliza that she had a visitor,

leaving Chaloner standing in a place that was no drier than outside. The rain hammered on the glass above, and there were at least twenty buckets scattered around the floor, placed to catch the worst of the drips. A red-faced, panting footman was struggling to empty them before they overflowed.

'The butler will not find Eliza, because she has gone to White Hall with the Duchess,' whispered a voice from the shadows. It was Molly, cuddling one of her hens. 'To spend the day with the Queen.'

'Goodness!' muttered Chaloner, not liking the notion of one of his murder suspects being in company with the woman who would – if she recovered from her latest miscarriage – provide the country with its next monarch.

'What are you doing in here, child?' came Baron Lucas's booming voice. 'You know you are not supposed to take shortcuts through the house with your birds.'

He was coming down the stairs with the Duke, who appeared frail and unsteady next to him. Glancing up, Chaloner saw Mansfield leaning over the banister on the top floor, clearly aiming to eavesdrop on what his father and step-uncle had to say to each other.

'I wanted to show everyone how I can curtsy,' explained Molly, and gave a rather ungainly demonstration. 'Eliza taught me last night, so as to be ready for tomorrow, when so many people of quality will visit.'

'Run along now, girl,' ordered Lucas. 'And do not bring chickens into the house again. My sister might defend them against those who think they are stupid, but that does not mean she wants their droppings all over her floors.'

Molly scuttled away, giving Chaloner a quick smile as she went.

'You have made a friend,' said the Duke to Chaloner. 'Now you will enjoy her affection for ever. Being kind to servants is wise, because you get better service from happy staff than ones who cannot bear the sight of you.'

Chaloner knew the advice was really intended for the listening Mansfield, and wondered if the son and heir was clever enough to heed it. He suspected not.

'I came to report that Topp was seen this morning,' he said. 'Alive.'

The Duke gaped, then gave a whoop of delight. 'I *knew* he was not a man for suicide!'

'So where is he?' demanded Lucas, who seemed less pleased by the news. 'Tell him to report to us at once and explain what the devil is going on.'

'I will, if I see him,' promised Chaloner. 'Although if he really did make off with three hundred pounds, he may be reluctant to oblige.'

The Duke's merry grin faded. 'I am sure he will have a good explanation for that.'

'He will: he stole it,' said Lucas shortly. 'I was fooled by him, too – considered him an honest and loyal fellow. But we were both wrong. He was . . . he *is* a rogue.'

On the landing above, Mansfield murmured heartfelt agreement.

'But he was also accused of seducing my wife,' countered the Duke. 'And we know *that* to be a lie. What if the missing money is just another sly plot against him? If so, I do not blame him for making an escape.'

'He did not "make an escape",' argued Lucas. 'He pretended to be dead, and Eliza and my sister have been distraught. How could he do that to them? Or to you, for that matter?'

The Duke had no answer, and mumbled something

317

about fetching a warmer hat. He turned to walk back up the stairs. With a hiss of alarm, Mansfield tried to duck out of sight before he was spotted. Unfortunately, he had leaned so far forward that his wig had snagged on the chandelier, and he was obliged to leave it swinging there as he scuttled away.

'I had better take your news to my sister and Eliza in White Hall,' said Lucas to Chaloner, smirking when he saw what had happened. 'Will you come with me?'

While Chaloner and Lucas waited for the Baron's personal coach to be readied – a time-consuming process that meant it would have been quicker to walk – the spy took the opportunity to slip away and question Sarah Shawe about the oysters she had sold to White Hall. She was on the green with her barrow, huddled under the tarpaulin that protected her wares from the rain.

Rather than launch straight into an interrogation, which was unlikely to secure the cooperation of so prickly an individual, he told her about Topp being seen alive.

'I knew *he* would never have hurt himself,' she spat, clearly disappointed. 'He is not a remorseful man. So what did he do? Buy a corpse to stand in for him? There are people who trade in such things – not from choice, but to put food on the table.'

Before he could be steered into a conversation about social injustice, Chaloner asked, 'Were you aware that your oysters were used to kill Chiffinch?'

Sarah glared at him. 'I did hear something to that effect. However, they were perfectly wholesome when they left me. I sold dozens of them that day, and even ate some myself. None of my other customers had a problem.'

318

'Did you follow the girl – Millicent – back to White Hall to see what she did with them?'

Sarah regarded him askance. 'Why would I do that? My time is too precious to waste on pointless errands. I sold the child my last two dozen oysters, then went home to prepare myself for an evening of teaching and debating in the Red Bull.'

'Did you—'

'I repeat,' interrupted Sarah angrily, 'the oysters left me in perfect health. However, that was hours before they were devoured by the man who died, so investigate what happened to them at the palace. Do not pester *me* with your impertinent questions.'

On that note, Chaloner returned to Newcastle House to see if the coach was ready.

As they swayed towards White Hall in Lucas's over-sprung carriage, Chaloner asked about Topp, hoping to learn something that would point to the steward as the White Hall poisoner – it would be a far more convenient solution than most of the other suspects on the list. Unfortunately, all Lucas could say was that Topp had appeared to be loyal and honest, and the family had left most of their financial and business affairs in his hands.

'They deserve better,' he growled. 'The Duke and my sister are good people, but what does fate hand them? Treacherous servants and the snivelling Mansfield as an heir.'

They alighted at White Hall, and were immediately aware of an atmosphere. The falling statue of Death in Westminster Abbey had convinced many courtiers that Mother Broughton was a genuine prophet, and there were now serious concerns about what would happen in three days' time. More than a few had discovered pressing business at their country estates. Thus if Friday the thirteenth 1666 did presage a great weeping and gnashing of teeth in London they would not be part of it.

The moment Chaloner and Lucas started walking across the Great Court, two men hailed them. The first was Samuel Pepys, an ambitious navy clerk, who nodded to Chaloner, then began to press Lucas for his opinion about a new weave of canvas. The second was Swaddell.

'You told me that Pamphlin was a Page of the Presence,' began Chaloner accusingly. 'But I learned – in my coffee house, of all places – that he is a Yeoman of the Larder. That is the same post that Tooley and Ashley held.'

Swaddell's surprise was quickly replaced by frustration. 'I looked him up in Williamson's files, but our record-keeping has been less assiduous since our clerks have been busy with the Dutch war. Damn it! If we had known . . .'

'I was also told that he raced away in a great hurry this morning.'

'He did – I saw him myself.' Swaddell was thoughtful. 'Which means that either he is the killer and feels the net tightening, or he knows the culprit's identity and elected to vanish before he could follow his friends to the grave.'

'Either way, we need to find him. Do you have any idea where he went?'

'I asked around, but the only person to venture an opinion was Captain Rolt. He said that Pamphlin has parents in Woolwich, but no other kin and no friends outside White Hall.'

Chaloner determined to ride to Woolwich as soon as he had made sure that the Duchess was not left alone with the Queen all day. And if Pamphlin proved to be a waste of time, he would hurry back and concentrate on Topp. He told Swaddell his plan, along with all he had learned since they had last met.

'Do not worry about the Queen,' said the assassin. 'Barbara Chiffinch has vowed not to leave her side until she is completely well again. She is appalled that Her Majesty learned the news of her mother's death from a careless-tongued courtier, and has promised to stay and protect her. You know you can trust her to keep the Queen safe – from the Duchess and everyone else.'

'Yes,' said Chaloner, relieved. 'Now we need to tell Eliza that she is not a widow.'

'Lucas will get there first,' said Swaddell, and Chaloner saw that the Baron had escaped from Pepys and was already entering the Queen's apartments. 'Not that the likes of us would have been allowed in there anyway. Still, it is a pity we shall not witness Eliza's reaction to the news ourselves. It occurs to me that she was Topp's accomplice.'

'Her grief seemed genuine to me.' Chaloner turned towards the palace stables. 'So now we ride to Woolwich.'

'I will stay here and make enquiries about Topp,' said Swaddell. 'I know I said we would be more efficient working together, but time is short, and we are no nearer to finding the truth now than we were when we started. We have no choice but to separate.'

'Of course we have a choice,' countered Chaloner, suspicious of the assassin's sudden desire to ditch him. Had he decided that Topp was indeed the culprit, and aimed to find the steward and slit his throat, to avoid the inconvenience of a public trial?

'Not if you want to make good time to Woolwich,'

said Swaddell sheepishly. 'I am not a skilled rider. I will slow you down. Go now, Tom. I will be here when you return.'

Unsettled and unhappy, Chaloner hurried to the stables and used the Earl's authority to requisition a horse, aware as he did so of the grooms' unfriendly stares. They looked away when he glared back.

'Where are you going?' came a familiar voice. It was Barker, although Chaloner took a second glance to be sure, as the Earl's clerk was unshaven, grey-faced and oddly rumpled.

'Woolwich.' Chaloner regarded him in concern. 'Are you ill?'

'Just worn out from the strain of working for a man who is rumoured to be a killer,' replied Barker. 'I keep wondering if there is any truth to the claims – that he really did order the deaths of three critics. Four, if Mushey is to be included.'

'You should know him better than that,' chided Chaloner. 'Besides, who would oblige him? You know it was not me, because you proved my alibi for when Chiffinch died.'

'I did,' acknowledged Barker. 'But that was before I learned that the oysters were poisoned on Thursday night, which means your whereabouts on Friday morning are irrelevant.'

Chaloner had wondered how long it would be before someone worked that one out. 'So you believe me to be an assassin,' he said heavily.

'Of course not! You would have done a much better job at concealing your handiwork.'

Chaloner felt this was no compliment. 'So who is the culprit?'

'That is what unnerves me,' replied Barker, glancing around in agitation. 'I do not know, and I find myself regarding everyone with terrified suspicion.'

At that point, Chaloner realised that the grooms were saddling his horse in such a way that he would be thrown the moment he urged it into a trot, revealing that *they* did not consider the murders too clumsy to be laid at his door. He drove them off with an irritable scowl, and buckled the straps himself. Barker came to watch, so Chaloner continued to quiz him.

'A few days ago, you told me that Tooley caught a fatal fever in the Red Bull. However, not only had he never been there, but nor did he die of a sickness.'

Barker shrugged. 'Blame Bess Widdrington – I got that tale from her. I have never been to the Red Bull either, so how was I to know it was false? I only mentioned the gossip because I thought you might find it helpful.'

'Have you heard that Pamphlin has fled the city?'

'Him and two dozen others. More will follow as Good Friday looms, particularly as the King has expressed a sudden desire to visit Dover. The Queen is too ill to travel with him, but he will not mind abandoning her to whatever fate lies in store for London.'

'Easy!' breathed Chaloner, aware that the grooms had not gone far, and that sort of remark from one of the Earl's retainers to another was dangerous.

'I shall resign today,' whispered Barker. 'The Earl will fall from grace soon, whether innocent of murder or not, and when he does, his staff will share his fate. I recommend that you look for another employer, too, before it is too late.'

And with that, he hurried away, leaving Chaloner staring after him worriedly. Did the clerk know more about the looming crisis than he was willing to admit? Such knowledge would certainly explain his sudden attack of anxiety. Chaloner started after him to ask, but the horse began to fuss, and by the time he had quietened it, Barker had disappeared into the maze of alleys near the kitchens.

Before Chaloner could mount up, he was approached by a courtier named Cotton, who was distantly related to him by virtue of his second marriage.

'You should be wary of Barker,' Cotton muttered. 'He has some odd friends.'

'Any you are willing to name?' asked Chaloner.

'Ask in the Red Bull,' replied Cotton, glancing around to make sure no one else was listening. 'And do not believe him when he says he has never been there, because he has.'

Chaloner clattered out of White Hall, aware that he needed to ride hard if he wanted to find Pamphlin and return home with answers the same day. It was a round journey of roughly twenty miles, mostly on good roads, although there was always the risk of delays from floods, defective bridges, fallen trees or broken-down carts. Even so, he reined in on King Street when he saw Kersey, feeling that the charnel-house keeper owed him an explanation.

Kersey was looking especially trim that morning. He was with a woman he introduced as his wife, although she was different from the last one. She was taller, older and more refined, leading Chaloner to suppose she was a gentlewoman, perhaps one whose family had been beggared by the wars, who had been delighted to forge an alliance with a wealthy man.

'There may have been a mistake,' conceded Kersey, when Chaloner informed him that Topp had been seen alive that morning. 'I based my identification on the papers found in the fellow's pockets, which is usually good enough.'

Chaloner rubbed his eyes, wishing he had taken the trouble to look at the corpse himself. 'So do we have yet another murder to investigate? The "Topp" in your care was dispatched to provide a body?'

'Wiseman examined him, and his verdict was drowning by accident or suicide – there is nothing to suggest foul play. Ergo, if Topp did stage his own death, he probably bought a corpse for the purpose. Then he dressed it in his own clothes, careful to leave "identifying" documents in the pockets. It has been done before.'

'Has it? You should have said so.'

Kersey smiled patiently. 'Why would I? There was no reason to suspect anything amiss, and there are limits to what I can be expected to do.'

'Did anyone come to view the body? His wife? The Duchess?'

'Both, but I advised against it, as the river had not been kind to their loved one's face. The Duchess left money for a coffin, and I was to have delivered the corpse to Clerkenwell today. Obviously, that will no longer be necessary, so she may have a refund.'

'Do you think they are party to the deception?' Chaloner still thought Eliza's grief was genuine, but Swaddell's remarks had sown a seed of doubt, and he wanted the opinion of a man who dealt with bereavement on a daily basis.

'I could not read the Duchess, but Eliza's distress was real.' Kersey's usually amiable face turned stern. 'It is a

325

terrible, selfish thing to have done. I hope he is ashamed of himself.'

Chaloner rode at a rapid clip towards London Bridge, recalling how eerily silent it had been at the height of the plague. He was glad to see it busy again, and to hear the familiar cacophony of curses as drivers bulled their rattling vehicles down a road that was not really wide enough to accommodate traffic in both directions. Above it all was the roar of the river, swollen with recent rains as it thundered through the arches below.

He ignored the grisly sight of the traitors' heads that adorned the entrance to the Southwark end, then turned along the Woolwich road. It was not long before he left the city behind, and was cantering through open country.

It was a miserable journey, with rain slanting into his face the whole way. It was a slow one, too, as churned mud made the road treacherously slick, and he did not want to injure the horse. He reached Woolwich eventually, only to be told that the Pamphlins had moved away during the plague.

'To Deptford,' elaborated the vicar he had hailed. 'Near the dockyards.'

Chaloner rode on, acutely aware of the passing time, even though the sun was hidden behind a bank of thick grey clouds. The rain grew harder still, so he was thoroughly drenched by the time he arrived in the village and found the right house. But his efforts were for nothing, because although the family was happy to co-operate, they had not seen Pamphlin in weeks.

'He prefers his lively friends at Court, and we are not good enough for him now,' confided the father bitterly.

'He has just been made a Yeoman of the Larder, you know.'

'Yes, I do,' growled Chaloner. 'And it was in this larder that another courtier's food was poisoned. It is a serious matter, so if you see him, tell him to return to White Hall at once.'

There was no more to be said, so Chaloner began to ride back to London, disgusted to discover that the wind had changed direction, and was in his face for the homeward journey as well. By the time he reached White Hall, he was cold, wet and weary, and day was turning to night. He stabled the horse, and jumped when Swaddell materialised at his side.

'I learned nothing about Topp, no one told me anything useful about Pamphlin, and our killer remains at large,' reported the assassin glumly. 'You?'

'It was a waste of time,' replied Chaloner dolefully. 'Did you say it was Captain Rolt who told you that Pamphlin had gone to Woolwich?'

Swaddell nodded. 'And there he is now, strutting across the Great Court like a pheasant. Shall we put a blade to his throat, and see if his memory serves him any better?'

Rolt started to run when he spotted Chaloner and Swaddell bearing down on him, but quickly realised this looked suspicious, so he stopped and pretended to be pleased to see them.

'You are very wet, Chaloner,' he remarked, all friendly concern. 'Has it been raining? I would not know, as I have been with the King all day, helping him pack for Dover.'

'You and a hundred others,' muttered Swaddell, thus telling Chaloner that the cosy image of His Majesty and

Rolt sorting through stockings and nether-garments together was a gross misrepresentation. 'Why did you send Tom on a wild-goose chase to Woolwich? You knew Pamphlin would not be there.'

Rolt regarded him askance. 'I knew no such thing! Besides, you did not ask where I thought Pamphlin might be – you asked if he had family or friends outside the city. The fault lay in the question, not the answer.'

'So where is Pamphlin now?' asked Chaloner, fighting the urge to punch him.

Rolt shrugged. 'I have not seen him since early this morning. However, I can tell you that something upset him, because I have never seen a man look more frightened.'

'Perhaps he was afraid of you,' said Swaddell coldly. 'After all, you head our list of suspects for the crime of murder.'

Rolt gaped at him. 'Me? On what grounds?'

Swaddell began to list them. 'The deaths of Tooley and Ashley mean you rise higher in the Cockpit Club hierarchy. You belong to a cabal that Chiffinch threatened to suppress. And you were suspiciously fast on the scene when his body was found. I do not believe you were there looking for a button.'

'Well, I was,' stated Rolt shortly. 'It belonged to my father, and so was of sentimental value. I have explained this to you already.'

But Chaloner recalled what he had read about Rolt in the report that Dutch Jane had left for her paymasters. 'Your father was a Puritan divine. Such men consider buttons sinful fripperies, and refuse to use them.'

'Hah!' exclaimed Swaddell triumphantly. 'You are caught in a lie! The button never existed, and your purpose in visiting the cockpit was to ensure that you had left nothing incriminating at the scene of the murder *you* committed. It was unfortunate that Fanny Clarke decided to rescue cockerels that morning and caught you.'

'You are mistaken!' cried Rolt, beginning to be alarmed. 'The button *does* exist. And if you must know why I was so keen to have it back, it is because it was gold.'

Chaloner regarded him thoughtfully. 'And you could not afford to lose such a thing, because you have no money.'

'Nonsense!' blustered Rolt. 'I am a wealthy man, like all my friends here.'

Chaloner summarised why he knew this to be untrue. 'You live in shabby Kensington, and you walk everywhere because you cannot afford to replace the horse that was killed. But you dare not admit your indigence, lest you are ousted from the Cockpit Club.'

'And it is through your Cockpit Club connections that you hope to land a lucrative post,' finished Swaddell. 'Without them, you will fade into impoverished oblivion.'

Rolt eyed them with dislike. 'So now you know. What are you going to do about it? Tell everyone? Obviously, I have no money to buy your discretion.'

'The name of the killer will ensure our silence,' said Swaddell silkily.

'But I do not know it!' cried Rolt, agitated. 'If I did, I would have informed you already. I do not want a murderer loose in White Hall, as it makes everyone wary of everyone else, and no one will hire me in an atmosphere of unease. The best I can do is tell you who is *not* responsible. I have been helping Cobbe look into the matter, you see.'

He proceeded to list some forty or so courtiers who had alibis for one or more of the murders, thus revealing that Cobbe's list of suspects had been a lot longer than Chaloner and Swaddell's, and that he had been working extremely diligently on the case.

'You can discount Widdrington and Bess as well,' Rolt finished. 'They were with me during the drinking game where Tooley was poisoned. We were discussing a task that Widdrington wants me to conduct on his Cornish estates. Neither slipped away to poison wine.'

'What task?' asked Swaddell disbelievingly.

Rolt eyed him with dislike. 'A review of his stables, if you must know. I am to travel there soon, stopping several places en route to deliver letters to his Devonshire farms. When I hand my finished report to his Cornwall steward, I shall be paid a handsome commission.'

He could tell them no more, so Swaddell indicated that he could leave. There was a nasty gleam in the assassin's eye.

'He will spend the last of his own money delivering all these missives, but will gain nothing in return,' he said, 'because Widdrington owns no Cornish estates.'

'Then why did you not warn him?' asked Chaloner curiously. 'It is a long way down there, and he may never raise the funds to come back again.'

'Almost certainly not,' agreed Swaddell smugly. 'But it serves him right. Have you noticed that people regard you with unease? Well, it is because of him. He smiles to your face, but all the while he whispers that you are the Earl's assassin.'

Chaloner was bemused. 'Why would he do such a thing? I barely know him.'

'Because maligning the Earl's retainers is an easy way

to ingratiate himself with his Cockpit Club cronies. I doubt it is anything personal.'

Chaloner pushed the treacherous captain from his mind. 'So our most likely suspects for the murders are now narrowed down to the Duchess, Topp and Clarke.'

'And the Cockpit Club,' said Swaddell. 'We may have eliminated Widdrington, Bess, Rolt, Cobbe and two dozen more, but Pamphlin and several others remain.'

As he was cold, wet, tired and dispirited, Chaloner was grateful when Swaddell offered to remain in White Hall alone that evening, to question their remaining suspects.

'And if you learn nothing new, we will go to the soirée in Newcastle House tomorrow,' he said. 'The Duchess will be there, and perhaps Topp will have slunk home by then, too, now that his nasty ruse has been exposed.'

'Do not hold your breath,' muttered Swaddell sourly.

Chapter 13

Despite being worn out by his hard ride to Woolwich and back, Chaloner slept poorly, kept awake by worry and the rain that pounded on the roof all night. He rose early, sluiced away the muck of travel in a bucket of warm water, and donned his favourite grey long-coat, feeling that if its drab colour made him look like an assassin, then that was too bad.

In the garden, he tended his poultry, pleased when the goose trustingly ate grain from his hand. Then he went to the parlour, where Wiseman, dressed in his best scarlet doublet, was entertaining Veriana and Ursula with the story of how he had heroically removed a cake of soap that had lodged in the Earl of Bristol's throat. Chaloner had heard the tale before, but still failed to understand what Bristol had been doing to land himself in such a predicament. While the spy helped himself to coddled eggs, Wiseman segued to his plans for the near future.

'The King is going to Dover tomorrow, so I shall join him there in a day or two. He says he does not believe these prophecies about the wicked getting their comeuppance, but he is also cognisant of the fact that one can never be too careful.'

'So His Majesty considers himself sinful?' breathed Ursula, wide-eyed.

'He *knows* he is sinful,' corrected Wiseman with a wink. 'But he does not want to change his ways, so he aims to be well away from the capital until the danger is over.'

'Leaving tomorrow will not make him very popular with Londoners,' remarked Chaloner. 'It is Maundy Thursday, when the monarch always distributes money to the poor.'

'He will fling a few handfuls to the milling masses before he goes,' said Wiseman with a careless wave of his hand. 'It will suffice.'

Chaloner hoped he was right. He finished his eggs and addressed his cousins. 'Are you ready to go to Fanny Clarke?'

'Must we?' groaned Ursula. 'Yesterday, she made us mend stockings with a lot of tedious ladies whose notion of excitement is discussing hems and gussets. I thought I would *die* of boredom. Fanny may be respectable, but she is about as interesting as a dead fish.'

'Besides, we have heard that Clerkenwell will be at the centre of Good Friday's trouble,' put in Veriana slyly. 'You do not want us in such a place, surely?'

'True,' acknowledged Chaloner. 'Which means you had better not go to Newcastle House this afternoon either.'

Ursula's face fell, and she shot her sister an exasperated glance. 'Nothing will happen until the day after tomorrow,' she said hastily. 'However, you will want us to look our best when we meet these wealthy nobles today, so we must stay here this morning, preparing.'

'Let us do that, and in exchange, we will endure Mrs

Boring with no complaints until we go to Lady Clarendon,' promised Veriana. 'We even swear not to laugh when she informs us that the secret of a happy marriage is to ensure our husbands always have clean underwear.'

Feeling he had just been manipulated in ways he could not begin to fathom, Chaloner nodded, then walked to Muscat's Coffee House, where he had arranged to meet Swaddell.

Much of the talk on the streets was of the crisis that would strike the city – starting in Clerkenwell – in less than forty-eight hours. There was no particular sense of fear, as most people seemed to think they were among the godly, and that it was everyone else who would be in trouble. Chaloner met William Prynne on Fleet Street, where the pamphleteer informed him that he was looking forward to the wicked getting their just deserts, as he expected to play a major role in running the country once they had been eradicated.

'But the last time we met,' Chaloner pointed out archly, 'you were dismissive of Mother Broughton's predictions, because she was a woman.'

'She still is a woman,' said Prynne with a moue of distaste. 'However, she was right about the walking corpses, so I have chosen to give her the benefit of the doubt.'

'Has she predicted anything else?'

'Just that tomorrow – Maundy Thursday – will be full of tears, a messenger will die, and the Fleet River will run red with blood. Then on Good Friday, there will be a rain of fire, followed by darkness all over the city, and a lot of wailing and gnashing of teeth.'

'I know about those. Has she said anything new?'

'There was something about the rain of fire coming from a clear blue sky, but I think she may have been

334

drunk at that point. I went to hear her in person last night, you see, and her supporters had been rather generous with the ale. But do not worry about it, Chaloner. By Easter Day, we shall all be in Paradise, and the Sun itself will dance for joy.'

Grumpily, Chaloner retorted that the Sun was not supposed to dance, and that he would far rather it stayed put.

Swaddell was waiting when Chaloner arrived at Muscat's, and although time was short they stayed long enough to down two dishes of coffee apiece, both feeling they needed the mental stimulation the beverage was alleged to provide.

'I loitered in White Hall until well past midnight,' said Swaddell, stifling a yawn. 'It was all but deserted. I think everyone was tired after Chiffinch's funeral feast, which went on well into the small hours of yesterday morning.'

'Did it?' asked Chaloner, signalling for Muscat to bring more coffee.

'Did you hear that halfway through it Will distributed three hundred mourning rings? It was to remind everyone who received one that his brother was a great man. Hypocrite! It is a pity he is no longer a suspect, because I have never liked him.'

Chaloner agreed. 'But of our remaining ones, three live in Clerkenwell: the Duchess, Clarke and Topp, who may or may not have had help from Eliza. And Clerkenwell seems to be where all this trouble will start – trouble that you, as the Spymaster's man, should prevent.'

'Then I suggest we go there now. We will concentrate on Clarke until it is time for the Newcastle House soirée, at which point we will turn our attention to the Duchess and Topp. And if we have no luck with them, we will consider the others on our list.'

'What list?' asked Chaloner with asperity. 'Of the Cockpit Club, we have eliminated everyone except one or two lesser members and Pamphlin, who has disappeared. Of course, it was not just them that Chiffinch alienated with his harsh tongue. Most of White Hall came under attack, too, so where do we start?'

'Perhaps we are wrong to assume Chiffinch was killed because he was critical of other people. He – and then the others – may have been dispatched because someone is unhappy with courtiers in general. So, I repeat: we shall tackle Clarke first, then see what we can learn at Newcastle House. If we are still floundering after, we shall turn our eyes to the palace servants.'

It seemed hopeless to Chaloner, but he hurried to Clerkenwell, aware that Mother Broughton was not the only soothsayer who had things to say about Good Friday. Others were also out in force, although none commanded audiences as large as hers, and traffic around the green came to a standstill when she stood on her box to hold forth. She was still tipsy from the previous night, and her disciples had to hold her arms to prevent her from toppling off.

While Swaddell went to hear what she had to say in the hope of learning something to stop it, Chaloner knocked on Clarke's door, only to be told that the physician was at White Hall and Fanny was out buying thread. Unwilling to waste time waiting for them to return, he trotted to the Red Bull, desperate enough to hope that its patrons might gossip to him about the looming crisis. There were no guards on the door this time, and the budding scholars within glanced up uneasily when he entered. Some recognised him from his previous visit and relaxed, murmuring to the rest that he was a friend of Eliza.

'Mr Barker speaks highly of him, too,' added Joan Cole the tobacco-seller, jerking a thick thumb at Chaloner. 'They work together at Clarendon House, see.'

'Barker comes here?' pounced Chaloner.

'Joan!' cried one of her friends. 'He begged our silence in exchange for free Latin lessons, and we agreed. You have broken his trust!'

So Cotton was right to suggest asking about Barker in the Red Bull, thought Chaloner, and here were the clerk's 'odd' friends – women determined to educate themselves.

'But Mr Barker likes *him*, Mary,' argued Joan, pointing at Chaloner again. 'He will not mind *him* knowing how he helps us with our grammar. Besides, he says he is tired of lying about visiting his mother, because too many people know she is dead.'

'Perhaps so, but he said his Earl would dismiss him if it ever became known that he was teaching us the language of religion and the law,' argued Mary. 'So we cannot—'

'His Earl no longer matters, because Mr Barker has resigned,' interrupted Joan, all smug triumph. 'He does not want to work for a man who cannot see that women are important members of society.'

'He is a saint, coming here to educate us,' said Mary. 'Especially after Bess Widdrington threatened to destroy anyone who teaches us things she thinks we should not know.'

'She is a hypocrite,' spat Joan. '*She* has these skills, but she cannot bear the thought of us having them too. She wants us tied down at home, having babies and toiling over the cooking fire. Pah! As if she ever does a lick of work!'

'Have you come to talk to Sarah?' asked Mary of Chaloner, once the chorus of angry indignation had died down. 'She said you quizzed her about poisoned oysters yesterday, and she has been pondering the matter ever since. She has some theories, and plans to share them with you today.'

Chaloner brightened. 'Where does she live?'

Joan heaved herself to her feet. 'Come. I will show you. It is not far.'

Sarah lived near Mother Broughton. There was no reply to their knock, but Joan had a key. She opened the door and stepped inside. Chaloner wrinkled his nose as he followed: the place was a pit. Discarded clothes and dirty plates sat on every available surface, and there was an eye-watering stench of rancid fat. On the table and in boxes on the floor were glass bottles with bulbous bottoms.

'Those are for pickling cockles,' said Joan, seeing him look at them. 'Now, where is she? Hah! Here she comes. Where have you been, Sarah? You said you would be home all morning.'

'Newcastle House,' replied Sarah smugly. 'I demanded an audience with that wretched little Mansfield, and when he slunk in, I ordered him to put things right with our Duchess.'

'What things?' asked Chaloner, surprised the servants had allowed her anywhere near the Viscount.

'The Duchess agreed to fund a *respectable* gathering of women,' explained Joan, 'but nasty old Mansfield told

338

her that the Red Bull is a brothel and we are all harlots, Shocked, the Duchess immediately withdrew her support.'

Sarah scowled. 'So I went to tell him that he had better tell her the truth, or else.'

'Or else what?' pressed Chaloner, astounded by her audacity.

'I reveal a secret about him.' Sarah made a moue of disdain. 'He capitulated, of course.'

'What secret?'

Sarah's expression turned haughty. 'If I told you, it would not be a secret, and he would then be free to encourage the Duchess to end her affiliation with our school.'

The determined jut of her chin told Chaloner that convincing her to confide in him would be a waste of time, so he let the matter drop. 'It is good of her to help you,' he said instead.

Sarah sniffed. 'Yes and no. She is very rich, so could easily give us more, but she would rather spend it on books for herself. I wish Eliza had a different mistress. She deserves better.'

'You do not like the Duchess?'

'Eliza is worth ten of her. Moreover, she is not half as clever as she thinks she is. Her logic is poor, she has no idea of grammar, and her spelling is as eccentric as her dress.'

It did not take a genius to see that Sarah was deeply jealous of the friendship between Eliza and her mistress. He changed the subject, aware that time was passing.

'Joan said you might have some theories about the poisoned oysters.'

Sarah frowned, evidently having relegated such an unimportant matter to the back of her mind. Then her expression cleared. 'Oh, yes. Your visit prompted me to reflect on it, and I remembered something I had forgotten – namely that someone was watching the girl who came to buy them. I do not believe she noticed, and I assumed at the time that it was some kindly soul who aimed to make sure she came to no harm in deadly Clerkenwell.'

'And now?'

'And now it occurs to me that this someone might have watched her with a view to poisoning the oysters the moment they were left unattended.'

'Can you describe this person?'

'Not really. All I can say is that it could have been a woman.'

'Thank you,' said Chaloner, although he was troubled. Did this mean the Duchess was the culprit after all?

As the Newcastle House soirée was likely to be a stylish affair, Chaloner hurried home and donned black breeches, white stockings and a pearl-grey vest – a loose, collarless, silk-lined garment with short sleeves, gathered at the waist with a belt. Then he borrowed a dark-red long-coat that no longer fitted Wiseman and grabbed his best hat.

When he was dressed, he went to the parlour, and found Ursula and Veriana talking to Temperance. They were so excited about visiting Newcastle House that they had been ready since breakfast, their hair crimped into the corkscrew curls that were currently popular at Court.

Unfortunately, Temperance had lent them some clothes that her prostitutes no longer needed, and Chaloner recoiled when he saw what she considered to be suitable attire. Ursula's neckline was so low-cut that she would have to keep very still or risk an embarrassing spillage, while Veriana's close-fitting bodice left nothing

340

to the imagination. And both had used so many black face-patches that they looked diseased.

'They are perfect,' announced Temperance. 'Do not look horrified, Thomas. I know a lot more about fashion than you do.'

'They are here to find husbands, not clients,' objected Chaloner. 'And I am *not* taking them looking like that.'

There followed a spat of the kind with which Chaloner, who had three older sisters and Puritan parents, was very familiar: his cousins declared they had the right to dress as they pleased, while he maintained that they would not leave the house until they had put on something more appropriate. Eventually, a compromise was reached: the dresses remained, but both girls wore shawls to protect their modesty, kept firmly in place with strong-pinned brooches. The face-patches were reduced to two apiece.

He was about to send Wiseman's groom for a hackney when there was a knock on the door and Swaddell was ushered in. The assassin had also been to some trouble with his toilette, and Chaloner had never seen him look so elegant. He had exchanged his trademark black for a long-coat of pale blue, complemented by an apricot falling-band. His shirt frothed with French lace and matching ribbons, and his slick black hair was concealed under a fine blond wig.

Chaloner gazed at him in surprise, not sure he would have recognised him, although the beady eyes were something of a giveaway. These were fixed unblinkingly on Ursula.

'I have borrowed Williamson's personal coach,' the assassin said before Chaloner could suggest he ogled someone else. 'I thought the ladies should arrive in style. After all, first impressions are important, are they not?'

Ursula gave an excited squeal before darting over to Swaddell and kissing his cheek. Swaddell's pallid face flushed red and he dropped his gloves in a fluster. Temperance smirked.

Chaloner started to point out that it would do his cousins – or him, for that matter – no good whatsoever if they rolled up outside Newcastle House in a carriage emblazoned with the arms of the Spymaster General, but Ursula had already raced out to see it. Veriana was hot on her heels. When he followed, more sedately, Chaloner was relieved to note that the vehicle was tastefully understated, and although there was a crest on the door, it was very small. No one would recognise it unless they looked closely.

'Do not bother fetching your viol, Tom,' advised Temperance, coming to see them off. 'There will be no playing for you today, because if you take your eyes off your wards for an instant, there will be trouble. They are sweet girls, but unversed in the ways of the world.'

'I am not so sure about that,' muttered Chaloner, watching Ursula simper at Swaddell; this time the assassin dropped his peach-coloured handkerchief. 'I have a bad feeling that I have underestimated them.'

Temperance laughed. 'I doubt Mr Swaddell has been on the receiving end of this sort of attention before, and he will propose to one of them unless you take steps to prevent it. And you do not want him in the family. It is bad enough having a lot of regicides, but you will be doomed for certain if you are related to Williamson's creature.'

During the journey from Covent Garden to Clerkenwell, Chaloner pondered the best way to gain access to the

342

Duchess's private quarters, surprised to find himself looking forward to the challenge. His only concern was whether Swaddell was equal to keeping watch for him and monitoring Veriana and Ursula at the same time.

While Chaloner planned, Swaddell entertained the girls. He told them about the omens and portents of doom predicted for two days' hence, and Ursula responded by declaring an intention to enjoy every moment of the coming afternoon, lest it was her first and only foray into high society. Then Veriana began to talk about Chiffinch and the poisoned oysters.

'It was the Duchess of Newcastle who urged him to gobble them all up,' she announced. 'He had had enough after a dozen, but she insisted that he finish them all, on the grounds that if they were going to die on his behalf, then the least he could do was eat them.'

'How do you know?' asked Chaloner, tearing his thoughts from spying.

'Because Lucy Bodvil told us while we were sewing in Chaloner Court,' replied Veriana. 'She disapproved, because gluttony is a sin, and she thinks that if Mr Chiffinch had eaten enough, he should not have been encouraged to overindulge.'

'Did Lucy Bodvil hear this conversation herself?'

'No, she had the tale from some other Court lady. It was unfortunate that these shellfish happened to be poisoned, though, as it looks as if the Duchess is involved in a murder.'

'Not as unfortunate for her as it was for the victim,' murmured Swaddell, and turned the discussion to the latest fashion in wigs.

They rattled along Holborn at a decent lick, but as they turned north, the number of private carriages increased, until there were so many that there was a jam all along Clerkenwell Road. They inched towards the green, at which point Chaloner realised that every one of the vehicles was aiming for Newcastle House.

'I thought this was to be a small gathering,' he said, peering out of the window and recognising coaches belonging to four earls, a bishop and six high-ranking courtiers.

'So did I,' said Swaddell. 'But a large one is better, as it will be easier for us to work.'

'But what about the music?' objected Chaloner, who had been looking forward to hearing the Duchess's matching viols a lot more than invading her boudoir and making sure his cousins did not attract the wrong kind of attention.

'You said you would not be playing anyway,' shrugged Swaddell. 'Which is good news for the rest of us. as you tend to rate technical difficulty above a good tune, which means you are not much fun to listen to. I much prefer a pretty jig to a complex fugue.'

'Lucy Bodvil was shocked that the Duchess should hold a party in Holy Week,' gossiped Ursula, thus preventing Chaloner from calling Swaddell a philistine. 'She thinks we should all refuse to attend. Fortunately, Fanny said that would be rude – that we *should* come, but that we should make a point of behaving with proper decorum.'

She could barely conceal her excitement as they inched closer to the gate, although Veriana strove for an air of worldly indifference. Eventually, it was their turn to alight, and liveried footmen came to open the coach door. Chaloner and his party walked up the steps to the main door, where the Duke and his Duchess stood to greet their guests. The ducal couple had positioned

344

themselves at either end of what appeared to be a horse trough. Then Chaloner saw it *was* a horse trough, set to catch the drips from the leaky ceiling.

The Duke had evidently decided that, as he was at home, he could wear what was most comfortable, so was clad in muddy riding boots and a tatty old coat. By contrast, the Duchess had donned attire more suitable for a coronation. Together, they appeared bizarre.

To enliven the task of welcoming a lot of people he did not know, the Duke was amusing himself by quizzing his guests on the pedigree of their horses. He gaped his disbelief when Swaddell informed him that one nag looked much like another, with four legs and two ends that were equally dangerous. Then he forced a polite smile because, even in his finery, Swaddell was obviously not a man to offend.

Meanwhile, the Duchess embraced Ursula and Veriana like long-lost friends, causing them to gaze pleadingly at Chaloner for guidance on how to respond. Then she returned Chaloner's bow, which was an odd thing for a lady to do, while Swaddell was treated to a smacking kiss on the cheek that made him reach for his dagger.

'We shall eat an olio later,' she informed them with an unnerving grin. 'Which is a stew containing a fine mixture of items. I banned certain spices, though, as they are known to inflame fierce passions. Do you know why I chose an olio as our fare today?'

'Because you wrote a book with "olio" in the title?' suggested Chaloner, although he knew he could not be right, as no one would be that self-serving.

'Yes!' she exclaimed, clapping her hands in girlish delight. '*The World's Olio*. It is clever of me, do you not think?'

345

'Oh, very,' said Swaddell, when Chaloner was too taken aback to reply.

'Now, Chiffinch's poisoner,' she said, sobering abruptly and regarding both men with disconcerting intensity. 'Have you found him yet?'

'No,' replied Chaloner, and as she had broached the subject, he seized the opportunity to ask some questions of his own. 'But we understand that you told one of the kitchen children where to buy the oysters. Is it true?'

The Duchess nodded. 'I happened to spot the child weeping, because White Hall's usual supplier had sold out, so I stepped in to save the day. The brat was very grateful, and deeply impressed that I, a lady of noble birth, should know about shellfish.'

Chaloner could not read her at all. Was she the cunning killer, toying with the dim-witted investigator? Or was she genuinely careless of the fact that she had played a role – inadvertent or otherwise – in a murder?

'Do you eat Sarah Shawe's wares yourself?'

She regarded him in distaste. 'Oysters are for commoners, so no. Besides, I feel for the creatures. How would you like to be swallowed alive, to die in someone else's stomach?'

'Then why did you facilitate the demise of two dozen of them by sending the child to Sarah?' Chaloner was aware that the question was insolent, and was glad the Duke was busily holding forth on dressage to Ursula and Veriana, sure he would object if he heard.

'I did not think of that at the time,' shrugged the Duchess. 'I regretted it later.'

'But you urged him to eat the ones on his plate, even though he said he was full.'

The Duchess's gaze did not waver. 'I did no such thing.

However, as they had been doused in lemon and salt, the least he could do was put the poor things out of their misery.'

'You must be pleased to learn that Topp is alive,' said Chaloner, in a final, desperate effort to shake her from her exasperating equanimity. 'That he is a thief but not a suicide.'

'I am glad for Eliza. I do not care for myself.'

At that point, the next guests bustled forward to make their obeisance. Chaloner was uncomfortably aware of the Duchess watching him as they gabbled polite nonsense, and he was under the impression that she would have liked to spar a little longer.

Newcastle House was full to bursting and very noisy. Fanny came to whisk Ursula and Veriana away to join her sewing circle, much to their dismay, leaving Chaloner and Swaddell to mingle. The first person to hail them was Clayton, resplendent in a set of new clothes. Viscount Mansfield was with him.

'You and your viol will not be needed today,' the steward said apologetically. 'Once I found out how many people were coming, I had to hire the entire troupe of the King's Private Musick instead.'

'But even they cannot make themselves heard over the rumpus,' sniggered Mansfield. 'My stepmother has invited half of London to share her stupid olio.'

He slithered away into the throng, where he began to murmur disparaging remarks about the Duchess to anyone who would listen. Clayton followed dutifully.

After a while, when the public rooms had become hotter and even more crowded, Chaloner went in search of his cousins. He tracked them down to a quiet

347

antechamber, where a group of middle-aged ladies were admiring the stitches on each other's lace. Ursula's face was a mask of despair, as every time she attempted to slip away, one of the matrons contrived to stop her. Veriana had given up trying, and sat with her arms folded and a pout on her face.

'*Please*, Thomas,' begged Ursula, leaping up to hiss desperately in his ear. 'We cannot stay in here all afternoon. If we are to find good husbands, we must be *noticed*.'

But Chaloner did not want them noticed by the Newcastles' guests. True, the gathering was mostly free of rakes, but there were still enough there to make it dangerous. Baron Lucas had brought friends from the Royal Society, who included several earls of dubious moral reputation, while Cobbe, clad in an eye-catching outfit of purple silk, had also contrived to get inside, despite his affiliation with the Cockpit Club.

The olio was served soon after, and did not induce 'fierce passions' as much as a fierce desire for water. Lucas spat his on the floor with a roar of shock, although others were more genteel and used handkerchiefs or disappeared behind curtains to get rid of theirs. Ursula and Veriana wanted a taste, but Fanny forbade it after her husband, who had gamely taken a very large mouthful, was compelled to glug a pint of wine to soothe the resulting burning.

'Do not touch it,' he gasped, tears running down his cheeks. 'It is toxic – and that is my professional medical opinion.'

'It is very nice,' countered Swaddell, and proceeded to devour an entire bowl without so much as a wince. It was a tactical mistake, as whispers began almost immediately that Satan and his familiars were partial to highly spicy food. Then Chaloner's attention was taken by Brodrick, who bustled up angrily.

'There will be no decent music,' he snarled. 'And that is the only reason I came. I am tempted to don a disguise and go to the cockpit instead, where Bess has organised a bear-fight.'

'You enjoy that sort of thing?' asked Chaloner in distaste.

'Not really, but it is better than being plied with in-edible olios here. Or reading law books in Clarendon House, which is my cousin's idea of light entertainment. And at least I would be among my own kind at the cockpit, because look around at who is here – physicians, dowdy matrons, natural philosophers, horse-traders, the rougher kind of cleric . . .'

'True,' agreed Chaloner.

'Worse, I think the Newcastles have let the servants bring their friends,' Brodrick went on in a shocked whisper. 'Because I am sure the ladies next to the refresh-ments are common traders.'

Chaloner looked to where a small, uncertain gaggle of women from the Red Bull stood. Sarah was in their midst, tall, proud and defiant, as if daring anyone to challenge her right to be there. No one did, so she and her cronies began to help themselves to wine, tentatively at first, then with increasing enthusiasm. Eliza arrived soon after, and Sarah strode forward to greet her, not caring that she jostled other guests as she went. Eliza looked haggard, worn out by the emotional upheavals of a husband missing, then dead, then alive again.

'We shall not stay long,' declared Sarah in a loud, self-important voice. 'We are busy women with hectic lives. But we wanted you to know that you have friends.'

'Er . . . yes,' said Eliza, flustered and embarrassed in

349

equal measure. 'Thank you. Yet I am surprised to see you here . . .'

'I told Molly to let us in,' explained Sarah. 'We thought you might need our support while you are obliged to move among . . . these individuals.' She gazed around in distaste.

'You see what happens when the established order of things is flouted?' Chaloner heard Fanny whisper to her friends. 'Boundaries are blurred, and no one knows where they stand.'

At that point, Baron Lucas swept the Red Bull contingent away to meet his Royal Society cronies, but the company suited neither party, so it was not long before they went their separate ways. Sarah led her coterie to the door, pausing just long enough to murmur something to Eliza, and any discomfiture she might have caused her friend was clearly forgiven, as the glance that she received was one of deep affection.

Eventually, Swaddell sidled up to Chaloner. 'I have just ascertained that the Duchess's boudoir is on the first floor, second door on the right. While you have a poke around, I will pretend to be watching the soirée over the banister. If anyone comes up the stairs, I will rap on it three times with my ring.'

Chaloner could see a lot wrong with that plan, not least of which was that he would be unlikely to hear such a sound once he was where he needed to be. But with luck, the Duchess would be too busy with her guests to return to her private quarters, so the warning would not be needed. He waited until he was sure no one was looking, then ran quickly up the staircase.

The Duchess's half of the house was decorated with an eclectic collection of artwork, and the furniture had been chosen for comfort, rather than style. Her boudoir was a messy, cluttered room, dominated by hanging picture frames. A glance told him that all held enlarged copies of the frontispieces in her books. Clearly, false modesty was not one of her vices.

As the room was so chaotic – table, chairs and floor were covered in papers and books – Chaloner realised a full search would be impossible, so he decided to concentrate on the desk, in the feeble hope that she had been careless enough to leave something incriminating lying out.

The first thing he saw was a list of Mother Broughton's prophecies, accompanied by notes outlining what the Duchess planned to do about them. For example, she aimed to neutralise Good Friday's rain of fire by gathering nice people under her roof, so that their combined virtue would render them all safe. She was also of the opinion that the joy scheduled for Easter Day would be the delight that would burst forth when she announced the publication of her next book.

Aware that folk might need some persuading before they agreed to fall in with her schemes, she had turned to tomes on religion to 'prove' that she was right. One lay open at a page depicting the motifs assigned to various saints. Chaloner frowned at one of the symbols – it was familiar, but he could not recall why. As he puzzled over it, he heard a sound from the closet in the corner. He whipped around, hand on his sword, but before he could draw it, the door flung open and someone jumped out with a gun.

It was Topp.

'Do not come any closer,' the steward hissed. 'If you do, I will shoot you.'

Chapter 14

There was silence in the Duchess's boudoir as Topp pointed the gun at Chaloner. The steward was so frightened by the situation in which he found himself that his hands shook violently, and Chaloner knew he was in more danger of being shot by accident than deliberately.

'Put it down,' he ordered. 'Before you hurt yourself.'

'I will hurt you,' blustered Topp, struggling to keep the tremor from his voice. 'You should not have come here. You are trespassing.'

'So are you,' retorted Chaloner. 'You stole three hundred pounds from people who trusted you, then you staged your own death. I cannot see you being welcomed back with open arms.'

Topp swallowed hard. 'I had no choice. That anonymous letter to the Duke . . . Thirty years of faithful service, destroyed by one spiteful pen. And it was lies! I *do* love the Duchess, but as a father loves a daughter. I would never take her as a lover. The very idea is repulsive.'

'The Duke knows that. He did not believe the accusations for a moment.'

'No?' asked Topp, startled and hopeful in equal measure.

'He charged one of the best investigators in the country to find out who wrote it – a man who is visiting the posthouse from which it was sent as we speak. Your employer remained loyal to you, and you repaid him by stealing.'

'I stole nothing,' countered Topp, licking his lips nervously. 'The three hundred pounds was mine – money I am owed for purchases made on his behalf. I am not a thief.'

'Is that so,' said Chaloner, before darting forward to grab the gun. As Topp's pockets and coat bulged suspiciously, he gave the man a shake, and was disgusted but not surprised when all manner of valuable items showered down on to the floor. 'I suppose these are your brooches, necklaces and jewels, then, are they?'

Even with the evidence of his perfidy scattered around his feet, Topp continued to bleat his innocence: the Duchess had promised him these things; he had just taken what was rightfully his; he had only availed himself of a fraction of what she had said he might have . . .

'Enough!' snapped Chaloner, tiring of the self-justifying tirade. 'You are a thief and a killer, and it is time for you to accept responsibility for what you have done.'

Topp regarded him in horror. 'A killer? What are you talking about? I accept that I might have been a little zealous in claiming what I am owed, but I have never hurt anyone.'

Chaloner indicated the gun. It had a distinctively engraved barrel, and he recalled it vividly from White Hall, when it and its partner had poked around the door to Mushey's room and blasted at him and Swaddell.

353

'You are the White Hall killer, who poisoned Chiffinch's oysters, then dispatched Mushey to ensure he never revealed that *you* were the one he let into the palace larder.'

The blood drained from Topp's face. 'No, Your Honour! I have never been inside the larder and I never met this Mushey. I swear on my mother's grave.'

'Then explain how you come to be in possession of this particular handgun.'

'I found it right there.' Topp pointed to a table. 'And there is a matching one under that copy of *The World's Olio*. I snatched it up when I heard you coming, because I thought I might have to protect myself. I had no choice but to wave it at you, although I would never have used it. You *must* believe me, Your Magnificence.'

A quick check revealed that the gun was unloaded, but as the steward seemed unaware of the fact, Chaloner was willing to accept that the weapons did not belong to him. So whose were they? The Duchess's, and it had been she who had shot at him and Swaddell in White Hall? He thought about Sarah's testimony that someone had watched Millicent buy the oysters from her; and Millicent's claim that a woman had lurked outside the larder that same day. Then there was the Duchess's peculiar request to watch Chiffinch dissected. She had been a suspect from the start, so did the pistols prove her guilt?

Topp saw Chaloner's hesitation and sought to capitalise on it. 'On the day the oysters were poisoned, I was off trying to purchase a corpse. It took hours, as I kept being offered ones that were unsuitable. Half were the wrong sex, for a start.'

Chaloner believed him, feeling that no one would admit to buying cadavers unless it was true. And if Topp

354

had not poisoned Chiffinch, then he had not killed the others either.

'So your Duchess murdered Chiffinch,' he said, purely to see if Topp would defend the lady he claimed to love. 'She must have done, given that the guns are hers.'

Topp licked his lips, and Chaloner could almost hear the wheels turning in his head as he pondered how blaming her might benefit himself. 'It is possible, Your Worship,' he hedged eventually, 'but there are far better suspects. Clayton, for example, who is a vile rogue.'

'He certainly does not like you. Indeed, I am surprised you have not accused him of sending that slanderous missive to the Duke.'

'I assumed he had, but when I looked at the Bishop-mark to see when it was posted, it transpires that he was with me at the time. Moreover, I know his handwriting as well as my own. He is not responsible for the letter.'

Answers to that particular mystery were beginning to form in Chaloner's mind, but while he was sure that Thurloe would be pleased to see it solved – assuming the ex-Spymaster had not already done it himself, of course – it was irrelevant to the more pressing matter of murder.

'What is your evidence for accusing Clayton of being the White Hall killer?' he asked.

'I do not have any, Your Worship,' admitted Topp wretchedly. 'But I will find some if you let me go. I will just gather up these baubles, and send word once I have what you need.'

Chaloner laughed. 'I do not think so! But why did you not leave the city after staging your "death"? No one questioned it, and you could have escaped scot-free.'

Topp pulled a disagreeable face. 'Because I realised I would need more than three hundred pounds to build a new life, so I had to come back to see what else was available. It is not theft, though – it is compensation for all the agony and inconvenience I have endured.'

'*You* have endured?' echoed Chaloner, amazed by the unabashed selfishness. 'What about Eliza, who mourned you?'

Topp had the grace to blush. 'I am sorry for that, but she is a loyal wife, and I have explained why I had to do it. She will forgive me eventually. Now, if there is nothing else, Your Eminence, I shall see about getting you some evidence to see Clayton hanged.'

'Stop,' ordered Chaloner, as the steward began to scoop up handfuls of jewellery from the floor. 'I imagine the Duke would like a word with you. Then he can decide how to proceed.'

Finding Topp had put Chaloner in an awkward situation, as he could hardly reveal that he had caught the steward while he had been searching the Duchess's private chambers for evidence that she was a murderer. He had just decided to say that he had met Topp in the hall – the steward would denounce the lie, but who would believe him? – when the door was flung open.

Chaloner's hand tightened around the gun as Eliza and Sarah walked in. Both women stopped dead in their tracks when they saw him, then Eliza turned to her husband with a muted whimper of distress.

'You promised to stay out of sight! Now you will be accused of terrible things, and I shall have to bear the pain of losing you all over again.'

'Do not worry,' said Sarah, who had drawn a dagger. 'I will not allow you to suffer a second time.' She addressed Topp. 'Has anyone else seen you since your "suicide"?'

'Just the Rector of St Dunstan-in-the-West,' replied Topp miserably. 'It was raining, and I ducked into his church for shelter. I did not think he would notice me, but he did.'

'Then I shall put it about that he was drunk at the time.' Sarah regarded Chaloner appraisingly, fingering her knife. 'That just leaves you.'

'You cannot stab him here,' gulped Eliza. 'The Duchess likes these rugs.'

'I will clean up the blood,' offered Topp, while Chaloner wondered why they thought they could best him, when he was not only bigger and stronger, but likely far better armed. 'This man means to destroy me, and I will pay you handsomely if you . . . dissuade him.'

'Pay her with what?' asked Chaloner archly. 'The Duchess's jewellery? If you do, she will be caught and hanged the moment she tries to exchange it for money.'

'My husband would *never* touch the Duchess's things,' declared Eliza stoutly. 'He is her most loyal servant – or he was, until someone wrote that nasty letter. It has destroyed our lives, because things have spiralled out of control since, and now he must leave the country.'

'You will miss him, I am sure,' muttered Chaloner, glancing at Sarah, who was looking delighted by the prospect of the steward being out of the way.

'I will.' Eliza's expression was anguished. 'And I shall spend every waking moment persuading the Duchess of his innocence. Then he can come home.'

'I am afraid his sticky fingers have destroyed all hope of a pardon,' said Chaloner. 'It is a pity he could not control them, because all might have ended well otherwise.'

'We shall return the money Francis *borrowed*,' said Eliza with quiet dignity, 'and I will find a way to exonerate him. Clayton will not win this war – and I am sure he *did* send that letter, no matter what the Bishop-mark says.'

'Clayton is the White Hall killer,' Topp declared confidently, and then indicated Chaloner. 'He accused me of it at first, but I convinced him that he was mistaken.'

'You *are* mistaken,' Eliza told Chaloner firmly. 'Francis was out buying a corpse when the oysters would have been poisoned, and has witnesses to prove it. And do not accuse Sarah or me of the crime either, because we were here in Newcastle House with the Duke, Mansfield and a hundred others. Baron Lucas gave a talk on air pressure that evening, you see, and he locked the doors to make sure no one sneaked out.'

'Although a few people managed to escape regardless,' put in Sarah. 'Namely Clayton and his two unsavoury friends. And the Duchess, of course, who went to visit John Milton, before heading for White Hall to defeat Chiffinch at backgammon. When Baron Lucas and Mansfield arrived there later – they travelled together, so have alibis in each other – she was already in the Shield Gallery. Lucas told me so himself.'

Eliza gave her an irritable glance, then glared at Chaloner. 'But do not even think of accusing My Lady. She is an angel, who has never hurt anyone in her life.'

Chaloner appreciated her loyalty, but dogged devotion was not proof. He said so.

Eliza was silent for a moment, thinking. Gradually, she began to smile, first with relief, then in jubilation. 'But Francis is right – Clayton *is* the White Hall killer! And I can prove it. Sarah, go and make sure no one is listening. We cannot risk eavesdroppers, because I do not want what I am about to say made public, twisted and embellished with every telling.'

'I would rather stay here,' countered Sarah, irked by what was effectively a dismissal. 'You need me to protect you. In case you have not noticed, Chaloner holds a gun.'

'He would have used it by now if he meant us harm,' said Eliza. 'So do as I ask.'

Sarah slouched, very reluctantly, through the door, while Topp looked from Chaloner to Eliza and back again, frightened and anxious about what was about to be revealed.

'When that anonymous letter arrived,' began Eliza, 'the first thing the Duke did was show it to Chiffinch.'

'Why would he do that?' asked Chaloner sceptically.

'Because Chiffinch received lots of applications from people wanting Court posts, so was familiar with their handwriting. He said he could not help, and sent the Duke to a man called William Prynne, who also deals with lots of official correspondence. Prynne did not recognise the writing, but he introduced the Duke to a man who promised to investigate.'

'Who?' asked Topp suspiciously, while Chaloner held his breath.

'The Duke refused to say,' replied Eliza.

Thank God for that, thought Chaloner in relief. 'So there is a link between the letter and one of the murder victims. That is interesting, but it does not prove Clayton is the killer.'

'You are not *listening*. Chiffinch said he "could not help" – he did not say the handwriting was unknown to him. I later overheard him gossiping to Widdrington, and I was under the impression that he *had* recognised it, but had decided to keep the information from the Duke. Perhaps he aimed to blackmail the culprit. Regardless, a few hours later, he was dead.'

'So you think the killer and the author of the letter are one and the same?' asked Chaloner. 'Then it cannot be Clayton, because he was with your husband when the letter was mailed from Grantham.'

Eliza smiled. 'But *you* know that alibi is meaningless – I can see it in your face. Clayton is a clever man, who not only disguised his handwriting – although there are experts who will see past that sort of thing – but sent someone to post the letter in his stead.'

She was right. The culprit would not have taken his missive to the posthouse in person, as Thurloe was likely to discover when he questioned its officials. But Clayton had two good friends: Booth and Liddell. One of them might do his bidding.

'Unfortunately, that is not evidence either,' warned Chaloner.

'It will be if Widdrington tells you what Chiffinch said about it,' argued Eliza. 'Or at least, enough to arrest Clayton for formal questioning.'

Chaloner doubted Widdrington would cooperate, and thought Eliza was clutching at straws. 'It is a fine theory, but I cannot see Clayton perpetrating such an elaborate scheme.'

'I can, Your Worship,' put in Topp eagerly. 'He hates the Duchess and he hates me. He always has, ever since we first met, and I saw through his sly, greedy manners.'

'I understand why he dislikes you,' said Chaloner. 'But why the Duchess?'

'Because he has thrown his eggs in Mansfield's basket, and aims to be sole steward when Mansfield inherits his father's estate,' explained Eliza earnestly. 'The Viscount loathes his stepmother, but would never dare plot against her while the Duke is alive. However, he will not object to someone else doing it on his behalf . . .'

Chaloner was far from convinced, but he had no other leads to follow, and Eliza's suggestion was better than nothing.

'I will look into Clayton,' he said eventually. 'But on two conditions: Topp will return everything he stole – including the three hundred pounds – and he will leave the country tonight.'

'He will,' promised Eliza, sagging in relief. 'You can trust us.'

Her, perhaps, thought Chaloner, but not her devious husband.

The soirée was in full swing when Chaloner rejoined Swaddell on the stairs. The assassin was dismayed, because Fanny's defences had been breached by the flamboyant Cobbe and the handsome young Earl of Lincoln. The pair sat next to Ursula and Veriana, who were delighted to have attracted such charming company, while Fanny fretted and flapped uselessly to one side, openly distressed by her failure to send the manly invaders packing.

Meanwhile, the ballroom was full of people trying to dance, although there were too many even for that great space, and the music was impossible to hear over the roar of lively conversation and laughter.

'You took your time,' said Swaddell accusingly. 'I hope you have something to show for it, because it kept me here when I should have been driving those peacocks from your cousins.'

'You might as well have gone for all the use you were,' retorted Chaloner curtly. 'You let Eliza and Sarah past, and they caught me.'

Swaddell blinked. 'Did they? They told me they were going to fetch some books.'

'They probably were,' said Chaloner acidly. 'From the Duchess's boudoir.'

'Oh,' said Swaddell guiltily. 'I suppose that should have been obvious. But my attention was on our ladies, and how I might save them from those two devious rakes.'

There was no point in berating him further, so Chaloner confined himself to recounting what had happened in the Duchess's rooms. Swaddell was unimpressed.

'You should not have let Topp go! He is a thief and should pay for his crimes.'

'Then you can pursue him later,' said Chaloner shortly. 'But first, we must prove that Clayton was responsible for the anonymous letter and that Chiffinch knew it. Then we can charge him with poisoning Chiffinch, and ask about the other victims once we have him in custody.'

'I hope you are sure about this,' grumbled Swaddell, 'because time is running out. It is Maundy Thursday tomorrow, after which Good Friday will be upon us. We will be too busy ducking rains of fire and gnashing our teeth to investigate murder.'

'Clerkenwell,' mused Chaloner. 'Everything comes back to Clerkenwell. The disasters will begin here, the prophet who predicted them lives here, our prime suspect works here . . .'

'So does our second: the Duchess,' put in Swaddell. 'And if Clayton transpires to be innocent, we shall have to look at her. Eliza is fiercely loyal to her mistress, and may have misled you deliberately. However, before we do anything else, we must remove your cousins from the clutches of those swaggering lotharios.'

Chaloner agreed that a dalliance with Cobbe was not

362

to be to encouraged, although he had no objection to the Earl of Lincoln. But before he could say so, the Duchess blew three long, shrill blasts on a ceremonial hunting horn that had been hanging on the ballroom wall. Startled, the musicians faltered into silence, the dancers tottered to a standstill, and the bellow of conversation faded away.

'It is time for you all to go home,' she announced, and Chaloner might have laughed at the astonished expressions on her guests' faces if he had not been so taken aback himself. 'This gathering has achieved its purpose, and your presence here is no longer required. Besides, it is Holy Week, so you should not be jigging about like monkeys anyway.'

'But it was you who provided the facilities, ma'am,' objected Brodrick, the only one bold – or drunk – enough to say what everyone else was thinking.

'I did,' acknowledged the Duchess. 'But it was a test, to see who would avail themselves of them, even though dancing is inappropriate for such a solemn day in the Church year. Those people will *not* be invited back again. However, those who restrained themselves will be expected to join me here any time after ten o'clock on Good Friday morning.'

'I do not understand,' snapped Brodrick waspishly. 'What—'

'You must have heard that a great calamity will befall London the day after tomorrow,' interrupted the Duchess, 'after which all evil will be wiped from the face of the Earth. However, the godly will be spared this destruction, so it makes sense for all us righteous types to gather in one place. Then we can enjoy the spectacle together.'

'Goodness!' breathed Swaddell, while the guests –

revellers and sobersides alike – exchanged glances of disbelief. 'I always thought the Almighty would have the task of weighing our souls. Since when did it become the role of the aristocracy?'

'So go home,' the Duchess continued. 'If you are among the fortunate few who will come on Friday, I shall see you then. As for the rest, all I can do is warn you to mend your debauched ways before it is too late.'

'I would not come back here anyway,' muttered Brodrick, as he plonked his glass down hard enough to break it. 'She belongs in Bedlam, and is not fit for proper society.'

Most guests agreed, especially when she elected to stand at the door and inform each person individually whether or not they had won her approbation.

'What manner of gathering will it be on Friday?' asked the Earl of Lincoln, who had passed the test only because Fanny had refused to let him whisk Ursula on to the dance floor.

'We shall read my books until the rain of fire begins, then we will watch the display through the upstairs windows,' replied the Duchess. 'Do not worry – you will be in no danger, and when you are old, you can tell your grandchildren about the Day the World Changed.'

The young nobleman bowed and left, although it was clear that he had no intention of spending what might be his last few hours with the eccentric Duchess of Newcastle.

'*You* may return,' she decreed, as Chaloner, Swaddell, Veriana and Ursula filed past. 'I commend you on your sobriety. I predicted you would fail, but I was wrong.'

Before they could respond, she had turned to inform Brodrick that *he* need not darken her doors again.

364

Chaloner began to laugh once they were outside, although he was the only one who did. All around, people were outraged that she should dare pass judgement on others, especially as news of the anonymous letter had seeped out, so there were rumours that she strayed outside the marriage bed.

'And she has pronounced her disgusting brother as one of the godly,' hissed Lady Muskerry furiously. 'The man who pawed shamelessly at me all afternoon. His Royal Society cronies qualified, too, but only because they were too busy arguing to dance.'

It was some time before Swaddell's coach arrived, because the Duchess's decision to end the soirée so abruptly meant that all the carriages were needed at once, causing a huge jam.

'Will you come here on Good Friday, Thomas?' asked Fanny, as they waited.

She was standing with the ladies from her sewing circle, all reeling from the news that they were not invited back. Apparently, being staid was not the same as being righteous, and the Duchess had decided to lump them in with the wicked. Dr Clarke was similarly condemned, because he had been spotted making a pass at Lady Muskerry.

'I doubt it,' replied Chaloner. 'What will you do?'

'Go to church,' replied Fanny with a shrug. 'Then invite my friends to sit with me while this rain of fire destroys the sinful.'

Chaloner regarded her askance. 'Surely you do not really believe that will happen?'

'I do not know what to think,' sighed Fanny unhappily. 'But perhaps the King has the right idea, and we should all go to Dover, just in case. But here is my coach at last. Good evening to you.'

Swaddell's carriage appeared eventually, but it was dark by the time it reached Covent Garden. Swaddell inveigled an invitation to stay for a cup of wine, and Wiseman was there to entertain everyone with an account of the King's bowels, so Chaloner decided to leave Clayton until the following day. He wrote a note to Kersey at the charnel house, asked one of Wiseman's servants to deliver it, and went to bed.

Chapter 15

It was just growing light when Chaloner rose the next morning. He went to the garden to let out the hens and the goose, then roused his cousins and told them to prepare for a day with Fanny. They grumbled bitterly, both about the early start and the prospect of such dull company, but they did as they were told.

He was just availing himself of bread and boiled eggs in the parlour when Swaddell was shown in. The assassin had reverted to his trademark black, although there were dark rings under his eyes – Chaloner was not the only one who had been kept awake by churning thoughts the previous night.

'What first?' Swaddell asked, craning his neck to see if he could spot Ursula or Veriana coming down the stairs. 'We must catch the killer today, Tom, because there will be no time tomorrow. I have offered to stay with Ursula then, lest she needs my protection from walking corpses or rains of fire.'

Chaloner would allow neither cousin to spend Good Friday with Swaddell, but it was no time to say so. He hailed a hackney, bundled his still-protesting kinswomen inside, and delivered them to Chaloner Court. Swaddell was at his most charming during the journey, but not even his promise of a visit to the cherry trees at Rotherhithe could distract them from the horrors of a day with middle-aged ladies whose idea of fun was comparing bone and metal pins.

Fanny was waiting for them, and Chaloner experienced a pang of guilt when she informed the girls that, as a change from needlework, they would read the Bible all morning, then cut up old newsbooks for compost in the afternoon.

'We may not be safe with her,' Ursula whispered in a last, desperate attempt to escape the ordeal. 'Not when terrible things will start in Clerkenwell tomorrow – things that will change the world for ever.'

'I shall be with you,' promised Swaddell gallantly. 'Do not worry.'

Veriana nodded polite thanks, but Ursula was much more effusive, and Chaloner saw that he needed to keep the two apart, lest Swaddell took warm-heartedness as a sign of affection. He did not fancy dealing with a Swaddell spurned in love.

He climbed back into the carriage and told the driver to take them to Westminster. While they lurched along the rutted streets, he told Swaddell his plans for the day.

'First, we must visit the charnel house, where I believe we will find proof that Clayton wrote the anonymous letter accusing the Duchess of adultery. Afterwards, we will speak to Widdrington, and ask what Chiffinch told *him* about it. Between the two, I think we might have answers at last.'

'And if Widdrington refuses to cooperate?' asked Swaddell.

'Oh, I am sure you can persuade him,' replied

Chaloner, feeling the time for gentleness was past now that Good Friday was almost upon them.

They travelled the rest of the way in silence, Chaloner thinking about the murders and the solutions that were emerging at last, while Swaddell smiled rather dreamily. They reached the charnel house at the same time as Kersey, who rolled up in his private carriage. Chaloner glanced inside and saw a woman there, although she was neither of his two wives. Kersey alighted, then poked his head back through the window to murmur thanks for a wonderful night.

'You are bold,' Swaddell told him admiringly. 'I would never dare.'

'Never dare what?' asked Kersey blandly.

Secrets and favours, thought Chaloner, reflecting on how many there were in his current investigation. Swaddell knew something about Bishop Morley that meant the prelate was willing to lie for him, while the Duchess had once done Thurloe such an important favour that the ex-Spymaster had gone to Grantham on her behalf. Chiffinch had whispered something to Widdrington that might have a bearing on his murder, and Chaloner himself had done the Topps a favour by letting the steward go in exchange for information.

He followed Kersey inside the charnel house, aware of a mounting sense of unease about the whole affair. There were connections he still did not understand, and he had the sense that if he pulled too hard on one thread, the lot would come crashing down around him. Perhaps *that* was what Mother Broughton thought was about to happen in Clerkenwell – one strand of discontent tweaked, beginning a chain of events that would not stop until the world was upside down again.

'I wonder if the messenger will come to me today,' said Kersey conversationally, and elaborated when Chaloner and Swaddell looked blank. 'Mother Broughton predicted that a "messenger" will die on Thursday and the Fleet River will run red with blood. Or have you taken steps to prevent that from happening?'

'How?' asked Swaddell wearily. 'We do not know who the prediction is for. However, I can tell you that it will not be Ambassador Downing. He has decided to stay in Dover until the danger is past.'

'Wise man,' said Kersey. 'But how may I help you today? I received the note you sent me last night, and did what you asked, but it made no sense.'

'When I was last here,' began Chaloner, 'you showed me the body of a man who had walked around after his brain had stopped working, along with items you had recovered from his pockets. You hoped he might be identified from them, so you could inform his family.'

Kersey inclined his head. 'There was a book by the Duchess of Newcastle, annotated with unflattering remarks, along with some coded messages and a few illegally clipped coins. I was going to send the messages to Spymaster Williamson, but your note arrived just in time, so they are still here. Do you want to see them?'

Chaloner nodded. 'I saw a list of saints' symbols in the Duchess's boudoir last night. One was familiar, although it took me a while to remember why.'

'It was in the messages?' asked Kersey, as he led the way inside, where the box containing the dead man's effects was waiting on the desk in his office.

Chaloner unfolded one of the pieces of paper. 'Yes, here it is – the broken wheel, which appears to be how the sender addresses the recipient.'

'So the dead man identified himself with a saint?' asked Swaddell warily. 'Which one?'

'A broken wheel signifies St Quentin, who was pinned to one during his martyrdom.' Chaloner waited for Swaddell to make the connection, but the assassin remained perplexed, obliging him to spell it out. 'Booth is the vicar of St *Quentin's* near Nottingham.'

'Yes, he did say that is where he has his living,' acknowledged Swaddell. 'He mentioned that it had caught fire recently . . .'

'Which is why he was so angry when he was attacked,' said Chaloner, watching understanding dawn on the assassin's face. 'He cannot afford to lose money to thieves.'

'This Vicar Booth was robbed?' asked Kersey, intrigued.

'A thief ambushed him and ran off with his purse,' explained Chaloner. 'He gave chase, and pursued the culprit into Newcastle House's stables – into the stall occupied by the high-spirited Henrietta Florence. She lunged at Booth when he tried to lay hold of the villain, which allowed him to escape. But the robber later went back – I suspect he had dropped his loot, and thought it would be easy to retrieve. Unfortunately, Henrietta Florence is dangerous . . .'

'My guest's head could have been damaged by a flying hoof,' mused Kersey. 'Indeed, it would explain the injury perfectly.'

'I saw the letter that accused the Duchess of infidelity,' said Chaloner, although he was not about to confide that Thurloe had shown it to him. 'The sender had tried to disguise his hand, but he neglected to change his distinctive *f*s. Now, look at the annotations in the book.'

'The *f*s are unusual,' said Kersey, fascinated.

'They are identical to the ones in the letter, which

371

means its author and the owner of this book are one and the same. A person whose identifying mark is St Quentin's broken wheel. There cannot be many churches dedicated to St Quentin in England . . .'

'So my guest is not a rebel dealing in coded letters,' surmised Kersey. 'He is just a common thief, and everything in his pockets came from Vicar Booth?'

'Yes,' said Chaloner. 'Now consider the clipped coins. If the thief stole the book and the letters from Booth, the chances are that the money came from Booth, too. Coin-clipping is a capital offence, which is why Booth risked haring after the thief – he *had* to get them back.'

'So Booth is guilty not only of devaluing the King's currency, but also of sending libellous letters to the Duke,' concluded Swaddell. 'Interesting. But I thought we were hoping for evidence that would prove *Clayton's* guilt.'

Chaloner could only assume that Swaddell was muddle-headed from a poor night's sleep, because he was not usually slow-witted. 'Booth is Clayton's friend – they are in it together. Indeed, I wager anything you please that St Quentin's is near Grantham, where the letter was posted. Booth will be the easier nut to crack, so I suggest we tackle him first.'

'No,' said Swaddell. 'We should speak to Widdrington before going to Newcastle House. We need to find out exactly what Chiffinch said to him about the anonymous letter. *Then* we will corner this criminal cleric, because if you are right about these connections, whatever Chiffinch said was what drove Clayton to poison his oysters.'

In the event, they were obliged to follow Chaloner's suggestion, because they arrived at White Hall only to discover that Widdrington had gone to buy a horse in

Hampstead, and was not expected back until the evening. Swaddell wanted to go after him, but Chaloner refused, remembering the hours he had squandered chasing Pamphlin.

'Booth, then,' conceded Swaddell, flagging down a hackney to take them to Clerkenwell. 'But you had better hope we have enough to force a confession, because otherwise all we will do is warn Clayton that we are closing in on him.'

Again, the journey was made in silence, with the assassin staring out of the window, one hand playing idly with his dagger. When they were stopped by a jam on Fleet Street, they heard passers-by talking in excited voices about Good Friday. Most seemed to be looking forward to it, on the grounds that they, as righteous individuals, would be spared. Folk were irked anew with the King, though. He had discharged his Maundy Thursday obligations by giving away coins, but had started – and finished – so early that most people had missed it. Then he had set out for Dover without a backward glance.

Eventually, Chaloner and Swaddell reached Newcastle House, which was busy, as an army of servants laboured to put all back to rights after the Duchess's soirée. Wine stains were being scrubbed from tables, scuff marks polished off floors, and goblets and jugs collected for washing. Chaloner wondered why it had not been done sooner, but had his answer from Molly, who told him that, after most of the guests had gone home, Baron Lucas had taken over the public rooms for an experiment with his Royal Society cronies. She had been his assistant.

'But it did not go according to plan, and everyone ended up covered in chicken muck,' she finished. 'He and I laughed our heads off, but his friends were cross.'

373

'What kind of experiment?' asked Chaloner, unable to imagine one that entailed manure being brought inside the house. He glanced up, and saw the glass ceiling high above was spattered with brown goo, and as there was no easy way to reach it, it might be there to stay.

'One involving explosions,' replied Molly, not very helpfully. 'They were only little ones, but Baron Lucas said he could easily make them much bigger.'

'Explosions?' asked Swaddell sharply. 'Why would he do such a thing?'

'It is called al-chem-y,' explained Molly, speaking the word slowly to ensure she got it right. 'Learning how things can be mixed up to make loud noises and nasty smells. He loves it, and wanted to show his friends what he can do with droppings, oil and some other stuff.'

Chaloner and Swaddell exchanged an uneasy glance, but before they could question her further, there was a commotion as some of her feathered charges invaded the hall. She scampered away to round them up, amid angry grumbles from the other servants who felt the birds were getting out of control.

'Dutch Jane has a lot to answer for,' muttered the butler. 'If she had not tried to steal one, the Duchess would never have given Molly sole control over the wretched things. Molly is wholly unequal to the task of keeping them in the garden.'

'What a mess!' muttered a cook, looking around in despair. 'And to think we shall have to clean up all over again tomorrow, after the Duchess hosts her next gathering.'

'It will not be as bad then,' predicted the butler, 'because she has only invited the godly. *They* will not spill wine or spoil the floor by dancing.'

As everyone was busy, Chaloner and Swaddell went in search of Vicar Booth themselves. They walked through the hall and into the ballroom, where Eliza was giving instructions to a carpenter – one of Lucas's experiments had involved a hot cauldron, which had burned a black circle on the beautiful oak floorboards. She looked pale and tired, although there was a sparkle in her eye that had been missing when she thought she was a widow. When she saw Chaloner, she came to greet him.

'Thank you for what you did last night,' she said in a low voice. 'The money and jewels have been returned, and my husband is already sailing down the Thames. He will live in France until I have convinced the Duke and Duchess to forgive him. But we all make mistakes, and I am grateful to you for allowing us to put this one right.'

'You are welcome,' mumbled Chaloner, aware of Swaddell's disapproving glare.

'Of course,' Eliza went on wryly, 'Francis will have to work hard to win back *my* good graces. It will not be easy to forget the distress he caused me by pretending to be dead.'

'Perhaps he thought you would be happier with Sarah,' said Swaddell baldly.

Eliza blushed. 'I am fond of Sarah, but Francis is my husband, and will always claim the best part of my heart. Him and my Duchess.'

'We need to talk to Booth,' said Chaloner, feeling the press of time upon him. 'Where might we find him?'

'Hiding in the church next door, lest he is put to work. Personally, I suspect he set fire to his own parish church himself, to give him licence to abandon his flock and loaf about with Clayton and Liddell.'

375

'We shall ask him,' said Swaddell crisply. 'Because that is entirely possible.'

Clerkenwell's church was peaceful after the busy bustle of Newcastle House, and they found Booth fast asleep on one of its pews. Swaddell woke him with a prod of his dagger. The vicar's eyes were bleary at first, but they snapped into alertness at the sight of the assassin looming over him with a blade.

'What do you want?' he gulped. 'I have done nothing wrong!'

'An interesting way to begin a conversation,' mused Swaddell. 'And one that reveals a guilty conscience as far as I am concerned. Now, time is of the essence, so do not waste mine with pointless denials. We want the truth about the letter you sent to the Duke.'

'What letter?' demanded Booth, although his terrified face revealed the truth.

'We know you wrote it,' said Swaddell. 'You see, we have the thief who relieved you of your purse – the purse that held an annotated book and notes addressed to a man who identifies himself with St Quentin.'

'Many people do,' objected Booth, struggling for defiance. 'He is a popular martyr.'

'Not in this country,' said Chaloner. 'It is an unusual dedication for an English church.'

'So why did you burn it down?' asked Swaddell, quietly menacing. 'In order to come to London and help Clayton malign the Duchess? It seems an extreme way to escape your pastoral duties, but—'

'It was struck by lightning,' bleated Booth. 'I was not even there when it happened! I was in Grantham.'

'Grantham?' pounced Chaloner. 'That is where this

letter was posted. So which crime will you admit – arson or mailing the slanderous missive?'

'Neither!' cried Booth, frightened. 'I am a man of God, not a criminal.'

'Oh, you are a criminal,' countered Swaddell softly, 'and the clipped coins in your purse will see you hanged, drawn and quartered. Debasing the King's currency is treason, and I will make sure you face the full extent of the law.'

The blood drained from Booth's face. 'Those coins are not mine! The thief must have robbed someone else before attacking me.'

'So if we search your lodgings, we will no find more of them?' asked Chaloner.

Booth deflated before their eyes. 'Damn that thief! This is his fault, and if I hang, he will dangle next to me.'

'He is beyond any vengeance of yours,' said Swaddell. 'Henrietta Florence saw to that.'

'The horse killed him?' asked Booth, and his expression turned vindictive. 'Good! But I did not clip those coins for my own benefit. I did it for my parishioners.'

'Really,' said Chaloner flatly. 'And why would you break the law for them?'

Booth hung his head. 'Because they blame me for the loss of their church. You see, it was not lightning that caused the fire, but the candle I forgot and left burning in the vestry when I went to Grantham. To pacify them, I agreed to provide a certain sum . . .'

'Which you decided to raise by shaving the silver from the King's shillings,' finished Swaddell in distaste. 'Very noble.'

Booth licked dry lips. 'I will tell you everything about

377

the letter if you agree to overlook the coins. Then I will disappear and you will never see me again.'

'You will tell us what you know and I will recommend leniency from the judge,' said Swaddell indignantly. 'Which is more than you deserve.'

Booth opened his mouth to argue, but a glance at the assassin's face warned him against it. He sagged in defeat.

'It was Clayton's idea,' he began wretchedly. 'He hates the Duchess, because she has started to check his accounts, which means he can no longer adjust them to his advantage. It has cost him hundreds of pounds a year. It is bad for Liddell, too, as he is obliged to pay full rent on his stud farm, rather than the half that Clayton always charged him.'

'Does her diligence affect you as well?' asked Chaloner.

Booth nodded miserably. 'Clayton sent me a little bonus each quarter for running a school that does not exist, but she put a stop to that, too. Rather than let her impoverish us, we decided to get rid of her.'

'You mean you plotted her death?' Swaddell's voice was cold and angry.

'No, not that!' gulped Booth. 'Clayton said we should get the Duke to divorce her for adultery. He picked Topp as her fictitious lover, because he wants to be sole steward. Two birds with one stone.'

'Fine behaviour for a cleric,' said Swaddell in distaste.

Booth managed to bristle. 'You no doubt think that Topp is charming, with all his "Your Worships" and "Your Honours". But beneath that oily exterior lies a very sly individual.'

Chaloner wanted to tell him that Topp's unctuousness was not charming at all, but the floodgates were open, and Booth could not stop talking – about how Clayton had asked him to pen the letter because he knew how to disguise his handwriting; how he, Clayton and Liddell had pondered long and hard over the wording; and how he had gone to Grantham to post it, because it was a place where no one knew him.

'And now,' said Swaddell, when the vicar eventually faltered into silence, 'you can tell us why Clayton – no doubt with help from you – murdered Chiffinch. Was it because Chiffinch recognised your distinctive *f*s, and guessed who sent this poisonous tirade?'

Booth gaped at him. 'You cannot lay *that* at my door! I am an innocent man!'

'Of course you are,' muttered Chaloner, 'as long as we overlook coin-clipping, libel, forgery and theft.'

When they had finished with Booth, Chaloner marched him to the stables, and shut him in the stall with Henrietta Florence. The vicar scuttled to the furthest corner and cowered, hands over his head as he wailed his terror. The horse was eating and ignored him, although her ears flicked every time Booth released a fresh howl.

'Do not annoy her by making an unseemly racket,' advised Swaddell, 'or we may return to discover you dead of a crushed skull, too.'

Booth went silent at once. Chaloner ordered a groom to stand guard over him, then he and Swaddell went in search of Clayton. The steward was in the tack room with Liddell. The horse-trader guessed at once that something was amiss, and bolted. Chaloner hared after him, chasing him clear across Clerkenwell Green to the Fleet River. He marched him back to Newcastle House, where they arrived to find Clayton slumped in a chair in defeat and Swaddell leaning against a wall, paring his fingernails with one of his sharp little daggers.

'Clayton has something he would like to tell you, Tom,' the assassin said mildly.

Chaloner had no idea what Swaddell had said or done, but the steward immediately gabbled a confession. It was almost identical to Booth's, the only difference being that it was Liddell who had masterminded the plan, while he and Booth were unwilling helpmeets. Naturally, Liddell objected to this version of events.

'Lies!' he cried. 'It is *you* who devised this—'

'The plan was yours,' snarled Clayton. 'Every last detail of it.'

'You are all in it together,' interrupted Chaloner, tired of their treachery. 'And you will all suffer the consequences. So, now we have dealt with the letter, we can discuss murder. First, you poisoned Chiffinch. We know you have access to White Hall, because I met you there myself. Then you dispatched Tooley, Ashley and Mushey—'

'No!' shouted Clayton, thoroughly rattled. 'I had never even heard of Mushey before Mr Swaddell mentioned him to me just now.'

'Moreover, two of the courtiers died on Sunday,' put in Liddell quickly, 'and we have an alibi for then. It was the day of the fox-tossing, and the Duke remained here in protest. He kept us busy all day with his horses. The Viscount was with us, too.'

Chaloner knew the Duke and his son had stayed home all day, because the Duchess had said so. However, no mention had been made of Clayton and Liddell.

'Then you shot at us in Mushey's room,' Swaddell forged on. 'You—'

'How can we have shot at you?' interrupted Clayton,

terrified. 'We have no guns. And if we had, we would not have needed to resort to poison. Your logic is flawed.'

'But you three, alone of everyone at Newcastle House, were not listening to Lucas's lecture when the toxin was added to Chiffinch's oysters,' argued Chaloner, although he was beginning to fear that he might have made a mistake in accepting Eliza's assumption that the authors of the letter and the White Hall killer were one and the same.

'We did manage to avoid his dull monologue,' acknowledged Liddell, 'but we did not use the time to kill a courtier we had never met. We were in our coffee house – ask anyone at Myddleton's. They will remember us there, because we had a fine debate on chocolate.'

'He is right,' said Clayton, and cunning flared in his eyes. 'We have a solid alibi. The Duchess, however, does not – at least, not one that can be proved. Ask *her* these questions.'

Chaloner experienced a bitter sense of defeat as he finally accepted that the unsavoury trio had nothing to do with Chiffinch's murder, and that he and Swaddell had wasted valuable time solving a crime that was irrelevant. Thurloe would be pleased to know the libellers had been caught, but that was the only positive outcome from their efforts that morning.

Swaddell pulled him to one side. 'There are still other Newcastle House connections to unravel,' he murmured. 'Namely, the Duchess. And her brother – perhaps Baron Lucas persuaded some of his Red Bull friends to go to White Hall and kill on his behalf.'

'But how will we prise answers from that pair?' asked Chaloner dejectedly. 'You cannot sit two nobles down and wave sharp knives at their throats. The only way to

381

catch them is with hard evidence, which we do not have.'

'Widdrington,' said Swaddell, unwilling to concede defeat. 'We can ask him—'

'His testimony is irrelevant,' snapped Chaloner. 'We do not need to know if Chiffinch told him who wrote the libellous letter, because we have worked it out for ourselves. We are back right where we started.'

'Not quite,' said Swaddell. 'We have exposed this rabble, and that counts for something.'

'Unfortunately, that pales into insignificance when compared to a poisoner at large and a city that will descend into chaos tomorrow.'

While Swaddell went to report their findings to the Duke, then summon soldiers to march Clayton and his helpmeets to the nearest gaol, Chaloner stood guard over the prisoners. He resented the wasted time, but dared not delegate the duty to anyone else, sure their slippery tongues would see them escape. Booth wept and pleaded, Liddell brayed threats, and Clayton opted for bribery. Chaloner was glad when Swaddell returned and the unpalatable trio were bundled away. He and the assassin were about to leave themselves when Eliza hailed them.

'I am in your debt more deeply than ever,' she said sincerely. 'You have thwarted this horrible plan to hurt my Duchess and Francis. Now everyone will know that they are the victims of a wicked lie.'

'Yes,' acknowledged Swaddell. 'Although our real purpose in coming here today was to catch whoever killed the courtiers.'

'Perhaps *that* is what Chiffinch and Widdrington were discussing when I saw them in White Hall on Thursday,' said Eliza. 'I assumed it was the letter, as the Duke had approached Chiffinch for help that day, but perhaps it was something else . . .'

'Regardless, it is unlikely to have been the murders,' Chaloner pointed out glumly, 'given that none of the four victims were dead when this conversation took place.'

Eliza frowned. 'Yet it was about something important, because they kept looking around to make sure no one else could hear. They did not consider me a threat, because I am effectively a servant. I still think you should speak to Widdrington about it.'

'Perhaps,' said Chaloner, although he was not about to squander more time following irrelevant leads. He changed the subject. 'The pair of handguns we found in the Duchess's boudoir last night – have you ever seen them before?'

Eliza blinked her surprise. 'You cannot have found them there, because she does not allow firearms in the house. You were holding one, so I assumed they were yours.'

'But Topp told me that he picked it up from her table,' said Chaloner. 'And I believe him, because if it had been his, he would have known it was not loaded when he threatened to shoot me with it. Ergo, it belongs to her.'

'It does not,' insisted Eliza. 'I told you: they are banned. The Duke has a palsy, and she is afraid that he might seize one and have an accident. There have been no guns of any description in their houses for years.'

Chaloner was about to retort that the Duchess had been wearing a brace of pistols when he had first met her, when he remembered that they had been wooden replicas. 'Then how did they get into her private quarters?'

Eliza shrugged. 'Planted there by someone who means her harm, I suppose. And you know there are plenty of those, because you have just arrested three of them. Clearly, someone left the things in the hope that they would see her accused of a crime she did not commit.'

'Well, it was not Clayton and his helpmeets,' averred Swaddell. 'They confined their malice to venomous missives.'

'Then the culprit will be someone she invited to her soirée,' persisted Eliza. 'God knows, there were enough rogues among them. Very few were asked to come back tomorrow, meaning that the majority are sinners and debauchees. You are spoiled for choice.'

'Where was the Duchess on Sunday?' Chaloner's fists were clenched in agitation, as he felt a solution slip further away with every word Eliza spoke. 'We know the Duke stayed here with Mansfield, because he disapproved of the fox-tossing . . .'

'We all did. The Duchess and I were here all morning, sometimes with the Duke, sometimes in the garden with the other ladies. We rode to White Hall in the afternoon to visit the Queen. And in the evening, she and I went to church, returning here about eight o'clock, just as the Viscount was leaving. If you want witnesses, I can provide dozens – for both of us, for every moment of the day. But why do you want to know?'

'Just a routine question,' replied Swaddell smoothly, when Chaloner was too disgusted to speak. In an earlier conversation, the Duchess had intimated that a mysterious errand had taken her out in the evening, but now it transpired that she had just gone to her devotions. Why could she not just have said so, instead of playing games to keep them guessing?

'Mother Broughton!' came a wail, and they turned to see Molly the chicken girl running towards them, her face wet with tears. 'She is dead!'

Clerkenwell's soothsayer was indeed dead. She lay on the bank of the River Fleet, not far from her cosy home. Blood seeped from a gash in her throat while her face was caked in mud. There was a strong smell of ale around her, and Chaloner noticed that her hands were clean, but that there was a deep skid-mark in the silt near her feet.

'I suspect she was walking home from a tavern when she slipped and fell,' he said to Swaddell, who was inspecting the neck wound with the disdain of a man who would have done it much more neatly. 'Her throat was cut when she was unconscious or drunk.'

'How do you know?' asked Swaddell curiously.

'Because there is no blood on her hands. She did not try to staunch the flow – which she certainly would have done, had she known what was happening to her.'

'True,' acknowledged Swaddell. 'People always scrabble at their necks when I apply my blade, although they waste their time. I should have deduced this for myself.'

'So that prophecy came true,' mused Chaloner, trying to dispel the image of Swaddell calmly watching his victims bleed to death. 'She predicted that the Fleet would run red with blood today and it has, although I doubt she thought she would be the one supplying it.'

'The *bank* is stained,' corrected Swaddell, 'but I would not say the river ran red, although I imagine her fanatical disciples will argue the point.'

'She also said a "messenger" would die. *She* is the

messenger – a person who informs others about what is going to happen. However, again, I doubt she thought she would be the one to perish. She told me that she expected to be part of the new government.'

'She was not a very good seer,' agreed Swaddell, and smirked, 'although I shall revise my opinion if you ever embark on a career in cheese.'

Chaloner ignored his levity. 'I think we can safely conclude that Mother Broughton was killed by someone who wants folk to think her projections about tomorrow will come true as well. We had the dead walking in Bunhill and Westminster Abbey – they did no such thing, but that is not what folk believe. Now we have the dead messenger and the blood.'

'And tomorrow we shall have a rain of fire, darkness and gnashing of teeth,' mused Swaddell. 'Followed by an Easter Sunday when the Sun will dance for joy. However, if all this does come to pass, it will have nothing to do with God. A human hand will have directed it and we need to make it stop. It is rebellion of the most insidious kind.'

Idly, Chaloner thought of the many other plots he had helped to thwart since entering the Earl's employ. Most were the King's own fault. If he at least tried to be upright, hardworking and just, his subjects would be less inclined to want him replaced.

'It is Holy Week,' he said, 'a time of sobriety and reflection. But the Court has organised fox-tossing, goose-pulling and dog-racing. Such secularism makes people uneasy. Good Friday falls on the thirteenth day of the month in the year with three sixes. It is superstitious claptrap, but folk are worried by it. The Court should not poke a hornets' nest.'

'Well, it has,' said Swaddell, 'and we must deal with the consequences.'

'No, our remit is to catch Chiffinch's killer,' said Chaloner. 'So I suggest we go to White Hall as we agreed and—'

'Forget Chiffinch,' interrupted Swaddell. 'Preventing a coup is far more important. We *must* prevent these insurgents from harming our city. If we allow them to succeed, it will not matter whether we have caught the killer or not.'

'But we do not know where to begin,' objected Chaloner. His head ached from tension, and he could not recall when he had last enjoyed a full night's sleep.

'By investigating *her* death,' replied Swaddell, nodding down at Mother Broughton. 'Someone will have seen something, because there are dozens of houses over-looking this part of the river. We shall question the residents of every one, and if that yields no results, we shall trawl the taverns. And pray we learn something, because otherwise . . .'

But it was hopeless. Not only were the people who lived in the hovels along the Fleet unwilling to talk to strangers, particularly ones from the government, but enquiries at the Red Bull told them that Mother Broughton had left in the small hours of the morning when it had been pitch dark. Ergo, it would have taken a miracle for anyone to have seen more than shadows anyway. Even so, Chaloner and Swaddell persisted until they were bone-weary and their voices were hoarse from asking questions.

'I just heard the nightwatchman call three o'clock,' said Swaddell eventually. 'It is Good Friday, Tom.'

Chaloner rubbed his eyes, which were sore and gritty

387

from being in so many smoky taverns. 'And we have learned nothing to help us stop whatever is going to happen.'

'I have never felt so helpless in my life,' sighed Swaddell. 'It is like trying to stem the flow of the Fleet. *Think*, Tom! There must be something we can do to prevent our city from erupting into flames around us.'

But Chaloner's mind was blank.

Chapter 16

Neither Chaloner nor Swaddell felt like going home when the Clerkenwell crisis loomed so close, so they went to the Red Bull, where they bought bread, cold meat and breakfast ale. Chaloner's stomach churned, and he kept coming back to the conviction that there *was* something they could do to prevent trouble – he just had to work out what it was. Unfortunately, he was too tired to think clearly, and he wondered if he and Swaddell should have opted for a good night's sleep, rather than wear themselves out with futile enquiries.

He dashed off a note to his cousins, ordering them to stay inside with Wiseman until further notice, politely declining Swaddell's offer to deliver it for him. Instead, he paid John Milton to do it – the blind Puritan poet was desperate for money, and could be trusted to place the letter in their hands. He felt better when it was done, knowing that at least they would be safe from whatever happened that day.

'I promised Ursula my protection,' said Swaddell worriedly. 'I should go to Covent Garden and sit with her, or she will see me as a man whose word cannot be trusted.'

'Your duty lies here,' said Chaloner tiredly, not about to stand by while the assassin foisted himself on his cousins all day. 'She will understand.'

'I did not expect to find you here,' came a voice from behind him. Chaloner leapt up with his hand on his sword, but Widdrington laughed derisively. 'If I had meant you harm, Earl's man, you would be dead already. I could have run you through where you sat.'

'No, you could not,' countered Swaddell in his most dangerous hiss.

'Oh,' gulped Widdrington, unsettled. 'I did not see you in the shadows, Swaddell.'

'Why are you here?' asked Chaloner, aware that he needed to be more careful if he wanted to see the Sun dance on Sunday.

'Pamphlin told me to come,' replied Widdrington, sitting uninvited at their table. 'Before he died, of course. I do not commune with corpses.'

'Pamphlin is dead?' blurted Chaloner, shocked. 'When?'

'Probably on Tuesday,' replied Widdrington, and smirked. 'The day you raced off to Woolwich in the hope of interrogating him, although the truth is that he never left London. He hid in my attic, and might still be alive if he had done what I advised and stayed put.'

'So why didn't he?' asked Swaddell shortly, irked by the gloating.

'Because Bess found out he was there, and he was afraid she would give him away. She is not very good with secrets. He decided to move in with Rolt instead, but he never got there and died on Piccadilly. Near Clarendon House, in fact.'

'Died of what?' asked Chaloner, hating to imagine

what his employer's enemies would make of that unfortunate happenstance.

'Poison, like the others, according to Wiseman. He had a wine-flask with him, and the toxin must have been in that. My guess is that he took a gulp from it, to give him the courage to pass Clarendon House, and that was the end of him.'

'If he was hiding in your attic, then the likelihood is that his wine-flask was filled before he left,' said Swaddell coldly. 'Which means you or Bess killed him.'

Widdrington shrugged. 'We both assumed he was with Rolt until news came last night that his body had been found in a ditch. Naturally, we were horrified to hear it. However, before he left my house, he told me to come here on Good Friday morning. So here I am.'

'If you aim to add to the mayhem,' said Swaddell coldly, 'you will be stopped.'

'Oh, use your wits, man,' snapped Widdrington irritably. 'Do I look like a rabble-rouser to you? I am here to *prevent* trouble – in my capacity as a member of the Artillery Company. My soldiers are outside, ready to swing into action and keep the King's peace.'

Chaloner regarded him incredulously. 'And Pamphlin suggested you do this?'

'Not quite. I told him my plan to mobilise the men today, ready to defend the King from any bother, and *he* said that if there is trouble, it will start in this tavern. He thought it would be the best place to nip anything untoward in the bud.'

'And how would he know?' demanded Swaddell, eyes narrowed.

'Because we decided to monitor it after we failed to get it shut down last Sunday, which we would have succeeded in doing if Baron Lucas had not interfered. Pamphlin took spying duty on Monday night, and heard something that terrified him. Indeed, it was what drove him to take refuge in my attic.'

'What did he hear?' asked Chaloner sceptically.

'That the rain of fire predicted for today is not figurative but literal. In other words, someone aims to bombard the city with fireballs.'

Chaloner gestured around him. 'I see no fireballs. I cannot smell them either, and I would if they were here, because gunpowder reeks.'

Widdrington settled himself more comfortably. 'Then perhaps whoever aims to lob them will bring them here later. If they do, I shall be waiting.'

'But Cockpit Club members are not welcome here,' said Chaloner, and nodded to where the other patrons were glaring in their direction. 'Ergo, Pamphlin cannot have heard anything terrifying here on Monday, because he would not have been allowed inside. Just as Tooley was not, no matter what Bess later claimed.'

'He donned a disguise – we all did when it was our turn to spy. And do not regard *me* in distaste, Chaloner. We did what was right. You may be willing to look the other way while whores are taught to read seditious broadsheets, but we are not. The very idea is anathema.'

'You sound like your wife,' said Swaddell coolly, and Chaloner saw he was not the only one whose dislike of the courtier had intensified during the discussion.

'Bess will not be in a position to bray her opinions soon,' said Widdrington with enormous satisfaction. 'She sails for Ireland in two days, and while the Sun may not dance for joy at her departure, I certainly shall. I am tired of her cloying, clinging presence.'

'You will break her heart,' said Chaloner reproachfully.

'So what? I do not love her and I never will.'

It was no time to discuss Widdrington's marital problems, so Chaloner returned to the matter of the Red Bull. 'Who started the tale that Tooley died of a fever that he caught here?'

'I did, but I believed it was true until Wiseman said otherwise. We were all afraid of catching the plague, especially the time when we tried to get this place shut down by starting a fracas. Why do you think we wore masks?'

'Is that why Baron Lucas was able to order you away so easily?' asked Chaloner. 'Because you were all frightened of catching a fatal fever? None of you really wanted to be here, so when he told you to go . . .'

'We were only too glad to take our leave,' finished Widdrington sheepishly. 'Yes, it was cowardly, but only a fool does not fear the plague.' He forced a smile. 'But Wiseman assures me that Clerkenwell has seen no new cases in months, so I am terrified no longer. And you need not worry about any other trouble erupting here today, because I will prevent it.'

'Will you indeed?' said Chaloner sceptically. 'And why should we believe you?'

The smug arrogance left Widdrington's face. 'You may not think much of me, but I am a patriot. I *will* protect London from whatever is brewing around here.'

'Very honourable,' sneered Swaddell. 'So where are your Cockpit Club friends? Are they ready to defend the King's peace, too?'

Widdrington looked away uncomfortably. 'The only one brave enough to rally to my call is Cobbe. He is outside with the troops. The remainder prefer to see the

393

blood of animals spilled than risk their own. Are you still interested in catching the White Hall killer, by the way?'

'Why?' asked Chaloner suspiciously. 'Do you know who it is?'

'I might,' replied Widdrington smoothly. 'I certainly have a theory to share with you.'

'Does this theory stem from whatever Chiffinch whispered to you on Thursday?' Chaloner shrugged at Widdrington's bemused frown. 'Eliza Topp saw the two of you together.'

Widdrington waved an impatient hand. 'Yes, Chiffinch did accost me, but only to relate some infantile gossip about the Duchess of Newcastle sleeping with her steward. No, my thesis concerns Dr Clarke, who comes here a lot. I assumed it was to ogle the women, but then Pamphlin told me something interesting . . .'

'Yes?' asked Chaloner warily, wondering if Widdrington's sudden burst of helpfulness was intended to keep him and Swaddell occupied while the rest of the Cockpit Club ignited the very trouble he claimed he was there to prevent.

'He saw Clarke buy a phial of poison from another Red Bull customer – a substance that the seller assured him would kill quickly and cleanly.'

Chaloner did not believe him. 'Clarke is a physician with powerful potions of his own. He has no need to buy more in taverns. And who sold it to him anyway?'

Widdrington shrugged. 'These are questions to ask Clarke, not me. There is something else, too: you may recall that Chiffinch was in the Shield Gallery the night he died, after which he went to his apartments. He remained there from four o'clock until shortly before six

394

– I saw him emerge myself, and a few of us walked across the Great Court with him.'

'What of it?'

'Cobbe has discovered that Chiffinch was not alone during those two hours – *Clarke* was with him. Now, should you decide to act on my information, you can start in Newcastle House. I saw Clarke go in there not half an hour ago.'

It was still dark outside, although dawn was not far off, and there was enough light for Chaloner and Swaddell to see where they were going. Shadows showed where Cobbe sat with Widdrington's soldiers, waiting for orders, while in the street there was an air of anticipation as folk whispered about what would happen that day. Chaloner wondered how many of them would be alive at the end of it, or if their families would be wailing over their broken bodies.

Cobbe came to exchange polite greetings as they passed, so despite the urgency of the situation, Chaloner took the opportunity to ask something that had been niggling at him ever since he had learned that Cobbe and Will had alibis in each other for Chiffinch's murder.

'I know you and Will were together in Chelsea last week,' he began. 'But he returned to the city on Thursday evening, whereas you did not arrive back until Friday morning. Why did you not travel together?'

Cobbe winced. 'You may have noticed that Will is not the most considerate of men. He rattled off in his private carriage without a backward glance, leaving me to make my own way home. It was nothing malicious – it just never occurred to him that not everyone keeps his own coach and four. And the next public coach was not until the following day.'

'You told Widdrington that Clarke followed Chiffinch into his apartments on the morning Chiffinch died,' said Chaloner. 'Is it true?'

Cobbe nodded. 'I had the tale from three different witnesses. Why? Do you think he—'

'Tom,' growled Swaddell impatiently. 'We do not have time for this. Come.'

He was right – they would have to speak to Cobbe properly later, should they still be alive. Chaloner hurried after Swaddell without another word, aware of bells tolling in the distance to mark this most sombre day of the Christian calendar. All over the city the faithful entered their parish churches to find the altars stripped, and all statues, paintings and symbols draped in purple cloth. It gave the impression that God had moved out.

'Do you believe Widdrington?' Swaddell asked, as he and Chaloner approached Newcastle House. 'I do – about Clarke, at least. We neglected our incompetent physician as we pursued more promising candidates, but I have a feeling that was a serious mistake.'

Chaloner agreed. 'If anyone knows about poisons, it is a *medicus*. But are you sure you want to challenge him now? You said earlier that we should forget about the killer and concentrate on preventing the crisis.'

'How can we, when we do not know what form it will take?' asked Swaddell bitterly. 'At least by cornering Clarke I shall feel as though we are doing something useful. However, while I *believe* Widdrington, I do not trust him. I doubt he is here for honourable purposes.'

'No,' agreed Chaloner. 'So I will tackle Clarke while you organise some troops of your own. We might need them later.'

Swaddell shot him a pitying glance. 'I did that hours

ago. They are in Bishop Morley's garden, ready to spring into action the moment I send for them. I wanted to impose a curfew on Clerkenwell today, but he said that would ignite a riot for certain.'

With despair, Chaloner saw they were damned whatever they did. The sight of armed men on the streets probably would provoke an angry reaction, but to leave the area unsupervised was an invitation for anyone to do as he pleased.

Chaloner was about to knock on Newcastle House's door, when he saw someone sneaking out through the stable gate, hooded and with a heavy sack over his shoulder. He ran forward and grabbed the culprit by the scruff of his neck. His captive shrieked his outrage, then began to kick and struggle.

'Let me go, you filthy commoner! How dare you lay hands on me!'

Recognising the voice, Chaloner released him. 'Viscount Mansfield. Forgive me. I thought you were a burglar.'

Mansfield clutched the sack to his chest, where a telltale clank revealed it was full of silver plate. 'This is mine,' he declared defiantly. 'I am not a thief.'

'Of course not,' said Chaloner, wondering how a bold and charismatic warrior like the Duke had sired such a miserable specimen. 'What are you doing out at such an hour?'

'Leaving,' replied Mansfield, brushing himself down in a feeble attempt to restore his dignity. 'I have a coach waiting in Aldgate, and I shall only return to the city when peace reigns again. My father is quite capable of defending Newcastle House, so my military skills are surplus to requirements.'

'I am sure they are,' said Chaloner ambiguously. 'Have you seen Clarke?'

'Clarke?' squeaked Mansfield, alarmed again. 'Why? He knows nothing that will interest you. Leave him alone. I *order* you to stay away from him on pain of death!'

Chaloner and Swaddell exchanged bemused glances.

'Everything I told him is private,' Mansfield gabbled on. 'You *cannot* ask him about it. But how did you guess?' His eyes narrowed. 'I know! It was *her*.'

'Who?' asked Chaloner warily.

'Sarah Shawe! She promised to keep her mouth shut if the Duchess continues to fund her seditious little school, but she is friends with Eliza, who hates me because she thinks I was behind that anonymous letter. *Sarah* told you my secret!'

'Yes, she did,' lied Chaloner, to see what would emerge. 'So now you are exposed.'

'I made *one* pass at her,' cried Mansfield in agitation. 'I thought she would welcome a fine man like me taking an interest, but she was livid and has never let me forget it.' He looked away. 'She keeps threatening to tell my wife unless I do what she says.'

So that was how Sarah kept him in line, mused Chaloner, recalling that she had forced him to retract his accusation about the Red Bull's pupils being prostitutes, thus ensuring that the Duchess continued to provide them with money and books.

'Do not look at *me* reprovingly,' the Viscount snapped sullenly. 'It was a moment of weakness, and I am a red-blooded man. However, I am sure we can reach an accommodation. If you keep my secret, I will tell you another in return.'

'What secret?' asked Swaddell cautiously.

'It is about Sarah. She does not buy pens and paper with the money that my stepmother gives her, but straw and crates. I saw her doing it with my own eyes.'

'Why would she want those?' asked Chaloner, nonplussed.

'Ask her,' suggested Mansfield, 'although expect untruths in return. And while we are on the subject of untruths, if Clayton tells you that it was my idea to send that letter about my stepmother's infidelity, you should not believe him. He will say anything to save himself.'

'He is not the only one,' muttered Chaloner, watching the Viscount scuttle away.

Despite the early hour, Newcastle House was busy as servants prepared to receive those people the Duchess had deemed worthy of her company on the day that the world would change. The lady herself was still abed, but everyone else was in a whirlwind of activity. Chaloner noted that although the staff were expected to remain, the Duke was arranging for his horses to be sent somewhere safe. He declined to speak to Chaloner and Swaddell on the grounds of being too busy, but Baron Lucas strode over to greet them.

'My sister is in your debt,' he said quietly. 'It beggars belief that Clayton – a man we treated and loved like family – would betray her in so sordid a manner. But you have restored her good name.'

'Yes,' said Chaloner impatiently. 'But we need to—'

'Courtiers are falling over themselves to make amends for gossiping about that letter,' Lucas went on, 'and she is inundated with requests to join her here today. Unfortunately, some are from folk she cannot refuse, such as the Duke of York and half the Privy

Council, although no one could possibly rate them as godly individuals.'

'No,' agreed Swaddell. 'But never mind that. We want—'

'I told her to let them all in.' Lucas waved an expansive arm. 'The servants worked hard to get this place shipshape, so we may as well put it to good use.'

'Is Clarke here?' demanded Chaloner, speaking quickly to make himself heard.

'Yes, he came to tend my nephew.' Lucas sneered. 'The boy was in a dreadful state after Clayton's arrest, and needed medicine to calm his nerves. He is afraid we will think the letter was his idea, although he would be wrong. He has neither the wits nor the courage.'

Chaloner was not so sure about that. 'Clarke,' he prompted urgently.

'Still with Mansfield,' replied Lucas. 'Why? Do you suspect him of something remiss? Hah! I knew it. There had to be some reason why that charlatan has been here all hours of the day and night. Come, I shall take you to them.'

He ran up the stairs so fast that Chaloner and Swaddell had no time to say that Mansfield had already left, which meant that the physician could not be with him. They hesitated, so he bawled at them to follow. When they caught up with him, he was hammering on the door to a first-floor bedchamber.

'The brat has locked himself in,' he growled, grabbing the handle and giving it a vigorous shake. 'Do you have a gun? If so, blast the thing open. We do not lock doors in Newcastle House – it smacks of unsavoury doings.'

Unwilling to wait while Lucas sent a servant out to

find one, Chaloner quickly picked the lock, although he hated wasting his time when he knew Clarke was not going to be in there. The moment it was done, Lucas stormed inside – and stopped in astonishment.

The room had been stripped completely bare. Marks on the walls showed where paintings had hung, and every stick of furniture was gone. The window was wide open, and scratches on the sill revealed exactly how everything had been removed with no one noticing.

'Lowered on to a cart below and driven away,' said Swaddell unnecessarily.

'The cowardly dog!' bellowed Lucas furiously. 'He thinks the house will be set alight by rioters, but rather than risk himself by fighting at his father's side, he has fled with everything he could lay his hands on.'

'Not quite everything,' said Chaloner, hearing a sound from inside the closet, and so striding towards it and hauling open the door so quickly that Clarke tumbled out on to the floor. 'He left his accomplice behind.'

'Accomplice?' gulped Clarke, scrambling quickly to his feet. 'I am merely helping a patient in acute mental distress. Mansfield is extremely agitated, so I have been humouring him in an effort to calm him down.'

'And does "humouring him" entail stealing the Duke's property?' demanded Lucas.

'Not steal – protect,' corrected Clarke firmly. 'I am sure he will share it with his father if this place goes up in flames.'

'Do you have any particular reason to think it will?' asked Chaloner anxiously.

'Just the seers' claims, although I hope they are wrong. But to return to Mansfield, I dropped the last bag of silver plate out of the window, and he promised to return

401

and unlock the door once it was safely stowed on his wagon. He will verify my tale when he arrives.'

'He has no intention of coming back,' said Swaddell. 'He left you shut in here so it will appear as if you are the thief. I imagine he will deny any involvement when he is questioned.'

Clarke gaped at him. 'But why would he do such a thing? I have answered his every summons for days, no matter what the hour or inconvenience to myself.'

'Which explains the comings and goings you noticed,' said Chaloner to Lucas, feeling his agitation rise as it became obvious that the physician did not possess the raw cunning to be the White Hall killer, and they should be looking elsewhere. Swaddell was unwilling to give up on Clarke as their culprit, though.

'You have a lot of explaining to do,' he said with soft menace. 'You were alone with Chiffinch in his quarters just before he died, and you bought poison in the Red Bull.'

Clarke's jaw tightened. 'I did not *buy* poison – it was given to me in lieu of payment by a patient. I aim to use it on those wretched cockerels. They let Fanny into the orangery, but whenever I try to follow, they fly at me.'

'You would kill her pet birds?' asked Chaloner, regarding the physician in distaste.

'I have a right to go where I choose in my own home,' flashed Clarke defensively.

'Never mind this,' snapped Swaddell. 'Tell us why you killed Chiffinch.'

Clarke's eyes went wide with alarm. 'I did nothing of the kind! I admit I followed him to his rooms on that fatal morning, but it was to beg a reprieve on the money

I owed him after the backgammon. I offered him free medical treatment instead, but he declined, so I left. He should have accepted – I might have been able to save his life.'

'I doubt it,' said Lucas, eyeing him with disdain. 'You could not save Tooley when I found him sick and reeling in White Hall on Sunday evening. I helped him home and sent for you, but your advice was to let him sleep it off.'

'Wait a moment,' said Chaloner. 'You two were with Tooley when he died?'

Lucas continued to glare at Clarke. 'No, we left before he breathed his last. I suspected something was seriously amiss, but this charlatan said he was just drunk. To my shame, I chose to accept his opinion, because I was eager to join the clever ladies at the Red Bull. It cost Tooley his life.'

'How was I supposed to know he had been poisoned?' demanded Clarke. 'He reeked of wine, his eyes were glazed, and he could not form a coherent sentence. He *was* drunk!'

'I think we can discount this bumbling ass as our sly killer,' murmured Swaddell, and Chaloner saw the defeat in his eyes. 'I have no more suspects left.'

'You want to arrest a killer?' asked Clarke, straining to hear what was being said. 'Then go and talk to Sarah Shawe. I have never liked her, and my wife fears for the safety of Clerkenwell as long as she is in it. She is a menace.'

'And now you shift the blame on to an innocent woman,' sneered Lucas in distaste. 'What kind of man are you?'

'One who aims to be alive on Easter Day,' retorted

Clarke. 'Which means I shall leave the city today. I am sure the King will welcome me in Dover.'

'You will stay here,' countered Lucas dangerously. 'You and those of your ilk claim to be the superior sex, so prove it. Go home and do your duty as a man by defending Fanny from whatever happens today.'

'Goodness!' gulped Clarke, daunted.

Chaloner and Swaddell hurried out of Newcastle House. It was now fully light, and the air of excited anticipation was a palpable thing, visible in the people who strode past with a spring in their step, and in the hordes who flocked to the church next door, hoping that a spell on their knees might make the difference between annihilation and survival.

'Perhaps we should join them,' said Swaddell, hoarse from fatigue. 'Because I cannot think of anything else to do.'

'We should go to see Sarah Shawe.'

Swaddell blinked. 'Surely you do not intend to act on Clarke's testimony? He spoke out of malice – he has no evidence against her.'

'Perhaps,' said Chaloner. 'But there are three other reasons why we should speak to her. First, because she has a large collection of glass bottles in her house. Second, because Mansfield told us that she has been buying crates and straw. And third, because she is one of Mother Broughton's strongest advocates.'

'You are speaking in riddles, and I am too weary to decipher them.'

'She has ensured – through Mother Broughton – that everyone knows there will be a rain of fire today, and what Pamphlin overheard in the Red Bull suggests that it will be a real one. I have a bad feeling that she is the person who intends to provide it.'

'What?' Swaddell was incredulous. 'How in God's name have you deduced that?'

Chaloner struggled to rally his tumbling thoughts. 'Crates and straw are used to transport fragile or dangerous items. And her friend Joan Cole said all those glass jars were for pickling cockles. But who bottles shellfish?'

'I still do not understand.'

'Sarah has made fireballs with them. And I know exactly how she learned to do it.'

'You do?' Swaddell sounded too tired to care, but Chaloner was suddenly imbued with energy as answers came at last.

'I overheard her and Lucas in the Red Bull on Sunday, discussing some aspect of combustion. I assumed it was just an academic debate, but she was actually pumping him for information, although I doubt he was aware of it. He was just delighted to converse with someone intelligent.'

'So you think she has made some bombs?' asked Swaddell warily. 'And will rain them down on those she deems to be unworthy, so that she can establish a new world order? It all sounds very unlikely, Tom.'

'Then we will look inside her house. If the bottles are full of cockles, we will know her intentions are innocent. But if they are gone or contain something else . . .'

They hurried to Sarah's unkempt little home, aware of the tension that permeated the alleys through which they ran. They knocked on the front door. There was no reply, so they trotted to the back one, only to find it was bolted from the inside. Chaloner kicked it down.

'She is not coming back,' said Swaddell unnecessarily, looking around and noting the absence of anything portable.

'Lest her plan fails and she is forced to flee,' agreed Chaloner. 'The bottles are gone, too.'

'And not a cockle in sight. However, I recognise that stench.'

'The last time I was here, this place absolutely reeked of rancid fat,' said Chaloner, 'but now the scent is different . . . sharper and stronger.'

'It is saltpetre,' provided Swaddell, and pointed to an open trapdoor leading to a cellar. 'It was probably stored down there, and your rancid fat was used to disguise the smell of it.'

Chaloner groaned. 'Of course! The Earl told me days ago that a quantity of saltpetre was stolen when *Royal Oak* was moored at Tower Wharf. It is why he wants me to sail with the Fleet on Sunday – to find out what happened to it.'

'Saltpetre is one of the ingredients in gunpowder,' said Swaddell soberly.

'Yes! The one that is most difficult to obtain, especially during a war, when the military needs every grain it can lay its hands on. She will also need brimstone and charcoal, but they are more readily available. I am right: she *has* devised some kind of fireball.'

'So Mother Broughton's prophecy will come true after all,' said Swaddell in despair. 'Because Sarah will see to it.'

'I think I can guess where she will start,' said Chaloner. 'The Duchess invited "godly" people to witness the Good Friday catastrophe with her, but a number of high-ranking courtiers and members of the Privy Council have decided to come, too.'

Swaddell's eyes were huge in his exhausted face. 'Well, blowing up the King's closest advisors will certainly usher in a new world order. We had better stop her before she ignites another civil war.'

Stomach churning as he considered the enormity of what Sarah was planning, Chaloner raced back to Newcastle House, Swaddell panting at his heels. They reached it to find guests arriving in droves, although it transpired that the Duchess was still in bed, while the Duke had elected to accompany his horses to the country. With Mansfield also gone, the only noble available to greet them all was Lucas, but he was more interested in conversing with the erudite Bishop of Oxford. The result was pandemonium, as the visitors – invited and otherwise – took the liberty of wandering wherever they pleased.

'Half the government and most of White Hall have turned up,' breathed Swaddell in horror. 'We must warn them to get out. Now!'

'Tell Lucas to do it,' said Chaloner, knowing that no one would obey orders from the Spymaster's assassin and a retainer of the hated Clarendon. 'I will start looking for Sarah. The servants will help.'

But the servants remembered Dutch Jane being dismissed for disobeying the Duchess's orders, and none were willing to risk the same fate by abandoning their assigned duties that day. His frantic pleas fell on deaf ears, and he saw he was on his own.

Reasoning that Sarah could not launch her attack from the public rooms – she would be seen and stopped – he aimed for the cellars. There were a lot of them, all so full that they were a nightmare to search. Sweat trickled down his back as he scrambled over piles of old wood,

407

broken furniture and disused tools. Above his head, he heard the tap of footsteps on wooden floorboards, telling him that Lucas had not yet started the evacuation.

The cellars were clear, so Chaloner aimed for the kitchens. These were frantic with activity, as the cook and his assistants prepared to feed far more people than they had been told to expect. Chaloner hurried on, aiming for the bedrooms on the first floor.

'What are you doing here?' demanded Eliza indignantly, when Chaloner had finished his search on the Duke's side of the house and was about to begin on the Duchess's. 'My Lady is asleep.'

'Then wake her,' ordered Chaloner. 'And tell her to make everyone leave. The rain of fire will start here – missiles that will ignite an inferno that may spread far beyond Clerkenwell.'

'I hope so,' said Eliza, and he saw she held a handgun, cocked and ready to shoot. 'It is what we have been working towards all these weeks.'

Chapter 17

With a sick sense of defeat, Chaloner realised he should have guessed that Sarah's lover would be involved in the plot. Now it was too late. The gun in Eliza's hand was steady, and there was an air of quiet determination about her. She indicated that he was to disarm.

'You cannot allow this to happen,' he said, feeling every bone in his body burn with fatigue as he unbuckled his sword and dropped three knives next to it. He kept a blade in his sleeve, sure she would never guess it was there, although he would only be able to use it on her if she came within range. 'Innocents may die.'

'Innocents *will* die,' she acknowledged. 'But so will the guilty, and new life will rise from the ashes of the old. We shall unleash our rain of fire on all those who have swarmed here, after which it will sweep through Clerkenwell and then cleanse the rest of the city.'

Chaloner was appalled. 'You will kill the Duke and Duchess? I thought you loved them.'

'I do. That is why he is heading to Hampstead with his horses, while she is racing north in the mistaken belief that the plague is back. I would never put them in harm's way.'

'But that is *exactly* what you are doing,' argued Chaloner. 'If they survive and others perish, they will be accused of organising a massacre – the one that started in *their* home. You must stop this madness before it is too late.'

'It will not matter who accuses who after today, because we shall have a fresh start, with leaders who are just and honest, not vicious hedonists who squander our taxes on themselves.'

'The government *is* flawed,' acknowledged Chaloner desperately. 'But you cannot—'

'I do not have time to debate this with you,' interrupted Eliza. 'Now, you have two choices. I can shoot you here – no one will hear, given the racket they are making downstairs – or you can come up to the roof and sit quietly while we work. Well? Which will it be?'

He was tempted to call her bluff and tell her to shoot him, but had a bad feeling that she might actually do it. Slowly, he turned to the stairs, every fibre in his body tensed to whip around and grab the gun. Unfortunately, she read his mind and stayed out of reach. He had the uneasy sense that she, unlike her husband, was both familiar and comfortable with firearms.

He climbed slowly, playing for time as he wracked his brains for a way out of his predicament, but by the time he reached the top, his mind was still a blank. He opened the door and stepped out on to the paved part of the roof. The glass ceiling with its supporting iron brace lay before him. Rain had pooled on the panes, deeper on the ones that still sagged in their lead frames, and a flock of gulls bobbed about in places, but the roof was otherwise deserted.

410

He turned to reason with her again, but the birds took off en masse, forcing him to duck. While he staggered, off balance, Eliza slammed the door behind him, trapping him on the roof. He whipped around, but too late. He heard her drop a bar into place on the other side and then her footsteps hammering back down the stairs. Then he saw he was not alone: Swaddell lay in a crumpled black heap nearby, eyes closed.

For a moment, Chaloner was too shocked to move. Then he forced himself into action. He ran to Swaddell and shook his shoulder, relieved when the assassin's eyes flickered open. He helped him to sit up.

'It was Eliza,' whispered Swaddell, raising a tentative hand to a lump on his head. 'I ran into her while I was hunting for Lucas. She said people were more likely to heed an order from the Duchess, who was taking the air on the roof. Like a fool, I followed her up here . . .'

Chaloner had been just as trusting, and was appalled that their gullibility would see the start of a crisis from which the city – even the country – might never recover. He crossed the paved part of the roof, and leaned forward to peer through the glass. The pooled water on the outside – and chicken manure from Lucas's experiment on the inside – distorted his view, but he could still see that the hall and the ballroom were full of people. Indeed, the entire house was packed, and he hated to imagine what carnage would ensue when Sarah swung into action.

'We will smash a hole in the ceiling,' he determined. 'Then we can yell down a warning.'

'The glass is strengthened,' said Swaddell. 'Remember? Clayton told us.'

Chaloner thought fast. 'Then we will kick one of the panes out. A number of their frames are already buckled, which is why the Duchess installed that massive brace.'

He stepped on one and began to stamp on it. But the pooled water was knee deep, which made it difficult to put any power behind the blows. All he did was get himself wet.

'They are stronger than they look,' he said in agitation after trying several different places with no success. 'And the guests are making too much noise to hear me thumping. I think a couple looked up, but I doubt they saw me through the chicken muck.'

He hurried to the knee-high balustrade on his left, which overlooked the street, and yelled at the top of his voice at the people down there, but there was too much noise from the arriving carriages and general traffic, so no one looked up. Then he darted to the opposite wall and peered down into the back garden, but it was deserted due to the inclement weather.

Not yet ready to give up, he waded across to the central brace and studied it carefully. It comprised a towering wall of iron plates, and would be impossible to climb, because there were no hand- or footholds. It was anchored to the roof with cement buttresses, but these jutted out too far for squeezing around to reach the other side. Clayton had been right when he had claimed that the Duchess's brace cut one side of the roof off from the other.

'Hey!' bellowed Swaddell, who had followed him and was peering through a tiny slit between two of the metal plates. 'Stop what you are doing immediately!'

Chaloner joined him, and saw that the far side of the roof was a hive of activity. Sarah was there with four women and three men from the Red Bull, along with Eliza, who had gone down the stairs on the Duchess's half of the house, and up the ones of the Duke's to reach them. Their section was stacked with crates. One was open, revealing bottles nestled among a packing of straw. These had oil-soaked rags protruding from their necks, ready to be set alight and thrown. Sarah did indeed aim to rain fire down on the heads of those below.

'Do you hear me?' shouted Swaddell furiously. 'Stop that at once!'

Sarah glanced in his direction before giving a small, smug smile and turning away. Chaloner clenched his fists in impotent frustration. He and Swaddell could holler all they liked, but there was nothing they could do to prevent what was about to happen.

'Do you have a gun?' he asked tersely. 'If we shoot Sarah, the rest might give up. Or better yet, a bullet will shatter one of these panes, and we can warn everyone to get out.'

'I rarely carry firearms – they are too noisy for my requirements.' Swaddell patted himself down. 'And Eliza must have relieved me of my knives when she stunned me.'

Chaloner produced the blade from his sleeve. 'I managed to keep one, but it is useless. We could have aimed a gun through that gap, but tossing a knife through it is impossible.'

Swaddell's eyes were suddenly agleam as he snatched the weapon. 'Not *through* it, Tom – over it. It will be throwing blind, but I spend hours practising this sort of manoeuvre.'

Chaloner regarded him warily. 'You do?'

Swaddell shrugged. 'A single man with few friends

413

must find something to while away his free evenings. Pray God it works, because it is the only chance we will get.'

He took a deep breath, and his face went blank as he calculated distances and angles in his mind. Then he stepped back and the knife flew, arcing over the brace towards the rebels on the other side. His aim was true, but one of the men moved suddenly, so the blade that should have hit Sarah thudded into him instead. The fellow staggered and fell. There was immediate consternation among his cronies, all of whom dived behind the crates.

'I *told* you to kill them,' yelled Sarah at Eliza. 'But oh, no, you knew best! And now it transpires that you did not even bother to disarm them properly!'

'They gave Francis a chance, so it is only right that I return the favour,' Eliza snapped back. 'But do not worry. I might have missed one knife, but they will have no more.'

Chaloner did not hear Sarah's reply, but Eliza was the only one who did not crouch behind the boxes for protection as they continued to unpack their deadly creations.

'Now what?' he muttered, heart pounding. 'Do we wait here uselessly while they prepare to murder everyone?'

'I am afraid so,' replied Swaddell tersely. 'Unless you have another plan?'

It was agony for Chaloner to feel so helpless. He returned to the paved area near the stairs – the only part of the roof that was above water – and paced restlessly, stopping every so often to kick the glass, batter at the door, or yell in the hope that someone would look up. No one did. Worse, it was bitterly cold so high up, and he and

414

Swaddell were wet. Meanwhile, Swaddell bombarded the rebels with reasons to stop before it was too late. All ignored him.

'Why the delay?' the assassin muttered. 'Why not just start and get it over with?'

'I suspect they are waiting for three o'clock,' predicted Chaloner. 'The time of Jesus's death on the cross – a symbolic moment for putting their nasty scheme into action.'

'But that is hours away!' gulped Swaddell. 'We will freeze to death before then.'

Chaloner waded over to the brace again. The rebels had not listened to Swaddell, so he had no real hope that he could do better, but he had to do something.

'Eliza, please!' he called. 'Think of the servants. Will you kill them, too?'

'The decent ones are under orders to leave the house at a quarter to three,' replied Eliza, all brisk efficiency. 'They will come to no harm. As for the rest . . . well, who cares?'

'But you cannot murder *all* the Duchess's guests,' he cried. 'The Bishop of Winchester is among them, and he is a good man.'

'That is regrettable,' said Sarah, although she did not sound sorry at all. 'But you cannot bake a cake without breaking eggs.'

'You will fail,' shouted Swaddell. 'The ceiling is strong and will protect everyone from your fireballs. It—'

'We loosened a few of the panes weeks ago,' interrupted Eliza. 'Which is why the ceiling began to leak, of course. All we need to do today is pull them out and we shall be ready.'

'The house will be alight in no time,' put in Sarah

415

gloatingly. 'It is full of new, oily wood from its recent refurbishment. And when a building this size burns, it will ignite its neighbours.'

'But why?' asked Chaloner, shocked by her venom. 'Surely you cannot hate everyone who lives around the green?'

'We are tired of the way things are, and it is time for change,' explained Sarah shortly. 'You cannot stop us. You heard Mother Broughton's prophecies – all have come true so far.'

'Only because you made them. You knew Dutch spies were using Bunhill cemetery, so you concocted a tale around them. One of you also toppled the statue of Death at Chiffinch's funeral, and cut Mother Broughton's throat to provide blood for the Fleet River.'

'*You* killed her?' asked Eliza, regarding Sarah uneasily. 'Why? She was harmless.'

'She was dead when I found her,' lied Sarah. 'And we had to get some blood and a "messenger" from somewhere once Ambassador Downing decided to stay in Dover.'

'And Dutch Jane?' called Chaloner, looking around frantically for something – anything – that would help him stop them. 'You cut her throat, too. Your "alibi" for her murder was pickling cockles with your friends – or rather, making fireballs with them – but I imagine you slipped out for a while, and then declined to tell them why.'

'She was a traitor,' barked Sarah, while Eliza's jaw dropped in shock and the other women exchanged uneasy glances, which told Chaloner that his guess was right. 'She sold our country's secrets to the enemy. She deserved to die.'

'How did you know what she was doing?' demanded

416

Swaddell, and added in an undertone to Chaloner, 'Obviously, we knew she passed our false intelligence on, but we never understood how until you pursued her to Bunhill.'

'Sarah must have followed her to the cemetery once,' Chaloner whispered, 'where she saw the red lights used by Ambassador van Goch's spies. Cleverly, she wove it into one of Mother Broughton's prophecies.'

'I take note of what is happening in my city,' Sarah was declaring superiorly. 'Which is why I will make a better leader than those useless nobles. It was *I* who thwarted the Dutch spies.'

'Thwarted, but not caught,' called Swaddell acidly. 'Thanks to you, they were able to escape, which means they still pose a threat to our country.'

Sarah's only reply was a dismissive and unrepentant sniff, although her co-conspirators were unsettled to learn that she had acted without consulting them. The women, in particular, were uncomfortable with what she had done to Dutch Jane and Mother Broughton.

'What about Chiffinch?' Chaloner shouted in the hope of causing dissension in the ranks. 'Did he deserve to die, too?'

Sarah snorted her disdain. 'If I had wanted him dead, I would not have used my own oysters to dispatch him. And before you ask, I did not kill the Cockpit Club men either. They are beneath my notice.'

'Please!' cried Swaddell, his voice cracking as he peered through the ceiling and saw even more people cramming themselves into the rooms below. 'You cannot massacre—'

'Enough talk,' barked Sarah. 'We have work to do.'

Chaloner ignored her and addressed the others in the forlorn hope that one would see reason. 'What you do

417

today will make no difference. The King will still be in charge tomorrow, and if you kill these ministers, he will just appoint more of the same. Nothing will change.'

'It *will* change!' snarled Sarah, and whipped around to her helpmeets. 'Do not listen to him. He is so stupid that he still has not identified the White Hall killer, even though the answer is staring him in the face.'

'You lie!' snapped Swaddell. '*You* are the culprit.'

'Are you, Sarah?' asked Eliza uneasily. 'I had no great fondness for those men, but—'

'Of course it is not me,' spat Sarah impatiently. 'And I can prove it, although I should not have to. My word alone should be enough.'

'It is,' Eliza assured her, and smiled tentatively. 'Although if you do have proof . . .'

Sarah's face was a mixture of hurt, disappointment and scorn. 'Then stay here while I fetch the *real* culprit's accomplice. Then you will hear the truth and we can put this divisive mistrust and suspicion behind us.'

Chaloner and Swaddell exchanged a glance of mystification, and when they looked back through the slit between the plates, Sarah had disappeared down the stairs.

'Climb over, quickly!' whispered Chaloner, making a stirrup of his hands. 'The others are less likely to fight you if Sarah is not here.'

When Swaddell's foot was secure, Chaloner propelled him upwards until the assassin could stand on his shoulders.

'Higher!' hissed Swaddell. '*Lots* higher.'

Chaloner did his best, but even holding Swaddell's feet in his hands with his arms stretched as far as they could go, the assassin was still unable to reach the top and haul

418

himself over. They gave up in defeat, and Swaddell slid back down to the roof. Then there was a commotion on the conspirators' side, and they peered through the gap to see that Sarah was back, dragging someone by the hair.

'She was in your Duchess's bedroom,' she informed Eliza. 'Poking around.'

'What?' cried Eliza. 'She should be nowhere near Newcastle House, let alone in my Duchess's private quarters. She was not invited.'

'Very few people downstairs were,' drawled Sarah. 'But aristocrats sense entertainment like maggots to rotting meat, and they flock to enjoy it whether they are welcome or not.'

'Bess Widdrington!' breathed Swaddell, as Sarah's prisoner freed herself furiously and looked around with haughty eyes. 'Is Sarah about to claim that *she* is the White Hall killer?'

'I was looking for my husband,' Bess declared, all angry defiance. 'He said he plans to spend the day in Clerkenwell, so I assumed he meant in Newcastle House. But what are you doing up here? And what is in those flasks? I demand an explanation!'

'It is you who will provide the explanation,' said Sarah, drawing a dagger. Bess stepped back smartly, unnerved. 'You, who helped a poisoner. Go on, admit it.'

'Her confession is not necessary,' called Chaloner, watching Bess jump when she heard his disembodied voice. 'We know the identity of the killer. We have done for days.'

It was a barefaced lie, but he was not about to give Sarah the satisfaction of revealing that the solution had only snapped into his mind when she had produced Bess.

419

'Liar,' sneered Sarah. 'If you did, you would not have accused me of it.'

'We were testing you,' blustered Chaloner. 'The killer is Fanny Clarke.'

There was a short silence after Chaloner spoke, then Bess began to screech a litany of denials. Her spitting vitriol unsettled Sarah's helpmeets, who stopped unpacking fireballs to watch her in alarm. While they were distracted, Swaddell turned to Chaloner.

'The poisoner cannot be Fanny. She has an alibi for Tooley's death – in the Queen.'

'Her Majesty is ill and sleeps most of the time,' Chaloner murmured back. 'Wiseman told me. She would not know if Fanny was there or not, so the "alibi" is worthless.'

'But Fanny would never forge such an alliance with Bess – a debauchee in her own right and married to the leader of the Cockpit Club.'

'Well, she did,' hissed Chaloner, 'because they ultimately share the same beliefs – that educating women will turn the world upside down again. We know from their own admissions that they went to the Red Bull together.'

'You claim *that* as their motive?' Swaddell was far from convinced.

Chaloner nodded. 'And Bess has the added incentive of wanting to please her husband. He also deplores educating women, and she will do anything to win his approval.'

'Learning to read will not make you people of quality,' Bess was jeering at her listeners. 'You are scum with delusions of grandeur, and I shall see every last one of you hanged. My husband is right to say you are nothing.'

'Poison,' called Chaloner, before her intemperate

420

tongue could see her shoved off the roof. 'Fanny is married to a physician. Ergo, she knows about the toxins in his medical arsenal and how to put them in ingenious little capsules. *That* is how we guessed she was the culprit.'

'Is that your evidence?' sneered Sarah contemptuously. 'Pah!'

'We suspected her the moment she "found" Chiffinch's body,' bluffed Chaloner. 'You see, Captain Rolt had lost a gold button, and went to the cockpit to look for it, expecting to find the place deserted. He almost caught her with her victim.'

'So she pretended to be shocked and swooning,' put in Swaddell, deciding Chaloner needed help. 'Perhaps Rolt was sceptical, so she invented a tale about trapped wind escaping from the body, aiming to make him sympathetic to this unworldly, vulnerable lady.'

'But physicians' wives are used to corpses, and Fanny rescues injured cockerels,' Chaloner went on, watching Bess fold her arms and look away. 'It was all an act.'

'But why kill Chiffinch?' asked Sarah, her gloating tone suggesting that she thought they would not know the answer.

'It was all about the Duchess,' explained Chaloner. 'Chiffinch aimed to discredit her, because he felt her eccentric behaviour reflected badly on the King. Fanny decided—'

'Eccentric behaviour?' interrupted Eliza, her voice dangerously soft.

'In his eyes,' clarified Chaloner quickly. 'Funding the Red Bull school, dressing how she pleases, publishing books under her own name, considering herself the intellectual equal of men. He deplored it all, and said so.'

'He did more than say so,' interjected Eliza coldly. 'He

421

wrote letters to influential people claiming that she, the Earl of Clarendon and the Cockpit Club had united to overthrow the King. His first missive – to the Archbishop of Canterbury, no less – was penned five days before his death, and claimed that she planned to rule the country herself, like Cromwell did.'

'It meant the Duchess had a motive for wanting him dead,' Chaloner went on, although he suspected no one had believed such outlandish allegations; Chiffinch had seriously overstepped the bounds of credibility. 'Fanny's plan was to see her accused of the crime.'

'Then it failed,' murmured Swaddell, regarding him uneasily. 'The Duchess as the culprit may have crossed our minds, but I doubt anyone else made the connection.'

'Not yet, but they will,' said Chaloner, 'because Fanny has been leaving "clues" to implicate her. It is only a matter of time before everyone knows about them.'

'What clues?' asked Eliza in the same low, angry voice.

'For a start, she put the guns with the engraved barrels in the Duchess's boudoir,' replied Chaloner, 'although that was a mistake. Clearly, she had no way of knowing that firearms are banned from Newcastle House.'

'It was also Fanny who started the rumour about the Duchess urging Chiffinch to finish the poisoned oysters,' put in Swaddell, beginning to be convinced at last.

'And Fanny who left the letter for Mansfield to find,' finished Chaloner, recalling the discussion between the Viscount and Lucas in Westminster Abbey. 'The one informing the Duchess that Chiffinch was plotting against her. The Duchess probably never saw it, but Mansfield could be relied upon to bray that she had – and thus that she knew Chiffinch had been working against her.'

'Alone, each of these clues might be disregarded,' said

Swaddell. 'But added together . . . well, even loyal friends would begin to question her innocence.'

'Fanny and I are right to try to get rid of her,' spat Bess contemptuously. 'She gives White Hall a bad name.'

'Unlike fox-tossing and goose-pulling then,' muttered Swaddell.

Sarah was scowling, and Chaloner could tell she resented the fact that he and Swaddell had worked out some of the answers, because she wanted her friends to think that *she* was the only one with the intelligence to do it. Sulkily, she flung out another challenge.

'But you do not know *how* Fanny poisoned Chiffinch.'

'Of course we do,' Chaloner shot back. 'She had already prepared her toxic capsules, so when the Master Cook sent the kitchen child – Millicent – to buy oysters, she followed her, hoping for a chance to doctor them outside White Hall. The plan almost came to nothing when the fish market had sold out, but then along came the Duchess . . .'

'She played right into Fanny's hands.' Swaddell took up the tale. 'She told Millicent to come to Clerkenwell, which did two things. First, it ensured that there were oysters to poison; and second, it made it look as though she was involved in the crime. And if you want to know why Fanny elected to use poison as a means to dispatch her victim, that is obvious, too.'

'Is it?' asked Sarah, hands on her hips as she glowered in his direction.

'Her husband is a physician, so she knew exactly what to use and how – she chose a method she was comfortable with. You saw her follow Millicent back to White Hall, and Millicent spotted her loitering outside the larder, waiting for a corrupt guard to let her buy her way inside.'

423

'So why kill *Chiffinch* to strike at the Duchess?' asked Sarah, desperate to find something they had failed to understand. 'Why not just dispatch the Duchess herself?'

'Because that would have created a martyr,' shrugged Chaloner. 'Her books would have flown off the shelves, and others would have emulated her. The only way to be rid of her permanently was to shame her – to present her as a common criminal.'

'So Fanny and Bess aimed to destroy the Duchess because they disapprove of women who want more than a life of drudgery and servitude,' said Sarah to the others. 'If you harbour any doubts about what we do today, their vile scheme should banish them once and for all.'

Eliza regarded Bess icily. 'You plotted to hurt the cleverest, most generous and brilliant woman alive. We shall ensure that you and your ilk never try such a thing again.'

Hurt and indignation flashed in Sarah's eyes at the revelation that someone else ranked more highly in her lover's affections, but it was quickly masked.

'Her nonconformity encourages free-thinking in the masses, which is dangerous,' declared Bess, and pointed at the helpmeets. 'And *they* prove my point. Fanny and I are right to prevent the spread of radical ideas – notions that set us at each others' throats again.'

Eliza fingered her pistol, and Chaloner watched in despair, wishing Bess had the sense to shut up, and not just for her own sake. Gunning down an unarmed woman, setting Clerkenwell alight, plotting to murder Ambassador Downing . . . all would give blinkered traditionalists like Fanny an excuse to block reform for years to come.

'Their next victim was Tooley,' Sarah was calling to him. 'Do you know why?'

'Lemons,' replied Chaloner, although he was tiring of the game. 'Cobbe made some remark about Fanny's superior knowledge of them, which Tooley heard. I suspect it sparked a train of thought that eventually led him to connect Fanny with the poisoned oysters.'

'Really?' blurted Sarah, surprised. 'I assumed he saw her in the larder. He was working there on Thursday evening, when the killer did her deadly work.'

'No one saw her,' snarled Bess. 'She wore a disguise. And the lemons used on Chiffinch's meal were from the Master Cook's private hothouse, not Fanny's orangery.'

'It does not matter where they came from,' argued Chaloner. 'The point is that Cobbe's remark caused Tooley to *associate* Fanny with Chiffinch's death, and once he started to ponder, he began to see answers.'

It occurred to Chaloner that he should have seen them, too, and was disgusted with himself for failing to spot what had been right in front of his eyes.

'What happened then?' asked Swaddell. 'Did Tooley try to blackmail Fanny?'

Bess nodded reluctantly. 'And he was not very nice about it.'

'He won the fox-tossing,' said Chaloner, taking up the tale again, 'so you suggested a drinking game to celebrate. Did Fanny give you the poison for his wine? Rolt claims you were talking to him, but your husband was making lucrative promises, which would have snagged his un-divided attention. I doubt he would have noticed you slip away.'

Bess started to deny it, but Eliza raised the gun threat-eningly. 'All right! Yes, she convinced me that removing Tooley was in our best interests.'

'Ashley was next,' Chaloner continued. 'I imagine he

425

saw you tampering with Tooley's cup, so you enticed him to Bunhill cemetery, perhaps with the promise of some Cockpit Club jape. But there was no need to kill him – he never did understand the significance of what he had witnessed.'

Bess narrowed her eyes. 'How do you know?'

'Because if he had, he would not have accepted the wine you offered him. As it was, I suspect he gulped it down without question.'

'And Mushey?' asked Sarah, annoyed that they had answers for everything.

'Killed to make sure he never revealed who bribed her way into the larder that night. But Pamphlin, the third Yeoman of the Larder and Mushey's friend, put some of it together. He fled to Widdrington, not realising Bess's role in the affair. She found him hiding in their attic . . .'

'She poisoned the wine in his flask before he escaped,' finished Swaddell. 'So, Sarah, how did *you* guess that Fanny and Bess were the culprits?'

'I did not *guess*,' replied Sarah loftily. 'I applied logic, based on facts learned from Cobbe, who is also exploring these crimes. He was happy to share them with me in return for a favour.'

'I have heard enough nastiness,' said Eliza curtly. 'No more talking.'

Chaloner had never known a time when he had felt more powerless. He tried again and again to batter open the door, while Swaddell yelled himself hoarse trying to attract the attention of pedestrians in the street below. They took turns stamping on the glass, but all they did was drench themselves in dirty water. Then the wind picked up, making it even less likely that someone would hear them. Eventually, the church bells tolled for two o'clock, and people began to head to church for their Good Friday devotions.

On the other side of the roof, Sarah and her friends worked with a deft efficiency that showed they had practised hard for their moment of triumph. Bess was ordered to stand near the garden-side balustrade, out of the way. She was subdued at first, but her natural belligerence soon returned, and she began to taunt her captors.

'You will not succeed,' she sneered. 'And I will see you hang. You are nothing!'

'You will be dead yourself, woman,' retorted Joan Cole the tobacco-seller, who had just arrived with another crate of fireballs in her powerful arms. 'We will make sure you burn first.'

Bess turned her tongue on Eliza. 'Your Duchess will not thank you for destroying her home. She spent a fortune doing it up. She will hate you for ever.'

'She will never know who was responsible,' said Sarah to Eliza quickly. 'And it will not matter anyway, because we shall be living in a better, fairer world. No one will care about what happened before.' She whipped around to face Bess. 'One more word from you, and I will toss you off the roof myself.'

The Red Bull folk grew increasingly tense as the minutes ticked past. The wind blew harder, chilling them all, and Joan began to mutter about the dangers of delaying. They had been lucky so far, but what if some of the revellers decided to visit the roof? After all, it was common knowledge that the servants gave guided tours.

'Light the fire,' said Eliza, coming to a decision. 'And remove the loose panes. It is time.'

427

'It is not,' countered Sarah sharply. 'We agreed on three o'clock. We shall wait.'

'Joan is right,' snapped Eliza, and Chaloner saw she was near breaking point, emotionally exhausted by the strain of the plot, her husband's antics, and the revelations about Bess and Fanny. 'I think Lady Muskerry just glanced up here and pointed. Either she spotted something amiss, or she wants to come and admire the view. We must act *now*.'

She stepped forward to wrench up a pane before Sarah could stop her, and her cronies were quick to follow suit, eager for the waiting to be over. Water splattered on to the people below, resulting in a chorus of angry yells. There was an immediate rush for the doors, but howls of indignation turned to cries of alarm when it was discovered that all the exits were barred – the rebels had people below, as well as on the roof.

Meanwhile, Joan lit a fire. She grabbed a bottle, touched its oil-soaked cloth to the flame and ran to one of the newly made holes in the ceiling. Her arm went back to lob the fireball, but there was a dull thump and it exploded in her hand. She screamed in horror and pain.

'Begin the rain of fire!' yelled Sarah, leaping in to take charge before Joan's fate caused her helpmeets' resolve to waver. 'Hurry!'

They hesitated, frightened and shocked, so she shoved past them, and started to lob the missiles herself. Her example forced them to drag their eyes away from the dying Joan and concentrate on the task in hand. Bess was forgotten in the sudden frenzy of activity, and might have reached the door – and freedom – had she resisted the urge to gloat.

'Your plot will fail, because you are stupid, with ideas above your station,' she jeered. 'You will all hang and so will the Duchess. I will make sure of it.'

Eliza snapped. Rage suffused her face as she rushed at Bess, giving her an almighty shove that sent her staggering towards the balustrade.

'You will harm my Duchess, will you?' she snarled. 'The woman I love more than any other? Well, we shall see about *that*!'

She pushed Bess again. Bess's eyes opened wide with terror as the backs of her legs caught on the low wall and she began to topple. She flailed blindly, and snatched at Eliza's dress. Eliza tried to rip it free, but Bess's grip was made strong by fear. Screaming, Bess disappeared over the edge, dragging Eliza with her.

Chapter 18

Appalled, Chaloner ran to the balustrade on his side of the roof and looked down into the garden below. Eliza and Bess lay there, broken and bleeding. Sarah released a keening wail of grief, and for a moment, he thought the whole plot would grind to an abrupt halt. But his hope was short-lived. Eliza's death served to inspire Sarah to an even greater frenzy of rage and revenge. She tore into action, howling frantic orders at her remaining help-meets as she sent fireball after fireball hurtling down to the rooms below.

Chaloner knelt to peer through the glass. Now a lot of the water had drained away, he could see more clearly through Lucas's splattering of chicken manure. Dozens of terrified eyes gazed upwards, and there was a huge press around the doors as people tried to batter their way out. He also noticed that the rainwater had formed a thin layer over the floor, so that most of the fireballs fizzled out at once. He jumped up and went to shout through the brace again.

'It is not working,' he bellowed. 'Give this up before—'

'Do you think we have confined our assault to

Newcastle House?' screamed Sarah, beside herself with frustration and fury. 'The city will burn today no matter what happens here.'

'What else have you done?' demanded Chaloner, a cold coil of dread beginning to writhe in his innards.

Sarah's face was a mask of bitter malice. 'You will see at three o'clock – if you live that long. Fanny will pay for trying to destroy our hopes and dreams.'

'So you aim to strike at Chaloner Court,' surmised Swaddell heavily. 'What—'

'She considers herself godly,' sneered Sarah, 'and intends to watch the Good Friday crisis from her orangery with her like-minded sewing cronies. They will all die.'

'Lucy Bodvil and the others are not wicked,' objected Chaloner in alarm. 'On the contrary, they speak out against the excesses of—'

'They are Fanny's friends,' hissed Sarah. 'And there is a price to pay for that. The same is true of your silly cousins.'

'They are safe in Covent Garden,' said Swaddell quickly. 'With Wiseman.'

'The Queen summoned him,' said Sarah gloatingly. 'So I told Fanny that they were alone on this most holy of days, and she fetched them in her carriage.'

With an anguished cry, Swaddell raced to the door, and began thumping and kicking it for all he was worth. Chaloner only stared at Sarah in stunned disbelief.

'But why? They have never hurt you. Indeed, they want to teach at your school, because they applaud what you are doing there.'

'They came to London to get husbands,' spat Sarah. 'But they should make their own way in the world, not expect some man to support them. Girls like them are

431

responsible for perpetuating a system that is manifestly unjust.'

'It is not for you to dictate how other women choose to spend their lives,' argued Chaloner, horror giving way to anger at her presumption.

'Then stop me,' taunted Sarah viciously. 'Come on!'

But while she argued with him, her accomplices had realised that their fireballs were having scant effect: there was no serious blaze and no major massacre. They began edging towards the stairs, aiming to flee while they could.

'You will be caught,' Swaddell barked at them. 'But I will arrange for you to escape the noose if you help me rescue Ursula and Veriana.'

'Never!' shrieked Sarah. 'They are doomed. You are *all* doomed!'

'Eliza would not want this,' yelled Chaloner desperately. 'She was going to let us go once the rain of fire was over. She did not approve of cold-blooded murder.'

'Eliza,' sneered Sarah. 'She said she loved me, but it was a lie. She refused to leave her husband, even though he was a selfish coward and a thief, and what was the last thing she said? That she loved her Duchess above all others. Well, she can rot in hell!'

'Sarah,' hissed one of the women. 'We must go or they will catch us.'

Sarah laughed wildly and without humour. 'Of course they will catch us! That has been obvious since our first bomb failed to ignite.'

Her friends exchanged agitated glances. 'But what about our places in government?' demanded one. 'And the new world you promised we would lead?'

'You will not have them now.' Sarah shrugged bitterly.

'Baron Lucas must have given me the wrong formula for our missiles, and I fear all has been lost. Unless . . .'

She looked at the chaos below, then at the place where Eliza had gone over the parapet. The madness in her eyes faded, and was replaced by something darker and more dangerous. She snatched up a fireball, lit it, and allowed the flames to catch her skirts. Then she grabbed a bomb-loaded crate and let herself drop with it through the ceiling. There was a moment when Chaloner thought she had sacrificed herself in vain, but then there was a loud thump, followed by a blinding flash. When his vision cleared, he could see fire licking up the walls and the wooden staircase.

Newcastle House was alight.

Chaloner and Swaddell kicked, hammered and shoulder-charged the door with all their might, but it was no use. Smoke billowed through the roof, and the rooms below were pandemonium. One of the doors had been smashed open, and everyone was fighting to squeeze through it, pushing each other and blocking it shut in their frantic desperation to escape.

The fire spread fast, partly because the wood was new, dry and oily, but also because the holes in the ceiling acted like a chimney, drawing the flames upwards. The roar and crackle told Chaloner that it would not be long before the whole house became an inferno, at which point sparks would dance away to ignite other buildings, just as Sarah had intended.

'So this is how Mother Broughton's prophecy will come true,' whispered Swaddell, clenching his fists in impotent fury. 'Smoke *will* darken the skies, and there *will* be much weeping and gnashing of teeth if the whole city burns.'

433

Chaloner resumed his assault on the door, even though he knew it was futile. His knuckles were skinned, his shoulders were bruised, and he wondered if he had broken his toes, but he ignored the pain and continued to batter.

'Enough, Tom,' croaked Swaddell, dragging him away as smoke swirled more thickly around them. 'Decide now: a quick death by jumping or a lingering one in the flames.'

'Come this way,' came a familiar voice, and Chaloner spun around to see that the door was open. Molly the chicken girl stood inside it, beckoning. 'Come on!'

'How did you . . .' he began.

'I saw you from the garden,' she explained with one of her sweet but vacant smiles. 'So I came up to say hello. But the door was barred, so I—'

Chaloner shoved her and then Swaddell towards the stairwell. Before he followed, he glanced back to see the roof sag dangerously as the lead frames began to melt. He ran down the steps, only to hear an anguished shout from Swaddell.

'The stairs are alight. We are trapped!'

'Then we must take the *secret* route,' said Molly unperturbed. 'Come with me.'

She took Chaloner's hand and pulled him back up a few steps to where a small gap in the wall gave access to the roof-space. She went through it on all fours, then crawled along a series of rafters. Sincerely hoping she knew what she was doing, Chaloner and Swaddell followed.

She led them over to the eaves, where there was a ladder. It led to a hall in the attic, where there was a servants' staircase down to the kitchens. They arrived to find the cook and his staff throwing pots, pans and other utensils into travelling crates.

'What are you doing?' howled Swaddell in disbelief. 'Go and help the people trapped in the ballroom before—'

'We did,' interrupted the cook shortly. 'Everyone is out. Now our task is to save the tools of our trade.'

'Your task is the save the house,' countered Swaddell furiously. 'Fill these vessels with water and—'

'The Duke has a much nicer palace in the country,' interrupted the cook. 'So we hope this one *is* razed to the ground. None of us like it very much.'

'But if you let it blaze out of control, it will take Clerkenwell with it,' hissed Swaddell. 'And if that happens, I shall charge you with treason. Now *fill the vessels with water.*'

Chaloner had never seen him look more deadly, so was not surprised when the cook hastened to obey, calling his assistants to do likewise.

'Not you, Molly,' said Chaloner, afraid the child would be trampled in the commotion. 'Go and see to your birds – keep them safe from smoke and flying cinders.'

She scampered away, and he turned his mind to the choice he had to make: fight the blaze in Newcastle House before it spread to ignite the whole city, or race to Chaloner Court in the hope of rescuing his cousins. An anguished glance at a clock on the mantelpiece told him it was three minutes to three – nowhere near enough time to run across the green, find Ursula and Veriana, and whisk them to safety.

'Stay here and organise this rabble, Tom,' ordered Swaddell briskly. 'I will find Ursula . . . the girls.'

It was clear from his white face that the assassin thought any attempt to enter Chaloner Court now would be fatal. Even so, he was ready to try, to save the woman who had captured his attention.

435

'These people are more frightened of you than of me,' said Chaloner. 'You must make sure they stay and do as they are told. I will go to Chaloner Court.'

'But Sarah has likely set an explosion,' argued Swaddell hoarsely. 'How else could she predict that it would happen at three o'clock precisely?'

'Yes,' acknowledged Chaloner. 'Do your duty here. I will see you later.'

He could tell by Swaddell's touching distress that he did not expect them to meet again.

'Then God's speed, Tom, dear friend.'

Heart hammering, Chaloner tore across Clerkenwell Green, not caring that he collided with the spectators who had gathered there to gape at the fire. He was dimly aware of the murmurs that Mother Broughton was right yet again, and many folk were uneasy, beginning to wonder if they really were godly enough to escape the coming carnage.

Chaloner Court was peculiarly still and quiet compared to the other houses around the green, all of which had people leaning out of the windows, calling desperately for reliable reports on the fire. He reached the front door and hammered on it, but there was no reply.

He picked the lock, but something was wrong with the mechanism, and no amount of hammering and battering could budge it. He sprinted to the back of the house, just in time to see two women haring away at top speed. It did not take a genius to guess that they had just lit fuses and were dashing to safety. Then the church clock struck three.

The pair had left the garden gate swinging open, so he shot through it and aimed for the back door. This

436

had been jammed shut by having a bench braced against it. Terrified howls emanated from the hallway within. Through an adjacent window, he could see the ladies from Fanny's sewing circle, plus half a dozen servants.

'Help us!' screamed Lucy Bodvil. 'Those women . . . they told us we are about to be blown to kingdom come! They had knives . . . *Help us!*'

Chaloner hauled the bench away from the door, and was almost knocked from his feet as the prisoners scrambled out. Veriana and Ursula were not among them, and nor was Fanny. He grabbed Lucy's arm as she hurtled past.

'Where are my cousins?'

'Not with us,' replied Lucy, fighting to pull away from him. 'Ask Fanny.'

'So where is Fanny?' demanded Chaloner in agitation.

'She went to the orangery to save her cockerels. Now, let me *go*!'

She tore free of him and was gone. Chaloner hared along the hallway, aware of a powerful reek of gunpowder. Then there was a boom so loud and powerful that he felt the floor jerk beneath his feet. Sincerely hoping the explosion had not been in the orangery, he raced on, ignoring the dust that showered down from the ceiling. He hauled open the orangery door, then jerked backwards when he found himself at the wrong end of a sword.

'Where are my cousins?' he snarled, reaching for his own weapon before remembering that it was still on the floor in Newcastle House, where Eliza had made him leave it.

The expression on Fanny's face was a combination of resigned detachment and stunned disbelief. She shook

437

her head slowly, and began to talk in a flat whisper, as if she could scarcely credit what she was saying.

'Two women were just here. They informed me that my efforts to prevent our world from being turned upside down again have failed. That all I did was for nothing.'

'Where are Veriana and Ursula?' shouted Chaloner, panic-stricken as another blast rocked the house. Dust pattered down from the cracked lintel under which he stood. 'Please! Just tell me. Then you can escape through the back door.'

'Escape is not an option for me,' said Fanny, in the same oddly faraway voice. 'It would mean standing trial for what Bess and I did to Chiffinch and the others. None were good men, but we will be castigated for dispatching them, even so.'

'You will be castigated even more if my cousins die,' yelled Chaloner, his stomach churning. 'Now *tell me where they are!*'

'I did what I thought was right,' Fanny went on softly, although her hand tightened on the sword when Chaloner took an agitated step towards her. 'I wanted everyone to see the Duchess as a dangerous lunatic. We cannot have noblewomen setting that sort of example, and I am tired of upheaval. My country needs stability.'

'I know,' said Chaloner pleadingly. 'And we can discuss it later, but—'

'I suppose my downfall was impatience,' she interrupted. 'When Chiffinch was still alive hours after eating his first oyster, I grew worried. I enticed him to the cockpit – a place I thought would be deserted – with the intention of giving him poisoned wine. But I should have let him be, as he collapsed moments after arriving. I waited with him while he died.'

'It does not matter!' shouted Chaloner, beside himself. 'Tell me where—'

He was interrupted by the loudest boom yet, and he staggered as the blast shook the house. So did Fanny, so he lunged for her weapon. She jerked away, flailing wildly, forcing him to dodge away until their places were reversed – he was in the orangery and she stood in the doorway. He opened his mouth to beg again, but there was a groan from above, and the lintel gave way. Fanny disappeared under a deluge of rubble.

For a moment, Chaloner could only stare in horror. Then he darted forward and began to dig her free, tearing his fingernails in his frantic haste. After a moment, he excavated an arm, but there was no life-beat in it. Fanny was dead.

He looked around wildly. Rubble blocked his way back into the house. There was no door to the garden from the orangery, meaning he was trapped. He ran to the biggest window and kicked it with all his might. The lead frame buckled, so he did it again. And again, until he was able to knock the whole thing out. He scrambled through it, and was followed by an eager flurry of feathers – Fanny's rescued cockerels, flapping through the hole and scattering in all directions across the garden.

He limped after them, then turned to survey the house, assessing it for other ways in. What he saw filled him with despair. Smoke poured from every window, so thick that he doubted anyone could still be alive within. The right side of the building had already collapsed, and even as he watched, more of it toppled inwards with a groan and a great billow of dust.

'No,' he whispered hoarsely. 'No, no, no!'

439

Then he spotted someone in one of the windows, a vague shape blurred by smoke. The figure raised an arm, and he was sure it was Veriana. He took two steps towards her, but there was a deafening rumble, and the rest of the house fell. One moment, there was a window with a living person standing at it, the next there was nothing but empty sky. Stunned, Chaloner dropped to his knees.

'Tom! Tom!'

Dazed with grief and guilt, Chaloner looked up to see Swaddell running towards him.

'Newcastle House is lost?' he asked dully. 'You abandoned your efforts to save it?'

'What? Oh, no – Widdrington arrived with his troops, and as he transpires to be unexpectedly adept at fire-fighting, I left him to it. Someone told him that his wife started the blaze, so he is keen to prove his worth by dousing it, lest he is accused of being her accomplice.'

'So it is under control?'

'Not yet, but it will be. There is no trouble on the streets either, because everyone is more interested in watching him do clever things with pumps and fire-hooks. And the men I hid in Bishop Morley's garden will nip any bad behaviour in the bud, should it be necessary.'

'I was too late,' said Chaloner in a low, exhausted voice.

'Yes,' agreed Swaddell sadly. 'This poor old house is well beyond repair, but at least there is no inferno to contain. London is safe once more.'

'Fanny would not tell me where my cousins were,' said Chaloner bleakly. 'I could not reach them . . .'

Swaddell regarded him in surprise. 'You think Ursula and Veriana were inside? No, Tom! They are on the green, watching Widdrington's heroics with everyone else. Surely you saw them as you ran past?'

Chaloner gaped at him. 'They are alive?'

A beatific grin stole over the assassin's face. 'Yes, and Ursula kissed me when I told her we had been frantic for her safety. She called out to you as you ran past, but you ignored her.'

'I thought they were inside when . . . I saw someone at an upstairs window . . .'

'Clarke, probably. Lucy Bodvil said Fanny contrived to lock him in a bedroom when she caught him packing for Dover.'

Chaloner struggled to make sense of it all. 'But Sarah gloated to us that Fanny collected Ursula and Veriana from Covent Garden this morning . . .'

'She tried, but they had already gone out – with Cobbe.'

'With *Cobbe*?'

'Remember Sarah telling us that Cobbe gave her information about Fanny in exchange for "a favour"? I assumed she meant she lay with him, but that is not the boon he demanded. He wanted to know where your cousins were lodging. Somehow, she managed to find out for him.'

'Perhaps Molly told her – she delivered that rescued goose from White Hall to my home.'

'Yes, most likely. Then this morning, while he was lounging in the Red Bull with Widdrington, he somehow learned that they were home alone, with no guardian to fight him off. He abandoned Widdrington at once, and went to whisk them away for a jaunt.'

'What sort of jaunt?' asked Chaloner weakly.

'A pleasant drive around the city, finishing here to

441

watch the rain of fire.' Swaddell patted Chaloner's shoulder. 'Do not worry, Tom. All is well.'

At that moment, there was a deep groan that sounded as though it came from the very heart of the house. Then the last wall crumpled on to the orangery, crushing it so completely that nothing recognisable remained.

'I am so sorry,' said Swaddell softly. 'Your beautiful ancestral home . . .'

'It does not matter,' said Chaloner, feeling a sudden weight lifted from his shoulders as he saw the assassin was right: all *was* well. 'I never liked what the Clarkes did to it anyway.'

Epilogue

Easter Sunday, two days later

It was a beautiful morning. The sun shone, the sky was blue, and everywhere were signs that spring was well and truly under way. Lent lilies nodded in a gentle breeze, all pale gold and bright white, and fresh new growth greened the trees. Birds sang, and Chaloner's poultry had provided him with ten fine brown eggs and one huge white one.

He and Thurloe sat on a bench in Wiseman's garden. The ex-Spymaster had arrived back in London an hour earlier, and had hurried straight to Covent Garden to find out what had happened in his absence. He had been regaled with quite a tale.

'So Mother Broughton was wrong,' he said. 'The world did not change irrevocably on Good Friday, and Easter is here with all its promises of renewal and salvation. Yet I do believe the Sun is dancing for joy. She was right about that, at least.'

Chaloner squinted upwards. 'It is not! And the world almost changed irrevocably for my cousins. If Cobbe

443

had not taken a fancy to Veriana, they might have been locked up with Clarke when Fanny's house blew up.'

'True, but look on the bright side: their narrow escape will make other relatives think twice before entrusting their children to your tender care.'

Chaloner was not so sure about that, given that good marriages meant everything to a clan staving off poverty. They might decide the risk of explosions was an acceptable one.

He watched his hens hunting for grain and worms. 'Mother Broughton was a charlatan. The Fleet only ran with blood because Sarah cut her throat after she fell down in a drunken stupor; corpses never walked in Bunhill or Westminster Abbey; and there was no weeping and gnashing of teeth on Good Friday.'

'Actually, there was quite a bit of weeping and gnashing,' countered Thurloe. 'By folk who are disappointed that the wicked still run the country. By Sarah's friends because justice and equality remain an impossible dream. By Fanny and Bess because their scheme to prevent destabilising change had failed. By those injured during the attack on Newcastle House . . .'

'All right, all right,' conceded Chaloner. 'But Mother Broughton was still a fraud.'

'Oh, yes,' agreed Thurloe. 'I charged a couple of my former intelligencers to monitor her while I was away, and they inform me that Sarah told her exactly what to "predict" – in exchange for money.'

'Which explains why she lived in a hovel that was stuffed full of smart new furnishings,' sighed Chaloner. 'I should have guessed that was relevant.'

'You should, although it would have made no difference in the end. Yet I am astonished that Fanny was

444

the White Hall killer. She always seemed so dull and meek.'

'Dull, perhaps, meek no. She poisoned Chiffinch without a qualm; she provided Bess with the wherewithal to kill Tooley, Ashley, Mushey and Pamphlin; and she shot at Swaddell and me in White Hall. Of course, Sarah killed Mother Broughton and Dutch Jane with just as much ruthless indifference . . .'

'Thank you for resolving that anonymous letter business, by the way. My enquiries in Grantham revealed the sender as Vicar Booth, but it would have been difficult to prove the others were involved. I was pleased that you provided the Duke with a full cast of culprits.'

Chaloner regarded him curiously. 'What favour did the Duchess once do you, which saw you race to her rescue? I think I have earned the right to ask, after all the trouble that letter caused me.'

'I was sent to the Tower at the Restoration, as you know, and all my assets were seized. My wife and children were in London at the time, terrified and unprotected. The Duchess arranged for them to travel home to Oxfordshire in her own coach. She had no reason to help a Parliamentarian family, but she did – out of pure Christian charity. I shall always be grateful.'

'Do you know what favour Swaddell did for the Bishop of Winchester?' asked Chaloner. 'It was significant enough that Morley would have lied to give me an alibi. Not that he had to in the end, thankfully.'

'Swaddell used to be Morley's steward, and served him faithfully for years. Then Morley was made a bishop, and as prelates can hardly keep assassins on their staff, it was agreed that he would go to Williamson instead. But the pair remain friends.'

Chaloner regarded him askance. 'But Morley is a good man – ethical and decent. How can he have employed someone like Swaddell?'

'Swaddell is not all bad, and loyal servants do not grow on trees. Morley is fond of him. But you are lucky Swaddell likes you, because you do not want him as an enemy, believe me.'

'I know,' said Chaloner drily.

'Incidentally, Clarke's heirs plan to demolish the ruins of your ancestral home and build ten new houses on the site. It will earn them a fortune, as Clerkenwell is a popular location among the rich. They have plucked triumph out of disaster.'

'Speaking of disasters, I need your help to prevent one. Cobbe wants to marry Veriana. He has been offered the post of Receiver General in Southampton, and claims that while he will never be fabulously wealthy, he can keep her in relative comfort.'

'But you are concerned about his character,' surmised Thurloe. 'Perhaps he will become a better man once away from the tainting influence of White Hall.'

Chaloner was not much comforted by the 'perhaps'. 'But what if he does not? Veriana will be stuck with him for the rest of her life.'

'What does she think?'

'She is delighted by his proposal, and thinks she can make something of him.'

'Then I suggest you let her try. Better she marries someone of her own choosing than someone of yours. Then she cannot blame you if the liaison goes wrong.'

It was a good point, and Chaloner supposed he could always insist on a long betrothal, to ensure both parties knew what they were doing.

Thurloe glanced at him. 'More importantly, how do you feel about Swaddell marrying Ursula? He is head over heels in love with her, and she told me, when I arrived just now, that she is just as enamoured of him.'

'I will not allow it,' said Chaloner firmly. 'Never. And if she continues to insist that she considers him a fine catch, I shall ask Wiseman to examine her for signs of madness. No one in her right mind could want a union with Swaddell.'

'Love is a peculiar thing, Tom, and none of us can control who we fall for. Take yourself, for example. You married two women who were patently unsuitable.'

Chaloner disliked being reminded of this. 'That was different,' he said stiffly.

'How?' asked Thurloe gently.

Chaloner had no answer, and returned to the more pressing matter of Ursula. 'But Swaddell is an assassin, who has murdered more people than we can count, and who enjoys slitting throats.'

'True. However, he did share your revulsion for the bloodsports at White Hall, so perhaps there is hope for him yet. Moreover, he has been a loyal friend to you, while a virtuous bishop thinks the world of him . . .'

'But his eyes still gleam at the prospect of killing, and God only knows what he does for Williamson under cover of state secrecy. I do not want such a man in my family.'

'I appreciate that,' said Thurloe. 'However, it is hardly fair to let your opinions stand between two people and their future happiness. I suggest you send Swaddell to the Isle of Man to woo your aunt. Let her decide whether Ursula should accept him.'

Chaloner seized on the solution with relief, sure she

447

would take one look at the assassin and forbid the match on the spot. 'Thank you,' he said sincerely. 'I will suggest it when I meet him in Clarendon House this evening.'

'Why will he be there, of all places?'

'Because the Earl is holding a soirée to celebrate the fact that he is no longer suspected of poisoning Chiffinch, and as Swaddell and I unmasked the real culprit, we are invited. I am to play my viol.'

'Which I am sure you will enjoy,' said Thurloe indulgently. 'However, I can tell you one group of people who will have no entertainment tonight: the surviving members of the Cockpit Club. They had a bird fight scheduled, but it was cancelled when all their cocks were stolen.'

'Poor Widdrington,' said Chaloner flatly. 'He will be disappointed.'

'Widdrington is currently on his way to Ireland, on the ship that was to have carried his wife. He aims to lie low until the furore surrounding Bess's crimes dies down. Without him, the Cockpit Club will founder.'

'Good,' said Chaloner. 'London's foxes, geese, bulls, bears, dogs, horses and cockerels can breathe again.'

'Speaking of cockerels, I heard that a girl matching the description of Molly from Newcastle House was seen on a cart loaded with cages outside White Hall this morning. There is a rumour that the Cockpit Club's birds are on their way to a safer life in Buckinghamshire.'

'They should like it there,' said Chaloner serenely. 'I know I would.'

'I am surprised you did not go with them. I imagine your family would like to see you, and as you have already solved the case of the stolen saltpetre, it is no longer necessary for you to sail with *Royal Oak* today.'

Chaloner grimaced. 'Spymaster Williamson raced down to Dover in the belief that he was on the trail of a mysterious saltpetre buyer, but it transpires that the "clues" were left by Sarah – she wanted him out of the way, lest he became inconveniently interested in what she was doing. Swaddell says he is mortified to have been so easily deceived.'

'He should be,' said Thurloe, unimpressed. 'He should have delegated the matter to one of his people, not hared off in person. But you have not answered my question. Why did you not go with Molly to Buckinghamshire?'

'Because the Newcastles have accepted an invitation to stay with my Earl while their own house is being repaired, and the Duke has a great fondness for a particular Somerset cheese. I am to travel there and bring some back for him.'

Thurloe raised his eyebrows. 'Mother Broughton predicted cheese in your future, did she not?'

'Coincidence,' said Chaloner firmly.

Low Sunday, one week later

The Duchess was very happy. She sat in her new quarters in Clarendon House and laughed aloud. All the people who had schemed against her were either dead or discredited, and their antics had given her books a huge amount of publicity. In a few days, sales had gone through the roof, and her printer could not produce copies quickly enough to meet the demand.

She was fêted at White Hall, and other women now emulated her style of dress, claiming the clothes she chose were far more comfortable than the cumbersome skirts and bodices dictated by fashion. And the King had approached her the previous day to solicit her opinion on all manner of subjects, including bloodsports. He had listened carefully to her reasons as to why they should be banned, and promised to raise the matter at the next Privy Council meeting.

But better than all that was the loyalty her husband had shown over the letter accusing her of adultery. He had confided last night that, although Clayton had composed and sent the missive, using Booth and Liddell to help him, the whole scheme had been Mansfield's idea. Mansfield had denied it, of course, but her husband did not believe him.

She laughed again. Poor, stupid Mansfield! Of course it had not been his idea! The plot had been devised by a person of considerable intelligence, who could see beyond the inconvenience such accusations would cause in the short term, to the benefits that would accrue in the long. Relations between the Duke and his heir were irrevocably shattered, and she never need worry that the Duke might take Mansfield's side again. Now he would listen only to her.

Everything had worked out exactly as she had intended.

Historical Note

The story of the anonymous letter, in which the Duchess of Newcastle is alleged to have had an affair with her husband's steward Francis Topp, is true. The Duke did not believe a word of it, and immediately ordered an investigation. It eventually emerged that the letter had been sent by another steward, Andrew Clayton. Clayton was corrupt, and when the Duchess decided to inspect his household accounts, he realised that he needed to get rid of her fast. Clayton recruited two friends to help him: a dodgy clergyman named John Booth and a dishonest horse-breeder called Francis Liddell. Together, they composed the letter, taking care to disguise their handwriting, and dispatched a servant to mail it from a posthouse in Grantham where none of them were known.

Rather stupidly, Clayton later wrote Booth a note about the plot, but forgot to send it through anonymous channels. It was intercepted, and Booth confessed to everything in order to save himself. Clayton tried to wriggle out of his predicament by accusing Booth of coin-clipping, an offence punishable by death. Booth was actually convicted of this crime, but escaped execution when the Duke intervened on his behalf.

Fortunately for the scheming trio, the Duke did not want his wife's name dragged through the mud in a public trial, so the libel charges were quietly dropped. However, there is some suggestion that the plot may have been instigated by Viscount Mansfield, the Duke's weak and uninspiring son by his first marriage, who disliked his stepmother, and lived in constant fear that she would cheat him out of his inheritance.

The Duchess of Newcastle – Margaret Cavendish – was a remarkable lady. She was a poet, playwright and biographer, and is credited with writing one of the first ever science fiction novels. She was also a philosopher, and had opinions about religion, feminism, social rules and animals. Her academic reputation was such that she was permitted to attend a meeting of the Royal Society, then a men-only organisation. Her older brother, Baron Lucas, was a member of the Royal Society, although he may later have been expelled.

Unfortunately, while the Duchess's intellectual abilities may have impressed some of her contemporaries, there were many more who were terrified by them, as she challenged the precepts of Restoration male-dominated society. Some accused her of insanity, although her behaviour suggests she was eccentric rather than deranged – the eye-catching costume that she really did wear to a public theatre is a case in point. As a result, she suffered much ridicule, particularly from those who were less well endowed in the brain department.

The Duke was also accomplished, and was a playwright, soldier and equestrian. It is possible that he suffered from Parkinson's-like symptoms in his later years, which prevented him from pursuing the outdoor activities that he loved.

For all their cleverness the Newcastles made terrible choices regarding their staff. Not only did they employ the treacherous Clayton, but Francis Topp cheated them for years before he was caught, at which point he absconded with £300 and faked his own death to prevent them from looking for him (he eventually died in 1675). Topp's wife Elizabeth (Eliza) was the Duchess's lady-in-waiting, and perhaps her best friend. It is unclear if she knew what her husband was up to, but she was dismissed in disgrace in 1671. She died at a ripe old age in 1703. The Newcastles also had a maid called Dutch Jane.

Newcastle House, which was on Clerkenwell Green, was originally an H-plan building, started in 1630 on the orders of the Duke himself. It is not to be confused with the Newcastle House in Lincoln's Inn Fields, which still exists. However, the Duchess never designed a transparent ceiling for it, and if she had, reinforced glass would not have been available to her, as this was a much later invention.

Some liberty has also been taken with dates. For example, the chances are that the ducal couple were at their estates in Welbeck in April 1666, as Newcastle House was being renovated. Also, the letter plot took place in the early 1670s. More about the Newcastles and their lives can be found in the excellent *Mad Madge* by Katie Whitaker.

Clerkenwell was a rapidly developing suburb in the 1660s. It was a separate parish, and contained a number of open areas. These included Bunhill Fields, Charterhouse, and the Artillery Ground, not to mention the gardens of several great houses. Perhaps its best known public building was the Red Bull, once famous as a playhouse, but probably just a tavern by 1666.

When the plague of 1665 filled London's graveyards, it was decided to create a civic burial ground in Bunhill Fields. Whether it was ready in time to take the plague dead is not known, although it was provided with a surrounding wall and gates between 1665 and 1666. One Mr Tyndal undertook the cost of this, and the site was then leased to him as a private cemetery. Controversially, some of it was left unconsecrated, so that nonconformists could use it without compromising their religious beliefs. Edward Bagshaw, the quarrelsome nonconformist divine (he had a vicious dispute with George Morley, Bishop of Winchester, among others) was buried here, although not until 1671.

Other notable Clerkenwell worthies included the poet John Milton, the famous physician Dr Goddard, the eccentric philanthropist Erasmus Smith, and Izaak Walton of *The Compleat Angler* fame. More infamous residents include Mistress Shawe, who was charged at the Middlesex assizes for being in possession of fireballs with the intention of using them for seditious purposes; and Mother Broughton, who considered herself a prophet. No doubt she had plenty to say about the year containing three sixes, not to mention the fact that Good Friday in 1666 fell on 13 April. There was also a tobacco-seller named Joan Cole.

Other one-time residents of Clerkenwell include Thomas Chaloner the elder (1521–1565) and Thomas Chaloner the younger (1559-1615). The younger Chaloner was the father of Thomas and James the regicides. His Clerkenwell house seems to have come into

James's possession, but this was forfeit at the Restoration, along with all his other property. James and his wife Ursula had several children, one of whom was named Veriana; she married Thomas Cobbe, the Receiver General of Southampton. James Chaloner died on the Isle of Man shortly after the Restoration, leaving his wife and unmarried children in very straitened circumstances. There is some suggestion that he may have swallowed poison to avoid the horrors of a trial.

Other real people in *The Clerkenwell Affair* include the courtiers. Colonel George Widdrington married Elizabeth (Bess) Bertie, and was a close friend of Viscount Mansfield. Widdrington was an outspoken critic of the Earl of Clarendon, and it is interesting to note that he only rose to real power after Clarendon's fall in 1667. George Ashley was a Sergeant of the Larder who died in April 1666; Richard Pamphlin fades from the records after his appointment as Page of the Presence in 1660; Abraham Hubbert was appointed Clerk of the Larder in 1661; and Henry Barker was Clerk of the Crown in Chancery from the Restoration until 1692. Michael Mushey was a Yeoman of the Kitchen in the 1660s, and Millicent Lantravant was a Child of the Kitchen, although as these were usually appointments for boys, this may be a mistake in the records.

Timothy Clarke was Physician to the Household, and was later promoted as Physician to the Person. His wife was named Frances (called Fanny here to prevent confusion with Francis Topp), of whom the diarist Samuel Pepys wrote in April 1666: 'has grown mighty high, fine and proud'. She was allegedly followed to a brothel in Moor Fields by the lively Captain Edward Rolt. Rolt had been a prominent member of Cromwell's court, and was also related to him, but deftly flipped sides at the Restoration. Richard Wiseman was Surgeon to the Person.

James Tooley was not a courtier, but he was murdered in 1666 by William Legg, although the culprit is unlikely to have been the same William Legg who was Colonel of Artillery and had a son named George.

Finally, Thomas Chiffinch died on 6 April 1666, and was interred in Westminster Abbey four days later. He had been Keeper of the Closet and Keeper of the Jewels, two titles that were then claimed by his less respectable younger brother William. 'Will' Chiffinch was known as the Pimp-Master General, as his duties involved providing the King with female company. He was firmly associated with the less salubrious aspects of Court life – its debauchery, corruption and immorality. One biographer remarked that the unsavoury Will carried 'the abuse of backstairs influence to scientific perfection'.